KT-172-795

Desmond Bagley was born in 1923 in Kendal, Westmorland, and brought up in Blackpool. He began his working life, aged 14, in the printing industry and then did a variety of jobs until going into an aircraft factory at the start of the Second World War.

When the war ended he decided to travel to southern Africa, going overland through Europe and the Sahara. He worked en route, reaching South Africa in 1951.

He became a freelance journalist in Johannesburg and wrote his first published novel, *The Golden Keel*, in 1963. In 1964 he returned to England and lived in Totnes, Devon, for twelve years. He and his wife then moved to Guernsey in the Channel Islands. Here he found the ideal place for combining his writing with his other interests, which included computers, mathematics, military history, and entertaining friends from all over the world.

Desmond Bagley died in April 1983. *Juggernaut*, the second previously unpublished novel was published in June 1986: the first, *Night of Error*, was published in 1984 and was on the bestseller list for many weeks.

DESMOND BAGLEY

High Citadel

FONTANA/Collins

To John Donaldson
and Bob Knittel

First published by William Collins Sons & Co. Ltd 1965
First issued in Fontana Paperbacks 1967
Thirtieth impression September 1987

Made and printed in Great Britain by
William Collins Sons & Co. Ltd, Glasgow

Chapter I

The bell shrilled insistently.

O'Hara frowned in his sleep and burrowed deeper into the pillow. He dragged up the thin sheet which covered him, but that left his feet uncovered and there was a sleepy protest from his companion. Without opening his eyes he put his hand out to the bedside table, seized the alarm clock, and hurled it violently across the room. Then he snuggled into the pillow again.

The bell still rang.

At last he opened his eyes, coming to the realisation that it was the telephone ringing. He propped himself up on one elbow and stared hatefully into the darkness. Ever since he had been in the hotel he had been asking Ramón to transfer the telephone to the bedside, and every time he had been assured that it would be done to-morrow. It had been nearly a year.

He got out of bed and padded across the room to the dressing-table without bothering to switch on the light. As he picked up the telephone he tweaked aside the window curtain and glanced outside. It was still dark and the moon was setting—he estimated it was about two hours to dawn.

He grunted into the mouthpiece: "O'Hara."

"Goddammit, what's the matter with you?" said Filson. "I've been trying to get you for a quarter of an hour."

"I was asleep," said O'Hara. "I usually sleep at night —I believe most people do, with the exception of Yankee flight managers."

"Very funny," said Filson tiredly. "Well, drag your ass down here—there's a flight scheduled for dawn."

"What the hell—I just got back six hours ago. I'm tired."

"You think I'm not?" said Filson. "This is important —a Samair 727 touched down in an emergency landing and the flight inspector grounded it. The passengers are mad as hornets, so the skipper and the hostess have sorted out priorities and we've got to take passengers to the coast. You know what a connection with Samair means to us; it could be that if we treat 'em nice they'll use us as a regular feeder."

"In a pig's eye," said O'Hara. "They'll use you in an

emergency but they'll never put you on their time-tables. All you'll get are thanks."

"It's worth trying," insisted Filson. "So get the hell down here."

O'Hara debated whether to inform Filson that he had already exceeded his month's flying hours and that it was only two-thirds through the month. He sighed, and said, "All right, I'm coming." It would cut no ice with Filson to plead regulations; as far as that hard-hearted character was concerned, the I.A.T.A. regulations were meant to be bent, if not broken. If he conformed to every international regulation, his two-cent firm would be permanently in the red.

Besides, O'Hara thought, this was the end of the line for him. If he lost this job survival would be difficult. There were too many broken-down pilots in South America hunting too few jobs and Filson's string-and-sealing-wax outfit was about as low as you could get. Hell, he thought disgustedly, I'm on a bloody escalator going the wrong way—it takes all the running I can do to stay in the same place.

He put down the hand-set abruptly and looked again into the night, scanning the sky. It looked all right here, but what about the mountains? Always he thought about the mountains, those cruel mountains with their jagged white swords stretched skywards to impale him. Filson had better have a good met. report.

He walked to the door and stepped into the corridor, unlit as usual. They turned off all lights in the public rooms at eleven p.m.—it was that kind of hotel. For the millionth time he wondered what he was doing in this godforsaken country, in this tired town, in this sleazy hotel. Unconcernedly naked, he walked down towards the bathroom. In his philosophy if a woman had seen a naked man before then it didn't matter —if she hadn't, it was time she did. Anyway, it was dark.

He showered quickly, washing away the night sweat, and returned to his room and switched on the bedside lamp wondering if it would work. It was always a fifty per cent chance that it wouldn't—the town's electricity supply was very erratic. The filament glowed faintly and in the dim light he dressed—long woollen underwear, jeans, a thick shirt and a leather jacket. By the time he had finished he was sweating again in the warm tropical night. But it would be cold over the mountains.

From the dressing-table he took a metal flask and shook it tentatively. It was only half full and he frowned. He could

6

wake Ramón and get a refill but that was not politic; for one thing Ramón did not like being wakened at night, and for another he would ask cutting questions about when his bill was going to be paid. Perhaps he could get something at the airport.

O'Hara was just leaving when he paused at the door and turned back to look at the sprawling figure in the bed. The sheet had slipped revealing dark breasts tipped a darker colour. He looked at her critically. Her olive skin had an underlying coppery sheen and he thought there was a sizeable admixture of Indian in this one. With a rueful grimace he took a thin wallet from the inside pocket of his leathery jacket, extracted two notes and tossed them on the bedside table. Then he went out, closing the door quietly behind him.

I I

When he pulled his battered car into the parking bay he looked with interest at the unaccustomed bright lights of the airport. The field was low-grade, classed as an emergency strip by the big operators, although to Filson it was a main base. A Samair Boeing 727 lay sleekly in front of the control tower and O'Hara looked at it enviously for a while, then switched his attention to the hangar beyond.

A Dakota was being loaded and, even at that distance, the lights were bright enough for O'Hara to see the emblem on the tail—two intertwined " A's," painted artistically to look like mountain peaks. He smiled gently to himself. It was appropriate that he should fly a plane decorated with the Double-A; alcoholics of the world unite—it was a pity Filson didn't see the joke. But Filson was very proud of his Andes Airlift and never joked about it. A humourless man, altogether.

He got out of the car and walked around to the main building to find it was full of people, tired people rudely awakened and set down in the middle of nowhere in the middle of the night. He pushed his way through the crowd towards Filson's office. An American voice with a Western twang complained loudly and bitterly, " This is a damned disgrace—I'm going to speak to Mr. Coulson about it when I get back to Rio."

O'Hara grinned as he pushed open the door of the office. Filson was sitting at his desk in his shirt-sleeves, his face shiny with sweat. He always sweated, particularly in an emergency and since his life was in a continual state of crisis it was a wonder he didn't melt away altogether. He looked up.

"So you got here at last."

"I'm always pleased at the welcome I get," observed O'Hara.

Filson ignored that. "All right; this is the dope," he said. "I've contracted with Samair to take ten of their passengers to Santillana—they're the ones who have to make connections with a ship. You'll take number one—she's being serviced now." His voice was briskly businesslike and O'Hara could tell by the way he sonorously rolled out the words "contracted with Samair" that he saw himself as a big-time air operator doing business with his peers instead of what he really was —an ageing ex-pilot making a precarious living off two twenty-five-year-old rattling ex-army surplus planes.

O'Hara merely said, "Who's coming with me?"

"Grivas."

"That cocky little bastard."

"He volunteered—which is more than you did," snapped Filson.

"Oh?"

"He was here when the 727 touched down," said Filson. He smiled thinly at O'Hara. "It was his idea to put it to Samair that we take some of their more urgent passengers, so he phoned me right away. That's the kind of quick thinking we need in this organisation."

"I don't like him in a plane," said O'Hara.

"So you're a better pilot," said Filson reluctantly. "That's why you're skipper and he's going as co-pilot." He looked at the ceiling reflectively. "When this deal with Samair comes off maybe I'll promote Grivas to the office. He's too good to be a pilot."

Filson had delusions of grandeur. O'Hara said deliberately, "If you think that South American Air is going to give you a feeder contract, you're crazy. You'll get paid for taking their passengers and you'll get their thanks—for what they're worth—and they'll kiss you off fast."

Filson pointed a pen at O'Hara. "You're paid to jockey a plane—leave the heavy thinking to me."

O'Hara gave up. "What happened to the 727?"

"Something wrong with the fuel feed—they're looking at it now." Filson picked up a sheaf of papers. "There's a crate of machinery to go for servicing. Here's the manifest."

"Christ!" said O'Hara. "This is an unscheduled flight. Do you have to do this?"

"Unscheduled or not, you're going with a full load. Damned if I send a half empty plane when I can send a full one."

O'Hara was mournful. "It's just that I thought I'd have an easy trip for a change. You know you always overload and it's a hell of a job going through the passes. The old bitch wallows like a hippo."

"You're going at the best time," said Filson. "It'll be worse later in the day when the sun has warmed things up. Now get the hell out of here and stop bothering me."

O'Hara left the office. The main hall was emptying, a stream of disgruntled Samair passengers leaving for the antiquated airport bus. A few people still stood about—those would be the passengers for Santillana. O'Hara ignored them; passengers or freight, it was all one to him. He took them over the Andes and dumped them on the other side and there was no point in getting involved with them. A bus driver doesn't mix with his passengers, he thought; and that's all I am—a bloody vertical bus driver.

He glanced at the manifest. Filson had done it again—there were *two* crates and he was aghast at their weight. One of these days, he thought savagely, I'll get an I.A.T.A. inspector up here at the right time and Filson will go for a loop. He crushed the manifest in his fist and went to inspect the Dakota.

Grivas was by the plane, lounging gracefully against the undercarriage. He straightened when he saw O'Hara and flicked his cigarette across the tarmac but did not step forward to meet him. O'Hara crossed over and said, "Is the cargo aboard?"

Grivas smiled. "Yes."

"Did you check it? Is it secure?"

"Of course, Señor O'Hara. I saw to it myself."

O'Hara grunted. He did not like Grivas, neither as a man nor as a pilot. He distrusted his smoothness, the slick patina of pseudo good breeding that covered him like a sheen from his patent leather hair and trim toothbrush moustache to his highly polished shoes. Grivas was a slim wiry man, not very tall, who always wore a smile. O'Hara distrusted the smile most of all.

"What's the weather?" he asked.

9

Grivas looked at the sky. "It seems all right."

O'Hara let acid creep into his voice. "A met. report would be a good thing, don't you think?"

Grivas grinned. "I'll get it," he said.

O'Hara watched him go, then turned to the Dakota and walked round to the cargo doors. The Dakota had been one of the most successful planes ever designed, the work-horse of the Allied forces during the war. Over ten thousand of them had fought a good war, flying countless millions of ton-miles of precious freight about the world. It was a good plane in its time, but that was long ago.

This Dakota was twenty-five years old, battered by too many air hours with too little servicing. O'Hara knew the exact amount of play in the rudder cables; he knew how to nurse the worn-out engines so as to get the best out of them —and a poor best it was; he knew the delicate technique of landing so as not to put too much strain on the weakened undercarriage. And he knew that one day the whole sorry fabric would play a murderous trick on him high over the white spears of the Andes.

He climbed into the plane and looked about the cavernous interior. There were ten seats up front, not the luxurious reclining couches of Samair but uncomfortable hard leather chairs each fitted with the safety-belt that even Filson could not skip, although he had grumbled at the added cost. The rest of the fuselage was devoted to cargo space and was at present occupied by two large crates.

O'Hara went round them testing the anchoring straps with his hand. He had a horror that one day the cargo would slide forward if he made a bad landing or hit very bad turbulence. That would be the end of any passengers who had the ill-luck to be flying Andes Airlift. He cursed as he found a loose strap. Grivas and his slip-shod ways would be the end of him one day.

Having seen the cargo was secured he went forward into the cockpit and did a routine check of the instruments. A mechanic was working on the port engine so O'Hara leaned out of the side window and asked in Spanish if it was all right. The mechanic spat, then drew his finger across his throat and made a bloodcurdling sound. "De un momento a otro."

He finished the instrument check and went into the hangar to find Fernandez, the chief mechanic, who usually had a bottle or two stored away, strictly against Filson's orders.

O'Hara liked Fernandez and he knew that Fernandez liked him; they got on well together and O'Hara made a point of keeping it that way—to be at loggerheads with the chief mechanic would be a passport to eternity in this job.

He chatted for a while with Fernandez, then filled his flask and took a hasty gulp from the bottle before he passed it back. Dawn was breaking as he strode back to the Dakota, and Grivas was in the cockpit fussing with the disposal of his brief-case. It's a funny thing, thought O'Hara, that the brief-case is just as much a part of an airline pilot as it is of any city gent. His own was under his seat; all it contained was a packet of sandwiches which he had picked up at an all-night café.

" Got the met. report?" he asked Grivas.

Grivas passed over the sheet of paper and O'Hara said, " You can taxi her down to the apron."

He studied the report. It wasn't too bad—it wasn't bad at all. No storms, no anomalies, no trouble—just good weather over the mountains. But O'Hara had known the meteorologists to be wrong before and there was no release of the tension within him. It was that tension, never relaxed in the air, that had kept him alive when a lot of better men had died.

As the Dakota came to a halt on the apron outside the main building, he saw Filson leading the small group of passengers. " See they have their seat-belts properly fastened," he said to Grivas.

" I'm not a hostess," said Grivas sulkily.

" When you're sitting on this side of the cockpit you can give orders," said O'Hara coldly. " Right now you take them. And I'd like you to do a better job of securing the passengers than you did of the cargo."

The smile left Grivas's face, but he turned and went into the main cabin. Presently Filson came forward and thrust a form at O'Hara. " Sign this."

It was the I.A.T.A. certificate of weights and fuel. O'Hara saw that Filson had cheated on the weights as usual, but made no comment and scribbled his signature. Filson said, " As soon as you land give me a ring. There might be return cargo."

O'Hara nodded and Filson withdrew. There was the double slam as the door closed and O'Hara said, " Take her to the end of the strip." He switched on the radio, warming it up.

Grivas was still sulky and would not talk. He made no answer as he revved the engines and the Dakota waddled away from the main building into the darkness, ungainly and heavy on the ground. At the end of the runway O'Hara thought for a moment. Filson had not given him a flight number. To hell with it, he thought; control ought to know what's going on. He clicked on the microphone and said, "A.A. special flight, destination Santillana—A.A. to San Croce control—ready to take off."

A voice crackled tinnily in his ear. "San Croce control to Andes Airlift special. Permission given—time 2.33 G.M.T."

"Roger and out." He put his hand to the throttles and waggled the stick. There was a stickiness about it. Without looking at Grivas he said, "Take your hands off the controls." Then he pushed on the throttle levers and the engines roared. Four minutes later the Dakota was airborne after an excessively long run.

He stayed at the controls for an hour, personally supervising the long climb to the roof of the world. He liked to find out if the old bitch was going to spring a new surprise. Cautiously he carried out gentle, almost imperceptible evolutions, his senses attuned to the feel of the plane. Occasionally he glanced at Grivas who was sitting frozen-faced in the other seat, staring blankly through the windscreen.

At last he was satisfied and engaged the automatic pilot but spent another quarter-hour keeping a wary eye on it. It had behaved badly on the last flight but Fernandez had assured him that it was now all right. He trusted Fernandez, but not that much—it was always better to do the final check personally.

Then he relaxed and looked ahead. It was much lighter in the high air and, although the dawn was behind, the sky ahead was curiously light. O'Hara knew why; it was the snow blink as the first light of the sun caught the high white peaks of the Andes. The mountains themselves were as yet invisible, lost in the early haze rising from the jungle below.

He began to think about his passengers and he wondered if they knew what they had got themselves into. This was no pressurised jet aircraft and they were going to fly pretty high—it would be cold and the air would be thin and he hoped none of the passengers had heart trouble. Presumably Filson had warned them, although he wouldn't put it past that bastard to keep his mouth shut. He was even too stingy

12

to provide decent oxygen masks—there were only mouth tubes to the oxygen bottles to port and starboard.

He scratched his cheek thoughtfully. These weren't the ordinary passengers he was used to carrying—the American mining engineers flying to San Croce and the poorer type of local businessman proud to be flying even by Andes Airlift. These were the Samair type of passengers—wealthy and not over fond of hardship. They were in a hurry, too, or they would have had more sense than to fly Andes Airlift. Perhaps he had better break his rule and go back to talk to them. When they found they weren't going to fly over the Andes but *through* them they might get scared. It would be better to warn them first.

He pushed his uniform cap to the back of his head and said, "Take over, Grivas. I'm going to talk to the passengers."

Grivas lifted his eyebrows—so surprised that he forgot to be sulky. He shrugged. "Why? What is so important about the passengers? Is this Samair?" He laughed noiselessly. "But, yes, of course—you have seen the girl; you want to see her again, eh?"

"What girl?"

"Just a girl, a woman; very beautiful. I think I will get to know her and take her out when we arrive in—er—Santillana," said Grivas thoughtfully. He looked at O'Hara out of the corner of his eye.

O'Hara grunted and took the passenger manifest from his breast pocket. As he suspected, the majority were American. He went through the list rapidly. Mr. and Mrs. Coughlin of Challis, Idaho—tourists; Dr. James Armstrong, London, England—no profession stated; Raymond Forester of New York—businessman; Señor and Señorita Montes—Argentinian and no profession stated; Miss Jennifer Ponsky of South Bridge, Connecticut—tourist; Dr. Willis of California; Miguel Rohde—no stated nationality, profession—importer; Joseph Peabody of Chicago, Illinois—businessman.

He flicked his finger on the manifest and grinned at Grivas. "Jennifer's a nice name—but Ponsky? I can't see you going around with anyone called Ponsky."

Grivas looked startled, then laughed convulsively. "Ah, my friend, you can have the fair Ponsky—I'll stick to my girl."

O'Hara looked at the list again. "Then it must be Señorita Montes—unless it's Mrs. Coughlin."

13

Grivas chuckled, his good spirits recovered. "You find out for yourself."

"I'll do that," said O'Hara. "Take over."

He went back into the main cabin and was confronted by ten uplifted heads. He smiled genially, modelling himself on the Samair pilots to whom public relations was as important as flying ability. Lifting his voice above the roar of the engines, he said, "I suppose I ought to tell you that we'll be reaching the mountains in about an hour. It will get cold, so I suggest you wear your overcoats. Mr. Filson will have told you that this aircraft isn't pressurised, but we don't fly at any great height for more than an hour, so you'll be quite all right."

A burly man with a whisky complexion interjected, "No one told me that."

O'Hara cursed Filson under his breath and broadened his smile. "Well, not to worry, Mr.—er . . ."

"Peabody—Joe Peabody."

"Mr. Peabody. It will be quite all right. There is an oxygen mouthpiece next to every seat which I advise you to use if you feel breathing difficult. Now, it gets a bit wearying shouting like this above the engine noise, so I'll come round and talk to you individually." He smiled at Peabody, who glowered back at him.

He bent to the first pair of seats on the port side. "Could I have your names, please?"

The first man said, "I'm Forester." The other contributed, "Willis."

"Glad to have you aboard, Dr. Willis, Mr. Forester."

Forester said, "I didn't bargain for this, you know. I didn't think kites like this were still flying."

O'Hara smiled deprecatingly. "Well, this is an emergency flight and it was laid on in the devil of a hurry. I'm sure it was an oversight that Mr. Filson forgot to tell you that this isn't a pressurised plane." Privately he was not sure of anything of the kind.

Willis said with a smile, "I came here to study high altitude conditions. I'm certainly starting with a bang. How high do we fly, Captain?"

"Not more than seventeen thousand feet," said O'Hara. "We fly through the passes—we don't go over the top. You'll find the oxygen mouthpieces easy to use—all you do is suck." He smiled and turned away and found himself held.

14

Peabody was clutching his sleeve, leaning forward over the seat behind. " Hey, Skipper. . . ."

" I'll be with you in a moment, Mr. Peabody," said O'Hara, and held Peabody with his eye. Peabody blinked rapidly, released his grip and subsided into his seat, and O'Hara turned to starboard.

The man was elderly, with an aquiline nose and a short grey beard. With him was a young girl of startling beauty, judging by what O'Hara could see of her face, which was not much because she was huddled deep into a fur coat. He said, " Señor Montes?"

The man inclined his head. " Don't worry, Captain, we know what to expect." He waved a gloved hand. " You see we are well prepared. I know the Andes, señor, and I know these aircraft. I know the Andes well; I have been over them on foot and by mule—in my youth I climbed some of the high peaks—didn't I, Benedetta?"

" Si, tío," she said in a colourless voice. " But that was long ago. I don't know if your heart . . ."

He patted her on the leg. " I will be all right if I relax; is that not so, Captain?"

" Do you understand the use of this oxygen tube?" asked O'Hara.

Montes nodded confidently, and O'Hara said, " Your uncle will be quite all right, Señorita Montes." He waited for her to reply but she made no answer, so he passed on to the seats behind.

These couldn't be the Coughlins; they were too ill-assorted a pair to be American tourists, although the woman was undoubtedly American. O'Hara said inquiringly, " Miss Ponsky?"

She lifted a sharp nose and said, " I declare this is all wrong, Captain. You must turn back at once."

The fixed smile on O'Hara's face nearly slipped. " I fly this route regularly, Miss Ponsky," he said. " There is nothing to fear."

But there was naked fear on her face—air fear. Sealed in the air-conditioned quietness of a modern jet-liner she could subdue it, but the primitiveness of the Dakota brought it to the surface. There was no clever décor to deceive her into thinking that she was in a drawing-room, just the stark functionalism of unpainted aluminium, battered and scratched, and with the plumbing showing like a dissected body.

O'Hara said quietly, "What is your profession, Miss Ponsky?"

"I'm a school teacher back in South Bridge," she said. "I've been teaching there for thirty years."

He judged she was naturally garrulous and perhaps this could be a way of conquering her fear. He glanced at the man, who said, "Miguel Rohde."

He was a racial anomaly—a Spanish-German name and Spanish-German features—straw-coloured hair and beady black eyes. There had been German immigration into South America for many years and this was one of the results.

O'Hara said, "Do you know the Andes, Señor Rohde?"

"Very well," he replied in a grating voice. He nodded ahead. "I lived up there for many years—now I am going back."

O'Hara switched back to Miss Ponsky. "Do you teach geography, Miss Ponsky?"

She nodded. "Yes, I do. That's one of the reasons I came to South America on my vacation. It makes such a difference if you can describe things first-hand."

"Then here you have a marvellous opportunity," said O'Hara with enthusiasm. "You'll see the Andes as you never would if you'd flown Samair. And I'm sure that Señor Rohde will point out the interesting sights."

Rohde nodded understandingly. "Si, very interesting; I know it well, the mountain country."

O'Hara smiled reassuringly at Miss Ponsky, who offered him a glimmering, tremulous smile in return. He caught a twinkle in Rohde's black eyes as he turned to the port side again.

The man sitting next to Peabody was undoubtedly British, so O'Hara said, "Glad to have you with us, Dr. Armstrong —Mr. Peabody."

Armstrong said, "Nice to hear an English accent, Captain, after all this Spa——"

Peabody broke in. "I'm damned if I'm glad to be here, skipper. What in hell kind of an airline is this, for godsake?"

"One run by an American, Mr. Peabody," said O'Hara calmly. "As you were saying, Dr. Armstrong?"

"Never expected to see an English captain out here," said Armstrong.

"Well, I'm Irish, and we tend to get about," said O'Hara.

"I'd put on some warm clothing if I were you. You, too, Mr. Peabody."

Peabody laughed and suddenly burst into song. "'I've got my love to keep me warm'." He produced a hip flask and waved it. "This is as good as a top-coat."

For a moment O'Hara saw himself in Peabody and was shocked and afraid. "As you wish," he said bleakly, and passed on to the last pair of seats opposite the luggage racks.

The Coughlins were an elderly couple, very Darby and Joanish. He must have been pushing seventy and she was not far behind, but there was a suggestion of youth about their eyes, good-humoured and with a zest for life. O'Hara said, "Are you all right, Mrs. Coughlin?"

"Fine," she said. "Aren't we, Harry?"

"Sure," said Coughlin, and looked up at O'Hara. "Will we be flying through the Puerto de las Aguilas?"

"That's right," said O'Hara. "Do you know these parts?"

Coughlin laughed. "Last time I was round here was in 1912. I've just come down to show my wife where I spent my misspent youth." He turned to her. "That means Eagle Pass, you know; it took me two weeks to get across back in 1910, and here we are doing it in an hour or two. Isn't it wonderful?"

"It sure is," Mrs. Coughlin replied comfortably.

There was nothing wrong with the Coughlins, decided O'Hara, so after a few more words he went back to the cockpit. Grivas still had the plane on automatic pilot and was sitting relaxed, gazing forward at the mountains. O'Hara sat down and looked intently at the oncoming mountain wall. He checked the course and said, "Keep taking a bearing on Chimitaxl and let me know when it's two hundred and ten degrees true bearing. You know the drill."

He stared down at the ground looking for landmarks and nodded with satisfaction as he saw the sinuous, twisting course of the Rio Sangre and the railway bridge that crossed it. Flying this route by day and for so long he knew the ground by heart and knew immediately whether he was on time. He judged that the north-west wind predicted by the meteorologists was a little stronger than they had prophesied and altered course accordingly, then he jacked in the auto pilot again and relaxed. All would be quiet until Grivas came up with the required bearing on Chimitaxl. He sat in repose and watched the ground slide away behind—the dun and olive foothills, craggy bare rock, and then the shining snow-covered peaks. Presently he munched on the sandwiches he took from his brief-case. He thought of washing them down with a drink from his flask but then he thought of Peabody's whisky-sodden face. Something inside him seemed to burst and he found that he didn't need a drink after all.

Grivas suddenly put down the bearing compass. "Thirty seconds," he said.

O'Hara looked at the wilderness of high peaks before him, a familiar wilderness. Some of these mountains were his friends, like Chimitaxl; they pointed out his route. Others were his deadly enemies—devils and demons lurked among them compounded of down draughts, driving snow and mists. But he was not afraid because it was all familiar and he knew and understood the dangers and how to escape them.

Grivas said, "Now," and O'Hara swung the control column gently, experience telling him the correct turn. His feet automatically moved in conjunction with his hands and the Dakota swept to port in a wide, easy curve, heading for a gap in the towering wall ahead.

Grivas said softly, "Señor O'Hara."

"Don't bother me now."

"But I must," said Grivas, and there was a tiny metallic click.

O'Hara glanced at him out of the corner of his eye and stiffened as he saw that Grivas was pointing a gun at him—a compact automatic pistol.

He jerked his head, his eyes widening in disbelief. "Have you gone crazy?"

Grivas's smile widened. "Does it matter?" he said indifferently. "We do not go through the Puerto de las Aguilas this trip, Señor O'Hara, that is al' that matters." His voice hardened. "Now steer course one-eight-four on a true bearing."

O'Hara took a deep breath and held his course. "You must have gone out of your mind," he said. "Put down that gun, Grivas, and maybe we'll forget this. I suppose I have been bearing down on you a bit too much, but that's no reason to pull a gun. Put it away and we'll straighten things out when we get to Santillana."

Grivas's teeth flashed. "You're a stupid man, O'Hara; do you think I do this for personal reasons? But since you mention it, you said not long ago that sitting in the captain's seat gave you authority." He lifted the gun slightly. "You

18

were wrong—this gives authority; all the authority there is. Now change course or I'll blow your head off. I can fly this aircraft too, remember."

"They'd hear you inside," said O'Hara.

"I've locked the door, and what could they do? They wouldn't take the controls from the only pilot. But that would be of no consequence to you, O'Hara—you'd be dead."

O'Hara saw his finger tighten on the trigger and bit his lip before swinging the control column. The Dakota turned to fly south, parallel to the main backbone of the Andes. Grivas was right, damn him; there was no point in getting himself killed. But what the hell was he up to?

He settled on the bearing given by Grivas and reached forward to the auto pilot control. Grivas jerked the gun. "No, Señor O'Hara; you fly this aircraft—it will give you something to do."

O'Hara drew back his hand slowly and grasped the wheel. He looked out to starboard past Grivas at the high peaks drifting by. "Where are we going?" he asked grimly.

"That is of no consequence," said Grivas. "But it is not very far. We land at an air-strip in five minutes."

O'Hara thought about that. There was no air-strip that he knew of on this course. There were no air-strips at all this high in the mountains except for the military strips, and those were on the Pacific side of the Andes chain. He would have to wait and see.

His eyes flickered to the microphone set on its hook close to his left hand. He looked at Grivas and saw he was not wearing his earphones. If the microphone was switched on then any loud conversation would go on the air and Grivas would be unaware of it. It was definitely worth trying.

He said to Grivas. "There are no air-strips on this course." His left hand strayed from the wheel.

"You don't know everything, O'Hara."

His fingers touched the microphone and he leaned over to obstruct Grivas's vision as much as possible, pretending to study the instruments. His fingers found the switch and he snapped it over and then he leaned back and relaxed. In a loud voice he said, "You'll never get away with this, Grivas; you can't steal a whole aeroplane so easily. When this Dakota is overdue at Santillana they'll lay on a search—you know that as well as I do."

Grivas laughed. "Oh, you're clever, O'Hara—but I was

cleverer. The radio is not working, you know. I took out the tubes when you were talking to the passengers."

O'Hara felt a sudden emptiness in the pit of his stomach. He looked at the jumble of peaks ahead and felt frightened. This was country he did not know and there would be dangers he could not recognise. He felt frightened for himself and for his passengers.

III

It was cold in the passenger cabin, and the air was thin. Señor Montes had blue lips and his face had turned grey. He sucked on the oxygen tube and his niece fumbled in her bag and produced a small bottle of pills. He smiled painfully and put a pill in his mouth, letting it dissolve on his tongue. Slowly some colour came back into his face; not a lot, but he looked better than he had before taking the pill.

In the seat behind, Miss Ponsky's teeth were chattering, not with cold but with conversation. Already Miguel Rohde had learned much of her life history, in which he had not the slightest interest although he did not show it. He let her talk, prompting her occasionally, and all the time he regarded the back of Montes's head with lively black eyes. At a question from Miss Ponsky he looked out of the window and suddenly frowned.

The Coughlins were also looking out of the window. Mr. Coughlin said, "I'd have sworn we were going to head that way—through that pass. But we suddenly changed course south."

"It all looks the same to me," said Mrs. Coughlin. "Just a lot of mountains and snow."

Coughlin said, "From what I remember, El Puerto de las Aguilas is back there."

"Oh, Harry, I'm sure you don't really remember. It's nearly fifty years since you were here—and you never saw it from an airplane."

"Maybe," he said, unconvinced. "But it sure is funny."

"Now, Harry, the pilot knows what he's doing. He looked a nice efficient young man to me."

Coughlin continued to look from the window. He said nothing more.

James Armstrong of London, England, was becoming very bored with Joe Peabody of Chicago, Illinois. The man

20

was a positive menace. Already he had sunk half the contents of his flask, which seemed an extraordinarily large one, and he was getting combatively drunk. "Whadya think of the nerve of that goddam fly-boy, chokin' me off like that?" he demanded. "Actin' high an' mighty jus' like the goddam limey he is."

Armstrong smiled gently. "I'm a—er—goddam limey too, you know," he pointed out.

"Well, jeez, presen' comp'ny excepted," said Peabody. "That's always the rule, ain't it? I ain't got anything against you limeys really, excep' you keep draggin' us into your wars."

"I take it you read the *Chicago Tribune*," said Armstrong solemnly.

Forester and Willis did not talk much—they had nothing in common. Willis had produced a large book as soon as they exhausted their small talk and to Forester it looked heavy in all senses of the word, being mainly mathematical.

Forester had nothing to do. In front of him was an aluminium bulkhead on which an axe and a first-aid box were mounted. There was no profit in looking at that and consequently his eyes frequently strayed across the aisle to Señor Montes. His lips tightened as he noted the bad colour of Montes's face and he looked at the first aid-box reflectively.

I V

"There it is," said Grivas. "You land there."

O'Hara straightened up and looked over the nose of the Dakota. Dead ahead amid a jumble of rocks and snow was a short air-strip, a mere track cut on a ledge of a mountain. He had time for the merest glimpse before it was gone behind them.

Grivas waved the gun. "Circle it," he said.

O'Hara eased the plane into an orbit round the strip and looked down at it. There were buildings down there, rough cabins in a scattered group, and there was a road leading down the mountain, twisting and turning like a snake. Someone had thoughtfully cleared the air-strip of snow, but there was no sign of life.

He judged his distance from the ground and glanced at the altimeter. "You're crazy, Grivas," he said. "We can't land on that strip."

"You can, O'Hara," said Grivas.

21

"I'm damned if I'm going to. This plane's overloaded and that strip's at an altitude of seventeen thousand feet. It would need to be three times as long for this crate to land safely. The air's too thin to hold us up at a slow landing speed—we'll hit the ground at a hell of a lick and we won't be able to pull up. We'll shoot off the other end of the strip and crash on the side of the mountain."

"You can do it."

"To hell with you," said O'Hara.

Grivas lifted his gun. "All right, I'll do it," he said. "But I'll have to kill you first."

O'Hara looked at the black hole staring at him like an evil eye. He could see the rifling inside the muzzle and it looked as big as a howitzer. In spite of the cold, he was sweating and could feel rivulets of perspiration running down his back. He turned away from Grivas and studied the strip again. "Why are you doing this?" he asked.

"You would not know if I told you," said Grivas. "You would not understand—you are English."

O'Hara sighed. It was going to be very dicey; *he* might be able to get the Dakota down in approximately one piece, but Grivas wouldn't have a chance—he'd pile it up for sure. He said, "All right—warn the passengers; get them to the rear of the cabin."

"Never mind the passengers," said Grivas flatly. "You do not think that I am going to leave this cockpit?"

O'Hara said, "All right, you're calling the shots, but I warn you—don't touch the controls by as much as a finger. You're not a pilot's backside—and you know it. There can be only one man flying a plane."

"Get on with it," said Grivas shortly.

"I'll take my own time," said O'Hara. "I want a good look before I do a damn thing."

He orbited the air-strip four more times, watching it as it spun crazily beneath the Dakota. The passengers should know there was something wrong by this time, he thought. No ordinary airliner stood on its wingtip and twitched about like this. Maybe they'd get alarmed and someone would try to do something about it—that might give him a chance to get at Grivas. But what the passengers could do was problematical.

The strip was all too short; it was also very narrow and made for a much smaller aircraft. He would have to land on the extreme edge, his wingtip brushing a rock wall. Then there was the question of wind direction. He looked down at the cabins, hoping to detect a wisp of smoke from the chimneys, but there was nothing.

"I'm going to go in closer—over the strip," he said. "But I'm not landing this time."

He pulled out of orbit and circled widely to come in for a landing approach. He lined up the nose of the Dakota on the strip like a gunsight and the plane came in, fast and level. To starboard there was a blur of rock and snow and O'Hara held his breath. If the wingtip touched the rock wall that would be the end. Ahead, the strip wound underneath, as though it was being swallowed by the Dakota. There was nothing as the strip ended—just a deep valley and the blue sky. He hauled on the stick and the plane shot skyward.

The passengers will know damn well there's something wrong now, he thought. To Grivas he said, "We're not going to get this aircraft down in one piece."

"Just get me down safely," said Grivas. "I'm the only one who matters."

O'Hara grinned tightly. "You don't matter a damn to me."

"Then think of your own neck," said Grivas. "That will take care of mine, too."

But O'Hara was thinking of ten lives in the passenger cabin. He circled widely again to make another approach and debated with himself the best way of doing this. He could come in with the undercarriage up or down. A belly-landing would be rough at that speed, but the plane would slow down faster because of the increased friction. The question was: could he hold her straight? On the other hand if he came in with the undercarriage down he would lose airspeed before he hit the deck—that was an advantage too.

He smiled grimly and decided to do both. For the first time he blessed Filson and his lousy aeroplanes. He knew to a hair how much stress the undercarriage would take; hitherto his problem had been that of putting the Dakota down gently. This time he would come in with undercarriage down, losing speed, and slam her down hard—hard enough to break off the weakened struts like matchsticks. That would give him his belly-landing, too.

He sighted the nose of the Dakota on the strip again. "Well, here goes nothing," he said. "Flaps down; undercarriage down."

As the plane lost airspeed the controls felt mushy under his hands. He set his teeth and concentrated as never before.

As the plane tipped wing down and started to orbit the air-strip Armstrong was thrown violently against Peabody. Peabody was in the act of taking another mouthful of whisky and the neck of the flask suddenly jammed against his teeth. He spluttered and yelled incoherently and thrust hard against Armstrong.

Rohde was thrown out of his seat and found himself sitting in the aisle, together with Coughlin and Montes. He struggled to his feet, shaking his head violently, then he bent to help Montes, speaking quick Spanish. Mrs. Coughlin helped her husband back to his seat.

Willis had been making a note in the margin of his book and the point of his pencil snapped as Forester lurched against him. Forester made no attempt to regain his position but looked incredulously out of the window, ignoring Willis's feeble protests at being squashed. Forester was a big man.

The whole cabin was a babel of sound in English and Spanish, dominated by the sharp and scratchy voice of Miss Ponsky as she querulously complained. "I knew it," she screamed. "I knew it was all wrong." She began to laugh hysterically and Rohde turned from Montes and slapped her with a heavy hand. She looked at him in surprise and suddenly burst into tears.

Peabody shouted, "What in goddam. hell is that limey doing now?" He stared out of the window at the air-strip. "The bastard's going to land."

Rohde spoke rapidly to Montes, who seemed so shaken he was apathetic. There was a quick exchange in Spanish between Rohde and the girl, and he pointed to the door leading to the cockpit. She nodded violently and he stood up.

Mrs. Coughlin was leaning forward in her seat, comforting Miss Ponsky. "Nothing's going to happen," she kept saying. "Nothing bad is going to happen."

The aircraft straightened as O'Hara came in for his first approach run. Rohde leaned over Armstrong and looked through the window, but turned as Miss Ponsky screamed in fright, looking at the blur of rock streaming past the starboard window and seeing the wingtip brushing it so closely. Then Rohde lost his balance again as O'Hara pulled the Dakota into a climb.

It was Forester who made the first constructive move. He was nearest the door leading to the cockpit and he grabbed the door handle, turned and pushed. Nothing happened. He put his shoulder to the door but was thrown away as the plane turned rapidly. O'Hara was going into his final landing approach.

Forester grabbed the axe from its clips on the bulkhead and raised it to strike, but his arm was caught by Rohde. "This is quicker," said Rohde, and lifted a heavy pistol in his other hand. He stepped in front of Forester and fired three quick shots at the lock of the door.

V I

O'Hara heard the shots a fraction of a second before the Dakota touched down. He not only heard them but saw the altimeter and the turn-and-climb indicator shiver into fragments as the bullets smashed into the instrument panel. But he had no time to see what was happening behind him because just then the heavily overloaded Dakota settled soggily at the extreme end of the strip, moving at high speed.

There was a sickening crunch and the whole air frame shuddered as the undercarriage collapsed and the plane sank on to its belly and slid with a tearing, rending sound towards the far end of the strip. O'Hara fought frantically with the controls as they kicked against his hands and feet and tried to keep the aircraft sliding in a straight line.

Out of the corner of his eye he saw Grivas turn to the door, his pistol raised. O'Hara took a chance, lifted one hand from the stick and struck out blindly at Grivas. He just had time for one blow and luckily it connected somewhere; he felt the edge of his hand strike home and then he was too busy to see if he had incapacitated Grivas.

The Dakota was still moving too fast. Already it was more than half-way down the strip and O'Hara could see the emptiness ahead where the strip stopped at the lip of the valley. In desperation he swung the rudder hard over and the Dakota swerved with a loud grating sound.

He braced himself for the crash.

The starboard wingtip hit the rock wall and the Dakota spun sharply to the right. O'Hara kept the rudder forced right over and saw the rock wall coming right at him. The nose of the plane hit rock and crumpled and the safety glass in the windscreens shivered into opacity. Then something hit him on the head and he lost consciousness.

VII

He came round because someone was slapping his face. His head rocked from side to side and he wanted them to stop because it was so good to be asleep. The slapping went on and on and he moaned and tried to tell them to stop. But the slapping did not stop so he opened his eyes.

It was Forester who was administering the punishment, and, as O'Hara opened his eyes, he turned to Rohde who was standing behind him and said, "Keep your gun on him."

Rohde smiled. His gun was in his hand but hanging slackly and pointing to the floor. He made no attempt to bring it up. Forester said, "What the hell did you think you were doing?"

O'Hara painfully lifted his arm to his head. He had a bump on his skull the size of an egg. He said weakly, "Where's Grivas?"

"Who is Grivas?"

"My co-pilot."

"He's here—he's in a bad way."

"I hope the bastard dies," said O'Hara bitterly. "He pulled a gun on me."

"You were at the controls," said Forester, giving him a hard look. "You put this plane down here—and I want to know why."

"It was Grivas—he forced me to do it."

"The *señor capitan* is right," said Rohde. "This man Grivas was going to shoot me and the *señor capitan* hit him." He bowed stiffly. "*Muchos gracias.*"

Forester swung round and looked at Rohde, then beyond him to Grivas. "Is he conscious?"

O'Hara looked across the cockpit. The side of the fuselage was caved in and a blunt spike of rock had hit Grivas in the chest, smashing his rib cage. It looked as though he wasn't going to make it, after all. But he was conscious, all right; his eyes were open and he looked at them with hatred.

O'Hara could hear a woman screaming endlessly in the

passenger cabin and someone else was moaning mono-
tonously. "For Christ's sake, what's happened back there?"

No one answered because Grivas began to speak. He
mumbled in a low whisper and blood frothed round his mouth.
"They'll get you," he said. "They'll be here any minute
now." His lips parted in a ghastly smile. "I'll be all right;
they'll take me to hospital. But you—you'll . . ." He broke
off in a fit of coughing and then continued: ". . . they'll
kill the lot of you." He lifted up his arm, the fingers curling
into a fist. "*Vivaca. . . .*"

The arm dropped flaccidly and the look of hate in his eyes
deepened into surprise—surprise that he was dead.

Rohde grabbed him by the wrist and held it for a moment.
"He's gone," he said.

"He was a lunatic," said O'Hara. "Stark, staring mad."

The woman was still screaming and Forester said, "For
God's sake, let's get everybody out of here."

Just then the Dakota lurched sickeningly and the whole
cockpit rose in the air. There was a ripping sound as the
spike of rock that had killed Grivas tore at the aluminium
sheathing of the fuselage. O'Hara had a sudden and horrible
intuition of what was happening. "Nobody move," he shouted.
"Everyone keep still."

He turned to Forester. "Bash in those windows."

Forester looked in surprise at the axe he was still holding
as though he had forgotten it, then he raised it and struck
at the opaque windscreen. The plastic filling in the glass
sandwich could not withstand his assault and he made a hole
big enough for a man to climb through.

O'Hara said, "I'll go through—I think I know what I'll
find. Don't either of you go back there—not yet. And
call through and tell anyone who can move to come up front."

He squeezed through the narrow gap and was astonished
to find that the nose of the Dakota was missing. He twisted
and crawled out on to the top of the fuselage and looked aft.
The tail and one wing were hanging in space over the valley
where the runway ended. The whole aircraft was delicately
balanced and even as he looked the tail tipped a little and
there was a ripping sound from the cockpit.

He twisted on to his stomach and wriggled so that he could
look into the cockpit, his head upside-down. "We're in a jam,"
he said to Forester. "We're hanging over a two-hundred
foot drop, and the only thing that's keeping the whole

bloody aeroplane from tipping over is that bit of rock there."
He indicated the rock projection driven into the side of the
cockpit.

He said, " If anyone goes back there the extra weight
might send us over because we're balanced just like a see-saw."

Forester turned his head and bawled, " Anyone who can
move, come up here."

There was a movement and Willis staggered through the
door, his head bloody. Forester shouted, " Anyone else?"

Señora Montes called urgently, " Please help my uncle—
oh, please."

Rohde drew Willis out of the way and stepped through the
door. Forester said sharply, " Don't go in too far."

Rohde did not even look at him, but bent to pick up Montes
who was lying by the door. He half carried, half dragged him
into the cockpit and Señorita Montes followed.

Forester looked up at O'Hara. " It's getting crowded in
here; I think we'd better start getting people outside."

" We'll get them on top first," said O'Hara. " The more
weight we have at this end, the better. Let the girl come
first."

She shook her head. " My uncle first."

" For God's sake, he's unconscious," said Forester. " You
go out—I'll look after him."

She shook her head stubbornly and O'Hara broke in
impatiently, " All right, Willis, come on up here; let's not
waste time." His head ached and he was panting in the thin
air; he was not inclined to waste time over silly girls.

He helped Willis through the smashed windscreen and
saw him settle on top of the fuselage. When he looked into
the cockpit again it was evident that the girl had changed
her mind. Rohde was talking quietly but emphatically to her
and she crossed over and O'Hara helped her out.

Armstrong came next, having made his own way to the
cockpit. He said, " It's a bloody shambles back there. I
think the old man in the back seat is dead and his wife is
pretty badly hurt. I don't think it's safe to move her."

" What about Peabody?"

" The luggage was thrown forward on to both of us. He's
half buried under it. I tried to get him free but I couldn't."

O'Hara passed this on to Forester. Rohde was kneeling
by Montes, trying to bring him round. Forester hesitated,
then said, " Now we've got some weight at this end it might
be safe for me to go back."

O'Hara said, "Tread lightly."

Forester gave a mirthless grin and went back through the door. He looked at Miss Ponsky. She was sitting rigid, her arms clutched tightly about her, her eyes staring unblinkingly at nothing. He ignored her and began to heave suitcases from the top of Peabody, being careful to stow them in the front seats. Peabody stirred and Forester shook him into consciousness and as soon as he seemed to be able to understand, said, "Go into the cockpit—the cockpit, you understand."

Peabody nodded blearily and Forester stepped a little farther aft. "Christ Almighty!" he whispered, shocked at what he saw.

Coughlin was a bloody pulp. The cargo had shifted in the smash and had come forward, crushing the two back seats. Mrs. Coughlin was still alive but both her legs had been cut off just below the knee. It was only because she had been leaning forward to comfort Miss Ponsky that she hadn't been killed like her husband.

Forester felt something touch his back and turned. It was Peabody moving aft. "I said the cockpit, you damned fool," shouted Forester.

"I wanna get outa here," mumbled Peabody. "I wanna get out. The door's back there."

Forester wasted no time in argument. Abruptly he jabbed at Peabody's stomach and then brought his clenched fists down at the nape of his neck as he bent over gasping, knocking him cold. He dragged him forward to the door and said to Rohde, "Take care of this fool. If he causes trouble, knock him on the head."

He went back and took Miss Ponsky by the arm. "Come," he said gently.

She rose and followed him like a somnambulist and he led her right into the cockpit and delivered her to O'Hara. Montes was now conscious and would be ready to move soon.

As soon as O'Hara reappeared Forester said, "I don't think the old lady back there will make it."

"Get her out," said O'Hara tightly. "For God's sake, get her out."

So Forester went back. He didn't know whether Mrs. Coughlin was alive or dead; her body was still warm, however, so he picked her up in his arms. Blood was still spurting from her shattered shins, and when he stepped into the cockpit

Rohde drew in his breath with a hiss. "On the seat," he said. "She needs tourniquets now—immediately."

He took off his jacket and then his shirt and began to rip the shirt into strips, saying to Forester curtly, "Get the old man out."

Forester and O'Hara helped Montes through the windscreen and then Forester turned and regarded Rohde, noting the goose-pimples on his back. "Clothing," he said to O'Hara. "We'll need warm clothing. It'll be bad up here by nightfall."

"Hell!" said O'Hara. "That's adding to the risk. I don't——"

"He is right," said Rohde without turning his head. "If we do not have clothing we will all be dead by morning."

"All right," said O'Hara. "Are you willing to take the risk?"

"I'll chance it," said Forester.

"I'll get these people on the ground first," said O'Hara. "But while you're at it get the maps. There are some air charts of the area in that pocket next to my seat."

Rohde grunted. "I'll get those."

O'Hara got the people from the top of the fuselage to the ground and Forester began to bring suitcases into the cockpit. Unceremoniously he heaved Peabody through the windscreen and equally carelessly O'Hara dropped him to the ground, where he lay sprawling. Then Rohde handed through the unconscious Mrs. Coughlin and O'Hara was surprised at her lightness. Rohde climbed out and, taking her in his arms, jumped to the ground, cushioning the shock for her.

Forester began to hand out suitcases and O'Hara tossed them indiscriminately. Some burst open, but most survived the fall intact.

The Dakota lurched.

"Forester," yelled O'Hara. "Come out."

"There's still some more."

"Get out, you idiot," O'Hara bawled. "She's going."

He grabbed Forester's arms and hauled him out bodily and let him go thumping to the ground. Then he jumped himself and, as he did so, the nose rose straight into the air and the plane slid over the edge of the cliff with a grinding noise and in a cloud of dust. It crashed down two hundred feet and there was a long dying rumble and then silence.

O'Hara looked at the silent people about him, then turned his eyes to the harsh and savage mountains which surrounded them. He shivered with cold as he felt the keen wind which blew from the snowfields, and then shivered for a different reason as he locked eyes with Forester. They both knew that the odds against survival were heavy and that it was probable that the escape from the Dakota was merely the prelude to a more protracted death.

VIII

" Now, let's hear all this from the beginning," said Forester.

They had moved into the nearest of the cabins. It proved bare but weatherproof, and there was a fire-place in which Armstrong had made a fire, using wood which Willis had brought from another cabin. Montes was lying in a corner being looked after by his niece, and Peabody was nursing a hangover and looking daggers at Forester.

Miss Ponsky had recovered remarkably from the rigidity of fright. When she had been dropped to the ground she had collapsed, digging her fingers into the frozen gravel in an ecstasy of relief. O'Hara judged she would never have the guts to enter an aeroplane ever again in her life. But now she was showing remarkable aptitude for sick nursing, helping Rohde to care for Mrs. Coughlin.

Now there was a character, thought O'Hara; Rohde was a man of unsuspected depths. Although he was not a medical man, he had a good working knowledge of practical medicine which was now invaluable. O'Hara had immediately turned to Willis for help with Mrs. Coughlin, but Willis had said, " Sorry, I'm a physicist—not a physician."

" Dr. Armstrong?" O'Hara had appealed.

Regretfully Armstrong had also shaken his head. " I'm a historian."

So Rohde had taken over—the non-doctor with the medical background—and the man with the gun.

O'Hara turned his attention to Forester. " All right," he said. " This is the way it was."

He told everything that had happened, right back from the take-off in San Croce, dredging from his memory everything Grivas had said. " I think he went off his head," he concluded.

Forester frowned. " No, it was planned," he contradicted. " And lunacy isn't planned. Grivas knew this air-strip and

31

he knew the course to take. You say he was at San Croce airfield when the Samair plane was grounded?"

"That's right—I thought it was a bit odd at the time. I mean, it was out of character for Grivas to be haunting the field in the middle of the night—he wasn't that keen on his job."

"It sounds as though he *knew* the Samair Boeing was going to have engine trouble," commented Willis.

Forester looked up quickly and Willis said, "It's the only logical answer—he didn't just steal a plane, he stole the contents; and the contents of the plane were people from the Boeing. O'Hara says those big crates contain ordinary mining machinery and I doubt if Grivas would want that."

"That implies sabotage of the Boeing," said Forester. "If Grivas was expecting the Boeing to land at San Croce, it also implies a sizeable organisation behind him."

"We know that already," said O'Hara. "Grivas was expecting a reception committee here. He said 'They'll be here any minute.' But where are *they*?"

"And *who* are they?" asked Forester.

O'Hara thought of something else Grivas had said: ". . . they'll kill the lot of you." He kept quiet about that and asked instead, "Remember the last thing he said—'*Vivaca*'? It doesn't make sense to me. It sounds vaguely Spanish, but it's no word I know."

"My Spanish is good," said Forester deliberately. "There's no such word." He slapped the side of his leg irritably. "I'd give a lot to know what's been going on and who's responsible for all this."

A weak voice came from across the room. "I fear, gentlemen, that in a way I am responsible."

Everyone in the room, with the exception of Mrs. Coughlin, turned to look at Señor Montes.

Chapter II

Montes looked ill. He was worse than he had been in the air. His chest heaved violently as he sucked in the thin air and he had a ghastly pallor. As he opened his mouth to speak again the girl said, "Hush, *tio*, be quiet. I will tell them."

She turned and looked across the cabins at O'Hara and

Forester. "My uncle's name is not Montes," she said levelly. "It is Aguillar." She said it as though it was an explanation, entire and complete in itself.

There was a moment of blank silence, then O'Hara snapped his fingers and said softly, "By God, the old eagle himself." He stared at the sick man.

"Yes, Señor O'Hara," whispered Aguillar. "But a crippled eagle, I am afraid."

"Say, what the hell is this?" grumbled Peabody. "What's so special about him?"

Willis gave Peabody a look of dislike and got to his feet. "I wouldn't have put it that way myself," he said. "But I could bear to know more."

O'Hara said, "Señor Aguillar was possibly the best president this country ever had until the army took over five years ago. He got out of the country just one jump ahead of a firing squad."

"General Lopez always was a hasty man," agreed Aguillar with a weak smile.

"You mean the government arranged all this—this jam we're in now—just to get you?" Willis's voice was shrill with incredulity.

Aguillar shook his head and started to speak, but the girl said, "No, you must be quiet." She looked at O'Hara appealingly. "Do not question him now, señor. Can't you see he is ill?"

"Can you speak for your uncle?" asked Forester gently. She looked at the old man and he nodded. "What is it you want to know?" she asked.

"What is your uncle doing back in Cordillera?"

"We have come to bring back good government to our country," she said. "We have come to throw out Lopez."

O'Hara gave a short laugh. "To throw out Lopez," he said flatly. "Just like that. An old man and a girl are going to throw out a man with an army at his back." He shook his head disbelievingly.

The girl flared up. "What do you know about it; you are a foreigner—you know nothing. Lopez is finished—everyone in Cordillera knows it, even Lopez himself. He has been too greedy, too corrupt; and the country is sick of him."

Forester rubbed his chin reflectively. "She could be right," he said. "It would take just a puff of wind to blow Lopez over right now. He's run this country right into the ground in the last five years—just about milked it dry and salted enough money away in Swiss banks to last a couple of life-times. I don't think he'd risk losing out now if it came to a showdown—if someone pushed hard enough he'd fold up and get out. I think he'd take wealth and comfort instead of power and the chance of being shot by some gun-happy student with a grievance."

"Lopez has bankrupted Cordillera," the girl said. She held up her head proudly. "But when my uncle appears in Santillana the people will rise, and that will be the end of Lopez."

"It could work," agreed Forester. "Your uncle was well liked. I suppose you've prepared the ground in advance."

She nodded. "The Democratic Committee of Action has made all the arrangements. All that remains is for my uncle to appear in Santillana."

"He may not get there," said O'Hara. "Someone is trying to stop him, and if it isn't Lopez, then who the hell is it?"

"The *comunistas*," the girl spat out with loathing in her voice. "They cannot afford to let my uncle get into power again. They want Cordillera for their own."

Forester said, "It figures. Lopez is a dead duck, come what may; so it's Aguillar versus the communists with Cordillera as the stake."

"They are not quite ready," the girl said. "They do not have enough support among the people. During the last two years they have been infiltrating the government very cleverly and if they had their way the people would wake up one morning to find Lopez gone, leaving a communist government to take his place."

"Swapping one dictatorship for another," said Forester. "Very clever."

"But they are not yet ready to get rid of Lopez," she said. "My uncle would spoil their plans—he would get rid of Lopez and the government, too. He would hold elections for the first time in nine years. So the communists are trying to stop him."

"And you think Grivas was a communist?" queried O'Hara.

Forester snapped his fingers. "Of course he was. That explains his last words. He was a communist, all right— Latin-American blend; when he said '*vivaca*' he was trying to say '*Viva* Castro.'" His voice hardened. "And we can expect his buddies along any minute."

"We must leave here quickly," said the girl. "They must not find my uncle."

O'Hara suddenly swung round and regarded Rohde, who had remained conspicuously silent. He said, "What do you import, Señor Rohde?"

"It is all right, Señor O'Hara," said Aguillar weakly. "Miguel is my secretary."

Forester looked at Rohde. "More like your bodyguard."

Aguillar flapped his hand limply as though the distinction was of no consequence, and Forester said, "What put you on to him, O'Hara?"

"I don't like men who carry guns," said O'Hara shortly. "Especially men who could be communist." He looked around the cabin. "All right, are there any more jokers in the pack? What about you, Forester? You seem to know a hell of a lot about local politics for an American businessman."

"Don't be a damn fool," said Forester. "If I didn't take an interest in local politics my corporation would fire me. Having the right kind of government is important to us, and we sure as hell don't want a commie set-up in Cordillera."

He took out his wallet and extracted a business card which he handed to O'Hara. It informed him that Raymond Forester was the South American sales manager for the Fairfield Machine Tool Corporation.

O'Hara gave it back to him. "Was Grivas the only communist aboard?" he said. "That's what I'm getting at. When we were coming in to land, did any of the passengers take any special precautions for their safety?"

Forester thought about it, then shook his head. "Everyone seemed to be taken by surprise—I don't think any of us knew just what was happening." He looked at O'Hara with respect. "In the circumstances that was a good question to ask."

"Well, I'm not a communist," said Miss Ponsky sharply. "The very idea!"

O'Hara smiled. "My apologies, Miss Ponsky," he said politely.

Rohde had been tending to Mrs. Coughlin; now he stood up. "This lady is dying," he said. "She has lost much blood and she is in shock. And she has the *soroche*—the mountain-sickness. If she does not get oxygen she will surely die." His black eyes switched to Aguillar, who seemed to have fallen asleep. "The Señor also must have oxygen—he's in grave danger." He looked at them. "We must go down the mountain. To stay at this height is very dangerous."

O'Hara was conscious of a vicious headache and the fact that his heart was thumping rapidly. He had been long enough

35

in the country to have heard of *soroche* and its effects. The lower air pressure on the mountain heights meant less oxygen, the respiratory rate went up and so did the heart-beat rate, pumping the blood faster. It killed a weak constitution.

He said slowly, " There were oxygen cylinders in the plane —maybe they're not busted."

" Good," said Rohde. " We will look, you and I. It would be better not to move this lady if possible. But if we do not find the oxygen, then we must go down the mountain."

Forester said, " We must keep a fire going—the rest of us will look for wood." He paused. " Bring some petrol from the plane—we may need it."

" All right," said O'Hara.

" Come on," said Forester to Peabody. " Let's move."

Peabody lay where he was, gasping. " I'm beat," he said. " And my head's killing me."

" It's just a hangover," said Forester callously. " Get on your feet, man."

Rohde put his hand on Forester's arm. " *Soroche*," he said warningly. " He will not be able to do much. Come, Señor."

O'Hara followed Rohde from the cabin and shivered in the biting air. He looked around. The air-strip was built on the only piece of level ground in the vicinity; all else was steeply shelving mountainside, and all around were the pinnacles of the high Andes, clear-cut in the cold and crystal air. They soared skyward, blindingly white against the blue where the snows lay on their flanks, and where the slope was too steep for the snow to stay was the dark grey of the rock.

It was cold, desolate and utterly lifeless. There was no restful green of vegetation, or the flick of a bird's wing—just black, white and the blue of the sky, a hard, dark metallic blue as alien as the landscape.

O'Hara pulled his jacket closer about him and looked at the other huts. " What is this place?"

" It is a mine," said Rohde. " Copper and zinc—the tunnels are over there." He pointed to a cliff face at the end of the air-strip and O'Hara saw the dark mouths of several tunnels driven into the cliff face. Rohde shook his head. " But it is too high to work—they should never have tried. No man can work well at this height; not even our mountain *indios*."

" You know this place then?"

36

" I know these mountains well," said Rohde. " I was born not far from here."

They trudged along the air-strip and before they had gone a hundred yards O'Hara felt exhausted. His head ached and he felt nauseated. He sucked the thin air into his lungs and his chest heaved.

Rohde stopped and said, " You must not force your breathing."

" What else can I do?" asked O'Hara, panting. " I've got to get enough air."

" Breathe naturally, without effort," said Rohde. " You will get enough air. But if you force your breathing you will wash all the carbon dioxide from your lungs, and that will upset the acid base of your blood and you will get muscle cramps. And that is very bad."

O'Hara moderated his breathing and said, " You seem to know a lot about it."

" I studied medicine once," said Rohde briefly.

They reached the far end of the strip and looked over the edge of the cliff. The Dakota was pretty well smashed up; the port wing had broken off, as had the entire tail section. Rohde studied the terrain. " We need not climb down the cliff; it will be easier to go round."

It took them a long time to get to the plane and when they got there they found only one oxygen cylinder intact. It was difficult to get it free and out of the aircraft, but they managed it after chopping away a part of the fuselage with the axe that O'Hara found on the floor of the cockpit.

The gauge showed that the cylinder was only a third full and O'Hara cursed Filson and his cheese-paring, but Rohde seemed satisfied. " It will be enough," he said. " We can stay in the hut to-night."

" What happens if these communists turn up?" asked O'Hara.

Rohde seemed unperturbed. " Then we will defend ourselves," he said equably. " One thing at a time, Señor O'Hara."

" Grivas seemed to think they were already here," said O'Hara. " I wonder what held them up?"

Rohde shrugged. " Does it matter?"

They could not manhandle the oxygen cylinder back to the huts without help, so Rohde went back, taking with him some mouthpieces and a bottle of petrol tapped from a wing tank. O'Hara searched the fuselage, looking for anything that might be of value, particularly food. That, he thought, might turn out to be a major problem. All he found was half a slab of milk chocolate in Grivas's seat pocket.

Rohde came back with Forester, Willis and Armstrong and they took it in turns carrying the oxygen cylinder, two by two. It was very hard work and they could only manage to move it twenty yards at a time. O'Hara estimated that back in San Croce he could have picked it up and carried it a mile, but the altitude seemed to have sucked all the strength from their muscles and they could work only a few minutes at a time before they collapsed in exhaustion.

When they got it to the hut they found that Miss Ponsky was feeding the fire with wood from a door of one of the other huts that Willis and Armstrong had torn down and smashed up laboriously with rocks. Willis was particularly glad to see the axe. " It'll be easier now," he said.

Rohde administered oxygen to Mrs. Coughlin and Aguillar. She remained unconscious, but it made a startling difference to the old man. As the colour came back to his cheeks his niece smiled for the first time since the crash.

O'Hara sat before the fire, feeling the warmth soak into him, and produced his air charts. He spread the relevant chart on the floor and pin-pointed a position with a pencilled cross. " That's where we were when we changed course," he said. " We flew on a true course of one-eighty-four for a shade over five minutes." He drew a line on the chart. " We were flying at a little over two hundred knots—say, two hundred and forty miles an hour. That's about twenty miles —so that puts us about—*here*." He made another cross.

Forester looked over his shoulder. " The air-strip isn't marked on the map," he said.

" Rohde said it was abandoned," said O'Hara.

Rohde came over and looked at the map and nodded. " You are right," he said. " That is where we are. The road down the mountain leads to the refinery. That also is abandoned, but I think some *indios* live there still."

" How far is that?" asked Forester.

" About forty kilometres," said Rohde.

" Twenty-five miles," translated Forester. " That's a hell of a long way in these conditions."

" It will not be very bad," said Rohde. He put his finger on the map. " When we get to this valley where the river

38

runs we will be nearly five thousand feet lower and we will breathe more easily. That is about sixteen kilometres by the road."

"We'll start early to-morrow," said O'Hara.

Rohde agreed. "If we had no oxygen I would have said go now. But it would be better to stay in the shelter of this hut to-night."

"What about Mrs. Coughlin?" said O'Hara quietly. "Can we move her?"

"We will have to move her," said Rohde positively. "She cannot live at this altitude."

"We'll rig together some kind of stretcher," said Forester. "We can make a sling out of clothing and poles—or maybe use a door."

O'Hara looked across to where Mrs. Coughlin was breathing stertorously, closely watched by Miss Ponsky. His voice was harsh. "I'd rather that bastard Grivas was still alive if that would give her back her legs," he said.

II

Mrs. Coughlin died during the night without regaining consciousness. They found her in the morning cold and stiff. Miss Ponsky was in tears. "I should have stayed awake," she sniffled. "I *couldn't* sleep most of the night, and then I had to drop off."

Rohde shook his head gravely. "She would have died," he said. "We could not do anything for her—none of us."

Forester, O'Hara and Peabody scratched out a shallow grave. Peabody seemed better and O'Hara thought that maybe Forester had been right when he said that Peabody was only suffering from a hangover. However, he had to be prodded into helping to dig the grave.

It seemed that everyone had had a bad night, no one sleeping very well. Rohde said that it was another symptom of *soroche* and the sooner they got to a lower altitude the better. O'Hara still had a splitting headache and heartily concurred.

The oxygen cylinder was empty.

O'Hara tapped the gauge with his finger but the needle stubbornly remained at zero. He opened the cock and bent his head to listen but there was no sound from the valve. He had heard the gentle hiss of oxygen several times during the night and had assumed that Rohde had been tending to Mrs. Coughlin or Aguillar.

He beckoned to Rohde. "Did you use all the oxygen last night?"

Rohde looked incredulously at the gauge. "I was saving some for to-day," he said. "Señor Aguillar needs it."

O'Hara bit his lip and looked across to where Peabody sat. "I thought he looked pretty chipper this morning."

Rohde growled something under his breath and took a step forward, but O'Hara caught his arm. "It can't be proved," he said. "I could be wrong. And anyway, we don't want any rows right here. Let's get down this mountain." He kicked the cylinder and it clanged emptily. "At least we won't have to carry this."

He remembered the chocolate and brought it out. There were eight small squares to be divided between ten of them, so he, Rohde and Forester did without and Aguillar had two pieces. O'Hara thought that he must have had three because the girl did not appear to eat her ration.

Armstrong and Willis appeared to work well as a team. Using the axe, they had ripped some timber from one of the huts and made a rough stretcher by pushing lengths of wood through the sleeves of two overcoats. That was for Aguillar, who could not walk.

They put on all the clothes they could and left the rest in suitcases. Forester gave O'Hara a bulky overcoat. "Don't mess it about if you can help it," he said. "That's vicuna—it cost a lot of dough." He grinned. "The boss's wife asked me to get it this trip; it's the old man's birthday soon."

Peabody grumbled when he had to leave his luggage and grumbled more when O'Hara assigned him to a stretcher-carrying stint. O'Hara resisted taking a poke at him; for one thing he did not want open trouble, and for another he did not know whether he had the strength to do any damage. At the moment it was all he could do to put one foot in front of the other.

So they left the huts and went down the road, turning their backs on the high peaks. The road was merely a rough track cut out of the mountainside. It wound down in a series of hairpin bends and Willis pointed out where blasting had been done on the corners. It was just wide enough to take a single vehicle but, from time to time, they came across a wide part where two trucks could pass.

O'Hara asked Rohde, "Did they intend to truck all the ore from the mine?"

"They would have built a telfer," said Rohde. "An endless rope with buckets. But they were still proving the mine. Petrol engines do not work well up here—they need superchargers." He stopped suddenly and stared at the ground.

In a patch of snow was the track of a tyre.

"Someone's been up here lately," observed O'Hara. "Super-charged or not. But I knew that."

"How?" Rohde demanded.

"The air-strip had been cleared of snow."

Rohde patted his breast and moved away without saying anything. O'Hara remembered the pistol and wondered what would happen if they came up against opposition.

Although the path was downhill and the going comparatively good, it was only possible to carry the stretcher a hundred yards at a time. Forester organised relays, and as one set of carriers collapsed exhaustedly another took over. Aguillar was in a comatose condition and the girl walked next to the stretcher, anxiously watching him. After a mile they stopped for a rest and O'Hara said to Rohde, "I've got a flask of spirits. I've been saving it for when things really get tough. Do you think it would help the old man?"

"Let me have it," said Rohde.

O'Hara took the flask from his hip and gave it to Rohde, who took off the cap and sniffed the contents. "*Aguardiente*," he said. "Not the best drink but it will do." He looked at O'Hara curiously. "Do you drink this?"

"I'm a poor man," said O'Hara defensively.

Rohde smiled. "When I was a student I also was poor. I also drank *aguardiente*. But I do not recommend too much." He looked across at Aguillar. "I think we save this for later." He recapped the flask and handed it back to O'Hara. As O'Hara was replacing it in his pocket he saw Peabody staring at him. He smiled back pleasantly.

After a rest of half an hour they started off again. O'Hara in the lead, looked back and thought they looked like a bunch of war refugees. Willis and Armstrong were stumbling along with the stretcher, the girl keeping pace alongside; Miss Ponsky was sticking close to Rohde, chatting as though on a Sunday afternoon walk, despite her shortness of breath, and Forester was in the rear with Peabody shambling beside him.

After the third stop O'Hara found that things were going better. His step felt lighter and his breathing eased, although the headache stayed with him. The stretcher-bearers found that they could carry for longer periods, and Aguillar had come round and was taking notice.

O'Hara mentioned this to Rohde, who pointed at the steep slopes about them. "We are losing a lot of height," he said. "It will get better now."

After the fourth halt O'Hara and Forester were carrying the stretcher. Aguillar apologised in a weak voice for the inconvenience he was causing, but O'Hara forbore to answer —he needed all his breath for the job. Things weren't that much better.

Forester suddenly stopped and O'Hara thankfully laid down the stretcher. His legs felt rubbery and the breath rasped in his throat. He grinned at Forester, who was beating his hands against his chest. "Never mind," he said. "It should be warmer down in the valley."

Forester blew on his fingers. "I hope so." He looked up at O'Hara. "You're a pretty good pilot," he said. "I've done some flying in my time, but I don't think I could do what you did yesterday."

"You might if you had a pistol at your head," said O'Hara with a grimace. "Anyway, I couldn't leave it to Grivas— he'd have killed the lot of us, starting with me first."

He looked past Forester and saw Rohde coming back up the road at a stumbling run, his gun in his hand. "Something's happening."

He went forward to meet Rohde, who gasped, his chest heaving, "There are huts here—I had forgotten them."

O'Hara looked at the gun. "Do you need that?"

Rohde gave a stark smile. "It is possible, señor." He waved casually down the road with the pistol. "I think we should be careful. I think we should look first before doing anything. You, me, and Señor Forester."

"I think so too," said Forester. "Grivas said his pals would be around and this seems a likely place to meet them."

"All right," said O'Hara, and looked about. There was no cover on the road but there was a jumble of rocks a little way back. "I think everyone else had better stick behind that lot," he said. "If anything does break, there's no point in being caught in the open."

They went back to shelter behind the rocks and O'Hara

told everyone what was happening. He ended by saying, "If there's shooting you don't do a damned thing—you freeze and stay put. Now I know we're not an army but we're likely to come under fire all the same—so I'm naming Doctor Willis as second-in-command. If anything happens to us you take your orders from him." Willis nodded.

Aguillar's niece was talking to Rohde, and as O'Hara went to join Forester she touched him on the arm. "Señor."

He looked down at her. "Yes, señorita."

"Please be careful, you and Señor Forester. I would not want anything to happen to you because of us."

"I'll be careful," said O'Hara. "Tell me, is your name the same as your uncle's?"

"I am Benedetta Aguillar," she said.

He nodded. "I'm Tim O'Hara. I'll be careful."

He joined the other two and they walked down the road to the bend. Rohde said, "These huts were where the miners lived. This is just about as high as a man can live permanently—a man who is acclimatised such as our mountain *indios*. I think we should leave the road here and approach from the side. If Grivas did have friends, here is where we will find them."

They took to the mountainside and came upon the camp from the top. A level place had been roughly bulldozed out of the side of the mountain and there were about a dozen timber-built huts, very much like the huts by the air-strip.

"This is no good," said Forester. "We'll have to go over this miniature cliff before we can get at them."

"There's no smoke," O'Hara pointed out.

"Maybe that means something—maybe it doesn't," said Forester. "I think that Rohde and I will go round and come up from the bottom. If anything happens, maybe you can cause a diversion from up here."

"What do I do?" asked O'Hara. "Throw stones?"

Forester shook with silent laughter. He pointed down the slope to beyond the camp. "We'll come out about there. You can see us from here but we'll be out of sight of anyone in the camp. If all's clear you can give us the signal to come up." He looked at Rohde, who nodded.

Forester and Rohde left quietly and O'Hara lay on his belly, looking down at the camp. He did not think there was anyone there. It was less than five miles up to the air-strip by the road and there was nothing to stop anybody going up there. If Grivas's confederates were anywhere, it was not likely that they would be at this camp—but it was as well to make sure. He scanned the huts but saw no sign of movement.

Presently he saw Forester wave from the side of the rock he had indicated and he waved back. Rohde went up first, in a wide arc to come upon the camp at an angle. Then Forester moved forward in the peculiar scuttling, zigzagging run of the experienced soldier who expects to be shot at. O'Hara wondered about Forester; the man had said he could fly an aeroplane and now he was behaving like a trained infantryman. He had an eye for ground, too, and was obviously accustomed to command.

Forester disappeared behind one of the huts and then Rohde came into sight at the far end of the camp, moving warily with his gun in his hand. He too disappeared, and O'Hara felt tension. He waited for what seemed a very long time, then Forester walked out from behind the nearest hut, moving quite unconcernedly. " You can come down," he called. " There's no one here."

O'Hara let out his breath with a rush and stood up. " I'll go back and get the rest of the people down here," he shouted, and Forester waved in assent.

O'Hara went back up the road, collected the party and took them down to the camp. Forester and Rohde were waiting in the main " street " and Forester called out, " We've struck it lucky; there's a lot of food here."

Suddenly O'Hara realised that he hadn't eaten for a day and a half. He did not feel particularly hungry, but he knew that if he did not eat he could not last out much longer—and neither could any of the others. To have food would make a lot of difference on the next leg of the journey.

Forester said, " Most of the huts are empty, but three of them are fitted out as living quarters complete with kerosene heaters."

O'Hara looked down at the ground which was criss-crossed with tyre tracks. " There's something funny going on," he said. " Rohde told me that the mine has been abandoned for a long time, yet there's all these signs of life and no one around. What the hell's going on?"

Forester shrugged. " Maybe the commie organisation is slipping," he said. " The Latins have never been noted for good planning. Maybe someone's put a spoke in their wheel."

" Maybe," said O'Hara. " We might as well take advantage of it. What do you think we should do now—how long should we stay here?"

Forester looked at the group entering one of the huts, then up at the sky. "We're pretty beat," he said. "Maybe we ought to stay here until to-morrow. It'll take us a while to get fed and it'll be late before we can move out. We ought to stay here to-night and keep warm."

"We'll consult Rohde," said O'Hara. "He's the expert on mountains and altitude."

The huts were well fitted. There were paraffin stoves, bunks, plenty of blankets and a large assortment of canned foods. On the table in one of the huts there were the remnants of a meal, the plates dirty and unwashed and frozen dregs of coffee in the bottoms of tin mugs. O'Hara felt the thickness of the ice and it cracked beneath the pressure of his finger.

"They haven't been gone long," he said. "If the hut was unheated this stuff would have frozen to the bottom." He passed the mug to Rohde. "What do you think?"

Rohde looked at the ice closely. "If they turned off the heaters when they left, the hut would stay warm for a while," he said. He tested the ice and thought deeply. "I would say two days," he said finally.

"Say yesterday morning," suggested O'Hara. "That would be about the time we took off from San Croce."

Forester groaned in exasperation. "It doesn't make sense. Why did they go to all this trouble, make all these preparations, and then clear out? One thing's sure: Grivas expected a reception committee—and where the hell is it?"

O'Hara said to Rohde, "We are thinking of staying here to-night. What do you think?"

"It is better here than at the mine," said Rohde. "We have lost a lot of height. I would say that we are at an altitude of about four thousand metres here—or maybe a little more. That will not harm us for one night; it will be better to stay here in shelter than to stay in the open to-night, even if it is lower down the mountain." He contracted his brows. "But I suggest we keep a watch."

Forester nodded. "We'll take it in turns."

Miss Ponsky and Benedetta were busy on the pressure stoves making hot soup. Armstrong had already got the heater going and Willis was sorting out cans of food. He called O'Hara over. "I thought we'd better take something with us when we leave," he said. "It might come in useful."

"A good idea," said O'Hara.

Willis grinned. "That's all very well, but I can't read Spanish. I have to go by the pictures on the labels. Someone had better check on these when I've got them sorted out."

Forester and Rohde went on down the road to pick a good spot for a sentry, and when Forester came back he said, "Rohde's taking the first watch. We've got a good place where we can see bits of road a good two miles away. And if they come up at night they're sure to have their lights on."

He looked at his watch. "We've got six able-bodied men, so if we leave here early to-morrow, that means two-hour watches. That's not too bad—it gives us all enough sleep."

After they had eaten Benedetta took some food down to Rohde and O'Hara found himself next to Armstrong. "You said you were a historian. I suppose you're over here to check up on the Incas," he said.

"Oh, no," said Armstrong. "They're not my line of country at all. My line is medieval history."

"Oh," said O'Hara blankly.

"I don't know anything about the Incas and I don't particularly want to," said Armstrong frankly. He smiled gently. "For the past ten years I've never had a real holiday. I'd go on holiday like a normal man—perhaps to France or Italy—and then I'd see something interesting. I'd do a bit of investigating—and before I'd know it I'd be hard at work."

He produced a pipe and peered dubiously into his tobacco pouch. "This year I decided to come to South America for a holiday. All there is here is pre-European and modern history—no medieval history at all. Clever of me, wasn't it?"

O'Hara smiled, suspecting that Armstrong was indulging in a bit of gentle leg-pulling. "And what's your line, Doctor Willis?" he asked.

"I'm a physicist," said Willis. "I'm interested in cosmic rays at high altitudes. I'm not getting very far with it, though."

They were certainly a mixed lot, thought O'Hara, looking across at Miss Ponsky as she talked animatedly to Aguillar. Now there was a sight—a New England spinster schoolmarm lecturing a statesman. She would certainly have plenty to tell her pupils when she arrived back at the little schoolhouse.

"What was this place, anyway?" asked Willis.

"Living quarters for the mine up on top," said O'Hara. "That's what Rohde tells me."

Willis nodded. "They had their workshops down here, too," he said. "All the machinery has gone, of course, but there are still a few bits and pieces left." He shivered. "I can't say I'd like to work in a place like this."

O'Hara looked about the hut. "Neither would I." He caught sight of an electric conduit tube running down a wall. "Where did their electricity supply come from, I wonder?"

"They had their own plant; there's the remains of it out back. The generator has gone—they must have salvaged it when the mine closed down. They scavenged most everything, I guess; there's precious little left."

Armstrong drew the last of the smoke from his failing pipe with a disconsolate gurgle. "Well, that's the last of the tobacco until we get back to civilisation," he said as he knocked out the dottle. "Tell me, Captain; what are you doing in this part of the world?"

"Oh, I fly aeroplanes from anywhere to anywhere," said O'Hara. Not any more I don't, he thought. As far as Filson was concerned, he was finished. Filson would never forgive a pilot who wrote off one of his aircraft, no matter what the reason. I've lost my job, he thought. It was a lousy job but it had kept him going, and now he'd lost it.

The girl came back and he crossed over to her. "Anything doing down the road?" he asked.

She shook her head. "Nothing. Miguel says everything is quiet."

"He's quite a character," said O'Hara. "He certainly knows a lot about these mountains—and he knows a bit about medicine too."

"He was born near here," Benedetta said. "And he was a medical student until——" She stopped.

"Until what?" prompted O'Hara.

"Until the revolution." She looked at her hands. "All his family were killed—that is why he hates Lopez. That is why he works with my uncle—he knows that my uncle will ruin Lopez."

"I thought he had a chip on his shoulder," said O'Hara.

She sighed. "It is a great pity about Miguel; he was going to do so much. He was very interested in the *soroche*, you know; he intended to study it as soon as he had taken his degree. But when the revolution came he had to leave the country and he had no money so he could not continue his studies. He worked in the Argentine for a while, and then he met my uncle. He saved my uncle's life."

47

" Oh?" O'Hara raised his eyebrows.

" In the beginning Lopez knew that he was not safe while my uncle was alive. He knew that my uncle would organise an opposition—underground, you know. So wherever my uncle went he was in danger from the murderers hired by Lopez—even in the Argentine. There were several attempts to kill him, and it was one of these times that Miguel saved his life."

O'Hara said, " Your uncle must have felt like another Trotsky. Joe Stalin had him bumped off in Mexico."

" That is right," she said with a grimace of distaste. " But they were communists, both of them. Anyway, Miguel stayed with us after that. He said that all he wanted was food to eat and a bed to sleep in, and he would help my uncle come back to Cordillera. And here we are."

Yes, thought O'Hara; marooned up a bloody mountain with God knows what waiting at the bottom.

Presently, Armstrong went out to relieve Rohde. Miss Ponsky came across to talk to O'Hara. " I'm sorry I behaved so stupidly in the airplane," she said crossly. " I don't know what came over me."

O'Hara thought there was no need to apologise for being half frightened to death; he had been bloody scared himself. But he couldn't say that—he couldn't even mention the word *fear* to her. That would be unforgivable; no one likes to be reminded of a lapse of that nature—not even a maiden lady getting on in years. He smiled and said diplomatically, " Not everyone would have come through an experience like that as well as you have, Miss Ponsky."

She was mollified and he knew that she had been in fear of a rebuff. She was the kind of person who would bite on a sore tooth, not letting it alone. She smiled and said, " Well now, Captain O'Hara—what do you think of all this talk about communists?"

" I think they're capable of anything," said O'Hara grimly.

" I'm going to put in a report to the State Department when I get back," she said. " You ought to hear what Señor Aguillar has been telling me about General Lopez. I think the State Department should help Señor Aguillar against General Lopez *and* the communists."

" I'm inclined to agree with you," said O'Hara. " But perhaps your State Department doesn't believe in interfering in Cordilleran affairs."

" Stuff and nonsense," said Miss Ponsky with acerbity.

"We're supposed to be fighting the communists, aren't we? Besides, Señor Aguillar assures me that he'll hold elections as soon as General Lopez is kicked out. He's a *real* democrat just like you and me."

O'Hara wondered what would happen if another South American state did go communist. Cuban agents were filtering all through Latin America like woodworms in a piece of furniture. He tried to think of the strategic importance of Cordillera—it was on the Pacific coast and it straddled the Andes, a gun pointing to the heart of the continent. He thought the Americans would be very upset if Cordillera went communist.

Rohde came back and talked for a few minutes with Aguillar, then he crossed to O'Hara and said in a low voice, "Señor Aguillar would like to speak to you." He gestured to Forester and the three of them went to where Aguillar was resting in a bunk.

He had brightened considerably and was looking quite spry. His eyes were lively and no longer filmed with weariness, and there was a strength and authority in his voice that O'Hara had not heard before. He realised that this was a strong man; maybe not too strong in the body because he was becoming old and his body was wearing out, but he had a strong mind. O'Hara suspected that if the old man had not had a strong will, the body would have crumpled under the strain it had undergone.

Aguillar said, "First I must thank you gentlemen for all you have done, and I am truly sorry that I have brought this calamity upon you." He shook his head sadly. "It is the innocent bystander who always suffers in the clash of our Latin politics. I am sorry that this should have happened and that you should see my country in this sad light."

"What else could we do?" asked Forester. "We're all in the same boat."

"I'm glad you see it that way," said Aguillar. "Because of what may come next. What happens if we meet up with the communists who should be here and are not?"

"Before we come to that there's something I'd like to query," said O'Hara. Aguillar raised his eyebrows and motioned him to continue, so O'Hara said deliberately, "How do we know they are communists? Señorita Aguillar tells me that Lopez has tried to liquidate you several times. How do you know he hasn't got wind of your return and is having another crack at you?"

Aguillar shook his head. "Lopez has—in your English idiom—shot his bolt. I *know*. Do not forget that I am a practical politician and give me credit for knowing my own work. Lopez forgot about me several years ago and is only interested in how he can safely relinquish the reins of power and retire. As for the communists—for years I have watched them work in my country, undermining the government and wooing the people. They have not got far with the people, or they would have disposed of Lopez by now. I am their only danger and I am sure that our situation is their work."

Forester said casually, "Grivas was trying to make a clenched fist salute when he died."

"All right," said O'Hara. "But why all this rigmarole of Grivas in the first place? Why not just put a time bomb in the Dakota—that would have done the job very easily."

Aguillar smiled. "Señor O'Hara, in my life as a politician I have had four bombs thrown at me and every one was defective. Our politics out here are emotional and emotion does not make for careful workmanship, even of bombs. And I am sure that even communism cannot make any difference to the native characteristics of my people. They wanted to make very sure of me and so they chose the unfortunate Grivas as their instrument. Would you have called Grivas an emotional man?"

"I should think he was," said O'Hara, thinking of Grivas's exultation even in death. "And he was pretty slipshod too."

Aguillar spread his hands, certain he had made his point. But he drove it home. "Grivas would be happy to be given such work; it would appeal to his sense of drama—and my people have a great sense of drama. As for being—er—slipshod, Grivas bungled the first part of the operation by stupidly killing himself, and the others have bungled the rest of it by not being here to meet us."

O'Hara rubbed his chin. As Aguillar drew the picture it made a weird kind of sense.

Aguillar said, "Now, my friends, we come to the next point. Supposing, on the way down this mountain, we meet these men—these communists? What happens then?" He regarded O'Hara and Forester with bright eyes. "It is not your fight—you are not Cordillerans—and I am interested to know what you would do. Would you give this dago politician into the hands of his enemies or . . ."

"Would we fight?" finished Forester.

"It's my fight," said O'Hara bluntly. "I'm not a Cordilleran, but Grivas pulled a gun on me and made me crash my plane. I didn't like that, and I didn't like the sight of the Coughlins. Anyway, I don't like the sight of communists, and I think that, all in all, this is my fight."

"I concur," said Forester.

Aguillar raised his hand. "But it is not as easy as that, is it? There are others to take into account. Would it be fair on Miss—er—Ponsky, for instance? Now what I propose is this. Miguel, my niece and I will withdraw into another cabin while you talk it over—and I will abide by your joint decision."

Forester looked speculatively at Peabody, who was just leaving the hut. He glanced at O'Hara, then said, "I think we should leave the question of fighting until there's something to fight. It's possible that we might just walk out of here."

Aguillar had seen Forester's look at Peabody. He smiled sardonically. "I see that you are a politician yourself, Señor Forester." He made a gesture of resignation. "Very well, we will leave the problem for the moment—but I think we will have to return to it."

"It's a pity we had to come down the mountain," said Forester. "There's sure to be an air search, and it might have been better to stay by the Dakota."

"We could not have lived up there," said Rohde.

"I know, but it's a pity all the same."

"I don't think it makes much difference," said O'Hara. "The wreck will be difficult to spot from the air—it's right at the foot of a cliff." He hesitated. "And I don't know about an air search—not yet, anyway."

Forester jerked his head. "What the hell do you mean by that?"

"Andes Airlift isn't noted for its efficiency and Filson, my boss, isn't good at paperwork. This flight didn't even have a number—I remember wondering about it just before we took off. It's on the cards that San Croce control haven't bothered to notify Santillana to expect us." As he saw Forester's expression he added, "The whole set-up is shoestring and sealing-wax—it's only a small field."

"But surely your boss will get worried when he doesn't hear from you?"

"He'll worry," agreed O'Hara. "He told me to phone him from Santillana—but he won't worry too much at first. There have been times when I haven't phoned through on his say-so and had a rocket for losing cargo. But I don't
51

think he'll worry about losing the plane for a couple of days at least."

Forester blew out his cheeks. "Wow—what a Rube Goldberg organisation. Now I really feel lost."

Rohde said, "We must depend on our own efforts. I think we can be sure of that."

"We flew off course too," said O'Hara. "They'll start the search north of here—when they start."

Rohde looked at Aguillar whose eyes were closed. "There is nothing we can do now," he said. "But we must sleep. It will be a hard day to-morrow."

Again, O'Hara did not sleep very well, but at least he was resting on a mattress instead of a hard floor with a full belly. Peabody was on watch and O'Hara was due to relieve him at two o'clock; he was glad when the time came.

He donned his leather jacket and took the vicuna coat that Forester had given him. He suspected that he would be glad of it during the next two hours. Forester was awake and waved lazily as he went out, although he did not speak.

The night air was thin and cold and O'Hara shivered as he set off down the road. As Rohde had said, the conditions for survival were better here than up by the air-strip, but it was still pretty dicey. He was aware that his heart was thumping and that his respiration rate was up. It would be much better when they got down to the *quebrada,* as Rohde called the lateral valley to which they were heading.

He reached the corner where he had to leave the road and headed towards the looming outcrop of rock which Rohde had picked as a vantage point. Peabody should have been perched on top of the rock and should have heard him coming, but there was no sign of his presence.

O'Hara called softly, "Peabody!"

There was silence.

Cautiously he circled the outcrop to get it silhouetted against the night sky. There was a lump on top of the rock which he could not quite make out. He began to climb the rock and as he reached the top he heard a muffled snore. He shook Peabody and his foot clinked on a bottle—Peabody was drunk.

"You bloody fool," he said and started to slap Peabody's

face, but without appreciable result. Peabody muttered in his drunken stupor but did not recover consciousness. " I ought to let you die of exposure," whispered O'Hara viciously, but he knew he could not do that. He also knew that he could not hope to carry Peabody back to the camp by himself. He would have to get help.

He stared down the mountainside but all was quiet, so he climbed down the rock and headed back up the road. Forester was still awake and looked up inquiringly as O'Hara entered the hut. " What's the matter?" he asked, suddenly alert.

" Peabody's passed out," said O'Hara. " I'll need help to bring him up."

" Damn this altitude," said Forester, putting on his shoes.

" It wasn't the altitude," O'Hara said coldly. " The bastard's dead drunk."

Forester muffled an imprecation. " Where did he get the stuff?"

" I suppose he found it in one of the huts," said O'Hara. " I've still got my flask—I was saving it for Aguillar."

" All right," said Forester. " Let's lug the damn fool up here."

It wasn't an easy thing to do. Peabody was a big, flabby man and his body lolled unco-operatively, but they managed it at last and dumped him unceremoniously in a bunk. Forester gasped and said, " This idiot will be the death of us all if we don't watch him." He paused. " I'll come down with you—it might be better to have two pairs of eyes down there right now."

They went back and climbed up on to the rock, lying side by side and scanning the dark mountainside. For fifteen minutes they were silent, but saw and heard nothing. " I think it's okay," said Forester at last. He shifted his position to ease his bones. " What do you think of the old man?"

" He seems all right to me," said O'Hara.

" He's a good joe—a good liberal politician. If he lasts long enough he might end up by being a good liberal statesman —but liberals don't last long in this part of the world, and I think he's a shade too soft." Forester chuckled. " Even when it's a matter of life and death—*his* life and death, not to mention his niece's—he still sticks to democratic procedure. He wants us to vote on whether we shall hand him over to the commies. Imagine that!"

" I wouldn't hand anyone over to the communists," said O'Hara. He glanced sideways at the dark bulk of Forester.

"You said you could fly a plane—I suppose you do it as a matter of business; company plane and all that."

"Hell, no," said Forester. "My outfit's not big enough or advanced enough for that. I was in the Air Force—I flew in Korea."

"So did I," said O'Hara. "I was in the R.A.F."

"Well, what do you know." Forester was delighted. "Where were you based?"

O'Hara told him and he said, "Then you were flying Sabres like I was. We went on joint operations—hell, we must have flown together."

"Probably."

They lay in companionable silence for a while, then Forester said, "Did you knock down any of those Migs? I got four, then they pulled me out. I was mad about that —I wanted to be a war hero; an ace, you know."

"You've got to get five in the American Air Force, haven't you?"

"That's right," said Forester. "Did you get any?"

"A couple," said O'Hara. He had shot down eight Migs but it was a part of his life he preferred to forget, so he didn't elaborate. Forester sensed his reserve and was quiet. After a few minutes he said, "I think I'll go back and get some sleep—if I can. We'll be on our way early."

When he had gone O'Hara stared into the darkness and thought about Korea. That had been the turning point of his life: before Korea he had been on his way up; after Korea there was just the endless slide, down to Filson and now beyond. He wondered where he would end up.

Thinking of Korea brought back Margaret and the letter. He had read the letter while on ready call on a frozen airfield. The Americans had a name for that kind of letter—they called them "Dear Johns." She was quite matter-of-fact about it and said that they were adult and must be sensible about this thing—all the usual rationalisations which covered plain infidelity. Looking back on it afterwards O'Hara could see a little humour in it—not much, but some. He was one of the inglorious ten per cent of any army fighting away from home, and he had lost his wife to a civilian. But it wasn't funny at all reading that letter on the cold airfield in Korea.

Five minutes later there was a scramble and he was in the air and thirty minutes later he was fighting. He went into battle with cold ferocity and a total lack of judgment. In three minutes he shot down two Migs, surprising them by sheer recklessness. Then a Chinese pilot with a cooler mind shot *him* down and he spent the rest of the war in a prison cage.

He did not like to think of that period and what had happened to him. He had come out of it with honour, but the psychiatrists had a field day with him when he got back to England. They did what they could but they could not break down the shell he had built about himself—and neither, by that time, could he break out.

And so it went—invalided out of the Air Force with a pension which he promptly commuted; the good jobs—at first—and then the poorer jobs, until he got down to Filson. And always the drink—more and more booze which had less and less effect as he tried to fill and smother the aching emptiness inside him.

He moved restlessly on the rock and heard the bottle clink. He put out his hand, picked it up and held it to the sky. It was a quarter full. He smiled. He could not get drunk on that but it would be very welcome. Yet as the fiery fluid spread and warmed his gut he felt guilty.

IV

Peabody was blearily belligerent when he woke up and found O'Hara looking at him. At first he looked defensive, then his instinct for attack took over. " I'm not gonna take anything from you," he said shakily. " Not from any goddam limey."

O'Hara just looked at him. He had no wish to tax Peabody with anything. Weren't they members of the same club? he thought sardonically. Fellow drunks. Why, we even drink from the same bottle. He felt miserable.

Rohde took a step forward and Peabody screamed, " And I'm not gonna take anything from a dago either."

" Then perhaps you'll take it from me," snapped Forester. He took one stride and slapped Peabody hard on the side of the face. Peabody sagged back on the bed and looked into Forester's cold eyes with an expression of fear and bewilderment on his face. His hand came up to touch the red blotch on his cheek. He was just going to speak when Forester pushed a finger at him. " Shut up! One cheep out of you and I'll mash you into a pulp. Now get your big fat butt off that bed and get to work—and if you step out of line again I swear to God I'll kill you."

55

The ferocity in Forester's voice had a chilling effect on Peabody. All the belligerence drained out of him. "I didn't mean to——" he began.

"Shut up!" said Forester and turned his back on him. "Let's get this show on the road," he announced generally.

They took food and a pressure stove and fuel, carrying it in awkwardly contrived packs cobbled from their overcoats. O'Hara did not think that Forester's boss would thank him for the vicuna coat, already showing signs of hard use.

Aguillar said he could walk, provided he was not asked to go too fast, so Forester took the stretcher poles and lashed them together in what he called a *travois*. "The Plains Indians used this for transport," he said. "They got along without wheels—so can we." He grinned. "They pulled with horses and we have only manpower, but it's downhill all the way."

The *travois* held a lot, much more than a man could carry, and Forester and O'Hara took first turn at pulling the triangular contraption, the apex bumping and bouncing on the stony ground. The others fell into line behind them and once more they wound their way down the mountain.

O'Hara looked at his watch—it was six a.m. He began to calculate—they had not come very far the previous day, not more than four or five miles, but they had been rested, warmed and fed, and that was all to the good. He doubted if they could make more than ten miles a day, so that meant another two days to the refinery, but they had enough food for at least four days, so they would be all right even if Aguillar slowed them down. Things seemed immeasurably brighter.

The terrain around them began to change. There were tufts of grass scattered sparsely and an occasional wild flower, and as they went on these signs of life became more frequent. They were able to move faster, too, and O'Hara said to Rohde, "The low altitude seems to be doing us good."

"That—and acclimatisation," said Rohde. He smiled grimly. "If it does not kill you, you can get used to it—eventually."

They came to one of the inevitable curves in the road and Rohde stopped and pointed to a silvery thread. "That is the *quebrada*—where the river is. We cross the river and turn north. The refinery is about twenty-four kilometres from the bridge."

"What's the height above sea-level?" asked O'Hara. He was beginning to take a great interest in the air he breathed —more interest than he had ever taken in his life.

"About three thousand five hundred metres," said Rohde.

Twelve thousand feet, O'Hara thought. That's much better.

They made good time and decided they would be able to have their midday rest and some hot food on the other side of the bridge. "A little over five miles in half a day," said Forester, chewing on a piece of jerked beef. "That won't be bad going. But I hope to God that Rohde is right when he says that the refinery is still inhabited."

"We will be all right," said Rohde. "There is a village ten miles the other side of the refinery. Some of us can go on and bring back help if necessary."

They pushed on and found that suddenly they were in the valley. There was no more snow and the ground was rocky, with more clumps of tough grass. The road ceased to twist and they went past many small ponds. It was appreciably warmer too, and O'Hara found that he could stride out without losing his breath.

We've got it made, he thought exultantly.

Soon they heard the roar of the river which carried the melt-water from the snow fields behind them and suddenly they were all gay. Miss Ponsky chattered unceasingly, exclaiming once in her high-pitched voice as she saw a bird, the first living, moving thing they had seen in two days. O'Hara heard Aguillar's deep chuckle and even Peabody cheered up, recovering from Forester's tongue-lashing.

O'Hara found himself next to Benedetta. She smiled at him and said, "Who has the pressure stove? We are going to need it soon."

He pointed back to where Willis and Armstrong were pulling the *travois*. "I packed it in there," he said.

They were very near the river now and he estimated that the road would have one last turn before they came to the bridge. "Come on," he said. "Let's see what's round the corner."

They stepped out and round the curve and O'Hara suddenly stopped. There were men and vehicles on the other side of the swollen river and the bridge was down.

A faint babble of voices arose above the river's roar as they were seen and some of the men on the other side started to run. O'Hara saw a man reach into the back of a truck and lift out a rifle and there was a popping noise as others opened up with pistols.

He lurched violently into Benedetta, sending her flying

57

just as the rifle cracked, and she stumbled into cover, dropping some cans in the middle of the road. As O'Hara fell after her one of the cans suddenly leaped into the air as a bullet hit it, and leaked a tomato bloodiness.

Chapter III

O'Hara, Forester and Rohde looked down on the bridge from the cover of a group of large boulders near the edge of the river gorge. Below, the river rumbled, a green torrent of ice-water smoothly slipping past the walls it had cut over the æons. The gorge was about fifty yards wide.

O'Hara was still shaking from the shock of being unexpectedly fired upon. He had thrown himself into the side of the road, winding himself by falling on to a can in the pocket of his overcoat. When he recovered his breath he had looked with stupefaction at the punctured can in the middle of the road, bleeding a red tomato and meat gravy. That could have been me, he thought—or Benedetta.

It was then that he started to shake.

They had crept back round the corner, keeping in cover, while rifle bullets flicked chips of granite from the road surface. Rohde was waiting for them, his gun drawn and his face anxious. He looked at Benedetta's face and his lips drew back over his teeth in a snarl as he took a step forward.

"Hold it," said Forester quietly from behind him. "Let's not be too hasty." He put his hand on O'Hara's arm. "What's happening back there?"

O'Hara took a grip on himself. "I didn't have time to see much. I think the bridge is down; there are some trucks on the other side and there seemed to be a hell of a lot of men."

Forester scanned the ground with a practised eye. "There's plenty of cover by the river—we should be able to get a good view from among those rocks without being spotted. Let's go."

So here they were, looking at the ant-like activity on the other side of the river. There seemed to be about twenty men; some were busy unloading thick planks from a truck, others were cutting rope into lengths. Three men had apparently been detailed off as sentries; they were standing with rifles in their hands, scanning the bank of the gorge. As they watched, one of the men must have thought he saw something move, because he raised his rifle and fired a shot.

Forester said, " Nervous, aren't they? They're firing at shadows."

O'Hara studied the gorge. The river was deep and ran fast—it was obviously impossible to swim. One would be swept away helplessly in the grip of that rush of water and be frozen to death in ten minutes. Apart from that, there were the problems of climbing down the edge of the gorge to the water's edge and getting up the other side, not to mention the likelihood of being shot.

He crossed the river off his mental list of possibilities and turned his attention to the bridge. It was a primitive suspension contraption with two rope catenaries strung from massive stone buttresses on each side of the gorge. From the catenaries other ropes, graded in length, supported the main roadway of the bridge which was made of planks. But there was a gap in the middle where a lot of planks were missing and the ropes dangled in the breeze.

Forester said softly, " That's why they didn't meet us at the air-strip. See the truck in the river—downstream, slapped up against the side of the gorge?"

O'Hara looked and saw the truck in the water, almost totally submerged, with a standing wave of water swirling over the top of the cab. He looked back at the bridge. " It seems as though it was crossing from this side when it went over."

" That figures," said Forester. " I reckon they'd have a couple of men to make the preliminary arrangements— stocking up the camp and so on—in readiness for the main party. When the main party was due they came down to the bridge to cross—God knows for what reason. But they didn't make it—and they buggered the bridge, with the main party still on the other side."

" They're repairing it now," said O'Hara. " Look."

Two men crawled on to the swaying bridge pushing a plank before them. They lashed it into place with the aid of a barrage of shouted advice from terra-firma and then retreated. O'Hara looked at his watch; it had taken them half an hour.

" How many planks to go?" he asked.

Rohde grunted. " About thirty."

" That gives us fifteen hours before they're across," said O'Hara.

"More than that," said Forester. "They're not likely to do that trapeze act in the dark."

Rohde took out his pistol and carefully sighted on the bridge, using his forearm as a rest. Forester said, "That's no damned use—you won't hit anything at fifty yards with a pistol."

"I can try," said Rohde.

Forester sighed. "All right," he conceded. "But just one shot to see how it goes. How many slugs have you got?"

"I had two magazines with seven bullets in each," said Rohde. "I have fired three shots."

"You pop off another and that leaves ten. That's not too many."

Rohde tightened his lips stubbornly and kept the pistol where it was. Forester winked at O'Hara and said, "If you don't mind I'm going to retire now. As soon as you start shooting they're going to shoot right back."

He withdrew slowly, then turned and lay on his back and looked at the sky, gesturing for O'Hara to join him. "It looks as though the time is ripe to hold our council of war," he said. "Surrender or fight. But there may be a way out of it—have you got that air chart of yours?"

O'Hara produced it. "We can't cross the river—not here, at least," he said.

Forester spread out the chart and studied it. He put his finger down. "Here's the river—and this is where we are. This bridge isn't shown. What's this shading by the river?"

"That's the gorge."

Forester whistled. "Hell, it starts pretty high in the mountains, so we can't get around it upstream. What about the other way?"

O'Hara measured off the distance roughly. "The gorge stretches for about eighty miles down stream, but there's a bridge marked here—fifty miles away, as near as dammit."

"That's a hell of a long way," commented Forester. "I doubt if the old man could make it—not over mountain country."

O'Hara said, "And if that crowd over there have any sense they'll have another truckload of men waiting for us if we do try it. They have the advantage of being able to travel fast on the lower roads."

"The bastards have got us boxed in," said Forester. "So it's surrender or fight."

"I surrender to no communists," said O'Hara.

There was a flat report as Rohde fired his pistol and, almost immediately, an answering fusillade of rifle shots, the sound redoubled by echoes from the high ground behind. A bullet ricocheted from close by and whined over O'Hara's head.

Rohde came slithering down. "I missed," he said.

Forester refrained from saying, "I told you so," but his expression showed it. Rohde grinned. "But it stopped them working on the bridge—they went back fast and the plank dropped in the river."

"That's something," said O'Hara. "Maybe we can hold them off that way."

"For how long?" asked Forester. "We can't hold them off for ever—not with ten slugs. We'd better hold our council of war. You stay here, Miguel; but choose a different observation point—they might have spotted this one."

O'Hara and Forester went back to the group on the road. As they approached O'Hara said in a low voice, "We'd better do something to ginger this lot up; they look too bloody nervous."

There was a feeling of tension in the air. Peabody was muttering in a low voice to Miss Ponsky, who for once was silent herself. Willis was sitting on a rock, nervously tapping his foot on the ground, and Aguillar was speaking rapidly to Benedetta some little way removed from the group. The only one at ease seemed to be Armstrong, who was placidly sucking on an empty pipe, idly engaged in drawing patterns on the ground with a stick.

O'Hara crossed to Aguillar. "We're going to decide what to do," he said. "As you suggested."

Aguillar nodded gravely. "I said that it must happen."

O'Hara said, "You're going to be all right." He looked at Benedetta; her face was pale and her eyes were dark smudges in her head. He said, "I don't know how long this is going to take, but why don't you begin preparing a meal for us. We'll all feel better when we've eaten."

"Yes, child," said Aguillar. "I will help you. I am a good cook, Señor O'Hara."

O'Hara smiled at Benedetta. "I'll leave you to it, then." He walked over to where Forester was giving a pep talk. "And that's the position," he was saying. "We're boxed in and there doesn't seem to be any way out of it—but there is always a way out of anything, using brains and determination. Anyway, it's a case of surrender or fight. I'm going to fight—and so is Tim O'Hara here; aren't you, Tim?"

" I am," said O'Hara grimly.

" I'm going to go round and ask your views, and you must each make your own decision," continued Forester. " What about you, Doctor Willis?"

Willis looked up and his face was strained. " It's difficult, isn't it? You see, I'm not much of a fighter. Then again, it's a question of the odds—can we win? I don't see much reason in putting up a fight if we're certain of losing—and I don't see any chance at all of our winning out." He paused, then said hesitantly, " But I'll go with the majority vote."

Willis, you bastard, you're a fine example of a fence-sitter, thought O'Hara.

" Peabody?" Forester's voice cut like a lash.

" What the hell has this got to do with us?" exploded Peabody. " I'm damned if I'm going to risk my life for any wop politician. I say hand the bastard over and let's get the hell out of here."

" What do you say, Miss Ponsky?"

She gave Peabody a look of scorn, then hesitated. All the talk seemed to be knocked out of her, leaving her curiously deflated. At last she said in a small voice, " I know I'm only a woman and I can't do much in the way of fighting, and I'm scared to death—but I think we ought to fight." She ended in a rush and looked defiantly at Peabody. " And that's my vote."

Good for you, Miss Ponsky, cheered O'Hara silently. That's three to fight. It's now up to Armstrong—he can tip it for fighting or make a deadlock, depending on his vote.

" Doctor Armstrong, what do you have to say?" queried Forester.

Armstrong sucked on his pipe and it made an obscene noise. " I suppose I'm more an authority on this kind of situation than anyone present," he observed. " With the possible exception of Señor Aguillar, who at present is cooking our lunch, I see. Give me a couple of hours and I could quote a hundred parallel examples drawn from history."

Peabody muttered in exasperation. " What the hell!"

" The question at issue is whether to hand Señor Aguillar to the gentlemen on the other side of the river. The important point, as I see it affecting us, is what would they do with him? And I can't really see that there is anything they can do

62

with him other than kill him. Keeping high-standing politicians as prisoners went out of fashion a long time ago. Now, if they kill him they will automatically be forced to kill us. They would not dare take the risk of letting this story loose upon the world. They would be most painfully criticised, perhaps to the point of losing what they have set out to gain. In short, the people of Cordillera would not stand for it. So you see, we are not fighting for the life of Señor Aguillar; we are fighting for our own lives."

He put his pipe back into his mouth and made another rude noise.

"Does that mean that you are in favour of fighting?" asked Forester.

"Of course," said Armstrong in surprise. "Haven't you been listening to what I've been saying?"

Peabody looked at him in horror. "Jesus!" he said. "What have I got myself into?" He buried his head in his hands.

Forester grinned at O'Hara, and said, "Well, Doctor Willis?"

"I fight," said Willis briefly.

O'Hara chuckled. One academic man had convinced another.

Forester said, "Ready to change your mind, Peabody?"

Peabody looked up. "You really think they're going to rub us all out?"

"If they kill Aguillar I don't see what else they can do," said Armstrong reasonably. "And they will kill Aguillar, you know."

"Oh, hell," said Peabody in an anguish of indecision.

"Come on," Forester ordered harshly. "Put up or shut up."

"I guess I'll have to throw in with you," Peabody said morosely.

"That's it, then," said Forester. "A unanimous vote. I'll tell Aguillar and we'll discuss how to fight over some food." Miss Ponsky went to help the Aguillars with their cooking and O'Hara went back to the river to see what Rohde was doing. He looked back and saw that Armstrong was talking to Willis and again drawing on the ground with a stick. Willis looked interested.

Rohde had chosen a better place for observation and at first O'Hara could not find him. At last he saw the sole of a boot protruding from behind a rock and joined Rohde, who seemed pleased. "They have not yet come out of their holes," he said. "It has been an hour. One bullet that missed has held them up for an hour."

"That's great," said O'Hara sardonically. "Ten bullets —ten hours."

"It is better than that," protested Rohde. "They have thirty planks to put in—that would take them fifteen hours without my bullets. With the shooting it will take them twenty-five hours. They will not work at night—so that is two full days."

O'Hara nodded. "It gives us time to decide what to do next," he admitted. But when the bullets were finished and the bridge completed a score of armed and ruthless men would come boiling over the river. It would be a slaughter.

"I will stay here," said Rohde. "Send some food when it is ready." He nodded towards the bridge. "It takes a brave man to walk on that, knowing that someone will shoot at him. I do not think these men are very brave—maybe it will be more than one hour to a bullet."

O'Hara went back and told Forester what was happening and Forester grimaced. "Two days—maybe—two days to come up with something. But with what?"

O'Hara said, "I think a Committee of Ways and Means is indicated."

They all sat in a circle on the sparse grass and Benedetta and Miss Ponsky served the food on the aluminium plates they had found at the camp. Forester said, "This is a war council, so please stick to the point and let's have no idle chit-chat—we've no time to waste. Any sensible suggestions will be welcome."

There was a dead silence, then Miss Ponsky said, "I suppose the main problem is to stop them repairing the bridge. Well, couldn't we do something at this end—cut the ropes or something?"

"That's good in principle," said Forester. "Any objections to it?" He glanced at O'Hara, knowing what he would say.

O'Hara looked at Forester sourly; it seemed as though he was being cast as the cold-water expert and he did not fancy the role. He said deliberately, "The approaches to the bridge from this side are wide open; there's no cover for at least a hundred yards—you saw what happened to Benedetta and me this morning. Anyone who tried to get to the bridge along the road would be cut down before he'd got half-way. It's point blank range, you know—they don't have to be

64

crack shots." He paused. "Now I know it's the only way we *can* get at the bridge, but it seems impossible to me."

"What about a night attack?" asked Willis.

"That sounds good," said Forester.

O'Hara hated to do it, but he spoke up. "I don't want to sound pessimistic, but I don't think those chaps over there are entirely stupid. They've got two trucks and four jeeps, maybe more, and those vehicles have at least two headlights apiece. They'll keep the bridge well lit during the dark hours."

There was silence again.

Armstrong cleared his throat. "Willis and I have been doing a little thinking and maybe we have something that will help. Again I find myself in the position of being something of an expert. You know that my work is the study of medieval history, but it so happens that I'm a specialist, and my speciality is medieval warfare. The position as I see it is that we are in a castle with a moat and a drawbridge. The drawbridge is fortuitously pulled up, but our enemies are trying to rectify that state of affairs. Our job is to stop them."

"With what?" asked O'Hara. "A push of a pike?"

"I wouldn't despise medieval weapons too much, O'Hara," said Armstrong mildly. "I admit that the people of those days weren't as adept in the art of slaughter as we are, but still, they managed to kill each other off at a satisfactory rate. Now, Rohde's pistol is highly inaccurate at the range he is forced to use. What we want is a more efficient missile weapon than Rohde's pistol."

"So we all make like Robin Hood," said Peabody derisively. "With the jolly old longbow, what? For Christ's sake, Professor!"

"Oh, no," said Armstrong. "A longbow is very chancy in the hands of a novice. It takes five years at least to train a good bowman."

"I can use the bow," said Miss Ponsky unexpectedly. Everyone looked at her and she coloured. "I'm president of the South Bridge Ladies' Greenwood Club. Last year I won our own little championship in the Hereford Round."

"That's interesting," said Armstrong.

O'Hara said, "Can you use a longbow lying down, Miss Ponsky?"

"It would be difficult," she said. "Perhaps impossible."

O'Hara jerked his head at the gorge. "You stand up there with a longbow and you'll get filled full of holes."

She bridled. " I think you'd do better helping than pouring cold water on all our ideas, Mr. O'Hara."

" I've got to do it," said O'Hara evenly. " I don't want anyone killed uselessly."

" For God's sake," exclaimed Willis. " How did a long-bow come into this? That's out—we can't make one; we haven't the material. Now, will you listen to Armstrong; he has a point to make." His voice was unexpectedly firm.

The flat crack of Rohde's pistol echoed on the afternoon air and there was the answering rattle of shots from the other side of the gorge. Peabody ducked and O'Hara looked at his watch. It had been an hour and twenty minutes—and they had nine bullets left.

Forester said, " That's one good thing—we're safe here. Their rifles won't shoot round corners. Make your point, Doctor Armstrong."

" I was thinking of something more on the lines of a prodd or crossbow," said Armstrong. " Anyone who can use a rifle can use a crossbow and it has an effective range of over a hundred yards." He smiled at O'Hara. " You can shoot it lying down, too."

O'Hara's mind jumped at it. They could cover the bridge and also the road on the other side where it turned north and followed the edge of the gorge and where the enemy trucks were. He said, " Does it have any penetrative power?"

" A bolt will go through mail if it hits squarely," said Armstrong.

" What about a petrol tank?"

" Oh, it would penetrate a petrol tank quite easily."

" Now, take it easy," said Forester. " How in hell can we make a crossbow?"

" You must understand that I'm merely a theoretician where this is concerned," explained Armstrong. " I'm no mechanic or engineer. But I described what I want to Willis and he thinks we can make it."

" Armstrong and I were rooting round up at the camp," said Willis. " One of the huts had been a workshop and there was a lot of junk lying about—you know, the usual bits and pieces that you find in a metal-working shop. I reckon they didn't think it worthwhile carting the stuff away when they abandoned the place. There are some flat springs and odd bits of metal rod; and there's some of that concrete reinforcing steel that we can cut up to make arrows."

" Bolts," Armstrong corrected mildly. " Or quarrels, if

you prefer. I thought first of making a prodd, you know; that's a type of crossbow which fires bullets, but Willis has convinced me that we can manufacture bolts more easily."

"What about tools?" asked O'Hara. "Have you anything that will cut metal?"

"There are some old hacksaw blades," Willis said. "And I saw a couple of worn-out files. And there's a hand-powered grindstone that looks as though it came out of the Ark. I'll make out; I'm good with my hands and I can adapt Armstrong's designs with the material available."

O'Hara looked at Forester, who said slowly, "A weapon accurate to a hundred yards built out of junk seems too good to be true. Are you certain about this, Doctor Armstrong?"

"Oh, yes," said Armstrong cheerfully. "The crossbow has killed thousands of men in its time—I see no reason why it shouldn't kill a few more. And Willis seems to think he can make it." He smiled. "I've drawn the blueprints there." He pointed to a few lines scratched in the dust.

"If we're going to do this, we'd better do it quickly," said O'Hara.

"Right." Forester looked up at the sun. "You've got time to make it up to the camp by nightfall. It's uphill, but you'll be travelling light. You go too, Peabody; Willis can use another pair of hands."

Peabody nodded quickly. He had no taste for staying too near the bridge.

"One moment," said Aguillar, speaking for the first time. "The bridge is made of rope and wood—very combustible materials. Have you considered the use of fire? Señor O'Hara gave me the idea when he spoke of petrol tanks."

"Um," said O'Hara. "But how to get the fire to the bridge?"

"Everyone think of that," said Forester. "Now let's get things moving."

Armstrong, Willis and Peabody left immediately on the long trudge up to the camp. Forester said, "I didn't know what to make of Willis—he's not very forthcoming—but I've got him tagged now. He's the practical type; give him something to do and he'll get it done, come hell or high water. He'll do."

Aguillar smiled. "Armstrong is surprising, too."

"My God!" said Forester. "Crossbows in this day and age!"

O'Hara said, "We've got to think about making camp.
67

There's no water here, and besides, our main force is too close to the enemy. There's a pond about half a mile back—I think that's a good spot."

"Benedetta, you see to that," Aguillar commanded. "Miss Ponsky will help you." He watched the two women go, then turned with a grave face. "There is something we must discuss, together with Miguel. Let us go over there."

Rohde was happy. "They have not put a plank in the bridge yet. They ran again like the rabbits they are."

Aguillar told him what was happening and he said uncertainly, "A crossbow?"

"I think it's crazy, too," said Forester. "But Armstrong reckons it'll work."

"Armstrong is a good man," said Aguillar. "He is thinking of immediate necessities—but I think of the future. Suppose we hold off these men; suppose we destroy the bridge—what then?"

"We're not really any better off," said O'Hara reflectively. "They've got us pinned down anyway."

"Exactly," said Aguillar. "True, we have plenty of food, but that means nothing. Time is very valuable to these men, just as it is to me. They gain everything by keeping me inactive."

"By keeping you here they've removed you from the game," agreed Forester. "How long do you think it will be before they make their *coup d'état*?"

Aguillar shrugged. "One month—maybe two. Certainly not longer. We advanced our own preparations because the communists showed signs of moving. It is a race between us with the destiny of Cordillera as the prize—maybe the destiny of the whole of Latin America is at stake. And the time is short."

"Your map, Señor O'Hara," said Rohde suddenly.

O'Hara took out the chart and spread it on a rock, and Rohde traced the course of the river north and south, shaking his head. "This river—this gorge—is a trap, pinning us against the mountains," he said.

"We've agreed it's no use going for the bridge downstream," said Forester. "It's a hell of a long way and it's sure to be guarded."

"What's to stop *them* crossing that bridge and pushing up on this side of the river to outflank us?" asked O'Hara.

"As long as they think they can repair this bridge they won't do that," Aguillar said. "Communists are not supermen; they are as lazy as other people and they would not relish crossing eighty kilometres of mountain country—that would take at least four days. I think they will be content to stop the bolt hole."

Rohde's fingers swept across the map to the west. "That leaves the mountains."

Forester turned and looked at the mountain wall, at the icy peaks. "I don't like the sound of that. I don't think Señor Aguillar could make it."

"I know," said Rohde. "He must stay here. But someone must cross the mountains for help."

"Let's see if it's practicable," said O'Hara. "I was going to fly through the Puerto de las Águilas. That means that anyone going back would have to go twenty miles north before striking west through the pass. And he'd have to go pretty high to get round this bloody gorge. The pass isn't so bad—it's only about fourteen thousand feet."

"A total of about thirty miles before he got into the Santos Valley," said Forester. "That's on straight line courses. It would probably be fifty miles over the ground."

"There is another way," said Rohde quietly. He pointed to the mountains. "This range is high, but not very wide. On the other side lies the Santos Valley. If you draw a line on the map from here to Altemiros in the Santos Valley you will find that it is not more than twenty-five kilometres."

O'Hara bent over the map and measured the distance. "You're right; about fifteen miles—but it's all peaks."

"There is a pass about two miles north-west of the mine," said Rohde. "It has no name because no one is so foolish as to use it. It is about five thousand eight hundred metres."

Forester rapidly translated. "Wow! Nineteen thousand feet."

"What about lack of oxygen?" asked O'Hara. "We've had enough trouble with that already. Could a man go over that pass without oxygen?"

"I have done so," said Rohde. "Under more favourable conditions. It is a matter of acclimatisation. Mountaineers know this; they stay for days at one level and then move up the mountain to another camp and stay a few days there also before moving to a higher level. It is to attune their bodies to the changing conditions." He looked up at the mountains. "If I went up to the camp to-morrow and spent a day there then went to the mine and stayed a day there—I think I could cross that pass."

Forester said, "You couldn't go alone."

"I'll go with you," said O'Hara promptly.

"Hold on there," said Forester. "Are you a mountaineer?"

"No," said O'Hara.

"Well, I am. I mean, I've scrambled about in the Rockies—that should count for something." He appealed to Rohde. "Shouldn't it?"

Aguillar said, "You should not go alone, Miguel."

"Very well," said Rohde. "I will take one man—you." He nodded to Forester and smiled grimly. "But I promise you—you will be sorry."

Forester grinned cheerfully and said, "Well, Tim, that leaves you as garrison commander. You'll have your hands full."

"*Si*," said Rohde. "You must hold them off."

A new sound was added to the noise of the river and Rohde immediately wriggled up to his observation post, then beckoned to O'Hara. "They are starting their engines," he said. "I think they are going away."

But the vehicles did not move. "What are they doing?" asked Rohde in perplexity.

"They're charging their batteries," said O'Hara. "They're making sure that they'll have plenty of light to-night."

II

O'Hara and Aguillar went back to help the women make camp, leaving Rohde and Forester to watch the bridge. There was no immediate danger of the enemy forcing the crossing and any unusual move could soon be reported. Forester's attitude had changed as soon as the decision to cross the mountains had been made. He no longer drove hard for action, seemingly being content to leave it to O'Hara. It was as though he had tacitly decided that there could be only one commander and the man was O'Hara.

O'Hara's lips quirked as he mentally reviewed his garrison. An old man and a young girl; two sedentary academic types; a drunk and someone's maiden aunt; and himself—a broken-down pilot. On the other side of the river were at least twenty ruthless men—with God knows how many more to back them up. His muscles tensed at the thought that they were communists; sloppy South American communists, no doubt—but still communists.

Whatever happens, they're not going to get me again, he thought.

Benedetta was very quiet and O'Hara knew why. To be shot at for the first time took the pith out of a person—one came to the abrupt realisation that one was a soft bag of wind and liquids, vulnerable and defenceless against steel-jacketed bullets which could rend and tear. He remembered the first time he had been in action, and felt very sorry for Benedetta; at least he had been prepared, however inadequately, for the bullets—the bullets and the cannon shells.

He looked across at the scattered rocks on the bleak hillside. "I wonder if there's a cave over there?" he suggested. "That would come in handy right now." He glanced at Benedetta. "Let's explore a little."

She looked at her uncle who was helping Miss Ponsky check the cans of food. "All right," she said.

They crossed the road and struck off at right angles, making their way diagonally up the slope. The ground was covered with boulders and small pebbles and the going was difficult, their feet slipping as the stones shifted. O'Hara thought that one could break an ankle quite easily and a faint idea stirred at the back of his mind.

After a while they separated, O'Hara to the left and the girl to the right. For an hour they toiled among the rocks, searching for something that would give shelter against the night wind, however small. O'Hara found nothing, but he heard a faint shout from Benedetta and crossed the hillside to see what she had found.

It was not a cave, merely a fortuitous tumbling of the rocks. A large boulder had rolled from above and wedged itself between two others, forming a roof. It reminded O'Hara of a dolmen he had seen on Dartmoor, although the whole thing was very much bigger. He regarded it appreciatively. At least it would be shelter from snow and rain and it gave a little protection from the wind.

He went inside and found a hollow at the back. "This is good," he said. "This will hold a lot of water—maybe twenty gallons."

He turned and looked at Benedetta. The exercise had brought some colour into her cheeks and she looked better. He produced his cigarettes. "Smoke?"

She shook her head. "I don't."

"Good!" he said with satisfaction. "I was hoping you

71

didn't." He looked into the packet—there were eleven left. "I'm a selfish type, you know; I want these for myself."

He sat down on a rock and lit his cigarette, voluptuously inhaling the smoke. Benedetta sat beside him and said, " I'm glad you decided to help my uncle."

O'Hara grinned. " Some of us weren't too sure. It needed a little tough reasoning to bring them round. But it was finally unanimous."

She said in a low voice, " Do you think there's any chance of our coming out of this?"

O'Hara bit his lip and was silent for a time. Then he said, " There's no point in hiding the truth—I don't think we've got a cat in hell's chance. If they bust across the bridge and we're as defenceless as we are now, we won't have a hope." He waved his hand at the terrain. " There's just one chance—if we split up, every man for himself heading in a different direction, then they'll have to split up, too. This is rough country and one of us might get away to tell what happened to the rest. But that's pretty poor consolation."

" Then why did you decide to fight?" she said in wonder.

O'Hara chuckled. " Armstrong put up some pretty cogent arguments," he said, and told her about it. Then he added, " But I'd have fought anyway. I don't like those boys across the river; I don't like what they do to people. It makes no difference if their skins are yellow, white or brown—they're all of the same stripe."

" Señor Forester was telling me that you fought together in Korea," Benedetta said.

" We might have—we probably did. He was in an American squadron which we flew with sometimes. But I never met him."

" It must have been terrible," she said. " All that fighting."

" It wasn't too bad," said O'Hara. " The fighting part of it." He smiled. " You *do* get used to being shot at, you know. I think that people can get used to anything if it goes on long enough—most things, anyway. That's the only way wars can be fought—because people can adapt and treat the craziest things as normal. Otherwise they couldn't go through with it."

She nodded. " I know. Look at us here. Those men shoot at us and Miguel shoots back—he regards it as the normal thing to do."

" It *is* the normal thing to do," said O'Hara harshly. " The

72

human being is a fighting animal; it's that quality which has put him where he is—the king of this planet." His lips twisted. "It's also the thing that's maybe holding him back from bigger things." He laughed abruptly. "Christ, this is no time for the philosophy of war—I'd better leave that to Armstrong."

"You said something strange," said Benedetta. "You said that Korea wasn't too bad—the fighting part of it. What *was* bad, if it wasn't the fighting?"

O'Hara looked into the distance. "It was when the fighting stopped—when *I* stopped fighting—when I couldn't fight any more. Then it was bad."

"You were a prisoner? In the hands of the Chinese? Forester said something of that."

O'Hara said slowly, "I've killed men in combat—in hot blood—and I'll probably do it again, and soon, at that. But what those communist bastards can do intellectually and with cold purpose is beyond . . ." He shook his head irritably. "I prefer not to talk about it."

He had a sudden vision of the bland, expressionless features of the Chinese lieutenant, Feng. It was something that had haunted his dreams and woken him screaming ever since Korea. It was the reason he preferred to go to sleep in a sodden, dreamless and mindless coma. He said, "Let's talk about you. You speak good English—where did you learn it?"

She was aware that she had trodden on forbidden and shaky ground. "I'm sorry if I disturbed you, Señor O'Hara," she said contritely.

"That's all right. But less of the Señor O'Hara; my name is Tim."

She smiled quickly. "I was educated in the United States, Tim. My uncle sent me there after Lopez made the revolution." She laughed. "I was taught English by a teacher very like Miss Ponsky."

"Now there's a game old trout," said O'Hara. "Your uncle sent you? What about your parents?"

"My mother died when I was a child. My father—Lopez had him shot."

O'Hara sighed. "We both seem to be scraping on raw nerves, Benedetta. I'm sorry."

She said sadly, "It's the way the world is, Tim."

He agreed sombrely. "Anyone who expects fair play in this world is a damn fool. That's why we're in this jam.

73

Come on, let's get back; this isn't getting us anywhere."
He pinched off his cigarette and carefully put the stub back
in the packet.

As Benedetta rose she said, "Do you think that Señor
Armstrong's idea of a crossbow will work?"

"I don't," said O'Hara flatly. "I think that Armstrong
is a romantic. He's specialised as a theoretician in wars a
thousand years gone, and I can't think of anything more futile
than that. He's an ivory-tower man—an academician—bloodthirsty in a theoretical way, but the sight of blood will turn
his stomach. And I think he's a little bit nuts."

III

Armstrong's pipe gurgled as he watched Willis rooting about
in the rubbish of the workshop. His heart was beating rapidly
and he felt breathless, although the altitude did not seem to
affect him as much as the previous time he had been at the
hutted camp. His mind was turning over the minutiæ of
his profession—the science of killing without gunpowder. He
thought coldly and clearly about the ranges, trajectories and
penetrations that could be obtained from pieces of bent steel
and twisted gut, and he sought to adapt the ingenious
mechanisms so clearly diagrammed in his mind to the
materials and needs of the moment. He looked up at the
roof beams of the hut and a new idea dawned on him. But he
put it aside—the crossbow came first.

Willis straightened, holding a flat spring. "This came
from an auto—will it do for the bow?"

Armstrong tried to flex it and found it very stiff. "It's
very strong," he said. "Probably stronger than anything
they had in the Middle Ages. This will be a very powerful
weapon. Perhaps this is too strong—we must be able to bend
it."

"Let's go over that problem again," Willis said.

Armstrong drew on the back of an envelope. "For the
light sporting bows they had a goat's-foot lever, but that
is not strong enough for the weapon we are considering.
For the heavier military bows they had two methods of bending
—the cranequin, a ratchet arranged like this, which was de-
mounted for firing, and the other was a windlass built into the
bow which worked a series of pulleys."

Willis looked at the rough sketches and nodded. "The

windlass is our best bet," he said. "That ratchet thing would be difficult to make. And if necessary we can weaken the spring by grinding it down." He looked around. "Where's Peabody?"

"I don't know," said Armstrong. "Let's get on with this."

"You'd better find him," Willis said. "We'll put him on to making arrows—that should be an easy job."

"Bolts or quarrels," said Armstrong patiently.

"Whatever they're called, let's get on with it," Willis said. They found Peabody taking it easy in one of the huts, heating a can of beans. Reluctantly he went along to the workshop and they got to work. Armstrong marvelled at the dexterity of Willis's fingers as he contrived effective parts from impossible materials and worse tools. They found the old grindstone to be their most efficient cutting tool, although it tended to waste material. Armstrong sweated in turning the crank and could not keep it up for long, so they took it in turns, he and Willis silently, Peabody with much cursing.

They ripped out electric wiring from a hut and tore down conduit tubing. They cut up reinforcing steel into lengths and slotted the ends to take flights. It was cold and their hands were numb and the blood oozed from the cuts made when their makeshift tools slipped.

They worked all night and dawn was brightening the sky as Armstrong took the completed weapon in his hands and looked at it dubiously. "It's a bit different from how I imagined it, but I think it will do." He rubbed his eyes wearily. "I'll take it down now—they might need it."

Willis slumped against the side of the hut. "I've got an idea for a better one," he said. "That thing will be a bastard to cock. But I must get some sleep first—and food." His voice trailed to a mumble and he blinked his eyes rapidly.

All that night the bridge had been illuminated by the headlamps of the enemy vehicles and it was obviously hopeless to make a sortie in an attempt to cut the cables. The enemy did not work on the bridge at night, not relishing being in a spotlight when a shot could come out of the darkness.

Forester was contemptuous of them. "The goddam fools," he said. "If we can't hit them in daylight then it's sure we can't at night—but if they'd any sense they'd see that they could spot our shooting at night and they'd send a man on to the bridge to draw our fire—then they'd fill our man full of holes."

But during the daylight hours the enemy *had* worked on the bridge, and had been less frightened of the shots fired at them. No one had been hit and it had become obvious that there was little danger other than that from a freakishly lucky shot. By morning there were but six bullets left for Rohde's pistol and there were nine more planks in the bridge.

By nine o'clock Rohde had expended two more bullets and it was then that Armstrong stumbled down the road carrying a contraption. "Here it is," he said. "Here's your crossbow." He rubbed his eyes which were red-rimmed and tired. "Professionally speaking, I'd call it an arbalest."

"My God, that was quick," said O'Hara.

"We worked all night," Armstrong said tiredly. "We thought you'd need it in a hurry."

"How does it work?" asked O'Hara, eyeing it curiously.

"The metal loop on the business end is a stirrup," said Armstrong. "You put it on the ground and put your foot in it. Then you take this cord and clip the hook on to the bowstring and start winding on this handle. That draws back the bowstring until it engages on this sear. You drop a bolt in this trough and you're ready to shoot. Press the trigger and the sear drops to release the bowstring."

The crossbow was heavy in O'Hara's hands. The bow itself was made from a car spring and the bowstring was a length of electric wire woven into a six-strand cord to give it strength. The cord which drew it back was also electric wire woven of three strands. The seat and trigger were carved from wood, and the trough where the bolt went was made from a piece of electric conduit piping.

It was a triumph of improvisation.

"We had to weaken the spring," said Armstrong. "But it's still got a lot of bounce. Here's a bolt—we made a dozen."

The bolt was merely a length of round steel, three-eighths of an inch in diameter and fifteen inches long. It was very rusty. One end was slotted to hold metal flights cut from a dried-milk can and the other end was sharpened to a point. O'Hara hefted it thoughtfully; it was quite heavy. "If this thing doesn't kill immediately, anyone hit will surely die of blood-poisoning. Does it give the range you expected?"

"A little more," said Armstrong. "These bolts are heavier than the medieval originals because they're steel throughout instead of having a wooden shaft—but the bow is very powerful and that makes up for it. Why don't you try it out?"

O'Hara put his foot in the stirrup and cranked the windlass handle. He found it more difficult than he had anticipated —the bow was very strong. As he slipped a bolt into the trough he said, "What should I shoot at?"

"What about that earth bank over there?"

The bank was about sixty yards away. He raised the crossbow and Armstrong said quickly, "Try it lying down, the way we'll use it in action. The trajectory is very flat so you won't have much trouble with sighting. I thought we'd wait until we got down here before sighting in." He produced a couple of gadgets made of wire. "We'll use a ring-and-pin sight."

O'Hara lay down and fitted the rough wooden butt awkwardly into his shoulder. He peered along the trough and sighted as best he could upon a brown patch of earth on the bank. Then he squeezed the trigger and the crossbow bucked hard against his shoulder as the string was released.

There was a puff of dust from the extreme right of the target at which he had aimed. He got up and rubbed his shoulder. "My God!" he said with astonishment. "She's got a hell of a kick."

Armstrong smiled faintly. "Let's retrieve the bolt."

They walked over to the bank but O'Hara could not see it. "It went in about here," he said. "I saw the dust distinctly —but where is it?"

Armstrong grinned. "I told you this weapon was powerful. There's the bolt."

O'Hara grunted with amazement as he saw what Armstrong meant. The bolt had penetrated more than its own length into the earth and had buried itself completely. As Armstrong dug it out, O'Hara said, "We'd better all practise with this thing and find out who's the best shot." He looked at Armstrong. "You'd better get some sleep; you look pooped."

"I'll wait until I see the bow in action," said Armstrong. "Maybe it'll need some modification. Willis is making another —he has some ideas for improvements—and we put Peabody to making more bolts." He stood upright with the bolt in his hands. "And I've got to fix the sights."

All of them, excepting Aguillar and Rohde, practised with the crossbow, and—perhaps not surprisingly—Miss Ponsky turned out to be the best shot, with Forester coming next and O'Hara third. Shooting the bow was rough on Miss Ponsky's shoulder, but she made a soft shoulder-pad and eight times out of ten she put a bolt into a twelve-inch circle, clucking deprecatingly when she missed.

"She's not got the strength to crank it," said Forester. "But she's damned good with the trigger."

"That settles it," said O'Hara. "She gets first crack at the enemy—if she'll do it." He crossed over to her and said with a smile, "It looks as though you're elected to go into action first. Will you give it a go?"

Her face paled and her nose seemed even sharper. "Oh, my!" she said, flustered. "Do you think I can do it?"

"They've put in another four planks," said O'Hara quietly. "And Rohde's saving his last four bullets until he's reasonably certain of making a hit. This is the only other chance we've got—and you're the best shot."

Visibly she pulled herself together and her chin rose in determination. "All right," she said. "I'll do my best."

"Good! You'd better come and have a look at 'the bridge to get your range right—and maybe you'd better take a few practice shots at the same range."

He took her up to where Rohde was lying. "Miss Ponsky's going to have a go with the crossbow," he said.

Rohde looked at it with interest. "Does it work?"

"It's got the range and the velocity," O'Hara told him. "It should work all right." He turned his attention to the bridge. Two men had just put in another plank and were retreating. The gap in the bridge was getting very small— soon it would be narrow enough for a determined man to leap. "You'd better take the nearest man the next time they come out," he said. "What would you say the range is?"

Miss Ponsky considered. "A little less than the range I've been practising at," she said. "I don't think I need to practise any more." There was a tremor in her voice.

O'Hara regarded her. "This has got to be done, Miss Ponsky. Remember what they did to Mrs. Coughlin—and what they'll do to us if they get across the bridge."

"I'll be all right," she said in a low voice.

O'Hara nodded in satisfaction. "You take Rohde's place. I'll be a little way along. Take your time—you needn't hurry. Regard it as the target practice you've just been doing."

Forester had already cocked the bow and handed it up to Miss Ponsky. She put a bolt in the trough and slid forward on her stomach until she got a good view of the bridge. O'Hara waited until she was settled, then moved a little way farther along the edge of the gorge. He looked back and saw Forester talking to Armstrong, who was lying full-length on the ground, his eyes closed.

He found a good observation post and lay waiting. Presently the same two men appeared again, carrying a plank. They crawled the length of the bridge, pushing the plank before them until they reached the gap—even though none of them had been hit, they weren't taking unnecessary chances. Once at the gap they got busy, lashing the plank to the two main ropes.

O'Hara found his heart thumping and the wait seemed intolerably long. The nearest man was wearing a leather jacket similar to his own and O'Hara could see quite clearly the flicker of his eyes as he gazed apprehensively at the opposite bank from time to time. O'Hara clenched his fist. "Now!" he whispered. "For God's sake—now!"

He did not hear the twang as the crossbow fired, but he saw the spurt of dust from the man's jacket as the bolt hit him, and suddenly a shaft of steel sprouted from the man's back just between the shoulder blades. There was a faint cry above the roar of the river and the man jerked his legs convulsively. He thrust his arms forward, almost in an imploring gesture, then he toppled sideways and rolled off the edge of the bridge, to fall in a spinning tangle of arms and legs into the raging river.

The other man paused uncertainly, then ran back across the bridge to the other side of the gorge. The bridge swayed under his pounding feet and as he ran he looked back fearfully. He joined the group at the end of the bridge and O'Hara saw him indicate his own back and another man shaking his head in disbelief.

Gently he withdrew and ran back to the place from which Miss Ponsky had fired the shot. She was lying on the ground, her body racked with sobs, and Forester was bending over her. "It's all right, Miss Ponsky," he was saying. "It had to be done."

"But I've killed a man," she wailed. "I've taken a life."

Forester got her to her feet and led her away, talking softly to her all the time. O'Hara bent and picked up the crossbow. "What a secret weapon!" he said in admiration. "No noise, no flash—just *zing*." He laughed. "They still don't know what happened—not for certain. Armstrong, you're a bloody genius."

But Armstrong was asleep.

The enemy made no further attempts to repair the bridge that morning. Instead, they kept up a steady, if slow, light barrage of rifle fire, probing the tumble of rocks at the edge of the gorge in the hope of making hits. O'Hara withdrew everyone to safety, including Rohde. Then he borrowed a small mirror from Benedetta and contrived a makeshift periscope, being careful to keep the glass in the shadow of a rock so that it would not reflect direct sunlight. He fixed it so that an observer could lie on his back in perfect cover, but could still keep an eye on the bridge. Forester took first watch.

O'Hara said, " If they come on the bridge again use the gun—just one shot. We've got them off-balance now and a bit nervous. They don't know if that chap fell off the bridge by accident, whether he was shot and they didn't hear the report, or whether it was something else. *We* know it was something else and so does the other man who was on the bridge, but I don't think they believe him. There was a hell of an argument going on the last I saw of it. At any rate, I think they'll be leery of coming out now, and a shot ought to put them off."

Forester checked the pistol and looked glumly at the four remaining bullets. " I feel a hell of a soldier—firing off twenty-five per cent of the available ammunition at one bang."

" It's best this way," said O'Hara. " They don't know the state of our ammunition, the crossbow is our secret weapon, and by God we must make the best use of it. I have ideas about that, but I want to wait for the second crossbow." He paused. " Have you any idea how many of the bastards are across there?"

" I tried a rough count," said Forester. " I made it twenty-three. The leader seems to be a big guy with a Castro beard. He's wearing some kind of uniform—jungle-green pants and a bush-jacket." He rubbed his chin and said thoughtfully, " It's my guess that he's a Cuban specialist."

" I'll look out for him," said O'Hara. " Maybe if we can nail him, the rest will pack up."

" Maybe," said Forester non-committally.

O'Hara trudged back to the camp which had now been transferred to the rock shelter on the hillside. That was a better defensive position and could not be so easily rushed, the attackers having to move over broken ground. But O'Hara had no great faith in it; if the enemy crossed the bridge they could move up the road fast, outflanking the rock shelter to move in behind and surround them. He had cudgelled his brain to find a way of blocking the road but had not come up with anything.

But there it was—a better place than the camp by the pond and the roadside. The trouble was water, but the rock hollow at the rear of the shelter had been filled with twenty-five gallons of water, transported laboriously a canful at a time, much of it spilling on the way. And it was a good place to sleep, too.

Miss Ponsky had recovered from her hysteria but not from her remorse. She was unaccustomedly quiet and withdrawn, speaking to no one. She had helped to transport the water and the food but had done so mechanically, as if she did not care. Aguillar was grave. "It is not right that this should be," he said. "It is not right that a lady like Miss Ponsky should have to do these things."

O'Hara felt exasperated. "Dammit, we didn't start this fight," he said. "The Coughlins are dead, and Benedetta was nearly killed—not to mention me. I'll try not to let it happen again, but she *is* the best shot and we *are* fighting for our lives."

"You are a soldier," said Aguillar. "Almost I seem to hear you say, with Napoleon, that one cannot make an omelette without breaking eggs." His voice was gently sardonic.

O'Hara disregarded that. "We must all practise with the bow—we must learn to use it while we have time."

Aguillar tapped him on the arm. "Señor O'Hara, perhaps if I gave myself to these people they would be satisfied."

O'Hara stared at him. "You know they wouldn't; they can't let us go—knowing what we know."

Aguillar nodded. "I know that; I was wondering if you did." He shrugged half-humorously. "I wanted you to convince me there is nothing to gain by it—and you have. I am sorry to have brought this upon all these innocent people."

O'Hara made an impatient noise and Aguillar continued, "There comes a time when the soldier takes affairs out of the hands of the politician—all ways seem to lead to violence. So I must cease to be a politician and become a soldier. I will learn how to shoot this bow well, señor."

"I wouldn't do too much, Señor Aguillar," said O'Hara.

"You must conserve your strength in case we must move suddenly and quickly. You're not in good physical shape, you know."

Aguillar's voice was sharp. "Señor, I will do what I must."

O'Hara said no more, guessing he had touched on Spanish-American pride. He went to talk to Miss Ponsky.

She was kneeling in front of the pressure stove, apparently intent on watching a can of water boil, but her eyes were unfocused and staring far beyond. He knew what she was looking at—a steel bolt that had sprouted like a monstrous growth in the middle of a man's back.

He said, "Killing another human being is a terrible thing, Miss Ponsky. I know—I've done it, and I was sickened for days afterwards. The first time I shot down an enemy fighter in Korea I followed him down—it was a dangerous thing to do, but I was young and inexperienced then. The Mig went down in flames, and his ejector seat didn't work, so he opened the canopy manually and jumped out against the slipstream.

"It was brave or desperate of that man to do that. But he had the Chinese sort of courage—or maybe the Russian courage, for all I know. You see, I didn't know the nationality or even the colour of the man I had killed. He fell to earth, a spinning black speck. His parachute didn't open. I knew he was a dead man."

O'Hara moistened his lips. "I felt bad about that, Miss Ponsky; it sickened me. But then I thought that the same man had been trying to kill me—he nearly succeeded, too. He had pumped my plane full of holes before I got him and I crash-landed on the air-strip. I was lucky to get away with it—I spent three weeks in hospital. I finally worked it out that it was a case of him or me, and I was the lucky one. I don't know if he would have had regrets if he had killed me—I think probably not. Those people aren't trained to have much respect for life."

He regarded her closely. "These people across the river are the same that I fought in Korea, no matter that their skins are a different colour. We have no fight with them if they will let us go in peace—but they won't do that, Miss Ponsky. So it's back to basics; kill or be killed and the devil take the loser. You did all right, Miss Ponsky; what you did may have saved all our lives and maybe the lives of a lot of people in this country. Who knows?"

As he lapsed into silence she turned to him and said in a husky, broken voice, "I'm a silly old woman, Mr. O'Hara.

For years I've been talking big, like everyone else in America, about fighting the communists; but I didn't have to do it myself, and when it comes to doing it yourself it's a different matter. Oh, we women cheered our American boys when they went to fight—there's no one more bloodthirsty than one who doesn't have to do the fighting. But when you do your own killing, it's a dreadful thing, Mr. O'Hara."

"I know," he said. "The only thing that makes it bearable is that if you don't kill, then you are killed. It reduces to a simple choice in the end."

"I realise that now, Mr. O'Hara," she said. "I'll be all right now."

"My name is Tim," he said. "The English are pretty stuffy about getting on to first-name terms, but not we Irish."

She gave him a tremulous smile. "I'm Jennifer."

"All right, Jenny," said O'Hara. "I'll try not to put you in a spot like that again."

She turned her head away and said in a muffled voice, "I think I'm going to cry." Hastily she scrambled to her feet and ran out of the shelter.

Benedetta said from behind O'Hara, "That was well done, Tim."

He turned and looked at her stonily. "Was it? It was something that had to be done." He got up and stretched his legs. "Let's practise with that crossbow."

v

For the rest of the day they practised, learning to allow for wind and the effect of a change of range. Miss Ponsky tightened still further her wire-drawn nerves and became instructress, and the general level of performance improved enormously.

O'Hara went down to the gorge and, by triangulation, carefully measured the distance to the enemy vehicles and was satisfied that he had the range measured to a foot. Then he went back and measured the same distance on the ground and told everyone to practise with the bow at that range. It was one hundred and eight yards.

He said to Benedetta, "I'm making you my chief-of-staff—that's a sort of glorified secretary that a general has. Have you got pencil and paper?"

She smiled and nodded, whereupon he reeled off a dozen things that had to be done. " You pass on that stuff to the right people in case I forget—I've got a hell of a lot of things on my mind right now and I might slip up on something important when the action starts."

He set Aguillar to tying bunches of rags around half a dozen bolts, then shot them at the target to see if the rags made any difference to the accuracy of the flight. There was no appreciable difference, so he soaked one of them in paraffin and lit it before firing, but the flame was extinguished before it reached the target.

He swore and experimented further, letting the paraffin burn fiercely before he pulled the trigger. At the expense of a scorched face he finally landed three fiercely burning bolts squarely in the target and observed happily that they continued to burn.

" We'll have to do this in the day-time," he said. " It'll be bloody dangerous in the dark—they'd spot the flame before we shot." He looked up at the sun. " To-morrow," he said. " We've got to drag this thing out as long as we can."

It was late afternoon before the enemy ventured on to the bridge again and they scattered at a shot from Rohde who, after a long sleep, had taken over again from Forester. Rohde fired another shot before sunset and then stopped on instructions from O'Hara. " Keep the last two bullets," he said. " We'll need them."

So the enemy put in three more planks and stepped up their illumination that night, although they dared not move on the bridge.

Chapter IV

Forester awoke at dawn. He felt refreshed after having had a night's unbroken sleep. O'Hara had insisted that he and Rohde should not stand night watches but should get as much sleep as they could. This was the day that he and Rohde were to go up to the hutted camp to get acclimatised and the next day to go on up to the mine.

He looked up at the white mountains and felt a sudden chill in his bones. He had lied to O'Hara when he said he had mountaineered in the Rockies—the highest he had climbed was to the top of the Empire State Building in an elevator. The high peaks were blindingly bright as the sun touched them and he wrinkled his eyes to see the pass that Rohde had pointed out. Rohde had said he would be sorry and Forester judged he was right; Rohde was a tough cookie and not given to exaggeration.

After cleaning up he went down to the bridge. Armstrong was on watch, lying on his back beneath the mirror. He was busy sketching on a scrap of paper with a pencil stub, glancing up at the mirror every few minutes. He waved as he saw Forester crawling up and said, "All quiet. They've just switched off the lights."

Forester looked at the piece of paper. Armstrong had drawn what looked like a chemist's balance. "What's that?" he asked. "The scales of justice?"

Armstrong looked startled and then pleased. "Why, sir, you have identified it correctly," he said.

Forester did not press it further. He thought Armstrong was a nut—clever, but still a nut. That crossbow of his had turned out to be some weapon—but it took a nut to think it up. He smiled at Armstrong and crawled away to where he could get a good look at the bridge.

His mouth tightened when he saw how narrow the gap was. Maybe he wouldn't have to climb the pass after all; maybe he'd have to fight and die right where he was. He judged that by the afternoon the gap would be narrow enough for a man to jump and that O'Hara had better prepare himself for a shock. But O'Hara had seemed untroubled and talked of a plan, and Forester hoped to God that he knew what he was doing.

When he got back to the rock shelter he found that Willis had come down from the hutted camp. He had hauled a *travois* the whole way and it was now being unpacked. He had brought more food, some blankets and another crossbow which he was demonstrating to O'Hara.

"This will be faster loading," he said. "I found some small gears, so I built them into the windlass—they make the cranking a lot easier. How did the other bow work?"

"Bloody good," said O'Hara. "It killed a man."

Willis paled a little and the unshaven bristles stood out against his white skin. Forester smiled grimly. The backroom boys always felt squeamish when they heard the results of their tinkering.

O'Hara turned to Forester. "As soon as they start work

85

on the bridge we'll give them a surprise," he said. "It's time we put a bloody crimp in their style. We'll have breakfast and then go down to the bridge—you'd better stick around and see the fun; you can leave immediately afterwards."

He swung around. "Jenny, don't bother about helping with the breakfast. You're our star turn. Take a crossbow and have a few practice shots at the same range as yesterday." As she paled, he smiled and said gently. "We'll be going down to the bridge and you'll be firing at a stationary, inanimate target."

Forester said to Willis, "Where's Peabody?"

"Back at the camp—making more arrows."

"Have any trouble with him?"

Willis grinned briefly. "He's a lazy swine but a couple of kicks up the butt soon cured that," he said, unexpectedly coarsely. "Where's Armstrong?"

"On watch down by the bridge."

Willis rubbed his chin with a rasping noise. "That man's got ideas," he said. "He's a whole Manhattan Project by himself. I want to talk to him."

He headed down the hill and Forester turned to Rohde, who had been talking to Aguillar and Benedetta in Spanish. "What do we take with us?"

"Nothing from here," Rohde said. "We can get what we want at the camp; but we must take little from there—we travel light."

O'Hara looked up from the can of stew he was opening. "You'd better take warm clothing—you can have my leather jacket," he offered.

"Thanks," Forester said.

O'Hara grinned. "And you'd better take your boss's vicuna coat—he may need it. I hear it gets cold in New York."

Forester smiled and took the can of hot stew. "I doubt if he'll appreciate it," he said dryly.

They had just finished breakfast when Willis came running back. "They've started work on the bridge," he shouted. "Armstrong wants to know if he should shoot."

"Hell no," said O'Hara. "We've only got two bullets." He swung on Rohde. "Go down there, get the gun from Armstrong and find yourself a good spot for shooting—but don't shoot until I tell you."

Rohde plunged down the hill and O'Hara turned to the others. "Everyone gather round," he ordered. "Where's Jenny?"

"I'm here," called Miss Ponsky from inside the shelter.
"Come to the front, Jenny; you'll play a big part in all this." O'Hara squatted down and drew two parallel lines in the dust with a sharp stone. "That's the gorge and this is the bridge. Here is the road; it crosses the bridge, turns sharply on the other side and runs on the edge of the gorge, parallel to the river."

He placed a small stone on his rough diagram. "Just by the bridge there's a jeep, and behind it another jeep. Both are turned so that their lights illuminate the bridge. Behind the second jeep there's a big truck half full of timber." O'Hara placed a larger stone. "Behind the truck there's another jeep. There are some other vehicles farther down, but we're not concerned with those now."

He shifted his position. "Now for our side of the gorge. Miguel will be here, upstream of the bridge. He'll take one shot at the men on the bridge. He won't hit anyone—he hasn't yet, anyway—but that doesn't matter. It'll scare them and divert their attention, which is what I want.

"Jenny will be *here*, downstream of the bridge and immediately opposite the truck. The range is one hundred and eight yards, and we know the crossbow will do it because Jenny was shooting consistently well at that range all yesterday afternoon. As soon as she hears the shot she lets fly at the petrol tank of the truck."

He looked up at Forester. "You'll be right behind Jenny. As soon as she has fired she'll hand you the bow and tell you if she's hit the tank. If she hasn't, you crank the bow, reload it and hand it back to her for another shot. If she *has* hit it, then you crank it, run up to where Benedetta will be waiting and give it to her cocked but unloaded."

He placed another small stone. "I'll be there with Benedetta right behind me. She'll have the other crossbow ready cocked and with a fire-bolt in it." He looked up at her. "When I give you the signal you'll light the paraffin rags on the bolt and hand the crossbow to me, and I'll take a crack at the truck. We might need a bit of rapid fire at this point, so crank up the bows. You stick to seeing that the bolts are properly ignited before the bows are handed to me, just like we did yesterday in practice."

He stood up and stretched. "Is that clear to everyone?"
Willis said, "What do I do?"
"Anyone not directly concerned with this operation will keep his head down and stay out of the way." O'Hara paused.

"But stand by in case anything goes wrong with the bows."

"I've got some spare bowstrings," said Willis. "I'll have a look at that first bow to see if it's okay."

"Do that," said O'Hara. "Any more questions?"

There were no questions. Miss Ponsky held up her chin in a grimly determined manner; Benedetta turned immediately to collect the fire-bolts which were her care; Forester merely said, "Okay with me."

As they were going down the hill, though, he said to O'Hara, "It's a good plan, but your part is goddam risky. They'll see those fire-bolts before you shoot. You stand a good chance of being knocked off."

"You can't fight a war without risk," said O'Hara. "And that's what this is, you know; it's as much a war as any bigger conflict."

"Yeah," said Forester thoughtfully. He glanced at O'Hara sideways. "What about me doing this fire-bolt bit?"

O'Hara laughed. "You're going with Rohde—you picked it, you do it. You said I was garrison commander, so while you're here you'll bloody well obey orders."

Forester laughed too. "It was worth a try," he said.

Close to the gorge they met Armstrong. "What's going on?" he asked plaintively.

"Willis will tell you all about it," said O'Hara. "Where's Rohde?"

Armstrong pointed. "Over there."

O'Hara said to Forester, "See that Jenny has a good seat for the performance," and went to find Rohde.

As always, Rohde had picked a good spot. O'Hara wormed his way next to him and asked, "How much longer do you think they'll be fixing that plank?"

"About five minutes." Rohde lifted the pistol, obviously itching to take a shot.

"Hold it," O'Hara said sharply. "When they come with the next plank give them five minutes and then take a crack. We've got a surprise cooking for them."

Rohde raised his eyebrows but said nothing. O'Hara looked at the massive stone buttresses which carried the cables of the bridge. "It's a pity those abutments aren't made of timber —they'd have burnt nicely. What the hell did they want to build them so big for?"

"The Incas always built well," said Rohde.

"You mean this is Inca work?" said O'Hara, astonished. Rohde nodded. "It was here before the Spaniards came.

The bridge needs constant renewal, but the buttresses will last for ever."

"Well, I'm damned," said O'Hara. "I wonder why the Incas wanted a bridge here—in the middle of nowhere."

"The Incas did many strange things." Rohde paused. "I seem to remember that the ore deposit of this mine was found by tracing the surface workings of the Incas. They would need the bridge if they worked metals up here."

O'Hara watched the men on the other side of the gorge. He spotted the big man with the beard whom Forester thought was the leader, wearing a quasi-uniform and with a pistol at his waist. He walked about bellowing orders and when he shouted men certainly jumped to it. O'Hara smiled grimly as he saw that they did not bother to take cover at all. No one had been shot at while on the other side—only when on the bridge and that policy was now going to pay off.

He said to Rohde, "You know what to do. I'm going to see to the rest of it." He slid back cautiously until it was safe to stand, then ran to where the rest were waiting, skirting the dangerous open ground at the approach to the bridge.

He said to Benedetta, "I'll be posted there; you'd better get your stuff ready. Have you got matches?"

"I have Señor Forester's cigarette-lighter."

"Good. You'd better keep it burning all the time, once the action starts. I'm just going along to see Jenny, then I'll be back."

Miss Ponsky was waiting with Forester a little farther along. She was bright-eyed and a little excited and O'Hara knew that she'd be all right if she didn't have to kill anyone. Well, that was all right, too; she would prepare the way and he'd do the killing. He said, "Have you had a look?"

She nodded quickly. "The gas tank is that big cylinder fastened under the truck."

"That's right; it's a big target. But try to hit it squarely —a bolt might glance off unless you hit it in the middle."

"I'll hit it," she said confidently.

He said, "They've just about finished putting a plank in. When they start to fasten the next one Rohde is going to give them five minutes and then pop off. That's your signal."

She smiled at him. "Don't worry, Tim, I'll do it."

Forester said, "I'll keep watch. When they bring up the plank Jenny can take over."

"Right," said O'Hara and went back to Benedetta. Armstrong was cocking the crossbow and Benedetta had arranged the fire-bolts in an arc, their points stuck in the earth. She lifted a can. " This is the last of the kerosene; we'll need more for cooking."

O'Hara smiled at this incongruous domestic note, and Willis said, " There's plenty up at the camp; we found two forty-gallon drums."

" Did you, by God?" said O'Hara. " That opens up possibilities." He climbed up among the rocks to the place he had chosen and tried to figure what could be done with a forty-gallon drum of paraffin. But then two men walked on to the bridge carrying a plank and he froze in concentration. One thing at a time, Tim, my boy, he thought.

He turned his head and said to Benedetta who was standing below, " Five minutes."

He heard the click as she tested the cigarette-lighter and turned his attention to the other side of the gorge. The minutes ticked by and he found the palms of his hands sweating. He wiped them on his shirt and cursed suddenly. A man had walked by the truck and was standing negligently in front of it—dead in front of the petrol tank.

" For Christ's sake, move on," muttered O'Hara. He knew that Miss Ponsky must have the man in her sights—but would she have the nerve to pull the trigger? He doubted it.

Hell's teeth, I should have told Rohde what was going on, he thought. Rhode wouldn't know about the crossbow and would fire his shot on time, regardless of the man covering the petrol tank. O'Hara ground his teeth as the man, a short, thick-set Indian type, produced a cigarette and carelessly struck a match on the side of the truck.

Rohde fired his shot and there was a yell from the bridge. The man by the truck stood frozen for a long moment and then started to run. O'Hara ignored him from then on—the man disappeared, that was all he knew—and his attention was riveted on the petrol tank. He heard a dull *thunk* even at that distance, and saw a dark shadow suddenly appear in the side of the tank, and saw the tank itself shiver abruptly.

Miss Ponsky had done it!

O'Hara wiped the sweat from his eyes and wished he had binoculars. Was that petrol dropping on to the road? Was that dark patch in the dust beneath the truck the spreading stain of leaking petrol, or was it just imagination? The trigger-happy bandits on the other side were letting go with all they had in their usual futile barrage, but he ignored the racket and strained his aching eyes.

The Indian came back and looked with an air of puzzlement at the truck. He sniffed the air suspiciously and then bent down to look underneath the vehicle. Then he let out a yell and waved violently.

By God, thought O'Hara exultantly, it *is* petrol!

He turned and snapped his fingers at Benedetta who immediately lit the fire-bolt waiting ready in the crossbow. O'Hara thumped the rock impatiently with his fist while she waited until it got well alight. But he knew this was the right way—if the rags were not burning well the flame would be extinguished in flight.

She thrust the bow at him suddenly and he twisted with it in his hands, the flame scorching his face. Another man had run up and was looking incredulously under the truck. O'Hara peered through the crude wire sight and through the flames of the burning bolt and willed himself to take his time. Gently he squeezed the trigger.

The butt lurched against his shoulder and he quickly twisted over to pass the bow back into Benedetta's waiting hands, but he had time to see the flaming bolt arch well over the truck to bury itself in the earth on the other side of the road.

This new bow was shooting too high.

He grabbed the second bow and tried again, burning his fingers as he incautiously put his hand in the flame. He could feel his eyebrows shrivelling as he aimed and again the butt slammed his shoulder as he pulled the trigger. The shot went too far to the right and the bolt skidded on the road surface, sending up a shower of sparks.

The two men by the truck had looked up in alarm when the first bolt had gone over their heads. At the sight of the second bolt they both shouted and pointed across the gorge.

Let this one be it, prayed O'Hara, as he seized the bow from Benedetta. This is the one that shoots high, he thought, as he deliberately aimed for the lip of the gorge. As he squeezed the trigger a bullet clipped the rock by his head and a granite splinter scored a bloody line across his forehead. But the bolt went true, a flaming line drawn across the gorge which passed between the two men and beneath the truck.

With a soft thud the dripping petrol caught alight and the truck was suddenly enveloped in flames. The Indian staggered out of the inferno, his clothing on fire, and ran screaming down the road, his hands clawing at his eyes. O'Hara did not see the other man; he had turned and was grabbing for the second bow.

But he didn't get off another shot. He had barely lined up the sights on one of the jeeps when the bow slammed into him before he touched the trigger. He was thrown back violently and the bow must have sprung of its own volition, for he saw a fire-bolt arch into the sky. Then his head struck a rock and he was knocked unconscious.

11

He came round to find Benedetta bathing his head, looking worried. Beyond, he saw Forester talking animatedly to Willis and beyond them the sky, disfigured by a coil of black, greasy smoke. He put his hand to his head and winced. "What the hell hit me?"

"Hush," said Benedetta. "Don't move."

He grinned weakly and lifted himself up on his elbow. Forester saw that he was moving. "Are you all right, Tim?"

"I don't know," said O'Hara. "I don't think so." His head ached abominably. "What happened?"

Willis lifted the crossbow. "A rifle bullet hit this," he said. "It smashed the stirrup—you were lucky it didn't hit you. You batted your head against a rock and passed out."

O'Hara smiled painfully at Benedetta. "I'm all right," he said and sat up. "Did we do the job?"

Forester laughed delightedly. "Did we do the job? Oh, boy!" He knelt down next to O'Hara. "To begin with, Rohde actually hit his man on the bridge when he shot— plugged him neatly through the shoulder. That caused all the commotion we needed. Jenny Ponsky had a goddam tricky time with that guy in front of the gas tank, but she did her job in the end. She was shaking like a leaf when she gave me the bow."

"What about the truck?" asked O'Hara. "I saw it catch fire—that's about the last thing I did see."

"The truck's gone," said Forester. "It's still burning —and the jeep next to it caught fire when the second gas tank on the other side of the truck blew up. Hell, they were running about like ants across there." He lowered his voice.

"Both the men who were by the truck were killed. The Indian ran plumb over the edge of the gorge—I reckon he was blinded—and the other guy was burned to a crisp. Jenny didn't see it and I didn't tell her."

O'Hara nodded; it would be a nasty thing for her to live with.

"That's about it," said Forester. "They've lost all their timber—it burned with the truck. They've lost the truck and a jeep and they've abandoned the jeep by the bridge—they couldn't get it back past the burning truck. All the other vehicles they've withdrawn a hell of a long way down the road where it turns away from the gorge. I'd say it's a good half-mile. They were hopping mad, judging by the way they opened up on us. They set up the damnedest barrage of rifle fire—they must have all the ammunition in the world."

"Anybody hurt?" demanded O'Hara.

"You're our most serious casualty—no one else got a scratch."

"I must bandage your head, Tim," said Benedetta.

"We'll go up to the pond," said O'Hara.

As he got to his feet Aguillar approached. "You did well, Señor O'Hara," he said.

O'Hara swayed and leaned on Forester for support. "Well enough, but they won't fall for that trick again. All we've bought is time." His voice was sober.

"Time is what we need," said Forester. "Earlier this morning I wouldn't have given two cents for our scheme to cross the mountains. But now Rohde and I can leave with an easy conscience." He looked at his watch. "We'd better get on the road."

Miss Ponsky came up. "Are you all right, Mr. O'Hara —Tim?"

"I'm fine," he said. "You did all right, Jenny."

She blushed. "Why—thank you, Tim. But I had a dreadful moment. I really thought I'd have to shoot that man by the truck."

O'Hara looked at Forester and grinned weakly and Forester suppressed a macabre laugh. "You did just what you were supposed to do," said O'Hara, "and you did it very well." He looked around. "Willis, you stay down here—get the gun from Rohde and if anything happens fire the last bullet. But I don't think anything will happen—not yet a while. The rest of us will have a war council up by the pond. I'd like to do that before Ray goes off."

"Okay," said Forester.

They went up to the pond and O'Hara walked over to the water's edge. Before he took a cupped handful of water he caught sight of his own reflection and grimaced distastefully. He was unshaven and very dirty, his face blackened by smoke and dried blood and his eyes red-rimmed and sore from the heat of the fire-bolts. My God, I look like a tramp, he thought.

He dashed cold water at his face and shivered violently, then turned to find Benedetta behind him, a strip of cloth in her hands. "Your head," she said. "The skin was broken."

He put a hand to the back of his head and felt the stickiness of drying blood. "Hell, I must have hit hard," he said.

"You're lucky you weren't killed. Let me see to it."

Her fingers were cool on his temples as she washed the wound and bandaged his head. He rubbed his hand raspingly over his cheek; Armstrong is always clean-shaven, he thought; I must find out how he does it.

Benedetta tied a neat little knot and said, "You must take it easy to-day, Tim. I think you are concussed a little."

He nodded, then winced as a sharp pain stabbed through his head. "I think you're right. But as for taking it easy— that isn't up to me; that's up to the boys on the other side of the river. Let's get back to the others."

Forester rose up as they approached. "Miguel thinks we should get going," he said.

"In a moment," said O'Hara. "There are a few things I want to find out." He turned to Rohde. "You'll be spending a day at the camp and a day at the mine. That's two days used up. Is this lost time necessary?"

"It is necessary and barely enough," said Rohde. "It should be longer."

"You're the expert on mountains," said O'Hara. "I'll take your word for it. How long to get across?"

"Two days," said Rohde positively. "If we have to take longer we will not do it at all."

"That's four days," said O'Hara. "Add another day to convince someone that we're in trouble and another for that someone to do something about it. We've got to hold out for six days at least—maybe longer."

Forester looked grave. "Can you do it?"

"We've got to do it," said O'Hara. "I think we've gained one day. They've got to find some timber from somewhere, and that means going back at least fifty miles to a town. They might have to get another truck as well—and it all takes time. I don't think we'll be troubled until to-morrow—maybe not until the next day. But I'm thinking about your troubles— how are you going to handle things on the other side of the mountain?"

Miss Ponsky said, " I've been wondering about that, too. You can't go to the government of this man Lopez. He would help Señor Aguillar, would he?"

Forester smiled mirthlessly. " He wouldn't lift a finger. Are there any of your people in Altemiros, Señor Aguillar?"

" I will give you an address," said Aguillar. " And Miguel will know. But you may not have to go as far as Altemiros."

Forester looked interested and Aguillar said to Rohde, " The airfield."

" Ah," said Rohde. " But we must be careful."

" What's this about an airfield?" Forester asked.

" There is a high-level airfield in the mountains this side of Altemiros," said Aguillar. " It is a military installation which the fighter squadrons use in rotation. Cordillera has four squadrons of fighter aircraft—the eighth, the tenth, the fourteenth and the twenty-first squadrons. We—like the communists—have been infiltrating the armed forces. The fourteenth squadron is ours; the eighth is communist; and the other two still belong to Lopez."

" So the odds are three to one that any squadron at the airfield will be a rotten egg," commented Forester.

" That is right," said Aguillar. " But the airfield is directly on your way to Altemiros. You must tread carefully and act discreetly, and perhaps you can save much time. The commandant of the fourteenth squadron, Colonel Rodriguez, is an old friend of mine—he is safe."

" If he's there," said Forester. " But it's worth the chance. We'll make for this airfield as soon as we've crossed the mountains."

" That's settled," said O'Hara with finality. " Doctor Armstrong, have you any more tricks up your medieval sleeve?"

Armstrong removed his pipe from his mouth. " I think I have. I had an idea and I've been talking to Willis about it and he thinks he can make it work." He nodded towards the gorge. " Those people are going to be more prepared when they come back with their timber. They're not going to stand up and be shot at like tin ducks in a shooting gallery—they're going to have their defences against our crossbows. So what we need now is a trench mortar."

"For Christ's sake," exploded O'Hara. "Where the devil are we going to get a trench mortar?"

"Willis is going to make it," Armstrong said equably. "With the help of Señor Rohde, Mr. Forester and myself—and Mr. Peabody, of course, although he isn't much help, really."

"So I'm going to make a trench mortar," said Forester helplessly. He looked baffled. "What do we use for explosives? Something cleverly cooked up out of match-heads?"

"Oh, you misunderstand me," said Armstrong. "I mean the medieval equivalent of a trench mortar. We need a machine that will throw a missile in a high trajectory to lob *behind* the defences which our enemies will undoubtedly have when they make their next move. There are no really new principles in modern warfare, you know; merely new methods of applying the old principles. Medieval man knew all the principles."

He looked glumly at his empty pipe. "They had a variety of weapons. The onager is no use for our purpose, of course. I did think of the mangonel and the ballista, but I discarded those too, and finally settled on the trebuchet. Powered by gravity, you know, and very effective."

If the crossbows had not been such a great success O'Hara would have jeered at Armstrong, but now he held his peace, contenting himself with looking across at Forester ironically. Forester still looked baffled and shrugged his shoulders. "What sort of missile would the thing throw?" he asked.

"I was thinking of rocks," said Armstrong. "I explained the principle of the trebuchet to Willis and he has worked it all out. It's merely the application of simple mechanics, you know, and Willis has got all that at his fingertips. We'll probably make a better trebuchet than they could in the Middle Ages—we can apply the scientific principles with more understanding. Willis thinks we can throw a twenty-pound rock over a couple of hundred yards with no trouble at all."

"Wow!" said O'Hara. He visualised a twenty-pound boulder arching in a high trajectory—it would come out of the sky almost vertically at that range. "We can do the bridge a bit of no good with a thing like that."

"How long will it take to make?" asked Forester.

"Not long," said Armstrong. "Not more than twelve hours, Willis thinks. It's a very simple machine, really."

O'Hara felt in his pocket and found his cigarette packet. He took one of his last cigarettes and gave it to Armstrong. "Put that in your pipe and smoke it. You deserve it."

Armstrong smiled delightedly and began to shred the cigarette. "Thanks," he said. "I can think much better when I smoke."

O'Hara grinned. "I'll give you all my cigarettes if you can come up with the medieval version of the atom bomb."

"That was gunpowder," said Armstrong seriously. "I think that's beyond us at the moment."

"There's just one thing wrong with your idea," O'Hara commented. "We can't have too many people up at the camp. We must have somebody down at the bridge in case the enemy does anything unexpected. We've got to keep a fighting force down here."

"I'll stay," said Armstrong, puffing at his pipe contentedly. "I'm not very good with my hands—my fingers are all thumbs. Willis knows what to do; he doesn't need me."

"That's it, then," said O'Hara to Forester. "You and Miguel go up to the camp, help Willis and Peabody build this contraption, then push on to the mine to-morrow. I'll go down and relieve Willis at the bridge."

III

Forester found the going hard as they climbed up to the camp. His breath wheezed in his throat and he developed slight chest pains. Rohde was not so much affected and Willis apparently not at all. During the fifteen-minute rest at the half-way point he commented on it. "That is acclimatisation," Rohde explained. "Señor Willis has spent much time at the camp—to come down means nothing to him. For us going up it is different."

"That's right," said Willis. "Going down to the bridge was like going down to sea-level, although the bridge must be about twelve thousand feet up."

"How high is the camp?" asked Forester.

"I'd say about fourteen and a half thousand feet," said Willis. "I'd put the mine at a couple of thousand feet higher."

Forester looked up at the peaks. "And the pass is nineteen thousand. Too close to heaven for my liking, Miguel."

Rohde's lips twisted. "Not heaven—it is a cold hell."

When they arrived at the camp Forester was feeling bad and said so. "You will be better to-morrow," said Rohde.

"But to-morrow we're going higher," said Forester morosely.

"One day at each level is not enough to acclimatise," Rohde admitted. "But it is all the time we can afford."

Willis looked around the camp. "Where the hell is Peabody? I'll go and root him out."

He wandered off and Rohde said, "I think we should search this camp thoroughly. There may be many things that would be of use to O'Hara."

"There's the kerosene," said Forester. "Maybe Armstrong's gadget can throw fire bombs. That would be one way of getting at the bridge to burn it."

They began to search the huts. Most of them were empty and disused, but three of them had been fitted out for habitation and there was much equipment. In one of the huts they found Willis shaking a recumbent Peabody, who was stretched out on a bunk.

"Five arrows," said Willis bitterly. "That's all this bastard has done—made five arrows before he drank himself stupid."

"Where's he getting the booze?" asked Forester.

"There's a case of the stuff in one of the other huts."

"Lock it up if you can," said Forester. "If you can't, pour it away—I ought to have warned you about this, but I forgot. We can't do much about him now—he's too far gone."

Rohde who had been exploring the hut grunted suddenly as he took a small leather bag from a shelf. "This is good."

Forester looked with interest at the pale green leaves which Rohde shook out into the palm of his hand. "What's that?"

"Coca leaves," said Rohde. "They will help us when we cross the mountain."

"Coca?" said Forester blankly.

"The curse of the Andes," said Rohde. "This is where cocaine comes from. It has been the ruin of the *indios*—this and *aguardiente*. Señor Aguillar intends to restrict the growing of coca when he comes into power." He smiled slowly. "It would be asking too much to stop it altogether."

"How is it going to help us?" asked Forester.

"Look around for another bag like this one containing

a white powder," said Rohde. As they rummaged among the shelves, he continued, " In the great days of the Incas the use of coca was restricted to the nobles. Then the royal messengers were permitted to use it because it increased their running power and stamina. Now all the *indios* chew coca— it is cheaper than food."

" It isn't a substitute for food, is it?"

" It anæsthetises the stomach lining," said Rohde. " A starving man will do anything to avoid the pangs of hunger. It is also a narcotic, bringing calmness and tranquillity—at a price."

" Is this what you're looking for?" asked Forester. He opened a small bag he had found and tipped out some of the powder. " What is it?"

" Lime," said Rohde. " Cocaine is an alkaloid and needs a base for it to precipitate. While we are waiting for Señor Willis to tell us what to do, I will prepare this for us."

He poured the coca leaves into a saucer and began to grind them, using the back of a spoon as a pestle. The leaves were brittle and dry and broke up easily. When he had ground them to a powder he added lime and continued to grind until the two substances were thoroughly mixed. Then he put the mixture into an empty tin and added water, stirring until he had a light green paste. He took another tin and punched holes in the bottom, and, using it as a strainer, he forced the paste through.

He said, " In any of the villages round here you can see the old women doing this. Will you get me some small, smooth stones?"

Forester went out and got the stones and Rohde used them to roll and squeeze the paste like a pastrycook. Finally the paste was rolled out for the last time and Rohde cut it into rectangles with his pocket-knife. " These must dry in the sun," he said. " Then we put them back in the bags."

Forester looked dubiously at the small green squares. " Is this stuff habit-forming?"

" Indeed it is," said Rohde. " But do not worry; this amount will do us no harm. And it will give us the endurance to climb the mountains."

Willis came back. " We can swing it," he said. " We've got the material to make this—what did Armstrong call it?"

" A trebuchet," Forester said.

" Well, we can do it," said Willis. He stopped and looked down at the table. " What's that stuff?"

Forester grinned. "A substitute for prime steak; Miguel just cooked it up." He shook his head. "Medieval artillery and pep pills—what a hell of a mixture."

"Talking about steak reminds me that I'm hungry," said Willis. "We'll eat before we get started."

They opened some cans of stew and prepared a meal. As Forester took the first mouthful, he said, "Now, tell me—what the hell is a trebuchet?"

Willis smiled and produced a stub of pencil. "Just an application of the lever," he said. "Imagine a thing like an out-of-balance see-saw—like this." Rapidly he sketched on the soft pine top of the table. "The pivot is here and one arm is, say, four times as long as the other. On the short arm you sling a weight, of, say, five hundred pounds, and on the other end you have your missile—a twenty-pound rock."

He began to jot down calculations. "Those medieval fellows worked empirically—they didn't have the concepts of energy that we have. We can do the whole thing precisely from scratch. Assuming your five-hundred-pound weight drops ten feet. The acceleration of gravity is such that, taking into account frictional losses at the pivot, it will take half a second to fall. That's five thousand foot-pounds in a half-second, six hundred thousand foot-pounds to the minute, eighteen horse-power of energy applied instantaneously to a twenty-pound rock on the end of the long arm."

"That should make it move," said Forester.

"I can tell you the speed," said Willis. "Assuming the ratio between the two arms is four to one, then the . . . the . . ." He stopped, tapped on the table for a moment, then grinned. "Let's call it the muzzle velocity, although this thing hasn't a muzzle. The muzzle velocity will be eighty feet per second."

"Is there any way of altering the range?"

"Sure," said Willis. "Heavy stones won't go as far as light stones. You want to decrease the range, you use a heavier rock. I must tell O'Hara that—he'd better get busy collecting and grading ammunition."

He began to sketch on the table in more detail. "For the pivot we have the back axle of a wrecked truck that's back of the huts. The arms we make from the roof beams of a hut. There'll have to be a cup of some kind to hold the missile—we'll use a hub cap bolted on to the end of the long arm. The whole thing will need a mounting but we'll figure that out when we come to it."

Forester looked at the sketch critically. "It's going to be damned big and heavy. How are we going to get it down the mountain?"

Willis grinned. "I've figured that out too. The whole thing will pull apart and we'll use the axle to carry the rest of it. We'll wheel the damn thing down the mountain and assemble it again at the bridge."

"You've done well," said Forester.

"It was Armstrong who thought it up," said Willis. "For a scholar, he has the most murderous tendencies. He knows more ways of killing people—say, have you ever heard of Greek fire?"

"In a vague sort of way."

"Armstrong says it was as good as napalm, and that the ancients used to have flame-throwers mounted on the prows of their warships. We've done a bit of thinking along those lines and got nowhere." He looked broodingly at his sketch. "He says this thing is nothing to the siege weapons they had. They used to throw dead horses over city walls to start a plague. How heavy is a horse?"

"Maybe horses weren't as big in those days," said Forester.

"Any horse that could carry a man in full armour was no midget," Willis pointed out. He spooned the last of the gravy from his plate. "We'd better get started—I don't want to work all night again."

Rohde nodded briefly and Forester looked over at Peabody, snoring on the bunk. "I think we'll start with a bucket of the coldest water we can get," he said.

I V

O'Hara looked across the gorge.

Tendrils of smoke still curled from the burnt-out vehicles and he caught the stench of burning rubber. He looked speculatively at the intact jeep at the bridgehead and debated whether to do something about it, but discarded the idea almost as soon as it came to him. It would be useless to destroy a single vehicle—the enemy had plenty more—and he must husband his resources for more vital targets. It was not his intention to wage a war of attrition; the enemy could beat him hands down at that game.

He had been along the edge of the gorge downstream to where the road turned away, half a mile from the bridge, and had picked out spots from which crossbowmen could keep up a harassing fire. Glumly, he thought that Armstrong was right—the enemy would not be content to be docile targets; they would certainly take steps to protect themselves against further attack. The only reason for the present success was the unexpectedness of it all, as though a rabbit had taken a weasel by the throat.

The enemy was still vigilant by the bridge. Once, when O'Hara had incautiously exposed himself, he drew a concentrated fire that was unpleasantly accurate and it was only his quick reflexes and the fact that he was in sight for so short a time that saved him from a bullet in the head. We can take no chances, he thought; no chances at all.

Now he looked at the bridge with the twelve-foot gap yawning in the middle and thought of ways of getting at it. Fire still seemed the best bet and Willis had said that there were two drums of paraffin up at the camp. He measured with his eye the hundred-yard approach to the bridge; there was a slight incline and he thought that, given a good push, a drum would roll as far as the bridge. It was worth trying.

Presently Armstrong came down to relieve him. "Grub's up," he said.

O'Hara regarded Armstrong's smooth cheeks. "I didn't bring my shaving-kit," he said. "Apparently you did."

"I've got one of those Swiss wind-up dry shavers," said Armstrong. "You can borrow it if you like. It's up at the shelter in my coat pocket."

O'Hara thanked him and pointed out the enemy observation posts he had spotted. "I don't think they'll make an attempt on the bridge to-day," he said, "so I'm going up to the camp this afternoon. I want those drums of paraffin. But if anything happens while I'm gone and the bastards get across, then you scatter. Aguillar, Benedetta and Jenny rendezvous at the mine—not the camp—and they go up the mountain the hard way, steering clear of the road. You get up to the camp by the road as fast as you can—you'd better move fast because they'll be right on your tail."

Armstrong nodded. "I have the idea. We stall them off at the camp, giving the others time to get to the mine."

"That's right," said O'Hara. "But you're the boss in my absence and you'll have to use your own judgment."

He left Armstrong and went back to the shelter, where he found the professor's coat and rummaged in the pockets. Benedetta smiled at him and said, "Lunch is ready."

"I'll be back in a few minutes," he said, and went down the hill towards the pond, carrying the dry shaver.

Aguillar pulled his overcoat tighter about him and looked at O'Hara's retreating figure with curious eyes. "That one is strange," he said. "He is a fighter but he is too cold—too objective. There is no hot blood in him, and that is not good for a young man."

Benedetta bent her head and concentrated on the stew. "Perhaps he has suffered," she said.

Aguillar smiled slightly as he regarded Benedetta's averted face. "You say he was a prisoner in Korea?" he asked.

She nodded.

"Then he must have suffered," agreed Aguillar. "Perhaps not in the body, but certainly in the spirit. Have you asked him about it?"

"He will not talk about it."

Aguillar wagged his head. "That is also very bad. It is not good for a man to be so self-contained—to have his violence pent-up. It is like screwing down the safety-valve on a boiler—one can expect an explosion." He grimaced. "I hope I am not near when that young man explodes."

Benedetta's head jerked up. "You talk nonsense, Uncle. His anger is directed against those others across the river. He would do us no harm."

Aguillar looked at her sadly. "You think so, child? His anger is directed against himself as the power of a bomb is directed against its casing—but when the casing shatters everyone around is hurt. O'Hara is a dangerous man."

Benedetta's lips tightened and she was going to reply when Miss Ponsky approached, lugging a crossbow. She seemed unaccountably flurried and the red stain of a blush was ebbing from her cheeks. Her protection was volubility. "I've got both bows sighted in," she said rapidly. "They're both shooting the same now, and very accurately. They're very strong too—I was hitting a target at one hundred and twenty yards. I left the other with Doctor Armstrong; I thought he might need it."

"Have you seen Señor O'Hara?" asked Benedetta.

Miss Ponsky turned pink again. "I saw him at the pond," she said in a subdued voice. "What are we having for lunch?" she continued brightly.

Benedetta laughed. "As always—stew."

Miss Ponsky shuddered delicately. Benedetta said, "It is

all that Señor Willis brought from the camp—cans of stew. Perhaps it is his favourite food."

"He ought to have thought of the rest of us," complained Miss Ponsky.

Aguillar stirred. "What do you think of Señor Forester, madam?"

"I think he is a very brave man," she said simply. "He and Señor Rohde."

"I think so too," said Aguillar. "But also I think there is something strange about him. He is too much the man of action to be a simple businessman."

"Oh, I don't know," Miss Ponsky demurred. "A good businessman must be a man of action, at least in the States."

"Somehow I don't think Forester's idea is the pursuit of the dollar," Aguillar said reflectively. "He is not like Peabody."

Miss Ponsky flared. "I could *spit* when I think of that man. He makes me ashamed to be an American."

"Do not be ashamed," Aguillar said gently. "He is not a coward because he is an American; there are cowards among all people."

O'Hara came back. He looked better now that he had shaved the stubble from his cheeks. It had not been easy; the clockwork rotary shaver had protested when asked to attack the thicket of his beard, but he had persisted and was now smooth-cheeked and clean. The water in the pond had been too cold for bathing, but he had stripped and taken a sponge-bath and felt the better for it. Out of the corner of his eye he had seen Miss Ponsky toiling up the hill towards the shelter and hoped she had not seen him—he did not want to offend the susceptibilities of maiden ladies.

"What have we got?" he asked.

"More stew," said Aguillar wryly.

O'Hara groaned and Benedetta laughed. He accepted the aluminium plate and said, "Maybe I can bring something else when I go up to the camp this afternoon. But I won't have room for much—I'm more interested in the paraffin."

Miss Ponsky asked, "What is it like by the river?"

"Quiet," said O'Hara. "They can't do much to-day so they're contenting themselves with keeping the bridge covered. I think it's safe enough for me to go up to the camp."

"I'll come with you," said Benedetta quickly.

O'Hara paused, his fork in mid-air. "I don't know if . . ."

"We need food," she said. "And if you cannot carry it, somebody must."

O'Hara glanced at Aguillar, who nodded tranquilly. "It will be all right," he said.

O'Hara shrugged. "It will be a help," he admitted.

Benedetta sketched a curtsy at him, but there was a flash of something in her eyes that warned O'Hara he must tread gently. "Thank you," she said, a shade too sweetly. "I'll try not to get in the way."

He grinned at her. "I'll tell you when you are."

V

Like Forester, O'Hara found the going hard on the way up to the camp. When he and Benedetta took a rest half-way, he sucked in the thin, cold air greedily, and gasped, "My God, this is getting tough."

Benedetta's eyes went to the high peaks. "What about Miguel and Señor Forester? They will have it worse."

O'Hara nodded, then said, "I think your uncle ought to come up to the camp to-morrow. It is better that he should do it when he can do it in his own time, instead of being chased. And it will acclimatise him in case we have to retreat to the mine."

"I think that is good," she said. "I will go with him to help, and I can bring more food when I return."

"He might be able to help Willis with his bits and pieces," said O'Hara. "After all, he can't do much down at the bridge anyway, and Willis wouldn't mind another pair of hands."

Benedetta pulled her coat about her. "Was it as cold as this in Korea?"

"Sometimes," O'Hara said. He thought of the stone-walled cell in which he had been imprisoned. Water ran down the walls and froze into ice at night—and then the weather got worse and the walls were iced day and night. It was then that Lieutenant Feng had taken away all his clothing. "Sometimes," he repeated bleakly.

"I suppose you had warmer clothing than we have," said Benedetta. "I am worried about Forester and Miguel. It will be very cold up in the pass."

O'Hara felt suddenly ashamed of himself and his self-pity. He looked away quickly from Benedetta and stared at the snows above. "We must see if we can improvise a tent for them. They'll spend at least one night in the open up there." He stood up. "We'd better get on."

The camp was busy with the noise of hammering and the trebuchet was taking shape in the central clearing between the huts. O'Hara stood unnoticed for a moment and looked at it. It reminded him very much of something he had once seen in an avant-garde art magazine; a modern sculptor had assembled a lot of junk into a crazy structure and had given it some high-falutin' name, and the trebuchet had the same appearance of wild improbability.

Forester paused and leaned on the length of steel he was using as a crude hammer. As he wiped the sweat from his eyes he caught sight of the newcomers and hailed them. "What the hell are you doing here? Is anything wrong?"

"All's quiet," said O'Hara reassuringly. "I've come for one of the drums of paraffin—and some grub." He walked round the trebuchet. "Will this contraption work?"

"Willis is confident," said Forester. "That's good enough for me."

"You won't be here," O'Hara said stonily. "But I suppose I'll have to trust the boffins. By the way—it's going to be bloody cold up there—have you made any preparations?"

"Not yet. We've been too busy on this thing."

"That's not good enough," said O'Hara sternly. "We're depending on you to bring the good old U.S. cavalry to the rescue. You've *got* to get across that pass—if you don't, then this piece of silly artillery will be wasted. Is there anything out of which you can improvise a tent?"

"I suppose you're right," said Forester. "I'll have a look around."

"Do that. Where's the paraffin?"

"Paraffin? Oh, you mean the kerosene. It's in that hut there. Willis locked it up; he put all the booze in there—we had to keep Peabody sober somehow."

"Um," said O'Hara. "How's he doing?"

"He's not much good. He's out of condition and his disposition doesn't help. We've got to drive him."

"Doesn't the bloody fool realise that if the bridge is forced he'll get his throat cut?"

Forester sighed. "It doesn't seem to make any difference —logic isn't his strong-point. He goofs off at the slightest opportunity."

O'Hara saw Benedetta going into one of the huts. " I'd better get that paraffin. We must have it at the bridge before it gets dark."

He got the key of the hut from Willis and opened the door. Just inside was a crate, half-filled with bottles. There was a stir of longing in his guts as he looked at them, but he suppressed it firmly and switched his attention to the two drums of paraffin. He tested the weight of one of them, and thought, this is going to be a bastard to get down the mountain.

He heaved the drum on to its side and rolled it out of the hut. Across the clearing he saw Forester helping Benedetta to make a *travois,* and crossed over to them. " Is there any rope up here?"

" Rope we've got," replied Forester. " But Rohde was worried about that—he said we'll need it in the mountains, rotten though it is; and Willis needs it for the trebuchet, too. But there's plenty of electric wire that Willis ripped out to make crossbow-strings with."

" I'll need some to help me get that drum down the mountain—I suppose the electric wire will have to do."

Peabody wandered over. His face had a flabby, unhealthy look about it and he exuded the scent of fear. " Say, what is this?" he demanded. " Willis tells me that you and the spic are making a getaway over the mountains."

Forester's eyes were cold. " If you want to put it that way —yes."

" Well, I wanna come," said Peabody. " I'm not staying here to be shot by a bunch of commies."

" Are you crazy?" said Forester.

" What's so crazy about it? Willis says it's only fifteen miles to this place Altemiros."

Forester looked at O'Hara speechlessly. O'Hara said quietly, " Do you think it's going to be like a stroll in Central Park, Peabody?"

" Hell, I'd rather take my chance in the mountains than with the commies," said Peabody. " I think you're crazy if you think you can hold them off. What have you got? You've got an old man, a silly bitch of a school-marm, two nutty scientists and a girl. And you're fighting with bows and arrows, for God's sake." He tapped Forester on the chest. " If you're making a getaway, I'm coming along."

Forester slapped his hand away. " Now get this, Peabody; you'll do as you're damn well told."

"Who the hell are you to give orders?" said Peabody with venom. "To begin with I take no orders from a limey—and I don't see why you should be so high and mighty, either. I'll do as I damn well please."

O'Hara caught Forester's eye. "Let's see Rohde," he said hastily. He had seen Forester balling his fist and wanted to prevent trouble, for an idea was crystallising in his mind.

Rohde was positively against it. "This man is in no condition to cross the mountains," he said. "He will hold us back, and if he holds us back none of us will get across. We cannot spend more than one night in the open."

"What do you think?" Forester asked O'Hara.

"I don't like the man," said O'Hara. "He's weak and he'll break under pressure. If he breaks it might be the end of the lot of us. I can't trust him."

"That's fair enough," Forester agreed. "He's a weak sister, all right. I'm going to overrule you, Miguel; he comes with us. We can't afford to leave him with O'Hara."

Rohde opened his mouth to protest but stopped when he saw the expression on Forester's face. Forester grinned wolfishly and there was a hard edge to his voice when he said, "If he holds us up, we'll drop the bastard into the nearest crevasse. Peabody will have to put up or shut up."

He called Peabody over. "All right, you come with us. But let's get this straight right from the start. You take orders."

Peabody nodded. "All right," he mumbled. "I'll take orders from you."

Forester was merciless. "You'll take orders from anyone who damn well gives them from now on. Miguel is the expert round here and when he gives an order—you jump fast."

Peabody's eyes flickered, but he gave in. He had no option if he wanted to go with them. He shot a look of dislike at Rohde and said, "Okay, but when I get back Stateside the State Department is going to get an earful from me. What kind of place is this where good Americans can be pushed around by spics and commies?"

O'Hara looked at Rohde quickly. His face was as placid as though he had not heard. O'Hara admired his self-control —but he pitied Peabody when he got into the mountains.

Half an hour later he and Benedetta left. She was pulling the *travois* and he was clumsily steering the drum of paraffin.

There were two loops of wire round the drum in a sling so that he could have a measure of control. They had wasted little time in saying good-bye to Rohde and Forester, and still less on Peabody. Willis had said, "We'll need you up here to-morrow; the trebuchet will be ready then."

" I'll be here," promised O'Hara. " If I haven't any other engagements."

It was difficult going down the mountain, even though they were on the road. Benedetta hauled on the *travois* and had to stop frequently to rest, and more often to help O'Hara with the drum. It weighed nearly four hundred pounds and seemed to have a malevolent mind of its own. His idea of being able to steer it by pulling on the wires did not work well. The drum would take charge and go careering at an angle to wedge itself in the ditch at the side of the road. Then it would be a matter of sweat and strain to get it out, whereupon it would charge into the opposite ditch.

By the time they got down to the bottom O'Hara felt as though he had been wrestling with a malign and evil adversary. His muscles ached and it seemed as though someone had pounded him with a hammer all over his body. Worse, in order to get the drum down the mountain at all he had been obliged to lighten the load by jettisoning a quarter of the contents and had helplessly watched ten gallons of invaluable paraffin drain away into the thirsty dust.

When they reached the valley Benedetta abandoned the *travois* and went for help. O'Hara had looked at the sky and said, " I want this drum at the bridge before nightfall."

Night swoops early on the eastern slopes of the Andes. The mountain wall catches the setting sun, casting long shadows across the hot jungles of the interior. At five in the afternoon the sun was just touching the topmost peaks and O'Hara knew that in an hour it would be dark.

Armstrong came up to help and O'Hara immediately asked, " Who's on watch?"

" Jenny. She's all right. Besides, there's nothing doing at all."

With two men to control the erratic drum it went more easily and they manœuvred it to the bridgehead within half an hour. Miss Ponsky came running up. " They switched on their lights just now and I think I heard an auto engine from way back along there." She pointed downstream.

" I would have liked to try and put out the headlamps on

this jeep," she said. " But I didn't want to waste an arrow
—a quarrel—and in any case there's something in front of the
glass."

" They have stone guards in front of the lights," said
Armstrong. " Heavy mesh wire."

" Go easy on the bolts, anyway," said O'Hara. " Peabody
was supposed to be making some but he's been loafing on
the job." He carefully crept up and surveyed the bridgehead.
The jeep's headlights illuminated the whole bridge and its
approaches and he knew that at least a dozen sharp pairs of
eyes were watching. It would be suicidal to go out there.

He dropped back and looked at the drum in the fading
light. It was much dented by its careering trip down the
mountain road but he thought it would roll a little farther.
He said, " This is the plan. We're going to burn the bridge.
We're going to play the same trick that we played this morning but we'll apply it on this side of the bridge."

He put his foot on top of the drum and rocked it gently.
" If Armstrong gives this one good heave it should roll right
down to the bridge—if we're lucky. Jenny will be standing
up there with her crossbow and when it gets into the right
position she'll puncture it. I'll be in position too, with
Benedetta to hand me the other crossbow with a fire-bolt.
If the drum is placed right then we'll burn through the
ropes on this side and the whole bloody bridge will drop
into the water."

" That sounds all right," said Armstrong.

" Get the bows, Jenny," said O'Hara and took Armstrong
to one side, out of hearing of the others. " It's a bit more
tricky than that," he said. " In order to get the drum in the
right place you'll have to come into the open." He held
his head on one side; the noise of the vehicle had stopped.
" So I want to do it before they get any more lights on the
job."

Armstrong smiled gently. " I think your little bit is more
dangerous than mine. Shooting those fire-bolts in the dark
will make you a perfect target—it won't be as easy as this
morning, and then you nearly got shot."

" Maybe," said O'Hara. " But this has got to be done.
This is how we do it. When that other jeep—or whatever it
is—comes up, maybe the chaps on the other side won't be so
vigilant. My guess is that they'll tend to watch the vehicle
manœuvre into position; I don't think they're a very dis-

ciplined crowd. Now, while that's happening is the time to do your stuff. I'll give you the signal."

"All right, my boy," said Armstrong. "You can rely on me."

O'Hara helped him to push the drum into the position easiest for him, and then Miss Ponsky and Benedetta came up with the crossbows. He said to Benedetta, "When I give Armstrong the signal to push off the drum, you light the first fire-bolt. This has got to be done quickly if it's going to be done at all."

"All right, Tim," she said.

Miss Ponsky went to her post without a word.

He heard the engine again, this time louder. He saw nothing on the road downstream and guessed that the vehicle was coming slowly and without lights. He thought they'd be scared of being fired on during that half-mile journey. By God, he thought, if I had a dozen men with a dozen bows I'd make life difficult for them. He smiled sourly. Might as well wish for a machine-gun section—it was just as unlikely a possibility.

Suddenly the vehicle switched its lights on. It was quite near the bridge and O'Hara got ready to give Armstrong the signal. He held his hand until the vehicle—a jeep—drew level with the burnt-out truck, then he said in a whispered shout, "Now!"

He heard the rattle as the drum rolled over the rocks and out of the corner of his eye saw the flame as Benedetta ignited the fire-bolt. The drum came into sight on his left, bumping down the slight incline which led towards the bridge. It hit a larger stone which threw it off course. Christ, he whispered, we've bungled it.

Then he saw Armstrong run into the open, chasing after the drum. A few faint shouts came from across the river and there was a shot. "You damned fool," yelled O'Hara. "Get back." But Armstrong kept running forward until he had caught up with the drum and, straightening it on course again, he gave it another boost.

There was a *rafale* of rifle-fire and spurts of dust flew about Armstrong's feet as he ran back at full speed, then a metallic *thunk* as a bullet hit the drum and, as it turned, O'Hara saw a silver spurt of liquid rise in the air. The enemy were divided in their intentions—they did not know which was more dangerous, Armstrong or the drum. And so Armstrong got safely into cover.

Miss Ponsky raised the bow. "Forget it, Jenny," roared O'Hara. "They've done it for us."

Again and again the drum was hit as it rolled towards the bridge and the paraffin spurted out of more holes, rising in gleaming jets into the air until the drum looked like some strange kind of liquid catherine wheel. But the repeated impact of bullets was slowing it down and there must have been a slight and unnoticed rise in the ground before the bridge because the drum rolled to a halt just short of the abutments.

O'Hara swore and turned to grasp the crossbow which Benedetta was holding. Firing in the dark with a fire-bolt was difficult; the flame obscured his vision and he had to will himself consciously to take aim slowly. There was another babble of shouts from over the river and a bullet ricocheted from a rock nearby and screamed over his head.

He pressed the trigger gently and the scorching heat was abruptly released from his face as the bolt shot away into the opposing glare of headlamps. He ducked as another bullet clipped the rock by the side of his head and thrust the bow at Benedetta for reloading.

It was not necessary. There was a dull explosion and a violent flare of light as the paraffin around the drum caught fire. O'Hara, breathing heavily, moved to another place where he could see what was happening. It would have been very foolish to pop his head up in the same place from which he had fired his bolt.

It was with dejection that he saw a raging fire arising from a great pool of paraffin just short of the bridge. The drum had stopped too soon and although the fire was spectacular it would do the bridge no damage at all. He watched for a long time, hoping the drum would explode and scatter burning paraffin on the bridge, but nothing happened and slowly the fire went out.

He dropped back to join the others. "Well, we messed that one up," he said bitterly.

"I should have pushed it harder," Armstrong said.

O'Hara flared up in anger. "You damned fool, if you hadn't run out and given it another shove it wouldn't have gone as far as it did. Don't do an idiotic thing like that again —you nearly got killed!"

Armstrong said quietly, "We're all of us on the verge of getting killed. Someone has to risk something besides you."

"I should have surveyed the ground more carefully," said O'Hara self-accusingly.

Benedetta put a hand on his arm. "Don't worry, Tim; you did the best you could."

"Sure you did," said Miss Ponsky militantly. "And we've shown them we're still here and fighting. I bet they're scared to come across now for fear of being burned alive."

"Come," said Benedetta. "Come and eat." There was a flash of humour in her voice. "I didn't bring the *travois* all the way down, so it will be stew again."

Wearily O'Hara turned his back on the bridge. It was the third night since the plane crash—and six more to go!

Chapter V

Forester attacked his baked beans with gusto. The dawn light was breaking, dimming the bright glare of the Coleman lamp and smoothing out the harsh shadows on his face. He said, "One day at the mine—two days crossing the pass—another two days getting help. We must cut that down somehow. When we get to the other side we'll have to act quickly."

Peabody looked at the table morosely, ignoring Forester. He was wondering if he had made the right decision, done the right thing by Joe Peabody. The way these guys talked, crossing the mountains wasn't going to be so easy. Aw, to hell with it—he could do anything any other guy could do—especially any spic.

Rohde said, "I thought I heard rifle-fire last night—just at sunset." His face was haunted by the knowledge of his helplessness.

"They should be all right. I don't see how the commies could have repaired the bridge and got across so quickly," said Forester reasonably. "That O'Hara's a smart cookie. He must have been doing something with that drum of kerosene he took down the hill yesterday. He's probably cooked the bridge to a turn."

Rohde's face cracked into a faint smile. "I hope so."

Forester finished his beans. "Okay, let's get the show on the road." He turned round in his chair and looked at the huddle of blankets on the bunk. "What about Willis?"

113

"Let him sleep," said Rohde. "He worked harder and longer than any of us."

Forester got up and examined the packs they had made up the previous night. Their equipment was pitifully inadequate for the job they had to do. He remembered the books he had read about mountaineering expeditions—the special rations they had, the lightweight nylon ropes and tents, the windproof clothing and the specialised gear—climbing-boots, ice-axes, pitons. He smiled grimly—yes, and porters to help hump it.

There was none of that here. Their packs were roughly cobbled together from blankets; they had an ice-axe which Willis had made—a roughly shaped metal blade mounted on the end of an old broom handle; their ropes were rotten and none too plentiful, scavenged from the rubbish heap of the camp and with too many knots and splices for safety; their climbing-boots were clumsy miners' boots made of thick, unpliant leather, heavy and graceless. Willis had discovered the boots and Rohde had practically gone into raptures over them.

He lifted his pack and wished it was heavier—heavier with the equipment they needed. They had worked far into the night improvising, with Willis and Rohde being the most inventive. Rohde had torn blankets into long strips to make puttees, and Willis had practically torn down one of the huts single-handed in his search for extra long nails to use as pitons. Rohde shook his head wryly when he saw them. "The metal is too soft, but they will have to do."

Forester heaved the pack on to his back and fastened the crude electric wiring fastenings. Perhaps it's as well we're staying a day at the mine, he thought; maybe we can do better than this. There are suitcases up there with proper straps; there is the plane—surely we can find something in there we can use. He zipped up the front of the leather jacket and was grateful to O'Hara for the loan of it. He suspected it would be windy higher up, and the jacket was windproof.

As he stepped out of the hut he heard Peabody cursing at the weight of his pack. He took no notice but strode on through the camp, past the trebuchet which crouched like a prehistoric monster, and so to the road which led up the mountain. In two strides Rohde caught up and came abreast of him. He indicated Peabody trailing behind. "This one will make trouble," he said.

Forester's face was suddenly bleak. " I meant what I said, Miguel. If he makes trouble, we get rid of him."

It took them a long time to get up to the mine. The air became very thin and Forester could feel that his heartbeat had accelerated and his heart thumped in his chest like a swinging stone. He breathed faster and was cautioned by Rohde against forced breathing. My God, he thought; what is it going to be like in the pass?

They reached the air-strip and the mine at midday. Forester felt dizzy and a little nauseated and was glad to reach the first of the deserted huts and to collapse on the floor. Peabody had been left behind long ago; they had ignored his pleas for them to stop and he had straggled farther and farther behind on the trail until he had disappeared from sight. " He'll catch up," Forester said. " He's more scared of the commies than he is of me." He grinned with savage satisfaction. " But I'll change that before we're through."

Rohde was in nearly as bad shape as Forester, although he was more used to the mountains. He sat on the floor of the hut, gasping for breath, too weary to shrug off his pack. They both relaxed for over half an hour before Rohde made any constructive move. At last he fumbled with numb fingers at the fastenings of his pack, and said, " We must have warmth; get out the kerosene."

As Forester undid his pack Rohde took the small axe which had been brought from the Dakota and left the hut. Presently Forester heard him chopping at something in one of the other huts and guessed he had gone for the makings of a fire. He got out the bottle of kerosene and put it aside, ready for when Rohde came back.

An hour later they had a small fire going in the middle of the hut. Rohde had used the minimum of kerosene to start it and small chips of wood built up in a pyramid. Forester chuckled. " You must have been a boy scout."

" I was," said Rohde seriously. " That is a fine organisation." He stretched. " Now we must eat."

" I don't feel hungry," objected Forester.

" I know—neither do I. Nevertheless, we must eat." Rohde looked out of the window towards the pass. " We must fuel ourselves for to-morrow."

They warmed a can of beans and Forester choked down his share. He had not the slightest desire for food, nor for anything except quietness. His limbs felt flaccid and heavy and he felt incapable of the slightest exertion. His mind was affected, too, and he found it difficult to think clearly and to stick to a single line of thought. He just sat there in a corner of the hut, listlessly munching his lukewarm beans and hating every mouthful.

He said, " Christ, I feel terrible."

" It is the *soroche*," said Rohde with a shrug. " We must expect to feel like this." He shook his head regretfully. " We are not allowing enough time for acclimatisation."

" It wasn't as bad as this when we came out of the plane," said Forester.

" We had oxygen," Rohde pointed out. " And we went down the mountain quickly. You understand that this is dangerous?"

" Dangerous? I know I feel goddam sick."

" There was an American expedition here a few years ago, climbing mountains to the north of here. They went quickly to a level of five thousand metres—about as high as we are now. One of the Americans lost consciousness because of the *soroche*, and although they had a doctor, he died while being taken down the mountain. Yes, it is dangerous, Señor Forester."

Forester grinned weakly. " In a moment of danger we ought to be on a first-name basis, Miguel. My name is Ray."

After a while they heard Peabody moving outside. Rohde heaved himself to his feet and went to the door. " We are here, señor."

Peabody stumbled into the hut and collapsed on the floor. " You lousy bastards," he gasped. " Why didn't you wait?"

Forester grinned at him. " We'll be moving really fast when we leave here," he said. " Coming up from the camp was like a Sunday morning stroll compared to what's coming next. We'll not wait for you then, Peabody."

" You son of a bitch. I'll get even with you," Peabody threatened.

Forester laughed. " I'll ram those words down your throat —but not now. There'll be time enough later."

Rohde put out a can of beans. " You must eat, and we must work. Come, Ray."

" I don't wanna eat," moaned Peabody.

" Suit yourself," said Forester. " I don't care if you starve to death." He got up and went out of the hut, following Rohde. " This loss of appetite—is that *soroche*, too?"

Rohde nodded. " We will eat little from now on—we

must live on the reserves of our bodies. A fit man can do it —but that man . . .? I don't know if he can do it."

They walked slowly down the air-strip towards the crashed Dakota. To Forester it seemed incredible that O'Hara had found it too short on which to land because to him it now appeared to be several miles long. He plodded on, mechanically putting one foot in front of the other, while the cold air rasped in his throat and his chest heaved with the drudging effort he was making.

They left the air-strip and skirted the cliff over which the plane had plunged. There had been a fresh fall of snow which mantled the broken wings and softened the jagged outlines of the holes torn in the fuselage. Forester looked down over the cliff, and said, " I don't think this can be seen from the air—the snow makes perfect camouflage. If there is an air search I don't think they'll find us."

Walking with difficulty over the broken ground, they climbed to the wreck and got inside through the hole O'Hara had chopped when he and Rohde had retrieved the oxygen cylinder. It was dim and bleak inside the Dakota and Forester shivered, not from the cold which was becoming intense, but from the odd idea that this was the corpse of a once living and vibrant thing. He shook the idea from him, and said, "There were some straps on the luggage rack—complete with buckles. We could use those, and O'Hara says there are gloves in the cockpit."

" That is good," agreed Rohde. " I will look towards the front for what I can find."

Forester went aft and his breath hissed when he saw the body of old Coughlin, a shattered smear of frozen flesh and broken bones on the rear seat. He averted his eyes and turned to the luggage-rack and began to unbuckle the straps. His fingers were numb with the cold and his movements clumsy, but at last he managed to get them free—four broad canvas straps which could be used on the packs. That gave him an idea and he turned his attention to the seat belts, but they were anchored firmly and it was hopeless to try to remove them without tools.

Rohde came aft carrying the first-aid box which he had taken from the bulkhead. He placed it on a seat and opened it, carefully moving his fingers among the jumbled contents. He grunted. " Morphine."

"Damn," said Forester. " We could have used that on Mrs. Coughlin."

117

Rohde held up the shattered end of an ampoule. "It would have been no use; they are all broken."

He put some bandages away in his pocket, then said, "This will be useful—aspirin." The bottle was cracked, but it still held together and contained a hundred tablets. They both took two tablets and Rohde put the bottle in his pocket. There was nothing more in the first-aid box that was usable.

Forester went into the cockpit. The body of Grivas was there, tumbled into an obscene attitude, and still with the look of deep surprise frozen into the open eyes which were gazing at the shattered instrument panel. Forester moved forward, thinking that there must be something in the wreck of an aircraft that could be salvaged, when he kicked something hard that slid down the inclined floor of the cockpit.

He looked down and saw an automatic pistol.

My God, he thought; we'd forgotten that. It was Grivas's gun, left behind in the scramble to get out of the Dakota. It would have been of use down by the bridge, he thought, picking it up. But it was too late for that now. The metal was cold in his hand and he stood for a moment, undecided, then he slipped it into his pocket, thinking of Peabody and of what lay on the other side of the pass.

Equipment for well-dressed mountaineers, he thought sardonically; one automatic pistol.

They found nothing more that was of use in the Dakota, so they retraced their steps along the air-strip and back to the hut. Forester took the straps and a small suitcase belonging to Miss Ponsky which had been left behind. From these unlikely ingredients he contrived a serviceable pack which sat on his shoulders more comfortably than the one he had.

Rohde went to look at the mine and Peabody sat slackly in a corner of the hut watching Forester work with lacklustre eyes. He had not eaten his beans, nor had he attempted to keep the fire going. Forester, when he came into the hut, had looked at him with contempt but said nothing. He took the axe and chipped a few shavings from the baulk of wood that Rohde had brought in, and rebuilt the fire.

Rohde came in, stamping the snow from his boots. "I have selected a tunnel for O'Hara," he said. "If the enemy force the bridge then O'Hara must come up here; I think the camp is indefensible."

Forester nodded. "I didn't think much of it myself," he said, remembering how they had "assaulted" the empty camp on the way down the mountain.

"Most of the tunnels drive straight into the mountain," said Rohde. "But there is one which has a sharp bend about fifty metres from the entrance. It will give protection against rifle fire."

"Let's have a look at it," said Forester.

Rohde led the way to the cliff face behind the huts and pointed out the tunnels. There were six of them driven into the base of the cliff. "That is the one," he said.

Forester investigated. It was a little over ten feet high and not much wider, just a hole blasted into the hard rock of the mountainside. He walked inside, finding it deepening from gloom to darkness the farther he went. He put his hands before him and found the side wall. As Rohde had said, it bent to the left sharply and, looking back, he saw that the welcome blue sky at the entrance was out of sight.

He went no farther, but turned around and walked back until he saw the bulk of Rohde outlined against the entrance. He was surprised at the relief he felt on coming out into the daylight, and said, "Not much of a home from home—it gives me the creeps."

"Perhaps that is because men have died there."

"Died?"

"Too many men," said Rohde. "The government closed the mine—that was when Señor Aguillar was President."

"I'm surprised that Lopez didn't try to coin some money out of it," commented Forester.

Rohde shrugged. "It would have cost a lot of money to put back into operation. It was uneconomical when it ran—just an experiment in high-altitude mining. I think it would have closed anyway."

Forester looked around. "When O'Hara comes up here he'll be in a hell of a hurry. What about building him a wall at the entrance here? We can leave a note in the hut telling him which tunnel to take."

"That is well thought," said Rohde. "There are many rocks about."

"Three will do better than two," said Forester. "I'll roust out Peabody." He went back to the hut and found Peabody still in the same corner gazing blankly at the wall. "Come on, buster," Forester commanded. "Rise and shine; we've got a job of work on hand."

Peabody's eyelid twitched. "Leave me alone," he said thickly.

Forester stooped, grasped Peabody by the lapels and hauled

him to his feet. "Now, listen, you crummy bastard; I told you that you'd have to take orders and that you'd have to jump to it. I've got a lower boiling-point than Rohde, so you'd better watch it."

Peabody began to beat at him ineffectually and Forester shoved and slammed him against the wall. "I'm sick," gasped Peabody. "I can't breathe."

"You can walk and you can carry rocks," said Forester callously. "Whether you breathe or not while you do it is immaterial. Personally, I'll be goddam glad when you *do* stop breathing. Now, are you going to leave this hut on your own two feet or do I kick you out?"

Muttering obscenities Peabody staggered to the door. Forester followed him to the tunnel and told him to start gathering rocks and then he pitched to with a will. It was hard physical labour and he had to stop and rest frequently, but he made sure that Peabody kept at it, driving him unmercifully.

They carried the rocks to the tunnel entrance, where Rohde built a rough wall. When they had to stop because of encroaching darkness, they had built little more than a breastwork. Forester sagged to the ground and looked at it through swimming eyes. "It's not much, but it will have to do." He beat his arms against his body. "God, but it's cold."

"We will go back to the hut," said Rohde. "There is nothing more we can do here."

So they went back to the hut, relit the fire and prepared a meal of canned stew. Again, Peabody would not eat, but Rohde and Forester forced themselves, choking over the succulent meat and the rich gravy. Then they turned in for the night.

11

Oddly enough, Forester was not very tired when he got up at dawn and his breathing was much easier. He thought— if we could spend another day here it would be much better. I could look forward to the pass with confidence. Then he rejected the thought—there was no more time.

In the dim light he saw Rohde wrapping strips of blanket puttee-fashion around his legs and silently he began to do the same. Neither of them felt like talking. Once that was done he went across to the huddle in the corner and stirred Peabody gently with his foot.

"Lemme alone," mumbled Peabody indistinctly.

Forester sighed and dropped the tip of his boot into Peabody's ribs. That did the trick. Peabody sat up cursing and Forester turned away without saying anything.

"It seems all right," said Rohde from the doorway. He was staring up at the mountains.

Forester caught a note of doubt in his voice and went to join him. It was a clear crystal dawn and the peaks, caught by the rising sun, stood out brilliantly against the dark sky behind. Forester said, "Anything wrong?"

"It is very clear," said Rohde. Again there was a shadow of doubt in his voice. "Perhaps too clear."

"Which way do we go?" asked Forester.

Rohde pointed. "Beyond that mountain is the pass. We go round the base of the peak and then over the pass and down the other side. It is this side which will be difficult—the other side is nothing."

The mountain Rohde had indicated seemed so close in the clear morning air that Forester felt that he could put out his hand and touch it. He sighed with relief. "It doesn't look too bad."

Rohde snorted. "It will be worse than you ever dreamed," he said and turned away. "We must eat again."

Peabody refused food again and Forester, after a significant glance from Rohde, said, "You'll eat even if I have to cram the stuff down your gullet. I've stood enough nonsense from you, Peabody; you're not going to louse this up by passing out through lack of food. But I warn you, if you do—if you hold us up for as little as one minute—we'll leave you."

Peabody looked at him with venom but took the warmed-up can and began to eat with difficulty. Forester said, "How are your boots?"

"Okay, I guess," said Peabody ungraciously.

"Don't guess," said Forester sharply. "I don't care if they pinch your toes off and cut your feet to pieces—I don't care if they raise blisters as big as golf balls—I don't care as far as you're concerned. But I am concerned about you holding us up. If those boots d͏ fit properly, say so now."

"They're all right," said Peabody. "They fit all right."

Rohde said, "We must go. Get your packs on."

Forester picked up the suitcase and fastened the straps

121

about his body. He padded the side of the case with the blanket material of his old pack so that it fitted snugly against his back, and he felt very pleased with his ingenuity.

Rohde took the primitive ice-axe and stuck the short axe from the Dakota into his belt. He eased the pack on his back so that it rested comfortably and looked pointedly at Peabody, who scrambled over to the corner where his pack lay. As he did so, something dropped with a clatter to the floor.

It was O'Hara's flask.

Forester stooped and picked it up, then fixed Peabody with a cold stare. "So you're a goddam thief, too."

"I'm not," yelled Peabody. "O'Hara gave it to me."

"O'Hara wouldn't give you the time of day," snarled Forester. He shook the flask and found it empty. "You little shit," he shouted, and hurled the flask at Peabody. Peabody ducked, but was too late and the flask hit him over the right eye.

Rohde thumped the butt of the ice-axe on the floor. "Enough," he commanded. "This man cannot come with us—we cannot trust him."

Peabody looked at him in horror, his hand dabbing at his forehead. "But you gotta take me," he whispered. "You gotta. You can't leave me to those bastards down the mountain."

Rohde's lips tightened implacably and Peabody whimpered. Forester took a deep breath and said, "If we leave him here he'll only go back to O'Hara; and he's sure to ball things up down there."

"I don't like it," said Rohde. "He is likely to kill us on the mountain."

Forester felt the weight of the gun in his pocket and came to a decision. "You're coming with us, Peabody," he said harshly. "But one more fast move and you're a dead duck." He turned to Rohde. "He won't hold us up—not for one minute, I promise you." He looked Rohde in the eye and Rohde nodded with understanding.

"Get your pack on, Peabody," said Forester. "And get out of that door on the double."

Peabody lurched away from the wall and seemed to cringe as he picked up his pack. He scuttled across the hut, running wide of Forester, and bolted through the door. Forester pulled a scrap of paper and a pencil from his pocket. "I'll leave a note for Tim, telling him of the right tunnel. Then we'll go."

122

It was comparatively easy at first, at least to Forester's later recollection. Although they had left the road and were striking across the mountainside, they made good time. Rohde was in the lead with Peabody following and Forester at the rear, ready to flail Peabody if he lagged. But to begin with there was no need for that; Peabody walked as though he had the devil at his heels.

At first the snow was shallow, dry and powdery, but then it began to get deeper, with a hard crust on top. It was then that Rohde stopped. "We must use the ropes."

They got out their pitiful lengths of rotten rope and Rohde carefully tested every knot. Then they tied themselves together, still in the same order, and carried on. Forester looked up at the steep white slope which seemed to stretch unendingly to the sky and thought that Rohde had been right—this wasn't going to be easy.

They plodded on, Rohde as trailbreaker and the other two thankful that he had broken a path for them in the thickening snow. The slope they were crossing was steep and swept dizzyingly below them and Forester found himself wondering what would happen if one of them fell. It was likely that he would drag down the other two and they would all slide, a tangled string of men and ropes, down the thousands of feet to the sharp rocks below.

Then he shook himself irritably. It wouldn't be like that at all. That was the reason for the ropes, so that a man's fall could be arrested.

From ahead he heard a rumble like thunder and Rohde paused. "What is it?" shouted Forester.

"Avalanche," replied Rohde. He said no more and resumed his even pace.

My God, thought Forester; I hadn't thought of avalanches. This could be goddam dangerous. Then he laughed to himself. He was in no more danger than O'Hara and the others down by the bridge—possibly less. His mind played about with the relativity of things and presently he was not thinking at all, just putting one foot in front of the other with mindless precision, an automaton toiling across the vast white expanse of snow like an ant crawling across a bed sheet.

He was jolted into consciousness by stumbling over Peabody, who lay sprawled in the snow, panting stertorously, his mouth opening and closing like a goldfish. " Get up, Peabody," he mumbled. " I told you what would happen if you held us up. Get up, damn you."

" Rohde's . . . Rohde's stopped," panted Peabody.

Forester looked up and squinted against a vast dazzle. Specks danced in front of his eyes and coalesced into a vague shape moving towards him. " I am sorry," said Rohde, unexpectedly closely. " I am a fool. I forgot this."

Forester rubbed his eyes. I'm going blind, he thought in an access of terror; I'm losing my sight.

" Relax," said Rohde. " Close your eyes; rest them."

Forester sank into the snow and closed his eyes. It felt as though there were hundreds of grains of sand beneath the lids and he felt the cold touch of tears on his cheeks. " What is it?" he asked.

" Ice glare," said Rohde. " Don't worry; it will be all right. Just keep your eyes closed for a few minutes."

He kept his eyes closed and gradually felt his muscles lose tension and he was grateful for this pause. He felt tired—more tired than he had ever felt in his life—and he wondered how far they had come. " How far have we come?" he asked.

" Not far," said Rohde.

" What time is it?"

There was a pause, then Rohde said, " Nine o'clock."

Forester was shocked. " Is that all?" He felt as though he had been walking all day.

" I'm going to rub something on your eyes," said Rohde, and Forester felt cold fingers massaging his eyelids with a substance at once soft and gritty.

" What is it, Miguel?"

" Wood ash. It is black—it will cut the glare, I think. I have heard it is an old Eskimo practice; I hope it will work."

After a while Forester ventured to open his eyes. To his relief he could see, not as well as he could normally, but he was not as blind as during that first shocking moment when he thought he had lost his sight. He looked over to where Rohde was ministering to Peabody and thought—yes, that's another thing mountaineers have—dark glasses. He blinked painfully.

Rohde turned and Forester burst out laughing at the sight of him. He had a broad, black streak across his eyes and looked like a Red Indian painted to go on the warpath.

Rohde smiled. "You too look funny, Ray," he said. Then more soberly, "Wrap a blanket round your head like a hood, so that it cuts out some of the glare from the side." Forester unfastened his pack and regretfully tore out the blanket from the side of the case. His pack would not be so comfortable from now on. The blanket provided enough material to make hoods for the three of them, and then Rohde said, "We must go on."

Forester looked back. He could still see the huts and estimated that they had not gained more than five hundred feet of altitude although they had come a considerable distance. Then the rope tugged at his waist and he stepped out, following the stumbling figure of Peabody.

It was midday when they rounded the shoulder of the mountain and were able to see their way to the pass. Forester sank to his knees and sobbed with exhaustion and Peabody dropped in his tracks as though knocked on the head. Only Rohde remained on his feet, staring up towards the pass, squinting with sore eyes. "It is as I remembered it," he said. "We will rest here."

Ignoring Peabody, he squatted beside Forester. "Are you all right?"

"I'm a bit bushed," said Forester, "but a rest will make a lot of difference."

Rohde took off his pack and unfastened it. "We will eat now."

"My God, I couldn't," said Forester.

"You will be able to stomach this," said Rohde, and produced a can of fruit. "It is sweet for energy."

There was a cold wind sweeping across the mountainside and Forester pulled the jacket round him as he watched Rohde dig into the snow. "What are you doing?"

"Making a wind break." He took a Primus stove and put it into the hole he had dug where it was sheltered from the wind. He lit it, then handed an empty bean can to Forester. "Fill that with snow and melt it; we must drink something hot. I will see to Peabody."

At the low atmospheric pressure the snow took a long time to melt and the resulting water was merely tepid. Rohde dropped a bouillon cube into it, and said, "You first."

Forester gagged as he drank it, and then filled the can with snow again. Peabody had revived and took the next canful, then Forester melted more snow for Rohde. "I haven't looked up the pass," he said. "What's it like?"

Rohde looked up from the can of fruit he was opening. "Bad," he said. "But I expected that." He paused. "There is a glacier with many crevasses."

Forester took the proffered can silently and began to eat. He found the it acceptable to his taste and his stomach— it was the first food he had enjoyed since the plane crash and it put new life into him. He looked back; the mine was out of sight, but far away he could see the river gorge, many thousands of feet below. He could not see the bridge.

He got to his feet and trudged forward to where he could see the pass. Immediately below was the glacier, a jumble of ice blocks and a maze of crevasses. It ended perhaps three thousand feet lower and he could see the blue waters of a mountain lake. As he looked he heard a whip-crack as of a stroke of lightning and the mutter of distant thunder and saw a plume of white leap up from the blue of the lake.

Rohde spoke from behind him. "That is a *laguna*," he said. "The glaciers are slowly retreating here and there is always a lake between the glacier and the moraine. But that is of no interest to us; we must go there." He pointed across the glacier and swept his arm upwards.

Across the valley of the pass white smoke appeared suddenly on the mountainside and a good ten seconds afterwards came a low rumble. "There is always movement in the mountains," said Rohde. "The ice works on the rock and there are many avalanches."

Forester looked up. "How much higher do we have to climb?"

"About five hundred metres—but first we must go down a little to cross the glacier."

"I don't suppose we could go round it," said Forester.

Rohde pointed downwards towards the lake. "We would lose a thousand metres of altitude and that would mean another night on the mountain. Two nights up here would kill us."

Forester regarded the glacier with distaste; he did not like what he saw and for the first time a cold knot of fear formed in his belly. So far there had been nothing but exhausting work, the labour of pushing through thick snow in bad and unaccustomed conditions. But here he was confronted with danger itself—the danger of the toppling ice block warmed to the point of insecurity by the sun, the trap of the snow-covered crevasse. Even as he watched he saw a movement on the glacier, a sudden alteration of the scene, and he heard a dull rumble.

126

Rohde said, "We will go now."

They went back to get their packs. Peabody was sitting in the snow, gazing apathetically at his hands folded in his lap. Forester said, "Come on, man; get your pack on," but Peabody did not stir. Forester sighed regretfully and kicked him in the side, not too violently. Peabody seemed to react only to physical stimuli, to threats of violence.

Obediently he got up and put on his pack and Rohde refastened the rope about him, careful to see that all was secure. Then they went on in the same order. First the more experienced Rohde, then Peabody, and finally Forester.

The climb down to the glacier—a matter of about two hundred feet—was a nightmare to Forester, although it did not seem to trouble Rohde and Peabody was lost in the daze of his own devising and was oblivious of the danger. Here the rock was bare of snow, blown clean by the strong wind which swept down the pass. But it was rotten and covered with a slick layer of ice, so that any movement at all was dangerous. Forester cursed as his feet slithered on the ice; we should have spikes, he thought; this is madness.

It took an hour to descend to the glacier, the last forty feet by what Rohde called an *abseil*. There was a vertical ice-covered cliff and Rohde showed them what to do. He hammered four of their makeshift pitons into the rotten rock and looped the rope through them. They went down in reverse order, Forester first, with Rohde belaying the rope. He showed Forester how to loop the rope round his body so that he was almost sitting in it, and how to check his descent if he went too fast.

"Try to keep facing the cliff," he said. "Then you can use your feet to keep clear—and try not to get into a spin."

Forester was heartily glad when he reached the bottom—this was not his idea of fun. He made up his mind that he would spend his next vacation as far from mountains as he could, preferably in the middle of Kansas.

Then Peabody came down, mechanically following Rohde's instructions. He had no trace of fear about him—his face was as blank as his mind and all fear had been drained out of him long before, together with everything else. He was an automaton who did precisely what he was told.

Rohde came last with no one to guard the rope above him. He dropped heavily the last ten feet as the pitons gave way one after the other in rapid succession and the rope dropped in coils about his prostrate body. Forester helped him to his feet. "Are you okay?"

Rohde swayed. "I'm all right," he gasped. "The pitons —find the pitons."

Forester searched about in the snow and found three of the pitons; he could not find the fourth. Rohde smiled grimly. "It is as well I fell," he said. "Otherwise we would have had to leave the pitons up there, and I think we will need them later. But we must keep clear of rock; the *verglas*—the ice on the rock—is too much for us without crampons."

Forester agreed with him from the bottom of his heart, although he did not say so aloud. He recoiled the rope and made one end fast about his waist while Rohde attended to Peabody. Then he looked at the glacier.

It was as fantastic as a lunar landscape—and as dead and removed from humanity. The pressures from below had squeezed up great masses of ice which the wind and the sun had carved into grotesque shapes, all now mantled with thick snow. There were great cliffs with dangerous overhanging columns which threatened to topple, and there were crevasses, some open to the sky and some, as Forester knew, treacherously covered with snow. Through this wilderness, this maze of ice, they had to find their way.

Forester said, "How far to the other side?"

Rohde reflected. "Three-quarters of one of your North American miles." He took the ice-axe firmly in his hand. "Let us move—time is going fast."

He led the way, testing every foot with the butt of the ice-axe. Forester noticed that he had shortened the intervals between the members of the party and had doubled the ropes, and he did not like the implication. The three of them were now quite close together and Rohde kept urging Peabody to move faster as he felt the drag on the rope when Peabody lagged. Forester stooped and picked up some snow; it was powdery and did not make a good snowball, but every time Peabody dragged on Rohde's rope he pelted him with snow.

The way was tortuous and more than once Rohde led them into a dead end, the way blocked by vertical ice walls or wide crevasses, and they would have to retrace their steps and hunt for a better way. Once, when they were seemingly entrapped in a maze of ice passages, Forester totally lost his sense of direction and wondered hopelessly if they would be condemned to wander for ever in this cold hell.

His feet were numb and he had no feeling in his toes. He

mentioned this to Rohde, who stopped immediately. " Sit down," he said. " Take off your boots."

Forester stripped the puttees from his legs and tried to untie his boot-laces with stiff fingers. It took him nearly fifteen minutes to complete this simple task. The laces were stiffened with ice, his fingers were cold, and his mind did not seem able to control the actions of his body. At last he got his boots off and stripped off the two pairs of socks he wore.

Rohde closely examined his toes and said, " You have the beginning of frost-bite. Rub your left foot—I'll rub the right."

Forester rubbed away violently. His big toe was bone-white at the tip and had a complete lack of sensation. Rohde was merciless in his rubbing; he ignored Forester's yelp of anguish as the circulation returned to his foot and continued to massage with vigorous movements.

Forester's feet seemed to be on fire as the blood forced its way into the frozen flesh and he moaned with the pain. Rohde said sternly, " You must not let this happen. You must work your toes all the time—imagine you are playing a piano with your feet—your toes. Let me see your fingers."

Forester held out his hands and Rohde inspected them. " All right," he said. " But you must watch for this. Your toes, your fingers and the tips of your ears and the nose. Keep rubbing them." He turned to where Peabody was sitting slackly. " And what about him?"

With difficulty Forester thrust his feet into his frozen boots, retied the laces and wrapped the puttees round his legs. Then he helped Rohde to take off Peabody's boots. Handling him was like handling a dummy—he neither hindered nor helped, letting his limbs be moved flaccidly.

His toes were badly frostbitten and they began to massage his feet. After working on him for ten minutes he suddenly moaned and Forester looked up to see a glimmer of intelligence steal into the dead eyes. " Hell!" Peabody protested. " You're hurting me."

They took no notice of him and continued to work away. Suddenly Peabody screamed and began to thrash about, and Forester grabbed his arms. " Be sensible, man," he shouted. He looked up at Peabody. " Keep moving your toes. Move them all the time in your boots."

Peabody was moaning with pain but it seemed to have the effect of bringing him out of his private dream. He was able to put on his own socks and boots and wrap the puttees round his legs, and all the time he swore in a dull monotone, uttering a string of obscenities directed against the mountains, against Rohde and Forester for being uncaring brutes, and against the fates in general for having got him into this mess.

Forester looked across at Rohde and grinned faintly, and Rohde picked up the ice-axe and said, "We must move—we must get out of here."

Somewhere in the middle of the glacier Rohde, after casting fruitlessly in several directions, led them to a crevasse and said, "Here we must cross—there is no other way."

There was a snow bridge across the crevasse, a frail span connecting the two sides. Forester went to the edge and looked down into the dim green depths. He could not see the bottom.

Rohde said, "The snow will bear our weight if we go over lying flat so that the weight is spread." He tapped Forester on the shoulder. "You go first."

Peabody said suddenly, "I'm not going across there. You think I'm crazy?"

Forester had intended to say the same but the fact that a man like Peabody had said it put some spirit into him. He said harshly—and the harshness was directed at himself for his moment of weakness—"Do as you're damn well told."

Rohde re-roped them so that the line would be long enough to stretch across the crevasse, which was about fifteen feet wide, and Forester approached cautiously. "Not on hands and knees," said Rohde. "Lie flat and wriggle across with your arms and legs spread out."

With trepidation Forester lay down by the edge of the crevasse and wriggled forward on to the bridge. It was only six feet wide and, as he went forward on his belly in the way he had been taught during his army training, he saw the snow crumble from the edge of the bridge to fall with a soft sigh into the abyss.

He was very thankful for the rope which trailed behind him, even though he knew it was probably not strong enough to withstand a sudden jerk, and it was with deep thankfulness that he gained the other side to lie gasping in the snow, beads of sweat trickling into his eyes.

After a long moment he stood up and turned. "Are you all right?" asked Rohde.

"I'm fine," he said, and wiped the sweat from his forehead before it froze.

"To hell with this," shouted Peabody. "You're not going to get me on that thing."

"You'll be roped from both sides," said Forester. "You can't possibly fall—isn't that right, Miguel?"

"That is so," said Rohde.

Peabody had a hunted look about him. Forester said, "Oh, to hell with him. Come across, Miguel, and leave the stupid bastard."

Peabody's voice cracked. "You can't leave me *here*," he screamed.

"Can't we?" asked Forester callously. "I told you what would happen if you held us up."

"Oh, Jesus!" said Peabody tearfully, and approached the snow bridge slowly.

"Get down," said Rohde abruptly.

"On your belly," called Forester.

Peabody lay down and began to inch his way across. He was shaking violently and twice he stopped as he heard snow swish into the crevasse from the crumbling edge of the bridge. As he approached Forester he began to wriggle along faster and Forester became intent on keeping the rope taut, as did Rohde, paying out as Peabody moved away from him.

Suddenly Peabody lost his nerve and got up on to his hands and knees and scrambled towards the end of the bridge. "Get down, you goddam fool," Forester yelled.

Suddenly he was enveloped in a cloud of snow dust and Peabody cannoned into him, knocking him flat. There was a roar as the bridge collapsed into the crevasse in a series of diminishing echoes, and when Forester got to his feet he looked across through the swirling fog of powdery snow and saw Rohde standing helplessly on the other side.

He turned and grabbed Peabody, who was clutching at the snow in an ecstasy of delight at being on firm ground. Hauling him to his feet, Forester hit him with his open palm in a vicious double slap across the face. "You selfish bastard," he shouted. "Can't you ever do anything right?"

Peabody's head lolled on his shoulders and there was a vacant look in his eyes. When Forester let him go he dropped to the ground, muttering incomprehensibly, and grovelled at Forester's feet. Forester kicked him for good measure and turned to Rohde. "What the hell do we do now?"

Rohde seemed unperturbed. He hefted the ice-axe like a spar and said, "Stand aside." Then he threw it and it stuck into the snow in front of Forester. "I think I can swing across," he said. "Hammer the axe into the snow as deep as you can."

Forester felt the rope at his waist. "This stuff isn't too strong, you know. It won't bear much weight."

Rohde measured the gap with his eye. "I think there is enough to make a triple strand," he said. "That should take my weight."

"It's your neck," said Forester, and began to beat the ice-axe into the snow. But he knew that *all* their lives were at stake. He did not have the experience to make the rest of the trip alone—his chances were still less if he was hampered by Peabody. He doubted if he could find his way out of the glacier safely.

He hammered the axe into the snow and ice for three-quarters of its length and tugged at it to make sure it was firm. Then he turned to Peabody, who was sobbing and drooling into the snow and stripped the rope from him. He tossed the ends across to Rohde who tied them round his waist and sat on the edge of the crevasse, looking into the depths between his knees and appearing as unconcerned as though he was sitting in an arm-chair.

Forester fastened the triple rope to the ice-axe and belayed a loop around his body, kicking grooves in the snow for his heels. "I've taken as much of the strain as I can," he called.

Rohde tugged on the taut rope experimentally, and seemed satisfied. He paused. "Put something between the rope and the edge to stop any chafing." So Forester stripped off his hood and wadded it into a pad, jamming it between the rope and the icy edge of the crevasse.

Rohde tugged again and measured his probable point of impact fifteen feet down on the farther wall of the crevasse. Then he launched himself into space.

Forester saw him disappear and felt the sudden strain on the rope, then heard the clash of Rohde's boots on the ice wall beneath. Thankfully he saw that there was no sudden easing of the tension on the rope and knew that Rohde had made it. All that remained now was for him to climb up.

It seemed an age before Rohde's head appeared above the edge and Forester went forward to haul him up. This is one hell of a man, he thought; this is one hell of a good joe. Rohde sat down not far from the edge and wiped the sweat from his face. " That was not a good thing to do," he said.

Forester cocked his head at Peabody. " What do we do about him? He'll kill us all yet." He took the gun from his pocket and Rohde's eyes widened. " I think this is the end of the trail for Peabody."

Peabody lay in the snow muttering to himself and Forester spoke as though he were not there, and it is doubtful if Peabody heard what was being said about him.

Rohde looked Forester in the eye. " Can you shoot a defenceless man—even him?"

" You're damned right I can," snapped Forester. " We don't have only our own lives to think of—there are the others down at the bridge depending on us; this crazy fool will let us all down."

He lifted the pistol and aimed at the back of Peabody's head. He was just taking up the slack on the trigger when his wrist was caught by Rohde. " No, Ray; you are not a murderer."

Forester tensed the muscles of his arm and fought Rohde's grip for a moment, then relaxed, and said, " Okay, Miguel; but you'll see I'm right. He's selfish and he'll never do anything right—but I guess we're stuck with him."

I V

Altogether it took them three hours to cross the glacier and by then Forester was exhausted, but Rohde would allow no rest. " We must get as high as we can while there is still light," he said. " To-night will weaken us very much—it is not good to spend a night in the open without a tent or the right kind of clothing."

Forester managed a grin. Everything to Rohde was either *good* or *not good*; black and white with no shades of grey. He kicked Peabody to his feet and said tiredly, " Okay; lead on, MacDuff."

Rohde looked up at the pass. " We lost height in crossing the glacier; we still have to ascend between five and six hundred metres to get to the top."

Sixteen hundred to two thousand feet, Forester translated silently. He followed Rohde's gaze. To their left was the glacier, oozing imperceptibly down the mountain and scraping

133

itself by a rock wall. Above, the clean sweep of snow was broken by a line of cliffs half way up to the top of the pass. " Do we have to climb *that*?" he demanded.

Rohde scrutinised the terrain carefully, then shook his head. " I think we can go by the cliffs there—on the extreme right. That will bring us on top of the cliffs. We will bivouac there to-night."

He put his hand in his pocket and produced the small leather bag of coca quids he had compounded back in the camp. " Hold out your hand," he said. " You will need these now."

He shook a dozen of the green squares into Forester's palm and Forester put one into his mouth and chewed it. It had an acrid and pungent taste which pleasantly warmed the inside of his mouth. " Not too many," warned Rohde. " Or your mouth will become inflamed."

It was useless giving them to Peabody. He had relapsed into his state of automatism and followed Rohde like a dog on a lead, obedient to the tugs on the rope. As Rohde set out on the long climb up to the cliffs he followed, mechanically going through the proper climbing movements as though guided by something outside himself. Forester, watching him from behind, hoped there would be no crisis; as long as things went well Peabody would be all right, but in an emergency he would certainly break, as O'Hara had prophesied.

He did not remember much of that long and toilsome climb. Perhaps the coca contributed to that, for he found himself in much the same state as he imagined Peabody to be in. Rhythmically chewing the quid, he climbed automatically, following the trail broken by the indefatigable Rohde.

At first the snow was thick and crusted, and then, as they approached the extreme right of the line of cliffs, the slope steepened and the snow cover became thinner and they found that under it was a sheet of ice. Climbing in these conditions without crampons was difficult, and, as Rohde confessed a little time afterwards, would have been considered impossible by anyone who knew the mountains.

It took them two hours to get above the rock cliffs and to meet a great disappointment. Above the cliffs and set a few feet back was a continuous ice wall over twenty feet high, surmounted by an overhanging snow cornice. The wall stretched across the width of the pass in an unbroken line.

Forester, gasping for breath in the thin air, looked at it in dismay. We've had it, he thought; how can we get over this? But Rohde, gazing across the pass, did not lose hope. He pointed. "I think the ice wall is lower there in the middle. Come, but stay away from the edge of the cliff."

They started out along the ledge between the ice wall and the edge of the cliff. At first the ledge was narrow, only a matter of feet, but as they went on it became broader and Rohde advanced more confidently and faster. But he seemed worried. "We cannot stay here," he said. "It is very dangerous. We must get above this wall before nightfall."

"What's the hurry?" asked Forester. "If we stay here, the wall will shelter us from the wind—it's from the west and I think it's rising."

"It is," replied Rohde. He pointed upwards. "That is what I worry about—the cornice. We cannot stay below it —it might break away—and the wind in the west will build it to breaking-point. It is going to snow—look down."

Forester looked into the dizzying depths below the cliffs and saw a gathering greyness of mist. He shivered and retreated to safety, then followed the shambling figure of Peabody.

It was not five minutes later when he felt his feet suddenly slide on the ice. Frantically he tried to recover his balance but to no effect, and he found himself on his back, swooping towards the edge of the cliff. He tried to brake himself with his hands and momentarily saw the smear of blood on the ice as, with a despairing cry, he went over the edge.

Rohde, hearing the cry and feeling the tug of Peabody on the rope, automatically dug the ice-axe firmly into the ice and took the strain. When he turned his head he saw only Peabody scrabbling at the edge of the cliff, desperately trying to prevent himself from being pulled off. He was screaming incoherently, and of Forester there was no sign.

Forester found the world wheeling crazily before his eyes, first a vast expanse of sky and a sudden vista of valleys and mountains half obscured by wreaths of mist, then the grey rock close by as he spun and dangled on the end of the rope, suspended over a sheer drop of three hundred feet on the steep snow slopes beneath. His chest hurt and he found that the rope had worked itself under his armpits and was constricting his ribs. From above he heard the terrified yammerings of Peabody.

With a heave Rohde cracked the muscles of his back and hoped the rotten rope would not break. He yelled to Peabody, "Pull on the rope—get him up." Instead he saw the flash of steel and saw that Peabody had a clasp-knife and was sawing at the rope where it went over the edge of the cliff.

Rohde did not hesitate. His hand went to his side and found the small axe they had taken from the Dakota. He drew it from his belt, reversing it quickly so that he held it by the handle. He lifted it, poised, for a second, judging his aim, and then hurled it at Peabody's head.

It struck Peabody squarely on the nape of the neck, splitting his skull. The terrified yelping stopped and from below Forester was aware of the startling silence and looked up. A knife dropped over the edge of the cliff and the blade cut a gash in his cheek before it went spinning into the abyss below, and a steady drip of blood rained on him from above.

Chapter VI

O'Hara had lost his flask.

He thought that perhaps he had left it in the pocket of the leather jacket he had given Forester, but then he remembered going through the pockets first. He looked about the shelter, trying not to draw attention to himself, but still could not find it and decided that it must be up at the camp.

The loss worried him unreasonably. To have a full flask at his side had comforted him; he knew that whenever he wanted a drink then it was there ready to hand, and because it was there he had been able, in some odd way, to resist the temptation. But now he felt an aching longing in the centre of his being for a drink, for the blessed relief of alcohol and the oblivion it would bring.

It made him very short-tempered.

The night had been quiet. Since the abortive attempt to burn the bridge the previous evening, nothing had happened. Now, in the dawn light, he was wondering whether it would be safe to bring down the trebuchet. His resources in manpower were slender and to bring the trebuchet from the camp would leave the bridge virtually defenceless. True, the enemy was quiet, but that was no guarantee of future inactivity. He had no means of telling how long it would take them to obtain more timber and to transport it.

It was the common dilemma of the military man—trying to guess what the enemy was doing on the other side of the hill and balancing guesses against resources.

He heard the clatter of a stone and turned his head to find Benedetta coming towards him. He waved her back and slid down from his observation post. "Jenny has made coffee," she said. "I will keep watch. Has anything happened?"

He shook his head. "Everything's quiet. They're still there, of course; if you stick your neck out you'll get your head blown off—so be careful." He paused; he badly needed to discuss his problems with someone else, not to shrug off responsibility but to clarify the situation in his own mind. He missed Forester.

He told Benedetta what he was thinking and she said immediately, "But, of course, I will come up to the camp."

"I might have known," he said unreasonably. "You won't be separated from your precious uncle."

"It is not like that," she said sharply. "All you men are needed to bring down this machine, but what good can Jenny *and* I do down here? If we are attacked we can only run; and it does not take two to watch. Four can bring the machine from the camp quicker than three—even though one of them *is* a woman. If the enemy attacks in force Jenny will warn us."

He said slowly, "We'll have to take the risk, of course; we've got no choice. And the sooner we move the better."

"Send Jenny down quickly," said Benedetta. "I'll wait for you at the pond."

O'Hara went up to the shelter and was glad of the mug of steaming coffee that was thrust into his hands. In between gulps he rapidly detailed his plan and ended by saying, "It puts a great deal on your shoulders, Jenny. I'm sorry about that."

"I'll be all right," she said quietly.

"You can have two shots—no more," he said. "We'll leave both bows cocked for you. If they start to work on the bridge, fire two bolts and then get up to the camp as fast as you can. With luck, the shots will slow them down enough for us to get back in time to fight them off. And for God's sake don't fire them both from the same place. They're getting smart over there and they have all our favourite posts spotted."

He surveyed the small group. "Any questions?"

Aguillar stirred. "So I am to return to the camp. I feel I am a drag on you; so far I have done nothing—nothing."

137

"God in heaven!" exclaimed O'Hara. "You're our king-pin—you're the reason for all this. If we let them get you we'll have fought for nothing."

Aguillar smiled slowly. "You know as well as I do that I do not matter any more. True, it is me they want, but they cannot let you live as well. Did not Doctor Armstrong point out that very fact?"

Armstrong removed his pipe from his mouth. "That might be so, but you're in no condition to fight," he said bluntly. "And while you're down here you are taking O'Hara's mind off his job. You'd be better out of the way up at the camp where you can do something constructive, like making new bolts."

Aguillar bent his head. "I stand corrected and rightly so. I am sorry, Señor O'Hara, for making more trouble than I need."

"That's all right," said O'Hara awkwardly. He felt sorry for Aguillar; the man had courage, but courage was not enough—or perhaps it was not the right kind of courage. Intellectual bravery was all very well in its place.

It was nearer three hours than two before they arrived at the camp, the slowness being caused by Aguillar's physical weakness, and O'Hara was fretting about what could have happened at the bridge. At least he had heard no rifle fire, but the wind was blowing away from the mountains and he doubted if he would have heard it anyway. This added to his tension.

Willis met them. "Did Forester and Rohde get away all right—and our good friend Peabody?" asked O'Hara.

"They left before I awoke," said Willis. He looked up at the mountains. "They should be at the mine by now."

Armstrong circled the trebuchet, making pleasurable noises. "I say, you've done a good job here, Willis."

Willis coloured a little. "I did the best I could in the time we had—and with what we had."

"I can't see how it can possibly work," said O'Hara.

Willis smiled. "Well, it's stripped down for transport. It's more or less upside-down now; we can wheel it down the road on the axle."

Armstrong said, "I was thinking of the Russo-Finnish war; a bit out of my field, I know, but the Finns were in very much the same case as we are—dreadfully under-equipped and using their ingenuity to the utmost. I seem to remember they invented the Molotov Cocktail."

O'Hara's mind leapt immediately to the remaining drum of paraffin and to the empty bottles he had seen lying round the camp. "My God, you've done it again," he said. "Gather together all the bottles you can find."

He strode across to the hut where the paraffin was stored, and Willis called after him, "It's open—I was in there this morning."

He pushed open the door and paused as he saw the crate of liquor. Slowly he bent down and pulled out a bottle. He cradled it in his hand, then held it up to the light; the clear liquid could have been water, but he knew the deception. This was the water of Lethe which brought blessed forgetfulness, which untied the knots in his soul. His tongue crept out to lick his lips.

He heard someone approaching the hut and quickly put the bottle on a shelf, pushing it behind a box and out of sight. When Benedetta came in he was bending over the paraffin drum, unscrewing the cap.

She was laden with empty bottles. "Willis said you wanted these. What are they for?"

"We're making bombs of a sort. We'll need some strips of cloth to make wicks and stoppers; see if you can find something."

He began to fill the bottles and presently Benedetta came back with the cloth and he showed her how to stuff the necks of the bottles, leaving an easily ignitable wick. "Where are the others?" he asked.

"Willis had an idea," she said. "Armstrong and my uncle are helping him."

He filled another bottle. "Do you mind leaving your uncle up here alone?"

"What else can we do?" she asked. She bent her head. "He has always been alone. He never married, you know. And then he has known a different kind of loneliness—the loneliness of power."

"And have *you* been lonely—since . . ."

"Since my family were killed?" She looked up and there was something in her dark eyes that he could not fathom. "Yes, I have. I joined my uncle and we were two lonely people together in foreign countries." Her lip curved. "I think you are also a lonely man, Tim."

"I get along," he said shortly, and wiped his hands on a piece of rag.

She stood up. "What will you do when we leave here?"

"Don't you mean, *if* we leave here?" He stood too and looked down at her upraised face. "I think I'll move on; there's nothing for me in Cordillera now. Filson will never forgive me for bending one of his aeroplanes."

"Is there nothing you want to stay for?"

Her lips were parted and on impulse he bent his head and kissed her. She clung to him and after a long moment he sighed. A sudden wonder had burst upon him and he said in surprise, "Yes, I think there is something to stay for."

They stood together quietly for a few minutes, not speaking. It is in the nature of lovers to make plans, but what could they plan for? So there was nothing to say.

At last Benedetta said, "We must go, Tim. There is work to do."

He released her. "I'll see what the others are doing. You'd better throw the booze out of the liquor crate and put the paraffin bottles in it; we can strap it on to the trebuchet."

He walked out of the hut and up to the other end of the camp to see what was happening. Half way there he stopped in deep thought and cursed quietly. He had at last recognised the strange look in Benedetta's eyes. It had been compassion.

He took a deep breath, then straightened his shoulders and walked forward again, viciously kicking at a stone. He heard voices to his left and tramped over to the hillside, where he saw Willis, Armstrong and Aguillar grouped round an old cable drum.

"What's all this?" he asked abruptly.

"Insurance," said Armstrong cheerfully. "In case the enemy gets across the bridge."

Willis gave another bang with the rock he was holding and O'Hara saw he had hammered a wedge to hold the drum in position. "You know what this is," he said. "It's one of those wooden drums used to transport heavy cable—looks like a big cotton reel, doesn't it?"

It did indeed look like a cotton reel, eight feet in diameter. "Well?" said O'Hara.

"The wood is rotten, of course—it must have been standing in the open for years," said Willis. "But it's heavy and it will roll. Take a few steps down the hill and tell me what you see."

O'Hara walked down the hill and came to a steep drop, and found he was overlooking a cutting, blasted when the road was being made. Willis said from behind him, "The drum is out of sight of the road. We wait until a jeep or a truck is coming up, then we pull away the chocks and with a bit of luck we cause a smash and block the road."

O'Hara looked back at Aguillar, whose grey face told of the exertions he had made. He felt anger welling up inside him and jerked his head curtly to Willis and Armstrong. He walked out of earshot of Aguillar, then said evenly, suppressing his anger, " I think it would be a good idea if we didn't go off half-cocked on independent tracks."

Willis looked surprised and his face flushed. " But——"

O'Hara cut him short. " It's a bloody good idea, but you might have had some consultation about it. I could have helped to get the drum down into position and the old man could have filled paraffin bottles. You know he's got a heart condition, and if he drops dead on us those swine on the other side of the river have won." He tapped Willis on the chest. " And I don't intend to let that happen if I have to kill you, me and every other member of this party to get Aguillar away to safety."

Willis looked shocked. " Speak for yourself, O'Hara," he said angrily. " I'm fighting for my own life."

" Not while I'm in command, you're not. You'll bloody well obey orders and you'll consult me on everything you do."

Willis flared up. " And who put *you* in command?"

" I did," said O'Hara briefly. He stared at Willis. " Want to make an issue of it?"

" I might," said Willis tightly.

O'Hara stared him down. " You won't," he said with finality.

Willis's eyes flickered away. Armstrong said quietly, " It would be a good idea if we didn't fight among ourselves." He turned to Willis. " O'Hara is right, though; we shouldn't have let Aguillar push the drum."

" Okay, okay," said Willis impatiently. " But I don't go for this death-or-glory stuff."

" Look," said O'Hara. " You know what I think? I think I'm a dead man as I stand here right now. I don't think we've a hope in hell of stopping those communist bastards crossing the bridge; we might slow them down but we can't stop them. And once they get across they'll hunt us down and slaughter us like pigs—that's why I think I'm a dead man. It's not that I particularly like Aguillar, but the communists want him and I'm out to stop them—that's why I'm so tender of him."

Willis had gone pale. "But what about Forester and Rohde?"

"I think they're dead too," said O'Hara coldly. "Have you any idea what it's like up there? Look, Willis; I flew men and equipment for two Yankee mountaineering expeditions and one German. And with all their modern gadgets they failed in their objectives three-quarters of the time." He waved his arm at the mountains. "Hell, half these mountains don't even have names, they're so inaccessible."

Armstrong said, "You paint a black picture, O'Hara."

"Is it a true picture?"

"I fear it is," said Armstrong ruefully.

O'Hara shook his head irritably. "This isn't doing any good. Let's get that contraption down to the bridge."

II

It was not as difficult as O'Hara anticipated getting the trebuchet down the mountain road. Willis had done a good job in mounting it for ease of transportation and it took only three hours to get back, the main difficulty being to manœuvre the clumsy machine round the hairpin bends. At every bend he half expected to see Miss Ponsky running up to tell them that the communists had made their attack, but all was quiet and he did not even hear the crack of a rifle. Things were too quiet, he thought; maybe they were running out of ammunition—there was none of the desultory firing that had gone on the previous day.

They pushed the trebuchet off the road to the place indicated by Willis, and O'Hara said expressionlessly, "Benedetta, relieve Jenny; tell her to come up and see me."

She looked at him curiously, but he had turned away to help Willis and Armstrong dismantle the trebuchet preparatory to erecting it as a weapon. They were going to mount it on a small knoll in order to get the height, so that the heavy weight on the shorter arm could have a good fall.

Miss Ponsky came up to him and told him that everything had been quiet. He thought for a moment and then said, "Did you hear any trucks?"

"Not since they took away the jeep this morning."

142

He rubbed his chin. "Maybe we hit them harder than we thought. You're sure they're still there?"

"Oh, yes," she said brightly. "I had that thought myself some hours ago so I waggled something in full view." She blushed. "I put my hat on a stick—I've seen it done on old movies on TV."

He smiled. "Did they hit it?"

"No—but they came close."

"You're doing all right, Jenny."

"You must be hungry—I'll make a meal." Her lips twitched. "I think this is fun, you know." She turned and hurried up the road, leaving him standing dumbfounded. Fun!

Assembling the trebuchet took two hours and when it was completed Armstrong, begrimed but happy, said with satisfaction, "There, now; I never expected to see one of these in action." He turned to O'Hara. "Forester came upon me sketching a trebuchet for Willis; he asked if I were drawing the scales of justice and I said that I was. He must have thought me mad, but it was perceptive of him."

He closed his eyes and recited as though quoting a dictionary entry. "From the medieval Latin *trebuchetum*; old French, *trébuchet*; a pair of scales, an assay balance." He opened his eyes and pointed. "You see the resemblance?"

O'Hara did see. The trebuchet looked like a warped balance, very much out of proportion, with one arm much longer than the other. He said, "Does this thing have much of a kick—much recoil?"

"Nothing detectable; the impact is absorbed by the ground."

O'Hara looked at the crazy system of ropes and pulleys. "The question is now—will the beast work?"

There was an edge of irritability to Willis's voice. "Of course it will work. Let's chuck this thing." He pointed to a round boulder about the size of a man's head.

"All right," said O'Hara. "Let's give it a bang. What do we do?"

"First we haul like hell on this rope," said Willis.

The rope was connected, through a three-part pulley arrangement, to the end of the long arm. As O'Hara and Willis pulled, the arm came down and the shorter arm with the weight rose into the air. The weight was a big, rusty iron bucket which Willis had found and filled with stones. As the long arm came to the ground, Armstrong stepped forward and threw over a lever and a wooden block dropped over the

143

arm, holding it down. Willis picked up the boulder and placed it in the hub-cap which served as a cup.

"We're ready," he said. "I've already aligned the thing in the general direction of the bridge; we need someone down there to call the fall of the shot."

"I'll go," said O'Hara. He walked across to where Benedetta was keeping watch and slid down beside her, being careful to keep his head down. "They're going to let fly," he said.

She turned her head to look at the trebuchet. "Do you think this will work?"

"I don't know." He grimaced. "All I know is that it's a hell of a way to fight a war."

"We're ready," shouted Armstrong.

O'Hara waved and Armstrong pulled the firing lever sharply. The weight dropped and the long arm bearing the missile flipped up into the air. There was an almighty crash as the iron bucket hit the ground, but O'Hara's attention was on the rock as it arched over his head. It was in the air a long time and went very high; then it reached the top of its trajectory and started to fall to earth, gaining speed appreciably as it plummeted. It fell far on the other side of the bridge, beyond the road and the burned vehicles, into the mountainside. A plume of dust fountained from the side of the hill to mark its fall.

"Jesus!" whispered O'Hara. "The thing has range." He slipped from his place and ran back. "Thirty yards over —fifteen to the right. How heavy was that rock?"

"About thirty pounds," said Willis offhandedly. "We need a bigger one." He heaved on the trebuchet. "We'll swing her a bit to the left."

O'Hara could hear a babble of voices from across the river and there was a brief rattle of rifle fire. Or should I call it musketry? he thought, just to keep it in period. He laughed and smote Armstrong on the back. "You've done it again," he roared. "We'll pound that bridge to matchwood."

But it was not to prove as easy as he thought. It took an hour to fire the next six shots—and not one of them hit the bridge. They had two near misses and one that grazed the catenary rope on the left, making the bridge shiver from end to end. But there were no direct hits.

Curiously, too, there was no marked reaction from the enemy. A lot of running about and random shooting followed each attempt, but there was no coherent action. What could they do after all, O'Hara thought; nothing could stop the rocks once they were in flight.

"Why can't we get the range right—what the hell's the matter with this thing?" he demanded at last.

Armstrong said mildly, "I knew a trebuchet wasn't a precision weapon, in a general way, of course; but this brings it home. It does tend to scatter a bit, doesn't it?"

Willis looked worried. "There's a bit of a whip in the arm," he said. "It isn't stiff enough. Then again, we haven't a standard shot; there are variations in weight and that causes the overs and unders. It's the whip that's responsible for the variations from side to side."

"Can you do anything about the whip in the arm?"

Willis shook his head. "A steel girder would help," he said ironically.

"There must be some way of getting a standard weight of shot."

So the ingenious Willis made a rough balance which, he said, would match one rock against another to the nearest half-pound. And they started again. Four shots later, they made the best one of the afternoon.

The trebuchet crashed again and a cloud of dust rose from where the bucket smashed into the ground. The long arm came over, just like a fast bowler at cricket, thought O'Hara, and the rock soared into the sky, higher and higher. Over O'Hara's head it reached it highest point and began to fall, seeming to go true to its target. "This is it," said O'Hara urgently. "This is going to be a smash hit."

The rock dropped faster and faster under the tug of gravity and O'Hara held his breath. It dropped right between the catenary ropes of the bridge and, to O'Hara's disgust, fell plumb through the gap in the middle, sending a plume of white spray leaping from the boiling river to splash on the underside of the planking.

"God Almighty!" he howled. "A perfect shot—and in the wrong bloody place."

But he had a sudden hope that what he had said to Willis up at the camp would prove to be wrong; that he was *not* a dead man—that the enemy would *not* get over the bridge—that they all had a fighting chance. As hope surged in him a knot of tension tightened in his stomach. When he had no hope his nerves had been taut enough, but the offer of continued life made life itself seem more precious and not to be lost or thrown away—and so the tension was redoubled.

A man who considers himself dead has no fear of dying, but with hope came a trace of fear.

He went back to the trebuchet. "You're a bloody fine artillery man," he said to Willis in mock-bitter tones.

Willis bristled. "What do you mean?"

"I mean what I say—you're a bloody fine artillery man. That last shot was perfect—but the bridge wasn't there at that point. The rock went through the gap."

Willis grinned self-consciously and seemed pleased. "It looks as though we've got the range."

"Let's get at it," said O'Hara.

For the rest of the afternoon the trebuchet thumped and crashed at irregular intervals. They worked like slaves hauling on the ropes and bringing rocks to the balance. O'Hara put Miss Ponsky in charge of the balance and as the afternoon wore on they became expert at judging the weight—it was no fun to carry a forty-pound rock a matter of a couple of hundred yards, only to have it rejected by Miss Ponsky.

O'Hara kept an eye on his watch and recorded the number of shots, finding that the rate of fire had speeded up to above twelve an hour. In two and a half hours they fired twenty-six rocks and scored about seven hits; about one in four. O'Hara had seen only two of them land but what he saw convinced him that the bridge could not take that kind of pounding for long. It was a pity that the hits were scattered on the bridge —a concentration would have been better—but they had opened a new gap of two planks and several more were badly bent. It was not enough to worry a man crossing the bridge—not yet—but no one would take a chance with a vehicle.

He was delighted—as much by the fact that the enemy was helpless as by anything else. There was nothing they could do to stop the bridge being slowly pounded into fragments, short of bringing up a mortar to bombard the trebuchet. At first there had been the usual futile rifle-fire, but that soon ceased. Now there was merely a chorus of jeers from the opposite bank when a shot missed and a groan when a hit was scored.

It was half an hour from nightfall when Willis came to him and said, "We can't keep this up. The beast is taking a hell of a battering—she's shaking herself to pieces. Another two or three shots and she'll collapse."

O'Hara swore and looked at the grey man—Willis was covered in dust from head to foot. He said slowly, "I had

146

hoped to carry on through the night—I wanted to ruin the bridge beyond repair."

"We can't," said Willis flatly. "She's loosened up a lot and there's a split in the arm—it'll break off if we don't bind it up with something. If that happens the trebuchet is the pile of junk it started out as."

O'Hara felt impotent fury welling up inside him. He turned away without speaking and walked several paces before he said over his shoulder, "Can you fix it?"

"I can try," said Willis. "I think I can."

"Don't try—don't think. Fix it," said O'Hara harshly, as he walked away. He did not look back.

III

Night.

A sheath of thin mist filmed the moon, but O'Hara could still see as he picked his way among the rocks. He found a comfortable place in which to sit, his back resting against a vertical slab. In front of him was a rock shelf on which he carefully placed the bottle he carried. It reflected the misted moon deep in its white depths as though enclosing a nacreous pearl.

He looked at it for a long time.

He was tired; the strain of the last few days had told heavily on him and his sleep had been a matter of a few hours snatched here and there. But Miss Ponsky and Benedetta were now taking night watches and that eased the burden. Over by the bridge Willis and Armstrong were tinkering with the trebuchet, and O'Hara thought he should go and help them but he did not. To hell with it, he thought; let me have an hour to myself.

The enemy—the peculiarly faceless enemy—had once more brought up another jeep and the bridge was again well illuminated. They weren't taking any chances of losing the bridge by a sudden fire-burning sortie. For two days they had not made a single offensive move apart from their futile barrages of rifle-fire. They're cooking something up, he thought; and when it comes, it's going to surprise us.

He looked at the bottle thoughtfully.

Forester and Rohde would be leaving the mine for the pass at dawn and he wondered if they would make it. He had been quite honest with Willis up at the camp—he honestly did

147

not think they had a hope. It would be cold up there and they had no tent and, by the look of the sky, there was going to be a change in the weather. If they did not cross the pass —maybe even if they did—the enemy had won; the God of Battles was on their side because they had the bigger battalions.

With a deep sigh he picked up the bottle and unscrewed the cap, giving way to the lurking devils within him.

I V

Miss Ponsky said, "You know, I'm enjoying this—really I am."

Benedetta looked up, startled. "Enjoying it!"

"Yes, I am," said Miss Ponsky comfortably, "I never thought I'd have such an adventure."

Benedetta said carefully, "You know we might all be killed?"

"Oh, yes, child; I know that. But I know now why men go to war. It's the same reason that makes them gamble, but in war they play for the highest stake of all—their own lives. It adds a certain edge to living."

She pulled her coat closer about her and smiled. "I've been a school teacher for thirty years," she said. "And you know how folk think of spinster schoolmarms—they're supposed to be prissy and sexless and unromantic, but I was never like that. If anything I was too romantic, surely too much so for my own good. I saw life in terms of old legends and historical novels, and of course life isn't like that at all. There was a man, you know, once . . ."

Benedetta was silent, not wishing to break the thread of this curious revelation.

Miss Ponsky visibly pulled herself together. "Anyway, there I was—a very romantic young girl growing into middle age and rising a little in her profession. I became a head-mistress—a sort of dragon to a lot of children. I suppose my romanticism showed a little by what I did in my spare time; I was quite a good fencer when I was younger, and of course, later there was the archery. But I wished I could have been a man and gone away and had adventures—men are so much *freer*, you know. I had almost given up hope when this happened."

She chuckled happily. "And now here I am, rising fifty-

148

five and engaged in a desperate adventure. Of course I know I might be killed but it's all worth it, every bit of it; it makes up for such a lot."

Benedetta looked at her sadly. What was happening threatened to destroy her uncle's hopes for their country and Miss Ponsky saw it in the light of dream-like romanticism, something from Robert Louis Stevenson to relieve the sterility of her life. She had jibbed at killing a man, but now she was blooded and would never look upon human life in the same light again. And when—or if—she went back home again, dear safe old South Bridge, Connecticut, would always seem a little unreal to her—reality would be a bleak mountainside with death coming over a bridge and a sense of quickened life as her blood coursed faster through parched veins.

Miss Ponsky said briskly, " But I mustn't run on like this. I must go down to the bridge; I promised Mr. O'Hara I would. He's such a handsome young man, isn't he? But he looks so sad sometimes."

Benedetta said in a low voice, " I think he is unhappy."

Miss Ponsky nodded wisely. " There has been a great grief in his life," she said, and Benedetta knew that she was casting O'Hara as a dark Byronic hero in the legend she was living. But he's not like that, she cried to herself; he's a man of flesh and blood, and a stupid man too, who will not allow others to help him, to share his troubles. She thought of what had happened up at the camp, of O'Hara's kisses and the way she had been stirred by them—and then of his inexplicable coldness towards her soon afterwards. If he would not share himself, she thought, perhaps such a man was not for her—but she found herself wishing she was wrong.

Miss Ponsky went out of the shelter. " It's becoming a little misty," she said. " We must watch all the more carefully."

Benedetta said, " I'll come down in two hours."

" Good," said Miss Ponsky gaily, and clattered her way down to the bridge.

Benedetta sat for a while repairing a rent in her coat with threads drawn out of the hem and using the needle which she always carried stuck in the lining of her handbag. The small domestic task finished, she thought, Tim's shirt is torn —perhaps I can mend that.

He had been glumly morose during the evening meal and had gone away immediately afterwards to the right along the mountainside, away from the bridge. She had recognised that he had something on his mind and had not interrupted, but had marked the way he had gone. Now she got up and stepped out of the shelter.

She came upon him suddenly from behind after being guided by the clink of glass against stone. He was sitting gazing at the moon, the bottle in his hand, and was quietly humming a tune she did not know. The bottle was half-empty.

He turned as she stepped forward out of the shadows and held out the bottle. " Have a drink; it's good for what ails you." His voice was slurred and furry.

" No, thank you, Tim." She stepped down and sat beside him. " You have a tear in your shirt—I'll mend it if you come back to the shelter."

" Ah, the little woman. Domesticity in a cave." He laughed humourlessly.

She indicated the bottle. " Do you think this is good—at this time?"

" It's good at this or any other time—but especially at this time." He waved the bottle. " Eat, drink and be merry—for to-morrow we certainly die." He thrust it at her. " Come on, have a snort."

She took the proffered bottle and quickly smashed it against a rock. He made a movement as though to save it, and said, " What the hell did you do that for?" in an aggrieved voice.

" Your name is not Peabody," she said cuttingly.

" What do you know about it? Peabody and I are old pals—bottle-babies, both of us." He stooped and groped. " Maybe it's not all gone—there might be some to be saved." He jerked suddenly. " Damn, I've cut my bloody finger," he said and laughed hysterically. " Look, I've got a bloody finger."

She saw the blood dripping from his hand, black in the moonlight. " You're irresponsible," she said. " Give me your hand." She lifted her skirt and ripped at her slip, tearing off a strip of cloth for a bandage.

O'Hara laughed uproariously. " The classic situation," he said. " The heroine bandages the wounded hero and does all the usual things that Hollywood invented. I suppose I should turn away like the gent I'm supposed to be, but you've got nice legs and I like looking at them."

She was silent as she bandaged his finger. He looked down at her dark head and said, " Irresponsible? I suppose I am.

So what? What is there to be responsible for? The world can go to hell in a hand-basket for all I care." He crooned. "Naked came I into the world and naked I shall go out of it —and what lies between is just a lot of crap."

"That's a sad philosophy of life," she said, not raising her head.

He put his hand under her chin to lift her head and stared at her. "Life? What do you know about life? Here you are—fighting the good fight in this crummy country—and for what? So that a lot of stupid Indians can have something that, if they had any guts at all, they'd get for themselves. But there's a big world outside which is always interfering— and you'll kowtow to Russia or America in the long run; you can't escape that fate. If you think that you'll be masters in your own country, you're even more stupid than I thought you were."

She met his eyes steadily. In a quiet and tranquil voice she said, "We can try."

"You'll never do it," he answered, and dropped his hand. "This is a world of dog eat dog and this country is one of the scraps that the big dogs fight over. It's a world of eat or be eaten—kill or be killed."

"I don't believe that," she said.

He gave a short laugh. "Don't you? Then what the hell are we doing here? Why don't we pack up our things and just go home? Let's pretend there's no one on the other side of the river who wants to kill us on sight."

She had no answer to that. He put his arm round her and she felt his hand on her knee, moving up her thigh under her skirt. She struggled loose and hit him with her open palm as hard as she could. He looked at her and there was a shocked expression in his eyes as he rubbed his cheek.

She cried, "You are one of the weak ones, Tim O'Hara, you are one of those who are killed and eaten. You have no courage and you always seek refuge—in the bottom of a bottle, in the arms of a woman, what does it matter? You're a pitiful, twisted man."

"Christ, what do you know about me?" he said, stung by the contempt in her voice but knowing that he liked her contempt better than her compassion.

"Not much. And I don't particularly like what I know. But I do know that you're worse than Peabody—he's a weak man who can't help it; you're a strong man who refuses to be strong. You spend all your time staring at your own navel

151

in the belief that it's the centre of the universe, and you have no human compassion at all."

"Compassion?" he shouted. "I have no need of *your* compassion—I've no time for people who are sorry for me. I don't need it."

"Everyone needs it," she retorted. "We're all afraid—that's the human predicament, to be afraid, and any man who says he isn't is a liar." In a quieter voice she went on, "You weren't always like this, Tim—what caused it?"

He dropped his head into his hands. He could feel something breaking within him; there was a shattering and a crumbling of his defences, the walls he had hidden behind for so long. He had just realised the truth of what Benedetta said; that his fear was not an abnormality but the normal situation of mankind and that it was not weakness to admit it.

He said in a muffled voice, "Good Christ, Benedetta, I'm frightened—I'm scared of falling into their hands again."

"The communists?"

He nodded.

"What did they do to you?"

So he told her and in the telling her face went white. He told her of the weeks of lying naked in his own filth in that icy cell; of the enforced sleeplessness, the interminable interrogations; of the blinding lamps and the electric shocks; of Lieutenant Feng. "They wanted me to confess to spreading plague germs," he said. He raised his head and she saw the streaks of tears in the moonlight. "But I didn't; it wasn't true, so I didn't." He gulped. "But I nearly did."

In her innermost being she felt a scalding contempt for herself—she had called *this* man weak. She cradled his head to her breast and felt the deep shudders which racked him. "It's all right now, Tim," she said. "It's all right."

He felt a draining of himself, a purging of the soul in the catharsis of telling to another human being that which had been locked within him for so long. And in a strange way, he felt strengthened and uplifted as he got rid of all the psychic pus that had festered in his spirit. Benedetta took the brunt of this verbal torrent calmly, comforting him with disconnected, almost incoherent endearments. She felt at once older and younger than he, which confused her and made her uncertain of what to do.

At last the violence of his speech ebbed and gradually he fell silent, leaning back against the rock as though physically exhausted. She held both his hands and said, "I'm sorry, Tim—for what I said."

He managed a smile. "You were right—I *have* been a thorough bastard, haven't I?"

"With reason."

"I must apologise to the others," he said. "I've been riding everybody too hard."

She said carefully, "We aren't chess pieces, Tim, to be moved as though we had no feelings. And that's what you have been doing, you know; moving my uncle, Willis and Armstrong—Jenny, too—as though they were just there to solve the problem. You see, it isn't only your problem—it belongs to all of us. Willis has worked harder than any of us; there was no need to behave towards him as you did when the trebuchet broke down."

O'Hara sighed. "I know," he said. "But it seemed the last straw. I was feeling bloody-minded about everything just then. But I'll apologise to him."

"A better thing would be to help him."

He nodded. "I'll go now." He looked at her and wondered if he had alienated her for ever. It seemed to him that no woman could love him who knew about him what this woman knew. But then Benedetta smiled brilliantly at him, and he knew with relief that everything was going to be all right.

"Come," she said. "I'll walk with you as far as the shelter." She felt an almost physical swelling pain her bosom, a surge of wild, unreasonable happiness, and she knew that she had been wrong when she had felt that Tim was not for her. This was the man with whom she would share her life —for as long as her life lasted.

He left her at the shelter and she kissed him before he went on. As she saw the dark shadow going away down the mountain she suddenly remembered and called, "What about the tear in your shirt?"

His answer came back almost gaily. "To-morrow," he shouted, and went on to the glimmer of light where Willis was working against time.

v

The morning dawned mistily but the rising sun soon burned away the haze. They held a dawn conference by the trebuchet to decide what was to be done next. "What do you think?" O'Hara asked Willis. "How much longer will it take?"

Armstrong clenched his teeth round the stem of his pipe and observed O'Hara with interest. Something of note had happened to this young man; something good. He looked over to where Benedetta was keeping watch on the bridge—her radiance this morning had been unbelievable, a shining effulgence that cast an almost visible glow about her. Armstrong smiled—it was almost indecent how happy these two were.

Willis said, "It'll be better now we can see what we're doing. I give us another couple of hours." His face was drawn and tired.

"We'll get to it," said O'Hara. He was going to continue but he paused suddenly, his head on one side. After a few seconds Armstrong also caught what O'Hara was listening to—the banshee whine of a jet plane approaching fast.

It was on them suddenly, coming low up-river. There was a howl and a wink of shadow as the aircraft swept over them to pull up into a steep climb and a sharp turn. Willis yelled, "They've found us—they've found us." He began to jump up and down in a frenzy of excitement, waving his arms.

"It's a Sabre," O'Hara shouted. "And it's coming back." They watched the plane reach the top of its turning climb and come back at them in a shallow dive. Miss Ponsky screamed at the top of her voice, her arms going like a semaphore, but O'Hara said suddenly, "I don't like this—everyone scatter—take cover."

He had seen aircraft behave like that in Korea, and he had done it himself; it had all the hallmarks of the beginning of a strafing attack.

They scattered like chickens at the sudden onset of a hawk and again the Sabre roared over, but there was no chatter of guns—just the diminishing whine of the engine as it went away down river. Twice more it came over them and the tough grass standing in clumps trembled stiff stems in the wake of its passage. And then it was gone in a long, almost vertical climb heading west over the mountains.

They came out of cover and stood in a group looking towards the peaks. Willis was the first to speak. "Damn you," he shouted at O'Hara. "Why did you make us hide? That plane must have been searching for us."

"Was it?" asked O'Hara. "Benedetta, does Cordillera have Sabres in the Air Force?"

"That was an Air Force fighter," she said. "I don't know which squadron."

"I missed the markings," said O'Hara. "Did anyone get them?"

No one had.

"I'd like to know which squadron that was," mused O'Hara. "It could make a difference."

"I tell you it was part of the search," insisted Willis.

"Nothing doing," said O'Hara. "The pilot of that plane knew exactly where to come—he wasn't searching. Someone had given him a pinpoint map position. There was nothing uncertain about his passes over us. We didn't tell him; Forester didn't tell him—they're only just leaving the mine now—so who did?"

Armstrong used his pipe as a pointer. "They did," he said, and pointed across the river. "We must assume that it means nothing good."

O'Hara was galvanised into activity. "Let's get this bloody beast working again. I want that bridge ruined as soon as possible. Jenny, take a bow and go down-river to where you can get a good view of the road where it bends away. If anyone comes through, take a crack at them and then get back here as fast as you can. Benedetta, you watch the bridge—the rest of us will get cracking here."

Willis had been too optimistic, because two hours went by and the trebuchet was still in pieces and far from being in working order. He wiped a grimy hand across his face. "It's not so bad now—another hour will see it right."

But they did not get another hour. Benedetta called out, "I can hear trucks." Following immediately upon her words came the rattle of rifle shots from down-river and another sound that chilled O'Hara—the unmistakable rat-a-tat of a machine-gun. He ran over to Benedetta and said breathlessly, "Can you see anything?"

"No," she answered; then, "Wait—yes, three trucks—big ones."

"Come down," said O'Hara. "I want to see this."

She climbed down from among the rocks and he took her place. Coming up the road at a fast clip and trailing a cloud of dust was a big American truck and behind it another, and another. The first one was full of men, at least twenty of them, all armed with rifles. There was something odd about it that O'Hara could not at first place, then he saw the deep skirting of steel plate below the truck body which covered the petrol tank. The enemy was taking precautions.

The truck pulled to a halt by the bridge and the men piled out, being careful to keep the truck between themselves and the river. The second truck stopped behind; this was empty of men apart from two in the cab, and O'Hara could not see what the covered body contained. The third truck also contained men, though not as many, and O'Hara felt cold as he saw the light machine-gun being unloaded and taken hurriedly to cover.

He turned and said to Benedetta, "Give me that bow, and get the others over here." But when he turned back there was no target for him; the road and mountainside opposite seemed deserted of life, and the three trucks held no profit for him.

Armstrong and Willis came up and he told them what was happening. Willis said, "The machine-gun sounds bad, I know, but what can they do with it that they can't do with the rifles they've got? It doesn't make us much worse off."

"They can use it like a hose-pipe," said O'Hara. "They can squirt a stream of bullets and systematically hose down the side of the gorge. It's going to be bloody dangerous using the crossbow from now on."

"You say the second truck was empty," observed Armstrong thoughtfully.

"I didn't say that; I said it had no men. There must be something in there but the top of the body is swathed in canvas and I couldn't see." He smiled sourly. "They've probably got a demountable mountain howitzer or a mortar in there—and if they have anything like that we've had our chips."

Armstrong absently knocked his pipe against a rock, forgetting it was empty. "The thing to do now is have a parley," he said unexpectedly. "There never was a siege I studied where there wasn't a parley somewhere along the line."

"For God's sake, talk sense," said O'Hara. "You can only parley when you've got something to offer. These boys are on top and they know it; why should they parley? Come to that—why should *we*? We know they'll offer us the earth, and we know damned well they'll not keep their promises—so what's the use?"

"We have something to offer," said Armstrong calmly.

156

"We have Aguillar—they want him, so we'll offer him." He held up his hands to silence the others' protests. "We know what they'll offer us—our lives, and we know what their promises are worth, but that doesn't matter. Oh, we don't give them Aguillar, but with a bit of luck we can stretch the parley out into a few hours, and who knows what a few hours may mean later on?"

O'Hara thought about it. "What do you think, Willis?"

Willis shrugged. "We don't stand to lose anything," he said, "and we stand to gain time. Everything we've done so far has been to gain time."

"We could get the trebuchet into working order again," mused O'Hara. "That alone would be worth it. All right, let's try it out."

"Just a minute," said Armstrong. "Is anything happening across there yet?"

O'Hara looked across the gorge; everything was still and quiet. "Nothing."

"I think we'd better wait until they start to do something," counselled Armstrong. "It's my guess that the new arrivals and the old guard are in conference; they may take a while and there's no point in breaking it up. *Any* time we gain is to our advantage, so let's wait awhile."

Benedetta, who was standing by quietly, now spoke. "Jenny hasn't come back yet."

O'Hara whirled. "Hasn't she?"

Willis said, "Perhaps she'll have been hit; that machine-gun . . ." His voice tailed away.

"I'll go and see," said Benedetta.

"No," said O'Hara sharply. "I'll go—she may need to be carried and you can't do that. You'd better stay here on watch and the others can get on with repairing the trebuchet."

He plunged away and ran across the level ground, skirting the bridgehead where there was no cover and began to clamber among the rocks on the other side, making his way down-river. He had a fair idea of the place Miss Ponsky would have taken and he made straight for it. As he went he swore and cursed under his breath; if she had been killed he would never forgive himself.

It took him over twenty minutes to make the journey—good time considering the ground was rough—but when he arrived at the most likely spot she was not there. But there were three bolts stuck point first in the ground and a small pool of sticky blood staining the rock.

He bent down and saw another blood-spot and then another. He followed this bloody spoor and back-tracked a hundred yards before he heard a weak groan and saw Miss Ponsky lying in the shadow of a boulder, her hand clutching her left shoulder. He dropped to his knee beside her and lifted her head. " Where were you hit, Jenny? In the shoulder?"

Her eyes flickered open and she nodded weakly.

" Anywhere else?"

She shook her head and whispered, " Oh, Tim, I'm sorry. I lost the bow."

" Never mind that," he said, and ripped the blouse from her shoulder, careful not to jerk her. He sighed in relief; the wound was not too bad, being through the flesh part of the shoulder and not having broken the bone so far as he could judge. But she had lost a lot of blood and that had weakened her, as had the physical shock.

She said in a stronger voice, " But I shouldn't have lost it —I should have held on tight. It fell into the river, Tim; I'm so sorry."

" Damn the bow," he said. " You're more important." He plugged the wound on both sides with pieces torn from his shirt, and made a rough bandage. " Can you walk?"

She tried to walk and could not, so he said cheerfully, " Then I'll have to carry you—fireman's lift. Up you come." He slung her over his shoulder and slowly made his way back to the bridge. By the time he got to the shelter and delivered her to Benedetta she was unconscious again.

" All the more need for a parley," he said grimly to Armstrong. " We must get Jenny on her feet again and capable of making a run for it. Has anything happened across there?"

" Nothing. But we've nearly finished the trebuchet."

It was not much later that two men began to strip the canvas from the second truck and O'Hara said, " Now we give it a go." He filled his lungs and shouted in Spanish, " Señors—Señors! I wish to speak to your leader. Let him step forward—we will not shoot."

The two men stopped dead and looked at each other. Then they stared across the gorge, undecided. O'Hara said, in a sardonic aside to Armstrong, " Not that we've got much to shoot with."

The men appeared to make up their minds. One of them ran off and presently the big man with the beard appeared from among the rocks, climbed down and walked to the abutments of the bridge. He shouted, " Is that Señor Aguillar?"

" No," shouted O'Hara, changing into English. " It is O'Hara."

" Ah, the pilot." The big man responded in English, rather startling O'Hara with his obvious knowledge of their identities. " What do you want, Señor O'Hara?"

Benedetta had returned to join them and now said quickly, " This man is not a Cordilleran; his accent is Cuban."

O'Hara winked at her. " Señor Cuban, why do you shoot at us?"

The big man laughed jovially. " Have you not asked Señor Aguillar? Or does he still call himself Montes?"

" Aguillar is nothing to do with me," called O'Hara. " His fight is not mine—and I'm tired of being shot at."

The Cuban threw back his head and laughed again, slapping his thigh. " So?"

" I want to get out of here."

" And Aguillar?"

" You can have him. That's what you're here for, isn't it?"

The Cuban paused as though thinking deeply, and O'Hara said to Benedetta, " When I pinch you, scream your head off." She looked at him in astonishment, then nodded.

" Bring Aguillar to the bridge and you can go free, Señor O'Hara."

" What about the girl?" asked O'Hara.

" The girl we want too, of course."

O'Hara pinched Benedetta in the arm and she uttered a blood-curdling scream, artistically chopping it off as though a hand had been clapped to her mouth. O'Hara grinned at her and waited a few moments before he raised his voice. " Sorry, Señor Cuban; we had some trouble." He let caution appear in his tone. " I'm not the only one here—there are others."

" You will all go free," said the big man with an air of largesse. " I myself will escort you to San Croce. Bring Aguillar to the bridge now; let us have him and you can all go."

" That is impossible," O'Hara protested. " Aguillar is at the upper camp. He went there when he saw what was happening here at the bridge. It will take time to bring him down."

The Cuban lifted his head suspiciously. " Aguillar ran away?" he asked incredulously.

O'Hara swore silently; he had not thought that Aguillar

would be held in such respect by his enemies. He quickly improvised. " He was sent away by Rohde, his friend. But Rohde has been killed by your machine-gun."

" Ah, the man who shot at us on the road just now." The Cuban looked down at his tapping foot, apparently undecided. Then he lifted his head. " Wait, Señor O'Hara."

" How long?"

" A few minutes, that is all." He walked up the road and disappeared among the rocks.

Armstrong said, " He's gone to consult with his second-in-command."

" Do you think he'll fall for it?"

" He might," said Willis. " It's an attractive proposition. You baited it well—he thinks that Rohde has been keeping us in line and that now he's dead we're about to collapse. It was very well done."

The Cuban was away for ten minutes, then he came back to the bridge accompanied by another man, a slight, swarthy Indian type. " Very well," he called. " As the *norteamericanos* say, you have made a deal. How long to bring Aguillar?"

" It's a long way," shouted O'Hara. " It will take some time—say, five hours."

The two men conferred and then the Cuban shouted, " All right, five hours."

" And we have an armistice?" shouted O'Hara. " No shooting from either side?"

" No shooting," promised the Cuban.

O'Hara sighed. " That's it. We must get the trebuchet finished. We've got five hours' grace. How's Jenny, Benedetta?"

" She will be all right. I gave her some hot soup and wrapped her in a blanket. She must be kept warm."

" Five hours isn't a long time," said Armstrong. " I know we were lucky to get it, but it still isn't long. Maybe we can string it out a little longer."

" We can try," said O'Hara. " But not for much longer. They'll get bloody suspicious when the five hours have gone and we haven't produced Aguillar."

Armstrong shrugged. " What can they do that they haven't been trying to do for the last three days?"

The day wore on.

The trebuchet was repaired and O'Hara made plans for the rage that was to come. He said, "We have one crossbow and a pistol with one bullet—that limits us if it comes to in-fighting. Benedetta, you take Jenny up to the camp as soon as she can walk. She won't be able to move fast, so you'd better get a head start in case things blow up here. I still don't know what they've got in the second truck, but it certainly isn't intended to do us any good."

So Benedetta and Miss Ponsky went off, taking a load of Molotov cocktails with them. Armstrong and O'Hara watched the bridge, while Willis tinkered with the trebuchet, doing unnecessary jobs. On the other side of the river men had popped out from among the rocks, and the hillside seemed alive with them as they unconcernedly smoked and chatted. It reminded O'Hara of the stories he had heard of the first Christmas of the First World War.

He counted the men carefully and compared notes with Armstrong. "I make it thirty-three," he said.

"I get thirty-five," said Armstrong. "But I don't suppose the difference matters." He looked at the bowl of his pipe. "I wish I had some tobacco," he said irritably.

"Sorry, I'm out of cigarettes."

"You're a modern soldier," said Armstrong. "What would you do in their position? I mean, how would you handle the next stage of the operation?"

O'Hara considered. "We've done the bridge a bit of no good with the trebuchet, but not enough. Once they've got that main gap repaired they can start rushing men across, but not vehicles. I'd make a rush and form a bridgehead at this end, spreading out along this side of the gorge where we are now. Once they've got us away from here it won't be much trouble to repair the rest of the bridge to the point where they can bring a couple of jeeps over. Then I'd use the jeeps as tanks, ram them up to the mine as fast as possible—they'd be there before we could arrive on foot. Once they hold both ends of the road where can we retreat to? There's not a lot we can do about it—that's the hell of it."

"Um," said Armstrong glumly. "That's the appreciation

I made." He rolled over on his back. "Look, it's clouding over."

O'Hara turned and looked up at the mountains. A dirty grey cloud was forming and had already blotted out the higher peaks and now swirled in misty coils just above the mine. "That looks like snow," he said. "If there was ever a chance of a real air-search looking for and finding us, it's completely shot now. And it must have caught Ray flat-footed." He shivered. "I wouldn't like to be in their boots."

They watched the cloud for some time and suddenly Armstrong said, "It may be all right for us, though; I believe it's coming low. We could do with a good, thick mist."

When the truce had but one hour to go the first grey tendrils of mist began to curl about the bridge and O'Hara sat up as he heard a motor engine. A new arrival pulled up behind the trucks, a big Mercédès saloon car out of which got a man in trim civilian clothes. O'Hara stared across the gorge as the man walked to the bridge and noted the short square build and the broad features. He nudged Armstrong. "The commissar has arrived," he said.

"A Russian?"

"I'd bet you a pound to a pinch of snuff," said O'Hara.

The Russian—if such he was—conferred with the Cuban and an argument seemed to develop, the Cuban waving his arms violently and the Russian stolidly stone-walling with his hands thrust deep into his coat pockets. He won the argument for the Cuban suddenly turned away and issued a string of rapid orders and the hillside on the other side of the gorge became a sudden ants' nest of activity.

The idling men disappeared behind the rocks again and it was as though the mountain had swallowed them. With frantic speed four men finished stripping the canvas from the second truck and the Cuban shouted to the Russian and waved his arms. The Russian, after one long look over the gorge, nonchalantly turned his back and strolled towards his car.

"By God, they're going to break the truce," said O'Hara tightly. He grabbed the loaded crossbow as the machine-gun suddenly ripped out and stitched the air with bullets. "Get back to the trebuchet." He aimed the bow carefully at the Russian's back, squeezed the trigger and was mortified to miss. He ducked to reload and heard the crash of the trebuchet behind him as Willis pulled the firing lever.

When he raised his head again he found that the trebuchet shot had missed and he paled as he saw what had been pulled out of the truck. It was a prefabricated length of bridging carried by six men who had already set foot on the bridge itself. Following them was a squad of men running at full speed. There was nothing that a single crossbow bolt would do to stop them and there was no time to reload the trebuchet —they would be across the bridge in a matter of seconds.

He yelled at Willis and Armstrong. "Retreat! Get back up the road—to the camp!" and ran towards the bridgehead, bow at the ready.

The first man was already across, scuttling from side to side, a sub-machine-gun at the ready. O'Hara crouched behind a rock and took aim, waiting until the man came closer. The mist was thickening rapidly and it was difficult to judge distances, so he waited until he thought the man was twenty yards away before he pulled the trigger.

The bolt took the man full in the chest, driving home right to the fletching. He shouted in a bubbling voice and threw his hands up as he collapsed, and the tightening death grip on the gun pulled the trigger. O'Hara saw the rest of the squad coming up behind him and the last thing he saw before he turned and ran was the prone figure on the ground quivering as the sub-machine-gun fired its magazine at random.

Chapter VII

Rohde hacked vigorously at the ice wall with the small axe. He had retrieved it—a grisly job—and now it was coming in very useful, returning to its designed function as an instrument for survival. Forester was lying, a huddled heap of old clothing, next to the ice wall, well away from the edge of the cliff. Rohde had stripped the outer clothing from Peabody's corpse and used it to wrap up Forester as warmly as possible before he pushed the body into the oblivion of the gathering mists below.

They needed warmth because it was going to be a bad night. The ledge was now enveloped in mist and it had started to snow in brief flurries. A shelter was imperative. Rohde stopped for a moment to bend over Forester who was still conscious, and adjusted the hood which had fallen away from his face. Then he resumed his chopping at the ice wall.

Forester had never felt so cold in his life. His hands and

feet were numb and his teeth chattered uncontrollably. He was so cold that he welcomed the waves of pain which rose from his chest; they seemed to warm him and they prevented him from slipping into unconsciousness. He knew he must not let that happen because Rohde had warned him about it, slapping his face to drive the point home.

It had been a damned near thing, he thought. Another couple of slashes from Peabody's knife and the rope would have parted to send him plunging to his death on the snow slopes far below. Rohde had been quick enough to kill Peabody when the need for it arose, even though he had been squeamish earlier. Or perhaps it wasn't that; perhaps he believed in expending just the necessary energy and effort that the job required. Forester, watching Rohde's easy strokes and the flakes of ice falling one by one, suddenly chuckled—a time-and-motion-study killer; that was one for the books. His weak chuckle died away as another wave of pain hit him; he clenched his teeth and waited for it to leave.

When Rohde had killed Peabody he had waited rigidly for a long time, holding the rope taut for fear that Peabody's body would slide over the edge, taking Forester with it. Then he began to dig the ice-axe deeper into the snow, hoping to use it to belay the rope; but he encountered ice beneath the thin layer of snow and, using only one hand, he could not force the axe down.

He changed his tactics. He pulled up the axe and, frightened of being pulled forward on the slippery ice, first chipped two deep steps into which he could put his feet. That gave him the leverage to haul himself upright by the rope and he felt Peabody's body shift under the strain. He stopped because he did not know how far Peabody had succeeded in damaging the rope and he was afraid it might part and let Forester go.

He took the axe and began to chip at the ice, making a large circular groove about two feet in diameter. He found it a difficult task because the head of the axe, improvised by Willis, was set at an awkward angle on the shaft and it was not easy to use. After nearly an hour of chipping he deepened the groove enough to take the rope, and carefully unfastening it from round his waist he belayed it round the ice mushroom he had created.

That left him free to walk to the edge of the cliff. He did not go forward immediately but stood for a while, stamping his feet and flexing his muscles to get the blood going again.

He had been lying in a very cramped position. When he looked over the edge he saw that Forester was unconscious, dangling limply on the end of the rope, his head lolling.

The rope was badly frayed where Peabody had attacked it, so Rohde took a short length from round his waist and carefully knotted it above and below the potential break. That done, he began to haul up the sagging and heavy body of Forester. It was hopeless to think of going farther that day. Forester was in no condition to move; the fall had tightened the rope cruelly about his chest and Rohde, probing carefully, thought that some ribs were cracked, if not broken. So he rolled Forester up in warm clothing and relaxed on the ledge between the rock cliff and the ice wall, wondering what to do next.

It was a bad place to spend a night—even a good night—and this was going to be a bad one. He was afraid that if the wind rose to the battering strength that it did during a blizzard, then the overhanging cornice on the ice wall would topple—and if it did they would be buried without benefit of grave-diggers. Again, they must have shelter from the wind and the snow, so he took the small axe, wiped the blood and the viscous grey matter from the blade, and began to chip a shallow cave in the ice wall.

II

The wind rose just after nightfall and Rohde was still working. As the first fierce gusts came he stopped and looked around wearily; he had been working for nearly three hours, chipping away at the hard ice with a blunt and inadequate instrument more suited to chopping household firewood. The small cleft he had made in the ice would barely hold the two of them but it would have to do.

He dragged Forester into the ice cave and propped him up against the rear wall, then he went out and brought in the three packs, arranging them at the front of the cave to form a low and totally inadequate wall which, however, served as some sort of bulwark against the drifting snow. He fumbled in his pocket and turned to Forester. " Here," he said urgently. " Chew these."

Forester mumbled and Rohde slapped him. " You must not sleep—not yet," he said. " You must chew coca." He forced open Forester's mouth and thrust a coca quid into it.

It took him over half an hour to open a pack and assemble the Primus stove. His fingers were cold and he was suffering from the effects of high altitude—the loss of energy and the mental haziness which dragged the time of each task to many times its normal length. Finally, he got the stove working. It provided little heat and less light, but it was a definite improvement.

He improvised a windshield from some pitons and pieces of blanket. Fortunately the wind came from behind, from the top of the pass and over the ice wall, so that they were in a relatively sheltered position. But vicious side gusts occasionally swept into the cave, bringing a flurry of snowflakes and making the Primus flare and roar. Rohde was glum when he thought of the direction of the wind. It was good as far as their present shelter went, but the snow cornice on top of the wall would begin to build up and as it grew heavier it would be more likely to break off. And, in the morning when they set off again, they would be climbing in the teeth of a gale. He prayed the wind would change direction before then.

Presently he had melted enough snow to make a warm drink, but Forester found the taste of the bouillon nauseating and could not drink it, so he heated some more water and they drank that; at least it put some warmth into their bellies.

Then he got to work on Forester, examining his hands and feet and pummelling him violently over many protests. After this Forester was wide awake and in full possession of his senses and did the same for Rohde, rubbing hands and feet to bring back the circulation. "Do you think we'll make it, Miguel?" he asked.

"Yes," said Rohde shortly; but he was having his first doubts. Forester was not in good condition for the final assault on the pass and the descent of the other side. It was not a good thing for a man with cracked ribs. He said, "You must keep moving—your fingers and toes, move them all the time. You must rub your face, your nose and ears. You must not sleep."

"We'd better talk," suggested Forester. "Keep each other awake." He raised his head and listened to the howls of the wind. "It'll be more like shouting, though, if this racket keeps up. What shall we talk about?"

Rohde grunted and pulled the hood about his ears. "O'Hara told me you were an airman."

"Right," said Forester. "I flew towards the end of the

166

war—in Italy mostly. I was flying Lightnings. Then when Korea came I was dragged in again—I was in the Air Force Reserve, you see. I did a conversion on to jets and then I flew Sabres all during the Korean war, or at least until I was pulled out to go back Stateside as an instructor. I think I must have flown some missions with O'Hara in Korea."

"So he said. And after Korea?"

Forester shrugged. "I was still bitten with the airplane bug; the company I work for specialises in airplane maintenance." He grinned. "When all this happened I was on my way to Santillana to complete a deal with your Air Force for maintenance equipment. You still have Sabres, you know; I sometimes get to flying them if the squadron commandant is a good guy." He paused. "If Aguillar pulls off his *coup d'état* the deal may go sour—I don't know why the hell I'm taking all this trouble."

Rohde smiled, and said, "If Señor Aguillar comes into power your business will be all right—he will remember. And you will not have to pay the bribes you have already figured into your costing." His voice was a little bitter.

"Hell," said Forester. "You know what it's like in this part of the world—especially under Lopez. Make no mistake, I'm for Aguillar; we businessmen like an honest government—it makes things easier all round." He beat his hands together. "Why are you for Aguillar?"

"Cordillera is my country," said Rohde simply, as though that explained everything, and Forester thought that meeting an honest patriot in Cordillera was a little odd, like finding a hippopotamus in the Arctic.

They were silent for a while, then Forester said, "What time is it?"

Rohde fumbled at his wrist-watch. "A little after nine."

Forester shivered. "Another nine hours before sunrise." The cold was biting deep into his bones and the wind gusts which flailed into their narrow shelter struck right through his clothing, even through O'Hara's leather jacket. He wondered if they would be alive in the morning; he had heard and read too many tales of men dying of exposure, even back home and closer to civilisation, to have any illusions about the precariousness of their position.

Rohde stirred and began to empty two of the packs. Carefully he arranged the contents where they would not roll out of the cave, then gave an empty pack to Forester. "Put your feet in this," he said. "It will be some protection against the cold."

Forester took the pack and flexed the blanket material, breaking off the encrusted ice. He put his feet into it and pulled the draw-string about the calves of his legs. "Didn't you say you'd been up here before?" he asked.

"Under better conditions," answered Rohde. "It was when I was a student many years ago. There was a mountaineering expedition to climb this peak—the one to our right here."

"Did they make it?"

Rohde shook his head. "They tried three times—they were brave, those Frenchmen. Then one of them was killed and they gave up."

"Why did you join them?" asked Forester curiously.

Rohde shrugged. "I needed the money—students always need money—and they paid well for porters. And, as a medical student, I was interested in the *soroche*. Oh, the equipment those men had! Fleece-lined under-boots and thick leather over-boots with crampons for the ice; quilted jackets filled with down; strong tents of nylon and long lengths of nylon rope—and good steel pitons that did not bend when you hammered them into the rock." He was like a starving man voluptuously remembering a banquet he had once attended.

"And you came over the pass?"

"From the other side—it was easier that way. I looked down over this side from the top and was glad we did not have to climb it. We had a camp—camp three—on top of the pass; and we came up slowly, staying some days at each camp to avoid the *soroche*."

"I don't know why men climb mountains," said Forester, and there was a note of annoyance in his voice. "God knows I'm not doing it because I want to; it beats me that men do it for pleasure."

"Those Frenchmen were geologists," said Rohde. "They were not climbing for the sake of climbing. They took many rock samples from the mountains around here. I saw a map they had made—published in Paris—and I read they had found many rich minerals."

"What's the use?" queried Forester. "No one can work up here."

"Not now," agreed Rohde. "But later—who knows?" His voice was serenely confident.

They talked together for a long time, each endeavouring to urge along the lagging clock. After a time Rohde began to sing—folk-songs of Cordillera and later the half-forgotten German songs that his father had taught him. Forester contributed some American songs, avoiding the modern pop tunes and sticking to the songs of his youth. He was half-way through " I've Been Working on the Railroad " when there was a thunderous crash from the left which momentarily drowned even the howls of the gale.

" What's that?" he asked, startled.

" The snow cornice is falling," said Rohde. " It has built up because of the wind; now it is too heavy and not strong enough to bear its own weight." He raised his eyes to the roof of the ice cave. " Let us pray that it does not fall in this place; we would be buried."

" What time is it?"

" Midnight. How do you feel?"

Forester had his arms crossed over his chest. " Goddam cold."

" And your ribs—how are they?"

" Can't feel a thing."

Rohde was concerned. " That is bad. Move, my friend; move yourself. You must not allow yourself to freeze." He began to slap and pummel Forester until he howled for mercy and could feel the pain in his chest again.

Just after two in the morning the snow cornice over the cave collapsed. Both Rohde and Forester had become dangerously moribund, relapsing into a half-world of cold and numbness. Rohde heard the preliminary creaking and stirred feebly, then sagged back weakly. There was a noise as of a bomb exploding as the cornice broke and a cloud of dry, powdery snow was driven into the shelter, choking and cold.

Rohde struggled against it, waving his arms in swimming motions as the tide of snow covered his legs and crept up to his chest. He yelled to Forester, " Keep a space clear for yourself."

Forester moaned in protest and waved his hands ineffectually, and luckily the snow stopped its advance, leaving them buried to their shoulders. After a long, dying rumble which seemed to come from an immense distance they became aware that it was unnaturally quiet; the noise of the blizzard which had battered at their ears for so long that they had ceased to be aware of it had gone, and the silence was loud and ear-splitting.

"What's happened?" mumbled Forester. Something was holding his arms imprisoned and he could not get them free. In a panic he began to struggle wildly until Rohde shouted, "Keep still." His voice was very loud in the confined space.

For a while they lay still, then Rohde began to move cautiously, feeling for his ice-axe. The snow in which he was embedded was fluffy and uncompacted, and he found he could move his arms upwards. When he freed them he began to push the snow away from his face and to plaster and compress it against the wall of the cave. He told Forester to do the same and it was not long before they had scooped out enough space in which to move. Rohde groped in his pocket for matches and tried to strike one, but they were all wet, the soggy ends crumbling against the box.

Forester said painfully, "I've got a lighter," and Rohde heard a click and saw a bright point of blinding light. He averted his eyes from the flame and looked about him. The flame burned quite still without flickering and he knew that they were buried. In front, where the opening to the cave had been, was an unbroken wall of compacted snow.

He said, "We must make a hole or suffocate," and groped in the snow for the small axe. It took him a long time to find it and his fingers encountered several other items of their inadequate equipment before he succeeded. These he put carefully to one side—everything would be important from now on.

He took the axe and, sitting up with his legs weighed down with snow, he began to hew at the wall before him. Although it was compacted it was not as hard to cut as the ice from which he had chopped the cave and he made good progress. But he did not know how much snow he had to go through before he broke through to the other side. Perhaps the fall extended right across the ledge between the ice wall and the cliff edge and he would come out upon a dizzying drop.

He put the thought out of his mind and diligently worked with the axe, cutting a hole only of such size as he needed to work in. Forester took the snow as it was scooped out of the hole and packed it to one side, observing after a while, "We're not going to have much room if this goes on much longer."

Rohde kept silent, cutting away in the dark, for he had blown out the small flame. He worked by sense of touch and at last he had penetrated as far as he could with the small axe, thrusting his arm right up to the shoulder into the hole he had made. He had still not come to the other side of the snow fall, and said abruptly, " The ice-axe."

Forester handed it to him and Rohde thrust it into the hole, driving vigorously. There was no room to cut with this long axe, so he pushed, forcing it through by sheer muscle power. To his relief, something suddenly gave and there was a welcome draught of cold air. It was only then he realised how fœtid the atmosphere had become. He collapsed, half on top of Forester, panting with his exertions and taking deep breaths of air.

Forester pushed him and he rolled away. After a while he said, " The fall is about two metres thick—we should have no trouble in getting through."

" We'd better get at it, then," said Forester.

Rohde considered the proposition and decided against it. " This might be the best thing for us. It is warmer in here now, the snow is shielding us from the wind. All we have to do is to keep that hole clear. And there will not be another fall."

" Okay," said Forester. " You're the boss."

Warmth was a relative term. Cutting the hole had made Rohde sweat freely and now he could feel the sweat freezing to ice on his body under his clothing. Awkwardly he began to strip and had Forester rub his body all over. Forester gave a low chuckle as he massaged, and said, " A low-temperature Turkish bath—I'll have to introduce it to New York. We'll make a mint of money."

Rohde dressed again, and asked, " How are you feeling?"

" Goddam cold," said Forester. " But otherwise okay."

" That shock did us good," said Rohde. " We were sinking fast—we must not let that happen again. We have another three hours to go before dawn—let us talk and sing."

So they sang lustily, the sound reverberating from the hard and narrow confines of the ice cave, making them sound, as Forester put it, " like a pair of goddam bathroom Carusos."

III

Half an hour before dawn Rohde began to cut their way out and he emerged into a grey world of blustery wind and driving snow. Forester was shocked at the conditions outside the cave. Although it was daylight, visibility was restricted to less than ten yards and the wind seemed to pierce right through him. He put his lips to Rohde's ear and shouted, "Draughty, isn't it?"

Rohde turned, his lips curled back in a fierce grin. "How is your chest?"

Forester's chest hurt abominably, but his smile was amiable. "Okay. I'll follow where you go." He knew they could not survive another night on the mountain—they had to get over the pass this day or they would die.

Rohde pointed upward with the ice-axe. "The cornice is forming again, but it is not too bad; we can go up here. Get the packs together." He stepped to the ice wall and began to cut steps skilfully, while Forester repacked their equipment. There was not much—some had been lost, buried under the snow fall, and some Rohde had discarded as being unnecessary deadweight to carry on this last desperate dash. They were stripped down to essentials.

Rohde cut steps in the fifteen-foot ice wall as high as he could reach while standing on reasonably firm ground, then climbed up and roped himself to pitons and stood in the steps he had already cut, chopping vigorously. He cut the steps very deep, having Forester in mind, and it took him nearly an hour before he was satisfied that Forester could climb the wall safely.

The packs were hauled up on a rope and then Forester began the climb, roped to Rohde. It was the most difficult task he had faced in his life. Normally he could have almost run up the broad and deep steps that Rohde had cut but now the bare ice burned his hands, even through the gloves, his chest ached and stabbing pains pierced him as he lifted his arms above his head, and he felt weak and tired as though the very breath of life had been drained from him. But he made it and collapsed at Rohde's feet.

Here the wind was a howling devil driving down the pass and bearing with it great clouds of powdery snow and ice particles which stung the face and hands. The din was indescribable, a freezing pandemonium from an icy hell, deafening in its loudness. Rohde bent over Forester, shielding him from the worst of the blast, and made him sit up. "You can't stay here," he shouted. "We must keep moving. There is no more hard climbing—just the slope to the top and down the other side."

Forester flinched as the ice particles drove like splinters into his face and he looked up into Rohde's hard and indomitable eyes. "Okay, buster," he croaked harshly. "Where you go, so can I."

Rohde thrust some coca quids into his hand. "You will need these." He checked the rope round Forester's waist and then picked up both packs, tentatively feeling their weight. He ripped them open and consolidated the contents into one pack, which he slung on his back despite Forester's protests. The empty pack was snatched by the wind and disappeared into the grey reaches of the blizzard behind them.

Forester stumbled to his feet and followed in the tracks that Rohde broke. He hunched his shoulders and held his head down, staring at his feet in order to keep the painful wind from his face. He wrapped the blanket hood about the lower part of his face but could do nothing to protect his eyes, which became red and sore. Once he looked up and the wind caught him right in the mouth, knocking the breath out of him as effectively as if he had been punched in the solar plexus. Quickly he bent his head again and trudged on.

The slope was not very steep, much less so than below the cliffs, but it meant that to gain altitude they had that much farther to go. He tried to work it out; they had to gain a thousand feet of height and the slope was, say, thirty degrees —but then his bemused mind bogged down in the intricacies of trigonometry and he gave up the calculation.

Rohde plodded on, breaking the deep snow and always testing the ground ahead with the ice-axe, while the wind shrieked and plucked at him with icy fingers. He could not see more than ten yards ahead but he trusted to the slope of the mountainside as being sufficient guide to the top of the pass. He had never climbed this side of the pass but had looked down from the top, and he hoped his memory of it was true and that what he had told Forester was correct —that there would be no serious climbing—just this steady plod.

Had he been alone he could have moved much faster, but he deliberately reduced his pace to help Forester. Besides, it helped conserve his own energy, which was not inexhaustible, although he was in better condition than Forester. But then, he had not fallen over a cliff. Like Forester, he went forward bent almost double, the wind tearing at his clothing and the snow coating his hood with a thickening film of ice.

After an hour they came to a slight dip where the slope eased and found that the ground became almost level. Here the snow had drifted and was very deep, getting deeper the farther they went on. Rohde raised his head and stared upwards, shielding his eyes with his hand and looking through the slits made by his fingers. There was nothing to be seen beyond the grey whirling world in which they were enclosed. He waited until Forester came abreast of him and shouted, "Wait here; I will go ahead a little way."

Forester nodded wearily and sank to the snow, turning his back to the gale and hunching himself into a fœtus-like attitude. Rohde unfastened the rope around his waist and dropped it by Forester's side, then went on. He had gone a few paces when he turned to look back and saw the dim huddle of Forester and, between them, the broken crust of the snow. He was satisfied that he could find his way back by following his own trail, so he pressed on into the blizzard.

Forester put another coca quid into his mouth and chewed it slowly. His gloved hand was clumsy and he pulled off the glove to pick up the quid from the palm of his hand. He was cold, numb to the bone, and his mouth was the only part of him that was pleasantly warm, a synthetic warmth induced by the coca. He had lost all sense of time; his watch had stopped long ago and he had no way of knowing how long they had been trudging up the mountain since scaling the ice wall. The cold seemed to have frozen his mind as well as his body, and he had the distinct impression that they had been going for several hours—or perhaps it was only several minutes; he did not know. All he knew was that he did not care much. He felt he was condemned to walk and climb for ever in this cold and bleak mountain world.

He lay apathetically in the snow for a long time and then, as the coca took effect, he roused himself and turned to look in the direction Rohde had gone. The wind flailed his face and he jerked and held up his hand, noticing absently that his knuckles had turned a scaly lizard-blue and that his fingers were cut in a myriad places by the wind-driven ice.

There was no sign of Rohde and Forester turned away, feeling a little surge of panic in his belly. What if Rohde could not find him again? But his mind was too torpid, too drugged by the cold and the coca, to drive his body into any kind of constructive action, and he slumped down to the snow again, where Rohde found him when he came back.

He was aroused by Rohde shaking him violently by the shoulder. "Move, man. You must not sit there and freeze. Rub your face and put on your glove."

Mechanically he brought up his hand and dabbed ineffectually at his face. He could feel no contact at all, both hand and face were anæsthetised by the cold. Rhode struck his face twice with vigorous open hand slaps and Forester was annoyed. "All right," he croaked. "No need to hit me." He slapped his hands together until the circulation came back and then began to massage his face.

Rohde shouted, "I went about two hundred metres—the snow was waist-deep and getting deeper. We cannot go that way; we must go round."

Forester felt a moment of despair. Would this never end? He staggered to his feet and waited while Rohde tied the rope, then followed him in a direction at right-angles to the course they had previously pursued. The wind was now striking at them from the side and, walking as they were across the slope, the buffeting gusts threatened to knock them off their feet and they had to lean into the wind to maintain a precarious balance.

The route chosen by Rohde skirted the deep drifts, but he did not like the way they tended to lose altitude. Every so often he would move up again towards the pass, and every time was forced down again by deepening snow. At last he found a way upwards where the slope steepened and the snow cover was thinner, and once more they gained altitude in the teeth of the gale.

Forester followed in a half-conscious stupor, mechanically putting one foot in front of the other in an endless lurching progression. From time to time as he cautiously raised his eyes he saw the dim snow-shrouded figure of Rohde ahead, and after a time his mind was wiped clean of all other considerations but that of keeping Rohde in sight and the rope slack. Occasionally he stumbled and fell forward and the rope would tighten and Rohde would wait patiently until he recovered his feet, and then they would go on again, and upwards—always upwards.

Suddenly Rohde halted and Forester shuffled to his side. There was a hint of desperation in Rohde's voice as he pointed forward with the ice-axe. "Rock," he said slowly. "We have come upon rock again." He struck the ice-glazed outcrop with the axe and the ice shattered. He struck again at the bare rock and it crumbled, flakes falling away to dirty the white purity of the snow. "The rock is rotten," said Rohde. "It is most dangerous. And there is the *verglas*."

Forester forced his lagging brain into action. "How far up do you think it extends?"

"Who knows?" said Rhode. He turned and squatted with his back to the wind and Forester followed his example. "We cannot climb this. It was bad enough on the other side of the glacier yesterday when we were fresh and there was no wind. To attempt this now would be madness." He beat his hands together.

"Maybe it's just an isolated outcrop," suggested Forester. "We can't see very far, you know."

Rohde grasped the ice-axe. "Wait here. I will find out." Once again he left Forester and scrambled upwards. Forester heard the steady chipping of the axe above the noise of the wind and pieces of ice and flakes of rock fell down out of the grey obscurity. He paid out rope as Rohde tugged and the hood about his head flapped loose and the wind stung his cheeks smartly.

He had just lifted his hand to wrap the hood about his face when Rohde fell. Forester heard the faint shout and saw the shapeless figure hurtling towards him from above out of the screaming turmoil. He grabbed the rope, turned and dug his heels into the snow ready to take the shock. Rohde tumbled past him in an uncontrollable fall and slid down the slope until he was brought up sharply on the end of the rope by a jerk which almost pulled Forester off his feet.

Forester hung on until he was sure that Rohde would go no farther down the slope. He saw him stir and then roll over to sit up and rub his leg. He shouted, "Miguel, are you okay?" then began to descend.

Rohde turned his face upwards and Forester saw that each hair of his beard stubble was coated with rime. "My leg," he said. "I've hurt my leg."

Forester bent over him and straightened the leg, probing with his fingers. The trouser-leg was torn and, as Forester put his hand inside, he felt the sticky wetness of blood. After a while he said, "It's not broken, but you've scraped it badly."

"It is impossible up there," said Rohde, his face twisted in pain. "No man could climb that—even in good weather."

"How far does the rock go?"

"As far as I could see, but that was not far." He paused. "We must go back and try the other side."

Forester was appalled. "But the glacier is on the other side; we can't cross the glacier in this weather."

"Perhaps there is a good way up this side of the glacier," said Rohde. He turned his head and looked up towards the rocks from which he had fallen. "One thing is certain—that way is impossible."

"We want something to bind this trouser-leg together," said Forester. "I don't know much about it, but I don't think it would be a good thing if this torn flesh became frostbitten."

pack," said Rohde. "Help me with the pack."

Forester helped him take off the pack and he emptied the contents into the snow and tore up the blanket material into strips which he bound tightly round Rohde's leg. He said wryly, "Our equipment gets less and less. I can put some of this stuff into my pocket, but not much."

"Take the Primus," said Rohde. "And some kerosene. If we have to go as far as the glacier perhaps we can find a place beneath an ice fall that is sheltered from the wind, where we can make a hot drink."

Forester put the bottle of kerosene and a handful of bouillon cubes into his pocket and slung the pressure stove over his shoulder suspended by a length of electric wire. As he did so, Rhode sat up suddenly and winced as he put unexpected pressure on his leg. He groped in the snow with scrabbling fingers. "The ice-axe," he said frantically. "The ice-axe—where is it?"

"I didn't see it," said Forester.

They both looked into the whirling grey darkness down the slope and Rohde felt an empty sensation in the pit of his stomach. The ice-axe had been invaluable; without it they could not have come as far as they had, and without it he doubted if they could get to the top of the pass. He looked down and saw that his hands were shaking uncontrollably and he knew he was coming to the end of his strength—physical and mental.

But Forester felt a renewed access of spirit. He said, "Well, what of it? This goddam mountain has done its best to kill us and it hasn't succeeded yet—and my guess is that it won't. If we've come this far we can go the rest of the way. It's only another five hundred feet to the top—five hundred lousy feet—do you hear that, Miguel?"

Rohde smiled wearily. "But we have to go down again."

"So what? It's just another way of getting up speed. I'll lead off this time. I can follow our tracks back to where we turned off."

And it was in this spirit of unreasonable and unreasoning

177

optimism that Forester led the way down with Rohde limping behind. He found it fairly easy to follow their tracks and followed them faithfully, even when they wavered where Rohde had diverged. He had not the same faith in his own wilderness path-finding that he had in Rohde's, and he knew that if he got off track in this blizzard he would never find it again. As it was, when they reached where they had turned off to the right and struck across the slope, the track was so faint as to be almost indistinguishable, the wind having nearly obliterated it with drifting snow.

He stopped and let Rohde catch up. "How's the leg?"

Rohde's grin was a snarl. "The pain has stopped. It is numb with the cold—and very stiff."

"I'll break trail then," said Forester. "You'd better take it easy for a while." He smiled and felt the stiffness of his cheeks. "You can use the rope like a rein to guide me—one tug to go left, two tugs to go right."

Rohde nodded without speaking, and they pressed on again. Forester found the going harder in the unbroken snow, especially as he did not have the ice-axe to test the way ahead. It's not so bad here, he thought; there are no crevasses—but it'll be goddam tricky if we have to cross the glacier. In spite of the hard going, he was better mentally than he had been; the task of leadership kept him alert and forced his creaking brain to work.

It seemed to him that the wind was not as strong and he hoped it was dropping. From time to time he swerved to the right under instruction from Rohde, but each time came to deep drifts and had to return to the general line of march. They came to the jumbled ice columns of the glacier without finding a good route up to the pass.

Forester dropped to his knees in the snow and felt tears of frustration squeeze out on to his cheeks. "What now?" he asked—not that he expected a good answer.

Rohde fell beside him, half-sitting, half-lying, his stiff leg jutting out before him. "We go into the glacier a little way to find shelter. The wind will not be as bad in there." He looked at his watch then held it to his ear. "It is two o'clock—four hours to nightfall; we cannot spare the time but we must drink something hot, even if it is only hot water."

"Two o'clock," said Forester bitterly. "I feel as though I've been wandering round this mountain for a hundred years, and made personal acquaintance with every goddam snow-flake."

They pushed on into the tangled ice maze of the glacier and Forester was deathly afraid of hidden crevasses. Twice he plunged to his armpits in deep snow and was hauled out with difficulty by Rohde. At last they found what they were looking for—a small cranny in the ice sheltered from the wind—and they sank into the snow with relief, glad to be out of the cutting blast.

Rohde assembled the Primus and lit it and then melted some snow. As before, they found the rich meaty taste of the bouillon nauseating and had to content themselves with hot water. Forester felt the heat radiating from his belly and was curiously content. He said, "How far to the top from here?"

"Seven hundred feet, maybe," said Rohde.

"Yes, we slipped about two hundred feet by coming back." Forester yawned. "Christ, it's good to be out of the wind; I feel a good hundred per cent warmer—which brings me up to freezing-point." He pulled the jacket closer about him and regarded Rohde through half-closed eyes. Rohde was looking vacantly at the flaring Primus, his eyes glazed with fatigue.

Thus they lay in their ice shelter while the wind howled about them and flurries of driven snow eddied in small whirlpools in that haven of quiet.

I V

Rohde dreamed.

He dreamed, curiously enough, that he was asleep—asleep in a vast feather bed into which he sank with voluptuous enjoyment. The bed enfolded him in soft comfort, seeming to support his tired body and to let him sink at the same time. Both he and the bed were falling slowly into a great chasm, drifting down and down and down, and suddenly he knew to his horror that this was the comfort of death and that when he reached the bottom of the pit he would die.

Frantically he struggled to get up, but the bed would not let him go and held him back in cloying folds and he heard a quiet maniacal tittering of high-pitched voices laughing at him. He discovered that his hand held a long, sharp knife and he stabbed at the bed with repeated plunges of his arm, ripping the fabric and releasing a fountain of feathers which whirled in the air before his eyes.

He started and screamed and opened his eyes. The scream came out as a dismal croak and he saw that the feathers were snowflakes dancing in the wind and beyond was the wilderness of the glacier. He was benumbed with the cold and he knew that if he slept he would not wake again.

There was something strange about the scene that he could not place and he forced himself to analyse what it was, and suddenly he knew—the wind had dropped. He got up stiffly and with difficulty and looked at the sky; the mist was clearing rapidly and through the dissipating wreaths he saw a faint patch of blue sky.

He turned to Forester who was lying prostrate, his head on one side and his cheek touching the ice, and wondered if he was dead. He leaned over him and shook him and Forester's head flopped down on to his chest. " Wake up," said Rohde, the words coming rustily to his throat. " Wake up—come on, wake up."

He took Forester by the shoulder and shook him and Forester's head lolled about, almost as though his neck was broken. Rohde seized his wrist and felt for the pulse; there was a faint fluttering beneath the cold skin and he knew that Forester was still alive—but only just.

The Primus stove was empty—he had fallen asleep with it still burning—but there was a drain of kerosene left in the bottle. He poured it into the Primus and heated some water with which he bathed Forester's head, hoping that the warmth would penetrate somehow and unfreeze his brain. After a while Forester stirred weakly and mumbled something incoherently.

Rohde slapped his face. " Wake up; you cannot give in now." He dragged Forester to his feet and he promptly collapsed. Again Rohde hauled him up and supported him. " You must walk," he said. " You must not sleep." He felt in his pocket and found one last coca quid which he forced into Forester's mouth. " Chew," he shouted. " Chew and walk."

Gradually Forester came round—never fully conscious but able to use his legs in an automatic manner, and Rohde walked him to-and-fro in an effort to get the blood circulating again. He talked all the time, not because he thought Forester could understand him, but to break the deathly silence that held the mountain now that the wind had gone. "Two hours to nightfall," he said. "It will be dark in two hours. We must get to the top before then—long before then. Here, stand still while I fasten the rope."

Forester obediently stood still, swaying slightly on his feet, and Rohde fastened the rope around his waist. "Can you follow me? Can you?"

Forester nodded slowly, his eyes half open.

"Good," said Rohde. "Then come on."

He led the way out of the glacier and on to the mountain slopes. The mist had now gone and he could see right to the top of the pass, and it seemed but a step away—a long step. Below, there was an unbroken sea of white cloud, illumined by the late afternoon sun into a blinding glare. It seemed solid and firm enough to walk on.

He looked at the snow slopes ahead and immediately saw what they had missed in the darkness of the blizzard—a definite ridge running right to the top of the pass. The snow cover would be thin there and would make for easy travel. He twitched on the rope and plunged forward, then glanced back at Forester to see how he was doing.

Forester was in the middle of a cold nightmare. He had been so warm, so cosily and beautiful warm, until Rohde had so rudely brought him back to the mountains. What the devil was the matter with the guy? Why couldn't he let a man sleep when he wanted to instead of pulling him up a mountain? But Rohde was a good joe, so he'd do what he said—but why was he doing it? Why was he on this mountain?

He tried to think but the reason eluded him. He dimly remembered a fall over a cliff and that this guy Rohde had saved his life. Hell, that was enough, wasn't it? If a guy saves your life he was entitled to push you around a little afterwards. He didn't know what he wanted, but he was with him all the way.

And so Forester shambled on, not knowing where or why, but content to follow where Rohde led. He kept falling because his legs were rubbery and he could not make them do precisely what he wanted, and every time he fell Rohde would return the length of the rope and help him to his feet. Once he started to slide and Rohde almost lost his balance and they both nearly tumbled down the slope, but Rohde managed to dig his heels into the snow and so stopped them.

Although Rohde's stiff leg impeded him, Forester impeded him more. But even so they made good time and the top of

181

the pass came nearer and nearer. There was only two hundred feet of altitude to make when Forester collapsed for the last time. Rohde went back along the rope but Forester could not stand. Cold and exhaustion had done their work in sapping the life energy from a strong man, and he lay in the snow unable to move.

A glimmer of intelligence returned to him and he peered at Rohde through red-rimmed eyes. He swallowed painfully and whispered, " Leave me, Miguel; I can't make it. You've *got* to get over the pass."

Rohde stared down at him in silence.

Forester croaked, " Goddam it—get the hell out of here." Although his voice was almost inaudible it was as loud as he could shout and the violence of the effort was too much for him and he relapsed into unconsciousness.

Still in silence Rohde bent down and gathered Forester into his arms. It was very difficult to lift him on to his shoulder in a fireman's lift—there was the steepness of the slope, his stiff leg and his general weakness—but he managed it and, staggering a little under the weight, he put one foot in front of the other.

And then the other.

And so on up the mountain. The thin air wheezed in his throat and the muscles of his thighs cracked under the strain. His stiff leg did not hurt but it was a hindrance because he had to swing it awkwardly sideways in an arc in order to take a step. But it was beautifully firm when he took the weight on it. Forrester's arms swung limply, tapping against the backs of his legs with every movement and this irritated him for a while until he no longer felt the tapping. Until he no longer felt anything at all.

His body was dead and it was only a bright hot spark of will burning in his mind that kept him going. He looked dispassionately at this flame of will, urging it to burn brighter when it flickered and screening out all else that would quench it. He did not see the snow or the sky or the crags and peaks which flanked him. He saw nothing at all, just a haze of darkness-shot with tiny sparks of light flaring inside his eyeballs.

One foot forward easily—that was his good foot. The next foot brought round in a stiff semi-circle to grope for a footing. This was harder because the foot was dead and he could not feel the ground. Slowly, very slowly, take the weight. Right—that was good. Now the other foot—easy again.

He began to count, got up to eleven and lost count. He started again and this time got up to eight. After that he did not bother to count but just went forward, content to know that one foot was moving in front of the other.

Pace . . . halt . . . swing . . . grope . . . halt . . . pace . . . halt . . . swing . . . grope . . . halt . . . pace . . . halt . . . swing . . . grope . . . halt . . . swing . . . something glared against his closed eyes and he opened them to stare full into the sun.

He stopped and then closed his eyes painfully, but not before he had seen the silver streak on the horizon and knew it was the sea. He opened his eyes again and looked down on the green valley and the white scattering of houses that was Altemiros lying snugly between the mountain and the lesser foothills beyond.

His tongue came out to lick ice-cracked lips stiffly. "Forester," he whispered. "Forester, we are on top."

But Forester was past caring, hanging limply unconscious across Rohde's broad shoulder.

Chapter VIII

Aguillar looked dispassionately at a small cut on his hand—one of many—from which the blood was oozing. I will never be a mechanic, he thought; I can guide people, but not machines. He laid down the broken piece of hacksaw-blade and wiped away the blood, then sucked the wound. When the blood ceased to flow he picked up the blade and got to work on the slot he was cutting in the length of steel reinforcing rod.

He had made ten bolts for the crossbows, or at least he had slotted them and put in the metal flights. To sharpen them was beyond his powers; he could not turn the old grindstone and sharpen a bolt at the same time, but he was confident that, given another pair of hands, the ten bolts would be usable within the hour.

He had also made an inventory of the contents of the camp, checked the food supplies and the water, and in general had behaved like any army quartermaster. He had a bitter-sweet feeling about being sent to the camp. He recognised that he was no use in a fight; he was old and weak and had heart trouble

183

—but there was more to it than that. He knew that he was a man of ideas and not a man of action, and the fact irked him, making him feel inadequate.

His sphere of action lay in the making of decisions and in administration; in order to get into a position to make valid decisions and to have something to administer he had schemed and plotted and manipulated the minds of men, but he had never fought physically. He did not believe in fighting, but hitherto he had thought about it in the abstract and in terms of large-scale conflicts. This sudden plunge into the realities of death by battle had led him out of his depth.

So here he was, the eternal politician, with others, as always, doing the fighting and dying and suffering—even his own niece. As he thought of Benedetta the blade slipped and he cut his hand again. He muttered a brief imprecation and sucked the blood, then looked at the slot he had cut and decided it was deep enough. There would be no more bolts; the teeth of the hacksaw-blade were worn smooth and would hardly cut cheese, let alone steel.

He fitted the flight into the slot, wedging it as Willis had shown him, and then put the unsharpened bolt with the others. It was strange, he thought, that night was falling so suddenly, and went out of the hut to be surprised by the deepening mist. He looked up towards the mountains, now hidden from sight, and felt deep sorrow as he thought of Rohde. And of Forester, yes—he must not forget Forester and the other *norteamericano*, Peabody.

Faintly from the river he heard the sound of small-arms fire and his ears pricked. Was that a machine-gun? He had heard that sound when Lopez and the army had ruthlessly tightened their grip on Cordillera five years earlier, and he did not think he was mistaken. He listened again but it was only some freak of the mountain winds that had brought the sound to his ears and he heard nothing more. He hoped that it was not a machine-gun—the dice were already loaded enough.

He sighed and went back into the hut and selected a can of soup from the shelf for his belated midday meal. He had just finished eating the hot soup half an hour later when he heard his niece calling him. He went out of the hut, tightening his coat against the cold air, and found that the mist was very much thicker. He shouted to Benedetta to let her know where he was and soon a dim figure loomed through the fog, a strange figure, misshapen and humped, and for a moment he felt fear.

Then he saw that it was Benedetta supporting someone and he ran forward to help her. She was breathing painfully and gasped, " It's Jenny, she's hurt."

" Hurt? How?"

" She was shot," said Benedetta briefly.

He was outraged. " This American lady—shot! This is criminal."

" Help me take her inside," said Benedetta. They got Miss Ponsky into the hut and laid her in a bunk. She was conscious and smiled weakly as Benedetta tucked in a blanket, then closed her eyes in relief. Benedetta looked at her uncle. " She killed a man and helped to kill others—why shouldn't she be shot at? I wish I were like her."

Aguillar looked at her with pain in his eyes. He said slowly, " I find all this difficult to believe. I feel as though I am in a dream. Why should these people shoot a woman?"

" They didn't know she was a woman," said Benedetta impatiently. " And I don't suppose they cared. She was shooting at them when it happened, anyway. I wish I could kill some of them." She looked up at Aguillar. " Oh, I know you always preach the peaceful way, but how can you be peaceful when someone is coming at you with a gun? Do you bare your breast and say, ' Kill me and take all I have '?"

Aguillar did not answer. He looked down at Miss Ponsky and said, " Is she badly hurt?"

" Not dangerously," said Benedetta. " But she has lost a lot of blood." She paused. " As we were coming up the road I heard a machine-gun."

He nodded. " I thought I heard it—but I was not sure." He held her eyes. " Do you think they are across the bridge?"

" They might be," said Benedetta steadily. " We must prepare. Have you made bolts? Tim has the crossbow and he will need them."

" Tim? Ah—O'Hara." He raised his eyebrows slightly, then said, " The bolts need sharpening."

" I will help you."

She turned the crank on the grindstone while Aguillar sharpened the steel rods to a point. As he worked he said, " O'Hara is a strange man—a complicated man. I do not think I fully understand him." He smiled slightly. " That is an admission from me."

" I understand him—now," she said. Despite the cold, a film of sweat formed on her forehead as she turned the heavy crank.

"So? You have talked with him?"

While the showers of sparks flew and the acrid stink of burning metal filled the air she told Aguillar about O'Hara and his face grew pinched as he heard the story. "That is the enemy," she said at length. "The same who are on the other side of the river."

Aguilar said in a low voice, "There is so much evil in the world—so much evil in the hearts of men."

They said nothing more until all the bolts were sharpened and then Benedetta said, "I am going out on the road. Will you watch Jenny?"

He nodded silently and she walked along the street between the two rows of huts. The mist was getting even thicker so that she could not see very far ahead, and tiny droplets of moisture condensed on the fabric of her coat. If it gets colder it will snow, she thought.

It was very quiet on the road, and very lonely. She did not hear a sound except for the occasional splash of a drop of water falling from a rock. It was as though being in the middle of a cloud was like being wrapped in cotton-wool; this was very dirty cotton-wool, but she had done enough flying to know that from above the cloud bank would be clean and shining.

After some time she walked off the road and crossed the rocky hillside until the gigantic cable drum loomed through the mist. She paused by the enormous reel, then went forward to the road cutting and looked down. The road surface was barely visible in the pervading greyness and she stood there uncertainly, wondering what to do. Surely there was something she could be doing.

Fire, she thought suddenly, we can fight them with fire. The drum was already poised to crash into a vehicle coming up the road, and fire would add to the confusion. She hurried back to the camp and collected the bottles of paraffin she had brought back from the bridge, stopping briefly to see how Miss Ponsky was.

Aguillar looked up as she came in. "There is soup," he said. "It will be good in this cold, my dear."

Benedetta spread her hands gratefully to the warmth of the paraffin heater and was aware that she was colder than she had thought. "I would like some soup," she said. She looked over to Miss Ponsky. "How are you, Jenny?"

Miss Ponsky, now sitting up, said briskly, "Much better,

thank you. Wasn't it silly of me to get shot? I shouldn't have leaned out so far—and then I missed. And I lost the bow."

" I would not worry," said Benedetta with a quick smile. "Does your shoulder hurt?"

"Not much," said Miss Ponsky. "It will be all right if I keep my arm in a sling. Señor Aguillar helped me to make one."

Benedetta finished her soup quickly and mentioned the bottles, which she had left outside. "I must take them up to the road," she said.

"Let me help you," said Aguillar.

"It is too cold out there, tío," she said. "Stay with Jenny."

She took the bottles down to the cable drum and then sat on the edge of the cutting, listening. A wind was rising and the mist swirled in wreaths and coils, thinning and thickening in the vagaries of the breeze. Sometimes she could see as far as the bend in the road, and at other times she could not see the road at all although it was only a few feet below her. And everything was quiet.

She was about to leave, sure that nothing was going to happen, when she heard the faint clatter of a rock from far down the mountain. She felt a moment of apprehension and scrambled to her feet. The others would not be coming unless they were in retreat, and in that case it could just as well be an enemy as a friend. She turned and picked up one of the bottles and felt for matches in her pocket.

It was a long time before she heard anything else and then it was the thud of running feet on the road. The mist had thinned momentarily and she saw a dim figure come round the bend and up the road at a stumbling run. As the figure came closer she saw that it was Willis.

"What is happening?" she called.

He looked up, startled to hear a voice from above his head and in a slight panic until he recognised it. He stopped, his chest heaving, and went into a fit of coughing. "They've come across," he gasped. "They broke across." He coughed again, rackingly. "The others are just behind me," he said. "I heard them running—unless . . ."

"You'd better come up here," she said.

He looked up at Benedetta, vaguely outlined at the top of the fifteen-foot cutting. "I'll come round by the road," he said, and began to move away at a fast walk.

By the time he joined her she had already heard someone else coming up the road, and, remembering Willis's *unless,* she lay down by the edge and grasped the bottle. It was Armstrong, coming up at a fast clip. "Up here," she called. "To the drum."

He cast a brief glance upwards but wasted no time in greeting, nor did he slacken his pace. She watched him go until he was lost in the mist and waited for him to join them.

They were both exhausted, having made the five-mile journey uphill in a little over an hour and a half. She let them rest a while and get their breath before she asked them, "What happened?"

"I don't know," said Willis. "We were on the trebuchet; we'd let fly when O'Hara told us to—it was ready loaded—and then he yelled for us to clear out, so we took it on the run. There was a devil of a lot of noise going on—a lot of shooting, I mean."

She looked at Armstrong. He said, "That's about it. I think O'Hara got one of them—I heard a man scream in a choked sort of way. But they came across the bridge; I saw them as I looked back—and I saw O'Hara run into the rocks. He should be along any minute now."

She sighed with relief.

Willis said, "And he'll have the whole pack of them on his heels. What the hell are we going to do?" There was a hysterical note in his voice.

Armstrong was calmer. "I don't think so. O'Hara and I talked about this and we came to the conclusion that they'll play it safe and repair the bridge while they can, and then run jeeps up to the mine before we can get there." He looked up at the cable drum. "This is all we've got to stop them."

Benedetta held up the bottle. "And some of these."

"Oh, good," said Armstrong approvingly. "Those should help." He thought a little. "There's not much your uncle can do—or Miss Ponsky. I suggest that they get started for the mine right now—and if they hear anyone or anything coming up the road behind them to duck into the rocks until they're sure it's safe. Thank God for this mist."

Benedetta did not stir and he said, "Will you go and tell them?"

She said, "I'm staying here. I want to fight."

"I'll go," said Willis. He got up and faded into the mist.

Armstrong caught the desperate edge in Benedetta's voice and patted her hand in a kindly, fatherly manner. "We all have to do the best we can," he said. "Willis is frightened, just as I am, and you are, I'm sure." His voice was grimly humorous. "O'Hara was talking to me about the situation back at the bridge and I gathered he didn't think much of Willis. He said he wasn't a leader—in fact, his exact words were, 'He couldn't lead a troop of boy scouts across a street.' I think he was being a bit hard on poor Willis—but, come to that, I gathered that he didn't think much of me either, from the tone of his voice." He laughed.

"I'm sure he didn't mean it," said Benedetta. "He has been under a strain."

"Oh, he was right," said Armstrong. "I'm no man of action. I'm a man of ideas, just like Willis."

"And my uncle," said Benedetta. She sat up suddenly. "Where *is* Tim? He should have been here by now." She clutched Armstrong's arm. "*Where is he?*"

II

O'Hara was lying in a crack in the rocks watching a pair of stout boots that stamped not more than two feet from his head, and trying not to cough. Events had been confused just after the rush across the bridge, he had not been able to get to the road—he would have been cut down before going ten yards in the open—so he had taken to the rocks, scuttling like a rabbit for cover.

It was then that he had slipped on a mist-wetted stone and turned his ankle, to come crashing to the ground. He had lain there with all the wind knocked out of him, expecting to feel the thud of bullets that would mean his death, but nothing like that happened. He heard a lot of shouting and knew his analysis of the enemy intentions had proved correct; they were spreading out along the edge of the gorge and covering the approaches to the bridge.

The mist helped, of course. He still had the crossbow and was within hearing distance of the noisy crowd which surrounded the man he had shot through the chest. He judged that they did not relish the task of winkling out a man with a silent killing weapon from the hillside, especially when death could come from the mist. There was a nervous snapping edge to the voices out there and he smiled grimly; knives they knew and guns they understood, but this was something different, something they regarded with awe.

He felt his ankle. It was swollen and painful and he wondered if it would bear his weight, but this was neither the time nor the place to stand. He took his small pocket-knife and slit his trousers, cutting a long strip. He did not take off his shoe because he knew he would not be able to get it on again, so he tied the strip of cloth tightly around the swelling and under the instep of his shoe, supporting his ankle.

He was so intent on this that he did not see the man approach. The first indication was the slither of a kicked pebble and he froze rigid. From the corner of his eye he saw the man standing sideways to him, looking back towards the bridge. O'Hara kept very still, except for his arm which groped for a handy-sized rock. The man scratched his ribs in a reflective sort of way, moved on and was lost in the mist.

O'Hara let loose his pent-up breath in a silent sigh and prepared to move. He had the crossbow and three bolts which had a confounded tendency to clink together unless he was careful. He slid forward on his belly, worming his way among the rocks, trying to go upwards, away from the bridge. Again he was warned of imminent peril by the rattle of a rock and he rolled into a crack between two boulders and then he saw the boots appear before his face and struggled with a tickle in his throat, fighting to suppress the cough.

The man stamped his feet noisily and beat his hands together, breathing heavily. Suddenly he turned with a clatter of boots and O'Hara heard the metallic snap as a safety-catch went off. " *Quien?* "

" Santos."

O'Hara recognised the voice of the Cuban. So his name was Santos—he'd remember that and look him up if he ever got out of this mess.

The man put the rifle back on safety and Santos said in Spanish, " See anything?"

" Nothing."

Santos grunted in his throat. " Keep moving; go up the hill—they won't hang about here."

The other man said, " The Russian ˋsaid we must stay down here."

" To hell with him," growled Santos. " If he had not interfered we would have old Aguillar in our hands right now. Move up the hill—and get the others going too."

The other did not reply but obediently moved off, and O'Hara heard him climbing higher. Santos stayed only a moment and then clattered away noisily in his steel-shod boots, and again O'Hara let out his breath softly.

He waited a while and thought of what to do next. If Santos was moving the men away up the hill, then his obvious course was to go down. But the enemy seemed to be divided into two factions and the Russian might still have kept some men below. Still, he would have to take that chance.

He slid out of the crack and began to crawl back the way he had come, inching his way along on his belly and being careful of his injured ankle. He was pleased to see that the mist was thickening and through it he heard shouts from the bridge and the knocking of steel on wood. They were getting on with their repairs and traffic in the vicinity of the bridge would be heavy, so it was a good place to stay away from. He wanted to find a lone man far away from his fellows and preferably armed to the teeth. A crossbow was all very well, but he could do with something that had a faster rate of fire.

He altered course and headed for the trebuchet, stopping every few yards to listen and to peer through the mist. As he approached he heard laughter and a few derogatory comments shouted in Spanish. There was a crowd round the trebuchet and apparently they found it a humorous piece of machinery. He stopped and cocked the crossbow awkwardly, using the noise of the crowd as cover for any clinkings he might make. Then he crawled closer and took cover behind a boulder.

Presently he heard the bull-roar of Santos. "Up the hill, you lot. In the name of Jesus, what are you doing wasting time here? Juan, you stay here; the rest of you get moving."

O'Hara flattened behind the boulder as the men moved off to the accompaniment of many grumbles. None of them came close to him, but he waited a few minutes before he began to crawl in a wide circle round the trebuchet, looking for the man left on guard. The bridge was illuminated by headlights and their glow lit the mist with a ghostly radiance, and at last he crept up on the guard who was just in the right position—silhouetted against the light.

Juan, the guard, was very young—not more than twenty—and O'Hara hesitated. Then he steeled himself because there was more at stake here than the life of a misguided youth. He lifted the crossbow and aimed carefully, then hesitated again, his finger on the trigger. His hesitation this time was for a different reason; Juan was playing soldiers, strutting about with his sub-machine-gun at the ready, and, O'Hara suspected, with the safety-catch off. He remembered the man he had shot by the bridge and how a full magazine had emptied in a dead hand, so he waited, not wanting any noise when he pulled the trigger.

At last Juan got tired of standing sentry and became more interested in the trebuchet. He leaned over to look at the mechanism which held down the long arm, found his gun in his way and let it fall to be held by the shoulder-sling. He never knew what hit him as the heavy bolt struck him between the shoulders at a range of ten yards. It knocked him forward against the long arm, the bolt protruding through his chest and skewering him to the baulk of timber. He was quite dead when O'Hara reached him.

Ten minutes later O'Hara was again ensconced among the rocks, examining his booty. He had the sub-machine-gun, three full magazines of ammunition, a loaded pistol and a heavy broad-bladed knife. He grinned in satisfaction—now he was becoming dangerous, he had got himself some sharp teeth.

III

Benedetta, Armstrong and Willis waited in the cold mist by the cable drum. Willis fidgeted, examining the wedge-shaped chock that prevented the drum from rolling on to the road and estimated the amount of force needed to free it when the time came. But Benedetta and Armstrong were quite still, listening intently for any sound that might come up the hill.

Armstrong was thinking that they would have to be careful; any person coming up might be O'Hara and they would have to make absolutely sure before jumping him, something that would be difficult in this mist. Benedetta's mind was emptied of everything except a deep sorrow. Why else was O'Hara not at the camp unless he were dead, or worse, captured? She knew his feelings about being captured again and she knew he would resist that, come what may. That made the likelihood of his being dead even more certain, and something within her died at the thought.

Aguillar had been difficult about retreating to the mine. He had wanted to stay and fight, old and unfit as he was, but

Benedetta had overruled him. His eyes had widened in surprise as he heard the incisive tone of command in her voice. "There are only three of us fit to fight," she said. "We can't spare one to help Jenny up to the mine. Someone must help her and you are the one. Besides, it is even higher up there than here, remember—you will have to go slowly so you must get away right now."

Aguillar glanced at the other two men. Willis was morosely kicking at the ground and Armstrong smiled slightly, and Aguillar saw that they were content to let Benedetta take the lead and give the orders in the absence of O'Hara. She has turned into a young Amazon, he thought; a raging young lioness. He went up to the mine road with Miss Ponsky without further argument.

Willis stopped fiddling with the chock. "Where are they?" he demanded in a high voice. "Why don't they come and get it over with?"

Benedetta glanced at Armstrong who said, "Quiet! Not so loud."

"All right," said Willis, whispering. "But what's keeping them from attacking us?"

"We have already discussed that," said Benedetta. She turned to Armstrong. "Do you think we can defend the camp?"

He shook his head. "It's indefensible. We haven't a hope. If we can block the road, our next step is to retreat to the mine."

"Then the camp must be burned," said Benedetta decisively. "We must not leave it to give comfort and shelter to them." She looked at Willis. "Go back and splash kerosene in the huts—all of them. And when you hear noise and shooting from here, set everything on fire."

"And then what?" he asked.

"Then you make your way up to the mine as best you can." She smiled slightly. "I would not come up this way again—go straight up and find the road at a higher level. We will be coming up too—as fast as we can."

Willis withdrew and she said to Armstrong, "That one is frightened. He tries to hide it, but it shows. I cannot trust him here."

"I'm frightened too. Aren't you?" asked Armstrong curiously.

"I was," she said. "I was afraid when the airplane crashed and for a long time afterwards. My bones were jelly—

193

my legs were weak at the thought of fighting and dying. Then I had a talk with Tim and he taught me not to be that way." She paused. "That was when he told me how frightened he was."

"What a damned silly situation this is," said Armstrong in wonder. "Here we are waiting to kill men whom we don't know and who don't know us. But that's always the way in a war, of course." He grinned. "But it is damned silly all the same; a middle-aged professor and a young woman lurking on a mountain with murderous intent. I think——"

She put her hand on his arm. "Hush!"

He listened. "What is it?"

"I thought I heard something."

They lay quietly, their ears straining and hearing nothing but the sough of the wind on the mist-shrouded mountain. Then Benedetta's hand tightened on his arm as she heard, far away, the characteristic sound of a gear change. "Tim was right," she whispered. "They're coming up in a truck or a jeep. We must get ready."

"I'll release the drum," Armstrong said. "You stay on the edge here, and give a shout when you want it to go." He scrambled to his feet and ran back to the drum.

Benedetta ran along the edge of the cutting where she had placed the Molotov cocktails. She lit the wicks of three of them and each flamed with a halo in the mist. The rags, slightly damp with exposure, took a long time to catch alight well. She did not think their light could be seen from the road below; nevertheless, she put them well back from the edge.

The vehicle was labouring heavily, the engine coughing in the thin air. Twice it stopped and she heard the revving of the self-starter. This was no supercharged engine designed for high-altitude operation and the vehicle could not be making more than six or seven miles an hour up the steep slopes of the road. But it was moving much faster than a man could climb under the same conditions.

Benedetta lay on the edge of the cutting and looked down the road towards the bend. The mist was too thick to see that far and she hoped the vehicle had lights strong enough to give her an indication of its position. The growling of the engine increased and then faded as the vehicle twisted and turned round the hairpin bends, and she thought she heard a double note as of two engines. One or two, she thought; it does not matter.

Armstrong crouched by the cable drum, grasping the short

194

length of electric wire which was fastened to the chock. He peered towards the cutting but saw nothing but a blank wall of grey mist. His face was strained as he waited.

Down the road Benedetta saw a faint glow at the corner of the road and knew that the first vehicle was coming up on the other side of the bend. She glanced back to see if the paraffin wicks were still burning, then turned back and saw two misty eyes of headlamps as the first vehicle made the turn. She had already decided when to shout to Armstrong —a rock was her mark and when the headlights drew level with it, that was the time.

She drew her breath as the engine coughed and died away and the jeep—for through the mist she could now see what it was—drew to a halt. There was a whine from the starter and the jeep began to move again. Behind it two more headlights came into view as a second vehicle pulled round the bend.

Then the headlights of the jeep were level with the rock, and she jumped up, shouting, "Now! Now! Now!"

There was a startled shout from below as she turned and grabbed the paraffin bottles, easy to see as they flamed close at hand. There was a rumble as the drum plunged forward and she looked up to see it charging down the slope like a juggernaut to crash over the side of the cutting.

She heard the smash and rending of metal and a man screamed. Then she ran back to the edge and hurled a bottle into the confusion below.

The heavy drum had dropped fifteen feet on to the front of the jeep, crushing the forepart entirely and killing the driver. The bottle broke beside the dazed passenger in the wrecked front seat and the paraffin ignited in a great flare and he screamed again, beating at the flames that enveloped him and trying to release his trapped legs. The two men in the back tumbled out and ran off down the road towards the truck coming up behind.

Armstrong ran up to Benedetta just as she threw the second bottle. He had two more in his hand which he lit from the flaming wick of the remaining one and ran along the edge of the cutting towards the truck, which had drawn to a halt. There was a babble of shouts from below and a couple of wild shots which came nowhere near him as he stood on the rim and looked into the truck full of men.

Deliberately he threw one bottle hard at the top of the cab. It smashed and flaming paraffin spread and dripped down past the open window and there came an alarmed cry from the driver. The other bottle he tossed into the body of the truck and in the flickering light he saw the mad scramble to get clear. No one had the time or inclination to shoot at him.

He ran back to Benedetta who was attempting to light another bottle, her hand shaking and her breath coming in harsh gasps. Exertion and the reaction of shock were taking equal toll of her fortitude. "Enough," he panted. "Let's get out of here." As he spoke, there was an explosion and a great flaring light from the jeep and he grinned tightly. "That wasn't paraffin—that was petrol. Come on."

As they ran they saw a glow from the direction of the camp—and then another and another. Willis was doing his job of arson.

IV

O'Hara's ankle was very painful. Before making his move up the hill he had rebound it, trying to give it some support, but it still could not bear his full weight. It made clambering among the rocks difficult and he made more noise than he liked.

He was following in the line of beaters that Santos had organised and luckily they were making more noise than he as they stumbled and fell about in the mist, and he thought they weren't making too good a job of it. He had his own troubles; the crossbow and the sub-machine-gun together were hard to handle and he thought of discarding the bow, but then thought better of it. It was a good, silent weapon and he still had two bolts.

He had a shock when he heard the roar of Santos ordering his men to return to the road and he shrank behind a boulder in case any of the men came his way. None did, and he smiled as he thought of the note of exasperation in Santos's voice. Apparently the Russian was getting his own way after all, and he was certain of it when he heard the engines start up from the direction of the bridge.

That was what they should have done in the first place—this searching of the mountain in the mist was futile. The Russian was definitely a better tactician than Santos; he had not fallen for their trick of promising to give up Aguillar, and now he was preparing to ram his force home to the mine.

O'Hara grimaced as he wondered what would happen at the camp.

Now that the mountainside ahead of him was clear of the enemy he made better time, and deliberately stayed as close as he could to the road. Soon he heard the groan of engines again and knew that the communist mechanised division was on its way. He saw the headlights as a jeep and a truck went past and he paused, listening for what was coming next. Apparently that was all, so he boldly stepped out on to the road and started to hobble along on the smooth surface.

He thought it was safe enough; he could hear if another truck came up behind and there was plenty of time to take cover. Still, as he walked he kept close to the edge of the road, the sub-machine-gun at the ready and his eyes carefully scanning the greyness ahead.

It took him a very long time to get anywhere near the camp and long before that he heard a few scattered shots and what sounded like an explosion, and he thought he could detect a glow up the mountain but was not sure whether his eyes were playing tricks. He redoubled his caution, which was fortunate, because presently he heard the thud of boots ahead of him and he slipped in among the rocks on the roadside, sweating with exertion.

A man clattered past at a dead run, and O'Hara heard the wheezing of his breath. He stayed hidden until there was nothing more to be heard, then came on to the road again and resumed his hobbling climb. Half an hour later he heard the sound of an engine from behind him and took cover again and watched a jeep go by at a crawl. He thought he could see the Russian but was not sure, and the jeep had gone by before he thought to raise the gun.

He cursed himself at the missed opportunity. He knew there was no point in killing the rank-and-file indiscriminately —there were too many of them—but if he could knock out the king-pins, then the whole enemy attack would collapse. The Russian and the Cuban would be his targets in future, and all else would be subordinated to the task of getting them in his sights.

He knew that something must have happened up ahead and tried to quicken his pace. The Russian had been sent for and that meant the enemy had run into trouble. He wondered if Benedetta was safe and felt a quick anger at these ruthless men who were harrying them like animals.

As he climbed higher he found that his eyes had not

197

deceived him—there was a definite glow of fire from up ahead, reflected and subdued by the surrounding mist. He stopped and considered. The fire seemed to be localised in two patches; one small patch which seemed to be on the road and another, which was so large that he could not believe it. Then he smiled—of course, that was the camp; the whole bloody place was going up in flames.

He had better give both localities a wide berth, he thought; so he left the road again, intending to cast a wide circle and come upon the road again above the camp. But curiosity drew him back to where the smaller fire was and where he suspected the Russian had gone.

The mist was too thick to see exactly what had happened but from the shouts he gathered that the road was blocked. Hell, he thought; that's the cutting where Willis was going to dump the cable drum. It looks as though it's worked. But he could not explain the fire which was now guttering out, so he tried to get closer.

His ankle gave way suddenly and he fell heavily, the crossbow falling from his grasp with a terrifying loud noise as it hit a rock, and he came down hard on his elbow and gasped with pain. He lay there, just by the side of the road and close by the Russian's jeep, his lips drawn back from his teeth in agony as he tried to suppress the groan which he felt was coming, and waited for the surprised shout of discovery.

But the enemy were making too much noise themselves as they tried to clear the road and O'Hara heard the jeep start up and drive a little way forward. Slowly the pain ebbed away and cautiously he tried to get up, but to his horror he found that his arm seemed to be trapped in a crevice between the rocks. Carefully he pulled and heard the clink as the sub-machine-gun he was holding came up against stone, and he stopped. Then he pushed his arm down and felt nothing.

At any other time he would have found it funny. He was like a monkey that had put its hand in the narrow neck of a bottle to grasp an apple and could not withdraw it without releasing the apple. He could not withdraw his arm without letting go of the gun, and he dared not let it go in case it made a noise. He wriggled cautiously, then stopped as he heard voices from close by.

" I say my way was best." It was the Cuban.

The other voice was flat and hard, speaking in badly-accented Spanish. " What did it get you? Two sprained ankles and a broken leg. You were losing men faster than

198

Aguillar could possibly kill them for you. It was futile to think of searching the mountain in this weather. You've bungled this right from the start."

"Was your way any better?" demanded Santos in an aggrieved voice. "Look at what has happened here—a jeep and a truck destroyed, two men killed and the road blocked. I still say that men on foot are better."

The other man—the Russian—said coldly, "It happened because you are stupid—you came up here as though you were driving through Havana. Aguillar is making you look like a fool, and I think he is right. Look, Santos, here is a pack of defenceless airline passengers and they have held you up four days; they have killed six of your men and you have a lot more wounded and out of action because of your own stupidity. Right from the start you should have made certain of the bridge—you should have been at the mine when Grivas landed the plane—but you bungled even there. Well, I am taking over from now, and when I come to write my report you are not going to look very good in Havana—not to mention Moscow."

O'Hara heard him walk away and sweated as he tried to free his arm. Here he had the two of them together and he could not do a damn' thing about it. With one burst he could have killed them both and chanced getting away afterwards, but he was trapped. He heard Santos shuffle his feet indecisively and then walk quickly after the Russian, mumbling as he went.

O'Hara lay there while they hooked up the Russian's jeep to the burned-out truck and withdrew it, to push it off the road and send it plunging down the mountain. Then they dragged out the jeep and did the same with it, and finally got to work on the cable drum. It took them two hours and, to O'Hara, sweating it out not more than six yards from where they were working, it seemed like two days.

v

Willis struggled to get back his breath as he looked down at the burning camp, thankful for the long hours he had put in at that high altitude previously. He had left Benedetta and Armstrong, glad to get away from the certainty of a hand-to-hand fight, defenceless against the ruthless armed men who were coming to butcher them. He could see no prospect

199

of any success; they had fought for days against tremendous odds and the outlook seemed blacker than ever. He did not relish the fact of his imminent death.

With difficulty he had rolled out the drum of paraffin and went from hut to hut, soaking the interior woodwork as thoroughly as possible. While in the last hut he thought he heard an engine and stepped outside to listen, catching the sound of the grinding of gears.

He struck a match, then paused. Benedetta had told him to wait for the shooting or noise and that had not come yet. But it might take some time for the huts to catch alight properly and, from the expression he had seen on Benedetta's face, the shooting was bound to come.

He tossed the match near a pool of paraffin and it caught fire in a flare of creeping flame which ran quickly up the woodwork. Hastily he lit the bundle of paraffin-soaked rags he held and ran along the line of huts, tossing them inside. As he reached the end of the first line he heard a distant crash from the road and a couple of shots. Better make this quick, he thought; now's the time to get out of here.

By the time he left the first line of huts was well aflame, great gouts of fire leaping from the windows. He scrambled up among the rocks above the camp and headed for the road, and when he reached it looked back to see the volcano of the burning camp erupting below. He felt satisfaction at that—he always liked to see a job well done. The mist was too thick to see more than the violent red and yellow glow, but he could make out enough to know that all the huts were well alight and there were no significant gaps. They won't sleep in there to-night, he thought, and turned to run up the road.

He went on for a long time, stopping occasionally to catch his labouring breath and to listen. He heard nothing once he was out of earshot of the camp. At first he had heard a faint shouting, but now everything was silent on the mountainside apart from the eerie keening of the wind. He did not know whether Armstrong and Benedetta were ahead of him or behind, but he listened carefully for any sound coming from the road below. Hearing nothing, he turned and pushed on again, feeling the first faint intimation of lack of oxygen as he went higher.

He was nearing the mine when he caught up with the others, Armstrong turning on his heels with alarm as he heard Willis's footsteps. Aguillar and Miss Ponsky were there also, having made very slow progress up the road. Armstrong said, falsely cheerful, "Bloody spectacular, wasn't it?"

Willis stopped, his chest heaving. "They'll be cold to-night —maybe they'll call off the final attack until to-morrow."

Armstrong shook his head in the gathering darkness. "I doubt it. Their blood is up—they're close to the kill." He looked at Willis, who was panting like a dog. "You'd better take it easy and help Jenny here—she's pretty bad. Benedetta and I can push up to the mine and see what we can do up there."

Willis stared back. "Do you think they're far behind?"

"Does it matter?" asked Benedetta. "We fight here or we fight at the mine." She absently kissed Aguillar and said something to him in Spanish, then gestured to Armstrong and they went off fairly quickly.

It did not take them long to get to the mine, and as Armstrong surveyed the three huts he said bleakly, "These are as indefensible as the camp. However, let's see what we can do."

He entered one of the huts and looked about in the gloom despairingly. He touched the wooden wall and thought, bullets will go through these like paper—we'd be better off scattered on the hillside facing death by exposure. He was roused by a cry from Benedetta, so he went outside.

She was holding a piece of paper in her hand and peering at it in the light of a burning wooden torch. She said excitedly, "From Forester—they prepared one of the mine tunnels for us."

Armstrong jerked up his head. "Where?" He took the piece of paper and examined the sketch on it, then looked about. "Over there," he said, pointing.

He found the tunnel and the low wall of rocks which Forester and Rohde had built. "Not much, but it's home," he said, looking into the blackness. "You'd better go back and bring the others, and I'll see what it's like inside."

By the time they all assembled in the tunnel mouth he had explored it pretty thoroughly with the aid of a smoky torch. "A dead end," he said. "This is where we make our last stand." He pulled a pistol from his belt. "I've still got Rohde's gun—with one bullet; can anyone shoot better than me?" He offered the gun to Willis. "What about you, General Custer?"

Willis looked at the pistol. "I've never fired a gun in my life."

Armstrong sighed. "Neither have I, but it looks as though this is my chance." He thrust the pistol back in his belt and said to Benedetta, "What's that you've got?"

"Miguel left us some food," she said. "Enough for a cold meal."

"Well, we won't die hungry," said Armstrong sardonically.

Willis made a sudden movement. "For God's sake, don't talk that way."

"I'm sorry," said Armstrong. "How are Miss Ponsky and Señor Aguillar?"

"As well as might be expected," said Benedetta bitterly. "For a man with a heart condition and an elderly lady with a hole in her shoulder, trying to breathe air that is not there." She looked up at Armstrong. "You think there is any chance for Tim?"

He averted his head. "No," he said shortly, and went to the mouth of the tunnel, where he lay down behind the low breastwork of rocks and put the gun beside him. If I wait I might kill someone, he thought; but I must wait until they're very close.

It was beginning to snow.

VI

It was very quiet by the cutting, although O'Hara could hear voices from farther up the road by the burning camp. There was not much of a glow through the mist now, and he judged that the huts must just about have burned down to their foundations. Slowly he relaxed his hand and let the sub-machine-gun fall. It clattered to the rocks and he pulled up his arm and massaged it.

He felt very damp and cold and wished he had been able to strip the llama-skin coat from the sentry by the trebuchet —young Juan would not have needed it. But it would have taken too long, apart from being a gruesome job, and he had not wanted to waste the time. Now he wished he had taken the chance.

He stayed there, sitting quietly for some time, wondering if anyone had noticed the noise of metal on stone. Then he set himself to retrieve the gun. It took him ten minutes to fish it from the crevice with the aid of the crossbow, and then he set off up the mountain again, steering clear of the road. At least the enforced halt had rested him.

Three more trucks had come up. They had not gone straight up to the mine—not yet; the enemy had indulged in a futile attempt to quench the fires of the flaming camp and that had taken some time. Knowing that the trucks were parked above the camp, he circled so as to come out upon them. His ankle was bad, the flesh soft and puffy, and he knew he could not walk very much farther—certainly not up to the mine. It was in his mind to get himself a truck the same way he got himself a gun—by killing for it.

A crowd of men were climbing into the trucks when he got back to the road and he felt depressed but brightened a little when he saw that only two trucks were being used. The jeep was drawn up alongside and O'Hara heard the Russian giving orders in his pedantic Spanish and fretted because he was not within range. Then the jeep set off up the road and the trucks rolled after it with a crashing of gears, leaving the third parked.

He could not see whether a guard had been left so he began to prowl forward very cautiously. He did not think that there was a guard—the enemy would not think of taking such a precaution, as everyone was supposed to have been driven up to the mine. So he was very shocked when he literally fell over a sentry, who had left his post by the truck and was relieving himself among the rocks by the roadside.

The man grunted in surprise as O'Hara cannoned into him. "*Cuidado!*" he said, and then looked up. O'Hara dropped both his weapons as the man opened his mouth and clamped the palm of his hand over the other's jaw before he could shout. They strained against each other silently, O'Hara forcing back the man's head, his fingers clawing for the vulnerable eyes. His other arm was wrapped around the man's chest, clutching him tight.

His opponent flailed frantically with both arms and O'Hara knew that he was in no condition for a real knock-down-drag-out fight with this man. He remembered the knife in his belt and decided to take a chance, depending on swiftness of action to kill the man before he made a noise. He released him suddenly, pushing him away, and his hand went swiftly to his waist. The man staggered and opened his mouth again and O'Hara stepped forward and drove the knife in a straight stab into his chest just below the breastbone, giving it an upward turn as it went in.

The man coughed in a surprised hiccuping fashion and leaned forward, toppling straight into O'Hara's arms. As

203

O'Hara lowered him to the ground he gave a deep sigh and died. Breathing heavily, O'Hara plucked out the knife and a gush of hot blood spurted over his hand. He stood for a moment, listening, and then picked up the sub-machine-gun from where he had dropped it. He felt a sudden shock as his finger brushed the safety-catch—it was in the off position; the sudden jar could well have fired a warning shot.

But that was past and he was beyond caring. He knew he was living from minute to minute and past possibilities and actions meant nothing to him. All that mattered was to get up to the mine as quickly as possible—to nail the Cuban and the Russian—and to find Benedetta.

He looked into the cab of the truck and opened the door. It was a big truck and from where he sat when he pulled himself into the cab he could see the dying embers of the camp. He did not see any movement there, apart from a few low flames and a curl of black smoke which was lost immediately in the mist. He turned back, looked ahead and pressed the starter.

The engine fired and he put it into gear and drove up the road, feeling a little light-headed. In a very short space of time he had killed three men, the first he had ever killed face to face, and he was preparing to go on killing for as long as was necessary. His mind had returned to the tautness he remembered from Korea before he had been shot down; all his senses were razor-sharp and his mind emptied of everything but the task ahead.

After a while he switched off the lights. It was risky, but he had to take the chance. There was the possibility that in the mist he could lose the road on one of the bends and go down the mountain out of control; but far worse was the risk that the enemy in the trucks ahead would see him and lay an ambush.

The truck ground on and on and the wheel bucked against his hand as the jolts were transmitted from the road surface. He went as fast as he thought safe, which was really not fast at all, but at last, rounding a particularly hair-raising corner, he saw a red tail-light disappearing round the next bend. At once he slowed down, content to follow at a discreet distance. There was nothing he could do on the road—his time would come at the mine.

He put out his hand to the sub-machine-gun resting on the seat next to him and drew it closer. It felt very comforting.

He reached a bend he remembered, the final corner before

the level ground at the mine. He drew into the side of the road and put on the brake, but left the engine running. Taking the gun, he dropped to the ground, wincing as he felt the weight on his bad ankle, and hobbled up the road. From ahead he could hear the roar of engines stopping one by one, and when he found a place from where he could see, he discovered the other trucks parked by the huts and in the glare of headlights he saw the movement of men.

The jeep revved up and started to move, the beams of its lights stabbing through the mist and searching along the base of the cliff where the mine tunnels had been driven. First one black cavern was illuminated and then another, and then there was a raised shout of triumph, a howl of fierce joy, as the beams swept past the third tunnel and returned almost immediately to show a low rock wall at the entrance and the white face of a man who quickly dodged back out of sight.

O'Hara wasted no time in wondering who it was. He hobbled back to his truck and put it in gear. Now was the time to enter that bleak arena.

Chapter IX

Forester felt warm and at ease, and to him the two were synonymous. Strange that the snow is so warm and soft, he thought; and opened his eyes to see a glare of white before him. He sighed and closed his eyes again, feeling a sense of disappointment. It *was* snow, after all. He supposed he should make an effort to move and get out of this deliciously warm snow or he would die, but he decided it was not worth the effort. He just let the warmth lap him in comfort and for a second before he relapsed into unconsciousness he wondered vaguely where Rohde had got to.

The next time he opened his eyes the glare of white was still there but now he had recovered enough to see it for what it was—the brilliance of sunlight falling on the crisply laundered white counterpane that covered him. He blinked and looked again, but the glare hurt his eyes, so he closed them. He knew he should do something but what it was he could not remember, and he passed out again while struggling to keep awake long enough to remember what it was.

Vaguely, in his sleep, he was aware of the passage of time

and he knew he must fight against this, that he must stop the clock, hold the moving fingers, because he had something to do that was of prime urgency. He stirred and moaned, and a nurse in a trim white uniform gently sponged the sweat from his brow.

But she did not wake him.

At last he woke fully and stared at the ceiling. That was also white, plainly white-washed with thick wooden beams. He turned his head and found himself looking into kindly eyes. He licked dry lips and whispered, "What happened?"

"*No comprendo*," said the nurse. "No talk—I bring doctor."

She got up and his eyes moved as she went out of the room. He desperately wanted her to come back, to tell him where he was and what had happened and where to find Rohde. As he thought of Rohde it all came back to him—the night on the mountain and the frustrating attempts to find a way over the pass. Most of it he remembered, although the end bits were hazy—and he also remembered why that impossible thing had been attempted.

He tried to sit up but his muscles had no strength in them and he just lay there, breathing hard. He felt as though his body weighed a thousand pounds and as though he had been beaten all over with a rubber hose. Every muscle was loose and flabby, even the muscles of his neck, as he found when he tried to raise his head. And he felt very, very tired.

It was a long time before anyone came into the room, and then it was the nurse bearing a bowl of hot soup. She would not let him talk and he was too weak to insist, and every time he opened his mouth she ladled a spoonful of soup into it. The broth gave him new strength and he felt better, and when he had finished the bowl he said, "Where is the other man—*el otro hombre*?"

"Your friend will be all right," she said in Spanish, and whisked out of the room before he could ask anything else.

Again it was a long time before anyone came to see him. He had no watch, but by the position of the sun he judged it was about midday. But which day? How long had he been there? He put up his hand to scratch an intolerable itching in his chest and discovered why he felt so heavy and uncomfortable; he seemed to be wrapped in a couple of miles of adhesive tape.

A man entered the room and closed the door. He said in an American accent, "Well, Mr. Forester, I hear you're better." He was dressed in hospital white and could have been a doctor. He was elderly but still powerfully built, with a shock of white hair and the crowsfeet of frequent laughter around his eyes.

Forester relaxed. "Thank God—an American," he said. His voice was much stronger.

"I'm McGruder—Doctor McGruder."

"How did you know my name?" asked Forester.

"The papers in your pocket," said McGruder. "You carry an American passport."

"Look," said Forester urgently. "You've got to let me out of here. I've got things to do. I've got to——"

"You're not leaving here for a long time," said McGruder abruptly. "And you couldn't stand if you tried."

Forester sagged back in the bed. "Where is this place?"

"San Antonio Mission," said McGruder. "I'm the Big White Chief here. Presbyterian, you know."

"Anywhere near Altemiros?"

"Sure. Altemiros village is just down the road—almost two miles away."

"I want a message sent," said Forester rapidly. "Two messages—one to Ramón Sueguerra in Altemiros and one to Santillana to the——"

McGruder held up his hand. "Whoa up, there; you'll have a relapse if you're not careful. Take it easy."

"For God's sake," said Forester bitterly. "This is urgent."

"For God's sake nothing is urgent," said McGruder equably. "He has all the time there is. What I'm interested in right now is why one man should come over an impossible pass in a blizzard carrying another man."

"Did Rohde carry me? How is he?"

"As well as can be expected," said McGruder. "I'd be interested to know why he carried you."

"Because I was dying," said Forester. He looked at McGruder speculatively, sizing him up. He did not want to make a blunder—the communists had some very unexpected friends in the strangest places—but he did not think he could go wrong with a Presbyterian doctor, and McGruder *looked* all right. "All right," he said at last. "I suppose I'll have to tell you. You look okay to me."

McGruder raised his eyebrows but said nothing, and Forester told him what was happening on the other side of the mountains, beginning with the air crash but leaving out such irrelevancies as the killing of Peabody, which, he thought,

207

might harm his case. As he spoke McGruder's eyebrows crawled up his scalp until they were almost lost in his hair.

When Forester finished he said, "Now that's as improbable a story as I've ever heard. You see, Mr. Forester, I don't entirely trust you. I had a phone call from the Air Force base—there's one quite close—and they were looking for you. Moreover, you were carrying this." He put his hand in his pocket and pulled out a pistol. "I don't like people who carry guns—it's against my religion."

Forester watched as McGruder skilfully worked the action and the cartridges flipped out. He said, "For a man who doesn't like guns you know a bit too much about their workings."

"I was a Marine at Iwo Jima," said McGruder. "Now why would the Cordilleran military be interested in you?"

"Because they've gone communist."

"Tchah!" said McGruder disgustedly. "You talk like an old maid who sees burglars under every bed. Colonel Rodriguez is as communist as I am."

Forester felt a sudden hope. Rodriguez was the commandant of Fourteenth Squadron and the friend of Aguillar. "Did you speak to Rodriguez?" he asked.

"No," said McGruder. "It was some junior officer." He paused. "Look, Forester, the military want you and I'd like you to tell me why."

"Is Fourteenth Squadron still at the airfield?" countered Forester.

"I don't know. Rodriguez did say something about moving —but I haven't seen him for nearly a month."

So it was a toss-up, thought Forester disgustedly. The military were friend or foe and he had no immediate means of finding out—and it looked as though McGruder was quite prepared to hand him over. He said speculatively, "I suppose you try to keep your nose clean. I suppose you work in with the local authorities and you don't interfere in local politics."

"Indeed I don't," said McGruder. "I don't want this mission closed. We have enough trouble as it is."

"You *think* you have trouble with Lopez, but that's nothing to the trouble you'll have when the commies move in," snapped Forester. "Tell me, is it against your religion to stand by and wait while your fellow human beings—some of them fellow countrymen, not that that matters—are slaughtered not fifteen miles from where you are standing?"

McGruder whitened about the nostrils and the lines deepened about his mouth. " I almost think you are telling the truth," he said slowly.

" You're damn right I am."

Ignoring the profanity McGruder said, " You mentioned a name—Sueguerra. I know Señor Sueguerra very well. I play chess with him whenever I get into the village. He is a good man, so that is a point for you. What was the other message—to Santillana?"

" The same message to a different man," said Forester patiently. " Bob Addison of the United States Embassy. Tell them both what I've told you—and tell Addison to get the lead out of his breeches fast."

McGruder wrinkled his brow. " Addison? I believe I know all the Embassy staff, but I don't recall an Addison."

" You wouldn't," said Forester. " He's an officer of the Central Intelligence Agency of the United States. We don't advertise."

McGruder's eyebrows crawled up again. " We?"

Forester grinned weakly. " I'm a C.I.A. officer, too. But you'll have to take it on trust—I don't carry the information tattooed on my chest."

I I

Forester was shocked to hear that Rohde was likely to lose his leg. " Frostbite in a very bad open wound is not conducive to the best of health," said McGruder dryly. " I'm very sorry about this; I'll try to save the leg, of course—it's a pity that this should happen to so brave a man."

McGruder now appeared to have accepted Forester's story, although he had taken a lot of convincing and had doubts about the wisdom of the State Department. " They're stupid," he said. " We don't want open American interference down here—that's certain to stir up anti-Americanism. It's giving the communists a perfect opening."

" For God's sake, I'm not interfering actively," protested Forester. " We knew that Aguillar was going to make his move and my job was to keep a friendly eye on him, to see that he got through safely." He looked at the ceiling and said bitterly, " I seem to have balled it up, don't I?"

" I don't see that you could have done anything different,"

observed McGruder. He got up from the bedside. "I'll check up on which squadron is at the airfield, and I'll go to see Sueguerra myself."

"Don't forget the Embassy."

"I'll put a phone call through right away."

But that proved to be difficult because the line was not open. McGruder sat at his desk and fumed at the unresponsive telephone. This was something that happened about once a week and always at a critical moment. At last he put down the hand-set and turned to take off his white coat, but hesitated as he heard the squeal of brakes from the courtyard. He looked through his office window and saw a military staff car pull up followed by a truck and a military ambulance. A squad of uniformed and armed men debussed from the truck under the barked orders of an N.C.O., and an officer climbed casually out of the staff car.

McGruder hastily put on the white coat again and when the officer strode into the room he was busy writing at his desk. He looked up and said, "Good day—er—Major. To what do I owe this honour?"

The officer clicked his heels punctiliously. "Major Garcia, at your service."

The doctor leaned back in his chair and put both his hands flat on the desk. "I'm McGruder. What can I do for you, Major?"

Garcia flicked his glove against the side of his well-cut breeches. "We—the Cordilleran Air Force, that is—thought we might be of service," he said easily. "We understand that you have two badly injured men here—the men who came down from the mountain. We offer the use of our medical staff and the base hospital at the airfield." He waved. "The ambulance is waiting outside."

McGruder swivelled his eyes to the window and saw the soldiers taking up position outside. They looked stripped for action. He flicked his gaze back to Garcia. "And the escort!"

Garcia smiled. "*No es nada*," he said casually. "I was conducting a small exercise when I got my orders, and it was as easy to bring the men along as to dismiss them and let them idle."

McGruder did not believe a word of it. He said pleasantly, "Well, Major, I don't think we need trouble the military. I haven't been in your hospital at the airfield, but this place of mine is well enough equipped to take care of these men. I don't think they need to be moved."

Garcia lost his smile. "But we insist," he said icily.

McGruder's mobile eyebrows shot up. "Insist, Major Garcia? I don't think you're in a position to insist."

Garcia looked meaningly at the squad of soldiers in the courtyard. "No?" he asked silkily.

"No," said McGruder flatly. "As a doctor, I say that these men are too sick to be moved. If you don't believe me, then trot out your own doctor from that ambulance and let *him* have a look at them. I am sure he will tell you the same."

For the first time Garcia seemed to lose his self-possession. "Doctor?" he said uncertainly. "Er . . . we have brought no doctor."

"No doctor?" said McGruder in surprise. He wiggled his eyebrows at Garcia. "I am sure you have misinterpreted your orders, Major Garcia. I don't think your commanding officer would approve of these men leaving here unless under qualified supervision; and I certainly don't have the time to go with you to the airfield—I am a busy man."

Garcia hesitated and then said sullenly, "Your telephone —may I use it?"

"Help yourself," said McGruder. "But it isn't working —as usual."

Garcia smiled thinly and spoke into the mouthpiece. He got an answer too, which really surprised McGruder and told him of the seriousness of the position. This was not an ordinary breakdown of the telephone system—it was planned; and he guessed that the exchange was under military control.

When next Garcia spoke he came to attention and McGruder smiled humourlessly; that would be his commanding officer and it certainly wouldn't be Rodriguez—he didn't go in for that kind of spit-and-polish. Garcia explained McGruder's attitude concisely and then listened to the spate of words which followed. There was a grim smile on his face as he put down the telephone. "I regret to tell you, Doctor McGruder, that I must take those men."

He stepped to the window and called his sergeant as McGruder came to his feet in anger. "And I say the men are too ill to be moved. One of those men is an American, Major Garcia. Are you trying to cause an international incident?"

"I am obeying orders," said Garcia stiffly. His sergeant came to the window and he gave a rapid stream of instructions, then turned to McGruder. "I have to inform you that these men stand accused of plotting against the safety of the State. I am under instructions to arrest them."

"You're nuts," said McGruder. "You take these men and you'll be up to your neck in diplomats." He moved over to the door.

Garcia stood in front of him. "I must ask you to move away from the door, Doctor McGruder, or I will be forced to arrest you, too." He spoke over McGruder's shoulder to a corporal standing outside. "Escort the doctor into the courtyard."

"Well, if you're going to feel like that about it, there's nothing I can do," said McGruder, "But that commanding officer of yours—what's his name . . .?"

"Colonel Coello."

"Colonel Coello is going to find himself in a sticky position." He stood aside and let Garcia precede him into the corridor.

Garcia waited for him, slapping the side of his leg impatiently. "Where are the men?"

McGruder led the way down the corridor at a rapid pace. Outside Forester's room he paused and deliberately raised his voice. "You realise I am letting these men go under protest. The military have no jurisdiction here and I intend to protest to the Cordilleran government through the United States Embassy. And I further protest upon medical grounds—neither of these men is fit to be moved."

"Where are the men?" repeated Garcia.

"I have just operated on one of them—he is recovering from an anæsthetic. The other is also very ill and I insist on giving him a sedative before he is moved."

Garcia hesitated and McGruder pressed him. "Come, Major; military ambulances have never been noted for smooth running—you would not begrudge a man a pain-killer." He tapped Garcia on the chest. "This is going to make headlines in every paper across the United States. Do you want to make matters worse by appearing anti-humanitarian?"

"Very well," said Garcia unwillingly.

"I'll get the morphine from the surgery," said McGruder, and went back, leaving Garcia standing in the corridor.

Forester heard the raised voices as he was polishing the plate of the best meal he had ever enjoyed in his life. He realised that something was amiss and that McGruder was making him appear sicker than he was. He was willing to play along with that, so he hastily pushed the tray under the bed and when the door opened he was lying flat on his back with his eyes closed. As McGruder touched him he groaned.

McGruder said, " Mr. Forester, Major Garcia thinks you will be better looked after in another hospital, so you are being moved." As Forester opened his eyes McGruder frowned at him heavily. " I do not agree with this move, which is being done under *force majeure*, and I am going to consult the appropriate authorities. I am going to give you a sedative so that the journey will not harm you, although it is not far —merely to the airfield."

He rolled up the sleeve of Forester's pyjamas and dabbed at his arm with cotton-wool, then produced a hypodermic syringe which he filled from an ampoule. He spoke casually. " The tape round your chest will support your ribs but I wouldn't move around much—not unless you have to." There was a subtle emphasis on the last few words and he winked at Forester.

As he pushed home the needle in Forester's arm he leaned over and whispered, " It's a stimulant."

" What was that?" said Garcia sharply.

" What was what?" asked McGruder, turning and skewering Garcia with an icy glare. " I'll trouble you not to interfere with a doctor in his duties. Mr. Forester is a very sick man, and on behalf of the United States government I am holding you and Colonel Coello responsible for what happens to him. Now, where are your stretcher-bearers?"

Garcia snapped to the sergeant at the door, " *Una camilla.*" The sergeant bawled down the corridor and presently a stretcher was brought in. McGruder fussed about while Forester was transferred from the bed, and when he was settled said, " There, you can take him."

He stepped back and knocked a kidney basin to the floor with a clatter. The noise was startling in that quiet room, and while everyone's attention was diverted McGruder hastily thrust something hard under Forester's pillow.

Then Forester was borne down the corridor and into the open courtyard and he winced as the sun struck his eyes. Once in the ambulance he had to wait a long time before anything else happened and he closed his eyes, feigning sleep, because the soldier on guard kept peering at him. Slowly he brought his hand up under the coverlet towards the pillow and eventually touched the butt of a gun.

Good old McGruder, he thought; the Marines to the rescue. He hooked his finger in the trigger guard and gradually brought the gun down to his side, where he thrust it into the waistband of his pyjamas at the small of his back where it could not be seen when he was transferred to another bed. He smiled to himself; at other times lying on a hard piece of metal might be thought extremely uncomfortable, but he found the touch of the gun very comforting.

And what McGruder had said was comforting, too. The tape would hold him together and the stimulant would give him strength to move. Not that he thought he needed it; his strength had returned rapidly once he had eaten, but no doubt the doctor knew best.

Rohde was pushed into the ambulance and Forester looked across at the stretcher. He was unconscious and there was a hump under the coverlet where his legs were. His face was pale and covered with small beads of sweat and he breathed stertorously.

Two soldiers climbed into the ambulance and the doors were slammed, and after a few minutes it moved off. Forester kept his eyes closed at first—he wanted the soldiers to believe that the hypothetical sedative was taking effect. But after a while he decided that these rank and file would probably not know anything about a sedative being given to him, so he risked opening his eyes and turned his head to look out of the window.

He could not see much because of the restricted angle of view, but presently the ambulance stopped and he saw a wrought-iron gate and through the bars a large board. It depicted an eagle flying over a snow-capped mountain, and round this emblem in a scroll and written in ornate letters were the words: ESQUADRON OCTAVO.

He closed his eyes in pain. They had drawn the wrong straw; this was the communist squadron.

III

McGruder watched the ambulance leave the courtyard followed by the staff car. Then he went into his office, stripped off his white coat and put on his jacket. He took his car keys from a drawer and went round to the hospital garage, where he got a shock. Lounging outside the big doors was a soldier in a sloppy uniform—but there was nothing sloppy about the rifle he was holding, nor about the gleaming bayonet.

He walked over and barked authoritatively, " Let me pass."

214

The soldier looked at him through half-closed eyes and shook his head, then spat on the ground. McGruder got mad and tried to push his way past but found the tip of the bayonet pricking his throat. The soldier said, "You see the sergeant —if he says you can take a car, then you take a car."

McGruder backed away, rubbing his throat. He turned on his heel and went to look for the sergeant, but got nowhere with him. The sergeant was a sympathetic man when away from his officers and his broad Indian face was sorrowful. "I'm sorry, Doctor," he said. "I just obey orders—and my orders are that no one leaves the mission until I get contrary orders."

"And when will that be?" demanded ˉGruder.

The sergeant shrugged. "Who knows? ˉe said with the fatalism of one to whom officers were a race apart and their doings incomprehensible.

McGruder snorted and withdrew to his office, where he picked up the telephone. Apparently it was still dead, but when he snapped, "Get me Colonel Coello at the military airfield," it suddenly came to life and he was put through— not to Coello, but to some underling.

It took him over fifteen minutes before he got through to Coello and by then he was breathing hard with ill-suppressed rage. He said aggressively, "McGruder here. What's all this about closing down San Antonio Mission?"

Coello was suave. "But the mission is not closed, Doctor; anyone can enter."

"But I can't leave," said McGruder. "I have work to do."

"Then do it," said Coello. "Your work is in the mission, Doctor; stick to your job—like the cobbler. Do not interfere in things which do not concern you."

"I don't know what the hell you mean," snarled McGruder with a profanity he had not used since his Marine days. "I have to pick up a consignment of drugs at the railroad depot in Altemiros. I need them and the Cordilleran Air Force is stopping me getting them—that's how I see it. You're not going to look very good when this comes out, Colonel."

"But you should have said this earlier," said Coello soothingly. "I will send one of the airfield vehicles to pick them up for you. As you know, the Cordilleran Air Force is always ready to help your mission. I hear you run a very good hospital, Doctor McGruder. We are short of good hospitals in this country."

McGruder heard the cynical amusement in the voice. He

said irascibly, "All right," and banged the phone down. Mopping his brow he thought that it was indeed fortunate there *was* a consignment of drugs waiting in Altemiros. He paused, wondering what to do next, then he drew a sheet of blank paper from a drawer and began writing.

Half an hour later he had the gist of Forester's story on paper. He folded the sheets, sealed them in an envelope and put the envelope into his pocket. All the while he was conscious of the soldier posted just outside the window who was keeping discreet surveillance of him. He went out into the corridor to find another soldier lounging outside the office door whom he ignored, carrying on down towards the wards and the operating theatre. The soldier stared after him with incurious eyes and drifted down the corridor after him.

McGruder looked for Sánchez, his second-in-command, and found him in one of the wards. Sánchez looked at his face and raised his eyebrows. "What is happening, Doctor?"

"The local military have gone berserk," said McGruder unhappily. "And I seem to be mixed up in it—they won't let me leave the mission."

"They won't let *anyone* leave the mission," said Sánchez. "I tried."

"I must get to Altemiros," said McGruder. "Will you help me? I know I'm usually non-political, but this is different. There's murder going on across the mountains."

"Eight Squadron came to the airfield two days ago—I have heard strange stories about Eight Squadron," said Sánchez reflectively. "You may be non-political, Doctor McGruder, but I am not. Of course I will help you."

McGruder turned and saw the soldier gazing blankly at him from the entrance of the ward. "Let's go into your office," he said.

They went to the office and McGruder switched on an X-ray viewer and pointed out the salient features of an X-ray plate to Sánchez. He left the door open and the soldier leaned on the opposite wall of the corridor, solemnly picking his teeth. "This is what I want you to do," said McGruder in a low voice.

Fifteen minutes later he went to find the sergeant and spoke to him forthrightly. "What are your orders concerning the mission?" he demanded.

The sergeant said, "Not to let anyone leave—and to watch you, Doctor McGruder." He paused. "I'm sorry."

"I seem to have noticed that I've been watched," said

McGruder with heavy irony. "Now, I'm going to do an operation. Old Pedro must have his kidneys seen to or he will die. I can't have any of your men in the operating theatre, spitting all over the floor; we have enough trouble attaining asepsis as it is."

"We all know you *norteamericanos* are very clean," acknowledged the sergeant. He frowned. "This room—how many doors?"

"One door—no windows," said McGruder. "You can come and look at it if you like; but don't spit on the floor."

He took the sergeant into the operating theatre and satisfied him that there was only one entrance. "Very well," said the sergeant. "I will put two men outside the door—that will be all right."

McGruder went into the sluice room and prepared for the operation, putting on his gown and cap and fastening the mask loosely about his neck. Old Pedro was brought up on a stretcher and McGruder stood outside the door while he was pushed into the theatre. The sergeant said, "How long will this take?"

McGruder considered. "About two hours—maybe longer. It is a serious operation, Sergeant."

He went into the theatre and closed the door. Five minutes later the empty stretcher was pushed out and the sergeant looked through the open door and saw the doctor, masked and bending over the operating table, a scalpel in his hand. The door closed, the sergeant nodded to the sentries and wandered towards the courtyard to find a sunny spot. He quite ignored the empty stretcher being pushed by two chattering nurses down the corridor.

In the safety of the bottom ward McGruder dropped from under the stretcher where he had been clinging and flexed the muscles of his arms. Getting too old for these acrobatics, he thought, and nodded to the nurses who had pushed in the stretcher. They giggled and went out, and he changed his clothes quickly.

He knew of a place where the tide of prickly pear which covered the hillside overflowed into the mission grounds. For weeks he had intended to cut down the growth and tidy it up, but now he was glad that he had let it be. No sentry in his right mind would deliberately patrol in the middle of a grove of sharp-spined cactus, no matter what his orders, and McGruder thought he had a chance of getting through.

He was right. Twenty minutes later he was on the other

side of a low rise, the mission out of sight behind him and the houses of Altemiros spread in front. His clothes were torn and so was his flesh—the cactus had not been kind.

He began to run.

Forester was still on his stretcher. He had expected to be taken into a hospital ward and transferred to a bed, but instead the stretcher was taken into an office and laid across two chairs. Then he was left alone, but he could hear the shuffling feet of a sentry outside the door and knew he was well guarded.

It was a large office overlooking the airfield, and he guessed it belonged to the commanding officer. There were many maps on the walls and some aerial photographs, mainly of mountain country. He looked at the décor without interest; he had been in many offices like this when he was in the American Air Force and it was all very familiar, from the group photographs of the squadron to the clock let into the boss of an old wooden propeller.

What interested him was the scene outside. One complete wall of the office was a window and through it he could see the apron outside the control tower and, farther away, a group of hangars. He clicked his tongue as he recognised the aircraft standing on the apron—they were Sabres.

Good old Uncle Sam, he thought in disgust; always willing to give handouts, even military handouts, to potential enemies. He looked at the fighter planes with intense curiosity. They were early model Sabres, now obsolete in the major air forces, but quite adequate for the defence of a country like Cordillera which had no conceivable military enemies of any strength. As far as he could see, they were the identical model he had flown in Korea. I could fly one of those, he thought, if I could just get into the cockpit.

There were four of them standing in a neat line and he saw they were being serviced. Suddenly he sat up—no, not serviced—those were rockets going under the wings. And those men standing on the wings were not mechanics, they were armourers loading cannon shells. He did not have to be close enough to see the shells; he had seen this operation performed many times in Korea and he knew automatically that these planes were being readied for instant action.

Christ! he thought bitterly; it's like using a steam hammer to crack a nut. O'Hara and the others won't have a chance against this lot. But then he became aware of something else —this must mean that O'Hara was still holding out; that the communists across the bridge were still baffled. He felt exhilarated and depressed at the same time as he watched the planes being readied.

He lay back again and felt the gun pressing into the small of his back. This was the time to prepare for action, he realised, so he pulled out the gun, keeping a wary eye on the door, and examined it. It was the pistol he had brought over the mountain—Grivas's pistol. Cold and exposure to the elements had not done it any good—the oil had dried out and the action was stiff—but he thought it would work. He snapped the action several times, catching the rounds as they flipped from the breech, then he reloaded the magazine and worked the action again, putting a round in the breech ready for instant shooting.

He stowed the pistol by his side under the coverlet and laid his hand on the butt. Now he was ready—as ready as he could be.

He waited a long time and began to get edgy. He felt little tics all over his body as small muscles jumped and twitched, and he had never been so wide-awake in his life. That's McGruder's stimulant he thought; I wonder what it was and if it'll mix with all the coca I've taken.

He kept an eye on the Sabres outside. The ground crews had completed their work long before someone opened the door of the office, and Forester looked up to see a man with a long, saturnine face looking down at him. The man smiled. "*Colonel Coello, a sus ordines.*" He clicked his heels.

Forester blinked his eyes, endeavouring to simulate sleepiness. " Colonel who?" he mumbled.

The colonel sat behind the desk. " Coello," he said pleasantly. " I am the commandant of this fighter squadron."

" It's the damnedest thing," said Forester with a baffled look. " One minute I was in hospital, and the next minute I'm in this office. Familiar surroundings, too; I woke up and became interested in those Sabres."

" You have flown?" asked Coello politely.

" I sure have," said Forester. " I was in Korea—I flew Sabres there."

" Then we can talk together as comrades," said Coello heartily. " You remember Doctor McGruder?"

219

"Not much," said Forester. "I woke up and he pumped me full of stuff to put me to sleep again—then I found myself here. Say, shouldn't I be in hospital or something?"

"Then you did not talk to McGruder about anything—anything at all?"

"I didn't have the chance," said Forester. He did not want to implicate McGruder in this. "Say, Colonel, am I glad to see you. All hell is breaking loose on the other side of the mountains. There's a bunch of bandits trying to murder some stranded airline passengers. We were on our way here to tell you."

"On your way *here*?"

"That's right; there was a South American guy told us to come here—now, what was his name?" Forester wrinkled his brow.

"Aguillar—perhaps?"

"Never heard that name before," said Forester. "No, this guy was called Montes."

"And Montes told you to come *here*?" said Coello incredulously. "He must have thought that fool Rodriguez was here. You were two days too late, Mr. Forester." He began to laugh.

Forester felt a cold chill run through him but pressed on with his act of innocence. "What's so funny?" he asked plaintively. "Why the hell are you sitting there laughing instead of doing something about it?"

Coello wiped the tears of laughter from his eyes. "Do not worry, Señor Forester; we know all about it already. We are making preparations for . . . er . . . a rescue attempt."

I'll bet you are, thought Forester bitterly, looking at the Sabres drawn up on the apron. He said, "What the hell! Then I nearly killed myself on the mountain for nothing. What a damned fool I am."

Coello opened a folder on his desk. "Your name is Raymond Forester; you are South American Sales Manager for the Fairfield Machine Tool Corporation, and you were on your way to Santillana." He smiled as he looked down at the folder. "We have checked, of course; there is a Raymond Forester who works for this company, and he *is* sales manager in South America. The C.I.A. can be efficient in small matters, Mr. Forester."

"Huh!" said Forester. "C.I.A.? What the devil are you talking about?"

Coello waved his hand airily. "Espionage! Sabotage! Corruption of public officials! Undermining the will of the people! Name anything bad and you name the C.I.A.—and also yourself, Mr. Forester."

"You're nuts," said Forester disgustedly.

"You are a meddling American," said Coello sharply. "You are a plutocratic, capitalistic lackey. One could forgive you if you were but a tool; but you do your filthy work in full awareness of its evil. You came to Cordillera to foment an imperialistic revolution, putting up that scoundrel Aguillar as a figurehead for your machinations."

"Who?" said Forester. "You're still nuts."

"Give up, Forester; stop this pretence. We know all about the Fairfield Machine Tool Corporation. It is a cover that capitalistic Wall Street has erected to hide your imperialistic American secret service. We know all about you and we know all about Addison in Santillana. He has been removed from the game—and so have you, Forester."

Forester smiled crookedly. "The voice is Spanish-American, but the words come from Moscow—or is it Peking this time?" He nodded towards the armed aircraft. "Who is really doing the meddling round here?"

Coello smiled. "I am a servant of the present government of General Lopez. I am sure he would be happy to know that Aguillar will soon be dead."

"But I bet you won't tell him," said Forester. "Not if I know how you boys operate. You'll use the threat of Aguillar to drive Lopez out as soon as it suits you." He tried to scratch his itching chest but was unsuccessful. "You jumped me and Rohde pretty fast—how did you know we were at McGruder's hospital?"

"I am sure you are trying to sound more stupid than you really are," said Coello. "My dear Forester, we are in radio communication with our forces on the other side of the mountains." He sounded suddenly bitter. "Inefficient though they are, they have at least kept their radio working. You were seen by the bridge. And when men come over that pass, do you think the news can be kept quiet? The whole of Altemiros knows of the mad American who has done the impossible."

But they don't know why I did it, thought Forester savagely; and they'll never find out if this bastard has his way.

221

Coello held up a photograph. "We suspected that the C.I.A. might have someone with Aguillar. It was only a suspicion then, but now we know it to be a fact. This photograph was taken in Washington six months ago."

He skimmed it over and Forester looked at it. It was a glossy picture of himself and his immediate superior talking together on the steps of a building. He flicked the photograph with his fingernail. "Processed in Moscow?"

Coello smiled and asked silkily, "Can you give me any sound reasons why you should not be shot?"

"Not many," said Forester off-handedly. "But enough." He propped himself up on one elbow and tried to make it sound good. "You're killing Americans on the other side of those mountains, Coello. The American government is going to demand an explanation—an investigation."

"So? There is an air crash—there have been many such crashes even in North America. Especially can they occur on such ill-run air lines as Andes Airlift, which, incidentally, is owned by one of your own countrymen. An obsolete aircraft with a drunken pilot—what more natural? There will be no bodies to send back to the United States, I assure you. Regrettable, isn't it?"

"You don't know the facts of life," said Forester. "My government is going to be very interested. Now, don't get me wrong; they're not interested in air crashes as such. But *I* was in that airplane and they're going to be goddam suspicious. There'll be an official investigation—Uncle Sam will goose the I.A.T.A. into making one—and there'll be a concurrent under-cover investigation. This country will be full of operatives within a week—you can't stop them all and you can't hide all the evidence. The truth is going to come out and the U.S. government will be delighted to blow the lid off. Nothing would please them more."

He coughed, sweating a little—now it had to sound really good. "Now, there's a way round all that." He sat up on the stretcher. "Have you a cigarette?"

Coello's eyes narrowed as he picked up a cigarette-box from the desk and walked round to the stretcher. He offered the open box and said, "Am I to understand that you're trying to bargain for your life?"

"You're dead right," said Forester. He put a whine in his voice. "I've no hankering to wear a wooden overcoat, and I know how you boys operate on captured prisoners."

222

Thoughtfully Coello flicked his lighter and lit Forester's cigarette. "Well?"

Forester said, "Look, Colonel; supposing I was the only survivor of that crash—thrown clear by some miraculous chance. Then I could say that the crash was okay; that it was on the up-and-up. Why wouldn't they believe me? I'm one of their bright boys."

Coello nodded. "You are bright." He smiled. "What guarantee have we that you will do this for us?"

"Guarantee? You know damn well I can't give you one. But I tell you this, buddy-boy; you're not the boss round here—not by a long shot. And I'm stuffed full of information about the C.I.A.—operation areas, names, faces, addresses, covers—you ask for it, I've got it. And if your boss ever finds out that you've turned down a chance like this you're going to be in trouble. What have you got to lose? All you have to do is to put it to your boss and let him say 'yes' or 'no.' If anything goes wrong he'll have to take the rap from higher up, but you'll be in the clear."

Coello tapped his teeth with a fingernail. "I think you're playing for time, Forester." He thought deeply. "If you can give me a sensible answer to the next question I might believe you. You say you are afraid of dying. If you are so afraid, why did you risk your life in coming over the pass?"

Forester thought of Peabody and laughed outright. "Use your brains. I was being shot at over there by that goddam bridge. Have you ever tried to talk reasonably with someone who shoots at you if you bat an eyelid? But you're not shooting at me, Colonel; I can talk to you. Anyway, I reckoned it was a sight safer on the mountain than down by the bridge—and I've proved it, haven't I? I'm here and I'm still alive."

"Yes," said Coello pensively. "You are still alive." He went to his desk. "You might as well begin by proving your goodwill immediately. We sent a reconnaissance plane over to see what was happening and the pilot took these photographs. What do you make of them?"

He tossed a sheaf of glossy photographs on to the foot of the stretcher. Forester leaned over and gasped. "Have a heart, Colonel; I'm all bust up inside—I can't reach."

Coello leaned over with a ruler and flicked them within his reach, and Forester fanned them out. They were good; a little blurred because of the speed of the aircraft, but still sharp enough to make out details. He saw the bridge and a scattering of upturned faces, white blobs against a grey background. And he saw the trebuchet. So they'd got it down from the camp all right. " Interesting," he said.

Coello leaned over. " What is that?" he asked. " Our experts have been able to make nothing of it." His finger was pointing at the trebuchet.

Forester smiled. " I'm not surprised," he said. " There's a nut-case over there; a guy called Armstrong. He conned the others into building that gadget; it's called a trebuchet and it's for throwing stones. He said the last time it was used was when Cortes besieged Mexico City and then it didn't work properly. It's nothing to worry about."

" No?" said Coello. " They nearly broke down the bridge with it."

Forester gave a silent cheer, but said nothing. He was itching to pull out his gun and let Coello have it right where it hurt most, but he would gain nothing by that—just a bullet in the brain from the guard and no chance of doing anything more damaging.

Coello gathered the photographs together and tapped them on his hand. " Very well," he said. " We will not shoot you—yet. You have possibly gained yourself another hour of life—perhaps much longer. I will consult my superior and let him decide what to do with you."

He went to the door, then turned. " I would not do anything foolish; you realise you are well guarded."

" What the hell can I do?" growled Forester. " I'm bust up inside and all strapped up; I'm as weak as a kitten and full of dope. I'm safe enough."

When Coello closed the door behind him Forester broke out into a sweat. During the last half-hour Coello had nearly been relieved of the responsibility of him, for he had almost had a heart attack on three separate occasions. He hoped he had established the points he had tried to make; that he could be bought—something which might gain precious time; that he was too ill to move—Coello might get a shock on that one; and that Coello himself had nothing to lose by waiting a little—nothing but his life, Forester hoped.

He touched the butt of the gun and gazed out of the window. There was action about the Sabres on the apron; a truck had pulled up and a group of men in flying kit were getting out—three of them. They stood about talking for some time and then went to their aircraft and got settled in the cockpits with the assistance of the ground crews. Forester heard the whine of the engines as the starter truck rolled from one plane to another and, one by one, the planes slowly taxied forward until they went out of his sight.

He looked at the remaining Sabre. He knew nothing about the Cordilleran Air Force insignia, but the three stripes on the tail looked important. Perhaps the good colonel was going to lead this strike himself; it would be just his mark, thought Forester with animosity.

V

Ramón Sueguerra was the last person he would have expected to be involved in a desperate enterprise involving the overthrow of governments, thought McGruder, as he made his devious way through the back streets of Altemiros towards Sueguerra's office. What had a plump and comfortable merchant to do with revolution? Yet perhaps the Lopez régime was hurting him more than most—his profits were eaten up by bribes; his markets were increasingly more restricted; and the fibre of his business slackened as the general economic level of the country sagged under the misrule of Lopez. Not all revolutions were made by the starving proletariat.

He came upon the building which housed the multitudinous activities of Sueguerra from the rear and entered by the back door. The front door was, of course, impossible; directly across the street was the post and telegraph office, and McGruder suspected that the building would be occupied by men of Eighth Squadron. He went into Sueguerra's office as he had always done—with a cheery wave to his secretary—and found Sueguerra looking out of the window which faced the street.

He was surprised to see McGruder. "What brings you here?" he asked. "It's too early for chess, my friend." A truck roared in the street outside and his eyes flickered back to the window and McGruder saw that he was uneasy and worried.

"I won't waste your time," said McGruder, pulling the envelope from his pocket. "Read this—it will be quicker than my explanations."

As Sueguerra read he sank into his chair and his face whitened. "But this is incredible," he said. "Are you sure of this?"

"They took Forester and Rohde from the mission," said McGruder. "It was done by force."

"The man Forester I do not know—but Miguel Rohde should have been here two days ago," said Sueguerra. "He is supposed to take charge in the mountains when . . ."

"When the revolution begins?"

Sueguerra looked up. "All right—call it revolution if you will. How else can we get rid of Lopez?" He cocked his head to the street. "This explains what is happening over there; I was wondering about that."

He picked up a white telephone. "Send in Juan."

"What are you going to do?" asked McGruder.

Sueguerra stabbed his finger at the black telephone. "That is useless, my friend, as long as the post office is occupied. And this local telephone exchange controls all the communications in our mountain area. I will send Juan, my son, over the mountains, but he has a long way to go and it will take time—you know what our roads are like."

"It will take him four hours or more," agreed McGruder.

"Still, I will send him. But we will take more direct action." Sueguerra walked over to the window and looked across the street at the post office. "We must take the post office."

McGruder's head jerked up. "You will fight Eighth Squadron?"

Sueguerra swung round. "We must—there is more than telephones involved here." He walked over to his desk and sat down. "Doctor McGruder, we always knew that when the revolution came and if Eighth Squadron was stationed here, then Eighth Squadron would have to be removed from the game. But how to do it—that was the problem."

He smiled slightly. "The solution proved to be ridiculously easy. Colonel Rodriguez has mined all important installations on the airfield. The mines can be exploded electrically—and the wires lead from the airfield to Altemiros; they were installed under the guise of telephone cables. It just needs one touch on a plunger and Eighth Squadron is out of action."

Then he thumped the desk and said savagely, "An extra lead was supposed to be installed in my office this morning—as it is, the only way we can do it is to take the post office by force, because that is where the electrical connection is."

McGruder shook his head. "I'm no electrical engineer, but surely you can tap the wire *outside* the post office."

"It was done by Fourteenth Squadron engineers in a

hurry," said Sueguerra. "And they were pulled out when Eighth Squadron so unexpectedly moved in. There are hundreds of wires in the civil and military networks and no one knows which is the right one. But I know the right connection *inside* the post office—Rodriguez showed it to me."

They heard the high scream of a jet as it flew over Altemiros from the airfield, and Sueguerra said, "We must act quickly —Eighth Squadron must not be allowed to fly."

He burst into activity and McGruder paled when he saw the extent of his preparations. Men assembled in his warehouses as though by magic and innocent tea-chests and bales of hides disgorged an incredible number of arms—both rifles and automatic weapons. The lines deepened in McGruder's face and he said to Sueguerra, "I will not fight, you know."

Sueguerra clapped him on the back. "We do not need you —what is one extra man? And in any case we do not want a *norteamericano* involved. This is a home-grown revolution. But there may be some patching-up for you to do when this is over."

But there was little fighting at the post office. The attack was so unexpected and in such overwhelming strength that the Eighth Squadron detachment put up almost no resistance at all, and the only casualty was a corporal who got a bullet in his leg because an inexperienced and enthusiastic amateur rifleman had left off his safety-catch.

Sueguerra strode into the post office. "Jaime! Jaime! Where is that fool of an electrician? Jaime!"

"I'm here," said Jaime, and came forward carrying a large box under his arm. Sueguerra took him into the main switch-room and McGruder followed.

"It's the third bank of switches—fifteenth from the right and nineteenth from the bottom," said Sueguerra, consulting a scrap of paper.

Jaime counted carefully. "That's it," he said. "Those two screw connections there." He produced a screwdriver. "I'll be about two minutes."

As he worked a plane screamed over the town and then another and another. "I hope we're not too late," whispered Sueguerra.

McGruder put his hand on his arm. "What about Forester and Rohde?" he said in alarm. "They are at the airfield."

"We do not destroy hospitals," said Sueguerra. "Only the important installations are mined—the fuel and ammunition dumps, the hangars, the runways, the control tower. We only want to immobilise them—they are Cordillerans, you know."

Jaime said, "Ready," and Sueguerra lifted the plunger.

"It must be done," he said, and abruptly pushed down hard.

V I

It seemed that Coello *was* leading the strike because the next time he entered the office he was in full flying kit, parachute pack and all. He looked sour. "You have gained yourself more time, Forester. The decision on you will have to wait. I have other, more urgent, matters to attend to. However, I have something to show you—an educative demonstration." He snapped his fingers and two soldiers entered and picked up the stretcher.

"What sort of a demonstration?" asked Forester as he was carried out.

"A demonstration of the dangers of lacking patriotism," answered Coello, smiling. "Something you may be accused of by *your* government one day, Mr. Forester."

Forester lay limply on the stretcher as it was carried out of the building and wondered what the hell was going on. The bearers veered across the apron in front of the control tower, past the single Sabre fighter, and Coello called to a mechanic, "*Diez momentos*." The man saluted, and Forester thought, Ten minutes? Whatever it is, it won't take long.

He turned his head as he heard the whine of an aircraft taking off and saw a Sabre clearing the ground, its wheels retracting. Then there was another, and then the third. They disappeared over the horizon and he wondered where they were going—certainly in the wrong direction if they intended to strafe O'Hara.

The small party approached one of the hangars. The big sliding doors were closed and Coello opened the wicker door and went inside, the stretcher-bearers following. There were no aircraft in the hangar and their footfalls echoed hollowly in dull clangour from the metal walls. Coello went into a side room, waddling awkwardly in his flying gear, and motioned for the stretcher to be brought in. He saw the stretcher placed across two chairs, then told the soldiers to wait outside.

Forester looked up at him. "What the hell is this?" he demanded.

228

"You will see," said Coello calmly, and switched on the light. He went to the window and drew a cord and the curtains came across. "Now then," he said, and crossed the room to draw another cord and curtains parted on an internal window looking into the hangar. "The demonstration will begin almost immediately," he said, and cocked his head on one side as though listening for something.

Forester heard it too, and looked up. It was the banshee howl of a diving jet plane, growing louder and louder until it threatened to shatter the eardrums. With a shriek the plane passed over the hangar and Forester reckoned with professional interest that it could not have cleared the hangar roof by many feet.

"We begin," said Coello, and indicated the hangar.

Almost as though the diving plane had been a signal, a file of soldiers marched into the hangar and stood in a line, an officer barking at them until they trimmed the rank. Each man carried a rifle at the slope and Forester began to have a prickly foreknowledge of what was to come.

He looked at Coello coldly and began to speak but the howling racket of another diving plane drowned his words. When the plane had gone he turned and saw with rage in his heart that Rohde was being dragged in.

He could not walk and two soldiers were half dragging, half carrying him, his feet trailing on the concrete floor. Coello tapped on the window with a pencil and the soldiers brought Rohde forward. His face was dreadfully battered, both eyes were turning black and he had bruised cheeks. But his eyes were open and he regarded Forester with a lacklustre expression and opened his mouth and said a few words which Forester could not hear. He had some teeth missing.

"You've beaten him up, you bastard," exploded Forester.

Coello laughed. "The man is a Cordilleran national, a traitor to his country, a conspirator against his lawful government. What do you do with traitors in the United States, Forester?"

"You hypocritical son-of-a-bitch," said Forester with heat. "What else are *you* doing but subverting the government?"

Coello grinned. "That is different; *I* have not been caught. Besides, I regard myself as being on the right side—the stronger side is always right, is it not? We will crush all these puling, whining liberals like Miguel Rohde and Aguillar." He bared his teeth. "In fact, we will crush Rohde now—and Aguillar in not more than forty-five minutes."

He waved to the officer in the hangar and the soldiers began to drag Rohde away. Forester began to curse Coello, but his words were destroyed in the quivering air as another plane dived on the hangar. He looked after the pitiful figure of Rohde and waited until it was quiet, then he said, "Why are you doing this?"

"Perhaps to teach you a lesson," said Coello lightly. "Let this be a warning—if you cross us, this can happen to you."

"But you're not too certain of your squadron, are you?" said Forester. "You're going to shoot Rohde and your military vanity makes you relish a firing-squad, but you can't afford a public execution—the men of the squadron might not stand for it. I'm right, aren't I?"

Coello gestured irritably. "Leave these mental probings to your bourgeois psychoanalysts."

"And you've laid on a lot of noise to drown the shots," persisted Forester as he heard another plane begin its dive.

Coello said something which was lost in the roar and Forester looked at him in horror. He did not know what to do. He could shoot Coello, but that would not help Rohde; there were more than a dozen armed men outside, and some were watching through the window. Coello laughed silently and pointed. When Forester could hear what he was saying, he shuddered. "The poor fool cannot stand, he will be shot sitting down."

"God damn you," groaned out Forester. "God damn your lousy soul to hell."

A soldier had brought up an ordinary kitchen chair which he placed against the wall, and Rohde was dragged to it and seated, his stiff leg sticking out grotesquely in front of him. A noose of rope was tossed over his head and he was bound to the chair. The soldiers left him and the officer barked out a command. The firing-squad lifted their rifles as one man and aimed, and the officer lifted his arm in the air.

Forester looked on helplessly but with horrified fascination, unable to drag his eyes away. He talked loudly, directing a stream of vicious obscenities at Coello in English and Spanish, each one viler than the last.

Another Sabre started its dive, the hand of the officer twitched and, as the noise grew to its height, he dropped his arm sharply and there was a rippling flash along the line of men. Rohde jerked convulsively in the chair as the bullets slammed into him and his body toppled on one side, taking the chair with it. The officer drew his pistol and walked over to examine the body.

Coello pulled the drawstring and the curtains closed, shutting off the hideous sight. Forester snarled, "*Hijo de puta!*"

"It will do you no good calling me names," said Coello. "Although as a man of honour I resent them and will take the appropriate steps." He smiled. "Now I will tell you the reason for this demonstration. From your rather crude observations I gather you are in sympathy with the unfortunate Rohde—the late Rohde, I should say. I was instructed to give you this test by my superior and I regret to inform you that you have failed. I think you have proved that you were not entirely sincere in the offer you made earlier, so I am afraid that you must go the same way as Rohde." His hand went to the pistol at his belt. "And after you—Aguillar. He will come to his reckoning not long from now." He began to draw the pistol. "Really, Forester, you should have known better than to——"

His words were lost in the uproar of another diving Sabre and it was then that Forester shot him, very coldly and precisely, twice in the stomach. He did not pull out the gun, but fired through the coverlet.

Coello shouted in pain and surprise and put his hands to his belly, but nothing could be heard over the tremendous racket above. Forester shot him again, this time to kill, right through the heart, and Coello rocked back as the bullet hit him and fell against the desk, dragging the blotter and the inkwell to the floor with him. He stared up with blank eyes at the ceiling, seeming to listen to the departing aircraft.

Forester slid from the stretcher and went to the door, gun in hand. Softly he turned the key, locking himself in, then he cautiously parted the curtain and looked into the hangar. The file of men—the firing-squad—were marching out, followed by the officer, and two soldiers were throwing a piece of canvas over the body of Rohde.

Forester waited until they had gone, then went to the door again and heard a shuffling of feet outside. His personal guard was still there, waiting to take him back to Coello's office or wherever Coello should direct. Something would have to be done about that.

He began to strip Coello's body, bending awkwardly in the mummy-like wrappings of tape which constricted him. His ribs hurt, but not very much, and his body seemed to

231

glory in the prospect of action. The twitchiness had gone now that he was moving about and he blessed McGruder for that enlivening injection.

He and Coello were much of a size and the flying overalls and boots fitted well enough. He strapped on the parachute and then lifted Coello on to the stretcher, covering him with the sheet carefully so that the face could not be seen. Then he put on the heavy plastic flying helmet with the dangling oxygen mask, and picked up the pistol.

When he opened the door he appeared to be having some trouble with the fastenings of the mask, for he was fumbling with the straps, his hand and the mask obscuring his face. He gestured casually with the pistol held in his other hand and said to the sentries, "*Vaya usted por alli,*" pointing to the other end of the hangar. His voice was very indistinct.

He was prepared to shoot it out if either of the soldiers showed any sign of suspicion and his finger was nervous on the trigger. The eyes of one of the men flicked momentarily to the room behind Forester, and he must have seen the shrouded body on the stretcher. Forester was counting on military obedience and the natural fear these men had for their officers. They had already witnessed one execution and if that mad dog, Coello, had held another, more private, killing, what was it to them?

The soldier clicked to attention. "*Si, mio Colonel,*" he said, and they both marched stiffly down to the end of the hangar. Forester watched them go out by the bottom door, then locked the office, thrust the pistol into the thigh pocket of the overalls and strode out of the hangar, fastening the oxygen mask as he went.

He heard the whistle of jet planes overhead and looked up to see the three Sabres circling in tight formation. As he watched they broke off into a straight course, climbing eastward over the mountains. They're not waiting for Coello, he thought; and broke into a clumsy run.

The ground crew waiting by the Sabre saw him coming and were galvanised into action. As he approached he pointed to the departing aircraft and shouted, "*Rapidemente! Dése prisa!*" He ran up to the Sabre with averted face and scrambled up to the cockpit, being surprised when one of the ground crew gave him a boost from behind.

He settled himself before the controls and looked at them; they were familiar but at the same time strange through long absence. The starter truck was already plugged in, its crew looking up at him with expectant faces. Damn, he thought; I don't know the command routine in Spanish. He closed his eyes and his hands went to the proper switches and then he waved.

Apparently that was good enough; the engine burst into noisy song and the ground crew ran to uncouple the starter cable. Another man tapped him on the helmet and closed the canopy and Forester waved again, indicating that the wheels should be unchocked. Then he was rolling, and he turned to taxi up the runway, coupling up the oxygen as he went.

At the end of the runway he switched on the radio, hoping that it was already netted in to the control tower; not that he wanted to obey any damned instructions they gave, but he wanted to know what was going on. A voice crackled in the headphones. " Colonel Coello?"

" *Si*," he mumbled.

" You are cleared for take-off."

Forester grinned, and rammed the Sabre straight down the runway. His wheels were just off the ground when all hell broke loose. The runway seemed to erupt before him for its entire length and the Sabre staggered in the air. He went into a steep, climbing turn and looked down at the airfield in astonishment. The ground was alive with the deep red flashes of violent explosions and, even as he watched, he saw the control tower shiver and disintegrate into a pile of rubble and a pillar of smoke coiled up to reach him.

He fought with the controls as a particularly violent eruption shivered the air, making the plane swerve drunkenly. " Who's started the goddam war?" he demanded of no one in particular. There was just a nervous crackle in the earphones to answer him—the control tower had cut out.

He gave up the futile questioning. Whatever it was certainly did him no harm and Eighth Squadron looked as though it was hamstrung for a long time. With one last look at the amazing spectacle on the ground, he set the Sabre in a long climb to the westward and clicked switches on the radio, searching for the other three Sabres. Two channels were apparently not in use, but he got them on the third, carrying on an idle conversation and in total ignorance of the destruction of their base, having already travelled too far to have seen the débâcle.

A sloppy, undisciplined lot, he thought; but useful. He looked down as he eavesdropped and saw the pass drifting below him, the place where he had nearly died, and decided that flying beat walking. Then he scanned the sky ahead, looking for the rest of the flight. From their talk he gathered that they were orbiting a pre-selected point while waiting for Coello and he wondered if they were already briefed on the operation or whether Coello had intended to brief them in flight. That might make a difference to his tactics.

At last he saw them orbiting the mountain by the side of the pass, but very high. He pulled gently on the control column and went to meet them. These were going to be three very surprised communists.

Chapter X

Armstrong heard trucks grinding up the mountain road. "They're coming," he said, and looked out over the breast-work of rock, his fingers curling round the butt of the gun.

The mist seemed to be thinning and he could see as far as the huts quite clearly and to where the road debouched on to the level ground; but there was still enough mist to halo the headlights even before the trucks came into view.

Benedetta ran up the tunnel and lay beside him. He said, "You'd better get back; there's nothing you can do here." He lifted the pistol. "One bullet. That's all the fighting we can do."

"They don't know that," she retorted.

"How is your uncle?" he asked.

"Better, but the altitude is not good for him." She hesitated. "I am not happy about Jenny; she is in a fever."

He said nothing; what was a fever or altitude sickness when the chances were that they would all be dead within the hour? Benedetta said, "We delayed them about three hours at the camp."

She was not really speaking sense, just making inconsequential noises to drown her own thoughts—and all her thoughts were of O'Hara. Armstrong looked at her sideways. "I'm sorry to be pessimistic," he said. "But I think this is the last act. We've done very well considering what we had to fight with, but it couldn't go on for ever. Napoleon was right—God is on the side of the big battalions."

Her voice was savage. "We can still take some of them
234

with us." She grasped his arm. "Look, they're coming."

The first vehicle was breasting the top of the rise. It was quite small and Armstrong judged it was a jeep. It came forward, its headlights probing the mist, and behind it came a big truck, and then another. He heard shouted commands and the trucks rolled as far as the huts and stopped, and he saw men climbing out and heard the clatter of boots on rock.

The jeep curved in a great arc, its lights cutting a swathe like a scythe, and Armstrong suddenly realised that it was searching the base of the cliffs where the tunnels were. Before he knew it he was fully illuminated, and as he dodged back into cover, he heard the animal roar of triumph from the enemy as he was seen.

"Damn!" he said. "I was stupid."

"It does not matter," Benedetta said. "They would have found us soon." She lay down and cautiously pulled a rock from the pile. "I think I can see through here," she whispered. "There is no need to put your head up."

Armstrong heard steps from behind as Willis came up. "Keep down," he said quietly. "Flat on your stomach."

Willis wriggled alongside him. "What's going on?"

"They've spotted us," said Armstrong. "They're deploying out there; getting ready to attack." He laughed humourlessly. "If they knew what we had to defend ourselves with, they'd just walk in."

"There's another truck coming," said Benedetta bitterly. "I suppose it's bringing more men; they need an army to crush us."

"Let me see," said Armstrong. Benedetta rolled away from the spy-hole and Armstrong looked through. "It's got no lights—that's odd; and it's moving fast. Now it's changing direction and going towards the huts. It doesn't seem to be slowing down."

They could hear the roar of the engine, and Armstrong yelled, "It's going faster—it's going to smash into them." His voice cracked on a scream. "Do you think it could be O'Hara?"

O'Hara held tight to the jolting wheel and rammed the accelerator to the floorboards. He had been making for the jeep but then he had seen something much more important; in the light of the truck headlights a group of men were assembling a light machine-gun. He swung the wheel and the truck swerved, two wheels coming off the ground and then bouncing back with a spine-jolting crash. The truck swayed alarmingly, but he held it on its new course and switched on his lights and saw the white faces of men turn towards him and their hands go up to shield their eyes from the glare.

Then they were running aside but two of them were too late and he heard the squashy thumps as the front of the truck hit them. But he was not concerned with men—he wanted the gun—and the truck lifted a little as he drove the off-side wheels over the machine-gun, grinding it into the rock. Then he had gone past and there was a belated and thin scattering of shots from behind.

He looked for the jeep, hauled the wheel round again, and the careering truck swung and went forward like a projectile. The driver of the jeep saw him coming and tried to run for it; the jeep shot forward, but O'Hara swerved again and the jeep was fully illuminated as he made for a head-on crash. He saw the Russian point a pistol and there was a flash and the truck windscreen starred in front of his face. He ducked involuntarily.

The driver of the jeep swung his wheel desperately, but turned the wrong way and came up against the base of the cliff. The jeep spun again, but the mistake had given O'Hara his chance and he charged forward to ram the jeep broadside on. He saw the Russian throw up his arms and disappear from sight as the light vehicle was hurled on its side with a tearing and rending sound, and then O'Hara had slammed into reverse and was backing away.

He looked back towards the trucks and saw a mob of men running towards him, so he picked up the sub-machine-gun from the floor of the cab and steadied it on the edge of the window. He squeezed the trigger three times, altering his aim slightly between bursts, and the mob broke up into fragments, individual men rolling on the open ground and desperately seeking cover.

As O'Hara engaged in bottom gear, a bullet tore through the body of the truck, and then another, but he took no notice. The front of the truck slammed into the overturned jeep again, catching it on the underside of the chassis. Remorselessly O'Hara pushed forward using the truck as a bulldozer and mashed the jeep against the cliff face with a dull crunching noise. When he had finished no human sounds came from the crushed vehicle.

But that act of anger and revenge was nearly the end of

him. By the time he had reversed the truck and swung clear again he was under heavy fire. He rolled forward and tried to zigzag, but the truck was slow in picking up speed and a barrage of fire came from the semi-circle of men surrounding him. The windscreen shattered into opacity and he could not see where he was heading.

Benedetta, Armstrong and Willis were on their feet yelling, but no bullets came their way—they were not as dangerous as O'Hara. They watched the truck weaving drunkenly and saw sparks fly as steel-jacketed bullets ricocheted from the metal armour Santos had installed. Willis shouted, " He's in trouble," and before they could stop him he had vaulted the rock wall and was running for the truck.

O'Hara was steering with one hand and using the butt of the sub-machine-gun as a hammer in an attempt to smash the useless windscreen before him. Willis leaped on the running-board and just as his fingers grasped the edge of the door O'Hara was hit. A rifle bullet flew the width of the cab and smashed his shoulder, slamming him into the door and nearly upsetting Willis's balance. He gave a great cry and slumped down in his seat.

Willis grabbed the wheel with one hand, turned it awkwardly. He shouted, " Keep your foot on the accelerator," and O'Hara heard him through a dark mist of pain and pushed down with his foot. Willis turned the truck towards the cliff and tried to head for the tunnel. He saw the rear view mirror disintegrate and he knew that the bullet that had hit it had passed between his body and the truck. That did not seem to matter—all that mattered was to get the truck into cover.

Armstrong saw the truck turn and head towards him. "Run," he shouted to Benedetta, and took to his heels, dragging her by the hand and making down the tunnel.

Willis saw the mouth of the tunnel yawn darkly before him and pressed closer to the body of the truck. As the nose of the truck hit the low wall, rocks exploded into the interior, splintering against the tunnel sides.

Then Willis was hit. The bullet took him in the small of the back and he let go of the wheel and the edge of the door. In the next instant, as the truck roared into the tunnel to crash at the bend, Willis was wiped off the running-board by the rock face and was flung in a crumpled heap to the ground just by the entrance.

He stirred slightly as a bullet clipped the rock just above his

head and his hands groped forward helplessly, the fingers
scrabbling at the cold rock. Then two bullets hit him almost
simultaneously and he jerked once and was still.

II

It seemed enormously quiet as Armstrong and Benedetta dragged O'Hara from the cab of the truck. The shooting had
stopped and there was no sound at all apart from the creakings
of the cooling engine and the clatter as Armstrong kicked
something loose on the floor of the cab. They were working
in darkness because a well-directed shot straight down the
tunnel would be dangerous.

At last they got O'Hara into safety round the corner and
Benedetta lit the wick of the last paraffin bottle. O'Hara was
unconscious and badly injured; his right arm hung limp
and his shoulder was a ghastly mess of torn flesh and splintered
bone. His face was badly cut too, because he had been thrown
forward when the truck had crashed at the bend of the tunnel
and Benedetta looked at him with tears in her eyes and
wondered where to start.

Aguillar tottered forward, the breath wheezing in his
chest, and said with difficulty, " In the name of God, what has
happened?"

"You cannot help, tío," she said. "Lie down again."

Aguillar looked down at O'Hara with shocked eyes—it
was brought home to him that war is a bloody business. Then
he said, "Where is Señor Willis?"

"I think he's dead," said Armstrong quietly. "He didn't
come back."

Aguillar sank down silently next to O'Hara, his face grey.
"Let me help," he said.

"I'll go back on watch," said Armstrong. "Though what
use that will be I don't know. It'll be dark soon. I suppose
that's what they're waiting for."

He went away into the darkness towards the truck, and
Benedetta examined O'Hara's shattered shoulder. She looked
up at Aguillar helplessly. "What can I do? This needs a
doctor—a hospital; we cannot do anything here."

"We must do what we can," said Aguillar. "Before he
recovers consciousness. Bring the light closer."

He began to pick out fragments of bone from the bloody
flesh and by the time he had finished and Benedetta had

238

bandaged the wound and put the arm in a sling O'Hara was wide awake, suppressing his groans. He looked up at Benedetta and whispered, " Where's Willis?"

She shook her head slowly and O'Hara turned his face away. He felt a growing rage within him at the unfairness of things; just when he had found life again he must leave it—and what a way to leave; cooped up in a cold, dank tunnel at the mercy of human wolves. From nearby he could hear a woman babbling incoherently. " Who is that?"

" Jenny," said Benedetta. " She is delirious."

They made O'Hara as comfortable as possible and then Benedetta stood up. " I must help Armstrong." Aguillar looked up and saw that her face was taut with anger and fatigue, the skin drawn tightly over her cheekbones and dark smudges below her eyes. He sighed softly and nipped the guttering wick into darkness.

Armstrong was crouched by the truck. " I was waiting for someone," he said.

" Who were you expecting?" she said sarcastically. " We two are the only able-bodied left." Then she said in a low voice. " I'm sorry."

" That's all right," said Armstrong. " How's Tim?"

Her voice was bitter. " He'll live—if he's allowed to."

Armstrong said nothing for a long time, allowing the anger and frustration to seep from her, then he said, " Everything's quiet; they haven't made a move and I don't understand it. I'd like to go up there and have a look when it gets really dark outside."

" Don't be an idiot," said Benedetta in alarm. " What can a defenceless man do?"

" Oh, I wouldn't start anything," said Armstrong. " And I wouldn't be exactly defenceless. Tim had one of those little machine-guns with him, and I think there are some full magazines. I haven't been able to find out how it works in the dark; I think I'll go back and examine it in the light of our lamp. The crossbow is here, too; and a couple of bolts—I'll leave those here with you."

She took his arm. " Don't leave yet."

He caught the loneliness and desolation in her voice and subsided. Presently he said, " Who would have thought that Willis would do a thing like that? It was the act of a really brave man and I never thought he was that."

" Who knows what lies inside a man?" said Benedetta softly, and Armstrong knew she was thinking of O'Hara.

He stayed with her a while and talked the tension out of her, then went back and lit the lamp. O'Hara looked across at him with pain-filled eyes. " Has the truck had it?"

" I don't know," said Armstrong. " I haven't looked yet."

" I thought we might make a getaway in it," said O'Hara.

" I'll have a look at it. I don't think it took much damage from the knocks it had—those chaps had it pretty well armoured against our crossbow bolts. But I don't think the bullets did it any good; the armour wouldn't be proof against those."

Aguillar came closer. " Perhaps we might try in the darkness—to get away, I mean."

" Where to?" asked Armstrong practically. " They'll have the bridge covered—and I wouldn't like to take a truck across that at night—it would be suicidal. And they'll have plenty of light up here, too; they'll keep the entrance to the tunnel well covered." He rubbed the top of his head. " I don't know why they don't just come in and take us right now."

" I think I killed the top man," said O'Hara. " I hope I did. And I don't think Santos has the stomach to push in here—he's scared of what he might meet."

" Who is Santos?" asked Aguillar.

" The Cuban." O'Hara smiled weakly. " I got pretty close to him down below."

" You did a lot of damage when you came up in the truck," observed Armstrong. " I don't wonder they're scared. Maybe they'll give up."

" Not now," said O'Hara with conviction. " They're too close to success to give up now. Anyway, all they have to do now is to camp outside and starve us out."

They were silent for a long time thinking about that, then Armstrong said, " I'd rather go down in glory." He pulled forward the sub-machine-gun. " Do you know how this thing works?"

O'Hara showed him how to work the simple mechanism, and when he had gone back to his post Aguillar said, " I am sorry about your shoulder, señor."

O'Hara bared his teeth in a brief grin. " Not as sorry as I am—it hurts like the devil. But it doesn't matter, you know; I'm not likely to feel pain for long."

Aguillar's asthmatical wheezing stopped momentarily as he caught his breath. " Then you think this is the end?"

" I do."

" A pity, señor. I could have made much use of you in the

new Cordillera. A man in my position needs good men—they are as hard to find as the teeth of a hen."

"What use would a broken-down pilot be to you? Men like me come ten a penny."

"I do not think so," said Aguillar seriously. "You have shown much initiative in this engagement and that is a commodity which is scarce. As you know, the military forces of Cordillera are rotten with politics and I need men to lift them out of the political arena—especially the fighter squadrons. If you wish to stay in Cordillera, I think I can promise you a position in the Air Force."

For a moment O'Hara forgot that the hours—and perhaps minutes—of his life were measured. He said simply, "I'd like that."

"I'm glad," said Aguillar. "Your first task would be to straighten out Eighth Squadron. But you must not think that because you are marrying into the President's family that the way will be made easy for you." He chuckled as he felt O'Hara start. "I know my niece very well, Tim. Never has she felt about a man as she feels about you. I hope you will be very happy together."

"We will be," said O'Hara, then fell silent as reality flooded upon him once more—the realisation that all this talk of marriage and future plans was futile. After a while, he said wistfully, "These are pipe dreams, Señor Aguillar; reality is much more frightening. But I do wish . . ."

"We are still alive," said Aguillar. "And while the blood runs in a man nothing is impossible for him."

He said nothing more and O'Hara heard only the rasping of his breath in the darkness.

III

When Armstrong joined Benedetta he looked towards the entrance of the tunnel and saw that night had fallen and there was a bright glare of headlamps flooding the opening. He strained his eyes and said, "The mist seems to be thickening, don't you think?"

"I think so," said Benedetta listlessly.

"Now's the time to scout around," he said.

"Don't," Benedetta implored him. "They'll see you."

"I don't think they can; the mist is throwing the light back at them. They'd see me if I went outside, but I don't

241

intend to do that. I don't think they can see a damned thing in the tunnel."

"All right, then. But be careful."

He smiled as he crawled forward. In their circumstances the word "careful" seemed ridiculous. It was like telling a man who had jumped from an aeroplane without a parachute to be careful. All the same, he was most careful to make no noise as he inched his way towards the entrance, hampered by the shattered remnants of the rock wall.

He stopped some ten yards short of the opening, knowing that to go farther would be too risky, and peered into the misty brightness. At first he could see nothing, but by shielding his eyes from the worst of the glare he managed to pick out some details. Two trucks were parked at an angle to the cliff, one on each side of the tunnel, and when the light from the left truck flickered he knew someone had walked in front of it.

He stayed there for some time and twice he made deliberate movements, but it was as he thought—he could not be seen. After a while he began to crawl about gathering rocks, which he built up into a low wall, barely eighteen inches high. It was not much but it would give solid protection against rifle fire to anyone lying behind it. This took him a long time and there was no action from outside; occasionally he heard a man coughing, and sometimes the sound of voices, but apart from that there was nothing.

Eventually he picked up the sub-machine-gun and went back to the truck. Benedetta whispered from the darkness, "What are they doing?"

"Damned if I know," he said, and looked back. "It's too quiet out there. Keep a good watch; I'm going to have a look at the truck."

He squeezed her hand and then groped his way to the cab of the truck and climbed inside. Everything seemed to be all right, as far as he could judge, barring the windscreen which could not be seen through. He sat in the driving-seat and thought about what would happen if they had to make a break for it.

To begin with, he would be driving—there was no one else who could handle the truck—and he would have to reverse out of the tunnel. There would be one man in the passenger seat beside him and the others in the back.

He examined the rest of the truck, more by feel than sight. Two of the tyres had been badly scored by bullets but miraculously the inner tubes had not been penetrated. The petrol tanks, too, were intact, protected by the deep skirts of mild steel, added to guard against crossbow bolts.

He had fears about the radiator, but a groping journey under the truck revealed no fatal drip of water and he was reassured about that. His only worries were that the final crash might have damaged the steering or the engine, but those could not be tested until the time came to go. He did not want to start the engine now—let sleeping dogs lie, he thought.

He rejoined Benedetta. "That's that," he said with satisfaction. "She seems to be in good fettle. I'll take over here. You'd better see how the others are."

She turned immediately, and he knew she was eager to get back to O'Hara.

"Wait a minute," he said. "You'd better know the drill if we have to make a sudden move." He lifted the gun. "Can you use this?"

"I don't know."

Armstrong chuckled. "I don't know if I can, either—it's too modern for me. But O'Hara reckons it's easy enough; you just pull the trigger and let her go. He says it takes a bit of holding down and you must be careful to slip off the safety-catch. Now, I'll be driving, with your uncle sitting next to me on the floor of the cab. Tim and Jenny will be in the back, flat on the floor. And there'll be you in the back, too—with this gun. It'll be a bit dangerous—you'll have to show yourself if you shoot."

Her voice was stony. "I'll shoot."

"Good girl," he said, and patted her on the shoulder. "Give Tim my love when you give him yours." He heard her go, then moved up the tunnel to the wall he had built and lay behind it, the sub-machine-gun ready to hand. He put his hand in his pocket and felt for his pipe, then uttered a muffled "Damn!" It was broken, the two pieces separate in his hand. He put the stem in his mouth and chewed on the mouthpiece, never taking his eyes from the entrance.

IV

The day dawned mistily, a dazzling whiteness at the mouth of the tunnel, and Armstrong shifted his position for the hundredth time, trying to find a place to ease his aching bones. He glanced across at O'Hara on the other side of the tunnel and thought, it's worse for him than for me.

When O'Hara had heard of the rebuilt wall he had insisted on moving there. "I haven't a hope of sleep," he said. "Not with this shoulder. And I've got a fully loaded pistol. I might as well stand—or lie—sentry out there as just lie here. I should be of some use, even if only to allow everyone else to get some sleep."

But in spite of that Armstrong had not slept. He ached too much to sleep, even though he felt more exhausted than ever before in his life, but he smiled cheerily at O'Hara in the growing light and lifted his head above the low barricade.

There was nothing to be seen except the white swirling mist, an impenetrable curtain. He said softly, "Tim, why didn't they jump us in the night?"

"They know we have this gun," said O'Hara. "I wouldn't like to come running into this tunnel knowing that—especially at night."

"Um," said Armstrong in an unconvinced tone. "But why haven't they tried to soften us up with rifle fire? They must know that any fire directed into this tunnel will ricochet from the walls—they don't have to be too accurate."

O'Hara was silent, and Armstrong continued reflectively: "I wonder if there is anyone out there?"

"Don't be a damn' fool," said O'Hara. "That's something we can't take a chance on—not yet. Besides, there was someone to turn the lights off not very long ago."

"True," said Armstrong, and turned as he heard a movement in the tunnel, and Benedetta crawled up holding a bundle in her arms.

"The last of the food," she said. "There's not much—and we have no water at all."

Armstrong's mouth turned down. "That's bad."

As he and O'Hara shared the food they heard a stirring outside and the murmur of voices. "Changing the guard," said O'Hara. "I heard it before about four hours ago when you were asleep. They're still there, all right."

"Me! Asleep!" said Armstrong in an aggrieved voice. "I didn't sleep a wink all night."

O'Hara smiled. "You got three or four winks out of the forty." He became serious. "If we really need water we can drain some from the truck radiator, but I wouldn't do that unless absolutely necessary."

Benedetta regarded O'Hara with worry in her eyes. He had a hectic flush and looked too animated for a man who had nearly been shot to death. Miss Ponsky had had the same reaction, and now she was off her head with delirium, unable to eat and crying for water. She said, " I think we ought to have water now; Jenny needs it."

" In that case we'll tap the radiator," said Armstrong. " I hope the anti-freeze compound isn't poisonous; I think it's just alcohol, so it should be all right."

He crawled back with Benedetta and squeezed underneath the truck to unscrew the drain-cock. He tapped out half a can of rusty-looking water and passed it to her. " That will have to do," he said. " We can't take too much—we might need the truck."

The day wore on and nothing happened. Gradually the mist cleared under the strengthening sun and then they could see out of the tunnel, and Armstrong's hopes were shattered as he saw a group of men standing by the huts. Even from their restricted view they could see that the enemy was in full strength.

" But can they see us?" mused O'Hara. " I don't think they can. This cavern must look as dark as the Black Hole of Calcutta from outside."

" What the devil are they doing?" asked Armstrong, his eyes level with the top of a rock.

O'Hara watched for a long time, then he said in wonder, " They're piling rocks on the ground—apart from that they're doing nothing."

They watched for a long time and all the enemy did was to pile stones in a long line stretching away from the tunnel. After a while they appeared to tire of that and congregated into small groups, chatting and smoking. They seemed to have the appearance of men waiting for something, but why they were waiting or what the rocks were for neither O'Hara nor Armstrong could imagine.

It was midday when Armstrong, his nerves cracking under the strain, said, " For God's sake, let's do something—something constructive."

O'Hara's voice was flat and tired. " What?"

" If we're going to make a break in the truck we might have to do it quickly. I suggest we put Jenny in the back of the truck right away, and get the old man settled in the front seat. Come to think of it, he'll be a damn sight more comfortable on a soft seat."

O'Hara nodded. " All right. Leave that sub-machine-gun with me. I might need it."

Armstrong went back to the truck, walking upright. To

hell with crawling on my belly like a snake, he thought; let me walk like a man for once. The enemy either did not see or saw and did not care. No shots were fired.

He saw Miss Ponsky safely into the back of the truck and then he escorted Aguillar to the cab. Aguillar was in a bad way, much worse than he had been. His speech was incoherent and his breathing was bad; he was in a daze and did not appear to know where he was. Benedetta was pale and worried and stayed to look after him.

When Armstrong dropped behind the rock wall, he said, " If we don't get out of here soon that bloody crowd will have won."

O'Hara jerked his head in surprise. "Why?"

" Aguillar—he looks on the verge of a heart attack; if he doesn't get down to where he can breathe more easily he'll peg out."

O'Hara looked outside and gestured with his good arm. " There are nearly two dozen men within sight; they'd shoot hell out of us if we tried to break out now. Look at what happened to me yesterday when they were hampered by mist —there's no mist now and we wouldn't stand a chance. We'll have to wait."

So they waited—and so did the enemy. And the day went on, the sun sloping back overhead into mid-afternoon. It was three o'clock when O'Hara stirred and then relaxed and shook his head. " I thought . . . but no."

He settled himself down, but a moment later his head jerked up again. " It *is*—can't you hear it?"

" Hear what?" asked Armstrong.

" A plane—or planes," said O'Hara excitedly.

Armstrong listened and caught the shrill whine of a jet plane passing overhead, the noise muffled and distorted. " By God, you're right," he said. He looked at O'Hara in sudden consternation. " Ours or theirs?"

But O'Hara had already seen their doom. He leaned up and looked, horrified, to the mouth of the tunnel. Framed in the opening against the sky was a diving plane coming head on and, as he watched, he saw something drop from each wing, and a spurt of vapour.

" Rockets!" he screamed. " For Christ's sake, get down!"

Forester had climbed to meet the three Sabres and as he approached they saw him and fell into a loose formation and awaited him. He came in from behind and increased speed, getting the leader in his sights. He flicked off the safety switches and his thumb caressed the firing-button. This boy would never know what hit him.

All the time there was a continual jabber in his ear-phones as the leader called Coello. At last, assuming that Coello's radio was at fault, he said, "Since you are silent, *mio Colonel*, I will lead the attack." It was then that Forester knew that these men had been briefed on the ground—and he pressed the firing-button.

Once again he felt the familiar jolt in the air, almost a halt, and saw the tracer shells streaking and corkscrewing towards their target. The leading Sabre was a-dance with coruscations of light as the shells burst, and suddenly it blew up in a gout of black smoke with a red heart at the centre.

Forester weaved to avoid wreckage and then went into a sharp turn and climbed rapidly, listening to the horrified exclamations from the other pilots. They babbled for a few moments then one of them said, "Silence. I will take him."

Forester searched the skies and thought—he's quick off the mark. He felt chilled; these boys would be young and have fast reflexes and they would be trained to a hair. He had not flown for nearly ten years, beyond the few annual hours necessary to keep up his rating, and he wondered grimly how long he would last.

He found his enemies. One was swooping in a graceful dive towards the ground and the other was climbing in a wide circle to get behind him. As he watched, the pilot fired his rockets aimlessly. "Oh, no, you don't, you bastard," said Forester. "You don't catch me like that." He knew his opponent had jettisoned his rockets in order to reduce weight and drag and to gain speed. For a moment he was tempted to do the same and to fight it out up there in the clean sky, but he knew he could not take the chance. Besides he had a better use for his rockets.

Instead, he pushed the control column forward and went into a screaming dive. This was dangerous—his opponent would be faster in the dive and it had been drilled into Forester never, *never* to lose height while in combat. He kept his eyes on the mirror and soon the Sabre came into view behind, catching up fast. He waited until the very last moment, until he was sure he was about to be fired on, then pushed the stick forward again and went into a suicidal vertical dive.

His opponent overshot him, taken unaware by the craziness of this manœuvre performed so near the ground. Forester ignored him, confident that he had lost him for the time being; he was more concerned with preventing his plane from splattering itself all over the mountainside. He felt juddering begin as the Sabre approached the sound barrier; the whole fabric of the plane groaned as he dragged it out of the dive and he hoped the wings would not come off.

By the time he was flying level the ground was a scant two hundred feet below, snow and rock merging together in a grey blur. He lifted the Sabre up a few hundred feet and circled widely away from the mountains, looking for the gorge and the bridge. He spotted the gorge immediately—it was too unmistakable to be missed, and a minute later he saw the bridge. He turned over it, scanning the ground, but saw no one, and then it was gone behind and he lifted up to the slope of the mountain, flying over the winding road he had laboriously tramped so often.

Abruptly he changed course, wanting to approach the mine parallel to the mountainside, and as he did so he looked up and saw a Sabre a thousand feet higher, launching two rockets. That's the second one, he thought. I was too late.

He turned again and screamed over the mine, the air-strip unwinding close below. Ahead were the huts and some trucks and a great arrow made of piled rocks pointing to the cliff face. And at the head of the arrow a boiling cloud of smoke and dust where the rockets had driven home into the cliff. "Jesus!" he said involuntarily, "I hope they survived that."

Then he had flashed over and went into a turn to come back. Come back he did with an enemy hammering on his heels. The Sabre he had eluded high in the sky had found him again and its guns were already crackling. But the range was too great and he knew that the other pilot, tricked before, was now waiting for him to play some other trick. This sign of inexperience gave him hope, but the other Sabre was faster and he must drop his rockets.

He had seen a good, unsuspecting target, yet to hit it he would have to come in on a smooth dive and stood a good chance of being hit by his pursuer. His lips curled back over his teeth and he held his course, sighting on the trucks and the huts and the group of men standing in their shelter. With one hand he flicked the rocket-arming switches and then fired, almost in the same instant.

The salvo of rockets streaked from under his wings, spearing down towards the trucks and the men who were looking up and waving. At the last moment, when they saw death coming from the sky, they broke and ran—but it was too late. Eight rockets exploded among them and as Forester roared overhead he saw a three-ton truck heave bodily into the air to fall on its side. He laughed out loud; a rocket that would stop a tank dead in its tracks would certainly shatter a truck.

The Sabre felt more handy immediately the rockets were gone and he felt the increase in speed. He put the nose down and screamed along the airstrip at zero feet, not looking back to see the damage he had done and striving to elude his pursuer by flying as low as he dared. At the end of the runway he dipped even lower over the wreckage of the Dakota and skidded in a frantic sideslip round the mountainside.

He looked in the mirror and saw his opponent take the corner more widely and much higher. Forester grinned; the bastard hadn't dared to come down on the deck and so he couldn't bring his guns to bear and he'd lost distance by his wide turn. Now to do him.

He fled up the mountainside parallel with the slope and barely twenty feet from the ground. It was risky, for there were jutting outcrops of rock which stretched out black fangs to tear out the belly of the Sabre if he made the slightest miscalculation. During the brief half-minute it took to reach clear sky, sweat formed on his forehead.

Then he was free of the mountain, and his enemy stooped to make his kill, but Forester was expecting it and went into a soaring vertical climb with a quick roll on top of the loop and was heading away in the opposite direction. He glanced back and grinned in satisfaction; he had tested the enemy and found him wanting—that young man would not take risks and Forester knew he could take him, so he went in for the kill.

It was brief and brutal. He turned to meet the oncoming plane and made as though to ram deliberately. At the closing speed of nearly fifteen hundred miles an hour the other pilot flinched as Forester knew he would, and swerved aside. By the time he had recovered Forester was on his tail and the end was mercifully quick—a sharp burst from the cannons at

minimum range and the inevitable explosion in mid-air
Again Forester swerved to avoid wreckage. As he climbed to
get his bearings, he reflected that battle experience still counted
for a lot and the assessment of personality for still more.

Armstrong was deaf; the echoes of that vast explosion still
rumbled in the innermost recesses of the tunnel but he did not
hear them. Nor could he see much because of the coils of dust
which thickened the air. His hands were vainly clutching the
hard rock of the tunnel floor as he pressed himself to the
ground and his mind felt shattered.

It was O'Hara who recovered first. Finding himself still
alive and able to move, he raised his head to look at the
tunnel entrance. Light showed dimly through the dust. He
missed, he thought vacantly; the rockets missed—but not by
much. Then he shook his head to clear it and stumbled across
to Armstrong who was still grovelling on the ground. He
shook him by the shoulder. "Back to the truck," he shouted.
"We've got to get out. He won't miss the second time
round."

Armstrong lifted his head and gazed at O'Hara dumbly,
and O'Hara pointed back to the truck and made a dumb show
of driving. He got to his feet shakily and followed O'Hara,
still feeling his head ringing from the violence of the explosion.

O'Hara yelled, "Benedetta—into the truck." He saw her
in and handed her the sub-machine-gun, then climbed in
himself with her aid and lay down next to Miss Ponsky.
Outside he heard the scream of a jet going by and a series of
explosions in the distance. He hoped that Armstrong was in
a condition to drive.

Armstrong climbed into the cab and felt the presence of
Aguillar in the next seat. "On the floor," he said, pushing
him down, and then his attention was wholly absorbed by
the task before him. He pressed the starter-button and the
starter whined and groaned. He stabbed it again and again
until, just as he was giving up hope, the engine fired with
a coughing roar.

Putting the gears into reverse, he leaned out of the cab and
gazed back towards the entrance and let out the clutch. The
truck bumped backwards clumsily and scraped the side wall.
He hauled on the wheel and tried to steer a straight course

for the entrance—as far as he could tell the steering had not been damaged and it did not take long to do the fifty yards. Then he stopped just short of the mouth of the tunnel in preparation for the dash into the open.

Benedetta gripped the unfamiliar weapon in her hands and held it ready, crouching down in the back of the truck. O'Hara was sitting up, a pistol in his good hand; he knew that if he lay down he would have difficulty in getting up again—he could only use one arm for leverage. Miss Ponsky was mercifully unaware of what was going on; she babbled a little in her stupor and then fell silent as the truck backed jerkily into the open and turned.

O'Hara heard Armstrong battering at the useless windscreen and prepared himself for a fusillade of rifle fire. Nothing came and he looked round and what he saw made him blink incredulously. It was a sight he had seen before but he had not expected to see it here. The huts and the trucks were shattered and wrecked and bodies lay about them. From a wounded man there came a mournful keening and there were only two men left on their feet, staggering about blindly and in a daze. He looked the awful scene over with a professional eye and knew that an aircraft had fired a ripple of eight rockets at this target, blasting it thoroughly.

He yelled, "Armstrong—get the hell out of here while we can," then sagged back and grinned at Benedetta. "One of those fighter boys made a mistake and hammered the wrong target; he's going to get a strip torn off him when he gets back to base."

Armstrong smashed enough of the windscreen away so that he could see ahead, then put the truck into gear and went forward, turning to go past the huts and down the road. He looked in fascinated horror at the wreckage until it was past and then applied himself to the task of driving an unfamiliar and awkward vehicle down a rough mountain road with its multitude of hairpin bends. As he went, he heard a jet plane whine overhead very low and he tensed, waiting for the slam of more explosions, but nothing happened and the plane went out of hearing.

Above, Forester saw the truck move off. One of them still left, he thought; and dived, his thumb ready on the firing-button. At the last moment he saw the streaming hair of a woman standing in the back and hastily removed his thumb as he screamed over the truck. My God, that was Benedetta—they've got themselves a truck.

He pulled the Sabre into a climb and looked about. He had not forgotten the third plane and hoped it had been scared off because a strange lassitude was creeping over him and he knew that the effects of McGruder's stimulant were wearing off. He tried to ease the ache in his chest while circling to keep an eye on the truck as it bounced down the mountain road.

O'Hara looked up at the circling Sabre. "I don't know what to make of that chap," he said. "He must know we're here, but he's doing nothing about it."

"He must think we're on his side," said Benedetta. "He must think that of anyone in a truck."

"That sounds logical," O'Hara agreed. "But someone did a good job of working over our friends up on top and it wasn't a mistake an experienced pilot would make." He winced as the truck jolted his shoulder. "We'd better prepare to pile out if he shows signs of coming in to strafe us. Can you arrange signals with Armstrong?"

Benedetta turned and hung over the side, craning her neck to see Armstrong at the wheel. "We might be attacked from the air," she shouted. "How can we stop you?"

Armstrong slowed for a nasty corner. "Thump like hell on top of the cab—I'll stop quick enough. I'm going to stop before we get to the camp, anyway; there might be someone laying for us down there."

Benedetta relayed this to O'Hara and he nodded. "A pity I can't use that thing," he said, indicating the sub-machine-gun. "If you have to shoot, hold it down; it kicks like the devil and you'll find yourself spraying the sky if you aren't careful."

He looked up at her. The wind was streaming her black hair and moulding the tattered dress to her body. She was cradling the sub-machine-gun in her hands and looking up at the plane and he thought in sudden astonishment, My God, a bloody Amazon—she looks like a recruiting poster for partisans. He thought of Aguillar's offer of an Air Force commission and had a sudden and irrational conviction that they would come through this nightmare safely.

Benedetta threw up her hand and cried in a voice of despair, "Another one—another plane."

O'Hara jerked his head and saw another Sabre curving overhead much higher and the first Sabre going to join it. Benedetta said bitterly, "Always they must hunt in packs—even when they know we are defenceless."

252

But O'Hara, studying the manœuvring of the two aircraft with a war-experienced eye, was not sure about that. "They're going to fight," he said with wonder. "They're jockeying for position. By God, they're going to fight each other." His raised and incredulous voice was sharply punctuated by the distant clatter of automatic cannon.

Forester had almost been caught napping. He had only seen the third enemy Sabre when it was much too close for comfort and he desperately climbed to get the advantage of height. As it was, the enemy fired first and there was a thump and a large, ragged hole magically appeared in his wing as a cannon shell exploded. He side-slipped evasively, then drove his plane into a sharp, climbing turn.

Below, O'Hara yelled excitedly and thumped with his free hand on the side of the cab. "Forester and Rohde—they've got across the mountain—they must have."

The truck jolted to a sudden stop and Armstrong shot out of the cab like a startled jack-rabbit and dived into the side of the road. From the other side Aguillar stepped down painfully into the road and was walking away slowly when he heard the excited shouts from the truck. He turned and then looked upwards to the embattled Sabres.

The fight was drifting westward and presently the two aircraft disappeared from sight over the mountain, leaving only the white inscription of vapour trails in the blue sky. Armstrong came up to the side of the truck. "What the devil's happening?" he asked with annoyance. "I got the fright of my life when you thumped on the cab."

"I'm damned if I know," said O'Hara helplessly. "But some of these planes seem to be on our side; a couple are having a dogfight now." He threw out his arm. "Look, here they come again."

The two Sabres were much lower as they came in sight round the mountain, one in hot pursuit of the other. There was a flickering on the wings of the rear plane as the cannon hammered and suddenly a stream of oily smoke burst from the leading craft. It dropped lower and a black speck shot upwards. "He's bailed out," said O'Hara. "He's had it."

The pursuing Sabre pulled up in a climb, but the crippled plane settled into a steepening dive to crash on the mountain-side. A pillar of black, greasy smoke marked the wreck and a parachute, suddenly opened, drifted across the sky like a blown dandelion seed.

Armstrong looked up and watched the departing victor

which was easing into a long turn, obviously intent on coming back. "That's all very well," he said worriedly. "But who won—us or them?"

"Everyone out," said O'Hara decisively. "Armstrong, give Benedetta a hand with Jenny."

But they had no time, for suddenly the Sabre was upon them, roaring overhead in a slow roll. O'Hara, who was cradling Miss Ponsky's head with his free arm, blew out his breath expressively. "Our side seems to have won that one," he said. "But I'd like to know who the hell our side is." He watched the Sabre coming back, dipping its wings from side to side. "Of course, it *couldn't* be Forester—that's impossible. A pity. He always wanted to become an ace, to make his fifth kill."

The plane dipped and turned as it came over again and headed down the mountain and presently they heard cannon-fire again. "Everyone in the truck," commanded O'Hara. "He's shooting up the camp—we'll have no trouble there. Armstrong, you get going and don't stop for a damned thing until we're on the other side of the bridge." He laughed delightedly. "We've got air cover now."

They pressed on and passed the camp. There was a fiercely burning truck by the side of the road, but no sign of anyone living. Half an hour later they approached the bridge and Armstrong drew to a slow halt by the abutments, looking about him anxiously. He heard the Sabre going over again and was reassured, so he put the truck into gear and slowly inched his way on to the frail and unsubstantial structure.

Overhead, Forester watched the slow progress of the truck as it crossed the bridge. He thought there was a wind blowing down there because the bridge seemed to sway and shiver, but perhaps it was only his tired eyes playing tricks. He cast an anxious eye on his fuel gauges and decided it was time to put the plane down—and he hoped he could put it down in one piece. He felt desperately tired and his whole body ached.

Making one last pass at the bridge to make sure that all was well, he headed away following the road, and had gone only a few miles when he saw a convoy of vehicles coming up, some of them conspicuously marked with the Red Cross. So that's that, he thought; McGruder got through and someone got on the phone to this side of the mountains and stirred things up. It couldn't possibly be another batch of communists—what would they want with ambulances?

He lifted his eyes and looked ahead for flat ground and a place to land.

Aguillar watched Armstrong's face lighten as the wheels of the truck rolled off the bridge and they were at last on the other side of the river. So many good people, he thought; and so many good ones dead—the Coughlins, Señor Willis—Miss Ponsky so dreadfully wounded and O'Hara also. But O'Hara would be all right; Benedetta would see to that. He smiled as he thought of them, of all the years of their future happiness. And then there were the others, too—Miguel and the two Americans, Forester and Peabody. The State of Cordillera would honour them all—yes, even Peabody, and especially Miguel Rohde.

It would be much later that he heard of what had happened to Peabody—and to Rohde.

O'Hara looked at Miss Ponsky. "Will she be all right?"

"The wound is clean—not as bad as yours, Tim. A hospital will do you both a lot of good." Benedetta fell silent. "What will you do now?"

"I suppose I should go back to San Croce to hand my resignation to Filson—and to punch him on the nose, too—but I don't think I will. He's not worth it, so I won't bother."

"You are returning to England, then?" She seemed despondent.

O'Hara smiled. "A future President of a South American country has offered me an interesting job. I think I might stick around if the pay is good enough."

He gasped as Benedetta rushed into his one-armed embrace. "Ouch! Careful of this shoulder! And for God's sake, drop that damned gun—you might cause an accident."

Armstrong was muttering to himself in a low chant and Aguillar turned his head. "What did you say, señor?"

Armstrong stopped and laughed. "Oh, it's something about a medieval battle; rather a famous one where the odds were against winning. Shakespeare said something about it which I've been trying to remember—he's not my line, really; he's weak on detail but he gets the spirit all right. It goes something like this." He lifted his voice and declaimed:

"'He that shall live this day, and see old age,
    Will yearly on the vigil feast his neighbours,
    And say, To-morrow is Saint Crispin's.
    Then will he strip his sleeve and show his scars,
    And say, These wounds I had on Crispin's day.

Old men forget; yet all shall be forgot,
But he'll remember with advantages
What feats he did that day . . .
We few, we happy few.' "

He fell silent and after a few minutes gave a low chuckle. "I think Jenny Ponsky will be able to teach that very well when she returns to her school. Do you think *she'll* 'strip her sleeve and show her scars'?"

The truck lurched down the road towards freedom.

THE END

THINGS I WISH I'D KNOWN

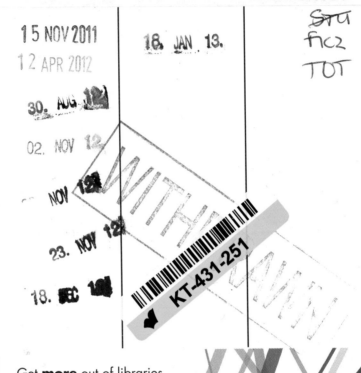

Get **more** out of libraries

Please return or renew this item by the last date shown.
You can renew online at www.hants.gov.uk/library
Or by phoning 0845 603 5631

Hampshire
County Council

THINGS I WISH I'D KNOWN

LINDA GREEN

ISIS
LARGE PRINT
Oxford

First published in Great Britain 2010
by
Headline Review
An imprint of Headline Publishing Group

Published in Large Print 2010 by ISIS Publishing Ltd.,
7 Centremead, Osney Mead, Oxford OX2 0ES
by arrangement with
Headline Publishing Group
An Hachette UK Company

British Library Cataloguing in Publication Data
Green, Linda, 1970–
    Things I wish I'd known.
    1. Divorced women - - Fiction.
    2. Ambition - - Fiction.
    3. Large type books.
    I. Title
    823.9'2–dc22

ISBN 978–0–7531–8710–4 (hb)
ISBN 978–0–7531–8711–1 (pb)

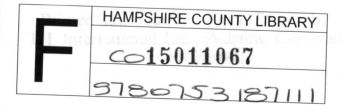

For Ian and Rohan

CHAPTER ONE

At first, I thought it was a joke, probably due to the unfeasibly large grin on Mark's face as we drew up outside the house. When he suggested we got out and took a closer look, a sense of unease spread over me. And at the point where I stepped on to the pavement and caught sight of the garish pink and orange "For Sale" sign in the front garden, I realised this was definitely no laughing matter.

"Well, what do you think?" Mark said, gesturing towards the large red-brick detached house which stood in front of us.

What I was thinking was that our happy, fun, not-going-anywhere-in-a-hurry carousel ride of a relationship was about to turn into the scariest rollercoaster at the fairground, the type where you had to choose between jumping off at the top while it was still moving or careering downhill into a lifetime of joint mortgage payments.

However, I also knew that in a relationship-defining moment like this, it paid to be non-committal until the other person had explained exactly what was going on. And that the last thing I wanted to do was wipe the deliriously excited expression off Mark's face.

"I think you may be about to audition for a presenter's job on *Location, Location, Location* and you'd like me to practise being an awkward, impossible-to-please house-hunter."

Mark laughed and shook his head, although I was aware I had still managed to turn the dimmer switch on his smile down a notch or two.

"I'm going to have to spell it out, aren't I?" he said.

"'Fraid so. I'm obviously being a bit dense here."

Mark took a moment to compose himself as he gazed down thoughtfully at his sandals. He didn't usually do hesitation.

"I'd like us to move in together. Somewhere new, not my place or yours. Somewhere we can be a proper couple and not have to have toothbrushes in two different places and dash home to get a change of clothes before work in the morning."

It sounded more like a proposal to merge two companies than to cement our future as a couple. But then Mark was not a romantic candlelit-dinner type of guy (he cited the fact that he'd once represented a client whose sleeve had caught fire in a restaurant). He was straightforward, practical and sometimes impulsive — as he had just demonstrated — but he was never going to sweep me off my feet and whisk me away to his castle on a white charger. Which was probably just as well, as I was in my thirties and still bearing the scars from two botched attempts at broken-heart surgery and had therefore long ago stopped believing in that sort of thing.

2

I glanced up and realised he was waiting for an answer. Not just any answer. The one he was desperate to hear.

"Oh," I said, totally inadequately, as my lips played for time while my head tried to come up with a more appropriate response.

"Have I finally succeeded in rendering you speechless? Can I make a note of this in my diary? 'Claire lost for words shocker'?"

I knew the joke was intended to cover up his disappointment. I smiled back at him, trying to make it clear that I wasn't about to blow him out. I couldn't; this was Mark, the man who had put a smile on my face for the past two years and had single-handedly restored my faith in men. It would have been unbearably cruel to extinguish the flame of optimism which burnt so brightly in him.

"Sorry. It's a bit of a shock, that's all."

"Lucky I didn't go the whole hog and propose, then." He was grinning, well aware of my view that it would be plain rude of me to expect my friends and family to shell out for wedding presents for a second time.

"It's just that I thought you were happy with things how they are," I said.

"I am," replied Mark, looking serious for once. "But I've realised I'd be even happier if we were living together." It was as near as he had ever got to declaring his undying love for me.

I smiled at him and kissed him on the lips. Because I wanted to and because I still wasn't sure what to say. It

3

wasn't that I didn't love him. I did. It was simply that loving someone and wanting to buy a house together were two very different things. But now Mark had bought me a ticket for the white-knuckle ride, I was well aware that continuing on the carousel wasn't really an option any more. I put my arms around his neck and kissed him again.

"Do I take that as a yes, then?" he asked when our lips finally parted.

"Argued so persuasively, how could I refuse?" I said.

The full cheek-to-cheek grin returned to his face. His greeny-blue eyes looked like they were celebrating a hat trick for England. Mark was happy. The panic was over. Air pressure in the cabin returned to normal. I took off the oxygen mask to find I could breathe again.

"There's just one thing I'm not sure about," I continued.

"Here we go," said Mark. "You're going to add in loads of conditions now, aren't you? Some sort of pre-nup for living together, where you get custody of the wok if I dare to pick my toenails in bed."

"No," I said. "It's, er, that." I pointed to the house with rather less aplomb than Mark had.

"What's wrong with it?" Mark sounded put out. I decided not to tell him that if he'd been trying to find my dream house, an Identikit new-build in a sought-after cul-de-sac in Littleborough couldn't have been further from it. I took a deep breath and tried to phrase it diplomatically.

"It's, er, a bit lacking in the charm department."

"OK, it's not chocolate-box thatched-cottage material, but if it was, it would also be cold, damp, dingy and draughty, be out in the sticks somewhere and cost us a fortune in running repairs over the years — if we could afford it to start off with, that is. Whereas what we have here, while admittedly not aesthetically appealing, is new, warm, solid, light, easy to maintain, has straight walls and ceilings, no vermin living beneath the floorboards or in the loft, is within walking distance of the station and I reckon we can get it for under two hundred and fifty thousand, so avoiding being stung for stamp duty."

I smiled. It was easy to see why Mark was capable of twisting anyone around his little finger in court. He possessed the true lawyer's knack of being able to paint black as white, and in such a way that you started to doubt whether it had ever been black in the first place (I was admittedly jealous of this, being the type of lawyer who somehow always got bogged down in the shades of grey in between). He was also right, of course. But as someone who had always been more head-in-the-clouds than practical, I was able to overlook that. My dream home was something older and weather-beaten, something I could fall in love with at first sight, something that oozed character from its crooked stone walls to its creaking floorboards. Something which would feel like home. My home. Not a show home.

"This is me you're speaking to, remember," I said, poking him playfully in the ribs. "You'll have to do better than that. I'm not going to agree to buy a house on the grounds that it hasn't got rats."

"That's all right," he said, pulling his sunglasses up on to the top of his head for a moment and squinting down the street. "Here's the very man to convince you." I followed his gaze to where a silver Saab had pulled up at the kerb and a man in his fifties, wearing an ill-fitting suit which refused to do up over his pot belly, was bounding towards us.

"What do you mean?" I said.

"That's Chris, the estate agent. He's going to show us around." I felt the perspiration break out on my brow. And it had nothing to do with it being the hottest day of the year so far. I wouldn't even buy a pair of shoes in the first shop I looked in, let alone snap up the very first house I viewed — especially when I hadn't even known we were looking until a few minutes ago.

"What, now?"

"Yeah, is that all right? I know it was a bit presumptuous of me, but I had a *carpe diem* moment. If you want me to put him off I can do."

Before I could answer, Chris was shaking my hand, positively foaming at the mouth at the prospect of a sale. He brought to mind a hound which hadn't been out on a hunt for weeks and had suddenly got wind of a fox. I guessed a recession did that to estate agents.

"Right," he said when the introductions were over. "Well, as you can see, it's a quiet but convenient location, only five minutes from the M62 and ten minutes' walk from the station. Where do you guys work?"

"Rochdale," we said in unison, me with a distinct lack of enthusiasm.

"Well, you're ideally situated here," he said, loosening his tie a touch as the sun reappeared from behind a cloud. "And of course, you're near excellent primary and secondary schools. It really is a perfect family home."

I nodded without saying anything and shifted my Birkenstock-clad feet on the pavement. The fact that he'd either assumed we already had kids or were planning to start a family made me a little uneasy. Where had he got the idea that it was a family home we were after?

I had been honest with Mark from very early on about my desire to remain "child-free" (as I preferred to call it). I didn't announce, "Now before we go any further, I need to make it clear that I don't want children," as we sat down for a meal on our first date. But to be honest, I didn't have to. Because even before we'd started going out together, during the prolonged wooing phase when Mark had tried his best to charm the knickers off me every time we'd bumped into each other in the café in Drake Street, where both of our practices were based, I'd made enough references to the fact that representing a steady stream of teenage delinquents and drug addicts was the career least likely to engender a burning desire in anyone to procreate, to get the message across.

To his credit, Mark had never pushed me on the matter or tried to persuade me of the joy to be derived from seeing your offspring in a miniature Blackburn

Rovers kit. But I'd long suspected he harboured a secret desire to be a father and now, suddenly, it occurred to me that this could be his first move in trying to get me to change my mind. I could see how his argument would go, something along the lines of, "Well, now we've got four bedrooms it would be a shame to waste the space. And being so near to some good schools, we may as well take advantage of them, otherwise we're simply paying taxes to educate other people's kids." Mark could convince anyone of anything. And before I knew it I'd have a toddler on one hip and a baby clamped to my breast.

I looked across at Mark. He gave a little shrug but made no attempt to correct Chris.

"Right, let's go inside," continued Chris. "This place is made for you. I have a feeling you're going to love it."

I shrugged back at Mark and followed Chris into the small hallway, the smell of "new" filling my nostrils.

"We'll start in the lounge," he said, pushing the door open to reveal an expanse of laminate flooring and magnolia walls. "Plenty of room for a big plasma screen in here," he grinned, turning to Mark. "Now, Claire, while Mark's watching the footie on TV, let me show you the fantastic kitchen which will make preparing meals so easy you'll have plenty of time to put your feet up with a magazine and catch up on all the latest celebrity gossip." I raised my eyebrows.

"Should I tell him women have the vote now?" I whispered to Mark.

"Perhaps he's used to dealing with bored housewives."

"Or maybe he's simply reading from the script," I replied. "In which case I'm about to get told about the state-of-the-art appliances in the beautifully appointed kitchen."

"Now then," said Chris, leading us into the kitchen, "there are some state-of-the-art appliances in here . . ."

I groaned inwardly and let Chris's sales patter drift over me as I looked around. It was one of those spot-the-difference kitchens where you don't know where anything is and would forever be opening doors and accidentally putting the milk in the dishwasher and the rubbish in the washing machine.

"Mmmm, great," I muttered unconvincingly as Chris led us back to the hallway.

"Why didn't you tell him that I hate all this hard-sell stuff?" I whispered to Mark as we climbed the stairs behind him.

"It's like telling a Jehovah's Witness you don't do religion; they simply try even harder. Anyway, some muppet showing us around isn't going to put us off, is it?"

What concerned me about Mark's reply was that it appeared to be a rhetorical question. He clearly didn't realise that I couldn't be put off because I'd never been keen on it in the first place.

"It's a beautifully appointed master bedroom, with en suite and dressing area — so plenty of room for all those designer frocks and Jimmy Choo shoes."

I forced out a smile to be polite, realising that we would get out of the place more quickly if I went along with Chris's notion that I was Victoria Beckham in disguise.

We moved on through the next three bedrooms, inspected the bathroom (the white was at least a refreshing change from magnolia), and were finally left on our own on the landing to "talk things through", while Chris went to open up the integral garage for our inspection.

I looked at Mark. The expression on his face suggested he would offer the asking price by the time we got downstairs.

"Well?" he said expectantly.

"You were right. The walls are straight and there's no vermin. However, I do have one concern."

"Which is?"

"Why is he under the impression we have more children than the Waltons?"

"Ah, yes, that," said Mark. "He's just got the wrong end of the stick. I said it was a long-term purchase we were looking for, that we wanted to put down some roots, and he's obviously interpreted that as meaning we wanted somewhere which would cater for a growing family."

"Right. So why do we need four bedrooms exactly?"

"Well, one of them can be a study, one room always ends up as a junk room so you may as well factor that in, and the other one can be a guest room."

He was doing it again. Making me doubt why I had ever questioned him in the first place. I stared at him intently, looking for any visible sign that he was talking grade-one lawyer bullshit.

10

"And you're sure you have no desire to fill the place with the patter of tiny feet and the smell of poo and vomit?"

Mark smiled. "I'd simply like some more space and I figured you'd feel the same way. It's the one thing neither of us has got."

He had a point. Mark lived in a one-bedroom flat in Littleborough which had one of those all-in-one kitchen/dining/living spaces that developers trying to maximise their profits seemed so fond of (presumably they didn't think anybody would mind if their sofa permanently smelt of last night's curry). And I lived in a small (poky was the word Mark used) two-bedroom terraced house a few miles down the road in Todmorden, just over the West Yorkshire border (something Mark used to rib me about as a born and bred Lancastrian who had come dangerously close to reigniting the War of the Roses on numerous occasions).

I glanced across at Mark. He was obviously desperate to buy the place. I felt mean for having such a downer on it. I needed to find something positive to say.

"I guess it would be nice to have a bathroom and an en suite."

"There speaks a woman with mildew on her over-the-bath shower curtain."

"At least I *have* a bath." Mark's flat only had a shower (presumably having been designed by a man who had no idea how tricky it was trying to shave your legs while standing up in a tiny shower cubicle).

"There, see, property snobbery already. Before you know it you'll be saying, 'Oh, don't you have an integral garage?'"

"Come on," I said, laughing uneasily. "Chris'll be wondering where we've got to."

We arrived downstairs to find Chris poised to give a demonstration of the up-and-over door.

"Obviously the garage is just as it's been finished at the moment, but if you wanted to decorate it in any way . . ."

"Great idea, I could paint it pink and do some nice floral stencilling," I said, managing to keep a straight face.

"I can see your little lady's been reading all the latest interior design magazines," said Chris, turning to Mark. I waited until he'd turned to lead us out of the garage before banging my head on the brick wall.

"Chin up, it's nearly over," whispered Mark.

"And of course, the garden is wonderfully low maintenance," said Chris, gesturing to the small square of lawn at the side of the property. "So, what do you think?" he asked, almost quivering with anticipation. He was looking at Mark, of course, clearly being of the view that the "little lady" would have no say on financial matters.

"It's great," said Mark. "Ticks all our boxes. Obviously we'll have to go away and have a think about it." I stared at him, relieved that he hadn't said yes on the spot but already aware that it was going to be very difficult for me to back out of it.

12

"Sure, I understand," said Chris, clearly gutted not to have finished off his prey. "Don't leave it too long, though. I have another viewing arranged next week. This is the only one left and the others have gone like hot cakes," he added.

I was about to point out that houses were in fact about as popular as three-day-old dried-up rolls in a baker's at the moment but decided not to put the boot in when he was so obviously desperate. Instead, I glanced around at the other properties in the cul-de-sac, a couple of which were occupied. There was a man washing his 4×4 in one drive, a woman swirling a Flymo across the lawn in a side garden and two kids on their bikes, trying desperately to outdo each other's skids. It reminded me of Potters Bar where I grew up. And of why I'd been so desperate to get out. We watched as Chris waved and drove off. At which point it was just me and Mark standing on the pavement, teetering on the brink of suburban hell.

"So," said Mark, turning to me. "If it was *Location, Location, Location*, what would you say now?"

"Show me the next property," I said. Mark laughed.

"How about a serious answer for once?"

I didn't have the heart to tell him that it had been. He was clearly already working out where his hi-fi and the giant yucca plant would go. The man who I loved had asked me to move in with him and had probably spent ages scouring the internet for the ideal home, which he had presented to me on a plate. OK, he couldn't have got it more wrong if he'd tried but I didn't want to appear an ungrateful wretch and I was well aware that a lot of people would have given anything to live in a house like that.

"It's not really the best time to buy a house, is it?" I said lamely. "Are you sure we can afford it?" Mark earned considerably more than me; he was a personal injury lawyer (or ambulance-chaser as my father insisted on referring to him), contracted by one of those national "no-win, no-fee" firms which advertised on daytime TV. Whereas I was a solicitor for a small family-owned business — and Legal Aid payments weren't all they could be.

"I'm recession-proof — people will always have accidents," said Mark. "Anyway, I've worked out the mortgage payments and everything. It's not a huge amount more than we both pay at the moment and we'll only have council tax and heating bills for one property. And I'll be covering the deposit and the stamp duty so you haven't got to worry about that. It actually makes huge financial sense."

I smiled at him, knowing again that he was right and trying to ignore the churning sensation in my stomach. The ride was going too fast already. I wanted to get off. I reached out for Mark's hand and clasped it tightly.

"OK, can I sleep on it?" I said. "Maybe a couple of nights, actually."

He grinned, sensing he almost had me.

Standing precariously on the top rung of my rickety stepladder, I pushed the loft cover to one side, rested the torch on the edge and prepared to haul myself upwards through the hatch, reassured by the fact that if

I did fall, I would at least have a personal injury lawyer on hand to try to get some compensation from the stepladder manufacturers.

As it was, the ladder — and my arms — held out and I scrambled unceremoniously on to the floorboards I'd laid across the joists to try to support the weight of the numerous boxes which were stacked there. I waited for the dust to settle and my eyes to get used to the dimness before picking up the torch and shining it around like some 1950s usherette who was a bit apprehensive about what might be going on in the back row of the cinema.

The cardboard boxes were piled high on top of each other. The building blocks of my life. They contained my DNA. Which was why they were taped shut; no one else was allowed to look at them and I would no sooner get rid of them than agree to sever my right arm. I hadn't been up there for ages, probably not since I'd moved in eight years previously. I stuck my head up there every Christmas to reach down the tree and decorations but it wasn't the same. I wasn't within touching distance. The memories were all out of reach. But not any longer. It was time. I was standing at a crossroads, wondering which way to go. Only I couldn't seem to work out where my future lay. Probably because I still hadn't come to terms with my past.

I walked over and ran my finger along the sealed top of the nearest box, which was marked "Photos". Making contact with the past. Acknowledging its existence while knowing I should keep it at arm's length. It was too tempting though. I peeled off the

15

parcel tape, feeling like a kid who had discovered her hidden Christmas presents on 23 December and decided to peek inside, even though she knew it was wrong. A pile of photo albums and bulging Kodak envelopes greeted me — a reminder of the days when photographs took up half of your household storage space instead of being contained in a few megabytes of computer hard drive. I pulled out the album on top and opened it up, immediately shutting it again as I caught sight of Andy grinning back at me. Even after all this time he still had the ability to do that to me. It wasn't as if I hadn't expected to see him; most of the boxes contained cardboard-to-cardboard Andy. It was simply that I hadn't expected him to look so good. I was sure that if most women dug out the photos of the idols who used to line their bedroom walls, they would cringe in horror at why they'd ever thought Nick Berry from *EastEnders* was good-looking just because he'd had a number-one single, or wonder how they hadn't noticed Simon Le Bon's double chin at the time. But in my case I had to compliment myself on having disturbingly good taste in men at the age of fifteen. Maybe that was what had got me into so much trouble.

I opened the album again and started flicking through it, in case I'd simply caught him on a good day, but no, whether he was standing shirtless outside the changing rooms with his arm around me on a summer's day or bent double in a baggy tracksuit doing hamstring stretches during a drizzly October half-term at the training ground, he still looked unnervingly good. Whereas I, it had to be said, looked bloody awful:

16

all hairsprayed flick, stick arms and highly dubious outfits. That was the weird thing about the eighties — how no one realised what a sight they looked at the time. Frankie, of course, looked gorgeous in every picture, but then she always was the exception to the rule. She probably still looked gorgeous now. It was a shame the photos hadn't continued past my sixteenth birthday, when I'd emerged from my ugly duckling phase. But by that time everything had changed and taking photos had been the last thing on my mind.

I leafed through every album and photo wallet, the vast majority full of snaps taken at the United training ground. Frankie and I must have doubled Kodak's profits in 1985. By the time I'd finished, I was on a full-blown nostalgia kick and didn't hesitate in removing the tape on the next box — the one marked "Diaries and Mementoes". It should have had some kind of emotional health warning on the side. Inside were piles of spiral-bound notepads (normal diaries had never had enough room for my teenage angst), many of them with doodles on the front, hearts with arrows through them declaring that CS loved AP for ever. I shook my head and smiled. It had all been so innocent back then. It was as I rummaged through the diaries that I noticed the envelope poking out from the side of one of them. A sealed pale blue envelope with "NOT TO BE OPENED UNTIL 31 JULY 2005" written on it in bold black letters. I knew what it was straight away, of course. What I couldn't work out was why I hadn't remembered it three years ago. I wondered if Frankie had opened hers then. Whether she still had it, even.

I slid my finger into the corner of the envelope and started to tear. It was like going back in time to visit a medium, armed with the hindsight necessary to know how accurate she was straight away. And, rather bizarrely, knowing that the medium had been me, aged fifteen.

I unfolded the single sheet of paper. "Twenty Years From Now" it read boldly at the top of the page.

Love life — Married to Andy Pailes.
Holidays — Florence, Italy.
Career — Partner in big city law firm.
Looks — Kind of the same but with shorter hair and bigger boobs.
Financial status — Well off but not super-rich.
Living — In a thatched cottage in the countryside, possibly in Yorkshire.
Children — Two, Steven and Lauren.
Best Friend — Frankie.
Interests — Football (United season-ticket holder, commute to games), politics (maybe a Labour councillor), law (making the world a better place).
Are you happy? — The happiest I've ever been.

I sat with the piece of paper in my hands, unable to decide for a moment whether to laugh or cry. But within a second or two the words on the page became blurred and I realised which option I'd chosen. It was silly really. How a fifteen-year-old version of me could be capable of cutting the adult model to the quick like that. But I'd had no idea back then how life doesn't always turn out the way you plan. How all your hopes and dreams can evaporate over time. Or sometimes be cruelly squashed in an instant. And no idea that one day I would sit in a dusty attic with tears streaming down my face wondering how my life had fallen so badly short of my expectations.

I sniffed, wiped my nose with my sleeve and re-read the list, inserting the real answers where the misplaced expectations had been.

Love life — Married law-school sweetheart David at 23. Divorced at 30. Boyfriend of two years, Mark, has asked me to move in with him.
Holidays — The Lake District or Cornwall (never been to Florence).
Career — Made redundant from my first job at a big Manchester law firm. Now a solicitor with small family-owned company Barnes and Co., on rota as duty solicitor for Rochdale Magistrates' Court dealing with a succession of career criminals and small-time crooks.
Looks — Filled out a bit (boobs did at least make it to an A cup), shoulder-length hair with fair highlights. Flick gone.
Financial status — Solvent but no savings or expectations of a pay rise.
Living — In a poky two-bed back-to-back Victorian terrace. Did end up in West Yorkshire but about to move into soulless new-build in a Lancashire cul-de-sac.

Children — None. Bit of luck bearing in mind the divorce.

Best friend — Fiona, one of the clerks at Rochdale Magistrates' Court. Lost touch with Frankie more than 17 years ago.

Interests — Gardening (have my own allotment), swimming (proper front crawl in the fast lane, not gossipy breaststroke without getting your hair wet), law (though I haven't even made Rochdale a better place, let alone the world). Went off United and football in general when all the money and prima donnas came in and ruined the game. Resigned from the Labour Party after Iraq invasion, without ever volunteering for leafleting duties, let alone running for election.

Are you happy?

I stopped abruptly at the last question, imagining for a moment what my fifteen-year-old self would have thought had she known the truth back then. How disillusioned and disappointed she would have been to see what had become of her. I knew that, compared to most of my classmates, I'd done all right for myself. But all right had never been good enough for me. I'd wanted the moon and stars. I'd even got close enough to touch them before plummeting back down to earth with an almighty bump. And suddenly I felt cheated by the consolation-prize life I had instead. I realised things had gone badly off course. But maybe I still had time to put that right. Maybe I wasn't past the "use-by" date for dreams.

Monday, 22 July 1985

As far as me and Frankie were concerned, it was nothing short of a crime. A crime which would shock the nation. A crime against humanity even.

We watched the gold BMW sweep through the gates of the training ground and park in the far corner as usual. We saw the familiar designer-tracksuited figure emerge, Rolex glistening in the bright morning sunlight.

It was only as he turned and began to stroll towards us, the other fans parting before him like that thing with Moses and the waves in the Bible, that we caught sight of it. And the full enormity of the situation became clear.

"Oh, shit," Frankie groaned. "Matt's had a perm."

We smiled politely in Matt Goodyear's direction as he glided swiftly past us into the clubhouse, the mass of tight curls sticking to his head like scrunched-up pieces of tissue paper on a school collage. And then we waited, bracing ourselves for the inevitable reaction.

"Bloody hell, it's Kevin Keegan." Gibbo's Welsh accent was the first voice we heard through the open dressing-room window above the predictable howls of laughter from Matt's teammates.

Frankie slumped on the low wall outside the dressing room, biting what was left of her scarlet-painted nails and scuffing the toe of her stiletto repeatedly against the wall.

I stood next to her, marvelling at the way she could still stick her boobs out even when she was slouching, while racking my brain for something to say that would make her feel better. When my grandad had died, my mum had tried to soften the blow by pointing out that I did at least have another grandfather. I didn't think the same tactic would work here, though. What with Matt only having the one head.

"Maybe he did it for a dare, or for charity or something."

I knew that twenty-eight year olds didn't do things for a dare. And I couldn't think of a single famous person who'd had a perm as a way of raising money for charity. They were much more likely to organise a big open-air pop concert and invite people like Sting and George Michael. It was less embarrassing that way.

Frankie gave me one of her looks.

"He's not Bob Geldof, you know. He hasn't done it to feed all the kids in Ethiopia."

"I was only trying to make you feel better."

"Well don't bother. I may as well get used to him being a laughing stock. The Arsenal fans are gonna love this, aren't they? 'Can you hear us, Matt Goodyear, you sad bastard with your girlie hair?' That's what they'll sing, you know. That's what John Motson will try and talk over on *Match of the Day*."

"So why do you think he had it done?"

"It's obvious, innit? Jane made him do it. The fat-arsed cow."

Frankie reckoned everything was Matt's wife's fault. If Russia ever nuked Potters Bar, she'd try to pin that one on her as well.

"Why would Jane want Matt to be a laughing stock?"

"'Cos she's jealous of all the attention he's been getting, you spaz. She can't stand the competition, can she? Thought she'd try and put his admirers off."

"So have you gone off him, then?"

Frankie thought about it for a moment, pursing her full scarlet lips as she did so.

"Nah, it'll take more than a perm," she said, tossing her own dark mane of long straight hair.

"You said you'd go off Simon Le Bon if he ever had a perm," I pointed out.

"Yeah, well. His legs aren't as good as Matt's, are they?"

"How do you know?"

Frankie gave a dramatic sigh.

"I just know, OK?"

I hated it when Frankie gave answers like that, acting as if she had some kind of inside information — which I knew she didn't. We waited in silence outside the clubhouse for five more minutes, until at last we heard the rasping sounds of studs hitting concrete. First one, then two and finally dozens of football boots pounded over the rough path to the dry, stubbly grass beyond.

This was it. The moment we had been waiting for. The real start of our school summer holidays. United, pride of north London, were coming out to play.

The tight blue shorts, the bulging, tanned thighs, the tantalising glimpse of chest hair beneath the silky sheen of their football shirts, I took it all in, my eyes straining to absorb every detail. If Michael Rodd off *Screen Test* had appeared and started asking me questions about the clip of footage I'd just seen, I'd have got every one right. Even the bonus question about who was the only player in a long-sleeved shirt. I took a deep breath, closing my eyes. Breathing in memories I could treasure for ever, instead of ones that kept me awake at night.

"This," whispered Frankie, "has got to be the best place on earth."

I nodded, still unable to believe that such a place existed. It was our first time at the training ground. Someone had told Frankie's dad that they let fans in to watch on Mondays and Wednesdays. For free as well, so my mum couldn't say we couldn't afford it. And there weren't going to be fans from any other club here, so she couldn't say there was going to be any trouble. Football hooligans weren't interested in watching players warming up and practising their half-volleys. Even my mum knew that.

We found a good vantage point on the grass banking at the side of the pitch, high enough that we could see over the crowds of fans, mostly little boys with bored-looking mums in tow, who were jostling for the best position on the touchline. The squad jogged off around the training ground, the first-team players still winding Matt up, the younger ones smirking, not daring to join in the banter but clearly smug in the knowledge that even an England star could commit a style faux pas of such monumental proportions.

I watched Matt as he jogged round, intermittently twisting and stretching from side to side. He'd been my favourite United player since I was twelve. Not because I fancied him (he looked a bit like Tony Hadley out of Spandau Ballet; I was more of a Martin Kemp kind of girl myself), but simply because he was our best player. He wasn't my favourite any more though. Not since we'd signed Andy Pailes last season, and I'd realised that I had no wish to idolise a man who stared up at me from my cornflakes box every morning. I wasn't a kid any more. I didn't want a superstar I had to share with everyone else. I wanted a precious but as yet undiscovered gemstone. One that I could claim as my very own.

Seconds later Andy jogged past, the sunlight catching the small gold ring in his left ear. I double-checked the hair but it was still the same — thick, dark, slightly spiky and not a curl in sight. I smiled to myself, happy that I had unearthed a rare thing of genuine beauty.

As Andy edged nearer — so near that I could see the beads of sweat forming on his forehead — the corners of my mouth crept upwards and somewhere inside me a vice tightened around my internal organs. My heart was pounding. Seriously pounding, as if it might burst right out of my ribcage. For a second I thought I was having a heart attack, until I realised that was unlikely, what with me being a skinny fifteen-year-old vegetarian and my mum having switched from butter to Flora. No, my pounding heart could mean only one thing. I was in love. Big time.

Having never been in love before (fancying Jason Pike at school for six months before he'd started going out with Angela Sutcliffe didn't count, as I was only thirteen at the time; that was just kids' stuff), I wanted to keep it to myself for a little while longer. But I blew it by going bright red as Andy jogged past me. Frankie never missed these things; she was much too sharp for that.

"You fancy him, don't you? You fancy Andy Pailes," she said, the collection of thin metal bangles on her wrist tinkling against each other as she waved her arms around.

"Shut up, will you," I pleaded, glancing at the other fans who were milling around below us. I didn't want a public announcement. This was a very private thing.

"So is it his bum or his legs?"

I sighed, wondering how I'd ended up with a best friend who didn't know the meaning of the word subtle.

"I think he's different, that's all. There's something intriguing about him."

"Something intriguing about him," mimicked Frankie. "What the hell's that s'posed to mean? You either fancy the pants off him or you don't."

"Some of us like to go a bit deeper than that."

"Bollocks. It's all right to admit you fancy him, you know. He's a good-looking bloke."

"D'you think so?" I asked.

"Nah, but you obviously do. So now we've got that sorted out, you can tell me all about it."

Frankie dragged me over to a quiet spot on the grassy bank, away from all the kids, and, with one eye still firmly on Matt, began bombarding me with questions about Andy. At first I tried to be coy, giving knowing smiles rather than detailed information as I fiddled with the badge on my canvas bag (it had one red arrow pointing in the opposite direction to lots of black arrows. I'd bought it so it looked as if being different to everyone else was a conscious decision I'd made, rather than an unfortunate turn of fate).

Eventually, under duress and in danger of losing Frankie's interest altogether, I was forced to admit I didn't know much about Andy at all.

"He's an enigma," I explained with the same flourish of the left hand that I'd seen an art critic on a late-night BBC2 programme give when he'd used the term. The silence that followed confirmed my hunch that Frankie wouldn't want to reveal her own ignorance by asking what the word actually meant. Which was just as well, as I wasn't altogether sure myself.

"Haven't you even found a fact file on him?" asked Frankie. As far as she was concerned, fact files were the football fan's equivalent of Letts revision notes. They told you all the key stuff you wanted to know without the need for hours of research.

"Give us a chance, will you? He's only been at United a few months."

"You mean he ain't famous enough to have one done on him."

I didn't bother rising to the bait. Sometimes arguing with Frankie was so easy it wasn't any fun.

"Look, do you want to know anything about him or not?" I said.

"Go on, I'm listening."

"Well, he's twenty-two, is from a place called Ponte-something in Yorkshire, started out at Huddersfield Town, played for the England under twenty-one team, signed for Leeds and had been there two years when we signed him."

"Yeah, yeah. Very interesting. But has he got a girlfriend?" asked Frankie.

"Er, I don't know."

Frankie gave another sigh.

"OK, let's see," she said, pushing her shades up for a second and squinting in the bright sunlight to get a better look at Andy. "I reckon you might be in there. He looks single to me."

"Oh, and you can tell, can you?"

"Come on, who would go out with a guy who looks like someone out of Echo and the Bunnymen? He doesn't look like a proper footballer at all."

"Just 'cos he hasn't got highlights and a poncey haircut, it doesn't mean he can't play football."

"I know. All I'm saying is he's not exactly in the Matt Goodyear mould, is he?" I was going to point out that at least that meant I wouldn't find a plastic Andy Pailes in my cornflakes, when I thought better of it. Frankie was having a tough day, what with the perm and that.

"Well no, but there's room for all tastes, isn't there?"

"Absolutely. So let's work this out: he's twenty-two and you're fourteen . . ."

"Fifteen, thank you," I said, annoyed that four months into my sixteenth year, Frankie still had to be reminded.

"OK, but that's still at least a seven-year age gap. Might be stretching it a bit."

"Oh, like the twelve years between you and Matt isn't, you mean?"

"Course not. It's different for me, innit? I don't look . . ."

Frankie's voice trailed off as I shifted from my crossed-leg position and stretched out my long legs in a desperate but ultimately futile attempt to look less like a *Blue Peter* viewer. She didn't need to finish the sentence. The brutal truth was that I did still look like a fourteen year old. Not even my heavily hair-sprayed flick (which looked so much more grown-up than my old straight-cut fringe) could distract from the stick-insect body poking out from beneath my pedal-pushers and tea-bag tank-top.

Whereas Frankie, while only eighteen months older than me, could easily pass for nineteen, thanks to her Mediterranean looks and page-three-girl figure. Sometimes I liked having a best friend who could put Samantha Fox in the shade. Other times I worried that hanging out with Frankie didn't do me any favours. No one noticed the foothills next to Mount Everest, did they?

"Cheer up," said Frankie, having finally noticed my bleak expression. "Maybe this will be the year it will all kick in for you. You've got to get boobs sometime, you know."

I wasn't so sure. Having been blessed with hormones that had forgotten the necessity for me to grow out in the right places as well as up, I was beginning to wonder if I would ever graduate from junior bras. It bothered me a lot. Every time I saw the AA sticker inside Mum's car I thought about it. And sometimes even when I changed the double-A batteries in my radio.

"Yeah, like never," I said, turning to face Frankie.

"Hey, don't get down about it. I wouldn't mind a few of your inches in height."

"At least you can wear high heels to make up for it. I don't fancy trying to pad my bra out. Do you remember that scene in *Little House on the Prairie*? The one where Laura Ingalls stuffed oranges down her top and they fell out in class? That would be me, that would."

"Maybe you're gonna be one of those late bloomers," said Frankie. "Today a tall, skinny kid, tomorrow a catwalk model."

"Yeah, right. And Maggie Thatcher will run off with Ken Livingstone. Dream on. Anyway, I don't wanna be a model, I want to be a lawyer, thank you."

"Oh, whatever. I was only trying to help. But you shouldn't let it get to you. Forget about it for the summer holidays. That's what I'm gonna do. Forget about my O-level results and starting college and all the crap at home. All I'm gonna think about this summer is United."

30

I liked the idea but wasn't sure that it would work for me. A lot of things that worked for Frankie didn't work for me. Like rah-rah skirts, for example. Frankie looked fantastic in hers, whereas I looked like an anaemic twiglet wearing a lampshade.

"It's all right for you. You haven't got anything to worry about."

"Yes I have," said Frankie. "My family are one big problem."

"At least you've got one. I can't remember the last time I even saw my dad."

"There you go then. You're halfway to forgetting about him already."

I wasn't convinced but I was prepared to give it a go.

"OK, but we'll have to come up here a lot if it's gonna work. Practically live here, I mean. I want to feel like one of the team."

"And I wanna feel up one of the team," Frankie replied with a smirk. She said stuff like that all the time, but I wasn't sure she actually meant it. She'd never had a boyfriend. I hadn't either but that was because I didn't look like Frankie. She didn't have an excuse.

When training was over we waited outside in the players' car park. It seemed to be where everyone else was gathering, autograph books at the ready.

"Come on," said Frankie, striding over to Matt's car. "I'm gonna have a look inside, see if I can find out what bands he's into at the moment." She ran her hands over the BMW's sleek bodywork before stooping to peer inside, pressing her nose against the warm glass and cupping her hands around her eyes to get a better look.

"You can't do that," I told her. "It looks like you're trying to break in or something."

"I'm checking out his tapes, that's all. I wanna see what he's got; maybe I could comment on his superb taste in music."

"I doubt it," I said, peering inside the window as my curiosity got the better of me. "There's a *Kids from Fame* tape in there for a start."

"You bitch, I don't believe you," said Frankie before her eyes settled on the offending cassette, tucked neatly away beside Elton John, the Eagles and Bread. All footballers over the age of twenty-seven seemed to list Bread as one of their favourite groups. I didn't have a clue who they were; I'd certainly never seen them on *Top of the Pops*. I wondered if they'd done the music to the Hovis advert.

"Well it must be Jane's," said Frankie. "I can't see Matt being into *Fame*. All that poxying around in leg-warmers and leotards and that Bruno guy with the awful perm . . ."

Frankie's voice trailed off as she heard the crunch of designer trainers on gravel. She spun round to see Matt standing there, looking at her with an irritated expression.

"Er, sorry, I was just, um, admiring your leather-trimmed interior," stuttered Frankie as she shuffled out of the way, thrusting her autograph book in Matt's face, presumably in an attempt to divert his attention from the smeary fingermarks she'd left on the driver's window. Matt signed his name and drove off without another word. I was embarrassed for Frankie. But I couldn't help feeling kind of pleased as well.

"Well, you made an impression all right," I said.

"Yeah, of a right joey."

Before I could say anything, the dressing-room door opened and I felt myself being nudged in the direction of the approaching Andy Pailes.

I started towards him before stopping abruptly, realising that I had no idea what I was going to say. It was too late though. Andy had seen me and was waiting expectantly. I was trapped in no-man's-land, knowing that I'd look a right prat if I retreated now.

For a second my mouth seemed to be moving but nothing came out, as if I was in a foreign film where the dubbing was out of sync. When the words did come, they rushed like a torrent, catching up with my mouth and overtaking it within a sentence.

"Hi, sorry to bother you, can you sign this 'To Claire' please, if you've got a second, that is, thank you very much."

"Sure, no problem," said Andy, taking the pen from my shaking outstretched hand. Everything after that was a bit of a blur, but somewhere along the line I registered him smiling at me, saying thank you, and handing the pen back before driving off, smiling at me again as he went.

I stood there for a second, wondering if I had imagined it all, before looking down and seeing Andy's signature in smudgy black biro in my autograph book.

The page wasn't even dry yet. But the impression, if not the ink, was indelible.

* ★ ★

The wrought-iron garden gate clanged shut behind me, announcing my return home. Not that there was anyone waiting for me. Mum was at work, doing the catering for some sixtieth birthday party where she would no doubt be trying to force feed her Tuscan pâté vol-au-vents to a generation who, if my nan was anything to go by, remained sceptical about anything that wasn't a sausage roll.

I let myself in and wandered into the newly fitted MFI kitchen, all gleaming stainless steel and spotless white Formica surfaces (Mum seemed to have this weird idea that a film crew wanting a location for a Jif advert could drop by at any moment). I glanced at the note that had been stuck to the fridge with a "Country Cousin" mouse magnet: "Cheese and tomato sandwich in here for you. Eat it quick or the mouse will have it! Back about six. Eek, eek!"

Mum's attempts at humour were so embarrassing. I used to tell her it was why I never brought any friends apart from Frankie back to the house (actually, it was because I didn't have any friends apart from Frankie, but I wasn't going to tell her that).

I poured myself a glass of Kia-ora and took the clingfilm-wrapped sandwich cut into neat triangles out of the fridge. She'd even taken the crusts off for me, as if I was three years old and hadn't learnt to chew properly.

Laura Ashley offered her usual greeting as I went into the living room, sniggering at me from each of the purple and blue flowers on the wallpaper, taunting me from behind the chintz curtains, and mocking me from the dark recesses of the sofa. Laura had been there the day I'd come home early from school because the heating had broken down. The day Dad had left home. She had provided the stage and the backdrop. She'd seen everything, and she'd never let me forget it. Mum had been talking recently about getting a new sofa. Something with a darker pattern, that didn't show the marks so easily. I thought it was a bit late for that.

I sat down at the square glass table (Mum liked to call that end the dining room, but it wasn't really, it was just a table), pointedly turning my back on Laura, staring instead at Torvill and Dean, poised on their knees, arms outstretched, ready to begin their Bolero routine. Mum never played the record. She said the music was too dreary. She'd only bought it to put on display at the front of the hi-fi cabinet. Because their costumes matched the colour scheme in the room.

I was halfway through my sandwich when the phone rang. I still had my mouth full when I answered it.

"Hi, Claire. It's Dad." He only ever seemed to call when Mum was working. I wondered if he had secret access to her bookings diary or something.

"Oh, hi. What do you want?"

"I just thought I'd call for a chat, if that's all right." It was weird, because he never usually called for a chat. He always said he was too busy at work.

"Oh, right." I decided to play it cool, not letting him know how pleased I was he'd phoned. Like women did in movies when they really liked some bloke but didn't want to show it in case he didn't feel the same way.

"What have you been up to?" Dad asked.

"I went to United's training ground today."

"Excellent. Looked fit and raring to go, did they? Up for the new season and all that?"

"Yep."

"What do you reckon then? Is this the year we're going to win the league?"

"'Course it is. We've got the best players in the world."

"That's what I like to hear. Healthy optimism, eh?"

No one said anything for a bit. It was always hard to think of something to say once we'd finished with United.

"How's the old revision going? Big year you've got coming up."

"I haven't started it yet. My mocks aren't till Christmas."

"I know. Nothing like getting ahead though, is there?"

I didn't say anything. Dad did this really weird laugh.

"Oh well, I'd better go, I suppose. People to see, places to go. It's, er, best to call me at work if you want to get in touch. I don't get home until late these days."

The last time I'd rung him at home a woman had answered. Dad had said it was the cleaner. Like I was really going to believe that. I hadn't wanted to know her name anyway. It was enough to know she was there.

"OK."

"I'll see you soon then. I'll have to get you tickets for a United game one of these days, won't I?" The first time he'd said that I hadn't slept for weeks. I'd given up believing he meant it now.

"Yeah, great. Bye then."

"Bye for now. Up the blues, eh." He did that weird laugh again and put the phone down.

I didn't think I'd ever get used to Dad not living with us. At first he'd made the effort to see me every other Saturday. It hadn't lasted long, though. When I went veggie he said there was no point him taking me to the Wimpy any more if I wasn't going to have a burger. I didn't see why that mattered. I'd have been perfectly happy with a Knickerbocker Glory.

I went upstairs. Laura Ashley was banned from my bedroom. The walls were painted in United blue, with matching United curtains, lampshade, duvet and pillowcase. Mum said it looked like a boy's room. Like that would really bother me.

I smiled up at the team poster which took pride of place above my bed. The walls were covered with pictures of the United players, cut out of *Shoot!* and *Match*. On the back of my door I had pictures of Spandau Ballet and George Michael, carefully torn out of *Smash Hits* and *Jackie* and stuck up with Blu-Tack. Although I fancied Martin Kemp (the cool one with the longish hair and the earring) I knew I didn't have a hope in hell with him. He was going out with one of the backing singers in Wham! Either Pepsi or Shirley, I could never remember which was which. I fancied George Michael as well (I used to imagine I was the rope he was holding on to in the "Careless Whispers" video). I didn't think he had a girlfriend, so maybe I was in with a chance there.

Frankie was a Duranie, like most of the girls at school. I'd tried my best to like them. I learnt all the lyrics to "Is There Something I Should Know?" I even wrote the line about nuclear war on my pencil case. But I lost interest when I found out Simon Le Bon hadn't meant it to be political; he'd just needed something to rhyme with "door".

I kicked off my trainers and flopped on to my bed, taking my autograph book out and turning immediately to Andy's page. I liked the way he'd signed his name. It wasn't one of those flashy, swirly signatures like Matt's that you couldn't read properly. It was very simple, a clear "Andy" with a big loop on the "y" and a little squiggle after the "s" at the end of Pailes. I traced the soft lines of his signature with my finger, holding the book up close to my face and sniffing the page as I detected the slight smell of aftershave, again very subtle, nothing flashy.

It was a nice name, Andy Pailes. Better than Claire Skidmore anyway. The other kids at school were always taking the piss out of my surname. If I was lucky they called me "Skidders", but more often it was "Skidmark".

I hoped Andy had a better nickname. All the players had nicknames, though sometimes it was quite difficult to find out what they were. According to the last fact file in *Match*, Mickey Squire didn't have one. But we knew he did and it was "Nobber". I guessed saying you didn't have one was like a code for it being too rude to print.

Rummaging in my bedside cabinet, I pulled out the United programme from the Nottm Forest game back in April. I hadn't been, of course. Mum said only hooligans and skinheads went to football matches. I'd considered having my head shaved and vandalising a phone box to try to further my cause but I'd decided against it in the end. She'd only have come up with another reason why I couldn't go. And now the Heysel thing had happened and the fire at Bradford, she had added getting trampled to death or burnt alive to the list of potential dangers. I couldn't see how she was ever going to let me go now.

I'd bought the programme from the end-of-season sale at the United shop, purely for the picture of Andy on the "New Faces" page. I'd had to look through at least half a dozen programmes before finding it, scanning each page while a queue had built up behind me. I looked again at those dark brown eyes and the shy half-smile. "Andy," I said out loud. "Andy, Andy, Andy, Andy, Andy." I was quite sure now. Quite sure I'd got the right one.

"Did you have a nice time today then?" said Mum.

We were eating tea (one of her nouvelle cuisine pasta creations, with the meat left out of my portion) when she said it. It wasn't that she was genuinely interested in my day, just that she had this thing about silence at mealtimes.

"Yeah. We got loads of autographs and one of the new players actually spoke to me."

"That's nice, love. I was wondering if you fancied going swimming this week? Only I bumped into Kim's mum in town. She said Kim and Debbie are going to the lido on Wednesday afternoon. Perhaps you could go with them."

Mum went to the same Tupperware parties as Kim and Debbie's mums and always made a point of saying what nice "normal" girls they were. I had a sneaking regard for Kim's ability to do handsprings over the box in gym club and I admired Debbie's knack of keeping her over-the-knee socks up without the need for elastic bands, but I didn't think that was any basis for a lasting and meaningful friendship. The fact that they'd never even heard of Matt Goodyear was clearly going to be a problem. Besides which, I had no doubt that I would be an unwelcome addition to their previously cosy twosome.

"No thanks, I'm going down the training ground on Wednesday."

"What, again? You've already been today. What do you want to go again for?"

"Because I like going there, OK?"

"I know you do, love, but it doesn't mean you have to go every day, does it?"

"You go jogging twice a week. I don't complain about that."

"I do that to keep fit."

"Well, it's a mile walk each way to the training ground. That keeps me fit. You'd moan if I sat about at home all day."

"That's not the point."

"What is the point then?" Sometimes I wished Mum would come straight out with it, instead of pretending like this.

"The point is you can't spend your entire summer holiday hanging around a bunch of footballers."

"Why not?"

Mum sighed and tucked a stray strand of her highlighted shoulder-length hair back behind her ear. "It's not normal."

"Oh, so I'm a freak now, am I?"

"Why do you always have to twist everything I say, Claire?"

"'Cos that's what lawyers have to do."

"I'm not a criminal, Claire. I'm your mother."

"Worse luck."

Mum shook her head and did that thing with her lips which she did when I'd said something to annoy her.

"It's your father's fault, of course. He should never have got you interested in that football team."

"You just don't like it that we share an interest," I said.

Mum snorted. "He doesn't share anything with you. He'd rather go in the firm's executive box with a bunch of blokes in suits than take you to a game."

"They don't let under-sixteens in the boxes," I said. "Anyway, Dad has to entertain clients so he can improve his promotion prospects." Mum snorted again, no doubt thinking about the career prospects she'd had until I came along. She'd told me I wasn't "planned". Which was a nice way of saying I was a mistake. The sort of mistake that had to be covered up under a loose-fitting wedding dress. Apparently, being a single mum hadn't been an option for her, not even at the end of the swinging sixties. She said the permissive society never got as far as Potters Bar. I guessed it must have stopped at Barnet — a bit like the travel zones on a Capital card.

We ate in silence for a while. I hadn't planned on telling her about Dad calling. But I was so mad about her having a go at him that it kind of came out.

"Dad rang today, actually."

"You didn't tell me."

"Yeah, well I'm telling you now, aren't I?"

"What did he want?"

"Said he was gonna try and get me some United tickets soon."

"Well, don't get your hopes up. You know what happened last time. He's hardly got a good track record of keeping promises, has he?"

I pushed my half-eaten dinner away and got up from the table.

"Aren't you going to finish that?"

"No," I said, heading for the door. "Not if it means listening to you."

I went straight up to my room, took the match programme with Andy's picture in it from under my pillow and kissed him on the lips.

Andy kisses me back. His lips are soft and velvety — just like I knew they would be.

"I came because you needed me," he says, his brown eyes searing through me. It is like he knows me, knows everything

42

about me, has known me all my life. I nod. My heart is about to spill over, the love bubbling out from inside me.

"I haven't got anyone, you see," I explain. "I'm not interested in anyone else. I only want you." He nods. I want him to know that this isn't some silly crush. That just because I'm only fifteen it doesn't mean it's not serious.

"I'll never stop loving you," I say. "Not ever. This is for keeps." He nods again. I pull him to my chest and lie there holding him until I go to sleep. Smiling in the knowledge that he is mine now. And I will never let him go.

CHAPTER
TWO

"Get me out of this fucking hole," Daz screamed at me from behind the glass partition of the interview room at Rochdale Magistrates' Court.

Most people hate going to work on Monday mornings. But for most people the worst that can happen is that the train is late and uncomfortably overcrowded, they forget their umbrella and get wet in the dash to the office only to find the coffee machine is out of order. Whereas I, on the other hand, stoically put up with all of those things then arrived at work, descended into the bowels of the building to be greeted by a burly Group 4 Security officer, who buzzed me through two locked doors and into a small, stuffy interview room where the person on the other side of the partition was hollering at me in a barely intelligible rant while sweating profusely due to going cold turkey from spending two nights in a police cell.

I could have done without it, bearing in mind the turmoil going on in my own head. But I knew that would have to wait. My clients' crises were more important than my own.

"All right, Daz," I said, speaking slowly and firmly. "I'll do my best. But you need to tell me how you got in here in the first place." Daz and I were well acquainted, of course. He was one of our regulars; a well-known heroin addict and persistent offender with a penchant for removing expensive jewellery from people's houses without asking.

Daz scraped himself off the glass partition and sat shaking in the chair as he struggled to string a few sentences together.

"Needed a fix, like. Fucking window was open. A bit of sunshine and they all lose their heads. Shocking it is, like. Should be bloody arrested for inciting a crime."

"What happened, Daz?"

"Climbed in over the sink, didn't break any dishes or anything, mind. Slipped upstairs, stuff was out on the dressing table on view, helped myself, like. Straight into me bag, that'll do nicely, thank you very much. Didn't make no mess. Even fed the cat on the way out 'cos he was making a fuss, starving hungry he was. Oh, and I shut the window behind me so no one else could get in, like."

Daz shook his head as if the owners of the house he had burgled should be ashamed of themselves for neglecting their cat and grateful to him for preventing any further crimes on their property, although admittedly there wouldn't have been much left to take, judging by the impressive haul of jewellery, including a particularly expensive Rolex, which the police had relieved him of barely an hour later when they'd spotted him trying to flog it on a street corner.

"The thing is, Daz, when you're out on bail, you need to keep yourself clean. The magistrates don't like it, you know that."

"You can get me out though, can't you? You've gotta get me fucking out. I need to see Mickey, get a fix, like."

I sighed. Although I'd long ago given up hope of Daz ever being anything other than a hardcore user, it still saddened me to hear him talk like that. The social worker within, who knew all about his chaotic childhood with his mentally ill mother, still wanted to save him from himself. But he never did anything bad enough to warrant more than a few months inside, and that was never enough to stop him falling straight back into his old ways when he came out. Mickey was usually waiting on the street corner for him when he was released, offering a free welcome-home present, knowing full well Daz would be back for more before the night was out. I ought to tell Daz to move up a league with his crimes, hold up a bank or something; that way he might earn a long enough stretch to get some proper help. As it was, he didn't stand a chance.

"I'll do my best, but no promises on this one. We'll go for an adjournment and I'll apply for bail, but it'll depend who's on the bench, OK?"

Daz nodded mournfully. He knew the score. If it was Martin "Mother 'em" Maddox, a former head teacher in a tough comprehensive, we were in with a chance. He was the only magistrate who seemed to have any idea what it was really like on the streets out there. But if it was any of the others, in particular Joan "Hang 'em" Silverman, we were stuffed. She was on a one-woman crusade to rid of the streets of the dirty homeless, the feckless unemployed and anyone who didn't keep a clean handkerchief in their pocket or handbag.

Daz was escorted from the room, still cursing and shaking, to be replaced by another of the usual suspects. I looked up at the ceiling, trying to hide my disillusionment. It really wasn't supposed to be like this.

Daz was in luck. Maddox was sitting in the remand court. Which meant he somehow got away with bail, albeit with a pile of conditions attached which effectively kept him under curfew in his flat. Not that he would take any notice of them, mind. He grinned at me as he left court, still shaking but in remarkably better spirits.

"Thanks very much, like," he said. "See ya soon."

"Not too soon I hope," I said. He smiled again as he got out his mobile phone and switched it on. I knew who the first person on his speed dial would be.

"Mickey," I heard him say as he went down the stairs. "Where are you, like?"

There was just time to grab a quick coffee before my first trial of the day, which had been put back half an hour while some missing documents were brought over from the Crown Prosecution Service's building. It was par for the course, really. I'd have been worried if I turned up one day and everything ran smoothly.

I went through to the staff side of the café, where Jill poured me my usual Monday-morning black with no sugar and passed it through the hatch.

"Given up mixing with the proletariat, have we?" Nigel Foster, one of the CPS prosecutors, asked, looking up from his copy of the *Daily Telegraph* at the table in the corner. It was the sort of jibe I'd come to expect from him, as he seemed to think I preferred the company of my clients to fellow solicitors (which it had to be said in his case was probably true). Nigel was firmly in the establishment camp and of the opinion that defence solicitors were only one very small step up in the world order from the defendants themselves.

"No, that's why I thought I'd come and talk to you."

"I do admire the fact that you retain a sense of humour despite the dreadful people you have to fraternise with," chortled Nigel. He was forever extolling the virtues of life with the CPS but I would no more cross to "the other side" than ask Hang 'em Silverman round for tea.

"Do I deduce that I have the pleasure of your company in court today?" I enquired.

"You do indeed. And I have to say I'm looking forward to hearing what sort of cock-and-bull story you concoct for this one. Should be most entertaining."

Sometimes I would happily humour Nigel; on other occasions I seriously contemplated asking one of my less salubrious "acquaintances" to wipe the smug smirk off his face. The trouble with Nigel — and all bar one of the magistrates for that matter — was that he existed in a world where he was simply unable or unwilling to

48

contemplate the possibility that the police might occasionally lie, fabricate evidence, fit someone up or simply get it wrong. Which inevitably led him to the conclusion that all of my clients were guilty, and that therefore I spent my entire time cooking up elaborate stories in an effort to get them off the hook. I had won enough cases against him over the years to cast doubt on his theory, of course. Although it had to be said that the case which was about to start was unlikely to be one of them. I didn't usually go into court assuming the worst, but on this occasion it was hard to do otherwise. I was representing a young man called Dean Chandler, who was known to the police, and had been arrested while queuing inside a building society. He had been loitering outside for some time with a carrier bag containing a child's water pistol and a note in his pocket which read, "Give me the money, please." Undeniably, this did not look good. And on top of that, Hang 'em Silverman was hearing the case. My only hope was to argue that the charge of attempted robbery could not be proved because he hadn't actually threatened anyone or demanded money. And to hope that Silverman, who was a stickler for good manners, was impressed by the fact that he had at least said please on the note.

"Don't worry," I said to Nigel, slurping down my coffee, before standing up to leave the café. "I'll give you a run for your money."

I strode into the courtroom, which was decorated in various shades of beige and mottled brown, as if the thought of any other colour would have been positively frivolous.

Fiona looked up from her clerk's desk, her short, choppy auburn hair as mad as ever and seemingly at odds with her sombre trouser suit.

"Have a good weekend?" she enquired, her lilting Glaswegian accent as pleasing to my ears as ever as I sat down in front of her.

"Eventful," I said.

"Good events or bad?" There was a rustling from the door behind her.

"I'll fill you in at lunch," I whispered as the door opened.

"Court rise," said Fiona. We stood to attention and Silverman, all neat coiffure with twinset and pearls, walked in with her two cronies. She nodded her approval and lowered herself slowly and deliberately on to her chair (she'd never been the same since the castors had gone from under her on one occasion and she'd ended up on the floor. Unfortunately I hadn't been in court that morning, but Fiona's account and slow-motion action replay when the court had been empty later that day had been enough to keep a smile on my face for weeks). We sat down, Fiona introduced the case and Nigel stood up next to me.

"Your worships, what we have here is a clear case of someone being caught red-handed. Dean Chandler went to the Bradford and Bingley Building Society in Middleton to carry out a robbery. It was only the alertness of a female cashier, who had spotted him loitering outside for some time and called the police, which prevented what could have been a very traumatic incident for staff and customers."

As Nigel droned on, trying to make out that Dean was somehow on a par with the Great Train Robbers, my mind wandered back to the Twenty Years From Now list. It had kept me awake half the night, trying to work out at what point exactly my dreams had all gone up in smoke. Some of the answers were obvious — the Andy one, for instance. But others were harder to pin down. The career dream had looked to be on course for a long time. Top marks at law school, a training contract with a large firm in Manchester and a job offer after I'd qualified, with the prospect of a partnership dangling tantalisingly ahead in the future. Until I'd been made redundant nine years ago as part of a "restructuring programme". I'd been out of work for six months, and when a temporary job had come up as maternity cover for a solicitor at Barnes and Co. in Rochdale, I thought I'd better take it. It was only supposed to be for nine months, but the woman I was covering for didn't return to work after having her baby so I was taken on full-time. And for some unknown reason, I'd never managed to escape.

Fiona's overstated cough and kick under the desk alerted me to the fact that the prosecution's first witness, PC Hough, was in the witness box and Nigel had come to the end of his tedious questioning. I shuffled my notes and scrambled to my feet.

"Officer Hough, when you entered the building society, can you describe what the defendant was doing?"

"He was standing in the queue."

"Was he behaving aggressively in any way?"

"No."

"And was he brandishing the child's water pistol which has been presented as Exhibit A?" I asked, gesturing at the orange and red toy on Nigel's desk.

"No, it was in his carrier bag."

"And was he holding it with the carrier bag wrapped around it tightly to make it look like it was a weapon?"

"No. It was concealed in the bottom of the bag, but he hadn't reached the front of the queue when I arrived."

"And did the defendant behave violently towards you or anyone in the building society before, during or after his arrest?"

"No."

"Thank you, Officer Hough."

I went through the same questions with the cashier who'd phoned the police. By the time Nigel was winding up his case I was beginning to feel I might actually pull this one out of the hat. It was all going to come down to Dean's performance. But as he rustled his way into the witness box, read the oath jauntily and chirped "All right, miss" as I stood up, I sensed that this was going to be hard work.

"Mr Chandler, can you explain why you had a note saying 'Give me the money, please' in your pocket on the day in question?"

"It was just for a dare, like. Me mate Spanner thought it would be a laugh, you know." I glanced up at

Silverman, who was clearly not seeing the funny side of this.

"And why were you carrying the water pistol?" I asked anxiously.

"Just for a laugh, like. There weren't even no water in it."

"So, just to be clear. You had been dared to rob a building society. You wrote a note which you put in your pocket and you placed a water pistol in your carrier bag. You were observed waiting outside the building society for almost an hour before you finally went in."

"That's right, miss."

"But the truth is you lost your nerve, didn't you?"

"Nah, I didn't. I was well up for it." I frowned at Dean. He'd pushed the sleeves of his shell suit up and looked like he was about to start a fight. I realised that he had forgotten I was on his side and had taken exception to me portraying him as a coward.

"Mr Chandler, I'm simply trying to make it clear to everyone in this room that you had no intention of carrying out or even attempting any kind of robbery, did you?"

"Are you calling me a bottler?" Dean snarled at me. I groaned inwardly. Nigel would never let me hear the end of this.

"I thought the wee lad was going to run over and lamp you one," chuckled Fiona as we sat in the café at lunchtime.

"Maybe I should start wearing a big badge in court which says 'Just agree with me, I'm on your side'."

"I daresay a lad like that isn't used to anyone in authority fighting his corner. Shame though, I thought you had Nigel on the ropes until that point." I shrugged. I'd thought that too. But Dean had managed to inadvertently shoot himself in the foot. I still thought Silverman had been harsh though. Sending him down for two months when he'd never actually touched or threatened anyone. But it could have been worse. As she'd said herself, the sentence would have been much longer if it wasn't for the fact that he'd waited politely in the queue.

"Anyway, fill me in about your weekend," said Fiona.

I finished my mouthful of jacket potato and took a glug of tea (I always switched to Earl Grey in the afternoon) before answering.

"Mark wants us to move in together," I said.

"Well that's great. Congratulations," she replied, before looking at my face and stopping. "You don't want to, do you?"

"It's not that I don't want to. It was all a bit sudden, that's all. He wants us to buy a new place together and he took me to view a house and I felt like I had to make a decision on the spot. It was a bit like being on *Deal or No Deal*."

"Don't tell me Mark's gone all Noel Edmonds on you and started tucking his shirt into his jeans."

"No, I mean I led him to believe I was going to accept his offer."

"And you're not?"

"I don't know. Part of me's wondering if I should have turned him down there and then and waited to see what was in my red box."

Fiona raised one of her eyebrows while stirring her coffee.

"What's brought this on? I thought you two were sorted. You always seem so happy together."

I put down my knife and fork with a big sigh.

"Did you ever have dreams, Fiona?"

"You haven't been reading one of those books that claims to interpret them, have you? Only I read one once which said that dreaming about eating chocolate finger biscuits was a sign of me wanting to escape my sexual repression. When actually it was because I went to bed bloody hungry because Neil had finished the packet himself."

I laughed and shook my head.

"No, I mean dreams, ambitions for the future. I found this list, you see. Something I wrote when I was fifteen about what I thought my life would be like in twenty years' time."

"And surprise, surprise, you're not the Lord Chancellor, you don't live in a palace and you're not married to a prince."

"They weren't that daft. Well, not quite. But they weren't about working here and living in a new-build in Littleborough, either," I said.

"What's wrong with Littleborough?" asked Fiona, who lived a few miles down the road in Wardle.

"You know what I mean. It's the whole idea of me signing up to this package deal for life. It's like an admission of failure. That I'm giving up on everything I once dreamt about."

Fiona thought for a moment as she chewed the last of her cheese and pickle roll.

"Neil wanted to be a Formula One racing driver when he was a kid," she said. "He did go-karting and all that stuff, won some junior competition for the north-west. He'd been promised his first rally car and then his parents split up and everything went out of the window. Which is why he had to make do with being a copper and occasionally doing eighty around the ring road with his blue light flashing."

"But he must wonder what could have been, if things had been different."

"Sometimes when he's watching Formula One on TV I catch him cornering in the armchair. He's pretty good at popping champagne bottles and maybe he still fantasises about living in Monaco with some stick-thin model. But that's all it is. A fantasy. He grew up, got a proper job and me and Aidan and he's happy with his lot. A damn sight happier than that miserable bunch of F1 drivers look, at any rate."

I smiled and nodded. Fiona was doing her usual Wise Woman of the North bit. Maybe she was right. Maybe I was being stupid, hankering after my teenage dreams instead of being grateful for what I had.

"You wouldn't gamble on what's in the red box then?" I said.

"The trouble with gambling," said Fiona as she stood up and took her empty plate over to the hatch, "is that sometimes you end up losing everything."

Wednesday, 31 July 1985

The knowledge that any attempt to find something even remotely fashionable in my wardrobe was ultimately doomed never actually stopped me trying. I guess I secretly hoped that by rummaging through the assortment of undesirable items Mum had bought from Kays catalogue and the home and wear section at Tesco, I could somehow trigger a miracle of C.S. Lewis proportions in my wardrobe. Only I was hoping to discover a magical world of Madonna's cast-offs rather than the kingdom of Narnia.

I may not have been a fashion guru like Frankie, but I was acutely aware that the Delamare label didn't exactly rank up there with Nike or Lacoste. And now I had Andy to impress, creating the right image had taken on a whole new significance.

Eventually I plumped for jeans and my tea-bag tank-top again, on the grounds that they were the least naff things I possessed. Though I was conscious that even my jeans weren't the right sort. They were straight leg but they weren't stretch so they were at least two inches too wide at the bottom. They didn't exactly flap in the breeze but I could get in and out of them without too much effort, which meant they failed the test. Frankie would break into a sweat trying to get into hers, but once she had, they looked like a second skin. Mum said jeans that tight weren't healthy. As if I cared about that.

I skipped breakfast, too nervous about the prospect of seeing Andy again to even contemplate eating, and set off for Frankie's. I strolled down the street, past the rows of neat semis with their pristine net curtains and immaculate front gardens with not a begonia out of place (I suspected the flower beds had been precision designed with the aid of a giant gardening version of my school geometry set). Even the cats, sunning themselves on front steps, seemed unnaturally clean, as if they had been put through the "delicates" cycle and left outside to dry.

I stopped off at Aspland's on the corner for my regular Wednesday-morning review of the latest *Shoot!*. I found it in the usual place under one of the "This is NOT a public library" signs written in thick red marker pen on grubby pieces of cardboard and stuck to the racks with Sellotape. I waited until Mr Aspland was busy serving someone then began flicking through the pages, past the team poster of Arsenal and the picture spread on Bryan Robson at home with his wife and daughters, until I got to the fact file. The one on Andy Pailes.

I drew a sharp intake of breath and shut the magazine, not wanting to read intimate details about Andy in such a public place, virtually threw the money at a startled Mr Aspland and ran the rest of the way to Frankie's.

58

"Hello, is she ready yet?" I asked breathlessly when Mrs Alberti opened the door, letting the smell of greasy bacon and burnt toast rush out to greet me.

"Hello, love. She shouldn't be long. Come in a sec while I give her a shout."

I squeezed past Mrs Alberti's dumpy frame into the narrow hallway beyond. It was like walking into a tiny second-hand junk shop. Bone-china figures of the Virgin Mary jostled for position with a collection of glass peacocks displaying their plumage on the crowded windowsill. The walls were lined with decorative china plates and tacky-looking mementoes of Italy. Laura Ashley would have run screaming from the house. I kind of liked it.

"Francesca, Claire's here for you," Mrs Alberti shouted from the bottom of the stairs, struggling to make herself heard above the sound of Radio One coming from Frankie's room.

"I think you'll have to go up, love," she said eventually. "Tell her to turn that racket down, will you?"

"Hey, what's up with you?" Frankie was putting the finishing touches to her make-up as I burst into her room.

"Andy P-Pailes, f-fact file, *Shoot!*," I stuttered, incapable of forming sentences.

"So, has he got a girlfriend then?" enquired Frankie, calmly dabbing her freshly applied red lipstick with a tissue before practising her pout in the dressing-table mirror.

"I dunno, I haven't read it yet, have I?"

"Here, give it to me. Let's see what this guy's made of."

Frankie snatched the magazine from me, turned down the radio and sprawled out on her belly on the bed, crossing her ankles in the air behind her and propping herself up on her elbows as I waited for her to begin reading.

FULL NAME: *Andrew Pailes*
BIRTHPLACE/DATE: *Pontefract, Yorkshire, 31.8.62*

"Hey, that means he's twenty-three next month," said Frankie. "You'd better get him a card or something."

HEIGHT/WEIGHT: *5ft 9ins, 11st*
MARITAL STATUS: *Single*

"See, told you," Frankie said. I tried hard not to grin too much as a surge of relief ran through me. Quickly followed by the realisation that it only meant he wasn't married or engaged, not that he didn't have a girlfriend.

LIVE: *Cuffley, Herts*
NICKNAME: *Haven't got one yet*

"Likely story," scoffed Frankie. "It's probably Andy Pandy or something."

MOST MEMORABLE MATCH: *The UEFA Cup Final victory last season*
MISCELLANEOUS LIKES: *Going for long walks*

in the country, polite people, Russian history, politics,
Yorkshire

"God, I'm nearly falling asleep," said Frankie.
"Where does he mention nightclubs?"

"There," I said, peering over Frankie's shoulder as I
pointed to Andy's answer to the next question.

MISCELLANEOUS DISLIKES: *Racism, hooligan-*
ism, Margaret Thatcher, nightclubs
FAVOURITE NEWSPAPER: *The* Guardian
FAVOURITE TV SHOW: Newsnight, Spitting Image,
Blackadder
TV SHOW YOU ALWAYS SWITCH OFF: Terry
and June
FAVOURITE PRE-MATCH MEAL: *Chicken and*
beans

"He's a bit old to be eating from the children's
menu, isn't he?" said Frankie. "I'm sorry, Claire, the
guy's got no sophistication whatsoever."

"Just 'cos he didn't put lasagne or something fancy
like Matt did. Anyway, I don't know what you're going
on about, there's nothing wrong with chicken and
beans."

"Said the vegetarian," said Frankie, throwing her
head back as she laughed out loud. I hated it when she
caught me out like that.

"When you've quite finished. I'd like to hear the rest
of it, thank you," I said. Frankie made a face at me
before continuing.

FAVOURITE MUSIC: *The Smiths, Echo and the Bunnymen, The Cure*

I nodded approvingly. I supported Morrissey's "Meat is Murder" stand, liked the song about the dancing horses and might have been a Goth if I'd only had the nerve to dye my hair black.

FAVOURITE FILM: *Reds*
BEST FRIEND IN FOOTBALL: *Mike Thompson at United*
WHICH PERSON IN THE WORLD WOULD YOU MOST LIKE TO MEET? *Nelson Mandela*
WHAT WILL YOU BE DOING IN 20 YEARS' TIME? *Working as a lawyer, living with my family somewhere rural, probably in Yorkshire*

The corners of my mouth curled up into a *Mona Lisa*-type smile as Frankie put the magazine down. I couldn't believe he wanted to be a lawyer too. Usually footballers either put "running a pub" or "being a manager" after they retired from playing. I knew for certain now. We were made for each other.

"He's absolutely perfect," I said, sitting down on the edge of the bed to steady myself.

"If you want to lead the most boring life imaginable," snorted Frankie.

"Come on then, what are you going to be doing in twenty years' time which is so great?"

"Lying on a Mediterranean beach, rubbing suntan lotion on to Matt's legs."

"What, the whole time? Life's not one big holiday, you know."

"God, you sound like my mother."

"I'm talking about what you'll really be doing, about your whole life."

"OK," said Frankie, going over to a cupboard in the corner of her room and pulling out some paper and a couple of pens. "Let's do our own Twenty Years From Now list. Five categories each and we'll both write down our answers." She handed me a pen. I took it from her, knowing how futile it was to argue with her and liking the idea of doing it anyway. Of seeing my life planned out before me like that.

"Right," said Frankie as she sat back down on the bed. "My categories are love life, where you go on holiday, career, what you look like and if you're rich or poor."

"You can't say love life, you have to put marital status like in the magazine."

"They're my questions, just write down your answers."

I tutted and started writing, looking up occasionally to try to glance over Frankie's shoulder.

"Come on then, your turn," she said a few minutes later.

"OK, where you'll be living, whether you've got kids, who your best friend is, what your interests are and whether you'll be happy."

"We're hardly gonna put we'll be miserable, are we?"

"I dunno. Morrissey seems to like it."

Frankie shrugged and started writing. I started thinking, keen not to rush it. If I was planning out my life like this I wanted to get it right. Frankie waited in silence for a few minutes after she'd finished before she started to hassle me.

"Hurry up, we'll never get to the training ground at this rate." I ignored her until I was certain I had it right.

"There," I said. "Finished."

"Come on then," said Frankie. "Let's hear it."

"You never said we were going to have to read it out."

"What else are we going to do with it?"

"I think we should put them in a sealed envelope only to be opened in twenty years' time."

"Why?"

The real reason was so that she didn't take the piss out of me until she knew whether it had come true or not, but I didn't want to admit that.

"Because it's what you do with stuff about the future," I said.

Frankie rolled her eyes. "I know what you've put anyway: married to Andy Pailes, working as a lawyer, living in Yorkshire, blah, blah, blah." I was perturbed to think I was that predictable. But there again I had a good idea what Frankie had put too: something which involved living with Matt, being a travel rep and having loads of dosh.

"No point reading them out then," I said. "Have you got an envelope?"

Frankie sighed, rummaged in a drawer and pulled out an unused writing set, the sort of thing great-aunts give you for Christmas without realising that fifteen-year-old girls don't send letters to anyone — apart from thank-you notes to great-aunts for writing sets. She handed me an envelope; I tucked the folded piece of paper inside and carefully sealed it.

"I still think you've been watching too many time capsules being buried on *Blue Peter*," said Frankie.

"We'd better write on the front," I said, choosing to ignore her. "So we don't forget what it is." I started writing in big bold letters: NOT TO BE OPENED UNTIL 31 JULY 2005.

"Fucking hell," said Frankie, "that's next millennium; we'll be ancient by then."

"You will," I said. "I'll always be eighteen months younger, remember."

Frankie pulled a face and stuffed her envelope into her knicker drawer. I put mine in my bag, safe in the knowledge I had everything mapped out now.

On the way to the training ground, I stopped off at the newsagent's to buy a copy of the *Guardian*, which I arranged in my bag so it could be clearly seen.

"Aren't you gonna buy some baked beans for him too?" sniggered Frankie.

"Piss off," I said. "Or I'll cross you off my list as being my best friend."

It was quiet when we arrived. The players were all getting ready in the clubhouse and there weren't as many fans as there had been on Monday. We made our way down to our vantage point on the grass banking. I'd been so excited at Andy's answers to the fact file, I hadn't stopped to think how it would go down with his teammates, most of whom read nothing more challenging than the *Sun* and the *Racing Post*. But as we watched the squad come out for the morning training session, it soon became clear that it wasn't only Frankie who thought Andy was weird.

"Are you coming with us, Trotsky, or do you fancy a nice long walk in the country?" Clubber shouted as Andy ran out. The other players started laughing. Frankie joined in too, though I don't think she understood why she was laughing. She dropped history before she did anything much about Russia.

Personally, I thought the jibe was a bit rich coming from someone who had listed *Porky's* as his favourite film in a recent fact file. Andy obviously thought so too.

"I'm surprised you've even heard of Trotsky. Did they name a racehorse after him or something?"

"Tell you one thing I wouldn't bet on," Clubber shouted back, "and that's your mate Mandela getting out of jail. He's got about as much chance of that as you have of getting my place in the first team."

"He'd better start packing then," said Andy.

I glowed with pride. Andy could give as good as he got. He didn't seem to care that he was different from all the others. I wished I could be like that.

We sprawled out in the sunshine on the grass banking, in the exact spot which Frankie had calculated gave her the best chance of seeing up Matt's shorts. Most of the players had taken their shirts off and were displaying the suntans they had acquired on various foreign holidays that summer. Frankie started trying to guess where each of them had been, as if she knew which beaches would produce a certain shade of tan (I knew for a fact this wasn't the case, as the only beach she had ever been to was Clacton).

The first strains of George Michael's "Careless Whisper" drifted across from the top of the bank, where a girl a bit older than us was sitting with her Walkman turned up loud enough for everyone to hear. Before I knew it, I was mouthing along to the words as I gazed down at Andy's glistening chest. When the saxophone kicked in, I felt myself begin to tingle in some weird places and let out a long, deep sigh.

"What do you think heaven's like?" I asked dreamily.

"Like this, I guess," Frankie said. "I reckon God's the referee in one huge, never-ending football match featuring United. And the only rule is that the players have to take their shirts off."

"I don't think the Pope would approve of that."

"What d'ya mean? The Pope would be in goal for the other side. He used to be a goalkeeper, you know," she said.

"No he didn't, you're having me on."

"He did. I swear on his life. He used to play for some Polish side, I read it somewhere."

"What, so girls like us in Poland used to fancy the Pope?"

"Yeah, I guess so. It's no more stupid than girls in Liverpool fancying Sammy Lee."

"No, I s'pose not. I wonder what his nickname was."

"Probably Nobber," said Frankie. "Now that would freak my mum out."

An hour or so later, United manager Ken Benson led the players over the other side of the grass bank, where the pitch they used for youth team games and practice matches was.

"They can't do that," complained Frankie, as the players disappeared from view and most of the other fans started wandering back towards the car park. "I haven't come up here to watch grass grow."

"They're probably practising tactics and things, stuff they want to keep secret," I informed her. Frankie didn't know much about that side of the game.

"Secret from who? We're hardly gonna be on a spying mission for Arsenal, are we?"

Frankie sat and fidgeted for five minutes before getting to her feet.

"It's no good, I'm going over the top to see what Matt's up to."

"Don't be a flid," I said, eyeing up the steep bank and Frankie's high heels and short skirt. "You'll never get up there in those shoes."

"Course I will. Watch me." Frankie started teetering up the bank. The grass was short and slippery where it had been scorched brown by the sun and she had to climb on all fours, clutching on to the odd clump of longer, straw-like grass as she went. As she scrambled triumphantly to the top of the bank she popped her head up, like an inquisitive meerkat, to look for Matt, only to come face-to-groin with him as he strode up the bank from the other side with the rest of the players.

"Oh, hi," she said lamely, craning her neck back to smile up at him before losing her footing and sliding back to the bottom of the bank, finishing in a crumpled heap with her skirt hitched up around her waist.

"They can see your knickers," I hissed, as the players jogged down the banking, barely concealed smirks on their faces.

"It's OK, I don't mind," whispered Frankie. "They're my best ones."

"Are you sure Matt didn't look at my arse?" Frankie asked for the fifth time, as we waited for the players to leave the clubhouse later.

"No, I told you, he kept looking straight ahead. What did you expect? He was hardly gonna jump on you after that performance, was he?"

"At least he'll have something to remember me by while we're away next week." Frankie's family were off to Clacton on holiday, while my mum was taking me to Great Yarmouth.

"If I were you, I'd hope he's got a very short memory," I said.

Matt certainly had very short shorts on when he emerged from the dressing room. I watched as a cluster of teenage girls, their tongues practically lolling out of their mouths, crowded round him, giving each other dirty sideways looks as they vied for his attention. Frankie turned to me and shook her head.

"Honestly, look at them," she said. "Have they no shame?" Seconds later she had rolled her already short skirt up at the waistband and was strutting across the car park towards him, dragging me behind her.

"Hi, Matt. Could I have my picture taken with you, please?" she said, flashing her best smile, which was nearly as dazzling as Matt's own Colgate-sponsored teeth. The crowd of girls parted grudgingly and Matt, who, if he did recognise her from earlier, was good enough not to say anything, turned to stand next to her with a fixed smile on his face. As I looked through the viewfinder I gasped as I saw Frankie's arm creep behind Matt before settling casually on his hip. A gentle breeze brought the overpowering smell of Paco Rabanne aftershave wafting through the air. Frankie's eyes glazed over and she appeared to swoon momentarily before regaining her composure just in time to smile for the shot to be taken.

"I thought you were gonna faint then," I said afterwards.

"Nah," replied Frankie. "I was having one of those no-sex orgasms."

I wasn't sure whether she was joking or whether this was actually possible. Maybe I'd missed that article in *Just Seventeen*.

With Matt departed, we turned our attention to the rest of the players. No member of the squad was allowed to get past us without signing something. It didn't even have to be a player; anyone who featured in the club handbook was deemed worthy of an autograph request. We got a "best wishes" from manager Ken Benson and an "all the best" from his number two Terry Dixon. Frankie even received a scrawled "good

70

luck" from Ray Moran, the youth-team coach, which caused great excitement at first when she deciphered it wrongly as "good fuck".

We were running out of people to ask when I spotted Albert Palmer, the club's balding kit manager, walking towards us with a crate under one arm. I approached him eagerly and asked for his autograph. There was a slight pause and a look of bewilderment crossed his face before it cracked into a broad smile.

"You can have it if you like, love, but I'm only Fred the baker. Still, you never know, I might make the first team yet."

Frankie collapsed in a fit of giggles. But for me, the embarrassment of having asked the baker for his autograph was nothing compared to the realisation that the whole thing had been witnessed by Andy, who had slipped unnoticed from the clubhouse and was waiting to squeeze past the bread van to get to his car.

I wondered if this day had been sent to test me in some way, to scientifically establish exactly what degree of embarrassment a fifteen-year-old girl could withstand. Andy gave an understanding shrug.

"Don't worry, I don't know who everyone here is yet, either."

"Yeah, but at least you don't go round asking the baker for his autograph," I said, feeling my face turn a shade not dissimilar to something called "pillar-box red" on the Dulux paint chart.

"True, but I might have asked the kit manager for a sliced loaf without realising."

I smiled. I was actually sharing a joke with Andy Pailes. Not in my head but in real life. Before I knew it, I was asking to have my photograph taken with him and edging towards him, not daring to be as bold as Frankie and place my arm around his waist, but feeling drawn to the point where our bodies almost touched.

"Did you forget to deliver that one this morning?" Andy asked, pointing to the copy of the *Guardian* sticking out of my bag.

"Oh no," I said, horrified that he should think I did a paper round. "It's mine, I get it every day."

"Great." Andy smiled. "That's two they sell round here then."

I turned back to smile at the camera. It took me a few seconds to realise that someone's hand was resting lightly on my shoulder. And a few more for it to sink in that the hand in question could only belong to one person. Andy Pailes had his arm round me. I knew straight away that this was the most significant moment in my life so far. More important even than winning the UEFA Cup last season. I just prayed that Frankie captured the photographic evidence I needed to prove it had actually happened. A second after the camera whirred, Andy said, "Thank you," slipped from my side and was gone, sending me plummeting back down to earth just as the real Albert Palmer, who it had to be said was a dead ringer for Fred the baker, strolled out of the clubhouse.

"Hey, Claire. Here's your man," giggled Frankie. "Aren't you going to ask for his autograph?"

"Piss off," I said. "You're only jealous 'cos Andy put his arm round me."

Frankie didn't say anything. But she sang "One Albert Palmer, there's only one Albert Palmer" quietly under her breath all the way home.

The pole felt cold and slippery under my sweaty palm. I looked up and realised I was gripping it so hard, my knuckles had turned white. I hadn't felt like this since I'd been on the rollercoaster at Thorpe Park. In comparison, the number 242 bus was cheaper and the queue for it had certainly been shorter. It wasn't being on the bus that was causing the stomach-churning, though. It was what I was going to do when I got off. I suspected there might actually be a law against it. I certainly hadn't told my mum where I was going, or even Frankie for that matter. This was something I wanted to keep to myself. I reached up and pressed the bell. It was a stop earlier than I had intended to get off, but as I wasn't sure where I was going anyway, it didn't seem to matter. The doors opened and folded back with a hiss. I glanced at the driver's face in the mirror. He might know, of course; I could always ask him. But it was too late now. The doors were open. I stepped off and walked purposefully in the direction the bus was going. As soon as it passed me, I stopped and took out the fact file from my bag.

Cuffley. That was all it said. Not much to go on, but Cuffley was a small place, much smaller than Potters Bar. I'd brought a map with me; it was simply a process of elimination. I had an idea in my head of what his home would look like. It would be individual, of course, like him. Something old and full of character — maybe even a thatched roof. I remembered the picture of Matt Goodyear's house which had featured in *Shoot!* It was big and modern and tasteless, like it had been made out of a "build a footballer's home" Identikit. The one thing I knew was that Andy's house would look nothing like that.

It smelt nice, Cuffley. Potters Bar smelt grey. But here it smelt fresh and welcoming; it was a different class of air. I walked on towards the village centre. Past a row of terraced cottages and up to a wooden gate which led into a churchyard. I hesitated before pushing it open and wandering up the cobbled path. The gravestones were the right sort. Lopsided and weathered with barely legible inscriptions. A few graves were dotted with fresh flowers; others were partially grown over with grass and weeds. But it was the church itself which I was drawn towards. It looked like the sort of church I'd painted as a child. A small stone chapel with a slate roof and stained-glass windows spaced at appropriate intervals. Towered over by a slightly crooked spire, reaching up past the tree-tops, oddly out of proportion with the rest of the structure. I walked around it, once in each direction. It was perfect.

I am wearing a huge dream of a wedding dress, one like Princess Di's. My mum didn't like it, of course. Tutted and said it looked like it needed a good iron. But it doesn't matter what she thinks. Not any more. I adore it. And more importantly, I know Andy will too. And that is all that matters. I gather the crumpled ball of ivory silk taffeta as I step down carefully from the horse-drawn carriage and watch it tumble on to the pavement, prompting gasps of delight from the well-wishers who have gathered outside. I smile at them and take my father's arm as I walk towards the front door of the church. I glance across at Dad's face. He is smiling broadly as if he is proud, really proud of his girl. Inside the church Andy is waiting, dressed in a charcoal-grey suit with a purple cravat, to match the colour of the tulips in my bouquet. He is thinking how lucky he is to be marrying the girl of his dreams. The girl who worships the ground he walks on. As I enter the church and the first shaky notes of the Bridal March ring out, he turns and catches his first glimpse of me. "Beautiful," he whispers, his eyes glistening with tears. I smile and glide on up the aisle as if I am on castors and the strength of his love is enough to pull me towards him.

"Hello. Can I help you?"

The voice was unfamiliar. I looked up. The vicar had twinkling eyes and a bushy beard. He was the right sort too.

"No, I'm fine, thanks. Just having a look round. Nice place you've got here."

The vicar smiled. He must get this sort of thing quite often. People popping in to see if it measured up to their requirements.

"Right, I'll leave you to it then," he said. "Take as long as you want."

"Thank you," I replied. "But I'm done now. I've seen everything I need to."

I started back down the aisle, before turning abruptly.

"How long in advance do you need to book? For weddings, I mean."

"Oh, I wouldn't worry for a while yet," he said, the twinkle getting brighter. "Come back a bit nearer the time. I'm sure we'll be able to fit you in."

I nodded appreciatively, wondering if he was a United fan.

I left the churchyard and crossed to the other side of the street. I could see a newsagent's on the corner. It would be a good place to start. I had no idea what I was going to say. But I knew the key was to sound casual about the whole thing.

The newsagent's was cramped, bulging magazine racks down one side and a central display crammed full of everything from greeting cards to Sindy vanity mirror sets. I flicked through the birthday cards, picking out something appropriate and edging it sideways as I held the other cards in place before taking it up to the till.

"That's seventy-nine pee, love," the woman behind the counter said. She was middle-aged and had hair which looked like it was set in curlers. I wasn't sure if she'd be any help but I handed over the money anyway before rummaging in my bag.

"Oh no."

"What's the matter, love?" The woman looked up from the till.

"I've only gone and forgotten my address book. The card's for a friend; it's his birthday tomorrow. I need to catch the last post."

"Does he live local?"

"Oh yeah, in Cuffley. It's just the name of the road I can't remember."

"Do you know what letter it begins with?"

"No, I can't even remember that. My mind's gone blank. Daft, isn't it? Oh well, he'll just have to get it a day late, I suppose."

I waited for an offer but it wasn't forthcoming. I was going to have to force the issue. Look casual, I reminded myself. I started to walk away before turning back.

"I've just thought. He probably gets his papers delivered from here. You couldn't have a look in your book for me, could you? Just in case."

The woman looked me up and down. For once I hoped that I did look like an innocent young thing. I did my big pleading eyes thing. It worked.

"Course I can, love. Hang on a sec."

She pulled out a large dog-eared black book from below the counter.

"Here we are, it's all done alphabetically. What's his surname?"

"Pailes," I said, hoping the newsagent couldn't hear the sound of my heart thumping. The woman flicked forward to the Ps.

"How about that? First one on the page. Monkton Road, it is. Number nine. Owes three weeks' papers, tell him."

The woman looked pleased with herself. But not half as pleased as I felt inside.

"Monkton, course it is. I remember now. Thanks ever so much. You've been a great help."

As I hurried out of the shop, I prayed that Andy wouldn't go to pay the papers the next day. Or that if he did, the woman wouldn't wish him a happy birthday.

According to my map, Monkton Road was on the far side of the village. My pace quickened as I drew nearer. It had to be right. It had to be how I'd imagined. I turned the corner and a smile slid across my face. The road was straight and narrow. A row of terraced cottages stretched down one side. Opposite were a mixture of shorter terraces and semi-detached cottages, set back slightly from the pavement. Not a hint of pebble-dash or white plastic window frames in sight. I breathed a sigh of relief. I counted along the odd side of the road. Number nine was one of the semi-detached cottages. It was painted white and had stone mullion windows. The solid wood front door had a brass knocker, the front step was satin black. It was Andy's home. It was everything I had dreamt it would be.

I blinked back the gathering tears. I hadn't realised how much it would hurt, being on the outside looking in. This was where I belonged. Where I was meant to be. I crossed the road and edged closer, one hesitant step at a time. His car wasn't there. And there was no sign of life inside. But it didn't matter, I could feel his presence. It was enough to be here. I stood for a long time, a few yards from his front door. Just watching. Taking it all in. A few people went past, a woman with a baby in a pushchair, an elderly man with a plastic shopping bag. They smiled at me in a neighbourly way. It would be a nice place to live. Much nicer than Potters Bar.

I was still standing there when the silver Golf pulled up on the other side of the road and the driver got out, casually slinging his jacket over one shoulder and jangling his keys in the other hand. I started walking, forcing my reluctant legs into action. Desperate that he shouldn't see me. Shouldn't get the wrong idea. I kept walking until I was safely out of sight round the corner. Taking a couple of deep breaths, I leant on a garden wall to steady myself. It was a few minutes before I stopped shaking. When I did, I took my address book and pen from my bag and carefully wrote, "9 Monkton Road, Cuffley" in big black capital letters. I didn't write it on the page marked "A" or "P". I wrote it under "H", for home.

CHAPTER
THREE

"Fat, greedy bastard," I said, scooping up the slug which had chomped its way through half of my lettuces and lobbing him high over the wall. The idea of getting the allotment had been to have somewhere to relax and unwind on my rare days off work. I'd envisaged ending up like Barbara from *The Good Life,* all chilled out, self-sufficient and earthily sexy. Instead I was stressed out, still having to buy most of my veg from Tesco, dirty and tired. It was hard work, this allotment lark, particularly as I'd vowed to do it all organically. I hadn't realised how mean and hungry the slugs were in Todmorden. And I suspected that the beer I'd poured into jam jars and sunk into the ground was actually encouraging them to my patch for a boozing and fast-food session, instead of drowning them in a drunken stupor.

"I've never seen a flying one before," said a voice from behind me. I looked up to see Tomato Ted (as he was known by all at the allotments) standing there holding a large slug which looked suspiciously like the one I'd just thrown (I couldn't tell for sure, as I hadn't yet found an efficient branding or microchip system)

80

between his thumb and forefinger. "Hit me on the head it did while I was on my way to the water butt."

I slapped my hand to my mouth. "Oh, Ted. I am so sorry. I hadn't realised you were there. I shouldn't have thrown it anyway, of course."

"It's all right. Didn't do me any lasting damage. I shan't be reporting you to the authorities." I grinned as I imagined coming up before Hang 'em Silverman on a charge of battering a pensioner with a slug. "I do have one request, though."

"Go on," I said.

"Permission to squash the blighter." Ted was not known for his sentimentality when it came to garden pests.

I surveyed the remains of my lettuces.

"I think on this occasion I won't be offering it a defence," I said.

"Good," said Ted. "And here's some advice." I drew closer; being offered advice by Tomato Ted was generally seen as acceptance into the inner allotment circle. "If you want rid of them, you'll have to throw them further than that. They can cover half a mile in one night, you know."

"Really? That's incredible," I said, annoyed at myself for not checking out the homing abilities of slugs before deciding where to dispose of them. And then I noticed Ted's shoulders shaking, and the hint of a smile on his weather-beaten face.

"Eh, I had you there," he chuckled, winking at me before walking off in the direction of his green and bountiful plot. I smiled. The trouble with being an allotment novice was that you never knew when someone was taking the piss.

I returned to my weeding, watering and wondering. The wondering wasn't anything to do with gardening, of course. It was about my answer. I was seeing Mark later when he'd finished work and I owed him one. Having managed to avoid the subject of the house every time we'd spoken on the phone since Saturday, I was well aware I wouldn't be able to get through a curry without it being raised. I suspected it would come up even before the poppadoms arrived. And although I knew what Mark wanted to hear, I was still unsure about saying it. I'd made mistakes in love before. Big ones. And I didn't know if saying yes was the sensible thing to do or the surest way of waving goodbye to my dreams.

The list was still on the coffee table when I got home. It had been there since I found it. Taunting me. Reminding me of the past. And the future which hadn't materialised.

I flipped up the lid of my laptop. I needed to know what had happened to Frankie's dreams. I wasn't sure whether I wanted them to have come true or not, but I felt a sudden urge to find out. I went straight to Friends Reunited. I'd looked her up once, when it had first started. She hadn't been on it then but that was a long time ago. I scrolled through the list of names from my old school, some familiar, others who I had no recollection of at all, until I found her. Francesca Alberti. I clicked on her profile and waited, scanning the brief information she'd provided. She was married with four children, still living in Potters Bar and running her own business. I nodded. The only part which surprised me was the number of children. Frankie had never struck me as the maternal type. I was relieved about the lack of a photo, because I suspected she'd still look fabulous. I imagined her suave, handsome husband by her side, the four adorable bambinos and the business she ran, probably some sort of travel firm specialising in villas in Italy.

The fifteen year old in me, who had always been somewhat in awe of her, felt a tiny bit jealous. Well, OK, a huge great bloody chunk jealous, actually. But the grown-up me was pleased for her. I also realised how much I missed her. I'd never intended to lose touch. But things had never been the same between us after what happened. And when I'd moved to Manchester to go to university we'd drifted even further apart. By the time I left, we were down to exchanging Christmas cards. And then I'd met David and everything had changed again. When I sent her the invite to my wedding, it came back to me marked "No longer at this address". Her family had obviously moved and I had no way of getting in touch with her. If she'd wanted to, she could have contacted me through my mum. She never did though. So I guessed she had a whole new life of her own.

And now? We could never go back to how we were. We would both have changed so much. She was a mum of four, for Christ's sake. It would be good to speak to her, though. To let her know I hadn't forgotten her.

And to find out how it felt to have all your dreams come true.

I clicked on "Send an e-mail". I had no idea what to say, so reverted to my fifteen-year-old self.

> Hi, Frankie, it's me. What have you been up to (apart from having four kids, that is)? I live in West Yorkshire now and I'm a lawyer (big surprise). Oh, and I finally made it into an A cup! Would be great to hear from you when you've got a moment.
> Love
> Claire
> X

I hesitated before pressing send. I was making contact with the past. A past which had lain dormant for a long time but was still capable of exploding in my face. I wanted to go there though. I wanted to find out what had become of Frankie. And what had become of me.

My message winged its way to Potters Bar. Before I knew it I was on a Google search screen, and my fingers had somehow typed in the name "Andy Pailes". That was the trouble with uncovering the past. It was hard to know when to stop digging.

The phone rang next to me. I jumped, my fingers fumbling for the green button.

"Hi, it's me." Mark's voice jolted me back to the present.

"Oh, hi."

"My case has just finished and I'm starving. So if you're up for eating earlier, they open at half five. Unless you've got enough stuff from the allotment for that curry you promised to make, that is."

I smiled. The chances of me successfully growing even a single pea now looked remote.

"No, 'fraid not. The bastard slugs have eaten it all. I'll meet you there at half five."

"Great. See you there. I'll probably have ordered my body weight in poppadoms."

I put the phone down, looked up at the screen, saw Andy's name, then deleted it and quickly returned to my inbox. It unnerved me, though. How close I had come.

"Hi. I take it you won," I said as I arrived at the Bay of Bengal to find Mark sitting in our usual booth, his shirt sleeves rolled up and tie loosened, a contented look on his face as he eyed the pile of poppadoms in front of him. He grinned at me, his eyes sparkling with aliveness, stood up and kissed me. The sort of kiss which reminded me how lucky I was to have him.

"Yep, Mrs Lupton is now considerably richer and the council will be a bit more careful about how they put up their Christmas lights this year." I laughed and shook my head. Mark's cases tended to range from the bizarre to the ridiculous. Often I felt his clients were trying their luck to cover up the fact that they'd been pretty stupid in the first place. But you really shouldn't have to worry about being hit on the head by an illuminated Christmas star while walking down the high street.

"I bet the press will have a field day with this one."

"I know," said Mark, breaking into the poppadoms as soon as I sat down. "Loads of 'Catch a Falling Star' headlines I should guess." I watched as he scooped up some raita. His whole body still wired with the thrill of the win, the scent of victory practically dripping off him. He was one of those people who it was impossible to separate from his job, it was so much a part of him. I'd seen it the first time I'd come up against him in court (I'd lost, of course): the sharpness of thought, the ability to twist and turn his way out of anything, the sheer love of playing the game. I sometimes thought he was wasted being a personal injury lawyer. He could have been a top criminal barrister if he'd put his mind to it. Or some hotshot corporate lawyer. But that was where he differed from David. He loved his work but he wanted a life outside of it. And he wasn't prepared to do that whole playing golf with the boss thing and being the chair of the Rotary Club simply to work his way up the greasy pole. He'd much rather have a kick-about with the lads from the pub footie team on a Sunday morning. And, amongst other things, that was why I'd fallen for him. Because he was good at what he did but he didn't take himself too seriously. He loved life. He wasn't a slave to anyone. And his enthusiasm for whatever he did was infectious. He was a very hard man to say no to.

"So," he said, sitting back on the plush bench seat and sweeping a stray wisp of his light brown hair back off his forehead, "have you had enough time yet? Only if you sleep on it any longer, you'll be developing bed sores."

I smiled. It was a fair enough point. I opened my mouth to say something but my insides were so twisted that they wouldn't let the words out. I looked up at Mark. Clouds of doubt were casting shadows over his face, his usual self-assurance momentarily obliterated.

"I do want to live with you," I managed finally. "I just don't want to rush into anything."

"Two years together is hardly what I'd call rushing," said Mark.

"I don't mean that. I mean being put on the spot about this house. I really appreciate all the effort you went to in finding it, but it just isn't me. I know you said it ticks all the boxes, but it doesn't tick any of my boxes."

Mark's eyebrows made a desperate bid for his hairline. He clearly hadn't been expecting that. I wasn't sure if I had. But now it was out, there was no taking it back.

"I see," he said, busying himself by trying to scoop up the last spoonful of raita from his plate in an effort to hide his disappointment. I reached out and took his other hand.

"This is not about you," I said. "So please don't take it personally. I'm simply suggesting that if we do this, we do it in a way that we're both happy with. That way we're not starting off with a problem, or with one of us resenting where we've ended up living."

"Is it because it's in Lancashire?" asked Mark. "Because if it is, I'd be willing to consider living just over the border, Walsden maybe. As long as I can see Lancashire on the horizon I should be all right. I could always get my air and water shipped in if my body can't stand the Yorkshire stuff."

I smiled, relieved he had at least retained his sense of humour.

"I've nothing against Lancashire. Not really. It's the house. It's too new, too lacking in character. I don't want to live in a road where every house looks the same. I'm not a great fan of cul-de-sacs. Something to do with there being no way out the other end, I think."

"OK," said Mark, visibly brightening. "There were some other houses on my shortlist. I'm sure there are some that aren't in cul-de-sacs. Why don't I arrange some viewings for next weekend?"

I sighed. I had tried so hard to avoid a straight "no". But I was going to have to put the brakes on before Mark's enthusiasm got the better of him and we skidded out of control.

"What I'm trying to suggest," I said, choosing to look at my plate rather than Mark, "is that we actually leave the whole house-hunting thing for the moment. It's pointless us finding something we love if we're not in a position to buy it. It would make a lot more sense to put both of our places on the market first and see what happens."

"And what if we get an offer on one of them?"

"We move in to whoever's is left while we start house-hunting. At least that way we can see how we get on together before we commit to a whopping great mortgage."

"So you're suggesting a sort of try-before-you-buy scheme?" said Mark, sounding a bit put out.

"It's a big step, living together. I want to make sure it's going to work."

"Why wouldn't it work?" Mark sounded stung. I looked up at him. Sometimes he forgot that I had previous. That I was uncomfortably familiar with the house and contents splitting process.

"You might be sick of me after a few months," I said. "Believe me, I'm not easy to live with."

Mark squeezed my hand, finally cottoning on to my reluctance.

"You're right. And if you change your mind about me, all you'll have to do is take me back to M and S for a refund. If you've still got the receipt, that is."

I grinned, relieved that I had bought the time I needed and we seemed to have survived the conversation. Though I suspected Mark was putting on a brave face for my benefit.

"Are you sure you're OK about all this?" I said. "I am sorry about the house. I know you really liked it."

"Hey, it's not me you should feel sorry for. It's Chris, the estate agent. I'll have to break it to him very gently. He's been ringing me every day."

We were interrupted by the waiter arriving at our table with an ice bucket and two champagne glasses. I looked at Mark. Clearly he hadn't anticipated my response.

"I wanted to celebrate in style," he shrugged. I winced as the waiter popped the cork and poured, knowing I had metaphorically kneed Mark in the balls.

"I'm sorry. I feel really bad now," I said, when the waiter had scuttled away. "I know this isn't what you had in mind."

"It's OK. We'll still get there in the end," Mark said. "It's just like you're taking me on the scenic route."

I nodded. Not wanting to admit that I didn't have a TomTom to back up my lousy navigational skills.

"Thanks," I said. "I do appreciate you being so good about it."

Mark smiled as our glasses collided with more of a thud than a clink. I noticed a tiny crack in mine as I raised it to my mouth, but decided not to say anything.

We got back to my house earlier than usual. The food had been good but the conversation a little strained and neither of us had poured another glass of champagne after the first one. Mark put the recorked bottle on the kitchen table.

"Would you like some?" I asked.

"No thanks. I could do with a coffee though."

"Sure, I'll put the kettle on. You go through." His hand stroked my waist as he squeezed past, but he barely seemed attached to it. He was gutted, I knew that. And I felt absolutely awful for being the one who had burst his balloon. But I also knew it would have been wrong to go along with buying the house simply because he wanted to. The whole "let's wait and see how it goes" thing really was, for me, a very sensible idea. And with the housing market the way it was, it could easily be a year before either of us had a buyer. Maybe by then I'd feel a lot clearer about everything. Maybe the list wouldn't be preying on my mind so much. Or maybe, if it was, I'd have done something about it.

I poured the boiling water into the cafetière and took two mugs from the tree. Only a few days ago I'd been swimming along quite contentedly in the slow lane. Vaguely aware that I could go faster if I wanted to but liking the feeling of not being rushed. Then someone had pulled me over into the fast lane. I'd so far managed to keep my head above water but knew I was well out of my depth.

I took the coffee through to the lounge. Mark was sprawled out on the sofa staring into space. The list was still on the coffee table where I'd left it. I hurriedly put the mugs down and repositioned my laptop to cover the list, hoping Mark wouldn't notice.

"I just need to check my e-mails a sec," I said, sitting down next to Mark.

There was one new message in my inbox. From someone called Francesca. I opened it up straight away, feeling the same kind of frisson I did when Frankie used to pass me notes in school.

Hi Claire,
And there was I thinking you must have emigrated! It was great to hear from you. I've got so much to fill you in on (and I'm sure you have too) that I don't know where to start and it would

probably take for ever, so I've got a better idea. I know I'm springing this on you at short notice but I've really missed you and I don't want to waste any time. So come and visit us. The weekend after next would be good, the kids will have just broken up for the summer holidays. We live in Potters Bar, not far from your mum's. Would be great to introduce you to my family and we could catch up properly. Oh, and my husband's a chef, so you'll even be fed and waited on. Please feel free to bring anyone you want — it'll be a bit of a squash but we do have a sofa bed! Really hope to see you soon.

Loads of love,

Frankie

X

I didn't realise that a tear was running down my face until I looked up and saw Mark staring at me.

"What is it?" he said, putting his hand on my knee.

"It's OK," I said. "Just my old school friend Frankie. I haven't heard from her for years. I guess I hadn't realised how much I missed her. She's got in touch through Friends Reunited, invited me down the weekend after next. She always was a bit impulsive."

"Great. It'll be really good for you to see her."

"You're sure you don't mind? You can come with me if you want. She said I could bring someone."

"What, and listen to you two going on about your school days? No, it sounds like a girl fest to me. I'll give it a miss if you don't mind."

I nodded and stroked his hand. Relieved he'd said no. Mark wasn't part of the past. He'd feel out of place, out of time. And to be honest, it was going to be hard for me to go back. So many memories. Good and bad. And an obvious topic of conversation which we couldn't discuss with Mark there. It was probably best that I did it on my own.

"No, of course not. I'll probably pop in and see Mum while I'm there. So at least you've got out of that."

"You make her out to be far worse than she actually is," said Mark, sipping his coffee.

"You didn't have to grow up with her. Anyway, she likes you. You have the official Skidmore seal of approval."

"God knows why." The real reasons were that he was the same age as me rather than several years older. And although he was undeniably attractive, there was a certain Hugh Grant-like, clean-cut innocence about him. Unlike the rugged stubble and chest-hair types I used to go for who reeked of carnal lust when they walked into a room. Mothers don't like that. Men who are obviously having rampant sex with their daughters. But I couldn't say that to Mark.

"You charmed the socks off her last Christmas, remember? She told me afterwards you were the only decent man I'd ever brought home," I said.

"God, shows what a lousy judge of character she is then," grinned Mark.

I laughed and leant over to kiss him. His lips were warm and welcoming but his arms stayed resolutely by his sides. Despite all his assurances, he obviously did feel rejected. Unsure of where he stood. Of where we stood.

"I love you," I whispered, keen to reassure him that nothing had changed, even though I knew it had.

"I love you too." His eyes were still shut when he said it. As if he couldn't bear for me to see the hurt.

I snuggled into him on the sofa, folding his arms around me. Letting him know it was still OK. We sat like that for a long time. Talking about nothing of importance. Neither of us wanting to reveal how we were really feeling. I knew that Mark wasn't going to stay the night long before he said it.

"Anyway, I'd better be going. You've got a long day tomorrow."

I nodded, deciding not to try to persuade him to change his mind. He had a right to go away and lick his wounds. And I needed some time to work out where we went from here.

He got up from the sofa and we walked through to the kitchen together.

"I'll call you tomorrow," I said.

"Sure." He kissed me on the lips, started to open the door and turned back to me.

"It'll be weird, won't it? Seeing the 'For Sale' sign outside here."

I nodded again, knowing he was looking for reassurance that I was at least going to go through with Plan B.

"Bet you I sell mine first," I said.

"I hope so," he said. "That way I get to stay in Lancashire."

"Away with you," I said, smiling. He waved and I shut the door. Wondering how long the champagne would last before it went flat.

Saturday, 3 August 1985

"Honestly, the face on you. Anyone would think I was taking you to a concentration camp not a holiday camp."

It was the first day of the new football season and I was on my way to Great Yarmouth. And for some reason, Mum expected me to be happy about it.

"Sorry for not jumping up and down in excitement."

"There's no need to be sarcastic, Claire. I don't ask for much, just that you don't sit there with a face like a wet weekend for the entire journey."

"But it is a wet weekend." The rain hadn't stopped since we'd left home. The windscreen wipers were in serious danger of overheating. "Anyway, I'd rather spend the week at the training ground."

"You could have told me before I booked."

"You didn't ask. You never do." It was easy arguing with Mum. I always seemed to win, sometimes on points, sometimes with a knockout blow. I was already ahead on points.

"So you didn't want to go on holiday at all?"

"Not to poxy Great Yarmouth."

"Ah, so where should I have taken you then?"

"Florence. It's in Italy."

"I know where it is, thank you. Why do you want to go there?"

"'Cos Andy Pailes has been there."

Mum shook her head. "I might have known it would be something daft like that. Well, you'll have to make do with Great Yarmouth."

"Can't wait."

"It's not that bad, Claire. You always used to enjoy our holidays there."

"Yeah, well, it was different then, wasn't it?"

"What do you mean?"

"Dad was with us."

Having delivered the knockout blow, I immediately wished I'd settled for a points win. We drove the rest of the way in silence. Apart from the hypnotic sound of the windscreen wipers swishing back and forth.

The woman in the red jacket who greeted us could hardly talk for smiling. We were shown into a chalet which looked identical to every other one we passed on the way from reception. The only good thing was that I did at least have my own little bedroom (Mum was sleeping on a sofa bed in the main living area). I took the photo of me and Andy out of my bag. It was my favourite picture of us together. Not the original, of course, that was in my photo album. This was a reprint. I had five more at home, each one hidden in a different place. You could never be too careful with photographs. I kissed the top of his head through the plastic wallet.

"Miss you already," I whispered. I stood the photo up against the lamp on the bedside table. Hoping the cleaner would think Andy was my boyfriend.

Mum was being all cheery at breakfast the next morning. This was generally a bad sign. And it particularly pissed me off because United had lost 1-0 away to Forest.

"How about a nice game of tennis this morning?" she said.

I was good at tennis. Dad had taught me when I was younger. We used to play together in the park. I'd kept practising after he'd left. Though it hadn't been the same on the Swingball in the garden.

"You don't play tennis."

"I didn't mean with me. There's a Teen Scene Club here."

"Yeah, right. I can really see myself teaming up with some zitty thirteen-year-old boy."

"There might be girls your own age around."

"I doubt it. Most people my age wouldn't be seen dead here."

Mum sighed, chased the last spoonful of Special K around her bowl and went off to the pool without saying another word.

I walk into my bedroom. Andy is lying in my bed.

"Come here," he says, pulling back the duvet. I slide in next to him and he wraps his muscular arms around me, holding me tight, protecting me, keeping me safe from harm.

"I've missed you so much," I say.

"I know, but I'm here now." I smile as he kisses the top of my head. We are on holiday together; everything is all right now. It doesn't matter where we are, as long as we are together.

The front door of the chalet burst open. I jumped up and pulled my clothes on quickly. I heard the clank of a bucket and the tap whooshing on and opened my bedroom door to find the chalet maid standing there in her Marigolds. I gave her a dirty look for not knocking first as I slipped out the front door. I wandered down to the pool. Mum was lying on a sun-lounger at the far end.

"Oh, so you've decided to grace me with your presence, have you?"

I think she was trying to be sarcastic. Adults are crap at being sarcastic.

"Didn't have much choice. The cleaner kicked me out."

Mum looked at my jeans and T-shirt.

"You could have put your cossie on, at least tried to look the part." I had packed my swimming costume under duress. I had no intention of wearing it in public.

"I'm OK as I am, thank you." I sat down on the lounger next to her, staring out across the pool, my face set to "I don't want to be here" mode. Everywhere I looked there were people enjoying themselves. Small children screaming excitedly as they splashed about on inflatables, parents laughing at their antics, couples lazing next to each other, rubbing sun cream into each other's backs. It was the worst bit of being a teenager. Having to watch everyone else being so bloody happy.

Mum looked across at me and sighed. "At least take your trainers off if you're stopping. They look ridiculous."

I looked at her. She was wearing a turquoise floral print swimsuit, matching eye shadow and clip-on dolphin earrings. And she was calling me ridiculous.

"Can I have the key, please?" I said. "I'm going back to the chalet to get my book."

When I returned five minutes later with my signed copy of United captain Dave Orton's autobiography tucked under my arm, there was a man sitting in the lounger next to Mum. He had slightly greying hair and a deep suntan and was wearing red swimming trunks that looked a size too small. Mum was leaning on one side, listening to him. I noticed that she was sucking her tummy in. When he finished talking, she threw back her head and laughed. It wasn't her normal laugh, either. It was deeper, dirtier. I didn't like it. As I approached, she looked up and immediately stopped laughing.

"I thought you were going back to the chalet?"

"No, you should try listening. I said I was gonna get my book."

I looked at the man on the lounger, who showed no sign of moving.

"Er, this is Brian, love. He only lives in Waltham Cross. I always say it's a small world, don't I?"

"Hello," said Brian, briefly acknowledging me before turning back to continue the conversation with Mum. I hovered above them for a few moments, but as soon as the laughing started again I headed back to the chalet. The cleaner had gone. Andy had gone too. I went straight to my room and picked up the photo of him.

"I wish I wasn't here," I said, kissing his forehead before clutching the photo to my chest. "I wish I was with you, where I belong."

When Mum came back at lunchtime she didn't mention Brian. She took a Jackie Collins book outside with her in the afternoon. It was called *The Bitch*. I didn't see Brian talking to her again.

"So, how bad was Clacton then? On a scale of one to ten."

We were sitting in Frankie's bedroom on the Sunday morning after United had beaten Watford 3-1 (Goodyear, Orton and Dodds). Neither of us usually got up in time to see Sunday mornings. But after a week with our families, I guess we were both desperate for some meaningful conversation.

"About a hundred," said Frankie, doing her usual drama-queen bit. "Aunt Josie kept going on about Connie's wedding preparations and saying things like, 'And when are you going to find yourself a nice Catholic boy, Francesca?'"

"What did you tell her?"

"When the Pope screws Madonna."

"You didn't."

"No. I didn't. Wish I had though. Stupid interfering cow." Frankie stabbed her pillow repeatedly with her hairbrush. She'd be scary if she was armed.

"So where's the virgin bride?" I asked, nodding in the direction of Connie's half of the room, which was suitably pink, prim and spotless. The Alberti sisters were a bit like rival animals, marking out their territory.

Only instead of peeing on her land, Frankie had stuck up pictures of Matt, Simon Le Bon and John Taylor to keep Connie at bay.

"Oh, she's downstairs somewhere. Probably sucking up to Mum by helping with the dinner. Proper little housewife she's turning into." Frankie went back to stabbing the pillow.

"Great Yawnmouth was fun," I said.

"I bet. What d'ya do all week?"

"Stayed in my room mostly."

"Yeah, I can see that." Frankie put her arm next to mine. She looked like she'd been grilled to a golden brown while I'd been put in the microwave on defrost.

"Well, I only burn, don't I?" I said. "Anyway, Mum was by the pool most of the time. I was trying to avoid her."

"Did she cop off with anyone?"

"She is thirty-nine, you know."

"Oh yeah. What about you, then?"

I stared at Frankie, unable to believe what I was hearing. I'd spent the entire week pining for Andy. Crying myself to sleep every night because I wanted to be with him so much it hurt. I wondered if she'd even thought about Matt while she'd been away.

"In case you've forgotten, I'm only interested in one man."

"I know, but he's not interested in you, is he?

"How do you know?"

"Well he hasn't invited you round for his birthday yet, has he?"

"No, but I'm still gonna see him. I'm going to the United centenary do on the thirty-first."

"Yeah, in your dreams."

"No, I'm gonna turn up outside the front gates so I can give him his card when he goes in. It'll be my last chance to see him before I go back to school. And I don't know why you're laughing, because you're coming with me."

"Now you are talking crap," said Frankie. "How the hell am I gonna wangle that one?" She had a point. Her mother's fear of her being murdered, raped or abducted by a marauding mob of tattooed skinheads meant that she wasn't allowed out the house at night on her own, not even to pop down the road. Frankie had to suffer the ultimate indignity of living in a permanent exclusion zone, which began two yards outside her house. If she dared to instigate an unauthorised incursion she was immediately shot down in flames. It was like the Falklands all over again.

"I have a cunning plan," I said in my best Baldrick voice.

"Oh God," said Frankie.

"Look, do you wanna see Matt in his tuxedo or not?"

"Course I do," she said.

"Right then, you'd better come downstairs with me."

Mrs Alberti was doing the ironing when we marched into the lounge. According to Frankie, her mum always got up at 4a.m. the day after they got back from holiday, so she could get everything washed, dried and ironed in one day. I thought it was taking the Catholic guilt-trip thing a bit far.

She looked up and smiled at me as we sat down. Frankie said her mum liked me. That she thought I was a good influence. Which goes to show what crap judges of character parents are.

"Hello, Claire love. Did you have a nice holiday?" she said.

"Yes, great, thanks. How about you?"

"Oh, smashing. My sister always makes us feel very welcome. And she was a great help with the wedding arrangements, wasn't she, Conchetta?"

Connie looked up from her copy of *Bride* magazine, gave a sickly-sweet smile and confirmed that Aunt Josie had helpfully pointed out the need to ensure the napkins at the reception were the same colour as the bridesmaids' dresses. Frankie rolled her eyes. I couldn't help wondering what odious sin she must have committed in a previous life to have been saddled with a sister who made Julie Andrews look positively depraved. I had suggested to Frankie that if she wanted to make some dosh she should grind Connie down into tiny granules and sell her as some kind of sugar substitute.

I looked at Mrs Alberti but she wasn't paying any attention to what was being said. She had stopped ironing and was staring at Frankie's T-shirt with a quizzical expression.

"Why didn't you get them to put 'Hello'?" she said.

"You what?" said Frankie.

"On your T-shirt. Why couldn't you have asked them to put 'Frankie says Hello' instead of 'Frankie says Relax'. Come to think of it, you could have got them to put Francesca instead of Frankie as well. I'll never understand why you don't use your proper name; you'd have complained if we hadn't given you one."

I turned to look at Frankie, who didn't seem to know whether to laugh or cry. "See what I mean?" she whispered. "They're all on another fucking planet in this house." As if to illustrate the point, a jingly rendition of "Pop Goes the Weasel" blared out from across the road, announcing the return of Frankie's older brother.

"Hello, love," said Mrs Alberti, visibly brightening as Alberto entered the room. "How was business?"

I thought the term "business" was stretching it a bit. Alberto had a dilapidated pink ice-cream van which sold Mr Whippies. And according to the rumour going round our school, he spent more time in his "ice-cream love machine" messing around with a box of 99 Flakes and a couple of slags from the sixth form than actually selling any ice creams.

"Bit quiet for this time of year," he said.

"Never mind, love, you go and get yourself cleaned up. Dinner will be ready soon." She smiled lovingly at him as he headed upstairs. I decided to take my chance.

"Mrs Alberti, my nan and grandad are having a golden wedding anniversary party next Saturday. And they've said I can bring a friend, so I wondered if Frankie could come."

"Oh, it's very nice of you to ask, Claire."

"It's only a quiet family do, see. It won't be late and my mum'll drop her off afterwards."

"Well, maybe just this once, seeing as it's a family thing."

"Thanks very much," I said. "I'll make sure they send some cake home for you."

Frankie came out to the front door to see me off.

"You lying cow," she laughed as soon as we were out of earshot.

"Sometimes, when you're a lawyer, you have to use your powers of persuasion," I said. "And anyway, Andy's worth lying for."

It had to be the right place. The Tesco near the training ground in Potters Bar would be far too busy, more chance of being stopped by a fan and asked for an autograph. I couldn't imagine him wanting that. The Co-op in Cuffley was nice and quiet. And it was right on his doorstep. But this was the sixth time now and still no sighting. It was costing me a fortune in bus fares. I was beginning to wonder whether he went shopping at all. Or whether someone else did it for him.

The shopping basket, already weighted down with orange juice, pineapple chunks, three tins of baked beans and the biggest block of mature Cheddar I'd been able to find, bashed awkwardly against my legs as I stopped to consult the crumpled shopping list my mum had left before dashing off to work (she hadn't questioned my newfound willingness to run shopping errands. She'd simply said how nice it was that I was pulling my weight at home these days). PG Tips it said on the list. But the Yorkshire Tea looked far more appealing. The chance to drink tea produced in Andy's birthplace was too good an opportunity to miss. Frankie took the mickey about the Yorkshire thing. Said that eating two Yorkshire puddings a day didn't turn you into a Yorkshire person, just like eating lots of Madeira cake didn't mean you could claim to be from Madeira, it just made you fat. I popped the Yorkshire Tea into the basket anyway, deciding Frankie was only jealous because she couldn't pin her colours to Matt in the same way. Nothing much came from Harlow in Essex.

Anything which could make me feel closer to Andy. That was what I wanted. If I could surround myself with him, eat the same food, drink the same tea, breathe the same air, I could shut my eyes and be with him whenever I wanted to. And one day I would wake up and it would be real. I wouldn't be in Potters Bar. I would be in Cuffley, in Andy's house. And he would be smiling down at me, bringing me breakfast in bed, kissing me softly on the top of my head. Telling me I was his special girl. That I meant the world to him.

I glanced down at the list. Only one thing left to get. I knew where everything was now. Had developed an encyclopaedic knowledge of the layout of the Co-op. But I chose to take the long way round, revisiting favourite haunts, lingering near the baked beans in the tinned goods aisle, browsing at the array of chicken breasts in the chiller cabinet, fingering the cans of Tetley's on special offer this week, all the time glancing around me, peeping down each aisle as I went.

Eventually I came to what Mum referred to as the "women's bits" and reached up for the large box of slightly perfumed Vespre sanitary towels. I presumed they were for me, as Mum still used the chunky, old-fashioned type that looked like they could absorb the contents of Lake Superior. Frankie said it must be like putting a brick in your knickers. But then Frankie was far more sophisticated in the sanitary provision department. She used tampons. I wanted to use them too but Mum had been horrified when I had suggested it, saying tampons were for when I was older. I wondered just how old you were supposed to be to use them. After all, Mum was thirty-nine but she still used towels. I had images of women skipping off to the chemist on their fortieth birthday to buy their first packet of tampons.

I started to work out how many sanitary towels I'd have to use over the next twenty-five years. I was still doing the calculation in my head as I approached the checkouts. Two women were on this afternoon. The dark-haired one with the boil on her chin and the young blonde girl with the wonky ponytail. Sometimes it was only one of them. It all depended how busy they were. They probably had all three tills working in the mornings. I was only guessing. I never came that early because I knew he'd be at training.

The queue for the dark-haired woman was shorter. I started towards her but stopped abruptly as something caught my eye in the other queue. It was the glint of gold from his earring I noticed first, followed, as my gaze dropped to the floor, by the flash of blue on his Adidas trainers. At last. I felt my hand tighten on the basket handle and a frown spread across my face as I struggled to work out how I could possibly have missed him in the aisles. But now was not the time for inquests. If I moved quickly, I could still sneak in behind him.

I turned on my heel and darted forward, narrowly beating an elderly lady with a blue rinse to the checkout. My hands were shaking as I began emptying the contents of my basket, so much so that a tin of baked beans slipped from my hand on to the conveyor belt with a thud. My gaze shot upwards, just as Andy turned and caught me staring at him. There was a flicker of recognition on his face before he smiled and said, "Hello. I know you from the training ground, don't I? It's Claire, isn't it?"

My eyes widened. He had noticed me. He knew who I was. He'd even made the first move.

"Hi," I said, smiling back at him. "Sorry, you took me by surprise."

"Even footballers have to go shopping sometimes," he said.

I nodded. Andy was still smiling. Still looking at me. I was caught between gazing into his eyes and trying to catch a glimpse of his shopping. To memorise each item on the conveyor belt as if I was a contestant on *The Generation Game*. And to see if the lasagne served one or two people.

"Excuse me, are you two together?"

The voice belonged to the checkout girl with the wonky ponytail. She was looking at us. At me and Andy. Together. That was what she thought. That the two of us belonged together. That we were an item. I felt a glow of warmth inside me.

"No," said Andy.

"Oh, so are, um . . . are these things yours?"

She was pointing to my shopping. To the cheese, the pineapple chunks, the tins of beans. And the box of Vespre. I clapped my hands to my face, my fingers cold against my hot cheeks.

"I'm so sorry," I said to Andy. "I was miles away. I forgot to put the bar thingy down. They're mine. All those things are mine. I'm really sorry."

"It's OK," he said. "No need to apologise. It's an easy mistake to make. Here, they won't be much use to me." He passed me the box of Vespre, which I realised were now of huge sentimental value and would be worth a fortune in years to come when he was an England star.

"I'm so sorry about that," I said.

"No problem," Andy said. "But next time you try to get someone else to pay for your shopping, at least pick someone of the right sex."

I started laughing. Andy was laughing too. I watched as he packed his shopping away. The lasagne was for one. And the pizza wasn't really big enough to share.

"See you then," he said, turning to say goodbye. "Thanks for brightening up my shopping trip."

"That's OK," I said. "Any time. See you soon."

I watched him walk out of the door and across the car park before disappearing from view. I had brightened up his day. It was only a matter of time now. Before I brightened up every day for him. I hadn't

110

dreamt of it starting this way, with a mix-up over sanitary towels. But it didn't matter how these things started. It was how they ended that was important.

CHAPTER
FOUR

The train pulled in to Potters Bar station. My life, not the station platform, flashed before me. The times I'd waited here, huddled up on one of the benches with Frankie when we were on our way to the United ground. And later, when I was a student, struggling down the steps with all my worldly goods, desperate to escape to my new life in Manchester.

I walked down the subway and squinted in the bright sunlight as I came out the other side. The bus station had been redeveloped but was still disturbingly familiar. Mum had said to ring when I arrived and she would come and pick me up. But now I was here I didn't want her to. I wanted to walk. I felt the need to acclimatise, like I'd just stepped off a plane somewhere in South America, thousands of feet above sea level.

The last time I'd been here, with Mark, the previous Christmas, we'd driven, arriving under cover of darkness and leaving at dusk the next day without having left the house. It was a long time since I'd walked these streets. I didn't get down much these days. I had the excuse of being on the duty rota to cover the police cells at weekends. But to be honest I think even my mum knew that it wasn't that which kept me away. It was a house full of memories. Most of which I'd rather forget.

I dialled Mark's number on my mobile as I walked along. Things were better between us but still not back to how they had been. The "For Sale" signs outside our homes a reminder that the market, like us, had stalled and we were waiting for things to start looking up.

"Hiya, I'm here," I said when he answered.

"Great. Journey all right?" I could hear the sound of water splashing in the background.

"Yeah, fine. Where are you?"

"I'm having my hair cut."

I frowned. The usual barber Mark went to was a confirmed dry-cut man.

"But Nathan doesn't wash hair."

"No, I'm, er, somewhere different. In Manchester, actually. Thought I'd have a look round the shops afterwards."

"Oh," I said, knowing Mark would usually balk at paying city salon prices or going anywhere near a shopping centre. "Well, I'll ring you tomorrow, when I'm on the train home."

"Sure," said Mark. "Have fun."

I put my phone back in my pocket. As I looked up I realised that I was only fifty yards away. The automatic pilot had clearly taken over. The front garden appeared the same as ever. I would no doubt be told there was a different variety of fuchsia or the crazy paving had been redone, but it looked the same to me. I stood on the doorstep and rang the bell. Remembering a time when

113

I had a key and could let in anyone I liked. Anyone at all.

My mother opened the door. She was a reluctant pensioner, her hair dyed the same shade of golden brown as I could always remember. It was worn pinned up now, her concession to the expectation that ladies of a certain age should have short hair. Although she still retained her dangly earrings and hid the wrinkled skin around her neck with a brightly coloured silk scarf.

"Claire, why didn't you ring?"

"I was halfway here by the time I remembered."

"It's silly struggling with that heavy bag on your own."

"Never mind, I'm here now, aren't I?" I always had to remind myself to continue being an adult, not to regress into that whole antagonistic mother and teenage daughter routine. We'd moved on from there. Not particularly far, but we had at least moved on.

"Yes," she said, kissing me on the cheek. "And it's lovely to see you. Come in and I'll put the kettle on."

I put my bag down in the hall and walked through to the kitchen. Mum chatted away about people and places I could barely remember, as if I had only left yesterday and was desperate for news of the machinations of the Potters Bar set. I followed her through to the lounge, cup and saucer in hand (my mother still resolutely held out against the onset of mugs). The Laura Ashley sofa had long disappeared, as had the wallpaper, but still the room held on to its secrets. Still it was uncomfortable for me to sit there, knowing what it had been a witness to.

114

"So, how's Mark?" said Mum, stirring her half-spoon of sugar around the cup with a dainty teaspoon.

"He's fine, thanks." I stopped myself saying we had some news because I knew my mother would leap to the wrong conclusion. As it turned out, she didn't even need prompting.

"I really like him, you know," she said, patting me on the hand. "I was wondering if you two had got any plans for the future?"

I smiled, knowing that a mention of the possibility of a fortnight's holiday somewhere warm next spring wasn't what she had in mind.

"We might be moving in together, actually."

"Why only might?"

I decided not to mention the possibility of buying somewhere new at this stage. I wanted to keep it as simple and low key as possible.

"Well, we've both put our places on the market; just depends how long it takes to sell one of them."

"Oh, well that's great. And it makes sense not to rush into anything." She might have omitted the words "this time" but I knew exactly what she was getting at. My propensity to fall hard and fast had got me into trouble before. She remembered only too well. Because she'd been there to help pick up the pieces.

"Good. I'm glad you approve," I said, deciding not to go into the whole business with the list and all the feelings it had brought up about the past. She didn't like to be reminded of any of that. And I knew full well what she'd say about it all.

"And how's Malcolm?" I asked instead, deciding it was safer to change the subject. Malcolm was, as my mother had once described him, her "man friend". He was a permanent fixture at Christmas and other family gatherings. I couldn't remember quite where he'd come from but equally it was getting hard to remember him not being there. She saw him most weekends, and often in the week now, since he'd retired. They were, to all intents and purposes, a couple. Except for the fact that they retained their separate houses and their own lives. And that was how it would stay, of course. For one simple reason. Because he wasn't Dad.

"Oh, much the same as ever. His back's playing him up at the moment. He won't bother the doctor with it though. Says you have to expect things like that at his age. He never complains about anything, you know."

I nodded. It was true. Malcolm was a salt-of-the-earth kind of guy. I liked him. Primarily because there was nothing about him to dislike. And because he was obviously devoted to Mum. There was a pause in the conversation. I knew what Mum was going to ask next way before she actually asked it. It always took her a few minutes to build up the courage. To steel herself for whatever news I might have.

"Have you heard from your father?" she asked. She didn't say seen him, of course, because he no longer lived in this country. He and his second wife had been running an English pub for ex-pats in Spain for about five years now. In the most recent photo he'd e-mailed he looked particularly bronzed and relaxed, one arm draped around the much paler Denise (her classic

116

redhead complexion had remained stubbornly un-Mediterranean). She still looked good for her age, mind. Though I wasn't going to tell Mum that, of course.

"Yeah, I had an e-mail from him a couple of months back. Saying that business is good and he's still enjoying the laid-back life over there." I knew better than to mention Denise. It was the fact that she'd now been married to Dad longer than he'd been married to Mum which really galled her. I remembered the look Mum had given her at my wedding. And the way she'd sucked her stomach in when she'd been asked to stand next to Dad for the family photographs. It was sad, really. How much she obviously still loved him. And ironic that I, the one who had once berated her for constantly attacking him, was the one who now had to remind her she was better off without him.

Mum nodded.

"I'm getting a new sofa delivered on Monday," she said, changing the subject.

"Oh, great."

"From that SCS place. You know, the ones that advertise on the telly with that chap with the nice smile."

"You mean Martin Kemp?"

"I think that's him. Lovely eyes he's got."

I shook my head, unsure whether to laugh or cry.

"I used to have his picture on my wall. He was the bass guitarist in Spandau Ballet."

"No, it's not him. This is the fella who used to be in *EastEnders*."

"Yeah, I know, it's the same guy."

"No, it can't be. He was scruffy with long hair and an earring. This chap's much more presentable. It must be a different Martin."

I opened my mouth to say something, decided against bothering to argue with her, and took a Bourbon biscuit from the plate she offered me instead.

"What time are you expected at Frankie's?"

"In about an hour," I said, glancing at my watch.

"It's a wonder I haven't seen her if she lives near me."

"Maybe you wouldn't recognise her now."

"Of course I would. She always stood out a mile. She wasn't exactly a plain Jane, was she?" It was strange to hear my mum say that. At fifteen I hadn't realised that she'd registered how stunning Frankie was. Although maybe that was why she'd always disapproved of her.

"Still, having four kids must have changed her a bit," I said, more in hope than expectation.

"Four, you say? Her mum must be thrilled. That's the thing about these Catholic families, there's never a shortage of grandchildren."

I smiled weakly, knowing it was a not-so-subtle dig at my failure to procreate. My cup clattered down on to my saucer.

"So," I said, keen to move things on again, "have you iced any good cakes lately?"

From the outside, Frankie's house looked like any other semi in Potters Bar. Certainly not as modern or swish as I had imagined. A selection of toys lay abandoned in the front garden: a battered tricycle, a bigger bike with football stickers plastered all over it and one of those rather evil-looking plastic baby dolls in a toy buggy. If Lloyd Grossman had been peering through the keyhole asking "Whose house is this?" I certainly wouldn't have guessed it was Frankie's.

I rang the bell and waited. The sound of children screaming and shouting came from inside. After a while the noise subsided slightly and I rang again. A young boy's voice called, "Someone's here," and seconds later footsteps approached and the door opened.

The woman who stood there was big. I mean seriously big; only politeness would have stopped me using the F word. She was clothed in black, stylishly so, her top cut to show off a little cleavage and her wide trousers skimming over her rounded hips. The body was entirely foreign but the face which was smiling at me was undeniably Frankie: fantastic cheekbones, full lips and dark, playful eyes, all exquisitely made up, shown off in a flawless complexion and framed by the same long dark hair she'd always had.

"Hi," said Frankie. "It's OK, you have got the right house. I guess I should have warned you that I'm twice the woman I used to be."

"No, I wasn't thinking that," I said, embarrassed that I must have let my surprise show.

"It may have been nearly twenty years, but I can still read your face like a book, you know," said Frankie. "And you were thinking, 'God, Frankie's turned into a fat cow,' or words to that effect."

I grinned at her, relieved to have instantly fallen back into the old banter.

"Actually, I was thinking about how you and Dawn French both prove you don't have to be a size zero to look gorgeous."

"Thank you," said Frankie. "Flattery will get you everywhere. Now come in and give me a hug, if you can still get your arms around me, you annoyingly skinny thing." I stepped forward and embraced Frankie. It felt weird to be holding her again. But a nice kind of weird, so nice that when we let go and grinned at each other I could see her eyes had welled up like mine.

"You're looking good, girl," said Frankie, touching my shoulder-length highlighted locks. "Relieved to see you got rid of the big hair."

"Ah, but I still have the tea-bag tank-top and pedal-pushers somewhere," I said.

There was a scream followed by a wailing sound from somewhere inside the house.

"Come on," said Frankie. "I'd better introduce you to the children before they kill each other."

I slipped off my sandals and followed her through to the lounge, where a small girl with long dark hair was lying on the floor bawling her eyes out, watched over by a similar-aged boy with glasses. An older boy with slightly spiky hair was looking daggers at her from the sofa.

"Paulo snatched the DS from me," screamed the girl.

"I did not. She snatched it from me," shouted the older boy, who presumably was Paulo.

"Right," said Frankie, clapping her hands, "someone's not telling the truth here." The small boy, who had so far kept out of the spat, ran up to Frankie, tapped her arm and when she bent down, whispered something into her ear. Frankie nodded, patted him on the head and said, "Right, Sophia, give the DS back to Paulo. Paulo, next time don't hog it for so long and if she snatches it from you, don't snatch it back, come and tell me, OK?" Paulo and Sophia scowled at each other then turned to scowl at the younger boy, who had obviously grassed them up. I couldn't help thinking he had excellent witness potential.

"Claire, I'd like you to meet my delightful children, Paulo, Sophia and Roberto. Kids, this is Claire, my old school friend I told you about who's come to visit."

"Has she brought us presents?" asked Sophia. "Most people who come bring us presents."

I winced, knowing I should have thought to get them something when I'd picked up the wine and chocolate truffles on the way. Although as I hadn't even known their ages it would have been hard to know what to get.

"They could share the chocolates I got you, if you like," I whispered to Frankie. The look she gave me in return made it quite clear that was not going to happen.

"Sophia, you know it's rude to ask people that. Besides which, it's not Christmas or your birthday. Claire's a guest and you guys love having people to stay. Though if you carry on behaving like this, she might turn around and go straight home."

I smiled, hoping to illustrate that this was not going to happen, but the children still looked suitably chastened. I crouched down next to Roberto.

"Hi, so how old are you?" I asked.

"Five and a half," he replied in a whisper.

"I'm five and a half too," chimed in Sophia. "But I'm older than him because I came out first."

Frankie nodded at me. "Twins," she said. "Although you'd never think so. They couldn't be more different."

"Hi, Sophia. Was that your doll I saw in the buggy outside?"

"Yes, but I'm getting a new Bratz one for Christmas."

"If she behaves herself," said Frankie.

"And you must be at least twenty-one," I said, turning to Paulo, who grinned back at me.

"I'm nearly eight. You support United, don't you? Mummy told me."

I glanced up at Frankie.

"Paulo's United's number one fan. He was very impressed when I told him you'd seen them play at Wembley."

"It was the old Wembley though, wasn't it?" said Paulo. "So you must be really old."

I laughed.

"Not so cheeky, you," said Frankie.

"Do you still go to the games?" asked Paulo.

"No, I haven't been for years, I'm afraid," I said, deciding not to add that the Wembley match had been my first and last United game.

"But you still support them?" asked Frankie.

I shook my head. "Not really. I could probably only name a handful of their players these days. I lost interest when they all turned into prima donnas and football became big business."

"What's a prima donna?" asked Paulo.

"Someone who's full of themselves, a bit of a show-off," said Frankie.

"A bit like Matt Goodyear," I laughed, digging Frankie in the ribs.

"He was Mummy's favourite player," said Paulo, turning to me. "Who was yours? Mummy said she couldn't remember."

I looked at Frankie and smiled, letting her know I appreciated her discretion, although it hadn't been necessary.

"Andy Pailes," I said. "The best left back we ever had."

"Never heard of him," said Paulo. "He can't be very famous."

"No, he wasn't," I replied. "Not really."

"Anyway," said Frankie, "I'm going to stick a DVD on for you kids so Claire and I can have some peace. What's it to be?"

"*Ben Ten*."

"*Fifi and the Flowertots*."

"*Bob the Builder*," came the replies from Paulo, Sophia and Roberto in turn.

"You see," said Frankie, turning to me. "There's just no pleasing them." She rummaged in a cabinet, pulled out a copy of *Lazy Town* and stuck it in the DVD player. "You can all sit together on the sofa; any arguing and it goes off. And guys . . ." the children looked up as Frankie pressed play, "enjoy the show!" She picked up Roberto and placed him strategically between Paulo and Sophia on the sofa.

"I take it he's the family mediator," I whispered as we left the room.

"The nearest I've got to one," said Frankie. "Joe calls him Supergrass but he's just naturally honest. He doesn't like it when the other two get away with stuff they shouldn't."

"Sounds like you've got a lawyer in the making."

"Well he's certainly not going to be a footballer. Joe named him after Roberto Baggio but I've never seen a child with less ability with a football. Which is weird, because Paulo, who's named after Paulo Maldini, is a complete natural. He can't stop scoring goals."

"So I guess you got to name Sophia after your favourite film star." I smiled.

"Yep, although as you may have noticed she doesn't appear to possess an ounce of Miss Loren's elegance or style. Maybe by the time she's a teenager she'll have stopped thumping boys and having tantrums."

"Can't think where she gets that temperament from," I grinned.

"Come on," said Frankie, leading the way upstairs. "There's one more to meet yet." She knocked on the door at the end of the landing, the one from where loud, whining music was emanating. "Can we come in?" she called.

"What?" came the reply.

"If you turned it down a bit, you might be able to hear me ask if we can come in," Frankie shouted. I smiled, remembering how Frankie's own mother used to say much the same thing.

The music stopped abruptly and the door opened to reveal Frankie standing there aged fifteen. It wasn't, of course. But I did have to do a double-take. In actual fact the girl standing before us was even more stunning than Frankie had been. She was taller and thinner for a start and she wore her long dark hair twisted round and tied to one side at the front, with a wispy fringe falling flatteringly over her forehead. I was doing the maths quickly in my head. Frankie had a teenage daughter, in which case she must have had her about the time we'd lost touch. When, as far as I knew, she hadn't even been going out with anyone. Certainly not Joe. It was weird to think that such a big thing had happened to her and I knew nothing about it. The girl's dark eyes looked up at me, her dangly hoop earrings jingling as she flicked back her fringe.

"Hi," she said. "I'm Emily."

"Pleased to meet you, Emily," I said, kissing her on both cheeks as Frankie's family used to do to me. "I expect you'll be wanting all the dirt about what your mum got up to as a teenager."

"Oh God, yeah. That'd be great. Then next time she tells me I can't do something, I can say 'But you used to do worse than that.'"

"Hey," said Frankie, turning to me. "Some friend you are."

"Don't worry," I said. "I won't tell her the story about you tricking your mum with the golden wedding cake."

"That was your idea," said Frankie. Emily giggled.

"So what were you up to, Emily, before we interrupted you?" I asked.

"Oh, nothing really."

"She was probably re-reading *Twilight* for the hundredth time and swooning at the pictures of the vampire fellow on her wall," said Frankie.

Emily's face flushed. "His name's Robert Pattinson," she said to me. "He plays Edward Cullen from the book in the new *Twilight* movie. My best mate Alia and me are going to the première in London in December."

"In her dreams," mumbled Frankie.

"Mum doesn't approve," said Emily, rolling her eyes.

"Let's see a photo of him then," I said.

Emily threw open the door behind her and I walked in. The first thing that struck me was how the room was split down the middle, just like Frankie and her sister's bedroom had been. On one side was a pink princess four-poster, which I took to be Sophia's, even though she didn't appear to be the slightest bit pink and princessy to me. On the other side was a cast-iron bed with a white duvet set, which I assumed was Emily's. The walls above the bed were adorned with a mass of posters and photos printed out from the internet, mainly of one particular man. Lean, dark, with heavy eyebrows, piercing eyes, a come-to-bed smile and hair which varied between floppy, spiky and plain wild.

"Wow, he's gorgeous," I said. "If I was twenty-odd years younger . . ."

"You'd be a geeky, flat-chested teenager with a flick from hell and he wouldn't give you a second look," cut in Frankie. I made a face at her.

"I've got no idea why she was my best friend," I said to Emily. "She always had rubbish taste in men as well." Emily giggled.

"Anyway," said Frankie to Emily, "we'll leave you to your vampire gazing. Make sure you're ready to go out in half an hour, and no bathroom hogging, Claire'll want to freshen up and get changed." Frankie shut the door behind her. I started laughing.

"What?" said Frankie.

"It's good to know that nothing's changed. You always used to do that, think I hadn't got dressed for wherever we were going when I actually had."

"Oh," said Frankie, looking at my frayed jeans and crumpled vest top. "It is Joe's restaurant we're going to, you know. Not Pizza Hut."

"I'll see if I can find something more suitable," I said, grinning as I followed her downstairs and picked up my overnight bag.

Frankie looked me up and down when I arrived back in the kitchen ten minutes later wearing cropped trousers and a square-necked top.

"Will I be allowed in?" I asked.

"I suppose so. Times are hard, they can't afford to be as choosy as normal," smiled Frankie, reaching for the kettle. "Tea or coffee?"

"Tea, please, milk, no sugar," I said, sitting down at the kitchen table as directed. "The kids are great. Emily's gorgeous."

"She's the fifteen year old from hell sometimes."

"She can't be harder work than you were."

"I never had a vampire fixation. She hardly ever leaves her room, you know. She looks bloody anaemic to me. And she's always complaining about being tired when all she does is lie there swooning at Robert what's-his-name or reading that bloody book."

"But isn't that what all the teenage girls are into these days?"

"To an extent, but she's more obsessive than the rest of them. She never goes out with other girls, no one apart from Alia, anyway, and she's as bad as her if not worse."

I grinned at Frankie. "You sound just like my mother used to."

"Yeah, well, she had a point, didn't she?"

"Maybe, but I didn't think that at the time. What does Emily say when you suggest she leaves her bedroom?"

"That vampires don't like sunshine."

I smiled, wishing I'd come up with a line that good when I was Emily's age.

"There you go then, you're fighting a losing battle. Give up and let her indulge it. She'll probably grow out of it soon."

"Like you did, you mean?" Frankie turned to look at me seriously for a moment.

128

"Is that what the problem is? You're worried she's going to do something daft?"

"You can't blame me, can you? For worrying about her. When I remember what happened to you . . ."

"That was me, not Emily. She appears to have her head screwed on a lot better than I did."

"I hope you're right," said Frankie, putting two mugs of tea on the table. "For all our sakes."

By the time we arrived outside Joe's restaurant in Waltham Cross, courtesy of Frankie's erratic driving in the people carrier, we were running considerably late (Emily did hog the bathroom) and were all rather frazzled (the younger kids argued about whether Stephanie or Sportacus was the best character in *Lazy Town* all the way there).

The restaurant was on the high street, not far from the station. I seemed to remember a carpet shop, a newsagent's and a dry cleaner's being there before, but the whole parade had now been taken over by convenience stores and fast-food outlets with neon lights. The London creep into Hertfordshire had become an onslaught. The restaurant itself had a stylish black and silver frontage. I looked up at the sign: Ristorante Ricotta.

"Was it named after your favourite cheese?" I asked Frankie as she got the younger children out of the car.

"Oh, I haven't told you that, have I? Ricotta's our surname."

I managed to hold my composure for a second before a snort, followed by a snigger, came out.

"Sorry," I said. "Very juvenile of me."

"It's all right," said Frankie. "I guess I gave you enough stick about being called Skidmore over the years. Time for you to get your own back. We've heard them all, mind. Joe's known as the big cheese at work and I've been called Mamma Ricotta on occasions."

I shook my head, imagining how horrified she'd have been at the prospect of the name change at sixteen. Joe had to be some guy for her to saddle herself with that surname. I imagined a Marco Pierre White type figure, a brooding mix of charm, temperament and dark Latin looks.

Frankie herded the children into the restaurant. We were early, it was mainly other families eating, but somehow I suspected our table was going to be noisier than anyone else's.

"Daddy," Sophia shouted and ran over to a man standing in the kitchen doorway, dressed in black and white checked trousers and a white top and hat. He was big, bigger than Frankie. On the short side, virtually bald and wearing dark-rimmed rectangular glasses. He couldn't have looked less like Matt Goodyear if he'd tried. Or less like the sort of man I'd imagined Frankie would marry. He bent down, scooped up Sophia in his arms and gave her a huge kiss before putting her down and coming over to greet Frankie with a kiss on the lips.

"Claire, this is my husband, Joe," said Frankie.

"Delighted to meet you, Claire," said Joe, kissing me on both cheeks. "From what I hear, you two were as thick as thieves when you were teenagers."

130

"Yeah, we were quite a double act."

"You'll have to fill me in later," said Joe, tapping his nose. "I pay good money for information, you know."

I laughed and looked over at Frankie. She was gazing at Joe with a look so warm, so loving on her face that it brought tears to my eyes. I wasn't sure if I'd ever loved anyone like that. Not even Andy.

The children clustered around Joe. He spoke to each in turn and gave them a wink or ruffled their hair. Sophia gazed up at him in utter adoration. Emily kissed him fondly on the cheek. Emily who, I guessed, was not his own but clearly regarded him as a father. He was indeed the big cheese. Frankie had found someone very special indeed.

Joe ushered us to a table. The children began arguing over who was going to sit next to him. "As soon as the food's ready I'll come and sit with you," he told them. "All of you in turn. We'll play musical chairs."

I leant across to Frankie. "I doubt if the Pope would get a better reception," I said.

"They all worship him," said Frankie. "Paulo even boasted in the playground once that his dad cooked better pizzas than anyone else's dad. He's a real hero. I'm just the one who shouts at them all the time."

"Hey, I'm sure they're proud of you as well," I said.

"Maybe, but you can't boast about your mum selling bras that are bigger than anyone else's bras."

"Is that what you do?" I laughed.

"Yep, I run an internet company selling luxury lingerie for larger ladies. Sexy stuff, not belly-warmers."

"What, peephole bras and crotchless knickers?"

"The works." Frankie winked. "Including stuff you certainly can't find in M and S."

"You'll have to show me later," I said.

"They won't fit you, I'm afraid. Cup sizes start at DD. We're not called Ample Bosoms for nothing."

I laughed and shook my head.

"You'll have to watch it," I said. "I might just launch a lingerie company of my own for the less well endowed."

"What will you call it?" asked Frankie.

"Fried Eggs," I replied.

"Now," said Frankie when she finally came downstairs later, having put the younger children to bed and left Emily reading by a nightlight, "what was that you said about wine and chocolates?"

"I thought you'd still be stuffed," I said, reaching into my overnight bag and passing Frankie a bottle of Cabernet Sauvignon and the truffles. The food, unsurprisingly, had been fantastic. Joe's house speciality spinach and ricotta cannelloni was the best I'd ever tasted. And the slice of wood-fired pizza which Emily had passed me (none of the other kids would give any of theirs up) had made me vow never to go to a pizza chain again.

"Thanks," said Frankie, ripping open the cellophane. "The thing is, chocolates aren't food, they're soft drugs for mums." She took a couple, passed the box back to me, grabbed two wine glasses from the kitchen (the large sort which lull you into thinking you can't be drunk when you are), plonked herself back down on

132

the sofa next to me and filled the glasses almost to the rim.

"And don't worry if I get pissed, because Joe will be able to carry me upstairs when he gets back from work." She raised her glass. "Cheers. So what are we drinking to?"

"Old times?"

"Nah, let's go for new beginnings," said Frankie, clinking her glass against mine and taking a large gulp. "The past's overrated if you ask me."

"What do you mean?"

"I only went on to Friends Reunited because I was nosy and wondered what you were up to. I'm not into all this looking back through rose-tinted spectacles lark; it wasn't that good as far as I can remember."

"We had some laughs, didn't we?"

"Yeah, but there was some pretty crap stuff as well. Or have you forgotten how horrible it was being a teenager?"

I took a sip of the wine. I hadn't forgotten the bad bits. But I hadn't forgotten the good parts either.

"I hated some of it. But I liked the hopes and the dreams. The idea that you could do anything, be anyone you wanted to be."

Frankie snorted a laugh. "Only it didn't turn out that way, did it?"

I hesitated, eyeing her over the top of my glass. Wondering if she still had hers.

"Have you read the list?" I asked.

"What list?"

"The 'Twenty Years From Now' list we did."

"Oh, that old tosh. I found it when I was having a clearout before the twins were born, had a good laugh and threw it away."

"You haven't got it any more?"

"No. Why would I keep it?"

"I wanted to know what you put."

Frankie laughed. "What, so you could take the piss?"

"No. Well, maybe a little bit. I was just interested. I found mine, you see. Only a couple of weeks ago. I'd forgotten all about it, and when I opened it . . ."

"You thought, 'What a sad, deluded teenager I was' and chucked yours in the bin too," finished Frankie.

"Well, er, no, actually. It made me think."

Frankie rolled her eyes and shook her head. "You haven't changed a bit, have you? You always did think too much. Analyse everything, worry yourself stupid."

"It was just weird, seeing this life I'd imagined for myself."

"Don't tell me, you said you were going to be married to Andy Pailes, living in some picture-book cottage with two adorable mini-Andy and mini-me kids while running the country and bringing the tyrants of the world to justice."

I shrugged. Put like that it did sound faintly ridiculous. Well, OK, highly ridiculous.

"Nothing seems to have turned out how I planned, that's all."

"Do you think I planned this?" Frankie said, gesturing around her. "Living in some chaotic semi with four kids and having to buy all my clothes from Evans."

"I guess not," I said, smiling. "But you're happy, aren't you?"

"I'm the happiest I've ever been. Joe's wonderful, he treats me like a princess and he's my best friend. I love being a mum — even if the kids do my head in at times. And I'm happy with myself — I wouldn't mind dropping a dress size or two but I'm not beating myself up about it, and I'm certainly not going to stop eating chocolates," she said, helping herself to another.

"And you don't ever think about what could have been?"

"I tried it, Claire. When I worked as a travel rep. I was living it up in the Costa del Sol. I fell in love with a tall, dark, handsome Spanish rep who made Matt look positively ordinary. I thought I'd found my dream man. Had my dream life."

"So what happened?"

"Emily's what happened."

"Oh." I nodded sympathetically. "I take it he didn't stick around?"

"Did a runner the morning after I told him I was up the duff. Never saw or heard from him again."

"What a bastard. That must have been so tough for you."

"It was. I came back here with my tail between my legs. Mum disowned me and kicked me out of the house."

"But that's awful. How could she do that to her own daughter?"

"I'd sinned, hadn't I? Gone against the Pope. Therefore I had to be excommunicated."

"What did you do?"

"Declared myself homeless and got a council flat in Cheshunt."

Something clicked inside my head.

"That must have been when we lost touch. I sent you an invite to my wedding . . ."

"Your wedding?"

"Yeah, David, the guy I was seeing." I noticed Frankie looking down at my left hand. For the ring which wasn't there. "Oh, we split up about eight years ago. Irreconcilable differences as us lawyers say. Anyway, the invite came back marked 'No longer at this address'. I thought your whole family must have moved. That you didn't want to stay in touch for some reason."

"No. Just my mum's way of sticking the knife in. It was like I no longer existed."

"Bloody hell. I'm so sorry. If I'd had any idea, I would have come and hammered on her door, demanded to know where you were."

Frankie shrugged. "Oh well, at least you've found me now."

I smiled and leant over to give her a hug. She stayed holding me for a long time.

"What about your dad?" I asked, when she eventually looked up.

"He couldn't stop her; you know how she ruled the place. He was caught in the middle. He made secret visits to the flat. Bought me stuff for Emily whenever he could spare the cash without Mum noticing. He doted on her but he died when she was one. Heart attack.

Not surprising really, considering the stress it all caused him."

I reached out and squeezed her hand, remembering how she'd always adored her father.

"And that wasn't enough to make your mum see sense?"

"Nope. She blanked me at the funeral. Connie said she blamed me for him dying. Wouldn't even so much as look at Emily."

"You must have been in bits."

"I was. Until Joe put me back together again. I met him at the funeral. He'd taken his father, who'd been an old friend of Dad's; they'd worked together at the council. He stopped to offer us a lift when he saw me and Emily waiting at the bus stop in the rain afterwards and that's where it all started. Well, how the friendship started. The rest just grew from there. And I know what you thought when you first met him because I thought that too. He wasn't the sort of guy I'd look twice at. But when you've been that low and someone comes along and treats you like you're the most amazing woman on earth, well, you start to believe it. And that's when you realise that looks count for nothing at the end of the day; it's what's inside that counts."

"You're right," I said. "But I never thought I'd hear you say that."

"I guess it's one of the lessons life teaches you. And here's another one," said Frankie, giggling as she leant closer. "The good-looking guys are crap at sex; they don't have to try, you see. But Joe, well, he's found places I never knew I had." We cracked up laughing on the sofa together, me nearly spilling my wine, Frankie almost dropping the chocolates.

"And I suppose you're going to tell me you couldn't possibly comment because you've only ever had the good-looking ones," Frankie grinned. "Your ex, David, what did he look like?"

"Pretty damn good, I guess. Dark hair, dark eyes, stubble, sporty body."

"You've just described Andy."

I hesitated, having always been in denial that David's physical similarity to Andy had been the attraction.

"Not really. David was a bit taller and his hair was different." Frankie looked unconvinced.

"Where did you meet him?"

"He was a solicitor at the firm I did my training contract with. A real hotshot corporate lawyer. He was nine years older than me, incredibly intelligent. I guess I was a bit in awe of him."

"Sounds familiar," said Frankie.

"Yeah, well, I couldn't believe it when he made a move for me. And I fell hook, line and sinker as usual. It was all very intense: he proposed six months after we got together and we were married within a year."

"So what went wrong?"

"He was a workaholic. Should have seen the warning signs really. We had a register office wedding and only a weekend away for a honeymoon because he had a big case on at work. He got a partnership at another firm not long after we married and I never saw him. He worked crazy hours, evenings, weekends, the lot. As Princess Di would have said, 'There were three people in our marriage and it was a bit crowded', only in my case it wasn't a person, it was his work which got in the way. And there's not much you can do to fight that."

"How long did it last?"

"Seven years. I was made redundant when we'd been married six years and it was downhill all the way from there. He was too busy to be supportive and it was like we were moving in different worlds. By the time I got the job where I am now, it was too late. He didn't even show up for the celebration takeout I'd ordered for us because he'd been too busy at work to go out for a meal. He phoned me from the office to offer me a divorce, like it was some kind of plea bargain."

Frankie shook her head. "I hope you took him to the cleaners."

"Not really. The only thing of his I kept was the surname. I'd put up with being a Skidmore for that long I couldn't face going back to it. Which is why I'm plain old Cooper now."

"So you're still single?" asked Frankie.

"Yeah, but I've been seeing a guy called Mark for two years. He's a solicitor too but he couldn't be more different from David. He's great. Makes me laugh, easy to talk to, doesn't mess me about and doesn't take work too seriously."

"What's the catch?"

"There isn't one. He wants us to buy a house together, actually."

"So why don't you sound very enthusiastic?"

I hadn't been aware it was so obvious. My finger traced the rim of my wine glass.

"I'm just not sure about it, that's all. Having already made a hash of things once, I want to make sure it's the right decision. And then when I read the list . . ."

"Fucking hell, Claire. You can't turn the guy down because he's not Andy Pailes."

"No, it's not that."

"So what is it?"

"It just feels like I'm kissing goodbye to all those hopes and dreams I had. Mark arranged for us to view this new build in a cul-de-sac, and I know he meant well but it scared the life out of me. I could see this future where we had net curtains and stayed in the same jobs for ever and had two point four children and a Volvo and . . ." My voice turned squeaky and trailed off. It was Frankie's turn to put her arm around me.

"You're a funny onion, you are. We grew up, Claire. We're nearly forty. It's time to get your head out of the clouds."

I nodded although I wasn't entirely sure I'd be able to breathe the air down below, so long it was since I'd been there.

"Anyway," I said, doing my best to pull myself together, "I bet you still get a tingle every week when you see Matt on Sky Sports."

"Not really. Joe and the kids just have a good laugh at him at my expense."

"You can't blame them, can you? Some of the things he wears . . ."

"It's not his fault. Jane always did have lousy fashion sense. I bet she buys all those shirts for him."

I gasped, about to berate her for still being on the hapless Jane's back, when I saw the grin spread across her face.

"Now who needs to grow up?" I laughed, reaching for another chocolate.

Saturday, 31 August 1985

The train pulled out of Potters Bar station. Jerking forward, taking me closer to Andy. I'd hardly slept the night before. Tossing and turning. Thinking about seeing him again. Praying he'd remember me.

Frankie settled back in her seat, crossing her miniskirted legs so exaggeratedly I could see her knickers and suspenders. It reminded me of that "all in the best possible taste" woman Kenny Everett did on TV. Except Frankie made it look sexy. I saw her gaze drop to my hands, which were fiddling with the handles of my bag.

"So, did you get Andy a birthday card then?" she asked.

"Yeah, but . . ."

"But what?"

"I dunno whether to give it to him. He might think I'm desperate."

"You are."

"I don't want him to know that, do I?"

"Show us what you've written inside, and I'll tell you whether it sounds desperate."

"I can't. I've stuck the envelope down now." I hadn't really. But I knew that if I showed Frankie the card and she held it up to the light she would see the indentation

142

of three kisses (which I'd decided had looked too familiar) beneath the Tipp-Ex.

"Suit yourself," Frankie said, turning to stare out of the window, her leather jacket squeaking with each jolt of the train. She looked good in that outfit. If she had been going to my nan and grandad's golden wedding she would probably have given Grandad a heart attack dressed like that. Sex appeal seemed to ooze from her pores. The only thing that came out of my pores was sweat.

"D'ya reckon Matt'll take Jane to the do?" I asked.

"S'pose he'll have to. She'll probably look a right state, mind. All lumpy thighs and fat arse."

"You shouldn't say that, it's not nice. She is nearly thirty."

"If I look like that by the time I'm thirty, you have permission to shoot me."

"OK," I said, laughing. I knew I wouldn't have to though. I couldn't imagine Frankie ever looking less than perfect.

"What'll you do if Andy has someone with him?" Frankie asked. "Some leggy model with big tits."

"He won't."

"How come you're so sure?"

"'Cos I know him. He's got more class than that."

By the time the train pulled into Hornsey station I had an unshakeable image in my head of Andy arriving with Sam Fox on one arm and Linda Lusardi on the other.

I loved Hornsey High Road. It was dirty and smelly and tatty. It was how London should be. I imagined how it would look on a match day, the crowd moving in one great swell, a sea of royal blue. The sound of fans chanting, of turnstiles clicking. One day, when I had my mum off my back, I'd be part of all that.

We didn't go to the main gates first. It was only five o'clock and the do didn't start till seven thirty. So we wandered down to the club shop. It was like stepping into Santa's grotto when you were a kid. Only the presents weren't wrapped up, they were displayed right in front of your eyes. Wall-to-wall United. You couldn't ask for anything more. Except maybe Andy Pailes in a little room somewhere, asking you to sit on his lap.

I had a fiver of saved pocket money with me, which I knew wouldn't go very far. So it was important to get as much of Andy as I could for my money. The shop was full of Matt stuff. Posters, Matt Goodyear fan club pencil cases, notebooks and key rings. I was glad Andy didn't have a fan club. I didn't want him cheapened like that. Eventually I found a programme containing an interview with Andy and a postcard-sized photo of him in action. Which just left me enough for the new team poster.

Frankie was still gazing at the array of Matt goods on offer.

"Are you getting anything?" I asked.

"Only that," she said, pointing to a baseball cap with Matt's picture on the front. It was last season's so the photo was pre-perm. I guessed that was why she was getting it.

We approached the counter. I recognised the woman serving from the training ground. She was in her thirties and wearing a high-necked cream blouse with a ruffle and a velvet bow and sporting a mousy Princess Di hairstyle that only served to accentuate the fact that wasn't nearly as pretty or young as Princess Di, and also happened to be at least six inches shorter and a good six inches wider (apart from which, the likeness was uncanny).

"Hello there," she said, nodding in recognition. "What can I get you two?"

Frankie asked for the cap.

"Oh, you're a fan of Matt's, are you?" she said. "He was in here with his wife only a couple of days ago, buying some of our United baby clothes they were."

"Baby clothes?" repeated Frankie.

"Yeah, Matt's going to be a dad. Right chuffed he seemed about it."

Frankie's face appeared to slip off her head and slide on to the floor, like something out of a cartoon. For a minute I thought she was going to burst into tears. Until I remembered that Frankie was much too stylish to cry.

"Well, thanks for breaking the good news," she snapped at the Princess Di look-nothing-like. "Remind me to spoil your day sometime." She picked up the cap, threw the money down on the counter and flounced out of the shop.

"She's Italian," I said by way of explanation as I paid for my stuff and hurried after her.

"Are you OK?" I said, when I caught up with Frankie outside.

"Never been better," she said, scraping her stiletto heels across the concrete.

"Nothing much you can do about that, is there?"

"Except hope Jane gets so fat she explodes," Frankie said over her shoulder as she set off back up the road.

When we got to the main gates, we saw another woman we recognised from the training ground leaning casually against the wall, fag in hand. She was called Dawn (if her gold name pendant was to be believed, and I'd never known anyone wear a false one) and she looked about twenty. She had long, peroxide-blonde hair, which needed the roots doing, and a heavily made-up face. The first time we'd seen her, Frankie had said that she looked as if she worked on the make-up counter at Boots, had taken the wrong turning and ended up at the training ground by mistake. Dawn eyed us both up and down without saying a word. I gave her a half-smile. Frankie scowled at her.

By seven o'clock there were a dozen or so fans waiting outside the gates. Mostly kids apart from us and Dawn. We were looking out expectantly for the first car when the woman who had served us in the shop came round the corner.

"You two still here?" she said. I wondered if she had some sort of affliction where she kept stating the obvious. "My name's Susan, by the way," she continued.

"I'm Claire," I said, deciding I might as well talk to her if she really did know the players.

"You calmed down yet?" she asked, turning to Frankie.

"I've had better days," Frankie replied.

146

"You were wasting your time there anyway, love," said Susan. "Matt's devoted to Jane, he'd never mess her around."

"How come you know all this?" said Frankie.

"You get to know all sorts, working at the shop."

"Like what?" I asked, wondering what she knew about Andy.

"Well," said Susan, lowering her voice, "Nobber went out with her over there." She nodded in the direction of Dawn.

"How long for?" I asked.

"Oh, only a few weeks. This is Nobber we're talking about."

A few minutes later Nobber swung round the corner in his black Escort XR3i. There was a woman sitting next to him. Long curly blonde hair, kind of pretty but tarty with it. My mum would have made some comment about her running out of material for her dress. The driver's window was down but as soon as Nobber caught sight of Dawn he wound it up and drove straight through with no more than a wave at the waiting fans.

I saw Dawn mouth the word "bastard" before turning on her heel and strutting off up the road, biting her bottom lip. I felt a bit sorry for her. But there again I couldn't understand anyone falling for Nobber in the first place.

The rest of the players started arriving in quick succession: Skip, Gibbo, Clubber, Thomo, each one accompanied by a glamorous wife or girlfriend. I wondered if there was some kind of designer footballer's girlfriend/wife shop in London that supplied all the players. Every model came with long legs, big tits, big hair, nice teeth and a little black dress. I could just about qualify on the long legs criteria but failed dismally on the others. I pictured myself in the reject basket outside the shop. Waiting for some non-league player from Barnet to come along.

"Hey, look," said Frankie, "here comes the birthday boy."

I looked up to see Andy's silver Golf edging towards us. I didn't look at him straight away. I looked at the passenger seat. It was empty. I gave a huge sigh. Andy was a vision in black. He even looked good in a bow tie, where most of the others had looked like complete dicks. He stopped just outside the gates. I let the kids go first. I didn't want them around cramping my style. As he signed the last autograph he looked up and flashed me a smile good enough to die for.

"Hi, Claire," he said. "How are you?" He'd remembered my name. We were on first-name terms. It was only a matter of time now.

"Fine, thanks," I said, holding out the photo of us; the original, not one of the reprints. "Could you sign this, please?"

"Sure. It's a nice photo is that."

"Thanks," I said, wondering if the compliment was meant for me, Frankie who'd taken it or Kodak who'd developed it.

"And, er, um, this is for you," I said, pulling the card from my bag and handing it to him. "Happy birthday."

He hesitated for a moment, as if he wasn't quite sure what to do.

"Oh, thanks very much. That's doubled my tally in one go."

I grinned, wondering who the other card was from, as Andy took the envelope, opened it, made a suitable "aahh" sound at the picture of the puppy in football boots on the front of the card, and thanked me again before putting it on the passenger seat. If he did notice the Tipp-Ex he was good enough not to say anything.

"Hope you have a good night," I said.

"Thanks, I'll do my best."

He flashed me another smile and was gone, sweeping through the gates into the car park, out of sight.

I strode back to Frankie triumphantly.

"See, I told you he was different."

"He's different all right," chipped in Susan. "Only one without a wife or girlfriend."

"So?" I said.

"Well, you've seen the earring, love. Work it out for yourself." Susan winked at me and walked off.

I turned to find Frankie laughing. "She's got a point," she said.

"Piss off," I said. "You're only jealous."

And she was, I knew that. Because I had Andy all to myself and Matt belonged to someone else. Someone who, far from looking a "right state", as Frankie put it, actually looked the best I'd ever seen her when she arrived with Matt a few minutes later. Frankie knew it too. She went up and got an autograph from Matt, but he didn't even bother to look up and see who he was signing for. He only had eyes for Jane.

We waited until we'd seen all the players arrive. I didn't want to leave. I wanted to stay all night, so I could feel close to Andy. Could say I'd spent his birthday night with him. We had to go though. Frankie had told her mum she'd be back by nine.

My mum picked us up from the station as we'd arranged.

"Have you got the cake?" I asked.

"Yes," she said, handing over a brown paper bag with the grease from the buttercream filling coming through it. "Though I wish I knew what you two are up to."

"Thanks," said Frankie, taking the bag. "It's just that Claire said you still had some of the golden wedding cake left, and you know how much my mum likes your baking."

Mum looked at us in the rear-view mirror. "Mmm," she said, sounding unconvinced. "I'd better get you home." We clambered into the back of the car and Mum drove off.

"Oh, I meant to tell you," she said as we were waiting at the traffic lights in the High Road. "My friend Rachel's doing the catering for that do at United tonight. Some last-minute job when it turned out the usual firm was double-booked."

I looked at Frankie and we both rolled our eyes at the same time. "Now she tells us," I hissed, rueing the lost chance of a ticket to the ball.

★　★　★

150

The room begins to fill with guests, mostly office staff and members of the supporters club. I self-consciously pull my skirt down and straighten my blouse. It is a simple uniform, black skirt and white top. I am relieved I don't have to wear an apron or a ridiculous hat like the waitresses in the Little Chef. I've had to wear my hair up but I don't mind that. It actually makes me look older, more sophisticated even.

I thread between the guests, smiling, tray of canapés in hand. Looking, searching everywhere. But still no Andy. The wives and girlfriends gather at one end of the room. Greeting each other with kisses on both cheeks, then laughing as they rub the lipstick marks off each other. They all stand in a certain way. One hip slightly out, the other leg (always the one with the split up the skirt), pointing diagonally outwards. Occasionally they throw back their heads and laugh, or toss their hair. They all look immaculate, they all look the same. A blur of black and blonde and gold, tinkling and shimmering. Knowing they have what everyone else in the room wants. A piece of United to call their own. I am not one of them yet but I will be soon. I want it more than anything else in the world. And if you want something badly enough it will come to you. I know that.

The guests are asked to take their seats. I return to the kitchen to collect the first of the starters. I am given tables three and four to look after. As I approach table three at the far end of the room I see Andy at last. He doesn't have anyone with him. He looks absolutely gorgeous in his dinner jacket. I reach over to give him his starter.

"Thanks," he says, looking up at me. He continues looking for several seconds before his face breaks into a smile.

"Hello again. I didn't know you worked here."

151

"I don't usually," I say. "I'm just helping out for the night."

"Well I'm glad you're here," Andy says. "I was dreading turning up to this on my own. But I'm not on my own now, am I?"

I blush and look down before hurrying away, smiling to myself. Every time I go back to the table Andy smiles at me. He can't say much, not with all the others there. But he doesn't need to. I can see it in his eyes.

I stand attentively behind his table during the after-dinner speeches. It is only when the dancing starts and the other players clear off to the bar that I finally get to be alone with him. "Move Closer" by Phyllis Nelson comes on. Andy reaches out for my hand.

"May I have the pleasure of this dance?" he says.

I smile and let him take my hand and lead me across to the centre of the dance floor. Other couples move out of the way. I hear whispers; one of the players' wives asking what he's doing dancing with a waitress. I don't care though. Because he has his arms around me. And I am not a waitress now. I am one of them. They just don't know it yet.

CHAPTER
FIVE

"Will you represent me, Miss Cooper?" My heart sank as I recognised Jake Dennison's voice. I turned around to see him standing there in his familiar Manchester City shirt and a pair of jeans which defied the laws of science by staying together despite the fact that there were clearly more holes than denim left in them.

"Hi, Jake," I said. "It only seems like five minutes since I last saw you."

"It was. I'm up for a breach of probation."

I let out a deep sigh. I had a soft spot for Jake. He had never hurt anyone; he'd just been brought up to believe that if you wanted something you simply went out and nicked it. This from his mother, only it turned out she was actually his grandmother. His real mother, who he'd always believed was his older sister, had got pregnant with him at thirteen. Coming from that sort of background, he'd done remarkably well to stay clean, sober, relatively sane and be nothing worse than a serial thief and occasional burglar.

"Oh Jake, it's not that I don't like you, but I was kind of hoping it might be a bit longer this time."

"I know. It was like one of those impulse purchases you ladies have. Only it wasn't in a shop, of course. And I didn't pay for it."

"What did you take, Jake?"

"A turkey," he said. I considered this statement for a moment before asking the obvious question.

"Dead or alive?"

"Alive."

I nodded. Jake's list of "previous" was fairly eclectic by Rochdale standards. But livestock was, as far as I was aware, a new venture for him.

"I feel quite a story coming on, Jake. I think I'm going to need a strong cup of coffee and a croissant. Can I get you anything?"

"How much is toast?" asked Jake.

"It doesn't matter, I'm buying. And I take it you'd like your usual cup of sugar with some tea thrown in?"

Jake grinned. "Nice one, Miss Cooper."

Jill did the honours and we settled down at a corner table in the public part of the café.

"Come on then," I said. "Let's hear it. From the beginning if you don't mind."

"I was walking along Catley Lane Head, minding me own business, like, when I saw this bird. A feathered one, like, I'm not being funny. Anyway, it was in a field, not tied down or anything. I didn't even know what sort of bird it was at first, but then it came nearer the fence and started making this gobbling noise and I realised it was a turkey." Jake took a break for a mouthful of toast and a slurp of tea. I braced myself for the next instalment.

154

"So, I looked around and I couldn't see any other turkeys or a farmer, like, and I wasn't even sure if it belonged to anyone." I decided against pointing out that wild turkeys were not common in that part of Rochdale. "And then I noticed some sort of sack in the corner of the field. And that's when I had the idea of nicking it."

"So it wasn't stolen to order?"

"Oh no. I was just using me head, like. What with Christmas being not too far away and that."

"Right," I said, nodding. "So what happened next?"

"Well I caught it and put it in the sack. Only trouble was, it was flapping around inside and I kept having to stop. And I'd only been walking about five minutes when a bloody cop car came past."

"And I take it that as you know the local cops pretty well, they stopped and asked what you had in the sack?"

"That's right. So I just said nothing, but the bloody bird started screeching and flapping its wings. That's when one of them got out the car and asked to have a look inside. I pretended I was surprised at first, that I hadn't realised there was a turkey in there, like. But I'm not sure they bought it."

I gazed down into my coffee, trying to keep a straight face as I imagined how anyone could inadvertently pick up a sack with a live turkey in it and carry it along the road for five minutes without realising it was in there.

"OK," I said. "I'm going to have my work cut out on this one but I'll give it a go. The first thing you'll have to do is apologise for trying to cover it up. And we'll need to stress that it was an opportunistic crime rather than a premeditated one and that you were not intending to do the bird any harm. That is right, isn't it?"

"Oh yeah, I wouldn't have killed it myself. I don't like turkey anyway. We usually have a KFC bucket for Christmas dinner."

I nodded and watched Jake drain the last dregs of tea from his mug. Somehow, I sensed this was going to be a long day.

"Is that a turkey roll you've got?" Fiona grinned when I joined her table at lunchtime. "Only don't gobble it all up at once."

"News travels fast round here," I said, sitting down with my cheese salad roll. Fiona hadn't even been in the same courtroom as me.

"Yeah, well I heard you did a bootiful job getting an adjournment."

"Am I going to get this for the rest of the year?" I asked.

"I suspect so. I'll certainly be putting my turkey order your way in the run-up to Christmas."

"You've got to hand it to the lad, he's nothing if not enterprising."

"I know. And I've got to thank you and your young friend for brightening up my morning. Boy, did I need it."

"Why, what's up?"

"Oh, just Aidan again." Fiona's fifteen-year-old son was going through some sort of rebellious stage and had fallen in with the wrong crowd. "He was out till 1a.m. on Friday night after they broke up from school. Wouldn't tell us where he'd been or who he'd been with."

"He's a teenager. That's what they do."

"No, this is different. It's this new bunch of kids he's been hanging out with. There was graffiti on some of the walls near us on Saturday morning. And the bus shelter had been smashed."

"Aidan wouldn't do anything like that, would he?"

"I don't know. His so-called mates could be putting him up to it. Goading him to get into trouble because he's a copper's son."

"What does Neil think?"

"He told Aidan to be big enough to tell his mates to fuck off if they tell him to do something he doesn't want to. But I don't think he's strong enough to do that."

"I wasn't when I was his age," I said.

"Did you get hassle from other kids at school then?"

"Yeah. Doesn't everyone?"

"I didn't," said Fiona.

"Yeah, but I bet you were a mouthy cow."

"Was that meant as an insult?"

"No, compliment actually. I can't imagine you taking any crap. And that's a good thing. I wish I'd been able to give as good as I got at that age."

"Trouble is I want to be Aidan's mouthy mum minder, but unfortunately I don't think that'd go down too well. I guess he'll have to sort it out for himself. I just worry he's going to end up in here one day. Give it a few years, he could be one of your failed criminals from hell."

"No, he'll sort himself out. You'll see. Just keep him well away from any untethered farm animals in the meantime."

My next case after lunch was adjourned — some cock-up with getting the right papers by the CPS — which meant I had a rare hour or so to myself.

I knew exactly what I was going to do. Something I should probably have done a long time ago. But the time was right now. The turkey case had tipped me over. I set up my laptop in a quiet corner of the café and went to the *Guardian*'s legal jobs website. It felt good simply to do it. Taking myself by the scruff of the neck and hauling myself towards the life I was supposed to be living. And maybe still could.

The first disappointment was how few jobs there were under the north-west and Yorkshire and Humberside sections. Five in total. And when I looked more closely, a couple of those were for legal secretaries and a couple more for legal caseworkers. There was only one job for a qualified solicitor. At a large corporate firm in Manchester. They wanted someone to specialise in employment law, which I'd had plenty of experience in at the previous firm I'd worked for. It was a proper job with a proper salary. And it wasn't in Rochdale. And I wouldn't be dealing with people who stole turkeys or were dared to rob a bank with an unloaded water pistol. I saved the page to favourites and opened up a Word document. "Curriculum Vitae" I typed at the top. Because I was actually going to do this. I was taking back control of my life.

My mind was still full of my job application when I got to Mark's after work. I pressed the intercom for flat number 7. Silence for a few seconds and then a click.

"Hi, come on up," said Mark.

"You're supposed to check who it is first. I could be a crazed bunny-boiler hitwoman for all you know," I said.

"OK," said Mark. "Tell me something about me that nobody else knows."

"You farted the first time we had sex," I said. Laughter from the other end of the intercom — and a cough from behind. I turned round to see a young man standing there with a broad smirk on his face.

"Beam me up, Scotty," I mumbled feebly into the intercom. I was still squirming in embarrassment when I arrived at the top of the stairs (I hadn't been able to face joining the smirking man in the lift). The door to Mark's flat was ajar, the smell of garlic and onions wafting out on to the landing.

"Hiya. You may want to avoid one of your neighbours for a while," I said as I walked in and shut the door behind me.

"Why?" asked Mark, turning around from the cooker to face me. It was his hair I noticed first. It had gone. Well, some of it anyway. The wispy, floppy strands shorn much closer to his head. It was only then that my gaze dropped to his clothes, none of which I'd ever seen before. In place of the usual jeans, T-shirt and trainers

159

was an expensive-looking grey shirt with oversized cuffs and collar, a pair of baggy black trousers with a twisted seam and some smart suede shoes with a large buckle on the front.

"Why?" I repeated.

"Yes, why avoid the neighbour?"

"Oh, he overheard my end of the conversation on the intercom. Must have sounded pretty weird. Er, what's the occasion?"

Mark shrugged as if it was no big deal that he'd entirely changed his appearance since the last time I'd seen him three days ago.

"I told you I went to a new hairdresser's on Saturday; fancied a bit of a change, that's all. Don't you like it?"

"Yeah, I do. At least I think I do. It may take me a while to get used to it, that's all. What about the gear? Where did you get that?"

"King Street."

I nodded, although still not quite understanding. Mark had spent a small fortune in shops frequented by Premiership footballers. The same Mark who usually balked at the idea of buying a new pair of trousers from Next unless they were in the sale.

"So what brought this on?"

"Just thought it was time I updated my image a bit," he said. "Made more of an effort. Though if I look like a complete prat, please tell me."

I put my briefcase down and walked over to him, noticing the smell as soon as I did so. Mark had aftershave on. He never wore aftershave.

160

"You look great," I said, running my fingers through what was left of his hair. "It suits you, reminds me a bit of Daniel Craig."

"Well, I'll settle for that. Still got a bit of work to do on the six-pack, mind," he said, sliding his arms around my waist.

"Don't worry, I'll make sure I don't take any photos of you emerging from the water in your Speedos."

"Thank you. Although I might be able to do my own stunts soon," he said.

"What do you mean?"

"I've joined a climbing club."

A laugh spilled out of my mouth before I could stop it.

"What?" he said.

"I'm sorry, but you were the one who famously said, 'I hate stairs', that time the lift was broken. You even talked about getting a ground-floor flat so you could avoid them altogether."

"I'm not climbing stairs. It's a climbing wall. A massive place in Rochdale. I did a taster session on Sunday and signed up on a beginners' course. Then when I get good enough they do trips out rock-climbing and abseiling. That sort of thing."

"Oh, right. Great," I said, trying desperately to be encouraging and supportive while wondering what the hell was going on. "Only I didn't think you had a head for heights?"

"Well, sometimes you have to push yourself a bit. Go outside your comfort zone."

I nodded again, convinced this wasn't Mark talking and he'd been brainwashed by some sort of trendy extreme-sports sect while I'd been at Frankie's.

"Sure, well as long as it's not a ploy to pick up clients when they fall and break their neck."

"I hadn't thought of that. Maybe I'll take some business cards with me next time," he grinned, brushing the hair out of my eyes. "Anyway, you chill out for a bit, you've had a long day. The lasagne's nearly ready."

I kissed him on the lips and went to sit down on the sofa. I kicked off my heels and put my feet up. It was then that I saw it. The book lying slap bang in the middle of the coffee table. *Gangs* by Ross Kemp.

"Why have you got this?" I said, holding it up in the air.

"A guy at the climbing club recommended it. There's some interesting stuff in it about gang culture around the world." If I'd compiled a list of "books least likely to be found on Mark's coffee table", the complete works of Ross Kemp would have been up there. The hair and the clothes and the rock-climbing I could put down to a rare weekend on his own with money to burn. But this took things to a whole different level.

"You're going to tell me you've joined the Territorial Army as well, aren't you?"

"Don't be daft," said Mark, walking over and sitting down next to me. "It's only a bloody book."

"I'm simply trying to get my head around why you've acquired a whole new look, wardrobe and set of hobbies and interests while I was away."

162

Mark looked stung. It occurred to me that this could be something to do with the house. With him feeling I'd rejected him. I reached out and stroked his hair. "You haven't done all this on my account, have you?"

"No, of course not. I simply fancied trying something new. Didn't want to get stuck in a rut."

"OK," I said, still unconvinced. "That makes two of us, then."

Mark looked worried for a moment.

"Have you taken up macrame on ice?" he asked.

I laughed, although I could see the potential for a celebrity version on Saturday nights.

"No. But I am applying for a new job."

Mark nodded as if he'd been expecting it, which surprised me. "So where is it?"

"A firm called Smith MacGuire in Manchester. They want an employment law specialist, corporate stuff I think. But it's got good career prospects and it's serious money as well."

"That'll come in handy with the new house then."

I was thrown for a second, aware that I was agitated because this wasn't supposed to be about the new house. It was about me doing something with my life. Besides, as neither of us had even had a viewing yet, the new house thing still seemed a very long way off.

"I've just got to the point where if I don't get out of Rochdale soon I'll stay there for ever."

"You're bloody good at it, though. Your regulars would really miss you. Having someone they can trust. Someone to fight their corner."

163

I hadn't really thought of it like that. But now I did I felt bad for even contemplating deserting them.

"I've done my time though, haven't I? It's been the longest maternity cover on record. Surely I'm allowed to move on at some point."

"Of course you are. And I know you have to put up with a lot of crap, but I do think you'd miss it more than you realise. And that this is more about what you think you should be doing than what you really want to do."

"Why do you say that?"

"I don't know. All this business with seeing Frankie again seems to have unsettled you. Made you want to change things."

He was right, of course. Unnervingly so. But I didn't want to admit that. Partly because I was embarrassed about how fixated I had become with the list and partly because I didn't want him to worry about where he stood in all this. I'd never told him about Andy. And I certainly didn't want to go into it all now. Me turning down the house had undoubtedly caused a wobble in our relationship. I didn't want to make things any worse.

"It just got me thinking, that's all. About how sometimes we can lose sight of what we want to do. End up drifting. Feeling a bit rudderless."

"Is that how you feel?" he asked, stroking my hair.

"I guess so. I always used to be so clear about where I was going, what I was going to do."

"But you said Frankie's life was nothing like you'd expected either."

164

"It isn't, but . . ." I broke off, realising I was about to say that she was happy. And that wouldn't sound good at all. "Are you sure you don't mind me inviting them up?" I'd suggested a return visit to Frankie, with the whole family. Now I'd found her again I wanted to make sure we did more than just send Christmas cards.

"Of course not. I'm looking forward to meeting her. Just as long as you don't both regress to your teens and start singing Spandau Ballet and Duran Duran songs."

"Don't worry," I said. "I am so over Martin Kemp."

I kept glancing at Mark all through dinner. Trying to get used to the new look as he explained the basics of rock-climbing to me. And wondering what the real reason behind his transformation was. Even when we snuggled up on the sofa afterwards, the aftershave was disconcerting. It was like I was with a new man. Only the old one was still with me as well. He leant over and started kissing my neck. Seriously kissing it, not simply a nuzzle.

"Steady on," I said. "Have you been watching those vampire films again?"

He smiled, but there was a distinctly odd look on his face, half excited, half frightened to death.

"Come on," he said, taking hold of my hand and pulling me up from the sofa. He led me past the bedroom to the front door.

"Where are you taking me?" I asked as he opened it and ushered me through.

"Out," he said.

"But *Newsnight*'s on in half an hour." It was kind of our week-night ritual. Curling up together on the sofa to watch Jeremy Paxman tearing some hapless politician to pieces with both of us point-scoring and seeing if we could come up with a better defence than they could for whatever it was they were alleged to have done wrong. I always insisted on staying up to see tomorrow morning's front pages at the end of the programme before we adjourned to the bedroom. Mark didn't know why. I simply told him that I didn't like getting surprises when I woke up.

"I know," he said now. "That's why we're going somewhere else."

"Don't I need my jacket and bag?" I asked as he pulled the door shut behind us and pressed the button for the lift.

"Nope," he said. "Not unless you're planning to make a run for it afterwards."

I looked at him, still not understanding, as we stepped inside the lift. And then a minute later the door shut, the lift stayed still and Mark started unbuttoning my shirt. Suddenly I understood all too well.

"We can't do it here," I said as he kissed my shoulders and let the shirt fall on to the floor. I wasn't sure whether it was a climbing instructor or Ross Kemp who had advocated sex in an unusual/exciting setting. But there was no way this was something Mark would do of his own accord

"Why not?" he asked breathlessly as he moved down to kiss my breasts.

"It's a bit *Fatal Attraction*," I said as he pushed me up against the lift wall.

"Well you're the one who started talking about bunny boilers, putting ideas in my head," he replied, unclasping my bra in one deft movement and circling and flicking with his tongue.

"Now, if you're quite finished," he said, looking up for a second with a wicked smile on his face, "I should very much like to ravish you." He hitched my skirt up and slipped his fingers inside my knickers. I let out a moan. He was good with his hands. Always had been. My eyes were shut, my breath rapid. Despite my initial reluctance I was actually getting turned on by this. Maybe a new man was just what I needed.

Some time later — and I mean some time — we sank down on to the floor in a damp, breathless heap.

"Jesus," I said. "Did you forget to mention the tantric sex course as well?"

"Yeah," said Mark with a grin. "Sting sends his regards."

I laughed, and as I did so I had the sensation that the earth was moving. Mark was good but not capable of that from where he was sitting.

"Fuck," I said. "Somebody's called the lift."

We scrambled to our feet as the lift descended to the ground floor. Mark pulled on his trousers. I stepped into my knickers, tugged my skirt down and, unable to locate my bra, threw my shirt back on and started buttoning fast.

The doors slid open at the bottom. A slim woman in her fifties in a buttoned-up cardigan was standing

167

there. Mark nodded and smiled at her. She stared at us for a second. I glanced down to check I didn't have a boob hanging out before realising she was waiting for us to get out. I nudged Mark and we shuffled out, Mark smiling and nodding so much that even if she hadn't suspected anything at the beginning, she probably did by now.

"Oh God," he said when the doors had closed behind us. "That was Miss Watson from upstairs. She does the Christian Aid collection for the local church."

"She's probably too prim to even suspect anything then," I said.

We walked back up the stairs to the third floor, giggling like a couple of teenagers. The lift was waiting outside Mark's flat. The doors open. A hand protruding from inside, holding between thumb and forefinger my missing black lacy bra.

"Yours, I presume," came a voice from inside.

I reached out and took the offending article.

"Thanks," I muttered. The hand disappeared, the doors shut again. "Oops, sorry," I said, turning to Mark. "I guess that's another neighbour you'll have to avoid for a while."

"Don't worry, it could have been worse." Mark grinned. "It could have been your knickers. Anyway, we'd better get back to the sofa."

"You're not up for it again, are you?" I said.

"No, but Jeremy Paxman will be wondering where you are, and you might just have made tomorrow morning's front pages."

Monday, 21 October 1985

I climbed out of bed, padded across the bedroom floor and went straight to my dressing-table mirror, pressing my face as close to it as I could while slowly curling back my top lip. The steel bar that ran across my top row of teeth gleamed menacingly back at me. I hated it, hated it more than I had ever hated anyone or anything in my life. Which was particularly worrying as I'd only had it for a few days. I couldn't help wondering how much I would hate it by the time I finished wearing it.

Six to nine months, the orthodontist had said. It might as well have been a life sentence as far as I was concerned. It was going to be a nightmare. I had decided that before I'd even got it. And nothing that had happened since had made me change my mind. The first day of wearing it at school last week had been even worse than I'd imagined. It hadn't exactly been going well before the brace. The downside of my best friend being in the year above me was that now she had left school and gone to college, I was Johnny-no-mates at break and lunchtime. It was tough getting used to not having her around. Throwing in a mouth full of metal to contend with was beyond a joke.

I'd tried to hide it at first, managing to smile with my mouth closed at the few people who said "awright" to me as I arrived. My vow of silence survived registration, due mainly to the fact that nobody had spoken to me, but finally succumbed to Mrs Osborne's persistent questioning in biology.

"Come on, Claire. The process by which plants turn sunlight into food. I'm sure you know the answer; perhaps you'd care to share it with us?"

The whole class had turned to look at me then, as if sensing there was some reason for my reticence.

"Photothynthethith," I'd lisped finally, the resulting "thank you" from Mrs Osborne drowned out by the laughter of my classmates.

By break time the news had spread. "Oi, Metal Mickey, give us a smile." "Hey, Skidmark, you shouldn't eat coat hangers for breakfast, they get stuck in your teeth." The jibes had come thick and fast. Each one making me clench my jaws ever tighter shut, until I'd begun to feel they had been wired together like my teeth.

I grimaced at my reflection in the mirror. And now today I was supposed to wear it to the training ground. Andy would never fancy me with it on. Not in a million years. It would be like asking someone to go out with the Elephant Man. And however nice he was, I couldn't expect him to do that.

"Do you want a straw for that orange juice, love, would it make it easier?" Mum asked as we sat in silence at the breakfast table. I glowered at her from under my flick.

"It just takes a bit longer than usual. I can't feel my mouth any more, it hurts so much."

"Never mind, it will get better."

"How do you know? You never wore one."

"The orthodontist said so, didn't he? You've just got to get used to it. The more you wear it, the easier it will get."

"I'm not wearing it to the training ground, if that's what you're getting at."

The very thought of turning up to see Andy with half of Sheffield steelworks in my gob was making me feel sick.

"I've told you already, Claire. If you don't wear it, you're not going. It's a brace, not a fashion accessory. You don't realise it now, but you'll thank me for making you wear it one day when you've got lovely straight teeth."

I couldn't imagine ever thanking my mum for anything. At that particular moment, I viewed her as nothing short of evil for having delivered me at the feet of Satan the orthodontist in the first place.

"Anyway," continued Mum, obviously not about to give up, "if it's a problem, don't go up there. Half-terms are supposed to be for doing things with your friends and family. Not mooning over some footballer on your own."

"It's not my fault Frankie's got her bridesmaid's dress fitting. Anyway, there's nothing wrong with me going to places on my own; it's called being independent," I said, glancing up from the back page of the *Daily Mirror*.

"It's because you want to do such strange things that no one else wants to do them with you," said Mum.

"Says the woman who goes to Tupperware parties on her own."

"That's completely different. It's to do with my work."

"So how come you get all done up before you go?"

"Oh, so I can't even make the effort to look my best now, can I?"

"I dunno why you bother. You're not going to meet any men at a Tupperware party, are you? Not unless you're planning to pin the organiser's husband to the settee."

It was only when I saw Mum's expression that I realised what I'd said. I opened my mouth to say sorry but nothing came out. The word remained stuck in my throat, in the exact place it had been for years. Threatening to choke me if I tried to dislodge it.

"Listen, young lady, I've had to sacrifice my personal life to work all the hours God sends to bring you up. So don't start making smart remarks like that, OK?"

"I'm gonna go up and get ready," I said. "I don't wanna miss them arriving."

I sat staring forlornly into the mirror. I'd been so busy looking at my brace that I hadn't noticed the huge zit which had appeared on my face overnight. I suspected Mum possessed secret powers, a bit like the wiggly-nosed woman in *Bewitched*, and must somehow be spiriting blemishes on to my face at crucial points in my life as a penance for my sins. I had no doubt that if Andy saw it, it would put him off me for life. The question was how to get rid of it. Squeezing it was not an option. Frankie did that and I considered it particularly gross.

Instead I reached for my medicated skin tonic, trying not to think about Frankie's assertion that it contained radioactive material. The liquid was blue, the same blue they used for National Health glasses. I wondered if they were linked in any way. I pressed the damp cotton wool pad hard against my chin, feeling the tingling sensation radiate across my face. When I removed the pad, the spot momentarily appeared to have diminished. But within seconds the fresh supply of oxygen had breathed new life into it, enabling it to return to its former splendour before my very eyes.

I resorted to the concealer stick I had bought for just such emergencies. It was shade 001, which the lady in Boots had assured me was the palest one available. But after applying a liberal covering I concluded that I must be anaemic, such was the difference between its colour and that of my skin. I tried dabbing some talc on top of the concealer to help blend it in, but only succeeded in creating an unsavoury looking growth that appeared to be in dire need of medical attention.

With a sigh, I wiped the mixture off, deciding that the original spot was less obtrusive than my botched attempt to conceal it, and opted instead for a diversionary tactic. Beads.

Beads were not really my thing. But I had noted how good they looked on Madonna, so when I'd spotted a long string of luminescent peach beads on sale in the market for £1.50, I'd decided to give them a go.

I had even practised dancing to "Into the Groove" with them on. Admittedly they didn't jangle about as much as Madonna's did (though neither did my boobs, for that matter), but they did look reasonably trendy. And if I teamed them up with my new short peach skirt, peach and cream vest top (bought after Frankie had informed me that horizontal stripes were the answer for the flat-chested) and cream jacket, I had what I considered a more than passable outfit. With a final twist of my beads in front of the mirror, I was ready. I hurried downstairs and out the front door before Mum had a chance to see me and make any comments about it being October and the need to dress sensibly. Yes, I'd be bloody freezing but that didn't matter. What mattered was looking good.

It felt strange, going to the training ground on my own. But I supposed I would have to get used to it. Frankie was always busy these days. Busy with preparations for Connie's wedding, busy with college work, busy with a whole new set of friends. All she ever talked about now was her mate Tara at college. I was thinking of getting her a T-shirt to replace her Frankie Goes to Hollywood one. Something with "Tara says . . ." on it.

And she kept on saying things like "You wouldn't understand" or "When you leave school". I was left feeling like some little kid who wasn't tall enough to go on the biggest ride at the theme park. Except that in my case I was plenty tall enough. I just couldn't seem to attract the attention of the man who was selling the tickets.

174

It wasn't until I was tottering down the garden path that I remembered how difficult it was to walk in proper heels. I'd had no choice but to wear my best white shoes; my usual blue pumps hadn't gone with the outfit, and on this occasion trainers were clearly out of the question. I knew Frankie would be proud of me though. For wearing such high heels.

"Nice legs, darling."

I was vaguely aware that the gruff voice and wolf whistle that had preceded it had come from a group of workmen to my left. I waited for Frankie to shout her usual colourful riposte. It was only after several seconds that I remembered Frankie wasn't with me. Which meant the comment, and whistle, had been directed at me.

I spun round.

"Sexist pig," I shouted at the nearest of a group of middle-aged workmen who were presiding over a large hole in the pavement.

"Give over, you love it really."

"In your dreams, Grandad," I yelled over my shoulder. But he'd hit a raw nerve. Deep down inside, way beyond the feminist pretensions, a tiny part of me was turning cartwheels of joy. For the first time in my life, someone had treated me as a sex object. A hint of a smile crossed my face as I walked on confidently to the training ground, occasionally sneaking a quick look down at my legs.

When I arrived, I was introduced to the novel experience of being disappointed not to see Susan from the club shop. Without Frankie, any familiar face would have been welcome. With no one I knew to talk to I tried to blend discreetly into the background. It was only when Andy pulled into the car park ten minutes later that I realised I didn't mind being on my own. Because it meant I could concentrate all my efforts on him.

I let the kids go up first. A dozen or so of them clustered around his car. He never used to get all that attention before. It was only because he was playing regularly in the first team now. He didn't seem to mind the fuss though. He looked as if he was enjoying it. Clubber didn't look so pleased, mind, when he came in and only one kid bothered to ask for his signature. He glared at Andy as he walked past. Andy was so busy signing autographs he didn't see it. I did though, so I gave Clubber a dirty look back on Andy's behalf. After what seemed like an age, the last of the kids scuttled off clutching his autograph book. Andy looked up, a smile lighting up his face.

"Hi, Claire, long time no see," he said. He remembered my name. Even after all this time. We were like old friends now. Me and Andy.

"I know. I've been busy."

I didn't want to say I'd been at school. It would have spoilt everything.

"You're looking great, anyway."

"Thanks," I said as he stopped in front of me. "Must be down to you guys being top of the league." I smiled at him and noticed his gaze drop to my mouth. I checked discreetly with my tongue to see if I'd got a bran flake stuck to my teeth, but there was nothing there — only my brace.

I snapped my mouth tight shut, cursing myself for being so concerned with covering up my spot and then getting the wolf whistle that I'd forgotten to take my brace out on the way as planned. I had mutated into Jaws with the metal teeth from the James Bond film and Andy was about to run screaming in the opposite direction. He didn't, of course, just smiled back politely before walking off towards the clubhouse.

As soon as his back was turned, I rushed to the ladies', where I yanked the brace from my mouth and rinsed it under the tap, hating the feel of the slippery plastic between my fingers. I briefly contemplated flushing it down the loo and telling my mum it had accidentally fallen out. But it would be pointless. The dentist had casts of my mouth and would simply make another one, possibly even more hideous than the first. I wrapped the brace in toilet paper, stuffed it into my bag and went back out to watch the training.

Even in the practice match, Andy played in the first team. Clubber didn't look very happy about playing with the reserves. But it was his own stupid fault for getting himself sent off and suspended in the first place. He couldn't expect to walk back into the first team, not with Andy playing as well as he had been.

"Hi. Where's your friend today?"

I looked up with a start to see Dawn, the girl who'd gone out with Nobber, standing next to me.

"She's busy. It's her sister's wedding on Saturday."

177

I still wasn't sure if that was the real reason Frankie hadn't come. But it sounded plausible enough. I wondered why Dawn didn't have a job to go to but felt it would be rude to ask. And remembered it was equally rude not to introduce myself.

"Oh, I'm Claire, by the way."

"Pleased to meet you. I'm Dawn."

"I know."

"Don't tell me, that Susan told you. And probably told you all sorts of other stuff about me as well. She's the worst gossip I've ever met, that woman."

"She didn't say anything bad. Only that you'd gone out with Nob . . . I mean, Mickey Squire."

"Don't worry, you can call him Nobber, everyone else does. It doesn't bother me. I knew his nickname before I went out with him so I s'pose it was my own stupid fault."

"Do you wanna get back with him?" I asked. Dawn snorted, obviously finding something amusing.

"Yeah, but it's not up to me, is it? It's up to him. Anyway," she continued, "you didn't come here to hear my sob story. Who've you got your eye on?"

"Oh, no one in particular," I said, immediately averting my eyes from Andy. "I like them all. It's the football I'm interested in actually."

Dawn looked doubtful but didn't push the point any further. I felt bad about lying to her after she'd walked away. But I didn't think it was right to tell her about me and Andy. It would be like rubbing her nose in it, because I had something she didn't. A United player who cared.

Nobber was the first to leave after training. I watched as Dawn checked her lipstick in her compact mirror, brushed a loose strand of hair from her eyes and strode across the car park towards him. He walked straight past her, without so much as a nod, let alone a kind word. Dawn stopped in her tracks and looked up at the sky for a second, before turning and marching out of the car park, lips pursed and head bowed.

I couldn't see the point of loving someone who treated you that badly. I gave silent thanks that I had better taste in men than Dawn. As if to prove the point, Andy came out and greeted me with a warm smile.

"Hiya, you still here? I thought you'd have had enough of us by now."

"Nah, you can never get too much of a good thing."

Andy laughed. "Is that right? So how come you're on your own today, then?"

"Oh, Frankie, my friend, she's having a bridesmaid's dress fitting."

"Whose wedding is it? Not yours, I hope."

I stared at him for a second, unable to believe what he'd just said. He was flirting with me. He'd practically asked me out. In fact he'd only just stopped short of proposing.

"No," I said, giggling as I tried not to blush. "It's her sister's. Big do she's having on Saturday. Three o'clock kick-off, same as you."

"Are you going?"

"Yeah, worse luck. I'd rather be listening to the commentary on the radio. I'll have to try and smuggle my trannie into the church."

"I'll tell the lads not to score in the first half then; we don't want the vicar throwing you out for cheering."

I laughed. It felt so normal, sharing a joke with him. As if we'd known each other for years. We were standing next to his car now. But he wasn't making any attempt to get in. He hadn't even opened the door. He was too busy talking to me.

"So what are you up to for the rest of half-term?"

I was mortified that my schoolgirl status was still so obvious.

"Oh, not much. Studying mainly. It's my final year. O levels and all that."

"God, don't remind me. My dad still hasn't forgiven me for flunking my maths."

"How many did you get then?" I asked.

"Oh, I managed eight, I think. Which isn't bad for a footballer, I guess."

I nodded. It was probably more than the rest of the team had put together. "So what are you planning to do afterwards?"

"I'll be off to college to do my A levels, then uni. I want to be a lawyer."

Andy grinned at me. "Fantastic. That's what I'm planning to do when I'm too old for this game."

"Really?" I said, deciding not to let on that I already knew in case he thought I'd just copied him.

"Yeah, it's what I was going to do before Huddersfield Town offered me a contract and football got in the way. I reckon I'd be a damn sight better at that than running a pub. I've just started an Open

180

University law course so I don't get left behind by bright young things like you."

I grinned, chuffed that he considered me bright. "It'll be ages before you have to give up playing though. You're not that old."

"Well thank you. Flattery will get you everywhere. Now, what can I sign for you today?"

"Um, I've got the Everton programme in here somewhere," I said, rummaging in my canvas shoulder bag before triumphantly producing it. I looked expectantly at Andy, who was staring down at the programme, seemingly reluctant to take it from me. I couldn't think why until I looked down and saw what had caught his eye. There, stuck rigidly to the picture of Dave Orton on the front, was a familiar-looking pink object with protruding wires and a decorative toilet-roll covering.

I stood, mouth wide open, eyes fixed firmly on my brace, as I rued the fact that I hadn't flushed it down the toilet when I'd had the chance.

"They're horrible things, aren't they?" said Andy, breaking the awkward silence. "Don't worry, I used to wear one, I know what it's like."

"Yeah, but I bet you never took it out to show people. I don't usually carry it around in my bag like this, honest," I said, prising the brace off the programme and taking a bit of Dave Orton's left knee with it as I did so.

"Are you sure you don't want me to sign it for you?" he asked.

181

I was already thinking how cool it would be to have Andy's autograph permanently in my mouth when I looked up at him and realised he was joking. A smile spread slowly across my face and I started laughing. Andy was laughing too. We were laughing together.

"How long did you have to wear yours for?" I asked eventually.

"Oh God, over a year, I think. I had awful fangs that stuck out here," he explained, pointing to the top corners of his mouth. "The kids at school used to call me Dracula, it was horrible. Still, believe it or not, it is worth it in the end."

"Right. I guess you just don't think that at the time."

"Anyway, don't worry about it. I'll pretend I never saw it. Now let me sign that programme of yours."

As I waited for Andy to drive off, I noticed him adjusting his rear view mirror. For a second I thought he was looking at my legs. I shook my head and smiled to myself. The wolf whistle must have gone to my head.

Frankie had told me Connie's dress was awful but I still gasped when I caught sight of her coming down the aisle looking for all the world like a crinoline lady toilet-roll holder. Frankie didn't look much better, mind, trussed up in an unflattering pink taffeta creation chosen by Connie, presumably because it was so hideous that she would find it impossible to upstage the bride on her big day.

A ripple of approving "aaahs" ran from the back of the church to the front pews as Connie made her way down the aisle. I couldn't decide whether the other guests were being polite or whether they genuinely had as bad taste as Connie. Frankie looked across at me as she trailed past. I grinned, so she thought I was being supportive. But actually it was quite funny, seeing her looking awful for a change.

The ceremony itself was tedious to the point of being painful. I shifted uncomfortably on the hard wooden pew, the words of the priest droning on fuzzily in the background like an irritating bluebottle. All I could think about was Andy and how he was doing. It was a big match today against Liverpool. A real test for him. I knew he'd pass it, I had every faith in him. But I wanted to help him through it, every minute, every second. Mum had said I couldn't take my radio into church. That it would be disrespectful. So all I could do was wait.

"Conchetta looks a picture, doesn't she, Claire?" Mrs Alberti said afterwards, brushing a tear away with a lace-edged handkerchief as we stood in the confetti-strewn churchyard, watching the official photographs being taken.

"Mmm," I replied, trying not to laugh. "She certainly does."

I looked at my watch. They'd be into the second half by now. These Catholic dos took so bloody long. I scoured the churchyard, sure I couldn't be the only one on tenterhooks. I was right. Mr Alberti was over in the far corner, trying to hide behind a tree, transistor radio pressed against his ear. He'd always been a big United fan; that was where Frankie had got it from. Every summer he created an entirely blue flower display along the central promenade in the park. Most people thought he had a thing about lobelias. Only me and Frankie knew it was a civic tribute to United. Such loyalty deserved to be rewarded. I'd told Frankie that should Percy Thrower ever forget to put a plastic cup on the top of one of his garden canes and accidentally poke his eye out, she should write in to *Blue Peter* nominating her father as his replacement.

"What's the score?" I whispered, sidling up to him.

"Nil-nil," he said. "But we're on top, should be two-nil up by now. Goodyear and Orton both missed sitters in the first half, apparently."

I smiled, remembering what Andy had said about telling the lads not to score before half-time. It was the first time I'd ever been pleased that United weren't winning.

"Can we have the bride's family now, please," the photographer shouted.

"Here," said Mr Alberti, thrusting the radio into my hand. "You'd better listen for me. Else I'm in big trouble."

I took the radio from him as he hurried off to join the rest of the family. When Matt scored a few moments later they must have seen me jumping up and down, because when the photographer took the next shot, Frankie (who had been looking decidedly pissed off) was actually smiling. And Mr Alberti's arm was raised aloft triumphantly.

"Isn't it lovely to see a man so proud of his daughter?" I heard a guest next to me say. I couldn't help thinking how much prouder Mr Alberti would look at the final whistle.

We won 1-0. Andy played a blinder, according to Alan Green on the radio. "A performance of considerable poise and maturity which will give the watching England manager Bobby Robson something to think about." That was what he actually said. I could have broken the school high-jump record at that moment. All the way through the speeches I kept thinking about it. My Andy playing for England. When we had to toast the bride and groom I said, "Andy for England" instead. Nobody heard me though. I only said it quietly.

When all the speeches and that were over, Frankie was finally allowed to leave the top table. She hurried over to join me, ignoring the smiles and greetings from other relatives who lined the route. She still looked uptight about the whole thing.

"Matt scored the goal," I said.

"Excellent."

"You don't seem very pleased."

"Course I am. I'm just fed up with having to wear this poxy dress and my dad going on about what a wonderful daughter Connie is. It made me wanna puke."

"You should have. It would have given you an excuse to take the dress off."

Frankie laughed. I liked it when she laughed at stuff I said. She hadn't done it so much lately. She usually only laughed at things Tara had said. Tara hadn't been invited to the wedding though, because Frankie had met her after the invites had gone out. I don't think Frankie wanted her there anyway. She wouldn't have wanted Tara to see her in that outfit.

"Hello, Francesca, how are you, love?"

A woman with a face that looked like a well-used piece of silver foil bent to embrace Frankie, almost falling out of her sequinned top as she did so, and planted a ring of mauve lipstick on her cheek. Frankie pulled away. The colour seemed to have drained from her face. The woman looked familiar but I couldn't place her.

"Have you got a kiss for your Uncle Tony, then?" she said, edging sideways to allow a small man with a suntanned face and wire-rimmed glasses to step forward. It was only when I heard his name and saw a flash of unnaturally white teeth that it clicked. The Maria Bellini School of Dancing in Potters Bar. Frankie had been a star pupil when she was younger; she'd won medals for it and everything. I'd gone to see her once in a show. She'd been brilliant; everyone had been talking about how good she was. Auntie Maria (the woman with the tinfoil skin) had marked her out for big things. Only Frankie had chucked it all in when she was twelve. Said it was kids' stuff. Her mum had never forgiven her.

Uncle Tony was still standing there flashing those teeth, his moustache twitching as he waited for a kiss. Only I could tell Frankie wasn't going to give him one. She'd taken a few steps backwards and her jaw had tightened. Her eyes seemed to have turned from brown to black.

186

"Excuse me," she said to Maria. "I've just got to show my friend to the toilets."

Frankie took hold of my arm and led me into the ladies' bogs. I was sure I could feel her shaking.

"Are you OK?" I said.

"Yeah, I'm fine."

"What was all that about?"

"He's not my real uncle."

"I know."

"Well he's got no fucking right, has he?"

"No," I said, having no idea what she was on about. Frankie disappeared into one of the cubicles, peed loudly, emerged without flushing and washed her hands twice under the hot tap.

"Are you all right now?" I asked. She didn't answer. Just wiped her hands on her dress and headed back into the hall.

"Francesca, I've found someone who wants to say hello to you," Mrs Alberti called from across the room as she spotted us making our way towards the bar. Frankie pretended she hadn't heard. A few moments later Mrs Alberti was tottering towards us, dragging a spotty-faced lad of about our age behind her.

"Who's that?" I asked.

Frankie rolled her eyes. "Oh God, it's this boy called Salvatore; he used to live next door when we were kids."

Mrs Alberti and Salvatore arrived in front of us, both of them grinning inanely.

"Go on, son," said Mrs Alberti, giving him a gentle poke in the ribs. "Don't be shy."

Salvatore took a deep breath and, in a shaky, out-of-key voice began to sing the opening lines from "Frankie" by Sister Sledge.

Mrs Alberti clapped her hands and the flap of skin hanging from her chin wobbled in delight.

"Well?" she said, looking at Frankie expectantly, when at last he had finished. "What do you think?"

Frankie didn't hesitate. "I think Sister Sledge are crap and he's a complete wanker," she said, before turning on her heel and flouncing out of the hall.

Mrs Alberti was still standing there, her mouth gaping open, when the first notes of "Tonight, I Celebrate My Love for You" brought Connie and Maurizio out into the centre of the dance floor. An appreciative audience gathered around them, cooing and taking photos. I decided to get some fresh air. Peabo Bryson and Roberta Flack always had that sort of effect on me.

I found Frankie sitting on the steps outside, like a dollop of dropped candyfloss.

"I can't believe you said that."

"She's always trying to fix me up with Italian boys. I'm sick of it."

"You should have seen that Salvatore's face. I thought he was gonna cry. Mind you, I'd cry if I had a voice like that."

Frankie started to laugh. We sat there for ages, just laughing and talking. She didn't mention Tara once.

CHAPTER
SIX

Mark pulled up outside my house just as I arrived back from the allotment. I sensed from the way he winced as he got out of the car and hobbled over towards me that his rock-climbing had not gone too well.

"What happened?" I asked.

"Just turned my ankle a bit on the way up. Nothing too serious."

I took hold of his hand and he winced again.

"Rope burns," he explained, holding up his palms. "Slipped a bit on the way down."

"What about the bit in between going up and coming down?"

"That was fine. I seem to be OK at the hanging around at the top bit. Just need to brush up my technique on the rest."

I nodded and kissed him. Despite his apparent enthusiasm, I still wasn't convinced that he was actually enjoying it. I liked the new hairstyle and had got used to some of the clothes, but I still couldn't get my head around the idea of someone who had been known to drive a couple of hundred yards to the newsagent's suddenly becoming some kind of action hero.

"Come in and stick your foot up on the sofa. I'll see if I can find some frozen peas."

"No, it's OK. I've eaten at the café, thanks."

I pulled a face at him.

"I hope you've got better lines than that if you're going to be the pre-meal entertainment tonight." Frankie and her family were due in an hour or so. I'd decided to cook a curry rather than take them to an Italian restaurant which wasn't anywhere near as good as Joe's. Although as I'd never cooked for a chef before, I was feeling slightly anxious about it.

"Don't worry, I'll do my utmost to charm and entertain your guests. I'll have to get back home tonight though. I've got a viewing for the flat first thing tomorrow morning."

I was thrown for a second. I hadn't expected either of us to get any viewings for months.

"Oh," was all I could manage.

"Does the prospect of me moving in fill you with that much excitement?"

"Sorry, I didn't mean it to sound like that. I was surprised, that's all."

"Well, you never know, we could be first time lucky."

"Yeah, let's hope so," I said, bending down to take off my muddy wellies. And secretly hoping that whoever was viewing Mark's flat wouldn't like it. Because if they did, we'd be back to looking at houses and the whole panicky "my life is turning into a cul-de-sac" thing would start again. I thought I'd bought some time with the "let's sell ours first" idea. But now the only person actively looking to buy in

Britain was going to sniff around Mark's flat, I realised the sand might run through rather quicker than I had expected.

We heard Frankie's family arrive long before they actually knocked on the door. Sophia's high-pitched scream was recognisable even from inside, and was followed by some sort of shouting match over who had been worst behaved on the journey. Mark looked up at me from the kitchen table.

"I never promised you a quiet weekend," I said.

"No, but you didn't tell me to bring my ear-protectors either."

"The kids are great. Just don't expect shy, retiring children."

Finally, the knock came. It was on the front door which was bolted and I never used. Southerners really had no idea how things worked north of the Watford Gap. I went out the back door and dashed around the end of the terrace to the front. They were standing huddled together on the pavement, all looking rather travel-weary.

"Hey," said Frankie, as she caught sight of me. "It's our friend up north. You never told me you lived in the hills. Or that you don't have proper summers up here."

I smiled, glancing up at the low grey clouds as the wind whipped my hair across my face.

"Well it's lovely to see you," I said, giving her a hug on the pavement. "And you're lucky it's not raining. Todmorden's the third wettest place in England. Usually it's chucking it down."

"Hi, Claire," said Joe, stepping forward to kiss me on both cheeks. "Good to see you again."

"And you. How was the journey, or shouldn't I ask?"

"Long," said Joe. "We resorted to telling the kids to look out for polar bears when we got to the M62."

"Can you see the Northern Lights from here?" asked Paulo. "We learnt about them at school."

"I'm afraid not," I said. "But I am planning tomorrow morning to take you to a fab children's museum where you can run around and touch everything." Paulo, Sophia and Roberto's faces lit up.

"Sorry," I said, turning to Emily, who was looking particularly trendy in a long layered dress and Aphrodite sandals. "I know it's not going to be much fun for you."

"It's OK, I'm used to it," she said with a shrug. "And at least it will keep them quiet so I'll get a chance to read."

"*Twilight* again?" I asked.

"No, the next one. *New Moon*. I read some of it on the way up and I can't wait to finish it."

"Anyway," interrupted Frankie. "Is the door broken or is there any chance of actually going inside to warm up a bit?"

"Sorry," I said. "Follow me. We use the back door, it's a northern thing." I led them round the side of the house and down through the back-to-back houses.

"Why do you put your washing up in the street?" asked Paulo.

"Because we don't have gardens. Just a back yard."

"Is that a northern thing as well?" asked Paulo.

"I guess so," I laughed.

It was only as I got to the back door that I noticed the clenching in my stomach. I was about to show Frankie my life, to hold it up for her scrutiny. And I couldn't help wondering what she'd make of it: Mark, the house and all my worldly goods. It was crazy, really. All those years I'd tried to impress Frankie, to measure up to her. And here I was at thirty-eight still doing the same thing.

Mark looked up from *The Times* sports section as we walked in and rose from his chair at the kitchen table.

"Hi," he said, smiling as the Ricotta clan shuffled inside. "I'm Mark, pleased to meet you all."

I looked at him hard as I did the introductions, trying to view him through fresh eyes, to see him as Frankie would. He looked good, actually. Somehow better than I remembered.

"Hi," said Frankie, stepping forward to kiss him. "Tough luck, eh? Ending up with Claire." Mark burst into laughter, glanced at me to check I was laughing too, then carried on.

"Watch it, you'll be sleeping in the shed if you're not careful," I said to Frankie.

"Is that a northern thing too?" asked Paulo.

"I think Claire was just joking," said Joe. "Anyway, good to meet you, Mark," he said, shaking his hand. It was weird seeing them standing there together. The two men in our lives. Two men who couldn't have been more different from the prototypes that were Matt and Andy. Frankie was obviously perfectly OK with that. So why did I still imagine Andy standing in this kitchen? why did I wonder what he was doing now? And whether he ever, in some quite unguarded moment, wondered about me.

"I'll stick the kettle on," I said. "You guys go through and chill out."

"Have you got biscuits?" Sophia asked Mark, tugging at the sleeve of his jumper.

"Loads," he said.

"Chocolate ones?"

"Are there any other kind?" replied Mark. Sophia grinned and followed him through to the lounge.

By the time I made it in there with a tea tray laden with drinks and biscuits (chocolate ones, of course), Sophia and Paulo were squabbling over who got to sit on the sofa next to Mark.

"Is he usually this popular?" asked Frankie, who had Roberto sitting quietly on her lap.

"No, usually people run a mile," I said, putting the tray down.

"It's not that I have a personal hygiene problem," said Mark. "It's because I'm a lawyer; scares people off." At which point Sophia and Paulo both jumped up and made a beeline for the biscuits.

"See?" he said.

"I think it was the lure of chocolate, actually," said Frankie, as she dived in to grab a biscuit before the children had scoffed them all.

"Paulo's is bigger than mine," whined Sophia.

"She's had more than me," said Paulo, squaring up to Sophia. There was a crash as Roberto held up an

194

arm to defend himself against the flailing arms and legs of his brother and sister and knocked an ornament off a shelf.

"Sorry," said Frankie, checking it wasn't broken before putting it back. "Do you have parks up north?"

"Yep, there's one ten minutes' walk away."

"Good. I think after being cooped up in the car so long they need to let off some steam."

"Can I take my football?" asked Paulo.

"Only if you let me go in goal," said Mark.

We all walked together down to the town centre, apart from Emily who'd said she was too tired to come and had opted to stay at home and read. Roberto was on a fold-up scooter he'd brought with him, Paulo had his football tucked under his arm and Sophia was being swung along by Joe and Mark.

"Are you sure your ankle's going to be OK?" I asked Mark. Joe had volunteered to take the children to the park so that Frankie and I could have some time to ourselves, and Mark had nobly offered to go with him.

"Yeah, I think it will hold up for a gentle kick-about."

Joe laughed. "Aah, you've never played football with Paulo before, have you?"

"Mark's not playing with Paulo, he's playing with me," said Sophia. Frankie rolled her eyes.

"See you back at the house, then," I called, as we stopped at the crossing and they carried on up towards the park. "Have fun."

I turned to Frankie, who was looking around as she pulled her silk scarf up around her neck.

"I don't suppose you've got an indoor shopping centre, have you?" she asked as we crossed the road.

"Nope, we have an indoor market but I guess that's not exactly what you had in mind."

Frankie laughed. "Not quite. I was thinking something more like the Trafford Centre."

"Twenty-five miles that way, I'm afraid," I said, pointing in the direction of Manchester. "You know, it's a shame you didn't end up with Matt."

"Why's that?"

"You would have made such a good WAG. The original and best. Victoria Beckham would have been a pale imitation of you."

Frankie grinned. "Yeah, and I could have had liposuction and a gastric band fitted after having the kids to lose weight. And let someone film it for reality TV."

I chuckled at the thought of it.

"I don't know why you're laughing," she said. "You'd have been the one they'd have done 'worst-dressed WAG' photo montages of in the Sunday magazines."

"Oh, cheers."

"Hey, it's a compliment. Most of them haven't got two brain cells to rub together. A lawyer WAG on a crusade to save the world and no interest in fashion would have been ripe for taking the piss out of."

"Bit of luck it didn't happen then," I said.

"Do you mean that?" asked Frankie.

I shrugged and pointed to the Bear café further down the road.

"That's a great place for coffee and cake," I said.

196

"Come on then," said Frankie. "Sounds much better than perusing hardware stalls and haberdasheries in the market."

We climbed the stairs to the first-floor café and approached the counter where a tempting array of cakes were on display.

"Hi, Pam," I said to the tall, dark-haired woman behind the serving hatch.

"Hiya, Claire, I'm glad you're here. I've been meaning to tell you, Incredible Edible Todmorden is having a harvest festival on the twenty-eighth of September. Wondered if you'd like to bring some stuff from your allotment?"

Frankie looked up from the cakes and started sniggering.

"I'll do my best," I said. "Although I think the word 'harvest' is a bit grand for two carrots and a couple of green tomatoes."

"That bad?" said Pam.

"I'm afraid so. Anyway," I said, turning to Frankie, "what are you having?"

"Don't tell me you're growing vegetables now," said Frankie as we sat down at a table by the window with our coffees and two large portions of chocolate cake.

"No, I'm not actually. Only slug food."

"It all sounds a bit like *The Good Life* to me."

"Oh, I thought it was quite trendy. Kim Wilde does that gardening programme and people think she's really cool."

"That's because every bloke had fantasies about her when she did the 'Kids in America' video. It's got nothing to do with gardening. WAGS definitely don't garden."

"Well, like I said. Bit of luck I'm not a WAG then."

Frankie stirred her coffee and took a bite of her cake. "Do you still think about him?"

"Who?"

"Come on. This is me you're talking to."

I rubbed a hole in the steam on the window with my sleeve and looked down to the street below. The people and cars passed by in a blur.

"He was everything to me," I said.

"I know," said Frankie, reaching out to squeeze my arm as I bit my lip hard. "You were so young, though. I look at Emily now and I can't believe you were the same age. It's scary."

I shrugged and went back to looking out of the window.

"What's he doing now, do you know?"

I shook my head. "It was always all or nothing with me and Andy. So I figure it's best to leave it at nothing. What I don't know can't hurt me."

"Still," said Frankie, "it doesn't matter now, does it? You've got Mark. He's great. I really like him."

I nodded and smiled, trying to pretend that I was fine with that. To give no sense that I still lay awake at night thinking about Andy. About what could have been if things had been different.

"So are you any closer to moving in together?"

"I guess so. He's got a viewing on his flat tomorrow."

"Don't sound so excited."

"That's what Mark said."

Frankie put her coffee mug down on the table. "So, what's the problem?"

"I don't know. Things have been a bit awkward since I told him I didn't want to buy that house with him."

"I'm not surprised. He probably felt rejected."

"I know. I've told him so many times it was about the house not him, but I don't think it's got through. And now he's gone all weird on me."

"What do you mean, weird?"

"He didn't used to have his hair like that or dress trendily. He had a sort of fashion makeover when I was down at yours."

Frankie giggled. "Well one of you has to be dragged into the current millennium."

"It's not just that. He's taken up rock-climbing. And bought a book by Ross Kemp."

"Jesus. That is serious. Have you lusted after someone macho in front of him?"

"No, not at all. And he's well aware that I still fancy George Michael, even though I understand now why he was never going to be interested."

"Such a disappointment for us girls," tutted Frankie, shaking her head. "If only it had been Andrew Ridgeley."

"One of those things I wish I'd known when I was fifteen."

"What are the others?"

"That Martin Kemp would end up doing sofa ads and my mum would say he had nice eyes."

"Your mum fancies Martin Kemp?"

"I know. I went off him straight away. Nothing worse than your mum fancying the same guy."

"So all we need now then," said Frankie, "is for your mum to confess she had the hots for Andy."

"Why do you say that?"

"Well that's what this is all about, isn't it? You've never really got over him. You married someone who reminded you of him and now you don't want to move in with Mark, simply because he's not Andy."

I sighed, not knowing what to say. And fearing she was getting uncomfortably close to the truth.

"It's not that. It's just all been a bit sudden. I feel I'm being pressured into it. Mark can be impulsive like that. He comes up with an idea and gets totally carried away with it."

"Sounds rather romantic."

I shook my head.

"He couldn't be less romantic if he tried. The living-together speech sounded more like a business plan."

"There's a lot to be said for being practical and sensible."

"Says she who was never either," I laughed. "Anyway, I bet Joe's a real romantic. He strikes me as a big softie."

"He is actually. He cried most of the way through our wedding service. Poor Emily kept asking what was wrong. She was only three, she didn't understand."

"He's great with the kids too."

"So is Mark. I bet he'd make a fantastic dad."

I looked out of the window again.

"Don't you want children?" asked Frankie.

"No, I never have."

"Yes you did. I bet it was on your list."

"I thought you said that was a load of old tosh?"

"It wasn't to you when you wrote it. Why did you change your mind?"

"David didn't want children. I guess I just got used to the idea of not having any. And when we split up, I was relieved we hadn't. I'd have hated to put my kids through what I went through when Mum and Dad split up."

"What about Mark?"

"I think he'd probably like to be a dad. But it's not a big issue for him. He knows how I feel."

"But things have changed. You and Mark might stay together for ever. Not everyone breaks up."

"Even if we did stay together, I'd be scared of screwing them up. Look at what our families did to us. They're hardly good role models, are they?"

"I know, but you have to break the chain somewhere, don't you? Be brave enough to give it a go, try to do things differently."

"When you found out you were pregnant, the first time, with Emily, did you ever think about . . ." I broke off, concerned from the look on Frankie's face that I shouldn't have asked. It was her turn to look out of the window

"I did, but not for very long. All that Catholic guilt stuff, I guess. I was terrified of giving birth and being a mum but I knew I couldn't get rid of it. And I'm so glad I didn't, even though it's still scary as hell being a mum. Especially when you know what teenagers are capable of."

"Well it looks to me like you're doing a great job. I don't think our mums had a clue, really. They were from a different generation, weren't they?"

"I guess so. But that doesn't stop me being concerned about Emily."

"How is she? She seemed a bit quiet."

"I'm really worried about her," said Frankie. "She's always tired and under the weather, picks up anything that's going around. And she's lost weight. Quite a bit, I think, although it's difficult to see under those baggy clothes she wears."

"You don't think she's got an eating disorder?"

"I don't know what to think. But I do know that with me and Joe being the size we are, she could get a hang-up about it. They get this whole body-image thing rammed down their throats these days."

"Have you spoken to her about it?"

"Not directly. And if she did have anorexia or something she'd only deny it anyway. But I have made an appointment for her to see the doctor next week. Told her it's just to find out if there's a reason for the weight loss. And why she always seems to be tired and going down with something."

"And what did she say?"

"She didn't protest. I think she quite likes the idea of them taking a blood sample. Thinks it will boost her vampire credentials."

I laughed as Frankie wiped the chocolate cake crumbs from her mouth.

"Well, hopefully it will put your mind at rest."

"Either that or I'll get a mouthful from her when she finds out the doctor isn't Robert Pattinson."

I watched Emily during the meal that evening. She did pick at her food but no more so than any other teenager. And she certainly rivalled Mark in her ability to demolish a pile of poppadoms. She was quieter than the last time I'd seen her, though, saying very little apart from thanking me for the meal at the end. At which point Joe declared that I must be a better cook than him because she never thanked him for his meals.

Frankie put the younger children to bed; Paulo and Roberto in the spare room and Sophia in my room, where she and Joe were going to sleep.

We stayed up talking for a while, Emily with her head still in *New Moon*, the rest of us sharing a bottle of wine and reminiscing about eighties TV shows and films. Until it was time for Mark to go home and Frankie and Joe turned in, knowing they'd get an early wake-up call from the kids in the morning.

Emily stifled a yawn and grinned at me as we were left alone in the room together.

"Come on, let's get ready for bed," I said. "I don't suppose we'll get a lie-in in the morning either."

Emily went to the bathroom first while I set up the sofa bed. It was only when she returned in her nightshirt that I noticed how skinny her legs were. And that they were covered in bruises.

"Have you been playing football with Paulo?" I asked. "Because if you have, I suggest you get some shin pads."

Emily frowned for a second before glancing down at her legs.

"Oh, those," she said. "I've got no idea where they all came from. I seem to collect them. A bit like spots, I guess."

I smiled and headed for the bathroom. By the time I returned, Emily was snuggled up under the duvet.

"Are you sure you don't mind sharing the sofa bed with me?" I asked. "I'll happily sleep on the floor if you'd rather."

"No, course not," said Emily. "It'll be fun. Like a sleepover."

"Except with a boring grown-up like me," I said, sliding in next to her. "You'll have to teach me what you talk about on sleepovers."

"I haven't been on that many really. Only at Alia's."

"So what's she like, Alia?"

"She's great. Really funny and a bit wacky. She's scene."

"Seen what?"

Emily laughed. "No, I mean she's a scene kid."

I looked at her blankly. "Go on, you'd better fill me in," I said.

"Scene kids like emo music but dress more colourfully and are quirkier. From what my mum says, if Cyndi Lauper were around today, she'd be scene."

"Right," I said, feeling positively ancient and uncool. "And what's emo music?"

"Emo means emotionally unstable. Emos dress a bit like goths did in your day and listen to depressing music, stuff by Paramore, Avenged Sevenfold and My Chemical Romance."

I nodded again, not wanting to admit that I'd never heard of any of them.

"So what are you?"

"That's the problem, I don't really fit into any one group. I like emo music, I dress like a bohemian, I'm a bit of a geek and my best friend's scene. The only things I'm definitely not are a plastic or a chav."

"I've heard of chavs," I said, triumphant to have scored at least one point on the "Are you cool enough to be a teenager?" scale.

"Plastics are obsessed with looks, like Girls Aloud," explained Emily.

"I've heard of them too. And seen them on telly, and I know that Cheryl Cole is married to Ashley Cole who plays for Chelsea."

Emily grinned. "Mum would have been a plastic."

I laughed. "God, she would, wouldn't she? I wonder what I'd have been."

"What were you like?"

"Swotty and uncool."

"A geek then, I guess. What music were you into?"

"Spandau Ballet."

"I've heard of them," laughed Emily, getting her own back.

"They were new romantics but I didn't wear frilly shirts or make-up like them."

"So what were you into?"

"United," I said. "Well, Andy Pailes really."

"Was he the guy on your bedroom wall?"

"Yeah, he was," I said, aware that it was the understatement of the year but deciding not to elaborate any further.

"Got any pictures of him?" asked Emily. I hesitated, embarrassed to admit I had enough pictures to fill an entire box.

"Just a few."

"Can I see them? I did show you my pics of Robert." This was true. Although she, of course, had no idea of the real reason for my reluctance to pass photos around.

"They're in the loft, I'm afraid. I'll have to dig one out for you another time." I reached out and turned the lamp off. Hoping Emily would recognise the signal but forgetting that she was fifteen.

"Were you totally and utterly in love with him?" she asked dreamily.

"Yeah, I was."

"Did you ever get to meet him? I've seen Mum's photos of her and that Matt guy she liked."

"Yeah, I've got some like that of me and Andy."

"And was he gorgeous in real life as well?"

I smiled, glad Emily couldn't see my pink cheeks in the dark.

"Yeah," I said. "He was."

"Robert will be gorgeous when I meet him at the premiere."

"You're still planning to go, then?"

"Me and Alia wouldn't miss it for the world. Just think, I might actually be able to touch him."

I shut my eyes for a second. Still feeling Andy's touch. And the ache it had left behind.

"It doesn't matter if you don't, though. Sometimes it's better that way. You won't end up disappointed."

"Robert will never be a disappointment to me. I know that."

"Night, Emily," I said, turning over on to one side so she didn't see the tear running down my cheek. And I didn't have to tell her that I had known that too.

Tuesday, 10 December 1985

I held the Immac bottle at arm's length and peered again at the instructions. It was the bit on the label that read, "Do NOT leave on for longer than 10 minutes" which particularly worried me. I couldn't help wondering what would happen if I did. Would my skin peel off with it? I had visions of looking like a napalm victim for the Junior Blues Christmas Disco. And that wasn't the idea at all.

The idea was that my stubbly legs, which had responded well to the ideal growing conditions under my thick over-the-knee socks during the winter, would be instantly transformed into super-smooth ones, enabling me to wear my shiny black ten-denier tights without any fear of the hairs sticking through.

That in turn would allow me to wear the black miniskirt I had bought for the occasion from Chelsea Girl. It wasn't that short. Only a couple of inches above the knee. But having long legs made it look shorter than it actually was. I hoped that the overall effect would be to make me look as sexy and sophisticated as the woman in the Immac adverts. I had decided that sexy and sophisticated was the image I needed to cultivate.

Sitting precariously on the edge of the bath, I undid the cap and squeezed the lotion out, smearing it thickly over my legs with the spatula provided. It didn't seem to go very far. I ended up using the entire bottle, which pissed me off because it had cost nearly three quid.

There was nothing to do then but sit there shivering in my bra and knickers, wishing Frankie was coming with me and wondering whether Andy would be there.

Frankie had been deemed too old to go. Under-sixteens only, they'd said. Not that she'd have gone even if she'd been allowed. She'd probably have said it was too childish for her. That was what she said about everything. Unless it was her college disco, of course. Which, as she kept telling me, was for adults only. Still, as long as Andy was there. That was all that mattered. I'd got him a card and a present. It was a pen — not a grotty old Bic or anything; a proper Papermate one in a box that had cost me ten quid. I'd decided it was personal enough without being over-familiar or too expensive. I didn't want him to feel bad that he hadn't got me anything.

Glancing at my watch, I realised I had daydreamed nine minutes away. My legs would be starting to fry. I scrambled to wet a chunk of cotton wool, and was about to begin the major deforestation exercise when I heard the phone ringing in the hall.

Ignoring it was not an option. A ringing phone always engendered a sense of urgency in me. It was the realisation that it could be a matter of life or death (I had never actually received a life-or-death phone call, but had seen plenty of them on TV and in the movies). Either that, or Andy offering me a lift to the disco.

I slithered off the edge of the bath and hurtled downstairs as quickly as my Immac-covered legs would allow.

"Hi, it's me."

"Oh, hi, Frankie."

"Don't sound so pleased."

"No, I was in the middle of doing my legs, that's all."

"What for?"

"The Junior Blues disco, it's tonight."

"Oh yeah, I'd forgotten. Do you want me to come round, do your make-up or anything?"

"I thought you were seeing Tara tonight?"

"Yeah, well I'm not now. Do you want me to come or not?"

"Yes please. Just give me half an hour to get myself sorted out."

As I turned to race back upstairs to the bathroom, fearing my legs might spontaneously combust at any moment, I was confronted with a telltale trail of Immac down the centre of my mum's much-loved red stair carpet.

I swore out loud, knowing the carpet would be scarred for life, even if I wasn't. I managed to salvage my own legs and was trying to mount a carpet clean-up operation by colouring in the stains with a red marker pen when Frankie arrived.

"It wouldn't wash off. It was the only thing I could think of. Mum'll do her nut if she sees it like this," I explained as I let her in.

Frankie started laughing, then stopped abruptly and caught her breath as she looked at me properly for the first time.

"Wow, your hair," she said. "It almost makes you look grown up."

"Thanks," I said, taking it as a compliment even if it was a sarky one. I'd forgotten that Frankie hadn't seen my new hairdo. It had been my mum's idea to get it done, which meant I now had to accept that she had made one worthwhile contribution to my teenage years. Initially, I had been reluctant. But when the hairdresser had shown me the finished look in the mirror I had been pleasantly surprised. The kid with the flick and the straggly split ends was gone, and in her place was a young woman with big, Farrah Fawcett style layered hair. The hairdresser had said I wouldn't have looked out of place on *Dynasty*. I had gone straight home and written that in my diary. In case no one ever paid me such a compliment again.

"So why aren't you seeing Tara then?" I asked Frankie.

"Oh, she's back together with her boyfriend. She's going out with him instead."

"Some friend she is."

"She did ask. I said I didn't mind."

I would never muck Frankie about like that. She knew it as well. I think that was why she was so touchy about it.

"Do you wanna see my outfit?" I asked, changing the subject to one I hoped she would be more comfortable with.

"Yeah, OK. Go and put it on."

I returned a few minutes later wearing a black top with a square neckline, the short black skirt, and slingbacks which Mum had lent me (the only decent thing she had in her wardrobe). Frankie stared at me without saying a word.

"Oh God, you hate it, don't you?"

She shook her head. "No. It looks great. I just hadn't noticed before, about you getting a figure, I mean."

I spun round to look in the mirror. Two pert mounds were visible where my washboard chest had once been, and my skirt curved in a soft arc around my hips. The top half could be put down to the padded bra I had bought with my savings especially for the occasion. But I could only conclude that the hips must have crept up on me overnight.

I turned back to Frankie and shrugged.

"You're gonna knock him dead," she said.

"I hope not. He's not much good to me or United dead."

"Come on, you daft cow," she said. "Let's get your face done."

Frankie spent ages applying my make-up. Pencilling the eyeliner as close to my lashes as she could get it, then smudging a deep copper tone across my eyelids, bringing the shimmering pools of blue below to life.

"There," she said when she'd finally finished. "Take a look at that."

I stared at the mirror. At the stylish young woman with the flawless complexion and a brace-free smile (for tonight at least) encased in honey-coloured lips. I wanted to give Frankie a huge hug. The sort of hug we used to share together all the time. But I wasn't sure if that was a bit childish.

"Thanks. Thanks a million," I grinned instead.

The huge black-and-white photographs of past United teams and triumphs towered over me as I made my way, wide-eyed, up the main staircase at Priory Park. I would have knelt and kissed the royal-blue carpet if there hadn't been anyone else around.

Inside the suite where the disco was being held, rows of blue and silver foil decorations hung from the ceiling and a giant glitterball twirled high above the makeshift dance floor. The DJ, a bearded man sporting a Pringle jumper worn over a silky lemon poloneck, was thumbing through a box of singles, no doubt putting aside anything by Frankie Goes to Hollywood deemed inappropriate for his audience. Most of the other guests were younger than me. Much younger. I imagined what Frankie would say if she was here. Wondered if I should slip out quietly now before anyone noticed. But I couldn't go — not without seeing Andy.

Matt was the first player to arrive. He was met by a surge of Junior Blues members, all squealing in excitement as they battled for his autograph. I stayed exactly where I was, relieved I was above that sort of thing.

"Hello, stranger."

I knew straight away who the voice belonged to. The faint smell of aftershave confirmed it if I'd had any doubts.

"Hiya," I said, turning to face Andy.

"I hardly recognised you," he said. "Your hair looks great. Really suits you."

I blushed. I'd hoped that he would notice my hair but hadn't for a moment thought he would actually comment on it.

"Oh, thanks. I didn't even realise you were here."

"Ah, I slipped in quietly through the back door. Didn't want to risk a stampede like that," he joked, gesturing towards Matt.

"I thought you'd be used to it by now, being our star player."

"I don't know about that. I'm sure Clubber will get his place back at some point."

"Not the way you're playing. You're gonna get an England call-up soon, that's what they said on *Saint and Greavsie* last Saturday."

"Oh, I wouldn't take too much notice of them."

"They said it in the *Daily Mirror* as well."

"OK, you win. I'm not going to argue with someone who thinks I'm the world's greatest footballer. Would you like to join my fan club?"

"I didn't know you had one."

"I didn't until just now. You're the first member. Congratulations."

I laughed. Aware that things seemed different between us tonight. Although I wasn't quite sure why.

"Do I get free membership then, for being the first?"

"You drive a hard bargain, you do. How about honorary life membership, will that do you?"

"Yeah, I guess so. But make sure you carry on playing for a long time. I want to get my money's worth."

Andy laughed again.

"Where's Thomo tonight?" I asked, looking around.

Andy hesitated before replying.

"He's not coming. His wife's not very well." He looked down, seeming thrown for a moment. "Where's your friend, anyway?" he said after a pause.

"What, Frankie? She's too old to come to Junior Blues events now. This is my last one, too."

"You're joking, over the hill at sixteen? That's really depressing. You're making me feel ancient."

"Sorry," I said. "Anyway, it's all right for you. You'll still be able to come to this next year."

"So I will. That's one date in my social calendar, then. Mind you, I'm not sure if I'll go, it wouldn't be the same without you."

"What do you mean?" I looked up, hardly daring to think about what Andy might say next.

"Well, there'd be no one to take the piss out of me for a start."

The disappointment lasted all of a few seconds. Then I started laughing. Andy was laughing too. Huge bellyaching laughs. The sort that made other people wonder what the joke was. I noticed Clubber and Nobber, who had just arrived, looking over at us. As soon as Andy saw them he stopped laughing.

"Anyway," he said, "I'd better go and sign some autographs. I'll catch up with you later. Come and rescue me if it looks like I need it."

"OK," I said. "I'll keep my eye out."

I stood at the edge of the room, watching a group of girls about my own age who were dancing round their handbags, tossing their hair and laughing hysterically at nothing in particular. They looked good, I could see that. But it didn't bother me. Because for once I knew I looked better. I had no desire to dance myself, particularly as "The Reflex" by Duran Duran was playing, I never knew what to do with my feet to the "fle-fle-fle-fle-flex" bit.

Every time I glanced over at Andy, he was surrounded by a cluster of fans. I hated having to share him with other people, wanted to shout at them all to leave him alone, that I had seen him first.

"OK, everyone, it's time for some fun," said Kay, the Junior Blues organiser (who looked like she truly had just stepped off the set of *Dynasty*), some time later as she announced that the promised party games were about to get under way. "First up is the balloon game. Can I introduce your team captains: Dave Orton, Barry Gibbons, Matt Goodyear and Jamie Kane."

A cheer went up as the players came forward and Kay began to explain the rules. You had to pass the balloon down the line between your teammates without using your hands or arms or letting it touch the ground. The DJ put on "Agadoo" and I started edging towards the door at the far end of the room, imagining what Frankie would say about it all.

"Hey, not so fast. Don't think I'm doing this if you're not."

I turned to look at the owner of the hand which had just grabbed my arm.

"Come on," said Andy. "You're on my team."

My heart was racing as I took my place in front of him in a long column of Junior Blues members and players who had lined up behind Dave Orton. Andy had picked me for his team. Without me even asking. I was desperate to know what it meant. Whether it was some kind of sign that he was interested or he was just being friendly.

"I'm not sure I'm going to be any good at this," I said. "I've never done it before.

"Good," said Andy. "That should make it more fun."

I turned to the front as Kay blew the whistle. We were squashed close enough together that I could feel the warmth of Andy's breath on the back of my neck. I daren't turn round in case he caught me looking. So I stood, eyes fixed forward, like a blinkered racehorse in the stalls, oblivious to everything going on around me.

"Quick." The squeal came from the little girl in front. She was standing facing me, a large red balloon wedged between her knees. I squatted down and, as instructed, inched the balloon from her. I shuffled round to face Andy while trying to prevent the balloon riding up towards my hemline.

"Here, let me help you," he said, taking hold of my hips to steady me and pulling me nearer. His thighs rubbed against mine as he grappled for the balloon, our bodies pressing against each other. I wondered if this counted as foreplay. I could feel a letter to *Just Seventeen* coming on. Nobody else seemed to realise what was happening; they all thought it was part of the game. Even Andy was acting like there was nothing going on, smiling and laughing as if it was all a bit of a joke. Maybe it was to him; maybe whatever it was I was feeling, he wasn't feeling at all. Or maybe he did feel it but he simply didn't want to let on in front of everyone else. Our foreheads were almost touching. I kept my eyes lowered because I knew that if I looked up, if my eyes met his, I might not be able to stop myself.

"There," he said, as he finally wrested the balloon from me. "That wasn't too bad, was it?"

He let go of me and turned to pass the balloon on. The beads of perspiration on my face turned to hot red blotches. I didn't know what to do, how I should react. I wasn't even sure what he'd meant about it not being that bad. All I did know was that I'd had a close encounter of the Andy Pailes kind. And I didn't think I'd ever be the same again. I straightened my skirt and stood waiting for the game to end. Our team came last, which was no surprise considering how long me and Andy had taken. As Kay called for volunteers for the next game, Andy whispered, "See you later," and slid out of the line behind me. I needed a minute to myself to get my head together. I headed straight for the toilets, shut the cubicle door behind me and leant heavily against it, taking long, deep breaths as I tried to stop myself shaking. My body still seemed to be in shock; nothing was functioning as it should be. My head was buzzing with it, the sight, the smell, the feel of him. I didn't understand why anyone bothered taking drugs when you could get a high like this from a man. But one fix wasn't enough. I needed to sort myself out and get back out there. I had to be near him, to touch him again. To give him a chance to say anything he might want to say.

I touched up my make-up, trying to powder over my flushed cheeks, and headed back out to the function suite. The next game had ended, "The Birdie Song" was being faded out and the DJ, seemingly forgetting the junior status of his audience, announced that he was going to "slow things down" for the final dance.

Whitney Houston started crooning about needing a few more minutes to get herself ready. I scanned the room for Andy. Eventually I found him, on the far corner of the dance floor, locked in the tight embrace of a chubby twelve-year-old girl, who was clinging on to him as if her very life depended on it. I was smiling to myself when Andy caught my eye.

"Help," he mouthed silently.

I didn't need asking twice. Putting my handbag down on a chair, I strode boldly across the dance floor, pausing only to consider how best to unlock my rival's vice-like grip.

"Excuse me, please," Andy said to the girl. "I think it's this young lady's turn now."

The girl looked up with a mean scowl on her face. For a second I feared I would get my face smashed in after school for this. Then I remembered I wasn't at school. I was at Priory Park and Andy Pailes had just asked me to dance. For real, not just in my head. I stood my ground, letting it be known that I wouldn't take no for an answer.

"Thanks," said Andy, as the girl reluctantly let go and I slipped smoothly into her place. "I could feel my

219

circulation beginning to cut off there. You may have just saved my life."

I felt Andy's hands on the back of my waist. I had an overwhelming desire to throw my arms around him and squeeze him tight, even tighter than the fat girl had done. I didn't though. I placed my hands lightly on his sides, barely touching his shirt at first, before slowly allowing my fingers to close around him. Although our bodies weren't quite touching, I could tell they fitted perfectly together, like interlocking parts of a jigsaw.

"So, have you recovered from all that excitement?" he asked.

I hesitated, unsure what he was getting at, whether he'd noticed my prolonged absence.

"Yeah, I just got a bit hot, that's all."

An awkward silence hung in the air.

"What'll you be doing for Christmas then?" Andy asked just as Whitney boomed her intention to make love the whole night through.

I tried to pretend I hadn't heard her. "Oh, nothing much, just the usual family stuff at home."

"You don't sound too keen."

"My mum does my head in."

"My dad's hard work as well," said Andy. "To be honest, it's a relief not to have to spend Christmas with him."

"So what'll you do on Christmas Day then?"

"I'll be with the rest of the lads at the training ground for a bit in the morning. Then Thomo's invited us round for Christmas lunch."

"What, the whole team?"

"No. I meant Ann . . . just, er, me and a friend, actually."

"Oh."

I flinched as if I'd been slapped across the cheek. He had a girlfriend. As much as he'd tried to cover it up, it was obvious. I'd been stupid enough to think he was flirting with me and all the time he had a girlfriend. My hands loosened their grip until I was barely touching his shirt. My feet felt like I was wearing huge, heavy football boots. And the studs were somehow sinking into the wooden dance floor. I looked up at the glitterball above us as I tried to blink back the tears. It didn't seem to be twirling any more. It was the rest of the world that was spinning. I tried to steady myself, scared I was about to keel over. I didn't even notice that the music had stopped. Neither did Andy.

"Party's over, Trotsky," said Clubber as he walked past. "And it's way past her bedtime."

Andy pulled away sharply, leaving us standing awkwardly together on the empty dance floor.

"Are you going to be OK getting home?" he said after a while. A few minutes ago I'd have thought he was making a move on me, but now I knew he was simply being polite.

"Yes thanks, my mum's picking me up."

Andy nodded and looked down at his feet. He seemed flustered. I wanted to get my handbag and give him the card and present but I knew I couldn't do that now. It wouldn't be right.

"Have a great Christmas then," he said as he started to walk away.

"Yeah, you too," I said.

I didn't mean it though. I hoped his girlfriend would choke to death on the five pence hidden in the Christmas pudding.

I stand at the end of my road waiting for him. I stamp my feet, kicking out against the cold, and blow a plume of warm breath into the air.

I recognise the car as soon as it appears round the bend on the main road. I wave a gloved hand as it glides to a halt in front of me and he leans over to open the passenger door.

"Merry Christmas," he says, the warmth from his smile shattering the brittle air.

I get in and turn to greet him. "Merry Christmas, you," I say, so overcome with emotion I can barely get the words out.

He leans over and kisses me on the lips. Just the once. But it is enough to chase the last vestige of coldness from my body.

We pull up outside his house and I step from the car like a princess, lifting my long skirt so it doesn't drag on the ground.

"Shut your eyes," he says as we step into the hall.

"Why? What are you up to?"

"Trust me," he says. "Just shut them."

I do as I am told. Trusting him more than I trust myself. He takes my hand and leads me through to the lounge. I can smell vanilla; warm and velvety. Hear the fire purring and popping, feel it radiating heat.

"OK, you can open them now."

I do it slowly. Letting my lids rise like a theatre curtain, revealing the scene inch by inch. I see the present under the tree first. A small box wrapped in shiny silver paper, the corners neatly square. Behind it the trunk rises tall and straight from the pot, the lowest branches dipping towards the floor as if weighed down with snow. Further up they shoot in all directions, the ends splaying out like fingers drawn by children on stick people. A helter-skelter of silver tinsel encircles the tree, with sparkly silver baubles dotted in between and on top a silver star, not too big, nor too small. Behind the tree, on the windowsill, a row of candles light the stage.

"It's perfect," I whisper, squeezing Andy's hand. "Absolutely perfect."

"Aren't you going to open it then?" he asks, nodding towards the present.

"What, now?"

"It'll be Boxing Day if you leave it much longer."

I bend down to pick up the present. It is light, and something rattles and moves inside as I turn it over and prise open the Sellotape before sliding out a velvet-covered box. I look up at Andy; he is smiling at me, willing me on. I lift the lid and peek inside. Hanging from a silver chain is a single sapphire, twinkling in the reflection from the lights. I take a sharp intake of breath.

"Thank you. It's beautiful."

"Good, just like you. Here, try it on."

He takes the necklace from me. I lift my hair up while he fastens the clasp and steps back to admire it.

"It goes with your eyes," he says. "I knew it would."

"I don't know what to say."

"You don't have to say anything."

223

We sit on the floor next to the fire. Andy wraps his legs and arms around me like tentacles, hugging me to his chest. I feel the softness of his jumper enveloping me, the roughness of his stubble against my face. It feels so good being held like this. I don't ever want him to let go. Nothing can happen to me while I am in his arms. I am safe here.

"I love you," I say, lifting a hand to stroke the side of his face.

"I know," he says. "I love you too."

I let the words seep into me. And smile as my tears blur the lights on the tree.

This is where I will spend every Christmas from now on. Next year I will wake up here on Christmas morning. Will pad downstairs in my bare feet before Andy has even stirred, to put his present under the tree. Then slip back into bed beside him, nestling up against his warm body, watching him breathing. Smiling as he sleeps.

By the following year the Christmas cards on the mantelpiece will say "To my Husband" and "To My Darling Wife". And one Christmas, not too long after that, it won't just be the two of us any more. There'll be a baby, the cutest face you've ever seen, sleeping soundly in a cot next to the Christmas tree. Lauren if it's a girl, Steven if a boy. With a "v" not a "ph". A little Pailes for me to love and cherish. A part of Andy and a part of me.

CHAPTER
SEVEN

"The thing is, Danny, I don't really think pleading not guilty is an option."

"Why not?" said Danny, who was slumped on a plastic chair in front of me in an interview room at court.

"Well, the fact that you signed your full name on the graffiti makes it very difficult."

Danny frowned and stared up at the ceiling.

"We could say someone else wrote it to get me into trouble."

"We could, if that was the truth, but it isn't, is it?"

Danny shook his head.

"In which case, I suggest you plead guilty. Admit you did it, apologise and hope they'll take your plea into consideration when sentencing."

Danny shrugged and went back to picking at a scab on his arm.

"And as much as I hope there won't be a next time, can I make a couple of suggestions?"

"If you like."

"There's a graffiti wall at the youth centre, a few streets away from where you were. You can do stuff all over that, you're allowed. And if, just supposing, you did fancy doing a bit of spraying somewhere else, don't use your full name next time. Make up a nickname for yourself."

"What like?"

"There's a famous graffiti artist called Banksy. He just signs that. Everyone admires his work but no one knows his real name."

"So I could call myself Dan the Man?"

"Something that hasn't got Dan in would be better."

"But then no one will know it's me."

"I know, Danny. That's the point. The police won't know it's you either."

A smile spread slowly over Danny's face.

"Nice one, miss. Thanks for the tip," he said with a wink.

I sighed as he left the room. This was what I'd been reduced to. It was a lousy, low-down job but I guessed someone had to do it.

Fiona was sitting down with her lunch when I made it through to the canteen.

"Have a good morning?" she asked.

"Not really. How about you?"

"Oh, the usual, adjournments, delays, chaos and confusion."

"You look wiped out," I said.

"Aidan didn't come home until the early hours again. Wouldn't say where he'd been this morning. If he carries on with this when they go back to school next week, he'll be falling asleep in the classroom."

"I seem to remember being able to function on a few hours' sleep at that age."

"Well I certainly can't. I used to worry about him when he was little, all the usual paranoid new-parent stuff. But I'd give anything to have that back again now. Teething and potty training were a breeze compared to this."

"At least he won't be a teenager for ever."

"True. Don't suppose I'll ever stop worrying though. Which reminds me, what happened to your Mark?"

"What do you mean?"

"I saw him this morning on my way to work. Had a real shiner around his left eye."

My stomach clenched as I had visions of him being caught up in some kind of brawl. Perhaps the interest in gang culture had gone too far. Ross Kemp had a lot to answer for.

"I've got no idea," I said. "He hasn't mentioned anything. Though I haven't seen him since the weekend. I'm on my way to meet him for a quick bit of lunch now."

"Well you'd better fill me in when you get back. If there's gossip and scandal around, I want to be the first to know."

I hurried off in the direction of the town centre, wondering what on earth had happened to him. What I couldn't understand was why he hadn't told me. The legal world in Rochdale was very small. Someone would have been bound to notice. When I arrived at Costa Coffee, he was sitting on one of the high stools facing the wall, as if anxious to go unnoticed. Yet even from the side profile I could see why Fiona had been so alarmed. It really was quite a shiner. The best approach would be to try to use humour to disarm him. A straight question would be sure to be met with a denial. He was a laywer, after all.

"Are you looking for legal representation?" I asked. "Only if you are, it's your lucky day. I know all the right people."

Mark grinned sheepishly at me.

"A snowboard did it."

"I've heard stories like this before," I said. "Far too many of them."

"No, really. You know I said I was going snowboarding at that Chill Factor place?"

I nodded, vaguely remembering a mention of the latest extreme sport he was going to try.

"It was great, I was doing really well until the point I went over a ridge and the board came up and smacked me in the face."

I looked at Mark and shook my head. "If one of my clients said that I'd think they were lying through their back teeth."

"If it's any help, I have a guilty plea from the snowboard." Mark joked.

"I think Daniel Craig will be doing his own stunts for a while longer, won't he?"

"I guess so."

"Does it still hurt?"

"Just a bit sore. I put some ice on it last night."

"Good. Well, lunch is on me. What are you having?"

I sat down on the stool next to Mark with our baguettes and coffees. Aware that I was irritated, not by him getting injured but by his insistence that he was enjoying something which I knew damn well he wasn't. I wanted to shake him, to shout at him to stop this pretence. But at the same time I couldn't help feeling it was my fault, that he was doing all this because I had made him feel insecure over the whole house thing. The immediate pressure had eased. The viewing on his flat had come to nothing and I still hadn't had any interest in mine. But sooner or later someone would put in an offer. And when they did, I needed to be ready to move in with Mark or have Mark move in with me while we started house-hunting. The trouble was, I didn't feel ready at all. If anything, seeing Frankie again and talking with Emily had brought everything to the surface. All the old memories and feelings. I was thinking about Andy more than ever. Thinking about the list.

"What case are you working on?" I asked, keen to break what felt to me like an awkward silence.

"Oh, a woman who cut herself opening a tin can at some council day centre."

"So who does she reckon's to blame for that?"

"The council, of course. For not providing her with training in opening cans correctly or putting up a warning notice that tins can be sharp when opened."

"Jesus. Does she have learning difficulties or anything?"

"Nope."

"Just plain stupid then. And trying to make a quick buck out of it."

"As her legal representative I couldn't possibly comment."

"You're never going to win that one though, are you?"

"I don't know. I won that other case where the guy complained that the council hadn't put a sign up warning that the fire could be hot."

I shook my head.

"What?" asked Mark.

"Don't you ever wonder what it's all about? If this is what we went through years of legal training for?"

"Sometimes. And then I remember that life doesn't always turn out how you planned and you just make the best of it. And that working for some big corporate company would be a nightmare, full of suits who are up their own arses."

"You don't think I should have applied for that job then?"

"No, I didn't mean it like that. I wasn't talking about you. Of course you should have applied if you feel you need a change. I know exactly how you feel. That's why I've done something about it too."

"Applied for something, you mean?"

"I've got it, actually."

"What, a new job?"

"No, not a paid one anyway. I've volunteered to do some casework for LawWorks in Manchester. They do free advice for people who don't qualify for Legal Aid."

I was gobsmacked. It wasn't quite up there with buying Ross Kemp books but it wasn't far off. Although in a totally different direction this time. To be honest, it was something I'd thought about doing myself, although never managed to get round to. The fact that Mark had beaten me to it not only perplexed me but also made me feel bad.

"But I'm the one with the social conscience." I realised as soon as I said it how bad it sounded. Mark started laughing.

"And you've got a monopoly on having one, I take it."

"I didn't mean it like that. I'm just surprised."

"You always seem to be surprised lately."

"That's because you keep doing surprising things." I lowered my voice as I glanced around the café. Aware that this was starting to sound like an argument.

"Aren't I allowed to try new things, broaden my horizons and all that?" asked Mark after a while.

"It's the reason why you're trying them that bothers me," I said.

"What do you mean?"

What I meant was that it felt like he was trying to please me or impress me. But I knew I couldn't say that without it sounding mean and ungrateful. Most women complained that their men weren't making enough effort. And here I was complaining that he was trying too hard.

"I don't want you to do stuff because you feel you should."

"I'm not. I'm doing it because you're right: sometimes this whole no-win-no-fee stuff does feels pretty hollow, even when I win the case. So if I can find a way I can use my legal skills to help people who really need it, well, that's great."

"So what's involved?" I asked, trying to sound more positive.

"Probably only a few hours a week, depending on what cases get referred to me. They do a lot of employment stuff, so I might have to pick your brains sometime."

"Of course, just let me know if I can help."

"So that's fine then?"

"Yeah," I said, deciding it was the only reasonable thing to say. "Any more surprises up your sleeve?"

"You'll have to wait and see," said Mark.

I gave the front door a good shove with my hip; the rain had made it stick again. A small pile of post lay on the doormat inside. I picked it up and flicked through: bills mostly, the odd circular. And a thick white envelope with a Manchester postmark addressed to Ms Claire Cooper.

I threw the rest of the post down on the kitchen table and tore open the envelope. As soon as I saw the Smith MacGuire letterhead I knew. I had an interview for the job in three weeks' time. I might not spend the rest of my life at Rochdale Magistrates' Court after all. I let out a whoop and did a little jig around the kitchen. It felt good to be wanted. And it made me think that maybe there was still time to turn my life around. That perhaps I could make a through road out of a cul-de-sac. But if that was the case, if there really was nothing stopping me apart from my own doubts, where did I draw the line? Because if I could find my way to getting at least one tick on the list, what was to stop me

232

trying for more? Even the one which seemed the most distant, the most out of reach. But which, like a glittering far-off jewel, held the greatest attraction.

It was only as I jigged back around the kitchen that I noticed the flashing light on the answering machine. It wouldn't be work, they always called my mobile. It occurred to me that it could be something to do with the interview. I pressed play and picked up a pen and pencil. It was Frankie's voice I heard. Although it wasn't her usual voice at all. It was a voice so empty, so devoid of any life or joy that it stopped me in my tracks.

"Claire, it's Frankie. Can you give me a call as soon as you get this." A pause, which although silent conveyed far more than the words. Then she left her phone number. Slow and deliberate, as if each number pained her. Followed by a click.

I called her back straight away. The phone rang several times. Her voice was flat when she answered, but as soon as I said hello it went high and squeaky.

"What's the matter? Are you OK?"

"It's Emily," she said. "The blood tests came back from the doctor. We had to go to hospital for some more tests. She's got leukaemia."

I shut my eyes and bit my lip as the sobs came from the other end of the phone. Frankie had been right to worry. Maternal instinct was obviously not to be doubted. Although the truth was far worse than even she had feared.

"Oh Frankie, I'm so sorry. How awful."

"I wish it had been anorexia now. I think I could have coped with that. But this . . ." Her voice trailed

233

off. I heard her blow her nose. Could picture her red-rimmed eyes.

"What do the doctors say? How bad is it?"

"It's bad. Something called acute lymphoblastic leukaemia, which progresses quickly. And she's got a high leukaemia cell count, which means it's already well advanced."

"So she'll have to have chemo?"

"Yeah. She's starting it tomorrow, but they've also found she's got something called a Philadelphia chromosome, which means there's a high risk of relapse. She could die, Claire. My beautiful Emily could die." The sobs came again. From both ends of the phone this time. I felt so helpless, so small and pathetic in the great big horrible world that had landed such a brutal blow.

"Try not to think that," I said. "You have to shut that out and believe she can get through this. Be strong for her."

"I know. And I try really hard when I'm with her, but it's so hard. Do you know what she said when the consultant asked if she had any questions? Would she still be able to go to the *Twilight* premiere? As if that's the only thing worth living for."

I smiled a watery smile. Remembering when I had thought like that. Unable to see anything more important than Andy.

"Where is she now?"

"In her room. She only got back from hospital this afternoon and she's going in first thing in the morning.

I don't know what she's doing. She's very quiet but she says she wants to be on her own."

I knew she'd be talking to Robert. Praying to him, no doubt. Because he was the closest thing to a God she had.

"What have you told the little ones?"

"Just that their big sister's very ill. That she needs to go to hospital. Sophia asked if the doctors would make her better so I said yes. I didn't see how I could say anything else."

"And Joe?"

"He's putting on a brave face but inside he's in bits. He had to walk out the room at the hospital when they took the bone marrow sample. They gave her a local anaesthetic but she still cried out with the pain. It was horrible."

"Oh Frankie. You poor thing. I don't know what to say. I just wish I could make this all go away for you. If there's anything I can do, however small."

"There is one thing. If I give you her e-mail address, will you drop her a line? She won't speak to anyone at the moment but she really took to you. She's been talking about you, a lot. Said you weren't like other grown-ups. You seemed to understand about her and Robert. Didn't make her feel silly about it."

I smiled and sniffed at the same time. Honoured to be thought of in that way. And desperately sad that we weren't communicating in different circumstances.

"Of course I can. It's the least I can do. Although I don't know if I'll find the right thing to say."

"You will," said Frankie. "I know you will."

"I'll do my best. But listen, if you need to talk. Or just cry down the phone at me. Any time, day or night. I'm on call, OK?"

"OK," said Frankie. There was a high-pitched scream and crying from somewhere in the house. It was a comforting sound in a way. Showing that life, in part of the Ricotta family at least, was continuing as normal. "I'd better go," she said. "You know what they're like."

I replaced the handset and sat down heavily on the chair. Feeling empty and winded and sick. The interview letter lay open on the table where I'd left it. Except, of course, it didn't seem nearly as important as it had done ten minutes ago. I put it back in the envelope and pulled my laptop out of my briefcase.

I sat for a long time before I wrote anything other than "Dear Emily". But when the words did finally come, they came in a flourish. Pouring out on to the screen. Full of Robert. Full of hopes and fears and dreams.

Friday, 10 January 1986

I gazed down at the latest picture of Andy in an England shirt in my United scrapbook. Even now, three days later, I still bristled with pride as I re-read the glowing newspaper testimonies to his impressive display on the hallowed Wembley turf. I had bought all the newspapers the day after and stuck each report firmly into place in my scrapbook, smoothing down the corners to ensure they didn't buckle or come unstuck when I turned the page. It was my way of paying homage to Andy, and, at the same time, reminding myself that good things did still happen — even if they were becoming increasingly few and far between.

The list of bad things in my life was getting pretty long and had now been extended to a second sheet of ruled A4 paper. The top one was, of course, "Andy going out with someone else". I'd found out what her name was. Annie, as in "Annie, I'm Not Your Daddy". That was how she introduced herself, apparently. Susan from the club shop had told me. I didn't see why anyone would resort to a Kid Creole and the Coconuts song when a simple "Annie" would do. But Susan said people in promotions were funny like that. Turned out that was what she was. A fucking United promotions girl. Just to rub it in, there was a photo of her with

Andy and the rest of the team in the United programme most weeks. Advertising the new range of leisure wear. She was dressed in a United vest top and shorts cut so high you could see her arse. And she was wearing ankle-warmers and stilettos. Like you'd really do a workout in high heels. She had big tits and big hair as well, of course (Susan reckoned you had to, to work in promotions). And the players were holding her up, like blokes used to do to dancing women in those old films. Skip, Gibbo and Matt were holding her shoulders, Nobber was by her feet and Andy was somewhere in the middle, near her arse. Susan said that was when they'd met. That she fell for him because he was polite and didn't try to chat her up like the others did. I couldn't work it out though, what Andy saw in her (apart from the obvious, I mean). Susan said she was as thick as shit. The sort of woman who thought the Gaza Strip was a club in Soho. I didn't get it. Andy was a *Guardian* reader; he watched *Newsnight*. I doubted if Annie could keep up with *John Craven's Newsround*.

I kept playing "Is She Really Going Out With Him?" at full volume over and over again, shouting out the words so loudly that I drowned out Joe Jackson.

I wished I'd never seen the photo or knew who she was. Whenever I closed my eyes, all I could see was her and Andy together. Holding hands, kissing, going for long walks in the country. All the things I'd dreamt of doing with him. That was the worst thing. Not that she was going out with him but that she'd stolen my dreams.

The most recent addition to the bad things list was Thomo's departure. It had all been very sudden. One minute he'd been talking about looking forward to a possible Wembley appearance with United in the Milk Cup Final. The next he'd been pictured in the papers proudly wearing an Aston Villa shirt and shaking hands with his new manager. I still couldn't get my head round it. I'd always imagined the team would stay together for ever. That Andy, Thomo and the rest of them would see out the remainder of their playing days at Priory Park before retiring to some home for ex-United players in the Hertfordshire countryside where I could go and visit them and reminisce about the good old days. Thomo's departure had forced me to confront the possibility that it wasn't going to be like that.

I kissed the picture of Andy and flicked through the scrapbook, counting the number of blank pages remaining. There were fourteen. I would be very happy indeed if fourteen pages' worth of good things happened between now and the end of the season.

"How do you fancy being taken out for a slap-up meal tonight?"

If it had been Andy asking me, I'd have jumped at it. But it wasn't, it was Dad on the phone. There had to be a catch.

"Why would you want to do that?"

"I don't need a reason to take my own daughter out, do I?"

"No, I s'pose not."

"So I'll take that as a yes then?"

"I'll have to ask Mum first but it should be OK."

"Good. I'll pick you up at seven thirty, on the corner as usual. Wear something nice, we're going somewhere a bit better than the Wimpy."

I enjoyed a couple of hours idly fantasising that Dad was going to announce he was moving back home, or at the very least getting me tickets for the Milk Cup semi-final, before Mum came home and brought me back down to earth.

"What's he done wrong then?"

"What d'ya mean?"

"Well he must be trying to soften you up for a reason. He wouldn't offer to take you out otherwise, would he?"

"He doesn't need an excuse to take his own daughter out, does he?" I said, repeating Dad's line with even less conviction than he had been able to muster.

"He's hardly made a habit of it in the past, has he? Don't you think it's strange that he should suddenly push the boat out like this? You're sure he's not emigrating to Australia or anything?"

"That's right, go and spoil it for me. You can't bear him making me happy, can you?"

"I just don't like him building up your expectations like this in case he lets you down, like he usually does."

"Oh, like you've never let me down."

Mum shook her head and walked a few steps towards me.

"I've always been there for you, Claire. I do at least try to make you happy."

"You won't even let me go to United matches, that's how much you care about my happiness."

"I don't want you getting caught up in the trouble, you know that."

"Well if anything happens to me you can always get Gerry Marsden or your mate Buddy Holly to make a charity record to raise some money for you, OK?"

"Buddy Holly's dead, Claire."

"Don't tell me, he was killed by hooligans at a football match."

"Don't be so facetious. I didn't bring you up to say things like that."

I wasn't sure what facetious meant, but guessed from the tone of Mum's voice that it was something bad.

"I must have got it from Dad then, mustn't I? Everything I do or say that's wrong is down to Dad."

I turned to walk out the room.

"Enjoy *Dempsey and Makepeace*, won't you?" I called back over my shoulder.

By the time I trotted down the road to meet Dad, I was so convinced he was about to emigrate to Australia that I expected to see him sitting in the car wearing a wide-brimmed hat with corks hanging from the rim and sipping a can of Foster's.

So, in a strange way, the fact that there was no hat and no can of Foster's but the passenger seat was occupied by a red-haired woman came as something of a relief at first. It was a good few seconds before I realised that Dad hadn't brought the woman along for decoration or to make up the numbers. She had to be there for a reason.

"Claire, I'd like you to meet Denise."

The introduction may have contained the bare minimum of information, but it was still more than I had wanted to know. The woman now had a name. And it was much harder to pretend someone didn't exist when you knew their name.

"Hiya, Claire, nice to meet you at last. Your father's told me a lot about you."

While aware that I was supposed to reply jovially, "All of it good, I hope," I did not feel inclined to observe social etiquette simply in order to put Denise at ease. Nor did I wish to let Dad off the hook by giving his girlfriend my seal of approval.

"What did he say?"

"I'm sorry?"

"What did he tell you about me?"

Denise was clearly thrown by such a direct question and looked to Dad for assistance.

"Honestly, Claire, what do you think I told her, that you were a raving lunatic or something?"

"No, I didn't think you knew much stuff about me, that's all."

"Well, I told her that you were a big United fan and a vegetarian and that you want to be a lawyer when you grow up. You do still want to be a lawyer, I take it?"

I resented the patronising tone in his voice, which implied that my desire to be a lawyer was as far-fetched as wanting to be an astronaut or a racing driver. I also

242

resented the phrase "when you grow up", which missed the fact that I already had.

"Yes, I do still want to be a lawyer. I'm doing work experience with the Crown Prosecution Service at Hornsey Magistrates' Court next month, actually."

"Good for you," Dad replied, obviously sensing this was going to be a very long evening. "At least we've got that one sorted out."

When we arrived at Valentino's, I forgot my animosity towards Denise and my anger at Dad for a few moments in the excitement of entering an establishment frequented by United players. I gazed at the three framed photographs which took pride of place in the plush reception area. They showed Matt Goodyear, Barry Gibbons and Dave Orton shaking hands with a rotund, slightly balding Italian man. Each photograph had been inscribed with a suitable message such as the "Thanks for a great night, Luigi" which Matt had written in black felt-tip pen. I hastily scanned the ranks of other diners, in case I could see any familiar faces amongst them.

"Hey, how about that then, Claire?" said Dad, following my gaze. "You might end up sitting next to Matt Goodyear."

"Is he your favourite player?" asked Denise, fiddling with the spaghetti-like straps of her red dress.

"No, Andy Pailes is, actually. Didn't my dad tell you that?"

Luigi seated us at a table by the window. I gathered from the conversation that Dad and Denise were regular clients. I couldn't remember him ever taking

243

Mum out to restaurants. Certainly not to ones that had proper tablecloths anyway.

"I expect this is all a bit of a drag for you, isn't it, Claire?" said Denise. "I bet you're usually out with your friends on a Saturday night."

I stared blankly at her, wondering why she was trying so hard to be friendly.

"Yeah, sometimes I am."

"So where do you go?"

I wished I hadn't lied now. It meant I would have to lie again.

"The pictures, things like that."

"Oh, I love the cinema. What was the last thing you saw?"

I hesitated. I wanted to say something cool like *St Elmo's Fire* or *The Breakfast Club*. But I didn't want to get caught out by any further questions from Denise which might expose the fact that I hadn't seen either of them. I decided to play it safe.

"*Gremlins*, I saw *Gremlins*. That was good."

"Oh God, yeah, I loved that. Weren't they cute at the beginning? I'm a sucker for kids' stuff like that. *Bambi* is my all-time favourite film, you know. I cried buckets when his mother got shot."

I had no idea why adults tried to pretend they liked kids' things. None of my classmates would be caught dead at anything less than a 15 certificate.

Luigi came back to take our order. We agreed to skip the starters, deciding to have desserts instead. I asked for the Napolitana pasta dish (mainly because it was the only vegetarian thing on the menu), Dad ordered the chicken and Denise plumped for the venison.

"She can't have the venison," I said.

Dad looked at me. He had one of those fixed smiles on his face.

"Why not? It's what she wants."

"Two minutes ago she said *Bambi* was her all-time favourite film. She said she cried when his mother got shot. And now she says she wants the venison."

"I'll have the fish if it's going to upset you," offered Denise, clearly embarrassed. Dad rolled his eyes and told Luigi to stick with the original order.

"For heaven's sake, Claire, there's no need to create a scene," he said, as Luigi returned to the kitchen scratching his head. "Just because you choose not to eat meat, it doesn't mean to say other people can't. Denise wants the venison and that's what she's having."

"Why did she say all that stuff about *Bambi* then? She's a hypocrite."

Dad gave me a look which meant "shut up". Denise started fiddling with the straps on her dress again. We sat in silence until the main courses arrived.

"Do you reckon they'll win the semi-final, then?" Dad asked as he tucked into his chicken breast.

"Yeah, easy. It's only QPR, isn't it?"

"They need to win something this year, even if it is only the Milk Cup. Doesn't look like they're going to win the league now, does it?"

"We're only six points behind Everton," I said.

"No chance of them slipping up, though. Not the way Lineker's playing. Still, now Roy Brown's come in as chairman we might be able to buy another decent striker ourselves. Best thing that's happened to United for years, that Brown is."

"How can you say that? He's a Tory MP. He's a complete fascist." I was still recovering from the shock of United's recent boardroom coup. I had visions of Maggie Thatcher being appointed honorary chairman of the club before the season was out.

"He could be Hitler's long-lost son for all I care; he's putting two million quid into the club, that's what matters."

"Money isn't everything, you know."

Dad laughed. "Are you sure you're a teenager?"

"What's that supposed to mean?"

"Oh, it doesn't matter. Money might not be everything to you, Claire, but it's pretty important to the rest of us. And it'll come in handy to buy a replacement for Thomo, won't it?"

"That's different. They should never have sold him in the first place."

"They didn't have much choice, did they? Not with that business with his wife."

"What did his wife have to do with it?"

"She had cancer, didn't she. That's why he went to Villa, so she could be near her family in Birmingham. Only they kept it all hush-hush because they didn't want it getting in the papers. That's what they were saying at the match last week anyway."

I pushed my half-eaten bowl of pasta away and stared out of the window. It all made sense now. I hated myself for ever having doubted Thomo's commitment,

246

for thinking he had let me down. My bottom lip started to tremble.

"Hey, come on, don't upset yourself," said Dad. "This is supposed to be a celebration."

"Is it?" I looked blankly at him. "What are we supposed to be celebrating?"

"Well, Denise and I have got something to tell you, actually." He paused for a second, shifting uncomfortably in his seat. "How do you fancy going to a wedding in September?"

"Depends if United are at home. And whose wedding it is."

"Ours, silly. It's going to be our wedding. We got engaged on New Year's Eve."

I felt as if a nuclear missile had exploded inside me, rendering all my vital organs useless and severing all communication links. My father was going to marry a hypocritical Fergie lookalike. I could only presume he must be having some kind of mid-life crisis, like the men in sitcoms.

I stared at Denise, who was looking down at her plate, chewing the same piece of food over and over again to avoid having to say anything. I couldn't believe that this woman was going to be my stepmother. She wasn't even wearing a bra, for Christ's sake. For all I knew she didn't have any knickers on either.

"Well, aren't you going to say anything?" Dad asked, clearly seeking my blessing.

"Actually, I've changed my mind," I said. "I don't want any pudding, thank you. I've kind of lost my appetite."

It wasn't until I got home that I was able to cry properly. The sound of the front door shutting behind me seemed to trigger my tear ducts back into life. A blurry vision of Mum appeared at the far end of the hall.

"What's he done now?"

"It's not his fault; it's hers."

"Whose fault, Claire? You're not making any sense."

"Denise, that's who. The stupid tart that Dad's gonna marry."

"Marry? Your father's getting married?"

"Yeah, in September. He wants me to go to the wedding. That'll be it then, I s'pose. He'll never want to see me again. Not once he's got her."

"Hey, don't be silly. Of course he'll want to see you." Mum went to put her arm around me but I pushed her away.

"How can you say that? You thought he was going to emigrate a few hours ago. That's how much you think he's bothered about me."

"You know I didn't mean that."

"Why bother saying something if you don't mean it?"

"I told you, love. I didn't want him building your hopes up, that was all. I didn't want him hurting you, like he obviously has done."

"You're as bad as her, you know. You say stuff you don't mean and you make things up 'cos you think it's what I want to hear. Why can't you tell the truth for once?"

Mum walked a few steps closer towards me.

"Because sometimes the truth hurts, love. Sometimes I think you need protecting from it."

"Is that why you never admit that you hate Dad?"

"I don't hate your father."

"There you go again, see, lying to me and saying stuff you don't mean. Just leave me alone, will you?"

I pushed past Mum and ran upstairs to my room, hurling myself on to my bed. The two men I loved most in the world had both deserted me for other women. I wished I could either rewind to being a little girl, so I could be the apple of Dad's eye again, or fast forward so I could have a chance of getting Andy back. I hated this awkward bit in the middle, where the tape machine appeared to be stuck on pause.

I popped out to the bathroom and pulled a string of sheets from the toilet roll. As I crept back across the landing, I heard Mum crying downstairs. I felt bad about what I'd said to her. I wasn't going to go down and tell her that, mind. Because I knew it wouldn't make any difference. She'd still hate me. Like she still hated Dad.

CHAPTER
EIGHT

"OK, you have fifteen minutes to get ready," announced Mark when he arrived at my house after work on Friday evening three weeks later. He had that look in his eye. He was up to something. And I had no idea what it was.

"Get ready for what?" I asked. "This doesn't involve getting rude in a lift by any chance, does it?"

"No," laughed Mark. "Not that I'm aware of. I'm taking you away for the weekend."

My instinctive reaction was to be thrilled. I couldn't remember the last time I'd been whisked off for a weekend away. In fact, when I thought about it, I realised it was because it had never actually happened before. Certainly Mark had never done it. And although David and I had managed a few odd nights away, he'd never spared the time off work for an entire weekend. And then I remembered Mark's behaviour of recent weeks. The words "odd" and "unpredictable" came to mind. Along with the realisation that his idea of a good weekend away might not necessarily be mine.

"Where are we going?" I asked.

"Aahh, that would be telling," he said, grabbing me around the waist and kissing me.

250

"But you have to give me some idea so I know what to pack."

"Three questions then," said Mark. "But only three, mind."

"OK, do I need my passport?"

"No."

I tried not to show my disappointment that the romantic weekend in Florence was out of the window.

"Formal or casual clothes?"

"Do I look like a guy who'd choose formal?" This was true. Even after his fashion makeover he could only be said to be in the smart-casual camp.

"You're right," I said. "Wasted question on my part. City or countryside, then?"

"Countryside."

"Should I be worried?"

"You've had your three. Not my fault if you wasted one." It wasn't the reassuring answer I'd been looking for. Still, the possibility of some gorgeous old country hotel with a roaring fire and four-poster bed had not been ruled out. And I was in need of a break. The whole thing with Emily had really got to me. I was emotionally drained, worried sick about her and could think about little else.

"OK," I said. "Can you give me twenty minutes?"

"Is this what you're like at plea bargaining?"

"I want to drop Emily a quick line first. Let her know that I'm going to be away for a couple of days." We'd been e-mailing back and forth on a regular basis. I didn't ask much about the chemo. Just left her to tell me what she wanted to. Mainly her worries that she wouldn't be able to go to the premiere. And I, of course, wasn't able to tell her that her mother was worried she might not even be alive by then. I'd told her bits about Andy to try to help. About me always getting spots when I was due to see him. And how much he'd liked my hair when I had it cut. All designed to make her laugh or give her hope that she'd look great with short hair while it grew back.

"Go on, then," he said. "And say hi from me." Mark had been upset when I'd told him. Though it was different for him. He didn't have the bond I had with Frankie. Or with Emily for that matter.

I went upstairs to the bedroom and bundled a variety of clothes into my suitcase. A pair of jeans and some combats, a couple of jumpers and a fleece. A nice outfit for dinner, some heels, jewellery and my best lingerie — just in case that country hotel turned out to be the secret destination. Then I sat down at my laptop to write to Emily. It felt wrong somehow, me going off to enjoy myself while she was going through a round of high-dose chemotherapy. But Frankie said she liked to hear about normal things, stuff that I was doing. That she got sick of everyone asking her how she was all the time. She wanted to hear about good things, happy things. Anything that could make her forget. Even for a moment or two.

"Ready," I said five minutes later as I arrived downstairs with my bulging suitcase.

"Come on, then," said Mark, ushering me outside. "Your chariot awaits."

252

We headed north to Burnley, then west, I crossed off potential destinations at each turn. By the time we got to the M6 I was pretty sure (although I did, admittedly, give a small sigh of relief as we passed the turning for Blackpool). We'd been to the Lake District together once before, the first holiday we'd had together if I remembered rightly. Just for a week, a village called Hawkshead, near where Beatrix Potter had lived. I remembered tea shops, the odd stroll around a lake, lock-ins at country pubs, a lot of sex (we were still in the honeymoon stage of our relationship) and a visit to the football museum in Ambleside (this after I'd told him I used to be a big United fan). We'd stayed in a nice hotel too, although I seemed to remember I'd booked it myself to make sure.

"Are we nearly there yet?" I asked as we approached junction 36.

"You're worse than a kid," laughed Mark.

"I'm not very good at surprises. I like to know. Do I get any clues?"

"It's not Scotland."

"OK, my guess is still on, then."

"What's your guess?"

"I can't tell you, can I? Otherwise if it's not there you'll think you've chosen the wrong place and worry I'll be disappointed."

"I'm worrying already now you've piled the pressure on like that."

"Well don't," I said. "I'm sure it'll be lovely, whatever it is. It's just nice to get away." What I didn't tell him was that I had my fingers crossed under my leg as I said it.

We left the motorway at junction 36 and headed west for some time. I was tired by now. It had been a busy week at work and I was still recovering from being on police cells duty rota the previous weekend. I had a disturbing knack of being called out at 2a.m. the night before a big trial. I was looking forward to a long hot bath, soft fluffy towels, a lie-in and maybe even breakfast in bed.

Mark turned off towards Grizedale Forest. He was heading up towards the hotel we'd first stayed at together, I was sure of it. But ten minutes later he took a sharp left and we started down a bumpy track. It was pitch black and had started to rain. All I could see in the headlights in front of the swishing windscreen wipers were trees.

"Are you sure this is the right way?" I asked.

"Pretty sure, yeah."

"It's not the way to Hawkshead."

"We're not going to Hawkshead."

"Oh. Well there don't even seem to be any buildings down here."

"I know. I wanted to find somewhere you could really get away from it all."

A feeling of unease spread over me. A sense that this was not going to be what I'd expected. We followed the track round to the left and pulled up sharply in a small gravelled car park.

"Come on," said Mark, leaping out of the car like some kid desperate to get to the beach. "Let me show you."

I quickly pulled on my waterproof jacket before he grabbed my hand and led me along a gravel track to a clearing in the woods. For a second I wondered if this was all an elaborate plan to have sex with me in the forest; if it was the next unusual venue to cross off after "lift". And then through the darkness I caught sight of a circle of soft lights. And in the middle, the tents. Half a dozen of them spaced out around the clearing. Large canvas bell tents. I glanced across at Mark to see if it was a joke, but the look on his face was one of pure unadulterated excitement.

"Camping," I said. "You've brought me camping."

"No," he said. "This is glamping."

"And what's that?"

"Glamorous camping. Luxury tent provided, complete with wooden floor, futon to sleep on and a wood-burning stove to keep us warm."

I nodded slowly, letting the information sink in. Deciding how best to react.

"Right, but no, er, bathroom facilities, I take it?"

"Yeah," said Mark, producing a torch from his jacket pocket and shining it across to a small hut at the edge of the clearing. "They've got a hot shower and a toilet. In there, I think."

I struggled for a moment not to burst into tears. His intentions, as always, were honourable. It was a really sweet thought to take me away, and no doubt this place sounded great on the internet. I could see why he was so enthusiastic about it. But the reality of turning up in the pitch black and pouring rain on a freezing-cold night at the end of September and being shown to a tent, however glamorous, rather than an en suite room with four-poster and whirlpool bath, was undeniably glum.

"You'll love it," Mark said, filling the awkward silence. "Just wait until morning when you wake up to birdsong and the wind rustling through the trees."

I smiled and nodded at him. Trying desperately not to let my disappointment show.

"You didn't tell me to pack my wellies," I said, looking down as my shoes started sinking into the mud.

"It's all right. I threw them in the boot while you were upstairs packing. And I've brought a double sleeping bag so we can keep each other warm. Not that it will be cold. There's a stove, like I said."

"So which one's ours?" I asked, trying to show willing.

"Er, I'm not too sure. The woman who runs it just said she'd leave the breakfast basket in it ready for the morning."

I was getting breakfast in bed after all. Or breakfast in futon at least. I felt myself start to soften, sensing how desperate Mark was for me to like it.

"Thank you," I said. His eyes lit up in relief.

"I knew you'd love it. I'll nip back to the car to get our wellies, then we'll go and find our tent." I stood there, rain dripping down my face, shivering in the cold. Concentrating hard on keeping the smile on my face.

I awoke in the early hours to what sounded like foxes fighting and the rain beating on the canvas above. It was still dark and the fire had gone out, leaving a distinct chill in the air. To which, as I was only wearing a flimsy camisole and shorts set (I hadn't wanted to be the passion killer who went to bed in a jumper), you had to add a buttock and nipple chill factor, in order to truly appreciate it. Mark, who had brought pyjamas, was sleeping soundly next to me. As much as I wanted to get back to sleep, I was aware I needed the toilet. It was just unfortunate that the only one in question was on the other side of the field. Quietly I unzipped my side of the sleeping bag and slid out. I fumbled around on the floor, feeling for the torch, then flicked it on to search for the waterproof to throw over me. I unzipped the flap to the tent and stepped into my wellies, like some mixed-up lingerie model who had gone to the wrong venue for the photo shoot. When I got to the hut I couldn't find a light inside and ended up squatting in the dark with the torch shining up at me as if I'd been caught in the act by a patrolling security guard.

I made my way gingerly back to the tent. It was only as I shone the torch around to establish the exact location of the futon that I noticed the man sitting bolt upright looking at me. The man who was not Mark.

"Sorry," I muttered. "They all look the same in the dark."

"Fine by me, love," he said, his eyes appearing to adjust to the torchlight in time to give my bare thighs a quick once-over. "I'm very happy to oblige."

I slunk back to the correct tent next door. Even on a weekend away, it seemed, we now had a neighbour to avoid.

★   ★   ★

257

"So what's the plan today then?"

We were sitting on the futon, huddled under the sleeping bag, having polished off our breakfast in record time in order to provide fuel for our freezing bodies. Mark hadn't admitted that, of course. Just said that having gone to the effort of making it on our two-ring camp stove, he didn't want to let it go cold. But I suspected his reason for shovelling the eggs and hash browns down so quickly was the same as mine. I was hoping that there was no plan. That we could have one of those lazy, wandering-around-doing-nothing kinds of days. But the excited expression on Mark's face indicated otherwise.

"Ahh, that would be telling."

I groaned inwardly, aware I was beginning to suffer from surprise fatigue.

"At least make sure I'm properly dressed for whatever we're doing this time."

"OK," said Mark. "Trainers, jeans, a fleece and your waterproof should do the job."

I nodded, resisting the temptation to ask whether my nice dress and heels were actually going to get an outing at any point.

"So we're going to be out in the elements. Will there be any pain or embarrassment involved?"

Mark considered the question for a moment.

"Hopefully no pain. Difficult to say on the embarrassment front due to it being uncharted territory."

"OK, not very reassuring, but as long as the guy in the next tent's not involved, I'll take a chance."

Mark looked at me, clearly waiting for an explanation.

"We had a night-time rendezvous," I said. "Of the unwanted and unexpected kind."

Mark shook his head and laughed. "Honestly, I can't take you anywhere, can I?"

An hour later I was standing in another clearing in the same forest, peering skywards as directed by Mark, unsure about exactly what I was supposed to be looking for.

"I can hear something in the trees," said Mark. "Keep your eyes peeled, I think it's coming." It wasn't a bird, or a plane, or Superman for that matter. It was some poor bastard hurtling through the trees hanging on to a zip-wire looking absolutely terrified. It was only a nanosecond after seeing him that it occurred to me that Mark hadn't brought me here to enjoy a spectator sport.

"That's what we're doing, isn't it?"

"Yep," said Mark, a huge grin on his face. "I've booked us on a three-hour hire-wire forest adventure." He said it in the same tone of voice you would say, "I've booked us on the Orient Express", or "I've booked us on a luxury cruise."

"And what gave you the impression I'd enjoy swinging through the trees like a monkey?" I said.

"Come on, it'll be great fun. You'll get a real kick out of it."

"I thought this was supposed to be a relaxing weekend away from it all?"

"It is. We'll relax later." Quite what was relaxing about going back to a tent in a muddy field I wasn't sure.

"Promise me you have no more surprises up your sleeve."

"Scout's honour," said Mark. "Now come on. We've got a safety session with an instructor before we set off."

Which was how, shortly afterwards, I came to be standing on a small wooden platform in the treetops, a harness around my body, being encouraged to jump by a young Australian woman with far too much energy and zest for life.

"Go, go, go," she whooped. The rest of our group were clapping and cheering. I felt like a kid at the top of the slide who desperately wanted to go back down the steps but didn't want to lose face with his peers. I shut my eyes and stepped off the platform. My stomach lurched, my hands gripped the rope for dear life and a few seconds later I swung into the cargo net which had been strategically placed to stop us on our short practice run. I could hear Mark and the instructor whooping. I waited for the sense of elation to wash over me but it didn't come. Probably because I knew that half an hour from now I was going to be standing on a much taller platform about to hurtle more than 275 metres through the trees with no cargo net at the end of it.

"See, I told you it was fun," said Mark, as we made our way to the start of the course proper. He appeared to be buzzing with the thrill of it all, unaware that the smile I had forced on to my face was only there for his sake.

Somehow or other I managed the first zip-wire. Mainly because I'd stumbled off the platform by accident and had my eyes shut for most of the way. I waited at the bottom for Mark to come down, ready to capture his descent on the video camera as instructed. He whizzed along, legs "running" while he sang the walking in the air song in his best Aled Jones voice and landed gracefully in the wood-chipped landing pit. I, of course, had forgotten to do the running bit with my legs, which might have explained why I'd landed bottom-first in an unceremonious bump-and-drag action.

I watched Mark as he dusted himself down and unclipped his harness from the wire. I still wasn't sure whether he was actually enjoying himself or simply putting on a brave front for me. What I did know was that there was no way I was going to let him turn the video camera on me.

"So what's next?" I enquired through gritted teeth.

"That thing up there," said Mark, pointing to a precarious-looking set of huge metal stirrups suspended high above our heads. I blamed Ant and Dec for this. Giving people the impression that putting someone through sheer terror in a wilderness hellhole was actually amusing in any way. Although I supposed I should be relieved that so far there had been no mention of eating creepy-crawlies.

The rope ladder up to the platform was the first challenge. An annoyingly agile teenager went first, powering his way up and practically leaping across the stirrups with barely a downward glance.

"Bastard," Mark whispered to me. "I hate it when the kids make it look easy."

Mark followed on behind. I watched him going up; he looked good, actually. Rather professional. No doubt the rock-climbing training had paid off. He clipped his safety harness on to the wire at the top and made his way steadily across the swinging stirrups, nowhere near as fast as the teenager but still managing to look assured. Which was the one thing I knew I didn't look as I clambered up the ladder behind him. Oddly, when I got to the top, I quite missed the Australian whooping woman. I could have done with a bit of that energy and enthusiasm washing off on me. Gingerly I reached out my left foot. "Harness," called someone from the ground. I smiled sheepishly and clipped myself on before trying again. Maybe I had a small stride, though how someone with long legs can have a small stride I'm not sure; something to do with my hips not working properly perhaps. But once I had one foot on the stirrup, all I could do was wobble wildly in the air as I tried to make contact with the next one.

"Try and go faster. You need to build up a bit of a momentum," yelled Mark from the far platform.

I grimaced at him, not wanting to have a domestic in the middle of this but feeling inclined to knee him somewhere soft and spongy when I got to the other side. Finally I managed to get my other foot in the next stirrup, only to find that as I tried to bring my rear leg forward I lost my footing. I gasped as I felt myself falling but a second later the safety harness pulled tight and I was left dangling in the air, one foot in a stirrup, the other flailing around in no-man's-land.

"Someone get the instructor," bellowed Mark from the platform. I heard footsteps below as a young lad ran off down the track.

After what seemed like an age (but was probably barely a minute or two), someone strong and reassuringly apelike was reaching out to me, telling me to keep calm as he hooked me on to his harness, instructed me to cling on to him and brought me back down to ground level within a few seconds.

"Thank you," I said feebly. "I'm obviously one of those rare people who appears not to have descended from apes."

"Are you OK?" asked Mark, who had climbed back along the stirrups and down the rope ladder to get to me.

"I guess so. Just a bit shaken."

"Perhaps you should skip this section," said the instructor.

"Yeah," I said, looking up at Mark. "And the next three as well, I think."

We sat in the tent drinking tea. The rain, which had mercifully eased off during our hire-wire adventure/disaster, was back to beating down on the canvas. Mark had the triumphant air of someone who had conquered Everest (he had offered to quit when I had but I'd told him to carry on, seeing that he really wanted to). I was, however, lacking anything like a shared sense of achievement. Having been bubbling quietly for much of the weekend, the volcano was in danger of erupting.

"Maybe we could come again another time," said Mark. "So you can get to finish the course." I looked at him wondering what planet he was currently inhabiting. Because it certainly wasn't mine.

"No thanks."

"You were just unlucky, that's all. It could have happened to anyone. I'm sure if you'd carried on you'd have really enjoyed it."

"Mark, I didn't enjoy it, OK? I could go back a hundred times and I still wouldn't enjoy it. A high-wire forest adventure is not my idea of fun. The only reason I never entered *The Krypton Factor* was because I knew I'd hate the assault course."

"You should have said."

I shook my head. "What chance did I have? It was all booked. I turned up and was told that was what I was doing, like I turned up here and was told we were camping . . ."

"Glamping," Mark interrupted.

I glared at him.

"The thing is, you never stop to think, do you? Or to ask what I'd like to do. You get totally carried away on some whim and assume that I'll like it simply because you do."

"That's not fair. I wanted to surprise you."

"Surprises aren't always good, you know. There are nasty ones too."

"But I did think about this. I booked it because you like the countryside."

"When have I ever said that?"

"It's on the list."

"What list?"

"Your list. The twenty years from now one. You said you wanted to live in the countryside. You said a lot of things."

I put my mug down on the floor and stared at Mark. It was like he'd knocked over the first domino and set a whole line of them toppling, splaying out in different directions. Revealing a pattern at the end which solved some cryptic puzzle. Or in this case explained everything about what had been going on over the past couple of months.

"When did you see it?"

"At your place, the night you said you didn't want to buy the house. You tried to hide it when you came in with the coffee but I'd already read it."

"Why didn't you tell me?"

"Guilt, I guess. It was like reading someone's secret diary without knowing what it was. By the time I realised, it was too late. I knew stuff I wasn't supposed to know."

"But you still should have said. It's not like you went rummaging through my drawers. It was my stupid fault for leaving it there on the bloody coffee table."

"To be honest, I didn't know what to say. It was pretty obvious why you'd been looking at it. Your life hadn't turned out like you'd planned and you wanted to get it back on track. I figured I'd be first on the list to go. That's why I kept quiet."

"Oh Mark," I said, leaning over to stroke his arm. "I wouldn't do that."

He shrugged. "Well I'm not Andy Pailes, am I? I never played football for England for a start."

I flinched as I heard his name. Coming from Mark's mouth it sounded cold and unfamiliar. I felt like the two halves of my life were about to collide.

"I'm surprised you've even heard of him."

"I only had a vague recollection. Probably had his sticker in my Panini album when I was at school. I had to look him up on the internet to find out more."

I heard the sound of car brakes screeching in my head. It was too late though to avert the full impact. All I could hope was that Mark hadn't got close enough to see the carnage. I decided to work on a damage limitation exercise in case there was still time.

"I'm surprised you found anything. He only played for England once."

"There wasn't much. Only a biography and photo on the United old boys page."

I breathed a silent sigh of relief, sure that United wouldn't have mentioned anything untoward.

"What did it say about him?" I asked, trying to appear casual.

"Just listed his appearances, goals and stuff. And a bit about what he's doing now."

I nodded. I wanted to ask what he was doing but I knew that would be one question too many. I needed to play it down. Feign lack of interest.

"He wasn't one of their star players or anything. Not really," I said.

"He must have been pretty special though, to be your favourite. Wasn't Matt Goodyear the big heartthrob in those days?"

"Yeah, well. I never like to follow a crowd, do I?"

"So were you some kind of groupie then?" Mark was smiling but my skin crawled. I still hated the word.

"He was my favourite player, that's all. It was no big deal."

"He was important enough for you to want to marry him."

"I was fifteen, for Christ's sake. I wanted to be prime minister as well."

"That was a narrow escape for Britain then."

I smiled at Mark and squeezed his hand, relieved at the first light moment in the conversation. He couldn't know. He would surely have said if he did. Certainly wouldn't have cracked a joke.

"You said you wanted kids as well," Mark continued.

"I guess I've changed my mind about a lot of things."

Mark nodded, his face serious again.

"Does it bother you?" I asked.

"Not enough to matter," he replied.

"So your trip to King Street," I said, deciding to take the opportunity of moving the conversation on. "You were trying to look more like a footballer, weren't you? That's why you did it. You were trying to be what I wanted. Or what I wanted when I was fifteen, anyway."

Mark looked down at the floor, the brave face crumpling, the confident façade cracking to reveal the inner child who I'd always known was inside.

"I was so scared you were going to leave me. I didn't want to lose you. I was prepared to turn myself into whatever it was you wanted me to be. Which I figured must be the opposite of me. Some adventurous, sporty, outdoor type."

"You didn't need to do that."

"I did, though. Because you're everything to me, even if I have never said it."

I rested my forehead against his, kissing him lightly on the nose. "You have now," I whispered. "And I don't want you to be someone you're not. I want you to be Mark."

He nodded and kissed me back. Although he still didn't seem convinced.

"But when you were looking at that list, you must have been thinking about Andy. Wondering what your life would have been like if you'd ended up with him."

I shook my head vehemently then stopped abruptly, aware that I was protesting too much. And I didn't want Mark to have any idea how much I still thought about Andy. Wondered what could have been.

"Only in the same way you might wonder what it would have been like being married to Madonna."

"I don't think I'm her type." Mark smiled.

"I don't know. I think you could be exactly what she needs."

"Look," he said, "if you do want out, now or at any point, please tell me. I'd rather know than have to face you slipping away gradually."

"The only thing I'm leaving," I said, "is this bloody campsite."

"I thought it would be romantic." He shrugged.

"Maybe it would, in June when it was twenty degrees warmer. And if you'd told me where we were going so I could pack the right kind of clothes."

"Sorry," said Mark. "I guess I wasn't thinking."

"Or maybe trying too hard."

"I want you to be happy."

"I am."

"So why do you seem to be so restless? Why are you applying for jobs and getting in touch with old friends and poring over lists you made twenty years ago?"

It was a fair point. And one which I wasn't really sure of the answer to myself.

"I found the list in the attic. It threw me, that's all. It was like a blast from the past. Knocked me off course, for a while."

"But you're back with me now? Full steam ahead and all that?"

"Yes. Yes I am." I wanted to believe it. And maybe if I said it enough it would become true.

"So are you going to cancel that job interview then?"

I shook my head. "No, because that's something I need to do. To see if I can still cut it out there."

Mark didn't appear to be convinced. I took his face in my hands and kissed him softly.

"But you can quit the worthy volunteering LawWorks stuff if you want to."

"No," he said. "That was the one good part of all this. Your list did make me think about where my life was going. And the fact that everything I do is for money. I've discovered I like helping people for the sake of it. I'm really enjoying it."

"More than you're enjoying the extreme sports?"

Mark looked up and smiled. "Is it that obvious?"

"It's just not you."

"I've never been so bloody petrified in my life, the first time I went up that climbing wall. Oddly enough, I am kind of getting used to it now. I actually enjoyed that today. Certainly more than the snowboarding. But I'd still rather go back to a lie-in and a kick-about with the lads on a Sunday morning."

"Good," I said. "And in that case, I request permission to donate *Gangs* to Oxfam."

Mark laughed. "There were a few good bits in it, honestly."

"That may be so. But I never could stand Grant Mitchell in *EastEnders*. He'd have been a natural out there today, you know. Swinging through the trees like an ape man. Now, can we start packing?"

"Do you want to go home?" Mark asked.

"No. We've still got one night left, and I know a really nice hotel in Hawkshead."

Friday, 14 February 1986

I hated February the fourteenth. It was the worst day of the year not to be going out with anyone. Even worse than Christmas. At least at Christmas you got cards from other people. It didn't matter that they were people you didn't give a stuff about, kids in your class who didn't bother speaking to you the rest of the year, and distant relatives you never even knew existed. You had something to put up. Something to hide your disappointment about not getting a Christmas card from someone special. But on Valentine's Day, if you didn't get a card from the person you wanted one from, there were no consolation prizes. No hiding place.

And it was worse than ever this year. Because I knew Andy would have sent one to her. To bloody Annie. And I still couldn't understand why and what the hell he was doing with her. I wanted to write to him, to bring him to his senses. Tell him he wasn't like the other players and that was no bad thing. He didn't have to try to be like them. Andy Pailes was different. At least he was supposed to be.

I don't know why, but I still dashed downstairs as soon as I heard the postman. A couple of envelopes were lying on the doormat. A large white one, which could have been a card, and a slim brown one which

271

looked like a bill, both with the addresses face down. Taking a deep breath, I picked up the white one and turned it over. It was addressed to Mrs Maureen Skidmore. So was the bill. I went into the kitchen, grunted a greeting to Mum and sat slumped over the kitchen table.

"Are those for me?" Mum asked, pointing to the envelopes I had tossed on to the table.

"Well they're not for me, are they?"

Mum sighed before opening the bill, shaking her head and picking up the white envelope. She tore across the top with her finger, started to pull out whatever was inside then stopped halfway, flushed bright red and pushed it back inside.

"What is it?" I said.

"Oh, nothing important, I'll look at it later."

She was lying through her teeth. I knew what it was. It was a Valentine's card. My forty-year-old mother had got a fucking Valentine's card. I finished my breakfast as quickly as I could and slunk off to school.

Kim and Debbie had got two each. If you asked me, that was being greedy. Not that I wanted one from some poxy kid at school. But at least if I'd got one it would have shut everyone else up. I told them I didn't believe in St Valentine's Day. That it was a commercial scam by card companies to boost their post-Christmas sales. That's what my mum used to say. Until she got one.

I went round to see Frankie after school. She had a half-day on Fridays. She'd got three cards from lads at college. But they didn't really count because it wasn't like she was bothered about them. To be honest, she seemed annoyed they'd sent them. Which was weird when you thought about it.

"My mum only went and got one, didn't she?"

"Who off?" asked Frankie.

"I dunno. Some perv down our road who gets off on middle-aged joggers, probably."

"That's really gross."

"Yeah, I know. So don't you fancy any of these lads then?" I asked.

"No, I told you. They're all stupid pricks. They go round trying to touch up half the girls in college."

"Have any of them asked you out?"

"What's it matter? I'm not interested."

I decided to let the subject drop.

"Oh God, I meant to tell you. Jane's had the baby. It was in the paper yesterday."

Frankie went quiet. I wondered if I should have broken the news more gently.

"I know," she said after a while. "They had a picture in ours today." She reached down by the bed and picked up a neatly folded copy of the *Daily Mirror*. On the back page was a big photo of Matt kissing the forehead of a tiny baby with a shock of dark hair. A little girl called Emma.

"Crap name," I said. "I bet Jane chose it."

"I like it," said Frankie. "I think it suits her. She's gorgeous, isn't she?"

I nodded. Aware that I always seemed to say the wrong thing to Frankie nowadays.

"So do you still like him, even though he's got a kid?"

"Course I do. Andy's screwing some tart at United but it hasn't put you off, has it?"

"That's different. I've still got a chance."

"Yeah, right."

"What do you mean by that?"

"Well he's hardly gonna dump her for you, is he?"

"You don't know that. You didn't see what he was like at the Christmas disco. I told you what he said to me."

"You probably imagined it. Heard what you wanted to hear."

I suspected Frankie was jealous of me and Andy. Because she knew nothing would ever happen with her and Matt now he was a dad. But I still didn't like the way she was making me out to be some little kid.

"Are you calling me a liar?" I demanded.

"No. I'm just saying grow up. Get real."

"That's not what you said last summer."

"Yeah, well. That was a long time ago."

We sat in silence for a while. I couldn't believe what she'd just said. I guessed she must have given up on Matt because of the baby. But I didn't see why she had to make out that I was being stupid for still loving Andy.

"I'd better go," I said. "Do you wanna come round and listen to the match with me tomorrow?"

"Nah, sorry. I can't. I've got a Saturday job."

"You never told me."

"It's only down the Little Chef."

I laughed. Frankie was the only person I knew who had failed her hostess badge in the Guides.

"What's so funny?"

"I just can't imagine you wearing that crappy uniform and serving people cups of tea and fry-ups."

"Yeah, well. I need the dosh, don't I? Tara and me wanna go on holiday in the summer. Abroad like."

"Your mum'll never let you go." I didn't mean for it to sound nasty. But I was hurt that she hadn't told me. And that I obviously wasn't invited.

"She'll have to get used to it. I'll be going abroad on my own next year."

"How come?"

"It's part of my course. You have to do a week's work experience, somewhere foreign."

Frankie was doing travel and tourism at college. She reckoned she was going to end up working as a travel rep in Florida, sipping cocktails with Matt Goodyear. One of my mum's friends was a travel agent. She worked in the Co-op, booking old biddies' day trips to Bognor.

"Oh, right," I said. I'd always imagined that me and Frankie would go away together when we were older. Only to somewhere in this country. But I guessed that wasn't going to happen now.

"Right, then. I'd better go," I said.

"See ya. Hope they win."

"Yeah," I said. Wondering why she'd said they instead of we.

"And Pailes is down and this looks serious."

The words sliced through my history revision like a cut-throat razor. I tossed the textbook to one side, the seriousness of the drama unfolding on the radio immediately taking precedence over the Russian

Revolution. I sat rocking to and fro on the edge of the bed as I pictured the scene being described by LBC's commentator. The physio kneeling attentively over Andy, the United supporters chanting "off, off, off", Robson protesting his innocence over the tackle and the referee seemingly happy to take his word for it. Just because he was the bloody England captain. I winced as the stretcher came on and Andy was lifted on to it, his face apparently etched with pain, and I burst into tears as he was carried off, applause ringing from the Old Trafford stands.

The rest of the match passed by in a blur. I was only vaguely aware that Manchester United went on to win 1–0. All I cared about was how badly Andy had been injured. The verdict came a few minutes after the final whistle.

"And the news from the visitors' dressing room is that Andy Pailes has torn his ankle ligaments and could be out of action for several weeks. That must make him doubtful for the Milk Cup Final next month. Now, other scores coming in from around the country . . ."

I thumped my pillow, a single blow first, followed by a volley of uppercuts and left hooks. I hoped Robson felt every punch. Three days ago I'd been celebrating us getting through to the Milk Cup Final. Now Andy probably wouldn't be able to play. The thought of him missing out on that was too much. I wanted to go to him and comfort him, but I knew that would be impossible. Because Annie would be with him. Fussing around and pretending that she cared, when I knew full well she didn't.

An hour went by and still I sat there, deep in thought and determined to maintain my bedside vigil. It didn't matter that it wasn't Andy's bedside; it was the gesture that was important. Shortly after six, Mum knocked on my bedroom door.

"Go away," I said, knowing that such a response was guaranteed to bring her into my room, where she could witness the full extent of my misery.

"What's the matter, love?" She sat down on the edge of the bed.

"Andy's been stretchered off. He's done his ankle ligaments in. He'll be out for ages; he'll probably miss the final."

Mum appeared to be unaware of the significance of this information.

"Never mind, it's not the end of the world. Try and cheer yourself up for tea. It's spaghetti tonight, your favourite."

I stared at her, wondering how she could possibly be so insensitive as to think a bowl of spaghetti was going to make everything better.

"I'm not hungry, can't you see that?"

"You've got to eat, Claire. There are starving children in Ethiopia who would be grateful for the food you waste."

"Well send my spaghetti to them, then. And stop making out that you care about them more than me. You didn't even buy the Band Aid single."

Mum stood up again.

"Listen, Claire, I haven't got time for this nonsense. I'm trying to cook a proper meal as well as sort you out. Do you want spaghetti or not?"

"No. I told you, I'm not hungry."

"Fine. Well I'll be in the kitchen. You're staying up here, are you? Only I've got a friend coming round later."

"OK."

"And I don't want to be disturbed."

"I'm staying up here. Just leave me alone, will you?"

Mum walked silently out of the room. I lay there brooding for the rest of the evening, until it was time for *Match of the Day*. Part of me couldn't bear the thought of seeing Andy in pain but another part of me felt a duty to be there for him, to share in his suffering.

I crept downstairs to the kitchen and stuffed a couple of digestive biscuits into my mouth, not wanting Mum to see that I was hungry after all. Still wiping the crumbs from my lips, I stood for a moment outside the living room door. I couldn't hear any voices so presumed her friend must have gone home. He hadn't though.

I walked in to find Mum sitting on the sofa next to a tall man with a moustache who had his arm draped around her shoulder. For a second I thought it was happening all over again. I was about to run from the room and dash full pelt down the road, to fling myself into my mother's arms, when I remembered that I couldn't do that. Because this time Mum was the one on the sofa.

"Who's he?"

"Oh, er, Claire." Mum's face was flushed. "This is my friend Malcolm. Malcolm, this is my daughter, Claire.

Malcolm looked decidedly awkward about the introductions and immediately withdrew his arm from Mum's shoulder.

"What's he doing here?"

"Honestly, have you no manners at all? Malcolm's here because I asked him round to dinner."

"You never said."

"I did, love." Mum was smiling one of those fake smiles. "I told you earlier I had a friend coming round."

"You didn't tell me it was a man though."

"For goodness' sake, does it make any difference?"

"Yes, it does. You don't normally have men round."

Mum turned to Malcolm. "I'm so sorry about this."

"It's OK. Maybe I should leave."

"No, please, there's no need for that. Claire's going back to her room now, aren't you?"

"But I want to watch *Match of the Day*."

"Well I'm sorry, you'll have to miss it for once. It won't kill you."

"That's not fair."

"I don't mind watching the football," said Malcolm, obviously trying his best to be accommodating. I eyed him suspiciously. I didn't like the shirt he had on. Or the way that he'd made himself so at home on the sofa. In fact I didn't like anything about him at all.

"It's OK, I know when I'm not wanted."

"Claire, please don't be like that."

But I was already heading for the door. I stopped to listen once I had slammed it behind me.

"I am so sorry about that. She's at an awkward age at the moment. To be honest, she's been at an awkward age for most of her life."

I heard Malcolm and my mother laugh. Both of them, together. Laughing at me. Laura Ashley was laughing too. I ran upstairs to my room and sat on the bed with my hands over my ears.

It was no good though. I could still hear the laughter. I took my Walkman from the bedside table, fitted the headphones snugly over my ears, and pressed the rewind button. I counted the seconds out in my head as the tape rewound, knowing exactly how long it took now. And sure enough when I pressed the play button Andy was there.

"Well, obviously, it was a great thrill for me to play for England. I didn't expect it at the beginning of the season but I'm determined to seize my chance . . ."

I knew the words off by heart now, I had replayed the radio interview so often. But I still loved listening to it, hearing Andy's voice so close to me. I shut my eyes, automatically hitting the rewind button every time the interview came to an end. When I finally drifted off to sleep, it was with Andy talking to me, whispering sweet nothings into my ear.

CHAPTER
NINE

"The thing I don't get, Kaz," I said, turning to the young skinny woman sitting across the table from me twiddling her hair, "is why you not only made no attempt to avoid the security cameras but seem to be positively smiling into them at one point."

Kaz shrugged and looked away. She was one of my regulars who I found particularly hard work. She had a drug habit, cocaine mainly, and a penchant for shoplifting. She was in this whole revolving-door thing of being in and out of prison on a frequent basis. From what I could gather her life was pretty chaotic; boyfriends coming and going, hassle from her family, moving about all the time. She was also rather uncommunicative, which wasn't a great help when I was trying to dig her out of holes she had got herself into.

"Kaz?"

"You never know, do you? Might get talent-spotted, like, if you're looking your best. For some modelling agency or a reality TV show."

"I don't think talent scouts tend to monitor CCTV pictures."

"Well, all sorts of stuff gets on to the internet. It could end up on YouTube. So I thought I'd do my hair and make-up and give it a go, like."

I shook my head. I didn't actually buy it. Despite her best efforts to appear otherwise, Kaz was a bright girl. Not academically so, but street-savvy and sharp. She certainly wasn't stupid. So I couldn't work out why she was pretending to be. I decided it was time to try to get to the bottom of it.

"How do you think that will go down in court, Kaz? Do you think it'll make you look good? Give the right impression?"

"Yeah, I think it'll give them a laugh."

"Or more likely send you back to prison."

"Good," she muttered.

"What did you say?"

"You heard me."

"You want to go to prison?" She shrugged and stared up at the ceiling. I could see her bottom lip trembling. "Why, Kaz?" I asked, my voice softening.

"If you must know, it's because it's better than my fucking life outside." She bit her lip, struggling to maintain the hard-girl act now she'd opened up.

I blew out and shook my head. It was a humbling thing to hear. I didn't want to believe that anyone's life could be worse outside than in jail. And I knew it wasn't because prison was cushy. I'd been to the women's establishment Kaz usually ended up at and it certainly didn't strike me as pleasant.

"So you got caught on camera on purpose, to go back inside?"

"Yeah. Seemed like the best option at the time. If I go in for a decent stretch I get help, see, with trying to come off. So I thought if I piss them off by smiling and laughing at the cameras it might even get in the papers and then they'd have to make an example of me."

"Are things really that bad?" I asked.

Kaz nodded and bit her lip again.

"Tell me," I said. "Tell me about all the crap in your life."

"Why, so you can have a good laugh?"

"No, Kaz, so I can help."

"Why would you wanna help me?"

"Because you're a fellow human being and no one should have to try to get sent to prison for a better life."

The dam wall burst and Kaz started to sob. I wanted to give her a hug but was worried she'd take it the wrong way, think I was pitying her. I delved into my bag and handed her a couple of tissues.

"Take your time," I said. "I've got all the time in the world."

She blew her nose, took a deep breath and started to talk. I listened intently, scribbling notes down as she spoke. She owed money. Lots of it. Her dealer was after her. Had threatened her. Suggested she could pay it off by letting him be her pimp. Her boyfriend was a user too. Stole off her, what little she had, and went missing for days on end. She suspected he was screwing around. She felt like a prostitute anyway when he turned up. That was all he used her for. Although instead of paying her, he took from her instead. She owed rent on her council flat. Had been threatened

283

with eviction. And she spent every minute of every day worrying about where she was going to get her next fix from. And how the hell she was going to pay for it. Apart from that, it seemed, everything was hunky-dory.

"OK," I said. "I'm going to go for an adjournment."

Kaz rolled her eyes.

"I'll be out on bail, won't I?"

"Not if I ask them to remand you."

"Can you do that?"

"I can try. I can say there's a risk of you absconding if you're bailed due to your chaotic lifestyle."

"And then what?"

"I'm going to try and get you a rehab place. Residential. Somewhere out of the area."

"There aren't any. That's what they always tell me."

"I'll be a pain in the arse then. Keep knocking on doors and hassling people until they get sick of me."

Kaz gave the faintest glimmer of a smile.

"Thanks," she said in a voice which was barely audible. "I still don't know why you're bothering for me."

"What is it that Jennifer Aniston says, in those adverts for the shampoo you keep nicking?"

"Because you're worth it." Kaz grinned.

"There you go then."

As soon as I got home I checked my e-mails. Emily managed to send one most days — even if it was just a quick one-liner. But it had been three days now since I'd heard from her. I'd texted Frankie to ask if everything was OK. Not OK in the normal meaning of the word, but rather a euphemistic way of checking Emily was at least still alive. The reply had come late at night. Frankie was staying with Emily in hospital while she underwent a particularly gruelling round of chemo. It was all taking its toll now. The sickness, the nausea, the constant stream of injections and blood tests. Emily was struggling to remain positive. And it was breaking Frankie's heart to watch her go through it all.

I felt so helpless being up in Yorkshire. I'd offered to go down the weekends I wasn't working to help out, but Frankie had been adamant that they could cope. Especially as Joe's family were doing a sterling job of looking after the younger children.

I was relieved to find something in my inbox. I opened up the message.

Hiya, Claire. It's OK. I am still here. Just had a really crappy few days spewing up and having loads of blood tests. Been like something out of a vampire movie — except without Robert, of course. I'm glad he can't see me at the moment, mind. I look like a right minger. Alia's gonna get me a Halloween witch's wig with long black hair — in case I need it for the premiere. Not that I'm robsessed you understand!
L8ers.
Emily Pattinson (I wish!)

I smiled as I read it. It was her optimism which always got to me. That and her failure to complain about what she was going through. To do the whole "why me?" bit. Maybe she did it inside her head. Or when she was talking to Robert. The way I used to do with Andy.

I looked at myself in the full-length bedroom mirror the next morning. What was good enough for Rochdale Magistrates' Court might not be good enough for Smith MacGuire in Manchester. I'd invested in a new pair of shoes for the occasion, but the suit still seemed to say "Rochdale" to me. Maybe I should have followed Mark's example and gone shopping in King Street for something new. It'd have to do for now though. The train was due in twenty minutes. I had an interview to go to.

I stood on the platform at Todmorden wondering why so many significant moments in my life involved railway stations. Maybe it was something to do with the sense that everyone else was moving on. That if I didn't jump on board a train to somewhere I'd get left behind.

The Manchester train pulled in, only a few minutes late. I found myself a window seat in a quiet part of the carriage. It was so much more pleasant travelling by train mid-morning rather than in the rush hour. I got a notebook out of my briefcase and re-read my questions and the answers I could give to theirs. Or what I thought theirs might be, at least. It was a long time since I'd been for an interview. I suspected I lacked the sharp edge of the type of go-getting career lawyers who probably clocked up several interviews a year. I knew the interview panel would probably ask me why I'd stayed in my present job so long. And I wasn't sure what to say. Loyalty didn't seem to be a desirable quality in an applicant any more. Only ambition.

By the time the train pulled into Victoria station I was convinced they'd only granted me an interview due to some bizarre quota system. Maybe they didn't have enough stuck-in-a-rut lawyers on the duty solicitor rota. I decided not to bother with the tram and walk instead. It was one of those beautiful crisp autumn mornings with the sun hanging low in the sky. Manchester bustled on around me: mums with runny-nosed kids in buggies, students hanging out because they had nothing better to do and no money to spend, and an army of grey shoppers intent on bagging some bargains while the younger, fitter crowd were at work. I cut through St Ann's Square, past the ever-hopeful buskers, who were definitely of a much higher quality than those in Rochdale. I could get used to this, I thought. An altogether more pleasant place to work (and shop if I happened to get the odd lunch hour).

I turned the corner into John Dalton Street. Smith MacGuire's offices loomed large in front of me, the imposing frontage doing nothing to quell my nerves. I opened the heavy glass door, walked up to the reception desk and stated my name and business.

"Lift B, third floor," the receptionist answered robotically as she slipped my name into a visitor's pass and handed it to me. "Please wear at all times and return before leaving." I was tempted to ask what the penalty was for not returning the pass and whether I'd require legal representation if I forgot but thought better of it. As far as I could remember, most people who worked for corporate law firms had undergone humour by-pass operations.

When I got out of the lift there was another reception desk, someone else to announce my arrival to.

"They're running slightly late," said the receptionist, "and you are early." Her tone suggested this was almost as big a crime as being late. "Please do take a seat while you wait."

I glanced around me at the swish waiting area with leather-upholstered seats and a water cooler. I decided to go to the toilet first to reduce the amount of time I would have to sit there pretending to be interested in glossy lifestyle magazines.

I followed the sign for the toilets to the end of the corridor. There were two doors, one with a picture of Barbie on and the other with Ken. Maybe someone here did have a sense of humour after all. I pushed the Barbie door and went through into a huge room, all black and steel with mirrored walls (someone had at least had the good sense to draw the line at a mirrored ceiling). I went through to a cubicle and shut the door. On the back was a sign saying "Are You Dehydrated?", below which was a colour chart depicting different shades of urine and the relevant medical assessment from "Optimum health" through "You need to drink at least two litres of water a day" down to "Seek an urgent medical assessment". My anxiety levels, which were already high, shot through the roof as I sat and peed, wondering if this was all part of the interview process and some machine was secretly extracting a sample from the toilet bowl which was to be shown to the interview panel for assessment before I even entered the room.

Flustered, I turned to flush, only to be greeted by a sign reading "Which level of flush do you require?" over two buttons, one marked "Two litres" and the other "Four litres". I was panicking now; the simple act of relieving myself had turned into some type of aptitude test. I had no idea how much water a normal flush contained but pressed "two", suspecting the "four" button would have triggered a black mark on my card for failing to conserve water. I walked over to the long trough-like washbasins, but as I finally worked out which of the several taps and dispensers contained the soap, a pair of large hairy hands appeared from the other side of the trough. I gasped and jumped back, fearing a spy for the interview panel was about to arrest me on suspicion of crimes related to personal hygiene.

"It's all right," said a male voice from behind the mirrors. "Just takes a bit of getting used to." It was only then I realised that this was where the Kens and Barbies came together on either side of the troughs to wash their hands. It reminded me of the communal toilets in *Ally McBeal*, which would have been enough to put me off working at Cage, Fish and Associates, despite the appeal of regular song-and-dance routines to break up the working day.

I dried my hands quickly and hurried back to the reception area, checking before I sat down in case the chair had a sign about optimum weight for height ratios and advice on a calorie reduction and exercise programme.

By the time I was called into the interview room, I was convinced Big Brother had been watching me and I was about to be voted off at any moment. The chair of the panel introduced himself as Ryan Kellerman, the MD. I recognised his voice instantly, and one glance down at his hirsute hands confirmed the worst. He was washbasin man. And I was dead in the water. He was flanked by two colleagues, a younger woman who looked unnervingly like the Barbie picture on the toilets and an older man with sophisticated streaks of silver in his hair. Kellerman started outlining Smith MacGuire's "raison d'être", using phrases such as "expanding corporate capabilities" and "streamlining management systems". He was so smooth I was surprised his clothes didn't simply slide off him. His first question to me was the obvious one.

"So, Claire, you work out of Rochdale Magistrates' Court, where you've been for, now let me see, yes, seven years. It must be interesting work, dealing with some rather difficult clients, I imagine. So what experience and qualities could you bring to Smith MacGuire?"

I was sorely tempted to shout, "Piss off, you patronising bastard" and leave the room. But I didn't want to give him the satisfaction. It was quite clear that what he was actually saying was "Why does a jumped-up duty solicitor from lowly Rochdale think she can make any sort of valid contribution to a slick, swanky corporate set-up?" So that was the question I decided to answer.

"Well, I said. "One of my clients yesterday was a low-life cocaine addict from a sink estate with an attitude problem and not a hope in hell of getting off." The Barbie woman exchanged anxious glances with Kellerman. "But I talked to her, tried to get under her skin. Found out what had prompted her to do it, what she wanted and how I could help her achieve it. She left me with a smile on her face and a belief that I could make a difference. I'm sure as a top-ranking corporate company you understand that you can't put a price on that sort of client satisfaction."

The Barbie woman raised an eyebrow, the silver-haired man nodded; even Kellerman was silenced for a moment. And I sat there, ready for the next question and trying not to think about what would happen to Kaz if I wasn't there.

"So, how did it go?" asked Mark when he arrived at my house after work.

"You were right," I said, giving him a kiss before letting him in. "They were a bunch of suits up their own arses."

Mark laughed. "I hope you gave as good as you got then."

"I think I did. Which means it could go either way. They'll either tell me where to go or be impressed by the fact that I put up a bit of a fight."

"But would you want to work for them if you did get offered the job?"

"I don't know," I said, sitting down at the kitchen table. "The money's good, career prospects excellent, very swanky offices."

"But you're Claire Cooper."

"What do you mean by that?"

"None of those things matter to you. You care about real things, real people. You always have."

"Some of the work would be useful, the employment rights stuff."

"You'd miss your clients, though. You know you would. You might complain about them sometimes but I've seen you when you've come home after getting someone off who the police had been trying to fit up. You're buzzing with it. That's what job satisfaction is for you."

I shrugged. He had a point. But this wasn't about what I enjoyed doing. It was about what I was capable of doing, what I should be doing.

"This is all about your list, isn't it?"

"I just think it's time I moved on."

"You're feeling you haven't fulfilled your destiny."

"I want to know if I can do it."

"It's getting in the way, Claire."

"What is?"

"This obsession with the way you wanted your life to be."

"It's not an obsession."

"It feels like it to me. You need to break it. Confront it head on and decide exactly what it is you want from your life."

I was taken aback by Mark's comments. He wasn't usually this perceptive. Or this assertive, come to that.

"And how am I supposed to do that?"

"You can start with this." He reached into his pocket, pulled out a folded piece of white paper and put it on the kitchen table.

"What's that?"

"Andy Pailes's address."

I stared at him, my eyes bulging, my lower jaw almost hitting the table.

"I don't understand."

"I want you to go and see him."

"Why?"

"To put the whole thing to rest. To see if that life you wanted for yourself is better than the one you've got."

"I've told you, he wasn't that important. I want you."

"And I've known you long enough to know when you're lying. I don't want to be second best, Claire. Someone you've settled for because you can't have the person you really want."

I shook my head, unsure how to react. Aware that it was the biggest gesture anyone had ever made to me. And that Mark was doing an incredibly brave thing.

"You don't have to do this."

"I know. But I want to. I want to get you back. Despite what you say, I don't feel you're with me at the moment, and I don't think you will be until you put this whole thing to rest. And the only way to do that is to go and see him."

"But that's a crazy thing to do."

"I'm hoping he'll be fat and bald and you'll wonder what you ever saw in him and come running back to me."

I smiled. The whole thing still felt surreal. I looked down at the piece of paper lying there between us.

"How did you get it?" I asked.

"A little bit of detective work. It wasn't hard. I had enough clues to go on from the United website."

I nodded. He knew more about Andy than I did. At least about what he was doing now, where he was. I wanted to know but still didn't feel it was right to ask or pick up the piece of paper. It would feel disloyal to Mark. Even though he had offered it to me on a plate.

"It might not be a good idea to go. I don't really want to rake up the past."

"It's not raking up the past, it's putting it to rest so you can concentrate on your future."

It was easy for Mark to say. He had no idea about what lay beneath if I disturbed the surface. And once I had, I might not be able to put things back how they were. Because I was scared that if I so much as caught a glimpse of him, I might lose control. Like I had done before.

"I'm asking you to do it for me," said Mark. "I'm prepared to live with the consequences, whatever happens. You have my permission. I want you to go and see him. What you do after that is up to you."

He got up from his chair, kissed me on the top of the head and walked out of the door. I sat looking at the piece of paper for a long time before I picked it up and unfolded it. When I did, I caught my breath as I read the address. All this time. And he was so close. Close enough now to be able to touch.

Monday, 7 April 1986

I peered down anxiously at the scuffmarks on the heel of my shoe and the metal rod poking through underneath where the plastic cap had come off. It hadn't mattered until I had arrived at court and noticed that all the sophisticated, professional women who hurried by, bulging briefcases at their sides, had immaculate shoes. Not a mark on them. I worried that mine were betraying my efforts to fit in, declaring to the world that the feet inside did not belong to a well-heeled lawyer but to a schoolgirl whose mother had said, "What do you need a new pair for? There's nothing wrong with the ones you've got."

It was a shame, because in all other respects I had brushed up fairly well. The neat black suit (which even had a proper lining) looked particularly impressive. The lady in the shop had said so when I'd tried it on. Even Mum had been forced to agree, saying it was classic and versatile and would come in handy for funerals. Quite whose funeral she'd had in mind, I hadn't liked to ask.

My hair was swept back off my face in a businesslike fashion, my make-up application skills had improved no end (I now understood that streaks of burnt-orange blusher applied liberally to my cheeks only succeeded in making me look like a fading new-romantic pop star), my teeth were almost straightened and were brace-free for the occasion and if I squeezed my shoulders in a bit you could even see a hint of cleavage.

It was quite ironic really. That at the point a few weeks past my sixteenth birthday where everything on the outside was finally coming together, inside everything was falling apart. Only my shoes gave the game away, affording a glimpse of the mess going on inside if you peeled back the outer layer.

"Miss Skidmore?"

I scrambled to my feet and grasped the outstretched hand of the tall, efficient-looking woman standing before me.

"Yes, that's me."

"I'm Miss Jenkins from the Crown Prosecution Service. You'll be shadowing me for the next week while you're with us. Now, if you'll come with me, I'd like to show you round the courtroom before the magistrates arrive."

I nodded and trotted obediently after Miss Jenkins, who had set off across the foyer before she'd even finished speaking. It was the smell of Court One that struck me first. Slightly musty, with an underlying aroma of leather-bound books and a hint of floor polish. The sort of smell that made you whisper without realising it. I marvelled at the austere surroundings, the oak-panelled walls, the coat of arms, the imposing magistrates' bench. I could start afresh here, be anyone I wanted to be. Could stop being Claire Skidmore, the lonely misfit who wandered the school corridors in constant fear of being noticed, and become Claire Skidmore, budding lawyer with the world at her feet. All I needed was the shoulder pads. And the shoes, of course.

The court rose as the magistrates entered the room. I followed Miss Jenkins's example and bowed my head solemnly before sitting again. The clerk called the first defendant and a timid-looking woman clutching a Superdrug carrier bag shuffled into the courtroom to face a charge of shoplifting eight pounds' worth of toiletries from Superdrug. I wondered if she had brought the carrier bag with her to prove that she did usually pay for her shopping. I smiled supportively at the woman. Miss Jenkins showed no such mercy.

The morning passed in a whirl of adjournments, fines and stiff sentences; the chairman of the bench sternly telling a succession of defendants that they were a burden upon society.

"Finding it interesting?" asked Miss Jenkins when we broke for lunch.

"Oh, definitely. You can't help feeling sorry for some of them, can you? He seems a bit mean."

"Well, it is a magistrates' court, not a holiday camp. There's no room for sentiment."

"No, of course not. I'm sure you're right."

"Good. Well, you go and grab something to eat and meet me back here at one fifty sharp."

For once, I didn't mind eating on my own. Real lawyers would never bring a bright orange lunchbox bearing the slogan "Chill Out" to court — I was quite sure of that. I sat on a bench outside the court building, munching my sandwiches and idly day dreaming about trying Maggie Thatcher for crimes against humanity.

"Are we ready for action then?"

Miss Jenkins was standing in front of me, with a shorter, jolly-looking man at her side. I slid my lunchbox discreetly behind me.

"Er, yes. Of course. I'm coming now."

Miss Jenkins's lunch companion followed us into the courtroom.

"Hi, I'm Gary Hurst, defence solicitor," he informed me as we settled into our places. "You'll have some company this afternoon. I've got someone shadowing me as well. You never know, you might even recognise him."

Before I could work out the reason for his cryptic comment, the door opened and Andy walked in, still limping heavily following his injury. The first thing that came into my head was that it was a late April Fool's joke. I was convinced the magistrate would walk in and reveal himself as Jeremy Beadle from *Game for a Laugh* at any second. But when I saw the equally surprised look on Andy's face, I realised that it wasn't a set-up at all.

"Andy, this is Miss Skidmore," said Mr Hurst. "She's going to be with the CPS this week."

"Pleased to meet you," said Andy with a mischievous grin on his face as he reached out to shake my hand. "You do look very familiar; are you sure we haven't met somewhere before?"

I had to stifle a giggle as the magistrates came back in and we all stood to attention.

"What are you doing here?" I whispered to Andy.

"I met Gary through the Open University. After I got injured I asked if I could shadow him one afternoon a week. Give me something useful to do while I'm out of action. What about you, is this your first day?"

"Yeah, I'm with her," I said, pointing to Miss Jenkins. "She's dead good but a bit mean. I think your Mr Hurst fancies her."

Andy raised his eyebrows and smiled. I noticed him look me up and down again.

"Nice suit," he said as he settled down next to me on the wooden bench. "You really look the part."

"Thanks," I said, positively glowing. "Sixteenth birthday present. I think I'll try for the briefcase for Christmas."

Andy stared hard at me, then broke into a smile, nodding to himself as if he'd finally solved the last clue in a particularly difficult crossword puzzle. I looked down and noticed his ankle was still bandaged. You could see the bulge under his sock.

The steady stream of defendants came and went in a blur. It was impossible to concentrate on the cases with Andy sitting there, inches away from me. Within touching distance but still out of bounds. I wondered if he could sense the atmosphere. It didn't feel like a one-way thing, though after what had happened at Christmas I couldn't be sure. But I did know he'd looked differently at me just now. Like he was seeing me through new eyes. It was as if Annie didn't exist in the courtroom. As if there was no one in the world apart from me and Andy.

"Any questions?" Miss Jenkins asked as she packed away her briefcase at the end of the afternoon.

"Er no, I don't think so. It all seemed pretty clear."

"Good, I'll see you tomorrow. Nine thirty prompt," she said before dashing off with Mr Hurst in hot pursuit.

Andy flashed a smile at me.

"So, how are you? How's it all going?"

I knew I couldn't possibly tell him the truth. I didn't see how I could explain how bad everything was. Not without mentioning Annie. And I didn't want to even say her name in case it broke the spell.

"Fine thanks," I said, deciding to swiftly change the subject. "What about you? How's your ankle? Are you gonna be fit for the Milk Cup Final?"

"Well, it's touch and go, but the physio thinks I'll make it."

"Really? That's fantastic. I can't wait. I've never seen us play at Wembley."

"Are you going?" he asked.

"No, couldn't get tickets. I'll watch it on telly, though. And I'll be shouting so loudly you'll be able to hear me at Wembley."

"I'd better play well then, if I've got you to answer to."

"Too right you had. A good performance should book your place in the World Cup squad."

"God, you've got it all worked out, haven't you? I wish I could be as confident as you are."

"What do you mean? Robson's bound to pick you, especially after the way you played last time."

"Tell you what, if I do get picked, I'll take you on as my agent."

"Great. I'm available from the end of June, soon as I've done my history O level."

"Right you are then, that's sorted," he said, grinning.

"Can you clear the courtroom now please, ladies and gents," the usher called.

I looked around the empty room and realised he must mean us. "Ladies" he'd said. I'd never been called a lady before. We made our way to the door, Andy holding it open for me. Like I really was a lady.

"How are you getting home?" he asked.

"I'll get the train. It doesn't take too long."

"Don't be daft. You live near the training ground, don't you?"

"Yeah, about a mile away."

"That's settled then, I'll give you a lift. As long as you don't mind me stopping off at the club on the way. I need to pick some post up."

"No, that's fine. If you're sure it's no trouble."

"It will be a pleasure," he said. "Come on."

I followed him out of the courtroom in a daze, praying that I wouldn't revert to my schoolgirl self the second I stepped outside the building.

"I'm sure that last defendant recognised me," Andy said as we walked together to the car park. "I thought for a moment he was going to ask for my autograph."

"I know, I don't think he could believe it. It could have been worse, mind. If he'd been an Arsenal fan he'd probably have tried to thump you."

Andy laughed as he unlocked the passenger door and held it open for me.

"All I need now is for one of our lads to come up for drink-driving while I'm there. Then I would be rumbled."

"The others don't know about you doing this then?"

"No," he said as we set off. "They wouldn't understand. I'd get some serious stick from them. You know what it's like."

I wondered how he knew that I got lots of stick too. It was as if he understood everything without me even having to tell him.

"Don't you get sick of them having a go at you all the time, just because you're a bit different?" I asked.

"I usually try and ignore it. Part and parcel of the game, that's what the gaffer would say. A bit of banter never hurt anyone."

"It does though, doesn't it?"

"Yeah," he said after a second. "Sometimes it does."

I smiled warmly and found myself reaching out to touch his hand, giving it a reassuring squeeze as we waited at the traffic lights.

Andy turned to look at me. I pulled my hand back. Neither of us said a word.

The lights turned to green and the car behind beeped its horn, cutting the silence in two. Andy dropped the handbrake and moved off.

The silence continued until we came within sight of Priory Park.

"You must miss having Thomo around," I said.

302

"Yeah, it's not the same without him. It was only him and Skip I could really talk to, to be honest."

"How's his wife?"

"Not too bad. She's still having chemotherapy; they think she's responding to it, but it's too early to say for sure."

"I was so upset when I heard. I didn't think it happened to people her age."

"Well it does. And it always happens to the good ones, people like Sarah. Thomo loves her so much, you know. I mean really loves her, not just . . ." His voice trailed off.

"It must be so scary for him," I said. "I don't know how I'd cope if something like that happened to someone I loved."

I could only think of one person I loved. I was sitting next to him.

"It's not easy," said Andy, pausing for a second. "My mum died of breast cancer when I was twelve."

"Oh God, I'm sorry, I'd no idea."

"That's OK, you weren't to know. I haven't told many people about it."

"Were you close, you and your mum?"

"Yeah, we were. Very close. She was lovely."

I tried to picture Andy's mum in my mind. I saw her with soft dark hair and warm rosy cheeks. The sort of mum who made big apple pies with lots of sugar sprinkled on top, not Tuscan pâté vol-au-vents.

"I bet she was. I bet she would have been very proud of you as well."

Andy smiled at me.

"I hope so," he said.

I wondered exactly how many other people Andy had told about his mum. Whether "not many" meant two, or twenty. I hoped it was more like two.

A few minutes later we were driving through the main gates at Priory Park, the security man nodding to Andy as he raised the barrier. It felt like he was nodding to me too. That I was part of it all. Part of Andy.

"Do you want to come in with me?" he asked. "You can wait here if you'd rather, it's up to you."

"I'll come in, if you're sure it's OK."

"Course it is. I don't think even Roy Brown charges for entry on non-match days."

"What's he like, Brown? Is he as bad as he comes over on telly?"

"Worse. I can't stand him. He's like something out of the dark ages, full of all this 'traditional family values' crap he's heading up for the Tories at moment."

"Does he have a lot of say, though, about the football side of things?"

"Most of the time he leaves it all to Ken. But every now and again he sticks his oar in, just to prove who's in charge."

Andy broke off as he held the glass door open and I slipped inside. The receptionist looked up, smiled at Andy and stared at me. The security man next to her followed my progress across the foyer. I felt like the mystery girl on the arm of someone famous in those Sunday magazine photographs. Everyone wondering who I was and what I was doing with him. I was so relieved I was wearing my little black suit and not my school uniform.

I looked up and caught Andy grinning at me.

"What?" I said.

"Just you. Turning heads without even realising it."

I hadn't imagined it this time. He was flirting with me. Andy Pailes was actually coming on to me. I floated up a flight of stairs and along a corridor, trying not to let the grin slip any further across my face. Andy paused in front of a panelled door and turned to me.

"Fancy a quick look at the UEFA Cup? Could be your last chance; it goes back in a few weeks."

I nodded, not needing convincing. Andy reached out and took my hand, his fingers curling around mine. It was like one of those science experiments at school, where the static electricity makes your hair stand on end. Only this wasn't some poxy physics lesson. It was me and Andy getting together. Like I always knew we would. My heart was in danger of overheating it was beating so fast as he led me into the room and I caught sight of the huge silver trophy which took pride of place in the long glass cabinet. He seemed to like it. Seeing my reaction. Making all my dreams come true. I looked down. He still had hold of my hand. I squeezed it to make sure it was real. He squeezed back.

"Let's get you a closer look," he said, disappearing for a minute before returning with a security man, who unlocked the cabinet.

"Cheers, Ted."

"No problem. Just give us a shout when you're done," he said, jingling the keys in his hand as he shut the door behind him.

Andy lifted the UEFA Cup up and passed it to me, laughing out loud as I buckled under the weight.

"Heavier than you thought, eh? Here, let me give you a hand." He moved closer to me, supporting the base.

His left hand touching mine. I could see our elongated reflections on the side of the cup, blurring into one.

"Can I kiss it?" I said.

"Sure, go on."

I turned my head sideways and kissed the cup, the shiny surface cold against my lips.

"My turn," said Andy.

"Haven't you kissed it already?"

"No," he said. "Never."

Andy leant over and kissed me. Right on the lips. They fizzed for a second like I'd just taken a mouthful of moon dust. He tasted so good, better than anything I'd ever tasted in my life. I let the sweetness seep into me, trickling down my throat like lemon and honey, soothing everything inside. Kissing it better. I couldn't take it in. Andy Pailes had just kissed me. For real, not in my head. My whole body had gone limp. If Andy hadn't been holding the cup as well, I would have dropped it.

"Did you like that?" he asked. I nodded, still unable to speak.

"Let's put this down," he said, taking the cup from me and placing it back in the cabinet. He turned round to face me. He had a look in his eyes, like he was possessed or something. No one had ever looked at me that way before. I took a step backwards, unsure what was coming next. My stomach was churning like a cement mixer. It was all happening so fast, and I wasn't sure where it was leading. I realised I'd never stopped to think about that. All the times I'd imagined our first kiss, it had always gone on for ever. Now it had happened for real. It had been and gone. We were on to the next bit. Something I hadn't dared think about in my dreams.

He moved towards me, his body colliding with mine and the momentum carrying me backwards until I hit the wall. He was kissing me hard, his chin like sandpaper, the rough edges scratching my skin. I didn't mind though. Not really. His hands were all over me, squeezing and rubbing, moulding me into shape. I could feel his thighs pressed against mine, his pelvis pushing into me. Like he couldn't get close enough. And I was gone, completely gone. Andy Pailes was doing this. Not to anyone else. To me.

"What about your girlfriend?" I said, when we broke for a second to breathe.

"I haven't got a girlfriend," he said. "Not any more."

It was like someone had turned off the hurt inside. Pulled the plug and let it all drain away. He had dumped Annie. For me. A huge smile spread across my face and we started kissing again. More frantic even than before. My arms were locked around him. My clothes sticking to me. The back of Andy's shirt was damp with sweat.

"I've got a confession to make," he whispered. "I'm getting turned on." Before I could say anything he unzipped his fly and slid my hand down. "Take hold of it," he said.

I didn't look down, just did as I was told. Taking hold of his prick, wishing I knew what to do with it. He put his hand over mine and started moving it up and down.

"Like this," he said. "That feels good."

I carried on. My fingers sliding over the ridges, feeling him getting harder. Hearing him groaning in my ear. Praying he was enjoying it as much as he seemed to be.

"Use your mouth," he said.

I wasn't sure what he meant for a second, until I felt his hand on my shoulder, pushing me down towards the floor.

"What if someone comes in?"

"They won't," he said. "Trust me."

I did trust him. I'd have done anything he asked. Anything to please him. I sank down on to my knees. I'd never seen a man's prick before. Not even on TV. I felt embarrassed just looking at it. I didn't dare look up and remind myself who it belonged to.

"Go on," he said. "Make me come."

I closed my eyes and took a deep breath before taking it in my mouth, trying to remember anything I knew about blow jobs. All I could think of was a girl at school mucking about with a cucumber in cookery, saying she was sucking it off. My lips closed around him and I started moving up and down, trying not to catch him with my teeth. I felt like I was going to suffocate; there was no room to breathe. Right at the point where I thought I might pass out, he came, warm

308

slimy liquid spurting into my mouth. It tasted disgusting, and I worried I was going to gag. I needed air. I did the only thing I could think of. I swallowed. The taste was still there afterwards. Like a medicine you couldn't get rid of. But at least I could breathe.

I leant back against the wall and discreetly wiped my mouth with the back of my hand. I didn't know where to look. The UEFA Cup was in the cabinet only a few feet away. It was all so weird. Ten minutes ago we'd never even held hands. Now I'd had his prick in my mouth. It was like I'd gone to the fair to go on the carousel and ended up being spun on the waltzer.

Andy did himself up and pulled me up towards him. He looked knackered, like he'd just finished extra time in a football match. He kissed me on the lips. I hoped he didn't mind the taste.

"Come on," he said. "We'd better get out of here. Ted'll be wondering what we're up to."

I didn't want to go. I wanted to stay and talk. To find out how long he'd felt like this. What it was that had made him fall in love with me. But I barely had time to tuck my blouse in and straighten my skirt before Andy ushered me along the corridor.

"I need to pop in here," I said as we came to a ladies' toilet.

"OK," said Andy. "I'll go and find Ted. I'll meet you back here in a couple of minutes."

I closed the door, grateful for a moment of privacy, and slid a pubic hair from my tongue. I held it up to the light, unsure what to do with it. The Claire who kept an Andy Pailes scrapbook would have saved it, framed it perhaps. The Claire who'd just given Andy Pailes a blow job dropped it in the bin. I had him for real now. I didn't need mementoes.

Andy was waiting for me outside. He didn't say anything. Just led me up the corridor to the post room. I stood in the doorway as he went in.

"Now then, Andy. You'll be getting as many as our Matt soon," the post lady chuckled, handing him a large bundle of letters before turning to me. "He's ever so popular, you know, your fella here. I hope you don't get jealous of all this."

I blushed and looked at my feet.

"Oh no, it's nothing like that," Andy said quickly. "Claire's just a friend."

The words tore at me like a knife in the back. I looked at Andy to see if he was joking but he wasn't. I didn't understand what was going on. It was as if he was embarrassed about what had just happened. Which was weird because he hadn't seemed embarrassed at the time. And half an hour ago he'd loved all the attention I was getting. I'd felt like he was showing me off as we'd walked in. But now it was like I had shown him up and he couldn't get me out of there quick enough.

He ushered me back along the corridor, down the stairs and out the main doors without a word. We got to the car park just as Clubber arrived.

"Weh-hey. School outing is it, Trotsky? Has she brought her lunchbox? Or are you providing that?"

"Leave it out, Clubber." Andy looked flustered.

310

"What's the matter? Can't she come out to play tonight? Annie's gonna love this. You taking up with a groupie. Wait till I tell her."

"I said drop it."

"Bit touchy today, aren't we? Must have a guilty conscience."

Andy glared at him as he walked past but said nothing more.

"I'm sorry about that," he said as we got into the car. I wasn't sure which bit of it all he was apologising for. The confusion must have shown on my face. "Clubber. He's a complete prat. Just ignore him."

"It's OK," I said. "It doesn't matter."

It did though. It mattered that Clubber had called me a groupie and that Andy didn't want to be seen in public with me. I wondered if my blow job had been crap. Or if he'd been lying about Annie and had a guilty conscience.

"Why did Clubber say he was going to tell Annie?" I said as we set off. "You said you're not going out with her any more."

"I'm not," Andy said. "But he is."

Neither of us said much on the way home. I wondered if Andy minded about Annie going out with Clubber. It must be weird, your ex going out with one of your teammates. I hadn't expected things to be this complicated. It was making my head hurt just thinking about it. Andy dropped me off on the corner of my road. I wanted to ask when I could see him again, but the look on his face stopped me. He seemed to be pissed off with me already. I didn't want to make things any worse.

"Bye then," I said.

"Yeah," he said. "See you around."

That was it. That was all he said. He didn't even ask for my phone number. It was as if the whole thing had been no big deal. But it had. It had been to me.

I walked down the road, the taste still lingering in my mouth. I felt like crying, which was stupid. This should have been the best day of my life. I tried to remember that first kiss, how good it had felt. But all I could think about was what had happened afterwards. I felt different. More grown up. I wondered if other people could see it, if my mum would be able to tell what I'd been up to as soon as she opened the door. And whether she'd be able to smell the evidence on my breath.

Andy squeezes my hand as we wait on the doorstep of Skip's house. I look up at him.

"You look gorgeous. Relax, they're going to love you."

I nod, trying to convince myself as much as anything. It's such a big step, being invited round for dinner. And by the club captain no less. It means we are officially a couple now. Andy and Claire, said in the same breath. Not a whisper but a statement of intent.

Skip's wife Gill opens the door. She's wearing a strappy red dress in a flimsy, expensive-looking material. Her hair and make-up are immaculate.

"Hi, Andy," she says, kissing him on both cheeks. "And you must be Claire," she adds, gripping my shoulder tightly

312

as she kisses me. "Lovely to meet you. Now I know why he's always got a smile on his face these days."

I feel myself blush. "Hi, these are for you," I say, handing her the wine and flowers.

"They're lovely, thank you. Come in. Let me take your coats."

I follow Gill through into the hall, my heels tapping across the polished black-and-white tiles, and hand over my jacket.

"Dave won't be a minute, he's just putting the kids to bed," Gill says.

Seconds later Skip comes downstairs holding a little girl wearing pink pyjamas.

"Hello, mate," he says, nodding to Andy. "Hi, Claire, nice to meet you properly at last. Sorry about that, I had my hands full."

"I can see that," I say. "What's her name?"

"Holly, we call her trouble for short. Her big brother's gone straight to bed but she seems to have different ideas."

I start playing peek-a-boo with Holly, laughing exaggeratedly every time she pops her face out from behind her hands.

"Holly, time for bed now," says Gill.

"I want the Cinderella lady to read me a bedtime story." She points straight at me. Everyone starts laughing.

"You are honoured," says Skip. "She's usually shy with new people."

"That's Claire, love," says Gill. "And she's come here to relax."

"It's OK, I'd love to read to her," I say.

"Please, Mummy."

"OK. But straight to sleep when Claire's finished, mind."

Holly claps excitedly and kisses Skip and Gill good night before running over to grab my hand.

"Looks like you're in demand," says Andy.

I grin. "Come on then," I say to Holly. "How about you take me up to your bedroom? What story are we going to read?"

"Cinderella."

"Fantastic, my favourite."

As we climb the stairs together, I hear laughter coming from the living room, and Gill's voice saying, "She's charming, Andy. A real breath of fresh air." I smile to myself, knowing I have been accepted.

"Can I take your dish, Claire?" Gill says later, when we've all finished.

"Yes thanks. That was lovely. Can I help at all?" I ask.

"You can give me a hand with the coffees if you like; save you listening to these two going on about the match."

"Claire knows more about football than I do," says Andy.

"Right, well she can explain the offside rule to me while we make the coffee."

I follow her out into the pine fitted kitchen.

"Andy can't take his eyes off you, you know. He's completely smitten," she says as she fills the kettle. I flush pink and look down at my shoes. "And I can see why. You're perfect for him. You make a great couple, you really do."

"Thanks," I say.

"I was only sixteen when I met Dave, you know."

"So you've been together since then?"

"Yeah, twelve years in August. I don't know where the time's gone."

"I hope we can be as happy as you two."

Gill pours the boiling water into the coffee percolator and turns to face me.

"You will be," she says. "I've seen the way he is with you. He's yours for life."

CHAPTER
TEN

I got off the train at Saltaire station. It hadn't taken much over an hour. Crazy really. That you could travel so far in such a short journey. Somehow as I'd walked between Bradford Interchange and Forster Square to catch the train the years had slipped away, each day torn off a calendar and thrown to the ground until I was wading knee-deep through dates from the past, feeling them crunch under my boots, watching the faded yellows and browns of my previous life. Until I'd emerged from the train here, a village rich in a past of its own. Salts Mill, looming large above everything, rejuvenated now as a trendy shopping, art gallery and dining venue for the chattering classes but once the employer of the mill workers who lived in the patchwork of terraced houses, built by Sir Titus Salt, which still surrounded it. I stood there feeling small and inconsequential in its shadow. And suddenly I was fifteen again, a piece of paper in my pocket, a house to find, an idol to locate. The word had been ruined now, hijacked by TV talent shows, cheapened and sullied. But I still remembered its true definition: an image of a deity, used as an object of worship, a person or thing that is the object of excessive or supreme adulation.

316

That was what he had been to me. And now I was going to find him. To see the future I never had. To see if it had turned out to be glittering and golden. Or whether the passage of time had rendered it dull and tarnished.

I started walking. Over the canal bridge, down the steps and on to the towpath. I put my hand into the pocket of my long chocolate-brown coat. The piece of paper with his address on was still there. It was all so much simpler now, of course. Google had taken all the fun out of finding your way somewhere. Removed the need for demonstrating initiative or communicating with your fellow human beings. Press print and you were there. I supposed it was just as well really. At least on this particular occasion. Because it gave me time to try to sort out the maelstrom inside my head. Had I driven Mark to do this by pushing him away? Why did I feel so disloyal to him for being here, when it was his idea in the first place? I'd left it a couple of weeks. Going any sooner would have demonstrated indecent haste; any longer would have been unkind to Mark by prolonging his agony. It was only now I was here that my questions moved on. Was Andy going to be here? Would he recognise me? Would he shut the door in my face? Or invite me in? And if he did, what was going to happen then? Could I trust myself? Or him?

I walked on, my legs unable to decide whether to be heavy and full of trepidation or to bounce with a spring in them and break into a trot. I pulled my woollen cap down firmly on my head as the wind swirled the autumn leaves in ever-increasing circles around my boots. The fields on the other side of the canal gave way to a wood. A lock was in front of me, the point where I had to turn right, away from the canal.

I made my way up a small lane past a row of cottages on one side. It was only at this point that I realised I had no idea what to say. I tried to remember how our last conversation had ended, but all I could recall was the lump in my throat and the tears which had followed it. I could hear water now, coming from a different direction to the canal. In front of me were two large mill buildings which appeared to have been turned into apartments. And standing on its own to one side of them, a low, sprawling stone building with a slate roof and mullion windows. On the wall next to the front door — a proper wooden door with a large black knocker — was a sign, "Mill Race Cottage".

This was it. This was where he lived. In my dream home. I shook my head. It was so bloody typical. If I'd drawn a picture of where I would be living in twenty years' time to go with the list, this was what it would have been. With Andy standing at the front door, of course. He was making it difficult for me already and I hadn't even seen him yet. It was a mistake. I shouldn't have come. It was all going to be too much. I stuffed my shaking hands into my pockets and walked on past the cottage, fifty yards or so to where the sound of roaring water was emanating from. I looked down over the stone wall to see the River Aire tumbling down a weir, the white foam crashing against the boulders. I couldn't do this. The ache I had carried around inside me for more than twenty years had reverted to the sharp pain it had once been. The hurt was being

318

reawakened. And I couldn't bear to feel its claws tearing at my heart again.

I turned and started walking. I even made it past his front door without so much as a sideways glance. I would have carried straight on and back the way I'd come to the train station. Told Mark he hadn't been in or maybe hadn't wanted to see me. Drawn a line under it for good. But then the dog came bounding up to me. A gorgeous black and white Border collie with mud-spattered fur and a lolling tongue. I smiled at it, the stupid way people do, before looking up to see its owner rounding the corner, one of those long ball-throwing sticks in his hand. I knew instantly, even at that distance. Something in his gait and the sound of his voice as he called to the dog.

"Titus, come here. Leave the lady alone."

I stopped, unable to walk another step. My legs feeling weak beneath me, my heart battering against my ribcage, trying desperately to escape as it remembered what had happened to it last time.

He carried on walking towards me, calling to Titus, who raced back to him only to dodge the attempt at putting him on a lead, perform a dog's equivalent of a handbrake turn and return to run circles around me, wagging his tail before stopping to have a good shake in front of me, sending mud flying everywhere.

"Titus." The tone of voice changed sharply. Titus's tail dropped and he stood solemnly still as the lead was clipped on to his collar.

"I'm so sorry," Andy said, finally arriving in front of me. "I hope he hasn't ruined your coat. I'll pay for you to get it cleaned if it needs it."

I stared at him, unable to speak or move. Slowly, silently, taking everything in. The hair was slightly sleeker and shorter than it used to be and flecked with grey now, as was his stubble. But he was still unmistakably Andy. The same chiselled features; only his face was weatherworn, his eyes heavier somehow. A slight frown creased his brow as he finished speaking and continued looking at me. As if peering at someone in the street who he knew he recognised but couldn't quite place. He looked for a long time before he said anything.

"Claire?" he uttered finally.

I nodded. "Hello, Andy."

Another silence. I couldn't work out whether he was pleased to see me or petrified. Maybe both.

"What are you doing here?"

"I needed to see you."

He nodded, as if that was a perfectly acceptable reason for turning up unannounced on his doorstep after twenty-odd years.

"Well you'd, er, better come in then." He smiled for the first time. A smile so achingly familiar that I found myself smiling back without even realising. Then rummaged in the pocket of his wax jacket and produced some keys. Titus was already jumping up at the door.

"Let me open it then," he said, squeezing past to unlock it and turn the handle. The door opened on to a flagstoned square hall with low oak beams. Andy held out his hand.

"After you," he said.

"Thanks." I stepped inside. Knowing that I was on his territory now. And under his spell. I watched him take off his boots on the doormat and bent to slip off my own.

"Here, let me take your coat," he said. "Is it OK? I meant what I said about getting it cleaned."

"It's fine, honestly. The mud'll brush straight off when it dries."

"He's just a bit excitable, I'm afraid. Not used to having house guests."

I glanced at the coat rack and down at the mat. Only men's jackets. And only men's boots and shoes. Andy lived on his own. I wasn't at all surprised. In fact, I realised I hadn't even considered the possibility that he would have a wife, or children. If I had, I wouldn't have come. Thinking about it, it was crazy to simply turn up like this. What would I have said if a woman had answered the door? How could Andy have explained my arrival to two inquisitive teenage children? I felt stupid. I'd been reckless, not stopping to think of the consequences of my actions. I was indeed sixteen again.

"I'm sorry," I said. "I shouldn't have turned up unannounced like this. Look, if you'd rather I go . . ."

"Don't be silly," said Andy. "It's good to see you. You're looking really well."

I was aware of his gaze on me as I took off my cap and scarf and hung them on the coat peg. And aware of the colour rising in my cheeks.

"Thanks," I said. "You're not looking too bad yourself."

"Considering I'm getting on a bit, you mean."

"Hey, I didn't say that."

We smiled at each other. Whatever it was that had been there, it hadn't gone away. Simply lain dormant all these years. Waiting to be ignited again.

"Have you come far?"

"Only Todmorden."

"Really? How did you end up there?"

"It's a long story," I said.

"How did you find me?"

"That's a long story too."

"You'd better come through then. I'll put the kettle on."

He led me into the kitchen: quarry-tiled floor, oak units, more beams, a butler's sink and an Aga, which Titus made a beeline for, curling up on the tiles underneath. My ideal kitchen. In my ideal home. Belonging to someone who, twenty-two years ago, was my ideal man. Was he my ideal man now? Lookswise he'd give George Clooney a run for his money. I'd never for a minute thought he would be fat and balding but nor did I think it was possible for him to get better-looking with age. As it stood, there was no sense of disappointment. And the lack of a wife and children meant there were no obvious "Warning: Keep Out" signs. Only the guilt I carried inside for even thinking about it when Mark was sitting at home, having been big enough and brave enough to ask me to do this.

"My boyfriend gave me your address," I said, feeling the need to draw a line between us very clearly in the sand.

"Oh, I see," said Andy, his face shielded from view as he filled the kettle and flicked it on. Only he didn't see, of course. It made no sense at all.

"I found a list I'd written when I was fifteen. About what I'd like to be doing in twenty years' time. Being married to you was number one."

"Looks like you had a lucky escape there then," Andy said, turning round to face me. I took it that he was joking, although it was hard to tell from his face. He was testing me. In the same way I was testing him.

"Maybe you're right," I said. "Mark just wanted me to make sure. Before we took things any further."

"Are you planning to get married?"

"No, just live together. Once bitten, twice shy and all that."

"You were married before?"

"Yeah. For seven years. Didn't work out though."

"I'm sorry," said Andy.

"No need to be. He was a workaholic lawyer."

Andy pursed his lips and blew out as he shook his head.

"Tea or coffee?"

"Coffee, please, white no sugar." It was only as I answered that I realised how absurd it was. Everything that had happened between us and he'd never even known how I took my coffee. It reminded me that we'd never had a grown-up relationship. Not really. Only in my head.

"So what does your boyfriend do?" Andy asked as he scooped some ground coffee into the cafetière.

"He's a lawyer too."

He turned to me and grinned.

"You're a sucker for punishment, aren't you? I take it you're a lawyer yourself?"

"Yep."

"Well that must be one thing ticked off on your list."

"I guess so. Though I don't think I envisaged working at Rochdale Magistrates' Court somehow."

"Obviously the work experience made quite an impression on you." He stopped short as soon as he said it, as if realising it had come out wrong. Sounding like a reference to what had gone on between us. He poured the coffee quickly, splashing some of it and having to wipe the surface down with a cloth. "I bet you're a defence solicitor," he continued.

"How did you guess?"

"I remember what you said about feeling sorry for the defendants. And about how hard-nosed that CPS woman was."

I smiled, wondering what else he remembered.

"Come on," he said, picking up the coffees. "Let's go through to the lounge." Titus jumped up as Andy opened the kitchen door. "I wasn't talking to you," Andy said. "Back in your basket. You're not going anywhere until you've had a good clean."

The lounge was just as I'd imagined it: oak floors and a fully beamed ceiling, some Hockney prints on the walls, including one of Salts Mill, a row of mullion windows and an open fire set in a stone fireplace.

"I love your house."

"Thanks. It's a former mill building. Used to be two cottages until they converted it into one before I bought it."

"How long ago was that?"

"About fifteen years now."

I nodded, starting to piece together Andy's post-me life in my mind.

"So you didn't stay down south for long?"

"No," he said, gesturing to me to sit down on the sofa. "As soon as the old knee gave way and I had to stop playing, I was back up here like a shot. West Yorkshire's my home. I wouldn't want to live anywhere else."

I nodded as I sat down, sinking into the plump cushion behind me. Andy sat in the armchair opposite, as if knowing that sitting next to me would have been pushing things a step too far.

"So come on," he continued. "How did you end up in West Yorkshire then?"

"I'm an adopted northerner." I smiled. "It kind of feels where I belong. I went to law school in Manchester and lived and worked there when I was married. After the divorce I moved to Todmorden. It was near enough to Rochdale where I work but I wanted to be out in the sticks a bit. I love the hills, the way you notice the colours changing during the seasons."

"You don't miss Potters Bar then?"

I shook my head. "I went back recently. My mum's still there. And my friend Frankie."

"The girl with long dark hair you used to come to the training ground with?"

325

"Yeah, that's her. She's got four kids now. She's happy living there. But I could never go back."

We sat for a moment without saying anything. I could hear Titus scratching at the door in the kitchen.

"Have you got any kids?" asked Andy.

"No. My husband didn't want any. Bit of luck, the way things worked out. What about you?"

Andy shook his head. "No. I did want them. That was the problem, I guess."

"What do you mean?"

"I lived with a woman for five years. Jennifer her name was. She was the first really serious girlfriend I'd had for a long time. I thought we were going to get married and have a family but it turned out she had other ideas. Went off to work in Abu Dhabi. Said she didn't want to be tied down or to live in Yorkshire for the rest of her life. So that was that. She was a lawyer too. Bloody unreliable bunch, aren't they?"

I nodded. All the times when I'd thought about him, wondered what he was doing, who he was with, I'd never for a moment imagined him being dumped. Idols were for ever. You didn't walk away from them. At least not in my case.

"And there's no one else?" I asked. I cringed as soon as I said it. Hoping he didn't take it the wrong way. Think that I was prying. Trying it on even.

"No, it's just me and Titus. Named after the man who built Salts Mill, by the way, not Titus Bramble the Wigan footballer."

I smiled. He still had the ability to make me laugh.

"Do you regret it?" I asked. "Not having a family, I mean."

"I guess so. Though not as much as I regret other things."

I shifted on the sofa, made a point of rearranging the cushions behind me. Anything to deflect from what he had just said. And what he might have meant.

"What, like voting for New Labour?" I said, hoping to swiftly change the subject.

Andy grinned.

"It's crazy, isn't it? There we were moaning about Thatcher and Reagan, little knowing that we'd end up with Blair and Bush."

"Just another of life's disappointments, I guess."

"Yeah," said Andy. "There seem to have been quite a few of those."

We sat in silence as we drank our coffee. The air heavy with things that hadn't been said.

"So what are you doing now?" I asked as I put my mug down.

"I'm a bloody lawyer too. Only a sports one, mind."

"Why do you say only?"

"It's all corporate and commercial stuff. Lining the pockets of football club chairmen mostly. Not really what I wanted to do at all."

"What did you want to do?"

"Criminal stuff. Helping people who really need it. Who appreciate what you're doing for them. Like you do, I guess."

I smiled.

"What?" he said.

"If you could hear some of the things my clients come out with you'd know why I was laughing."

"But it must have some rewarding moments."

"It does," I said, "but a lot of frustrating ones as well. That's why I'm trying to get out."

"To do what?"

"Employment law, corporate stuff at a big firm in Manchester. I've had an interview, I'm waiting to hear."

Andy shook his head. "It's funny, isn't it? Both of us wanting to do what the other one's doing."

"Didn't you try to get into criminal work?"

"No. I couldn't really, could I? Too many people remembered my name."

I nodded slowly. Embarrassed that I hadn't thought it through. There was an awkward silence. Now Andy had brought up the subject, it hung over us like a thundercloud waiting to burst.

"Does your boyfriend know what happened between us?"

I shook my head. "Not the sort of thing you can just drop into a conversation, is it?"

"I didn't think he did. He wouldn't have given you my address if he'd known."

I shrugged. "Maybe not. I don't know. He wants me to confront things head on. To see what could have been and walk away from it."

"It's not that easy, though, is it?"

"It is if you're happy with what you've got."

"You're not, though, are you? Otherwise you wouldn't be here."

I stared at him, the expression on my face hardening at his assumption.

"Maybe I'm only looking for closure."

It was Andy's turn to look stung. I hadn't realised I had the ability to hurt him. Now or ever. I gazed down at my feet, wishing I hadn't said it. But knowing his hurt didn't run as deep as mine.

"I've thought about you a lot, over the years."

I looked up to make sure it really was Andy's mouth the words had come out of. That was going to be my line.

"I thought you'd want to forget me."

"Don't be daft. You meant a lot to me, Claire. It wouldn't have happened otherwise."

"It didn't feel like that at the time."

Andy sighed. "Things were awkward for me. Professional footballers aren't supposed to do things like that. At least they weren't back then. I'd probably get away with it now. It would have been nothing compared to what most of them get up to."

I looked up at the ceiling, my bottom lip beginning to tremble. Hating the fact that he had cheapened it like that. Reduced what had happened between us to a minor misdemeanour.

"Sorry, that came out wrong. What I meant was that it was simply a case of being the wrong time for us. You were too young. I couldn't let things go any further."

I shrugged, wondering exactly how much further we could have gone.

"Look, if you'd have been five years older it might have been entirely different. Who knows, maybe we'd still be together."

I raised my eyebrows. He was making it hard for me now. Telling me I could have had everything I wanted. That my life could have been here with him. I felt the tears pricking at the corners of my eyes. I so didn't want to cry in front of him again.

"I'm sorry, Claire. I seem to be making things worse," he said, walking over and sitting down on the sofa next to me. I saw his hand reach out to squeeze mine. Felt his fingers on my skin. Caught the scent of him in my nostrils. I knew I had to put a stop to this. Couldn't risk letting him touch me a second longer. Because already my resistance was ebbing away. I was slipping down some deep, dark time-warp tunnel and if I got to the end I would be sixteen once more. And I would let it happen all over again.

"I think I should go," I said, pulling away and standing up in one swift movement.

"You're scared of how you're feeling, aren't you?"

"It was a bad idea to come here. It's stirred up a lot of emotions."

"That doesn't necessarily have to be a bad thing."

"It does in my case." I started walking towards the door. Andy followed silently, a few steps behind. Perhaps unsure of his next move, of which Claire he was dealing with. Which wasn't surprising because I wasn't sure either. The sixteen year old wanted him to grab me, to pin me up against the wall and start frantically kissing me. The thirty-eight year old, who

330

still bore the emotional scars from last time, knew that could only lead to trouble. And who carried Mark's love deep inside. Where it could prick at my conscience.

"Maybe we could meet up again sometime," I heard Andy say from behind. He hadn't lost it. The ability to bring me down one minute and up the next.

"Why?" I asked, swinging around to face him.

"Because I like you, Claire. I liked you then and I still like you now. And I remember how well we used to get on. Before all the shit happened, I mean."

"I don't know if that would be a good idea."

"It just seems a shame, after you've taken the trouble to come here and see me. To think that we'll never see each other again."

The pain was sharp this time. Maybe he'd known. Maybe that was why he'd said it. "Never" was a word I struggled with. It brought to mind the hurt of our last meeting. Of resigning myself to spending the rest of my life with nothing but painful memories.

I stopped with my hand on the doorknob. The hesitation was fatal. Showed him I wasn't so sure about walking away for good.

"Here," he said, handing me a piece of paper and a pen from the table in the hall. "At least give me your mobile number. Then if I ever need someone to tell me what a git I am, I know how to get hold of you."

I turned and smiled at him, successfully disarmed. I took the pen and scribbled down my number, my hand shaking as I did so.

331

"Thanks," he said, handing me a hastily scrawled mobile number in return. "That's so you can check to see if I'm in first before you come round next time."

I hesitated. Wanting to tell him that there wouldn't be a next time. That Mark's offer had only extended to the one visit. But something stopped the words coming out. The same thing which made me take the piece of paper and stuff it quickly into my pocket.

"It's been good to see you," he said, handing me my coat. "I'm really glad you came." He leant forward to kiss me. I turned away but it was too late. He still caught me on the cheek. The merest touch of his lips. But it was enough to let me know what had gone unsaid. That he was there if I wanted him. And now only a phone call away.

He saw me out to the pavement. My steps unsteady. My head light.

"Where's your car?" he asked.

"I came by train."

"Can I give you a lift to the station?"

"No thanks," I said. "I could do with some fresh air."

Somehow I got back home. I didn't remember any part of the journey. I must have switched to automatic pilot due to the numerous malfunctions in my head. Andy was back in my life. Part of me wished his wife had opened the door, two children playing behind her in the hall. In which case I would have apologised for having the wrong house and fled back home. Knowing it was not only over but dead and buried. A real sense of closure. Of putting the past to rest. Presumably that was what Mark had been hoping for. Certainly not this. All I could think of was that *Friends* episode. The one where they all put their idols' names on a laminated card on the understanding that if they ever got the opportunity, their partner would not stand in their way. And then Ross had been sitting in Central Perk when Isabella Rossellini walked into the room. Except in my case, Andy hadn't blown me out. He'd made it very clear what was available. And as Mark had given me his address, told me to go and see him in the first place, he couldn't complain if I took him up on the offer. He probably wouldn't either; he'd probably go so far as to wish us every happiness. Which was what made it even harder. You didn't take advantage of nice guys like that. It simply wasn't right.

I sat and sweated and stewed. I had a bath, feeling guilty enough to remove even the faintest whiff of Andy from my person. And then sat at the kitchen table staring into a knot in the wood so hard I expected it to split in two. Until seven thirty. When the knock on the door I had been expecting came.

Mark looked as if he was undergoing the most agonising wait of his life. His face was pale and drawn. His eyes implored me to put him out of his misery, one way or another. I felt his pain like a stab to my heart. I stood to one side to let him come in. Wanting to at least do this in private. And then before he could say a word I burst into tears, throwing my arms around him. Needing the warmth of him, the strength of him, the solidness of his love.

He held me close to him, until the point where there was a pause in my sobs and I looked up.

"You came back then," he said.

"Did you really think I wouldn't?"

"I didn't know what to think, to be honest. Did you see him?"

I nodded through my tears.

"But I take it he wasn't quite as you'd remembered."

I nodded again, unable to bring myself to dim his unfailing optimism.

"Can you throw away that list now?" said Mark. "Can we go back to how things were?"

I nodded once more.

"Thank you," I said. "For doing that for me."

"That's OK," he said. "It needed to be done. And I knew we'd both feel better afterwards."

He held me tighter than he'd ever held me. I didn't have the heart to tell him I felt far worse than I'd been before.

Friday, 11 April 1986

It was in the middle of the Hornsey riot case that Andy walked into court. It hadn't been a full-scale riot like the one last year, more a skirmish with baseball bats and one homemade petrol bomb which hadn't worked. But I liked to think of it as a riot. It sounded far more dramatic.

He simply strolled in and sat down next to me. As if it was a perfectly normal thing to do. No one in the courtroom would have guessed that the last time we'd seen each other I'd had his prick in my mouth. Gary Hurst turned round and nodded to him, very matter-of-fact. The magistrate gave him a quick glance and then turned his attention back to the unsavoury-looking collection of yobs standing before him. And everything carried on as it was before.

Apart from in my head, where Andy's unexpected arrival had caused some sort of malfunction. He wasn't supposed to be in court on a Friday, only on Monday afternoons. He could have changed his routine in order to witness the Hornsey not-quite-a-riot trial but it seemed unlikely. So he must have come to see me. Which, bearing in mind how we'd parted on Monday, didn't make sense at all.

The possible explanations for Andy's behaviour that day had been spinning around in my head like some kind of manic Rubik's Cube. No matter how hard I tried to unscramble it, I couldn't get the pieces to fit. Presumably he must have liked me to come on to me like that. But if he did like me, I didn't see why he'd been so off with me afterwards. Unless my blow job had been totally crap. But if it had been, surely he wouldn't have come in my mouth. Unless men could fake that stuff. I wasn't sure. I was beginning to feel out of my depth. All I did know was that the Andy I used to chat to at the training ground had never been off with me like that. That was who I wanted back, the Andy I used to know, not this new version. But I didn't know if he still existed. Or even if he ever had.

I could smell his aftershave; it was stronger than usual, freshly applied. He was turning me on without even trying. Or maybe he *was* trying. I looked across at him sitting there, only inches away from me. His hair still wet from the shower. He looked so good, I wanted him all over again. Wanted to show him I was better than Annie. That I could make him happier than she ever had. If only he'd give me another chance.

A commotion at the front of the court alerted me to the fact that the case had collapsed, the defendants grinning cockily and congratulating each other as they left the court. Miss Jenkins was standing over me, explaining about some legal technicality and the fact that things didn't always go to plan. Muttering something else about how impressed she'd been with me. And how I should get in touch next year to see about doing some more work experience.

I nodded and smiled and said something suitably appreciative, all on automatic pilot. I just wanted to get to the point where me and Andy could be alone. I watched as Miss Jenkins strode towards the door, not even waiting for Mr Hurst, who gathered his things and scuttled off after her, clearly having blotted his copybook by scuppering her case. He wasn't going to get anywhere with her now.

And then Andy was standing in front of me. Asking if I was OK. Smiling, as if everything was fine again, and offering me a lift home. It felt like it was happening all over again. Only I couldn't be sure because I'd got it so wrong before. It could be some kind of game. One I didn't know the rules to. And I couldn't learn because they were written in a foreign language.

"What are you doing here?" I said.

"Something's come up next Monday, so I thought I'd come this afternoon instead." He sounded about as unsure of the whole thing as I felt. "And anyway," he continued, "I wanted to give you this."

He handed me a small white envelope with my name written neatly in block capitals on the front. I looked at him blankly, wondering if it was a belated birthday card, before prising it open. Inside were two tickets for the Milk Cup Final at Wembley. My jaw dropped and my eyes bulged wide. I looked up at Andy. He was smiling at me expectantly.

"I don't know what to say."

"You do want to go, don't you?" he said.

"Course I do, I just can't believe that you'd do this for me."

"It was no trouble. Anyway, I felt bad about Monday. I wanted to say sorry."

"What for?"

"For putting you in an awkward situation. Afterwards . . . you know."

"It didn't matter."

"You were pretty quiet on the way home."

"I was worried, that was all. I felt like I'd done something wrong. Shown you up or something."

Andy stood for a moment, not saying anything, shaking his head slowly from side to side.

"You haven't done anything wrong, Claire. I just wasn't expecting any of that to happen. I hadn't thought things through."

The Rubik's Cube unscrambled in my head.

"So everything's fine between us?"

"Sure it is. I got you the tickets, didn't I?" He was laughing as he said it. Like the old Andy would have.

"Thank you," I said. "Thank you very much."

I tucked the tickets safely inside my bag and walked with Andy to the car park, feeling as though my shoes had developed huge air-cushioned soles. I still didn't understand exactly what was going on. Whether we were going back to how we were on Monday, or how we'd been before that. I wasn't even sure which I wanted. All I knew was that I had to be with Andy. Whatever that involved.

"So, how's it been going? Had any good cases since I saw you?" he asked.

"Oh God, loads. I don't know if good's the right word though; some of them have been pretty awful. The thing is, I get so angry about it when people aren't treated fairly. Sometimes I want to stand up in court and shout at the magistrates. Miss Jenkins says that if I want to be a lawyer, I've got to stop letting my heart rule my head."

"And what do you think?"

"I think that's crap. It's just a lousy excuse for not getting involved when you know you should do."

Andy nodded. Very slowly.

"It's like that last bloke," I said. "The one who was up for hitting his wife. I don't know how your Mr Hurst could have defended him. Going on about him being in the Rotary Club, as if that made it all right."

"I know. Gary says it's all part of the job, that he's there to give people the best defence possible, regardless of what he thinks of them."

"I dunno," I said, "I'm not sure if I'm cut out to be a lawyer."

"Nonsense," said Andy. "You've got years to go before you qualify. There's plenty of time for you to become hard and cynical like the rest of us."

I looked at him, unsure as to whether it was a joke or not.

"But I don't want to get like that."

"Then don't." He smiled gently. "Be yourself, Claire Skidmore, the lawyer with a conscience. You never know, it might even catch on."

"But what if it doesn't?"

Andy shook his head.

"You worry too much, you do."

"I can't help it, there's so much to worry about. Didn't you watch *Threads*? Thatcher and Reagan will probably nuke the world to pieces before I get the chance to become a lawyer."

"True. Worse things could happen, mind."

"How d'ya mean?"

"Well, Arsenal could do the double."

I elbowed Andy in the ribs as I started laughing. "Now you're taking the piss."

"Would I?" he said.

When we got to his car, he came round and unlocked the door for me. His body brushed against mine. I thought for a moment he was going to kiss me. He didn't though. It was only then that I knew for certain I wanted him to. I wished I knew what I had to do to get him to do it again. But the truth was I still didn't know what had made him kiss me in the first place.

Andy got in and turned the radio on. We didn't say much at first. It felt a bit awkward again, being back in the car with him. A few minutes later "Don't Stand So Close To Me" came on. Andy turned the radio off. Which was weird, because I was sure I'd read somewhere that he liked The Police.

"So, is it back to school for you next week?" Andy asked as we headed towards Potters Bar.

"'Fraid so. I wish I didn't have to but I've got my O levels to do before I can escape. At least it's only for a few months. I'll be going to college in September. It should be better there."

340

"A more adult environment, you mean?"

"Yeah, I guess so. I've never really fitted in at school. It's a bit like you and Clubber's lot, I s'pose. It's like I'm on a different planet to everyone else. I don't really belong there."

"So where do you belong?"

With you, Andy. With you. I looked at him in alarm, waiting for his reaction. And then realised I hadn't actually said it out loud. Only in my head.

"Oh, I dunno. I don't seem to belong anywhere right now, certainly not at home."

"Family giving you grief, are they?"

"You could say that. My dad's remarrying in the summer and my mum's started seeing some bloke called Malcolm. They don't care about me any more."

"Hey, come on. I'm sure that's not true."

"It is."

"Have you tried talking to them about it?"

"There's no point. I hardly ever see my dad, and my mum still treats me like I'm twelve years old."

"I know what you mean," said Andy. "My dad's like that. Sends me birthday cards with footballers on. Doesn't seem to realise that I'm one myself now."

I smiled at him.

"That's better. Just think of all the good things you've got to look forward to."

"What, like you playing in the World Cup?"

"No." Andy seemed irritated. "Your own stuff. Things you're going to be doing. I bet you've got holiday plans, you and Frankie."

I opened my mouth to say something but nothing came out. I didn't know how to explain that Frankie had better people to go on holiday with. Or that I'd kind of hoped he might ask me.

"Your road's next left, isn't it?"

I looked out of the window with a start. Aspland's newsagent's was looming large in front of us on the next corner. I bit my bottom lip to try to stop it trembling and clenched my fists, digging my nails into my palms so hard I thought they were going to bleed. I couldn't cope with this. Going back to being friends with Andy again. If that was what this was. Things had moved on and I couldn't pretend nothing had happened between us, even if he could. I knew that if I let him drive off now, that would be it. Nothing else would ever happen between us. I wouldn't even see him again for months. And I couldn't cope with that. Not on top of everything else.

My breath caught as the first sob arrived. The noise that came out was pitiful. A sharp, choking cry, like that of an animal, snared in a trap.

"Hey, what's the matter?" Andy turned in to my road and ground sharply to a halt as the tears began streaming down my cheeks. My head was bowed and my hair hung limply over my face, my shoulders shaking as I sobbed.

He undid his seat belt, leant over and brushed a soggy strand of hair back from my face, tucking it behind my ear. His hand went back to brush a tear away from my cheek. And back again, only this time

342

there wasn't even a tear. He stroked my face softly, as if I was a porcelain doll.

"It's all right," he said. "Come here, it's all right."

I flung my arms around him, burying my head in his shoulder.

"I'm sorry." My muffled voice drifted up from between the sobs below. "I was trying so hard not to cry. It's just I'm going through a rough time right now. And I don't think I can cope without you. You're the only one I can talk to."

I sniffed loudly. I didn't have any tissues. Andy reached over to the back seat and handed me a United shirt.

"I can't use that."

"Yes you can. I've only worn it once; it shouldn't be too smelly."

"Are you sure?"

"What, about it being smelly?"

"No. About me using it."

"Course I am. There's plenty more where that came from."

I took the shirt and blew my nose gingerly on the sleeve, apologising as I did so.

"Oh God," he said. "I didn't realise you were going to do that with it. I'd never have offered it to you if I'd known."

I smiled up at him, a thin, watery smile.

"So how come I'm the only one you can talk to?" asked Andy. "Why can't you talk to Frankie?"

"We had a row. She doesn't want to be my friend any more. She thinks I'm . . . Oh, it doesn't matter."

"No, come on, she thinks you're what?"

I hesitated, fearing it would sound ridiculous. But I knew I had to tell him, in case I never got the chance again.

"She thinks I'm stupid . . . for loving you so much."

I waited. Waited for Andy to start laughing. To tell me Frankie was right, I was being stupid. I should grow up. Get a life. Get real.

But he didn't laugh. He didn't say a word. He lifted my head towards his, looked at me for a moment and kissed me. Deep and hard and long. Drawing out the doubts and confusion, injecting pure ecstasy in their place. He loved me. He really did. It wasn't just a one-off, it was a real relationship. The whole thing on Monday must have been some kind of test. And I'd passed it because I hadn't given up on him or had a go at him or demanded to know what was going on. And now I was getting my reward. Everything I'd ever wanted. Andy. All to myself. In years to come I wouldn't even remember these past few days. The wobble in between. The first kiss and this one would melt seamlessly into each other. The start of our relationship. Of our life together. The tears dried instantly and a smile lit up my face.

"Don't ever stop smiling," Andy whispered. "You've got a beautiful smile."

I wished I'd had a tape recorder going. I would be able to replay it in my head over and over again. But it would have been nice to be able to play it back to Frankie.

344

"Is there anyone inside?" he asked, nodding towards the house. I hesitated for a moment, feeling my stomach clenching. It was what he wanted though. And it was the grown-up thing to do.

"No," I said. "No one at all."

Andy nodded. We scrambled out of the car and hurried up the front path. I fumbled with the key in the lock and led him into the lounge without saying a word. Andy threw his jacket down and yanked his tie off. Pulling me over to the sofa and laying me down. One by one he undid the buttons on my blouse, kissing me frantically as he did so. I was looking at him, staring into his eyes, trying to make myself believe that this was really happening. I wondered what Frankie would think if she could see us now. Whether she'd be jealous that it wasn't her and Matt. Andy slid my blouse off my shoulders.

"Your go," he whispered.

Andy Pailes was asking me to undress him. I had no idea what to do. I started to unbutton his shirt. But my hands were shaking so much I couldn't do it. He put his finger to his lips as I started to apologise. I watched as he pulled his shirt over his head and tossed it on the floor. The ache deep inside me got a whole lot worse.

Andy lowered himself on top of me. I flinched as his bare skin touched mine. Confirmation that he existed in the flesh, not just inside my head. I'd thought the hairs on his chest would tickle me but they didn't. Not really. He was breathing heavily now. Pushing against me, rubbing his hand up and down my thigh, getting closer and closer to the ache inside. I felt his fingers touch me, stroking me through my knickers, then slipping inside. I heard myself moan out loud. Laura Ashley started laughing.

I closed my eyes, trying to shut it out. But the laughter got louder. I could see myself now. Twelve years old, my hair tied in bunches, my dirty white socks sagging around my ankles, a bruise on my left knee. We'd been sent home early from school; the central heating had broken down. It was on at home though. I felt the warmth hit me as I let myself in and stepped inside the hall.

The laughter was the first thing I heard. It was a deep, throaty laugh, belonging to a woman. It wasn't my mum's laugh though. The laughter turned into a moan. A rhythmic, repetitive moan, which grew louder by the second. It was coming from the lounge. Slowly I pushed open the door. Pauline from next-door-but-one was lying on the sofa, her skirt hitched up around her waist, her legs splayed apart. She didn't have any knickers on. Dad was lying on top of her, or in between her, it was hard to work out which exactly. His trousers were lying in a crumpled heap on the floor. He still had his socks on. Pauline was still moaning. Writhing and wriggling, while Dad was thrusting into her, harder and harder each time.

"Stop!" I shouted.

They both looked up, startled. Pauline swore, Dad called my name. But I was gone, I was running; out of the house and down the street, all the way to the baker's where Mum worked. Where I threw myself at her, crying into her floury apron and beating my fists against her sides.

I opened my eyes with a start. Andy was looking at me in alarm. I realised I must have shouted out loud.

"Are you OK?" he said. "Do you want me to stop?"

"No," I said. "I want you to carry on. Not here though. The sofa's not comfortable. Can we go upstairs?"

Andy nodded and I led him hurriedly up to my room and shut the door behind us. I turned to face him. But he wasn't looking at me. He was staring at the pictures of himself which lined my bedroom walls. I stood, feeling naked and exposed in just my bra and skirt, waiting for him to carry on where he'd left off. He didn't move, though. Just kept staring at the pictures. I couldn't understand what the problem was. I thought he'd like them.

"Is everything all right?" I asked.

"Yeah," he said eventually. "Come here. Let's do this properly."

He slipped my skirt off and unfastened my bra. He knew now that it was padded. I froze for a second, bracing myself for the look of disappointment on his face. But he didn't falter, simply cupped what there was of my breasts in his hands as he kissed me hard on the neck. I knew he had done this before. Probably more times than I'd care to know about. But today he was doing it with me. And that was all that mattered.

He took his trousers and pants off. I noticed the lines where the suntan stopped, where his shorts usually were. I knew I was about to lose my virginity. Not to some boy from school but to Andy Pailes, United and England star. It was weird; all the times I'd imagined us together, I'd never imagined us doing this. I'd dreamt about waking up with him in the morning and lying next to him watching him sleeping. But that was all. I felt embarrassed, scared even. But above all, I felt absolutely elated that he should want me this much.

"You are so sexy," Andy whispered, pulling me down on to the bed. "That's what makes you so different, you know. You've got absolutely no idea how sexy you are."

I lay there basking in the glory. Knowing I'd never forget this moment. The thrill of Andy's heaving, sweating body pressing against me, a mass of taut skin and toned muscle. Every time he touched me a spurt of elation ran through me. He kissed my neck, then my shoulders, working his way down my body and showering me with compliments as he went. He turned me over and peeled off my knickers. "You've got a great bum," he said. "Where did you get a bum like that?"

I smiled, then hesitated for a second, wondering if I should say something, confess I'd never done this before, ask if he had a condom. But I couldn't remember Demi Moore ever stopping Rob Lowe in his tracks. Come to think of it, I couldn't remember anyone in the movies ever mentioning stuff like that. All they said were things like "Go on, baby" and "Take me." And anyway, I knew that if Andy didn't have a condom, I'd let him do it all the same. Just in case I never got the chance again.

His hand slid between my legs, his fingers quick and deft, sending my body into rhythmic contractions. I lifted my head and looked at him.

"Go on," I said, in my best Hollywood actress voice. "I'm all yours."

Afterwards, when it was all over, I lay there, a sticky wet substance trickling down my inner thigh, and wondered why you never got to see how messy it all was in the movies. Or hear the sort of strange squelching noises which had emanated from me.

I looked up at the pictures of Andy and the rest of the team on the wall. Suddenly I felt embarrassed, lying naked squashed up against him on the single bed. Which was weird because I hadn't felt embarrassed while we were doing it. I glanced across at Andy. He was looking at the pictures on the wall too. His face ashen.

I prayed I had been all right, done the right things. I began mentally trawling through all the magazine articles on sex I had ever read. I wished I'd cut them out and kept them now. Stored them in a series of ring binders, like those part-work magazines they advertised on TV. The ones that built up into a "remarkable collection for you to pass on to your grandchildren". Although obviously I wouldn't have been able to do that with this one.

I wasn't even sure if I'd had an orgasm. It had felt good. But there hadn't been one little bit which had been better than all the rest, a point where bells had rung or neon lights had flashed. I consoled myself with the fact that Andy had evidently enjoyed himself. What was it he'd said at the end? Just before he had collapsed on top of me and I'd realised that, far from getting going, it was actually all over.

"You are so good, you are so beautiful." That was what he'd said. And that was all I'd needed to hear.

I pulled the corner of the United duvet over me. I didn't want to get up. I wanted to lie with Andy for ever. Have a cuddle under the duvet, listen to music together, whatever it was other couples did afterwards. But before I could do any of that, Andy got out of bed. He didn't say anything to me. I figured I should get up too.

We dressed in silence, Andy keeping his head bowed. Not looking at me or anything around him. It was strange how putting clothes on was so much more embarrassing than taking them off. I hadn't expected things to feel this awkward, not after what we'd just done. When we got down to the lounge I saw his United shirt lying on the sofa. I hadn't even realised I'd brought it in with me.

"Here, don't forget this," I said.

"No, you have it."

"Are you sure?"

"Yeah. You blew your nose on it, didn't you?"

I smiled at him.

"It was all right, wasn't it?"

"Yeah, of course it was."

I didn't know what I was supposed to do now. How this kind of thing worked. It was like we'd skipped the bit where he asked me out and gone straight to the sex.

I wasn't sure if he was going to ask me out now, or whether I should just take it that we already were going out. That it went without saying. It seemed stupid to ask, but I realised he was about to walk away again. And I had to be sure this time.

"When can I see you again?"

"Soon, I'll sort something out." He didn't sound too sure.

"I'll give you my phone number," I said, jotting it down on a piece of paper and handing it to him. He put it in his pocket without saying anything.

"Can I have yours, please?" I said. It felt like asking for an autograph.

He hesitated, then took the piece of paper I'd just given him from his jacket pocket, tore the bottom half off, scribbled something on it and gave it to me.

"Thank you," I said.

I looked at Andy, feeling the tears pricking at the corners of my eyes again. I went to give him a kiss but he moved away. He seemed to be in a hurry. I stood in the doorway, waving to him as he drove off down the road. As I turned to go back inside I noticed two men sitting in a black Escort parked further down the road. One of them was holding something but I couldn't see what it was. As soon as he saw me looking at him he put it down. I shut the door and went back inside. Wondering how on earth I was going to be able to act normal when Mum came home.

I lay in bed, hugging Andy's shirt tightly to me. Certain I could still smell him on it, and still taste him on my lips. I gazed at the pictures of him on my wall. It was weird, if you thought about it. I had a picture of Spandau Ballet on my wall too. And yet I couldn't imagine any of them ever being naked in my bedroom, having sex with me.

I'd lain awake most of the night, thinking about what had happened. It hadn't sunk in yet. I wasn't sure it ever would. A week ago I'd never even kissed a boy. Now I'd lost my virginity to Andy Pailes. *The* Andy Pailes. It was like I'd skipped all the usual stuff, the getting off with lads at school, and gone from nothing to everything in one go. Having sex with someone famous. Someone who meant the world to me. You couldn't get much bigger than that. Part of me was elated, buzzing with the thrill of it all. Yet another part of me felt kind of flat, disappointed almost. It wasn't supposed to be like this. Me lying here, unsure what to do next, waiting for him to call. I could phone him myself. I'd memorised the number, but I didn't want to appear too desperate, even if I was. It was better to wait for him. I just wished I knew whether it would be this morning, tomorrow or the week after next.

I'd always thought that once you'd had sex with someone, that was it, you were kind of joined to them at the hip. I'd never expected it to be like this. To not even know when you were going to see them again. To have all these doubts and anxieties about the whole thing.

I could be pregnant, for all I knew. Michelle in *EastEnders* only had sex with Dirty Den once, but she'd got pregnant. The thought of giving birth frightened the life out of me (so did the thought of telling Mum I was up the duff). But there was no way I could get rid of a baby. I didn't like the anti-abortion people. They'd come to school once, done a talk and pulled a plastic foetus out of a shopping bag. Fucking loopy they were. But they'd got to me. Made me wonder if there had been some darker message behind Wham!'s "Choose Life" T-shirts. And if I was pregnant, it wouldn't be any old baby. It would be Andy's. So I couldn't possibly get rid of it. Because if I had his baby he wouldn't have any choice then. He'd have to love me back.

I needed to go to the loo. I threw back the duvet, catching sight of myself in the mirror. "Puppy Love", it said on my nightshirt, above a picture of a spaniel-type thing with floppy ears and its tongue hanging out. It looked stupid, like something a ten year old would wear. I wasn't a kid any more, I was a woman. I should be wearing a sexy negligée, something in black satin. I'd have to buy one. I didn't want Andy seeing me in some poxy nightshirt.

I padded along the landing. Mum was asleep, I heard her snoring as I passed her bedroom, but I still bolted the bathroom door behind me. As I started to pee, I noticed a strange stinging sensation. It was only then I realised how sore I was. It was like someone had punched me down there; I imagined everything red and puffy. I wondered if it always felt like this afterwards, or if it was only the first time. At least there wasn't any blood on the sheets. I could never have washed them or got rid of them without Mum knowing. The

353

bloodstained knickers had been easy. I'd wrapped them up inside three carrier bags and put them in the outside bin. If Mum noticed they'd gone I could always say I lost them in the changing rooms at school.

I'd just got back in bed when I heard the doorbell go. It was seven thirty on a Saturday morning. No one called at that time. Unless it was the postman, delivering a parcel. But I didn't think we were expecting anything. I lay there for a while, hoping whoever it was would go away. But they didn't. They rang again. That was when I realised it could be Andy. That he might want to see me before he left for the match.

I leapt out of bed, pulled on my dressing gown and dashed downstairs.

"Hang on a sec," I called to the blurred figure I could make out beyond the frosted glass panel as I fumbled with the look. The door finally jolted open. It wasn't Andy after all.

"Hello, it's Claire, isn't it?"

I stared at the man on the doorstep. He had a fat, squashed nose and wavy hair that looked as if it was fighting to pull free of his head. I had no idea how he knew my name. I didn't say anything, just nodded.

"Shaun Mackie, I'm a reporter with the *News of the World*. Sorry to trouble you so early, only I need to ask you a few questions about your boyfriend. How long have you been seeing Andy Pailes?"

For a split second it sounded good, hearing Andy described as my boyfriend. It made me feel all warm inside. Then I remembered that this wasn't Frankie I was talking to. It was some reporter who was trying to get Andy into trouble. Instinct took over, telling me to deny everything.

"I dunno what you're talking about."

"Would you like me to remind you? About Andy's little visit yesterday. We've got photographs, you see. Pictures of him kissing you. And then coming into this house."

My stomach turned over. What little colour I had drained from my face. My mum was going to go mental. I couldn't work out what had happened. How they'd found out about me and Andy. How they'd got the pictures.

"Nothing happened. He just came in for a chat."

The reporter was smiling. Like he didn't believe me.

"I take it he knows you're still at school. Did he have sex with you, Claire?"

The churning sensation in my stomach got a whole lot worse. I felt myself going red. The whirring of a camera motor-drive alerted me to the photographer standing at the gate. It was the man I'd seen in the car yesterday. That was what he'd been doing. Taking photos of me and Andy. He was taking photos of me again now, standing there in my fucking dressing gown. I started to close the door.

"Who is it, Claire?" Mum's voice called from the hallway. I hadn't heard her come downstairs.

"No one," I said, but it was too late. She came up behind me and poked her head round the door.

"If you're selling something you can go away and come back at a reasonable hour."

The reporter smirked.

"I'm from the *News of the World*. I'd like to ask you a few questions about your daughter's boyfriend."

"What are you talking about? She hasn't got a boyfriend. You've got the wrong house."

"I'm afraid we haven't, Mrs Skidmore. Your daughter's been seeing Andy Pailes, the footballer."

Mum started laughing. "In her dreams maybe. Her head's full of silly nonsense. You know what teenage girls are like."

The reporter took a photograph from a large brown envelope and held it up. It was a bit fuzzy. But you could still make out me and Andy kissing in the car.

"He came to this house yesterday, Mrs Skidmore. He was inside for over an hour. Do you condone your daughter having sex with an England footballer?"

Mum looked from me to the photo, and back to me. As if checking that it really was the same person.

"Claire?"

I looked down at my feet. "Shut the door, Mum."

"I really think you should answer, Mrs Skidmore. It's not going to look very good if you don't say anything. Perhaps you could tell me how long your daughter's been seeing him. We understand she was only fifteen when they first met."

I slammed the door shut and stood with my head leant back against the cold glass, breathing heavily. Desperate to block it all out, make it go away. It wouldn't though. Mum ushered me away from the door and into the living room, looking at me like I was a piece of dog shit stuck to her shoe.

"What the hell have you been up to?"

Her voice was quivering. I'd only ever heard her shout like that once before. The day Dad left home.

"It's not what you think."

"I've seen the bloody photo, Claire. I want to know what happened."

"I . . . I met him at court, he gave me lifts home a couple of times. He only came in once. Yesterday, when he dropped me off. It was only kisses and stuff. Nothing else."

"You must think I was born yesterday. Just came in for a chat, did he? Or a nice cup of tea and a biscuit."

"I was upset, I needed someone to talk to."

"You weren't doing much talking in the car."

"Yeah, well, we got a bit carried away."

"How far, exactly?"

"It doesn't matter."

"Yes it does. You're sixteen, for Christ's sake. And he's a bloody footballer. What are people going to think?"

"I don't care what they think. I love him."

"Don't be ridiculous. You don't even know him."

"I do. He's given me his phone number and everything. I'm kind of going out with him."

"Give me strength." Mum looked up at the ceiling, her whole body shaking. "He's taken advantage of you, that's what he's done. He's a dirty little bastard."

The words slapped me across the face. I wished she'd leave Andy out of it. None of this was his fault.

"He's not," I shouted. "He didn't sleep with me, OK?"

"That's what you say. I don't know that, do I? And nor does anyone else. If this gets in the papers, you're going to look like a slut. That's what that reporter thought of you. I could see it, the way he was looking at me. Wondering what sort of mother I was, bringing you up to behave like that."

"Is that what you think of me?"

"I don't know what to think of you any more, Claire. I really don't."

"That's because you don't know me. You never have done. Andy's the only one who listens to me. The only one who cares."

Mum threw her hands up into the air. "For goodness' sake, will you get it into your head. He won't want to know you, not now he's got what he wanted. Believe me, Claire. They're all the same."

I heard the letter box rattle and ran back into the hall as a note came through. I picked it up and went back into the living room.

"What does it say?" asked Mum.

"It says to call if we change our minds about talking. It's got the reporter's phone number on it."

"Well you can put that in the bin for a start."

I moved towards the phone.

"What are you doing?"

"I'm calling Andy. I'm going to warn him. They might go round there."

Mum darted forward, standing between me and the phone. I tried to reach it but she grabbed hold of my arm.

"This is going to stop right now. You're not to talk to him, to write to him. Nothing. And if you think you're ever going up that bloody training ground again, you've got another think coming."

"You can't do that, you can't stop me seeing him."

"Just you watch me."

I pulled away from her. "Why don't you fuck off and stop screwing up my life?"

I heard her burst into tears as I ran upstairs. I'd never sworn at her before. But then she'd never called me a slut before either. I threw myself on to my bed, gulping huge mouthfuls of air as I struggled to take it all in. It wasn't fair. This was the first time I'd ever kissed anyone or brought anyone back to the house, and now it was going to be in the papers. They were going to make me look like a real slag. And it hadn't been like that. It was me and Andy, who I loved more than anyone else in the world. It was special and he was special. Just because I was still at school, it didn't make it wrong. I started crying, huge, heavy tears that plopped on to my pillow. It had all gone horribly wrong. And I had no idea what to do.

I stayed in my room the rest of the day, listening to the radio. United lost 2–1 to Everton. Which meant we were nine points behind them, all dreams of winning the league over. Andy was substituted at half-time. The commentator said he'd had a nightmare, been at fault for both goals, that he seemed to be distracted. I guessed he'd had a visit from the paper as well. I wondered what he'd told them. And why he hadn't called me.

CHAPTER
ELEVEN

"Catherine wheels," whooped Fiona in delight as she peered inside the box I had just given her. "Your box has got Catherine wheels. I was only saying five minutes ago that you know the world's in a state when you can't find a decent Catherine wheel in a box of fireworks any more."

I laughed and shook my head. Fiona's enthusiasm for fireworks knew no bounds. I wasn't sure if it was because Guy Fawkes was a well-known Scots-hater or simply her stubborn refusal to stop behaving like a big kid, but 5 November was bigger than Christmas in the Walker household.

They'd started holding their fireworks parties when Aidan was a toddler. The fact that he was now fifteen years old and therefore wouldn't be seen dead at anything organised by his parents hadn't dented Fiona's enthusiasm or her resolve to continue the tradition.

"You've made a sad lady very happy," said Neil with a grin.

"Well this should make a sober man very drunk," said Mark, handling Neil a twelve-pack of lager.

"Thanks. Remind me to invite the two of you around for Hogmanay," said Neil. "We shall declare you honorary Scots."

Mark and I fought our way through to the already packed kitchen where jacket potatoes, chilli and hot dogs were being devoured by the guests.

"Get in quick before the gannets eat it all," said Fiona.

"Thanks," I said. "It smells fantastic."

"Hopefully it will taste good too. The chilli has the Aidan seal of approval, which is saying something."

"Where's he gone tonight?" I asked.

"Out," said Fiona, mimicking her son's gruff voice. "That's about as much as we get these days from the sullen and secretive one."

Mark nodded. "Yep, sounds like a normal teenager to me."

"I know, but if you could see the kids that hang out on the streets round here you'd understand why we're so worried. Neil knows some of the families. And let's just say he doesn't know them because they're pillars of the community."

"I went around with some dodgy kids for a bit when I was his age," said Mark. "Just to annoy my parents, I think. I soon got fed up of them and went back to my own mates."

"Yeah, but he's very impressionable. And he's got less than a year to go till his GCSEs. He's supposed to be doing work experience in a couple of weeks but he hasn't even sorted anything out."

"Why don't you take him into work with you?" Mark asked.

"He wouldn't be seen dead with me. He's at that age when your parents are the most embarrassing people on earth."

"I'll happily have him with me for a week," said Mark. "If you think he'd go for it."

"Would you really?" said Fiona.

"Of course. Might put him off being a lawyer, mind."

"No, I think it's a great idea. I reckon he might even go for that. I'll ask him tomorrow. Cheers, Mark."

Fiona hurried off to get some more potatoes out of the oven. I reached out to stroke Mark's arm.

"Thanks," I said. "That was really good of you."

"I hope he goes for it," said Mark. "Be good to have someone to keep me on my toes. Ask lots of difficult questions." He paused for a second. "Where did you go on work experience?"

"Hornsey Magistrates' Court," I said.

"Bloody hell, I pity the poor sod who got you. I bet you gave them a hard time."

I smiled uneasily. Mark put his arm around me, as if to make clear he'd only been joking. He'd seemed a lot happier the last couple of weeks. More at ease. More confident in our relationship. And I was trying. I was trying so hard to be happy too. But still it hung there in the air. Andy's apparent willingness to rekindle our relationship. And the knowledge that he could call me at any time. I wished I could talk to someone about it. But Mark was obviously out of the question, and Fiona was too close to Mark and not given to discussing

362

emotional affairs of the heart. The only person who might be able to understand what I was going through was Frankie, and I couldn't possibly bother her when she had far more important things on her mind. Emily was at the end of her intensive chemotherapy. They were waiting to hear if it had been a success. And what would happen next. Every phone call from Frankie was more frantic. Every e-mail from Emily more desperate about not being well enough to go to the *Twilight* premiere.

"Come on then," said Mark, reaching for the plates. "Let's tuck in, I'm starving."

"Ladies and gentlemen," shouted Fiona half an hour later when everyone had been fed and watered. "If you'd care to take your places on the patio, the main event is about to commence."

We joined the throng of party-goers huddling together outside as the first rocket went up. Fiona always liked to start with a bang. There was the usual mixture of successful fireworks, which gained a cheer from the onlookers and exaggerated oohhs and aahhs, and damp-squib ones presumably thrown in to make up the numbers in the box. I was enjoying Fiona's excitement at the first Catherine wheel when my mobile rang. It was a wonder I heard it above the noise. I guess I was on hyper-alert, as I had been every time it had rung for the past couple of weeks. Wondering if it would be Andy. Or whether having raised my hopes he'd got cold feet and thought better of it. I grabbed my mobile and looked at the screen. It was Frankie.

"I'd better take this inside," I said to Mark, hurrying back in through the patio door before answering.

"Hi," I said. "Are you OK?" There was a high-pitched sob from the other end of the line, followed by a bang as a rocket went off outside. "Frankie, what's wrong?"

"Emily's in remission," sniffed Frankie.

"But that's good, isn't it? That's what you wanted."

"The doctors say the risk of a relapse is so high because of this chromosome thing that she's got to have a bone marrow transplant straight away."

"Oh, Frankie. I'm so sorry."

"It just goes from bad to worse."

"You poor thing. What about donors? Can you do it?"

"No. Parents aren't compatible and Joe's not a match. They've tested the kids as well but they're not compatible either. And as I've got no idea where her father is or whether he's got any more children, there's not much I can do. Searching for a Gonzales in Spain would be a bit like looking for a Smith in England."

"What about that bone marrow register they have?"

"They've checked it for Europe and the rest of the world and it seems there's no match. Apparently that's not uncommon. It's unbelievable, isn't it? The whole fucking world to choose from and nothing for my Emily."

"So what happens now?"

"We wait and hope that someone compatible joins the register in time. And they won't say exactly how long she's got."

364

Another rocket exploded nearby, accompanied by the usual chorus of approving "oohhs". It felt wrong, people celebrating, having fun, when someone on the end of the phone was facing losing her daughter.

"Oh God. How's Emily taken it?"

"Pretty bad. She's back from hospital tonight. In her room as usual."

"I'll e-mail her later. Look, if there's anything I can do to help . . ."

"There is one thing. Although I know it's a lot to ask. You could register as a donor. They said to ask anyone we knew."

"Of course I will. I'll ask Mark too. Bloody hell, it's the least we can do."

"Thanks," said Frankie. "We really appreciate it. Anyway, I'd better go. Joe's working and Roberto's scared of the fireworks."

"Well you take care. Love to everyone. And a big hug from me. If you need to talk . . ."

"I will," said Frankie.

I slowly made my way back outside. Fiona was lighting a Roman candle. Mark clapped and whooped along with the rest of the crowd as the coloured flares popped up. And I knew that I had to go home straight away. Because all I wanted to do was yell at them to shut up, to show some respect. For a fifteen-year-old girl who might not be around to see Christmas.

"Hi, all set?" I asked when I met Mark outside his offices at lunchtime a couple of days later.

"Yeah, I guess so," he said, looking decidedly unsure about the whole thing. Admittedly giving a blood sample wasn't my idea of the best way to spend a lunch hour, but I wasn't going to complain when I knew what Emily was going through. Mark had agreed instantly to register as a donor when I'd told him what the situation was. Although he hadn't looked quite so keen when I'd explained it involved a blood test at the local hospital.

"So how was your morning?" I asked as we walked through town, trying to take his mind off what was in store.

"Quiet," he said. "So quiet I did some more work on that case. You know, the LawWorks one." He was representing an arts charity for adults with mental-health problems which faced losing its funding because it had been given notice to leave its premises by the end of the month. "The landlord of the building is being a complete arsehole. He wants to get planning permission for a commercial use for it. Obviously figures it will be easier with the charity out of the way."

"Is there anything you can do to stop him?"

"If there is I'm going to find it. The building's got a long history of community use, I'm ploughing through all the planning conditions and deeds at the moment."

I looked at him. He was really fired up.

"You're enjoying doing this, aren't you?"

"Yeah," he said, turning to face me with a grin. "I like sticking up for the little guys against the bullies."

We walked on towards the hospital, Mark talking enthusiastically about the case. It was great to see him like this: angry and passionate about something instead of appearing as if he was simply going through the motions. He even seemed to forget momentarily where we were heading — until we arrived at the clinic and the colour drained from his face again.

"Are you all right?" I asked.

"Yeah, I'm fine. Hospitals make me feel a bit queasy, that's all."

I nodded, still not convinced that he wanted to go through with this.

"Look, you don't have to, you know. Frankie would understand."

"No she wouldn't. I wouldn't understand if my daughter was dying of leukaemia and some wimp didn't want to give four measly millilitres of blood just because he had a thing about hospitals." It was a fair point. One I couldn't argue with.

"OK. Well if you need someone to hold on to while you're in there . . ."

"Don't worry, I'll dig my fingernails into the nurse. Maybe I can get some blood out of her at the same time." He was smiling as he said it, but I knew from the colour of his face that this wasn't a laughing matter at all for him. He'd never really explained why he had a fear of hospitals. Just said it was one of those things. It was clearly a big thing, though, for him to look as bad as he did.

"Twenty-six and twenty-seven," called a disturbingly efficient-looking nurse. We'd been given numbers when we came in. A bit like they did at the deli counter at the supermarket on a busy day. Except we weren't waiting for some pâté or half a pound of Somerset goat's cheese. We were about to be human pin cushions. We followed the nurse through to a small room with two wooden chairs facing various posters about giving blood and HIV screening. I appreciated the NHS didn't have money to spend on flowers or soft furnishings but any attempt to cheer the room up, even a poster of the Simpsons, would have been a help.

I handed the nurse my blood-testing kit which had been sent through by the Anthony Nolan Trust. She scanned the leaflet inside, got the needle ready and made some comment along the lines of being able to do this with her eyes shut. I hoped she didn't mean it literally.

"Right, arm out straight, clench your fist." I felt the prick before she said anything else. "OK, that's you done." Clearly there was no time for pleasantries. Perhaps she was on some kind of bonus depending on how many she got through in a lunch hour. I glanced over at Mark, who was being attended to by the other nurse in the room. If he'd looked pale earlier he looked distinctly green around the gills now.

"Are you OK?" I called over.

"Yes, I think she's drilling for oil," he said through gritted teeth as the needle was inserted.

I glanced up at the nurse. Not so much as a glimmer of a smile. She whacked a plaster on Mark's arm and went out to call the next number.

I shook my head and smiled as we made our way back along the corridor.

"You're not laughing at the nurse's friendly bedside manner, are you?" asked Mark.

"No, I'm thinking Emily will be so impressed when I tell her about this."

"What, because we did it for her?"

"No, because of this whole business with the vampires. I'll tell her Edward Cullen took our samples. Might even raise a laugh."

We were walking through the hospital car park when my mobile rang. My head was still full of Emily. So full that I didn't even think to check the screen before answering, as I'd been in the habit of doing for the past few weeks. I should have, though. To give myself a second or two to prepare.

"Hi, Claire."

I knew the voice instantly. Had gone to sleep with it playing through my Walkman so many times that I didn't have a doubt in my head that it was Andy. I hadn't actually thought he was going to ring now. Thought maybe I'd read the signs wrong, as I had so often in the past, and he'd simply asked for my number to be polite. Like when people who you haven't seen for years promise to stay in touch if you bump into them in the street, even though you both know damn well you won't.

"Oh, hi." I looked across at Mark as I said it. He was oblivious, of course, that I was speaking to the person he thought I'd put behind me.

"How are you fixed after work?" asked Andy. "Only I'm in the area this afternoon. Wondered if you fancied going for a drink?"

I was thrown for a second. Andy Pailes was asking me out for a drink. I had to rein myself back in. Maybe it was nothing. Maybe he was genuinely "in the area" and was simply being friendly. Or maybe it was the other "in the area". The one where you make a twenty-mile detour in order to get there.

"Oh, I see." I appeared to have been rendered incapable of giving proper answers to questions.

"You can't talk right now, can you?"

I glanced sideways at Mark. "Er, no. Not really."

"OK. So, as I don't know any pubs in Rochdale, how about I meet you at the magistrates' court at about half four? Will you be finished by then?"

"Yeah." I didn't recognise my own voice as I said it. Had even less idea where the answer had come from. My whole body felt weak, my head was spinning. And it had nothing to do with the nurse with the big needle.

"Great. See you then."

Somehow, without actually agreeing to anything, other than the time I finished work, I appeared to have arranged to meet Andy for a drink.

"Bye," I said, trying desperately to stop my voice coming out squeakily, not so much for Andy's sake but so as to stop Mark suspecting anything. And that was it. Andy said goodbye and was gone. Except he wasn't gone. He was everywhere again. Running through every vein in my body. I looked up at Mark. Feeling the need to deny something even though he had no reason to suspect.

"Just work," I said. And that was it. I had lied to him. It was a slippery slope from here on.

★ ★ ★

370

The rest of the afternoon passed by in a blur. It was a bit of luck I had nothing more taxing than a couple of adjournments; I certainly wouldn't have been capable of battling my way through a trial.

"Are you OK?" asked Fiona, as I gathered my things together at the end of the afternoon's session. "You seem a bit distracted."

"Do I?" I replied, struggling with the clasp on my briefcase. "I guess the blood clinic visit threw me a bit."

"All this business with your friend's daughter must be really worrying. I can't imagine what I'd do if anything happened to Aidan."

I nodded, feeling bad for using Emily as a cover when the actual reason for my distraction was Andy. I couldn't tell Fiona that, though. I was hoping she would be gone before Andy arrived. I didn't want the web of deceit spreading any further than it already had.

My mobile beeped a message. I knocked a folder from the top of the pile on my desk in my haste to check it. I hadn't listed Andy's name in my address book in case Mark saw it. Besides, there was no need. I knew the number anyway. I had it listed in my head alongside his home number from twenty-odd years ago. Which had stubbornly refused to be deleted.

"Hi. I'm in the foyer. A."

Fuck. He was early. I had two choices. I could either keep him waiting until everyone had gone or make a dash for it now.

"Right, I'm off," I said to Fiona as I put the folder back on my desk and grabbed my coat.

"A bit keen, aren't you?"

"Just getting out while the going's good. See you tomorrow."

I didn't even wait for her reply. I was already out of the door and careering down the corridor. Slowing my pace, I walked down the steps, trying to replace the inner fluster with an outward appearance of calm. I was doing quite well until I saw him. Standing there looking out of the window. His chiselled features marking him out from the round-faced security guards. His expensive-looking winter coat advertising the fact that he didn't belong in Rochdale.

He turned to look at me as my boots clopped down the stairs.

"Wow, get you," he said as I reached the bottom. "You're the genuine article now."

He was right, of course. The last time he'd seen me in court I'd been desperately trying to look like a solicitor. And now here I was. Bulging briefcase in hand and a fully paid up member of the Law Society. And here he was. Still looming large in my life. We were back in court again.

"I guess we've both come a long way," I said, trying to distance myself from the past. To break the sense of *déjà vu* which was flooding over me.

"Older and wiser, you mean?" said Andy.

"Yeah," I replied. Although I wasn't so sure about the wiser bit.

"Anyway, good to see you again," he said, greeting me with a peck on the cheek. I felt my face flush. Was suddenly conscious of the gaze of the security guards.

372

And of my desire to flee the environment which was so tied up with the past.

"You too. Let's make a move," I said, heading for the door.

"I hope you don't mind me turning up like this," said Andy, as we headed down the road. "It's a bit like buses, isn't it? Nothing for twenty-two years then two sightings in a few weeks."

"Where was your job?" I asked, eager to establish if he really had been "just passing".

"Blackburn Rovers. We're doing some work on their new sponsorship deal."

I nodded. Trying to visualise the surrounding road networks in my head. Pretty sure that there was a quicker way back to Leeds than via Rochdale.

"Here we are," I said, a few moments later, as we arrived outside the Flying Horse.

"Is this your regular watering hole, then?" asked Andy, holding the door open for me.

"Yeah. Although we don't usually make it here at lunchtime. Or that often after work, come to that. Everybody's busy with their families and stuff, I guess."

We walked in. It was quiet. Just a few clusters of suits around the tables. I scanned the room quickly in case there was anyone I knew. It was risky coming here, really. But there were so few decent pubs around that I hadn't felt like I had much choice.

"So, what can I get you?" asked Andy.

He had no idea, of course. Because back then, I hadn't even been old enough to drink.

"A dry white wine, please."

He nodded. "Sure. You grab a seat. I'll bring them over."

I made for a small table in the corner and sat down with my back to the rest of the pub. It was ridiculous, really. All the times I'd imagined doing something like this with Andy and, when it actually happened, I was far too worried about being spotted with him to enjoy it. All I could think of was that every time I came here from now on, I would look at this table and immediately be reminded of Andy. He was intruding into my life. On to my territory. Uninvited. Or so I liked to think.

Andy returned with the drinks and sat down opposite me.

"Thanks," I said.

"Were you with your boyfriend earlier when I called?" he asked, taking a swig from his bottle of Stella.

"Yeah." I didn't want to go into detail.

"I hope I didn't make things awkward for you."

"No, not at all," I said, trying hard not to spill any wine as I raised the glass to my lips.

"I take it he doesn't know you're with me now."

I didn't understand why Andy was doing this. It was as if he wanted to make me feel even more guilty than I already was. Maybe he was testing me. Seeing if he was still my Achilles heel.

"No, he doesn't. Not that it matters. I mean we're only having a drink, aren't we?"

I was testing him now.

"Yeah. We are. For now, at least."

"What do you mean by that?"

"You know what I mean, Claire. There can be as many meetings at Blackburn Rovers as you want there to be."

I looked down, fingering the stem of my glass, scared to look him in the eye in case I gave any inkling of the implosion his words had caused inside. I couldn't pretend it was all in my head any longer. He was right. It was up to me now. And that was the scary bit.

"That's not why I came here, Andy."

"Why did you come?"

"Because you asked me. Because I've never been very good at saying no to you."

"So why not just say yes?"

I could feel the word rising up in my throat. I swallowed hard, determined to thwart its progress. While I struggled for enough air to breathe. I glanced over my shoulder as the door opened and a large crowd of people walked in. I instantly recognised one of them from Mark's firm. Larry his name was. Or maybe Lenny. I'd only met him briefly at a Christmas do. But it was enough to make me reach for my coat.

"What are you doing?" asked Andy.

"Look, I've got to go."

"But you haven't even finished your drink."

"I'm sorry, OK? I can't stay here any longer."

"You've seen someone you know, haven't you?"

"What does it matter?"

"It matters because it's getting in the way."

"It was a bad idea to come here. I wasn't really thinking."

"So let's meet somewhere else then. Somewhere we can talk properly."

"I don't know. I need a bit of time to think things through."

"Fine. Let's leave it a couple of weeks. Why don't you come for Sunday lunch at Salts Mill? Say, the end of the month."

He was doing it again. Making it seem harmless. Making it hard to say no.

"I can't make it then," I said. It was a compromise. I wasn't able to say an outright no but at the same time I wasn't going to lie to Mark. Make up some story about where I was going.

"OK. When can you make it?"

"December the fourteenth," I heard myself saying. The day of Mark's football club Christmas lunch. They always lasted into the evening. I could be there and back without him knowing. It was still wrong, of course. But somehow it didn't seem as bad.

"Sure, no problem. Should be nice and festive. Shall we say about one?"

I nodded, glancing around anxiously as I heard Larry's group move away from the bar.

"I've got to go."

"OK. I'll see you on the fourteenth."

"Yeah. See you then," I said.

I picked up my briefcase and fled. Head down. Eyes firmly on the floor. Not once looking back. Knowing it was wrong to ever look back. But equally scared of what might lie ahead.

Sunday, 13 April 1986

I crept downstairs next morning before Mum was up and dialled Andy's number. I wanted to tell him he was in the clear. That I had denied everything. That it was all going to be OK. I let it ring for several minutes, in case he was still in bed. But he didn't answer. I hated this, not being able to talk to him. It wasn't supposed to be like this. Not now we were going out together. I put the phone down and sat at the bottom of the stairs waiting for our copy of the *News of the World* to be delivered. Telling myself they might not even use the photo. It wasn't really such a big deal, two young people kissing. If I'd been a year or so older, no one would have given a toss.

I heard the garden gate clink and the paperboy's footsteps coming up the path. As the letterbox opened I snatched the rolled-up paper from his hand and unfurled it, steeling myself to look at the back page. There was a photo of Gary Lineker scoring against us and a story about Arsenal sacking Don Howe. I flicked through the rest of the sports pages but there was nothing there, not even a paragraph. A wave of relief ran through me. Andy wasn't going to get in trouble at all. I turned the paper over. The picture of me and Andy kissing stared back at me from the front page.

Above it was the headline, "England Star in Schoolgirl Shame". Underneath, in smaller letters, it said: "Pailes denies under-age sex with teen fan."

"Fucking hell," I said out loud. It was there in front of me. In huge bloody great letters, on the front page of a national newspaper. I sat down on the stairs, my hands shaking, unable to take it all in. It didn't seem real. It was like there was another Claire Skidmore, one who had nothing to do with me. The story continued inside, over two more pages. There were more photos too. One of us going into my house and another of Andy leaving afterwards. And a photo of him at his front door which they said they'd taken yesterday. He looked shocked, bewildered. I knew how he felt.

I started reading the story. When I'd finished, I turned back to the front page and started from the beginning again, hoping it would sound better second time around. It didn't though; if anything it got worse. It wasn't the headline I found hard to stomach, or even the quote from an anonymous fan, presumably Susan, saying, "She tried to come over all innocent at the training ground, but I always knew there was something going on between them." It was the comments from Andy. The bit where he said I'd never been his girlfriend. That he wouldn't be seeing me again and it had all been a terrible misunderstanding.

I wondered which bit of it exactly I had misunderstood.

They started gathering outside our house within an hour of the paper arriving. The reporter and photographer from the *News of the World* came first. They rang the bell again but I didn't answer. Nor did Mum. I thought they'd go away but they didn't. Soon they were joined by others. Half a dozen photographers with long-lens cameras and bulging bags over their shoulders. And some others, presumably reporters, with spiral-bound notebooks in their hands. Even a bloke with a bloody TV camera with ITN written on the side. Outside our fucking house. Every now and again I peeked at them through the crack in my bedroom curtains. Each time I looked there were more than before. Lined up along the front garden wall. Chatting to each other, having a fag. Waiting for me to show my face. Content in the knowledge they had me cornered. I felt like a fox cowering in its lair. Knowing they could scent my blood. And that if I stepped outside I would be ripped to shreds.

I was surprised Mum hadn't been in. I still had the newspaper by the side of my bed. I guessed she couldn't face it. Seeing what a slut her little girl had turned into. I wondered if Frankie had seen it yet. And if she had, what she thought. I knew she'd be shocked. I hadn't even told her about the blow job. Let alone having sex with him. But at least she'd realise that I wasn't just some schoolkid any more. That I was a proper grown-up. Like her mate Tara.

Most of all I wondered why Andy hadn't answered the phone. Or called me. I needed to talk to him, to explain that I'd never meant for any of this to happen. To sort out what we were going to do. I was worried he blamed me. Maybe even thought it was my doing, some sort of kiss-and-tell thing I'd set him up for. I wondered if he'd meant what he said in the paper, that he was never going to see me again. I knew my Andy wouldn't do that, desert me at the very time I needed him most. But I wasn't sure if he was my Andy. Not any more.

It was halfway through the morning when I heard a commotion outside. People calling out, shouting to someone. I rushed to the window, craning my neck to see if it was Andy, scanning the road for a silver Golf. A second later the doorbell rang. Whoever it was didn't take their finger off the bell. Just left it ringing. I got up and crept to the top of the landing. The letterbox opened and a voice shouted through.

"Claire, it's your father. Let me in."

I dashed downstairs and opened the door a few inches, standing behind it so no one outside could see me. Dad squeezed through into the hall. He looked as if he hadn't shaved or brushed his hair. His eyes seemed to be flashing about all over the place, like he couldn't get them to focus.

"Hi," I said, as I shut the door. I wasn't sure what else to say. I didn't have to worry about it, though. Dad seemed to have plenty of things to say.

"Have you seen them out there? Have you got any idea what you've done? I always thought you had more sense than this. What on earth were you thinking of?"

I wasn't expected to answer any of his questions. He didn't provide the necessary gaps for me to do so. And anyway, before I could get a word in, Mum came out into the hall.

"What the hell are you doing here?" she said.

380

I wished everyone would stop asking questions and actually say something. Dad swung round to look at her.

"I'm trying to find out how my daughter's ended up on the front page of this fucking newspaper," he said, taking a copy out from inside his jacket and throwing it down on the hall table.

Mum's gaze dropped to the paper. I watched her scan the front page, brow furrowed, eyes bulging, before she looked back at him.

"There's no need to swear."

Dad snorted and shook his head. "What's the matter? Worried I might corrupt her? I think it's a bit late for that."

"Yeah, you're right. You already did that. About four years ago, if I remember."

Dad looked wounded. If I'd been scoring points I'd have given that one to Mum. But I wasn't refereeing. I was standing in between them, taking each punch squarely on the chin. To try and soften the blow for them.

"You can't pin this one on me, Maureen. You're the one who's supposed to have been bringing her up. Keeping an eye on her."

"Oh, and I suppose you think I've got nothing better to do than stay at home looking after her all day. It's not as if I need to go out and earn enough money to keep a roof over her head, is it?"

"You could have talked to her. Found out what was going on."

"And you think she'd have told me? For Christ's sake, Roger, you've got no idea what she's like."

"I am still here, you know," I said. They both turned to look at me. Then carried on arguing.

"Maybe if you hadn't encouraged her," Mum said. "Got her all worked up about football, none of this would have happened."

"I didn't tell her to screw her favourite player."

"Shut up, both of you," I shouted.

They turned to look at me again.

"She says she didn't sleep with him," Mum said.

"And you believe her?"

Mum shrugged.

"Oh, thanks," I said.

"Did he have sex with you, Claire?" Dad asked. "It's important that you tell us."

"Why? So that you can argue about whose fault it is?"

"No. So that if he did, we can report it to the club. I'm sure they'll have rules about players' conduct. And if this started before you were sixteen, well there are laws against under-age sex. You know that, don't you?"

"Course I do. I'm not stupid."

"You were stupid enough to get caught," he said.

"So were you," I replied.

They both fell silent. I knew I'd delivered the knockout blow. It didn't make me feel any better though. If anything, I felt worse.

"All you've done is have a go at each other," I continued. "You haven't asked how *I* feel. You don't care what I'm going through."

"We do. We're just worried that you're protecting him," Mum said.

"He has got a name, you know."

"I want you to tell the truth, Claire," she said.

"OK, I'll tell you. Andy listened to me. He wiped away my tears. Treated me like a woman. He made me feel more special than anyone else has ever done. And for a little while, an hour or so of my crappy life, he took the hurt away."

Mum started crying. Dad looked down at the floor.

"I'd better go," he said.

"That's right," Mum said. "Leave me to pick up the pieces."

Dad looked at her but didn't say anything. He smiled at me. A half-hearted sort of smile. And slipped out the front door.

The commotion started up again outside. I knew they were taking photos of Dad. I could hear him telling them to leave us alone. Mum was still standing there crying. I wanted her to take hold of me. To give me a hug. She didn't though. She went into the kitchen to put the kettle on.

I picked up the phone and called Andy. Still no answer. He must be avoiding me. Two days ago he'd been in this house, telling me how beautiful I was, making love to me. Now he couldn't even bring himself to speak to me on the phone. That was how badly I'd screwed this whole thing up. I needed to talk to someone, I pressed the button and dialled Frankie's number.

"Hello."

"Hello, Mr Alberti. It's Claire. Is Frankie there, please?"

"Just a minute."

I heard muffled voices in the background. A woman's voice whispering something. It sounded like her mum. After a long pause he came back to the phone.

"No, I'm sorry. She's not here at the moment."

"Oh," I said, not believing him for a moment. "Can you tell her I called then? I'll be in all day."

"OK. I'll tell her."

I went back to my room and sat on the end of the bed, staring at the photo of me and Andy on the wall. It was the first picture we'd ever had taken together. We were both smiling. Like we didn't have a care in the world. It had all been so simple then. If only things could be simple again now. I put my Thompson Twins tape on and fast forwarded to "Hold Me Now". I turned it up and sang the words out loud. My voice trembled through the bit about having a picture pinned to my wall and finally broke off when I got to "tattered and torn". I turned the tape off, sniffed loudly and wiped the tears away with the sleeve of Andy's shirt.

It was Trevor McDonald who broke the news the next night. In the past I'd always regarded him with affection; a sort of favourite-uncle figure whose friendly smile and soothing tones I welcomed into the living room. And yet here he was recast as the bearer of bad tidings, betraying my trust in much the same way as everyone else had.

384

"Disgraced England footballer Andy Pailes has been transfer-listed by his club and told he will not figure in the England World Cup squad due to be announced next week.

"United chairman and Conservative MP Roy Brown said Pailes, who is alleged to have had a relationship with a sixteen-year-old schoolgirl, would not play for the club again. It is thought Brown, who is heading up the government's family-values task force, came under pressure from Prime Minister Margaret Thatcher to take the tough action.

"The news came only hours after the Football Association revealed that Pailes would not be considered for England matches for the foreseeable future."

It took a good few seconds for everything to sink in, to process each piece of information, weigh up the implications and reach a logical conclusion: Andy's career was finished, I would never see him again — and it was all my fault.

The howl I let out was enough to bring Mum rushing in from the kitchen, still brandishing her icing bag.

"What on earth's the matter?"

"It's Andy," I said, tears pouring down my cheeks. "He's been transfer-listed."

"Does that mean he'll be leaving?"

"Yeah, he'll never play for us again."

"Good. Maybe it'll put an end to all this nonsense. Give us a chance to go back to being a normal family again."

I wondered what had given Mum the idea that we had ever been a normal family.

"How can you say that? Andy's the only person I care about and I've ruined everything for him. He's got to leave United and he's not going to be picked for the World Cup squad, and it's all because of me."

"It's not your fault. He ruined things for himself, so don't you start feeling sorry for him. Anyway, he can always play in the World Cup next year, can't he?"

"There isn't going to be a World Cup next year; they only play it every four years. This might have been his only chance."

Mum sighed and shook her head.

"For goodness' sake, Claire, this is *your* only chance to get your O levels; that's far more important. Now, I suggest you go upstairs and get yourself ready for school. Because you're not having another day off, even if those photographers are still outside in the morning. We're going to hold our heads up high and get on with our lives."

I sat on the toilet, staring at the array of air fresheners, odour neutralisers and disinfectants around me. I had never noticed them before. But now that I had, Mum's desire to forget all about it began to make sense. The slightest whiff of something unpleasant and she was there, can of Haze in hand, spraying frantically until the bad odours had dissipated and everything smelt of roses (or forest pine air freshener) again. Only this time she hadn't been able to do it. Because not even her formidable arsenal of ozone-depleting weapons could compete with the *News of the World* and *News at Ten*. So she was burying her head in the sand. Where she couldn't smell a thing.

I wasn't at all sure that living your life by the air-freshener philosophy was a good idea. But I could see that it allowed Mum to exist in a world where anything that caused pain, upset or embarrassment could be obliterated. And I couldn't help being rather envious of that.

I flushed the toilet and turned on the shower. I put the dial to the highest number. Wanting it hot enough to hurt worse than the pain inside. Afterwards I walked back to my bedroom, my skin raw and tingling, my brain struggling to take everything in. Trevor McDonald's words going round and round in my head until they became garbled and made no sense at all, not that they had in the first place. The very idea that Maggie Thatcher had got Andy transfer-listed was bordering on the surreal. I could only presume that it was some kind of divine retribution for me having been disappointed she'd survived the Brighton bombing.

My freshly pressed school uniform was hanging ominously from my wardrobe door. My stomach tightened at the thought of facing the world, of going to school in the morning, of even stepping outside the front door. I wasn't sure I could cope any more. And I didn't see the point of coping when all it would do was get me through another day without Andy.

He was leaving. I was never going to see him again. He hated me now. Probably wished he'd never set eyes on me. Not that I could blame him, after what I'd done. But I knew that however much he hated me, however much Mum and Dad and Frankie and everyone else hated me, they still didn't hate me as much as I hated myself.

"You don't have to do this, you know, Claire," says Andy, stroking my hair as we sit in Ken's office. "If you don't want to go through with it, I'll walk away, go somewhere else. You come first, you know that."

"I know, but I'm not going to let your career suffer because of me. And if this is what it takes, this is what I'll do."

Andy strokes my cheek with his hand.

"It means the world to me, you know. That you're prepared to do this."

I shrug. "It's a small price to pay really. If it means you can stay."

Andy pulls me towards him and kisses me on the forehead. I know it is going to be hard but I can do this for him. There is a picture of a dove on my wall at home, flying high above the sea. The words on it say, "If you love someone, set them free. If they come back to you, they are yours. If they don't, they never were." And Andy will come back, I know that. He will wait for me.

There is a knock and a pensive-looking Ken Benson, dressed in a suit rather than his usual tracksuit, sticks his head round the door.

"Are you ready for this?"

"Yes, boss," says Andy. "We're ready."

Ken turns to face me.

"You're something else, you are. There's not many would be prepared to make a sacrifice like this."

"You've fought to keep Andy here," I say. "This is the least I can do."

We follow Ken out of the room and along the brightly lit corridor towards United's main conference room. My hand tightens around Andy's. He gives it a quick squeeze. "Just remember, this will all be worth it in the end," he whispers.

Ken opens the door and flashes from dozens of cameras explode in our faces as we walk into the room. Andy puts his arm around me and guides me towards a chair, before sitting down next to me. Ken sits on the other side of him.

Andy pulls a sheet of paper out from his inside jacket pocket. I haven't read it but I know what he is going to say. He squeezes my knee under the table and mouths, "Are you OK?" I nod. He turns back to the sheet of paper and starts to read.

"Claire and I chose to come out and face you today for the simple reason that we have got nothing to hide. We have been in a relationship for several months now. However, the relationship is not and never has been of a sexual nature. In view of Claire's age, I understand the level of concern which has been expressed about our relationship but I wish to stress that nothing improper has taken place. It is a serious relationship and we are very much in love."

He pauses for a second. I feel a lump rising in my throat. I know what is coming next. Andy looks across at me. I nod and he continues.

"However, in order to ensure that there is no further negative publicity for this football club which we both love, we have taken the extremely difficult decision to put our relationship on hold until after Claire leaves school and the World Cup is over. We hope this will serve to demonstrate our appreciation to both Ken and the England manager for their continued support and the strength of our commitment to each other. I wish to stress we will simply not be seeing each other for a few months. We are not splitting up; indeed we have every intention of spending the rest of our lives together. And to that end, I want to give her this.

"I love you, Claire," he says, pulling a small box from his jacket pocket and opening it. "Will you marry me?"

The battery of flashes going off blinds me momentarily. But when I blink and begin to see again, there is a ring, a beautiful diamond engagement ring, twinkling up at me. I gaze across at Andy. I had no idea he was going to do this. I am floating in delight, barely able to keep my feet on the ground. He is waiting for an answer. He is smiling, though. Because he knows what I am going to say.

"Yes," I say, loud enough for everyone to hear. "Yes, I will."

Andy kisses me. The flashes go off again. The journalists start asking questions. Whose idea it had been. Whether we have my parents' blessing. Andy deals with them all effortlessly.

"Have you got anything to say, Claire?" asks a young woman scribbling furiously at the front. I look at Andy, waiting for his nod to go ahead.

"Just that I love Andy and United very much. And I'm looking forward to our future together."

Andy smiles at me. We walk out of the room together, hand in hand.

CHAPTER
TWELVE

It hadn't been so much of a harvest, more a humane way of putting what was left of my vegetables out of their misery. The truth was the runner bean plants were never actually going to produce runner beans and to pretend otherwise was positively cruel. Equally, any aspirations the carrots had of gracing a dinner plate some time were clearly fanciful. By the time I peeled them there wouldn't really be anything left worth eating. Even the handful of green tomatoes I'd picked would probably never ripen now. But I felt the need to take something home for my efforts, to place them on the windowsill and live in hope of a faint glow of orange appearing on their skin. I remembered watching the film *Fried Green Tomatoes* and wondered if they actually tasted any good like that.

I was still mulling it over when I noticed a familiar pair of size nines hovering on the edge of my patch.

"Hi," said Mark as I stood up.

I stared at him. His face looked pale and drawn. I felt dizzy. Maybe I had stood up too quickly. Or maybe I was scared that my whole world was going to come crashing down around my ears. Mark must have found

391

out something about me and Andy. Spoken to Lenny at work. It was all I could think of.

"What are you doing here?"

"That's a charming way to welcome me to your oasis of calm and tranquillity," he said.

"You know what I mean. You never come here. What's wrong?"

He hesitated for a second.

"I had a phone call from those Anthony Nolan bone marrow people."

He didn't know about Andy. And I felt awful for being relieved when what he was saying was far more important.

"Have you got something wrong with your blood?"

"No, they think I might be a match for someone."

"For Emily?"

"They don't tell you that. They just said someone who needs a transplant."

"God. That's all very quick."

"Yeah, it's a bit like winning the lottery, I guess. You do it but you don't really think it's going to be you."

I smiled at Mark, who it had to be said looked about as far removed as you could possibly be from celebrating a lottery win.

"So what happens now?"

"I need to give another blood sample at the clinic, a bigger one this time; they've sent me a special kit to post back to them. And I've got to go down to London for a medical at a private hospital on Wednesday." He looked down and kicked some earth with the toe of his boot. He was trying not to let me see his face. Because he was petrified.

I put my spade down and walked over. Wrapping my arms around him, letting him know he wasn't on his own.

"This is going to be really hard for you, isn't it?"

"You must think I'm a complete wimp," he said, still not looking me in the eye.

"Of course I don't. Lots of people are scared of hospitals."

"I can't help it, you see. It's to do with my dad."

"What do you mean?"

Mark let go of a big sigh. "He went into hospital when I was eight. It was only supposed to be an exploratory operation but they found something wrong with his bowel, so he had to have another op to remove part of it and they basically cocked it up, which meant he ended up having another major op to try to repair the damage. He was in hospital for nearly six months."

"God, that must have been hard for you all. Did you visit him and stuff?"

Mark nodded. "The thing was, nobody explained to me what was happening. You know what my parents are like about talking about anything remotely embarrassing. So I just assumed the worst. I thought he was dying."

"Oh, Mark."

He looked up, his eyes moist with tears. All I could see was the little boy inside, frightened and with no one to talk to.

393

"I remember one time we went in to visit him," he continued shakily, "and the old man in the bed next to him, who always used to talk to me and my brother, had gone. The bed was empty. No one told me he'd gone home so I thought he'd died and that Dad was next in line, because his was the next bed along."

"And you couldn't even talk to your mum?"

"I didn't want to upset her about it, so I never said anything. Until the day she told me Dad was coming home. I cried buckets. She thought I'd just missed him. She had no idea."

I shook my head and sighed.

"And that's why you don't like hospitals."

"Yeah. Stupid really. But I've never got over it."

"Look," I said, holding him tightly, "you don't have to go ahead with this. There's still time to back out if you don't want to do it."

"I can't, can I? It would be like signing up for the army and then saying you didn't want to go to war."

"Frankie would understand. I could explain to her about what you just said."

Mark pulled away and walked across to the other side of the patch, keeping his back to me, trying to hold it together.

"What if it's Emily?" he said. "What if it's her I match? I can't back out, can I? Imagine how Frankie would feel if I did that."

"I don't have to tell her."

"No, you don't," said Mark, his voice soft but firm. "Because I'm going ahead with it. Even if it does frighten the hell out of me. I hope it is for Emily, but if

394

it isn't then I still want to do it because someone out there is scared that someone they love is going to die and I might just be able to help them. I know they said it doesn't always work, but it's just about giving someone the chance, isn't it? If it was you, I'd want you to have the chance."

I stood and stared at him, shaking my head slowly. If I'd heard anyone else's boyfriend make that speech, I'd have been blown away. It wasn't anyone else's boyfriend though. It was my boyfriend. And perhaps it was about time I opened my eyes and saw him for the person he was.

"You're a good man, Mark Parry," I said, kissing him softly on the lips. "If I didn't know how insulting you'd find it as a Lancastrian, I'd say there was true Yorkshire grit in you."

"Thank you for not saying it then," he smiled.

"I'll come with you," I said. "Down to London for the medical."

"Don't be daft, you don't need to do that. It's only routine stuff and you've got a trial on this week. I'll be fine, honestly."

"Well at least let me come to the clinic with you for the blood test. Lend a bit of moral support."

"OK, as long as you promise to tell me some jokes to take my mind off it."

"Sure. Come on," I said. "Let's go back to mine. We're having fried green tomatoes for lunch."

I waited until Mark had gone to play football the next morning before phoning Frankie. I didn't want to embarrass him by praising his heroic gesture within earshot, or put added pressure on him in case he really was having second thoughts.

"Hi, it's me, how's things?" I asked when she answered. It was weird: all those years apart and here we were, within a couple of months of getting back in touch, reverting to saying "it's me" on the phone. Just as we used to do.

"Oh, up and down," said Frankie. "Mostly down, to tell you the truth."

"Is that you or Emily?"

"Well, me certainly. It's hard to tell with Emily. She says so little about it. I worry she's bottling it all up inside." I didn't want to tell Frankie the full extent of what Emily had been telling me. I was sworn to secrecy for one thing. And I didn't want her to feel in any way inadequate as a mother because she wasn't the one Emily was confiding in.

"I know she's talking to Alia," I said. "And to Robert, of course." Robert more than anyone. Hours spent simply looking at him, holding a picture of him, feeling the certainty of his love.

"I understand why it used to drive your mum crazy now," said Frankie. "She's not still talking about going to this stupid premiere, is she?"

"There is a plan in existence," I said. "Although I can reveal no more than that."

"Does it involve pulling the wool over my eyes with some limp story about Alia's grandparents' golden wedding party?"

396

"No," I laughed. "I've already warned her not to do that one. It'll be a bit more sophisticated, I think."

There was a long silence at the other end of the phone.

"She'll be heartbroken, won't she? When she's not well enough to go."

"I think she'll be OK, actually," I said. "I think she kind of knows already. This is simply a game she's playing to take her mind off everything that's going on. She's a hell of a lot wiser than I was at her age, you know."

"Well that wouldn't be hard, would it?" said Frankie.

"No, I mean her dreams really are just dreams. She knows she's not really going to end up with Robert Pattinson. She's not in the least bit deluded about it."

"It's crazy, isn't it?" sniffed Frankie. "Because all I want now is for her to have dreams which can come true."

I shut my eyes and sighed. Knowing exactly what she meant.

"Mark's tissue type looks like it's a match for someone," I said. "They want him to give another sample, go down for some tests."

There was a brief silence from Frankie's end.

"Really? That's fantastic. Oh Claire. That's the best news I've had in ages."

"It could be anyone," I said. "It doesn't mean it's Emily."

"I know. But it's just brilliant that he's doing it. That someone, somewhere will have some hope."

"It's funny. That's exactly what he said. He's terrified, you see. Got a real phobia about hospitals."

"Well you tell him from me that I think he's a complete star and Joe will probably offer to courier him up a pizza a day for life when I tell him."

"You'd better not then," I laughed. "I'm not sure his waistline can take it."

"Don't tell Emily yet though," continued Frankie. "I think it might be hard for her to take. That someone else is going to get a transplant when Mark only did it because of her."

"Of course, I understand. I won't say a word."

"You must be so proud of him," said Frankie.

"Yes. Yes I am." And as I put the phone down I realised I meant it too. So the realisation was swiftly followed by a pang of guilt. Because somewhere in my diary was a note of a 1p.m. lunch in Saltaire next month. And if I did mean it and I did love Mark, what the hell was I doing agreeing to see Andy again? The first visit had been officially sanctioned. I went because Mark wanted me to. But that was it. It was supposed to be a once-only opportunity. I'd already seen him once behind Mark's back; there could be no excuse for another meeting. Even if Andy's name had been on my laminated card for twenty-two years, it would still be utterly wrong.

Tuesday, 15 April 1986

I woke up with a bellyache. It wasn't just nerves. My period had come on. I felt sad, disappointed. Like I'd let the last bit of Andy slip away. If I'd been pregnant, he'd have had to see me again. We'd have been bonded together for the rest of our lives. But I wasn't. So that was that.

I put the radio on. America had bombed Libya during the night. I couldn't work out why, exactly. Other than that Reagan didn't like Colonel Gaddafi. I didn't like Bryan Robson but I had no intention of dropping a bomb on Manchester. I wondered if there'd be a nuclear war. It was about the only way my life could get any worse. Though I wasn't sure whether being fried alive would actually be worse than what I was about to go through.

I peered through the crack in the curtains. They were still there. Which was stupid, if you thought about it. The world was on the brink of a nuclear war and half of Fleet Street was standing outside my front garden. I wanted to open the window and shout down to them that they were in the wrong place; Colonel Gaddafi didn't live in Potters Bar.

Mum was already in the kitchen when I got downstairs. Doing her best to pretend that everything was normal. Her normal, not mine.

"Kettle's just boiled."

"Right."

"I've done your lunch. It's on the table."

"OK."

"I did you cheese and pickle for a change. It's a while since you had pickle, isn't it?"

I didn't waste my breath replying. I popped a tea bag into my United mug and poured water over it, watching the bag being dragged under by the current. I sat silently at the kitchen table, staring into my mug.

"Aren't you having any breakfast?"

"Nah."

"You have to eat, you know, Claire."

"Yeah."

Mum sat down opposite me, stirring her tea frantically, as if paddling for survival. I think I liked it better when she was shouting at me.

"Would you like me to run you to school in the car?"

I was relieved at the offer but didn't want to show it in case she thought it meant I still needed her.

"Yeah. If you want."

"Just this once, mind. I'm not going to do it every day."

I hoped there wouldn't be a need to do it every day. Though I was beginning to wonder what level of world disaster it would take to get rid of them.

I finished my tea in silence, picked up my lunchbox and went upstairs to get my bag. I glanced at myself in the bedroom mirror. I was back to being a schoolgirl again. It was like the other Claire had never existed.

Except in the photographs in the paper. I took a deep breath and went downstairs.

"All set, then?" said Mum, as if we were popping out for a nice little trip to the shops.

I nodded. I noticed she had her best jacket on. She never usually wore it to work. She turned the latch, opened the door a fraction and then shut it again.

"Now remember what I said. We hold our heads up high. Take no notice of them, OK?"

She was like a general telling the men about to go over the top not to worry about being shot. It was all right for her. She wasn't the one they were firing at. She opened the door and I blinked in the bright sunlight. It wasn't faces I saw. It was a mass of lenses pointing at me. Mum strode towards the car; I followed as close behind her as I could, head down, keeping my eyes on the ground.

"Claire, this way, Claire."

"Are you going to be seeing Andy again, Claire?"

"Has Andy called you?"

"Have you reported him to the police, Mrs Skidmore?"

"This way, Claire. Over here."

The barrage of questions and instructions was accompanied by a volley of camera shutters being fired and the whirring of motor drives from the cluster of bodies at the end of the drive. The noise battered against my head. I understood what Princess Di must feel like. Being watched and shouted at like that the whole time. Mum got in the car and leant over to unlock the passenger door. I felt myself shrinking as I stood there, as if my insides had collapsed and the outer shell was about to cave in. I fumbled for the door handle and clambered inside, fastening my seat belt, wishing it could protect me from what lurked at the end of the drive. Mum started the engine and edged forwards towards the waiting photographers. I glanced across at her. She looked flustered. I was trying hard not to cry.

"They're not moving," she said. "What shall I do?"

"Just go. Drive straight at them."

"What if I hit one of them?"

"I don't care. Just go."

The car lurched forward and the photographers parted, running round to my side of the car. I turned my head the other way but I could still see them out of the corner of my eye. Jostling for position, thrusting their cameras up against the car window, flashes going off again and again. I wondered if Andy would see these pictures in tomorrow's newspapers. Whether he'd look at me and think what a big mistake he'd made. I wished I wasn't wearing my school uniform. It made me look like a kid.

We eased through the gates and turned right on to the road. I could still see them behind us in the mirror. Mum accelerated away. I noticed her hands shaking on the wheel. It was all my fault again.

We didn't say anything to each other during the three-minute journey to school. I think we were both in shock. I could still see the flashes going off every time I closed my eyes. And hear the questions being fired out

402

like a machine gun. Mum pulled up about a hundred yards from the school gates.

"Is this OK?"

"Yeah, thanks."

"With any luck they'll be gone by tonight."

"Yeah."

"If you want, I can come and pick you up from school."

I imagined what my classmates would say if they knew my mum was waiting for me outside.

"No, it's all right."

I picked up my bag and opened the passenger door.

"Chin up, eh?" said Mum, managing a half-smile.

"Yeah," I said as I got out of the car, head bowed.

I watched the blue Fiesta disappear up the road and turned to start walking up towards the school gates. There were no photographers outside. Just masses of familiar faces. Inquisitive eyes and loud mouths at the ready. I knew it was only a matter of time.

"Slag." I didn't even know the owner of the first voice to speak out. Though I vaguely recognised a fourth-year face. The other lads around him started laughing and pointing. I didn't respond, just kept on walking, wishing I had a Teflon coating instead of an open flesh wound.

The closer I got to the school building, the more people pointed and stared. "That's her, the one that bonked that footballer," I heard one girl say as I walked past. I felt a hundred pairs of eyes on my back. I knew what they were thinking. She's nothing special. Whatever did he see in her?

I headed straight for my class room. It seemed the safest place to go. Debbie and Kim were already there. I sat down next to them.

"Awright," I said.

"Did you hear something?" Debbie said to Kim, looking animatedly around the room.

"Nah," she replied. "Nothing worth listening to."

"That's all right then. What were you saying? Something about that slapper in the papers."

Some of the lads at the back started laughing. I looked down at my desk. Fixing my stare on a knot in the wood.

"How much for a good knobbing?" shouted one of the boys. He reached into his pocket, produced a ten-pence piece and tossed it towards me.

"What do I get for that, Skidmark? Must be worth at least a blow job."

Some of the other lads started lobbing coins at me. Kim and Debbie were laughing, egging them on. I thought how unfair it was. I'd spent most of my school life being called a lezzie because I'd never had a boyfriend. Now, after one weekend, they were calling me a fucking prostitute.

"What's going on here?" Mr Butterworth's voice boomed from the doorway.

"Nothing, sir."

"It doesn't look like nothing to me. Sit down and shut up, the lot of you. I don't want to hear another word out of you."

When the bell went for first lesson, Mr Butterworth called me over.

"The head would like a word with you, Claire."

"What about?"

"I think you know what it's about."

"Now, sir?"

"Yes, now."

I hurried down the corridor, my shoes squeaking on the newly polished tiles. Mrs Millward, the secretary, looked up as I knocked on the door.

"Go straight in, Claire. Mr Burgess is waiting for you."

It was weird hearing his proper name. We always called him Birdshit.

I knocked on the door and went in. Birdshit was sitting behind his desk in a large swivel chair. His expression stern. Dark hairs bursting out of his tight collar and bristling under his cuffs.

"Sit down, Claire."

I did as I was told. I couldn't remember ever being in his office before. I noticed he had a photo of his wife and kids on his desk. It was facing towards me. As if he couldn't bear to look at them but wanted everyone else to know they existed.

"And what have you got to say for yourself, young lady?"

I looked at him blankly. It was a stupid question. I shrugged.

"Perhaps an apology would be a good place to start."

"Sorry, sir," I said. I wasn't sure what I was apologising for. It had fuck-all to do with him.

"When we send our pupils out on work experience, we expect them to behave in a way that is a credit to this school. We do not expect them to end up on the front page of a tabloid newspaper." He paused and looked at me over the top of his glasses.

"No, sir," I said. Deciding the quickest way out of the room would be to agree with everything he said.

"What's more, we do not take kindly to having the good name of this school dragged through the mud in this way. Under normal circumstances I would have no hesitation in suspending you. However, in view of the fact that you only have two months left at the school, I am going to allow you to continue as a pupil here in order that you may take the examinations which you have been entered for."

"Thank you, sir."

I didn't feel grateful at all. I would have been quite happy to have been kicked out. At least then I wouldn't have had to face going back to my classroom.

"Now I suggest you keep your head down, stay out of trouble and concentrate on your studies. No doubt your mother has already told you this, but I strongly advise that you have no further contact with the young man in question. Do I make myself clear?"

I wanted to knee him in the balls for being such an arsehole. Thinking he had any right to stop me seeing Andy.

"Yes, sir," I said.

"Good. That will be all."

I got up and walked out of his office. Mrs Millward smiled again and gestured me towards her.

"The school nurse is in at one o'clock today, dear," she said. "In case you need to see her about anything."

I stared at her, realising she'd read every word in the papers. And that she believed it all.

I went back to my lesson. It was double history. Everyone looked round when I walked in. I sat at the back and kept my head down. It was the same the rest of the morning. I didn't say a word to anyone. Just sat in silence. Knowing that every time someone laughed, they were laughing at me.

When the bell went for lunch, I let everyone else rush off while I packed my things away as slowly as possible, making sure it was a good five minutes before I left the classroom. I slunk down the corridor towards the canteen. I didn't like the place at the best of times. It smelt of disinfectant and mashed potato, which was strange because I'd never considered that mashed potato had a smell to it before I'd been in there. It was also far too exposed for my liking. The plastic-coated tables were laid out in neat, regimented rows with no more than a few feet between them. And the dining area was fronted by a huge wall of glass, looking out on to the playground, ensuring that no one was safe from prying eyes and pointing fingers, whether from inside or out.

I managed to find an empty table and sat down. Everyone in the canteen turned to look at me. I could see people outside pointing at me as well. And hear a wave of whispers and laughter rolling up from the far end. I eased my lunchbox from my bulging schoolbag, opened the silver-foil package containing my cheese and pickle sandwiches and took a large bite. I chewed it over and over again, but I couldn't seem to swallow.

Eventually I spat it out and sat there staring at the mangled mess I'd produced. Wondering whether Andy was able to eat, or whether I'd ruined his appetite too.

The trundling sound of the shutters being pulled down on the canteen brought me sharply back to reality. I was the only one left in the canteen. A dinner lady was standing over me, viewing the remains of my sandwiches with disdain.

"Are you eating them or what, love? Only we've got to get the tables cleaned up and put away."

"No, it's all right, you carry on. I'm not hungry. I'll put them in the bin on my way out."

I wrapped the sandwiches back up in the silver foil, squeezing them so tightly that some of the pickle oozed out and dripped on to the floor. The dinner lady tutted, her previously warm expression turning frosty.

"Not content with wasting good food, are you? Got to make a nice mess for us to clear up as well."

I mumbled an apology before sloping off down the corridor. I started calculating how many school days there were until I'd finished my exams. Getting through one lunch break was bad enough; the thought of surviving thirty-five more was daunting to say the least.

The girls' loos were empty when I pushed open the heavy wooden door. I slipped into the right-hand cubicle, locked the door and fished around in my bag for the slim beige plastic case that contained my spare Vespre. Nothing was written on it to indicate its use; it was its very discreetness which gave the game away. I held one end of my soiled sanitary towel with the very tip of my thumb and index finger and peeled it from my knickers. I looked behind me for the bin, only to discover it was missing, leaving me squatting there, knickers round my ankles, as I considered my next move.

There was a sternly worded notice on the door saying not to flush sanitary towels down the toilet, but short of walking out of the cubicle waving it about, I didn't see I had a choice. I chucked it down the loo, peed on it and flushed hard. The water gushed into the bowl, sending the towel swirling around before disappearing down the U-bend. But as the water rose slowly back up, so too did the towel.

I sighed, knowing I must now wait an eternity while the cistern refilled before I could try again. The main door opened and two pairs of heels clicked into the toilets.

"Fucking hell, it stinks in here. Be quick, will you."

"Yeah, all right. I've got to do me hair, it was blowing a right gale out there."

"I know. It was worth it, though. I didn't want her trying to sit next to us in the canteen. Never know what you might catch."

It was only when I heard the laughter that I recognised the voices. And realised that Debbie and Kim were talking about me.

"D'ya reckon she did bonk him then?" said Debbie.

"Yeah. I bet he wasn't the first, either. I always wondered why she went down that training ground."

"I can't work out what that Andy guy saw in her, mind. I mean, he's not bad-looking."

"He's probably got some schoolgirl fetish thing going on. He looks a bit of a perv to me."

"Maybe. He dumped her pretty sharpish though, didn't he?"

"Yeah," said Kim. "Probably took one look at her fried-egg tits and legged it."

There was another round of giggles.

"Come on," said Debbie. "I'm done in here. Let's go."

I flushed the toilet again to try and drown out the noise of my sobs. The sanitary towel went down this time. Not that I cared any more. I waited until I was sure Kim and Debbie had gone, then slipped out of the cubicle and splashed some cold water on my eyes, trying to cover up the redness. I tried telling myself it didn't matter. They were only jealous because they'd never been out with anyone older. But a tiny part of me still wanted to run after them, pleading for them to be my friends. I didn't though. Not because my pride wouldn't allow it. But because I was scared it might make them hate me even more.

I turned the corner into my road, my schoolbag banging against my legs. Most of the photographers had gone, pissed off to Libya hopefully. But there were still three left. Leant up against the garden wall, having a laugh about something, probably me. As far as they were concerned I was some silly little groupie who went around shagging footballers. That was what it must look like. I could see that now. As soon as they saw me walking down the road they picked up their cameras and started taking photos. It was like being one of those moving targets at the fairground. I looked down at the pavement, counting the cracks as I stepped between them. The breeze blew my hair over my eyes. I let it stay there. The photographers didn't call out or anything. Just kept on taking pictures. I couldn't believe they hadn't got enough by now.

I opened the gate. Mum's car was parked in the drive. She was home earlier than usual. I hurried up the garden path and let myself in, banging the door behind me. Shutting out the outside world. Mum came out of the lounge. She was fiddling with her rings. She looked like she'd been crying again.

"There's someone here to see you," she said.

For a split second I thought it might be Andy. Until I remembered there was no way Mum would have let him in. I followed her into the lounge. There was a woman sitting on the sofa wearing a navy suit and wide-rimmed glasses that looked too big for her. She got up when she saw me.

"Hello, Claire. I'm Sergeant Hopkins from the Child Protection Unit."

I spun round to look at my mum.

"Did you do this? Did you ring them?"

Mum looked away. She didn't say anything.

"I can't believe you called the cops. I thought you were supposed to be on my side."

"We are on your side," Sergeant Hopkins said. "We're here to protect you."

"I don't need protecting. And I'm not a child."

"I need to ask you a few questions, Claire. About your relationship with Andy Pailes before you turned sixteen."

"You wanna get him in trouble, don't you?"

"There are laws, Claire, to protect girls under sixteen. If Mr Pailes did something he shouldn't have, put any kind of pressure on you, you need to tell me. Please sit down, both of you."

I perched on the edge of the armchair. Mum sat down on the sofa, at the opposite end to the copper. Where me and Andy had been.

"Good. Now the questions I'm going to ask you may be difficult, Claire, but it is important that you answer truthfully. I want you to understand that this is a very serious matter."

I nodded. But I had no intention of hurting Andy any more than I already had done.

"How long have you known Mr Pailes, Claire?"

"Since last summer."

"And how would you describe your relationship with him?"

"We're friends. Very close. He's the best person I know."

"And has that relationship ever gone beyond friendship?"

"Only last week. When he kissed me."

"And nothing at all had happened before then?"

I could see Mum out of the corner of my eye, biting her lip. I decided not to mention the blow job.

"No."

412

"OK. So you're telling me there was no sexual contact between you while you were underage?"

"No. Nothing. He's not like that. You've got him all wrong."

The copper looked at Mum and raised her eyebrows before turning back to me.

"Claire, you do understand that if anything sexual did happen between you, you wouldn't get into trouble. And that you do have a duty to tell me if it did. To protect other girls like you."

I nodded.

"Right then. We'll leave it there for now. If I can just have a quick word with your mother."

I went into the hall and listened through the door. I could hear Mum saying she didn't believe me. But the copper said that without any evidence or a statement from me, there was nothing more they could do.

"Thank you for your co-operation, Claire," she said, shaking my hand as she came out. "If you do think of anything else you'd like to tell me, please give me a call."

She pressed a card with her name and number on into my hand.

"Are you going to interview Andy?" I asked.

"No. Not at the moment. Unless you think we should."

"No. Course not. I was just gonna ask you to say hi from me if you were. That's all."

The copper smiled at me, shook her head and let herself out.

CHAPTER
THIRTEEN

Fiona passed me the note with all due solemnity, seconds before the magistrates walked back into court. I nodded an acknowledgement, sat down and opened the piece of paper.

"Mother 'em Maddox is a secret hankie-waver. I have it on good authority that he was spotted morris-dancing at a festival last weekend."

I pursed my lips hard and stared intently at a crack in the top of the bench to try to prevent the huge guffaw brewing inside me from seeping out. I scribbled furiously on a piece of paper, "Thanks, you complete cow. How the hell am I supposed to keep a straight face now?" and handed it to her. Fiona read it, nodded slowly as if taking in a complex piece of legal information and filed it safely away in her folder, before turning to the assembled magistrates, including one Martin Maddox.

"Mr Foster is here for the CPS," she said, "and Miss Cooper is representing Miss Wilson."

Maddox nodded, I tried not to imagine the bells jingling as he did so. Instead I looked over at Kaz, who was standing in the witness box, fiddling with her hair.

"You OK?" I mouthed to her. Kaz shrugged. I was aware that her future was hanging in the balance. She had already pleaded guilty to the shoplifting charges. We were only here for sentencing. And although I would have liked to reassure her that everything would be fine, I couldn't. Because I was still waiting to hear if I'd got her the rehab place I'd been chasing for weeks. Dozens of phone calls back and forth between social services, the probation service and a particular rehab centre in York which had come highly recommended. The offer of a place had been due yesterday but had so far failed to materialise. I hadn't told Kaz, of course. There was no point upsetting her at this stage, because even if I did get an offer of a place, there was no guarantee Mother 'em Maddox would go for it. Especially if he'd had a bad day with the hankies.

Nigel rose from his seat next to me, the usual smug look on his face. He'd already told me he was going to ask for a custodial sentence. I hadn't bothered to try to persuade him otherwise. As there was no evidence he had a heart, it was pointless to ask him to use it.

"Your worships," he began, "Miss Wilson has pleaded guilty to several shoplifting charges. As you will have seen from the probation reports, she has a long history of previous shoplifting and drug-related offences. I am in no doubt that anything short of a custodial sentence will result in her being back before you within a very short space of time and for that reason urge you to impose the maximum custodial sentence available to you today."

I rolled my eyes. The trouble with Nigel's approach was that he was so sure of himself he didn't even see the holes in his own arguments. If prison was working for Kaz, she wouldn't keep coming back, would she? I got to my feet. I was going to adopt a different approach. It was risky and a long shot but it was my best bet. Although it would only work if Maddox truly did have a heart.

"Your worships," I began, "I'm going to do something unusual here. I'm going to break the confidentiality clause between myself and my client. Usually you don't get to hear what is said between us in private meetings. Quite right too. But I'm going to tell you what Miss Wilson said to me. Because I think you need to hear it."

I turned to look at Kaz. She nodded, having reluctantly agreed to what I wanted to do.

"Miss Wilson committed these crimes on purpose. Not, as my colleague from the CPS suggested, because she has a flagrant disregard for the law, but because she wanted to get caught. She wanted to get caught because she wanted to go to prison. Not because it's a soft option but because it's the only place she feels safe. From her dealer, from her drug-using boyfriend, from loan sharks who are out to get her. I know it's hard for us to believe with our nice houses and loving families, but that's the truth. Karen Wilson's life is so awful that she believes she is better off — and safer — inside prison."

I glanced up as I paused for a second. Maddox was listening intently, a slight frown on his forehead. I was in with a chance here.

"Prison is the only place where she has ever been given any help to come off the drugs which are behind

416

all of her offending. Only unfortunately, the three-month sentences she's received so far aren't long enough to do a proper detox and rehabilitation. So this time she thought she'd muck around, smile at the security cameras, make it look as if she had a flagrant disregard for the law so that you would make an example of her and bang her up for a long time."

I paused again. Nigel was staring up at me as if I had finally lost the plot.

"I think that's a damning indictment not of Miss Wilson but of our legal system and our society," I continued, turning to look at Kaz, who was cowering like a rabbit caught in the headlights. "I think she deserves better than that. I think she deserves a proper chance to build a drug- and crime-free life. And I don't believe prison is actually the best place for that.

"Since the probation reports were prepared, Miss Wilson has been offered a long-term placement at a drug rehabilitation centre in York. It's a good one. One of the best in the country." I handed Fiona a brochure about the centre and she passed it up to Maddox.

"What I'm asking you to do today is give her that chance. If she ends up back in front of you in a year's time, feel free to make an example of her. But I'm confident she won't let you down. And I'm confident that when you return to your nice homes in nice communities this evening you will sleep more soundly knowing that Karen Wilson is safe and is at last getting the help she needs."

It was only as I sat down that I realised my legs were shaking. Only as I glanced up at Fiona, her eyes

417

rimmed with red, that I had an inkling of the effect my speech had had on the courtroom. There was silence for a moment before Maddox called Fiona up to the bench. A second later she said, "The magistrates will retire to consider this matter." As soon as they did so I went up to Kaz.

"Hang on in there," I said. "I've nearly got this sorted for you." I dashed out of court number three, turned my mobile on and waited for the beep of a message. I was shaking when it came and as I dialled 123 to listen.

"Hi, it's Rob Dangerfield from Turning Point. Regarding the place you wanted for Karen Wilson, I have now confirmed to the probation service that we have one available and advised them to let me know by the end of the day whether she'll be taking it up."

I breathed a long sigh of relief and scuttled back into the courtroom just as the magistrates were returning, smiling at Kaz as she stood up.

"Miss Wilson," began Maddox, "your counsel has given a very moving account of your predicament. Although we were minded to give a custodial sentence, my colleagues and I have decided to impose a six-month suspended sentence on condition you take up the place at the Turning Point drug rehabilitation centre in York." Karen's face broke into a huge grin. "May we wish you the very best of luck," finished Maddox, nodding at me briefly before standing to leave the room. And instantly becoming my all-time favourite morris-dancer in the process.

"Court rise," said Fiona as the magistrates filed out. I walked over to Kaz, who still appeared to be in shock.

"Have I got the place?" she said.

"Yes, you've really got the place. I just had a call."

"I dunno what to say. I can't afford to get you anything and I can't even nick you anything now, can I?"

"Definitely not." I smiled. "The only present I want from you is to never see you in here again, OK?"

"You've got it."

"I'll visit you there," I said. "See how you're getting on. Have you got your stuff with you?" She nodded. "I'll speak to the probation service and we'll sort out some transport."

As I turned to leave the court, Fiona winked at me and walked over.

"Unorthodox, but you pulled it off," she whispered. "It's not like me to come over all emotional. You had us all wrung out there."

"Sometimes you just have to lay it on the line," I said.

"You know what? I wish Aidan had been here to see that. So he could understand that what you get out of work is what you put into it."

"Mark says he's been doing really well on work experience this week. Very responsible and showing a lot of interest."

"Well I'm glad to hear it," said Fiona, looking chuffed. "Maybe there's still time for him to turn things around."

"I probably shouldn't tell you this," I said, lowering my voice. "But as I'm on a roll of breaking client-lawyer confidentiality, I'll tell you something else Mark told me."

"What?"

"When Aidan's out late at night, he's not hanging out with those dodgy kids. He's seeing his girlfriend."

"Girlfriend? I didn't know he had one," said Fiona.

"I know, you're not supposed to. You're his mother, remember. She's got nice tits and a cute arse, apparently. That's what he told Mark."

Fiona rolled her eyes and laughed. "Lord, now I have got something to worry about."

"Not a word, though, remember. You're still playing the dumb parent."

"And that's exactly what I am," smiled Fiona.

I was about to leave when I noticed Nigel was still sitting there, shaking his head in disbelief. I walked over to him.

"Sometimes," I said, "you don't find the answers in textbooks. It has to come from the heart. I understand the Wizard of Oz can get you one. You have to follow the Yellow Brick Road." I turned and strode out of the courtroom, a huge bloody great smile on my face.

There was a letter for me on the mat when I got home. I recognised the thick cream stationery straight away. Smith MacGuire used nothing but the best. I put my briefcase down and tore open the envelope. Racing past all the niceties and the "thank you for coming to the interview" bit to get to the "I regret to inform you that

420

on this occasion you have not been successful" part. It didn't come though. Instead I read, "We are delighted to offer you the position of legal executive on a starting salary of £38,000 a year. Please contact our HR department at your earliest possible convenience to advise when you will be able to take up this position."

I read the letter again just to make sure, but the words remained the same. I'd been offered the job. A plum job at a top city firm with partnership prospects and a salary which dwarfed my present one. But instead of being elated, of dancing around the kitchen in delight, all I could think was that it felt absolutely nowhere near as good as the feeling I'd had in the courtroom earlier.

When Mark came round later after work, I didn't even mention the job offer at first. It was Kaz I wanted to tell him about.

"Hey, that's brilliant," he said, giving me a hug. "Sounds like you played a blinder. Do you think she can turn her life around?"

"Yeah. I do. She really wants to. And when you want something that badly I think you make sure you get it."

"I'd have loved to have seen the look on Nigel's face," said Mark, sitting down at the kitchen table.

"It was priceless," I said. "I suspect that I'll get extra flak from him next time we cross swords, but it will have been worth it."

"Well I've had a success too," he said. "That LawWorks case, the charity's safe; the project's got its funding."

"How come?"

"I found a condition in the original planning permission for the building, stipulating that part of it had to be retained for community use. The landlord's decided not to sell and withdrawn their notice."

"That's fantastic. You've completely saved the day for them."

"Yeah. The project leader was really chuffed. Said some of the group were in tears. Apparently they're busy making me some thank-you piece of artwork."

"Brilliant." I smiled at Mark, seeing someone different standing before me. Someone who appeared to be growing in stature before my very eyes.

"It feels good, doesn't it?"

"What?"

"Making a difference."

I nodded, knowing I needed to say something.

"I've had a job offer, actually."

"Smith MacGuire? When?"

"Just now," I said, pointing to the letter on the table.

"Bloody hell, that's great." Mark hesitated as he looked at me. "Well, it's great that they offered it to you."

"What do you mean?"

"You don't want it. You might have thought you did, but now you've got it, you don't, do you?"

"I wasn't expecting it, that's all. It's taken me by surprise. But I can't say no to a job like that, can I?"

"Why not?"

"It's got everything going for it. Ticks all the boxes. I'd be crazy to turn it down."

"You turned down a perfectly good house which ticked all my boxes because it wasn't what you wanted. That wasn't crazy. It was the right thing to do."

"You didn't think that at the time."

"No. Because like you said I'd got carried away with my plans and hadn't stopped to think that you might not want the same things as me."

"But what's that got to do with this job?"

"I think you're getting carried away with thinking this is your dream job and you're not stopping to ask yourself if what you used to want is the same as what you want now."

I looked down at the table, thrown for a minute by how perceptive he'd become.

"Sometimes you don't know what you want until you try it."

"And sometimes you don't realise you actually had what you wanted until you've lost it."

I got up and walked over to the sink, busying myself with filling the kettle. Playing for time while I tried to work out whether Mark was still talking about the job or had moved on to something else. The troubling thing was that I suspected he could be right. Although he had no idea exactly how right.

Everything I supposedly wanted was there for me on a plate. All I had to do was take it. And yet here I was with a sudden yearning to keep the things I had. Because I was seeing them in a new light. Or maybe the light hadn't changed, just something inside of me. I poured our teas and turned back to face Mark. He was sitting at the table, a crumpled envelope in his hand.

"What's that?" I said.

"I got a big letter too today. From the Anthony Nolan people. Confirming I am the best match for the person who needs the transplant. And I've passed the medical, so it's all systems go."

"What, the actual transplant?"

"Yeah. Apparently there's two ways you can donate these days: the traditional way where they give you a general anaesthetic and take the bone marrow from your pelvis, and some new technique involving blood stem cells, which is much easier and doesn't involve an overnight stay in hospital."

"So which are you doing?"

"The traditional way. The doctors say it will give the recipient the best chance in this case. So that's what I've said I'll do."

"How soon?"

"December the fifteenth."

"Jesus, that's only a couple of weeks away."

"Yeah. I've got to go down to London the day before. It's a private hospital. I'll only need to stay two nights. Means I'll miss our football club do, but hey, that's not important any more."

As soon as he said it I realised. The fourteenth was the day I was supposed to be meeting Andy for lunch. My first thought was that it was rotten timing. And then the wave of self-revulsion hit me as I cursed myself for being such a selfish cow. Besides, it was actually brilliant timing because it meant I'd have to cancel. And I knew damn well I should never have agreed to see him again in the first place.

"I'll go down with you," I said. "Lend some moral support."

Mark shook his head. "No thanks. I want to go on my own."

"Don't be ridiculous. You can't do that. I'm the one who got you into this in the first place by telling you about Emily. The least I can do is be there with you."

Mark reached out across the table and took hold of my hand.

"I know you want to and I know I'd want to be with you if it were the other way around. But actually, I really do think it's best if I do this on my own."

"Why?"

"Because of all the stuff I told you about. It was bad enough you seeing me being pathetic at the blood clinic; what I don't want is for you to see me in hospital, crapping myself before the op."

"I don't want you to go through that on your own. I want to be there for you. To help you."

"Then please do as I ask," Mark said. "I need to confront my demons on my own. You understand that, don't you?"

I nodded.

"If you can get the time off work, come down on Monday morning so you're there when I come round and I can revel in the glory of what I've done and have someone to help me home the next day. But let me do the first bit on my own."

I sighed and looked up at the ceiling. I didn't want to agree for two reasons, the first being that I genuinely did want to be with him, to support him through this incredible thing he was doing; the second that I didn't trust myself not to go and see Andy in Mark's absence. Too much time to think about the past, to mull over everything that was on the table was a dangerous thing. I looked back at Mark. It was what he wanted. I had to go along with it.

"OK, if you insist. But I will feel awful about not being there with you."

"Well don't sit about brooding. Go out and have some fun while you get the chance. You'll be stuck playing Nurse Cooper for the rest of the week."

I smiled the best smile I could muster. And started to worry.

I was still worrying at two o'clock in the morning. Lying next to Mark. Feeling the warmth of his body, the gentle rising and falling of his chest, the familiar light snoring sound he made when he was fast asleep. I swung my legs out of bed, pulled on my dressing gown and padded downstairs to the kitchen to make a cup of tea. I sat down with my mug at the table and flipped open the lid of my laptop. It was annoying, my desire to check my e-mails even at this hour in the morning, but if I couldn't sleep I figured I might as well do something useful with my time.

The only thing in my inbox was from someone whose e-mail address started with em4rob. I smiled and opened up Emily's missive.

So, what do you want first, the good news or the bad news? The bad news is that I'm going to miss the *Twilight* premiere, even though I'll only be a couple of miles away from it. The good news is that it's because I'll be getting ready for a bone marrow transplant on 15 December! They've found me a donor. The match is almost perfect, but there are no guarantees it will work and I've got to have another lot of chemo beforehand. They've given me this massive booklet listing all the things that can go wrong and side effects and stuff afterwards, but hey, what the hell. Someone's given me a chance. And although I'm really gutted about not seeing Robert (Alia's mum won't let her go on her own either), what matters is that I might just be around for the *New Moon* premiere next time. I can't believe that someone I don't even know would do this for me. Would give me this chance. Right now I love them almost as much as I love Robert!

L8ers.

Emily

X

I smiled and wiped the tears from my face as I closed the lid. I wasn't going to reply now. I would speak to Frankie first. Find out if it was OK for me to tell Emily. That it wasn't someone she didn't know after all.

I drank my tea, crept back upstairs and slid back under the duvet alongside Mark.

Sunday, 20 April 1986

The look in Mrs Alberti's eyes as she opened the door was familiar. It was the same look I had been seeing all week. The one of surprise and thinly veiled disapproval.

"Claire," she said, with none of her usual warmth, "I'll get Francesca." No invitation to step inside, no chitchat about how my mother was or how things were going at school. When Frankie appeared in the doorway a few moments later, she had the exact same look on her face.

"You'd better come in."

It was more an instruction than an invitation and Frankie led the way up to her bedroom without another word. I stared at the bare walls which greeted me.

"You've taken all your United posters down," I said.

"Yeah, well it was about time. I couldn't keep them up for ever, could I?"

Frankie looked uncomfortable, seemingly aware that she couldn't avoid the obvious topic of conversation any longer.

"I guess you've had a crap week," she said.

"Yeah. I was kind of hoping you'd come round, or at least call me back."

"To say what? Congratulations, you got what you wanted?"

"This isn't what I wanted."

"No? So how come it's all I've heard about for the past year. How you and Andy were made for each other."

"I wanted to go out with him. For him to love me back. Not for all this shit to happen."

"So why'd you have sex with him, then?"

"Who said we did? You're just taking the newspaper's word for it like everyone else."

"OK," she said, taking a few paces further towards me. "Tell me what really happened."

I looked down at my feet. I could lie to my mum and a copper but not to Frankie. And besides, I wanted her to know.

"We did have sex. Just the once. Unless blow jobs count, I don't know."

Frankie looked at me like I'd just told her I'd murdered my own granny.

"You dirty slag," she said, jabbing her finger in the air at me.

I couldn't believe it. I'd expected her to be impressed.

"What d'ya mean? You're the one who told me to grow up. Get real, you said."

"I meant to stop dreaming about him. Not to go and bloody bonk him or suck his cock off."

"I don't get you," I said. "You've spent half your life going on about how you'd like to screw Matt's brains out. And now you're sounding like the fucking Pope."

"Yeah, well, it was just words. I was never actually gonna do it with Matt, was I?"

"Oh I get it. You're jealous. Because Andy wanted me and Matt was never interested in you."

"It's not like that."

"Yes it is. You're all mouth and no action, you are. And now you're upset because I've done it and you haven't."

Frankie sat down on the bed and started to cry. I felt a massive pang of guilt.

"Look, I'm sorry it never worked out with you and Matt, OK?"

"It's nothing to do with him."

"Well what then?"

"You wouldn't understand," Frankie said, her eyes rimmed with red.

"You always do this," I said. "Make me out to be some stupid kid. But I'm not any more. Why can't you see that?"

Frankie was bawling her eyes out now, her shoulders shaking with each fresh sob. I didn't get it.

"I'm the one who should be crying," I said. "I came round here because everything's gone horribly wrong and I needed to talk to someone, and all you do is have a go at me and act like some drama queen."

"You wanna know why I'm upset?" she said, the tears turning to anger as she started jabbing her finger again. "I'm crying because you've spoilt it all for me. It was safe, me and Matt, you and Andy. Safe and innocent. It was all just a bit of fun, and now you've ruined it, made it dirty."

"It wasn't dirty. It was beautiful. I love him, you know that."

430

"That's bollocks. It was a dirty thing to do. Trust me, I should know."

"What d'ya mean by that?"

"Nothing."

"Yes you do. You wouldn't have said it otherwise."

"All I'm saying is you shouldn't have let him touch you, Claire. You'll regret it. I do."

"Regret what? You haven't done anything."

"That's what you think."

"You never said."

"Yeah, well, I wasn't exactly proud of it."

"Of what? You're not making any sense."

"It doesn't matter now."

"Yes it does. You can't do this big scene and then say that."

"OK, you wanna hear it? I'm a dirty slag, just like you."

I looked down at her, a frown creasing my brow.

"What d'ya mean?"

"Why d'ya think I packed in the tap-dancing?"

"You said it was boring kids' stuff."

"I had to make something up, didn't I?"

"So why did you leave?"

"I didn't have much choice. Not with him there, leering at me the whole time."

"Who? Uncle Tony?"

"He's not my uncle, OK?"

"What did he do to you?"

"Fucking hell, do I have to spell it out? He touched me, Claire. In places he shouldn't have. And made me touch him."

I slumped down on to the bed next to her, holding my head in my hands.

"I'm sorry. I had no idea."

"No, I know. I didn't tell anyone. Not even my mum."

"Why not?"

"Because nice little Catholic girls don't let things like that happen to them, do they? And anyway, Auntie Maria was my mum's friend."

"How long did it go on for?"

"A few months. Long enough to make me feel like a slag."

"It wasn't your fault, Frankie."

"Yes it was. I must have done something. Turned him on in some way. Because he didn't touch Connie, or any of the others. He told me that. Said I was his special favourite. It was our little secret."

"You can't blame yourself. You were only a kid."

"I still let him do it. I've had to live with that for four years."

"I wish you'd talked to me."

"I didn't even wanna think about it. I tried to put it out of my mind. Until I read all that stuff about you and Andy. And it brought it all back again. Made my skin crawl."

"But this was nothing like that. I knew what I was doing, Frankie. He didn't make me do anything I didn't want to."

"You don't see it, do you?" she said, standing up, her arms flailing in the air. "You're still a kid. And he's seven years older than you. He's a fucking pervert."

"No he isn't. He really cares about me. We would have been going out if all this crap hadn't happened."

"Oh yeah? So where is he now? Where is your precious Andy Pailes? Called you, has he? Or been to see you? Course he ain't. He got what he wanted and he doesn't give a toss about you. He's no better than bloody Tony."

I looked at her and shook my head. I was starting to feel sick inside.

"You can't say that. That's a horrible thing to say."

"It's true. You just can't face up to it. Like I couldn't. I just hope someone doesn't rake it all up again for you years later. 'Cos believe me, it's not very nice."

I sat there watching the tears streaming down Frankie's face and realised that she was right. It was all my fault. I'd screwed things up for all the people I really loved. It was no wonder everyone hated me. The trouble was I didn't know how to stop, to turn the clock back. Or how to live with myself. I got up and walked over to Frankie. I tried to put my arm around her but she pushed me away.

"I'm sorry, Frankie. I thought I was making everyone happy. Thought that was what you wanted me to do."

"Yeah, well. You thought wrong, didn't you?"

"I know that now. And I'm really sorry. I don't blame you for hating me."

"Claire, I don't . . ."

"No, it's all right. I'm going. You'll be better off without me."

I turned and walked out of the room, down the stairs and out the front door. Not once looking back.

The first thing that hit me when I got home was the smell of the chicken roasting in the oven, reminding me that Mum had invited Malcolm and my nan round for Sunday lunch. I wasn't sure I could cope with that. I wasn't sure I could cope with anything any more. The radio was playing to itself in the kitchen; upstairs I could hear the sound of the hot-water pipes whistling, confirming that Mum was having her usual Sunday-morning soak.

I hurried into the hall, picked up the phone and dialled the number again, feeling my warm breath hitting the mouthpiece and bouncing back to me as I waited, my hand tightening on the receiver as I heard the ringing tone. He would answer this time; he had to. He didn't though.

I put the phone down, more convinced than ever that Andy must hate me, really hate me, if he still didn't want to talk to me. He had every right to, I reminded myself. After what I'd done to him.

The smell of roast chicken wafted down the hall from the kitchen, wrapping itself around my throat and making me feel slightly queasy. "Chicken and beans, chicken and beans, chicken and beans," it taunted me as it swirled around my head. I'd never be able to forget him, I knew that now.

I followed the smell into the kitchen and opened the oven door. The heat hit me square in the face. I felt obliged to stand there and take it though, to suffer a little for Andy's sake. To make some kind of sacrifice.

I pulled the roasting tray towards me, feeling the heat pricking the tops of my fingers through the tea towel. In one quick movement I dragged the tray out and deposited it on top of the hob, watching the plumes of heat rising, turning the pattern on the kitchen tiles behind into a hazy blur.

It was three years since I'd gone veggie. I'd almost forgotten what chicken tasted like. I took the carving knife and prodded the bird. The skin came off easily, rolling back to reveal the white flesh beneath. I took the piece of skin in my hand, holding it between my thumb and forefinger. I licked it first, feeling the grease on my tongue, grimacing as it drizzled down my chin. Then popped it into my mouth, chewing for a few seconds before swallowing hard.

There, I had done it. Done something I'd hated doing, for Andy. I felt a brief spurt of elation before I realised the nasty taste was still there. Lingering on my tongue, seeping into my flesh.

I put the chicken back into the oven and ran to the sink as I started to retch. I could feel the spasms in my stomach. My throat tightening. But nothing came up. It was stuck deep inside of me, with all the other bad stuff; the things I shouldn't have done or said. I was rotten on the inside. And it was spreading, like some giant cancer. Soon it would be out of control.

I had to get out of the house, to breathe some fresh air. And I could only think of one place to go. I dashed up to my room and took the Milk Cup Final tickets from my top drawer. After everything that had happened, I'd decided it was best to stay away. But I realised now that if Andy had been good enough to get the tickets for me, I owed it to him to use them. I took something else out of the drawer as well. The letter I'd written the previous night. The one that explained how sorry I was. How much I hated myself for screwing up his life. I remembered the bundle of letters that had been waiting for Andy on the day I'd gone inside Priory Park with him. All of them from people who thought he was special, who maybe liked to think they were special to him. They weren't, though. I understood that now. They were nothing special at all.

I paused, looking around the room, before grabbing Andy's crumpled United shirt from my bed. I would wear it to Wembley. It was the least I could do.

"I'm going out," I called in the direction of the bathroom, before bolting down the stairs and out the front door before Mum could stop me. When I reached the post box on the corner I hesitated for a second. And then watched as the envelope slipped from my still greasy fingers and disappeared from view.

Walking up Wembley Way, I tried to blend in with the other fans. It should have been easy enough. I was wearing jeans and a United shirt like everyone else. But it didn't seem to make any difference. I still felt as if I had a huge neon sign above my head proclaiming, "I'm the girl in the papers, the one that ruined Andy's career, the one you all hate." I wished I'd worn my United cap so I could have pulled it down over my face and let myself be blindly pushed along by the crowd, up to the twin towers and through the turnstiles.

436

It was worse still inside. The laughter and the whispers. I caught a snatch of conversation from behind: "Brown's barmy, if you ask me, getting rid of Pailes instead of having a go at the girl for coming on to him. Stupid slag."

I felt it like a kick in the stomach. Part of me wanted to turn round and defend myself. But I knew it was pointless. The jury had given its verdict. I was guilty. Obliged to take any punishment thrown at me.

When United walked out on to the pitch, I looked for Andy. Even though I knew he wasn't there. Only his shadow, hanging over everything. I followed the match with my eyes, watching every pass, every header, every tackle. But my heart wasn't in it any more. The magic had gone. It was my fault. I'd wished for too much and had lost everything.

As Matt scored on the stroke of half-time, everyone around me leapt up in the air while my guilt nailed my feet to the ground. I watched them all bobbing up and down in delight, whooping and cheering. And I remembered how good it had once felt.

But although I hadn't felt the usual ecstasy when United scored, I still felt the agony when Forest equalised not long after the restart, and when they scored the winner in the last minute. Maybe I'd known all along that United would lose and had simply come to torture myself. To solemnly watch Forest's lap of honour while all the United fans around me were streaming out of the ground. I was the chief mourner, saying goodbye to a much-loved friend.

It was a long time before I began walking back to the tube station. It was true what they said as well. About it seeming a lot further on the way back when you'd lost. It was raining heavily. The raindrops mingled with my tears and washed them down my face, making room for the next ones.

When I got to the ticket barrier at Wembley Park I had to rummage deep in my bag for my Capital card, searching through the soggy tissues and discarded chocolate wrappers before I found it, stuck firmly to the picture of Andy. The one in the little plastic folder, protecting it from getting damaged or torn. I stopped dead in my tracks, staring at Andy's face smiling up at me. He hadn't known back then, of course. How I was going to ruin his life.

"Are you going through or not, love? We haven't got all day, you know."

I looked round apologetically at the middle-aged man who had spoken and shuffled to the side of the ticket barrier, letting everyone in the queue which had built up behind me go past. They had trains to catch. They had places to go.

A handful of people were still on the platform when I finally got there, mostly United fans who appeared to have been drowning their sorrows before beginning the journey home. A young man wearing an oversized United bobble hat looked straight at me. For a second I thought he was going to point, to shout, "That's her, that's the one whose fault it is." He didn't though; he just smiled knowingly.

438

"That is one depressed lady," he said to his friend, nodding in my direction. "It's all right, love," he called after me. "There's always next season."

There wasn't though. Not for Andy. And therefore not for me. Nothing left to look forward to. I wondered if people felt like this after they'd climbed Everest. That the view from the top hadn't been as good as they'd expected. And that now they'd stood at the summit, there was no place left worth going. Nothing to dream of any more. And without dreams all you had left was reality.

I tried to think of one good thing in my life. One person I loved who didn't hate me, one chance to put everything right, one glimmer of hope on the horizon. I thought for a long time. Nothing came.

I walked to the far end of the platform, past the covered section, and stood letting the rain beat down on me. I wanted it to beat harder, to make me suffer more. I needed a punishment that would fit the crime. Of ruining the life of the very person I loved most in the world.

As I heard the faint rumble of the train on the tracks, I knew what I had to do. It was the only option left. The only thing that would take the bad taste away. And prove how sorry I was for everything I had done. I started running back down the platform, faster and faster as the train came into view. The faces of the other fans flashed past me, as if I was watching them from the train. I heard voices. I couldn't make out what they said, but it was like everyone was talking to me, chanting, urging me to do it.

I stopped and steadied myself for a second on the edge of the platform, wrapping my arms around me as I hugged Andy's shirt, knowing he would give me the strength I needed. I remembered what he had said to me in the car.

"Don't ever stop smiling. You've got a beautiful smile."

It was all he'd ever asked of me but I hadn't even been able to manage that. I'd let him down. I wouldn't let him down now though. Not this time. I blinked away the tears and stared into the cab of the approaching train, waiting until the driver looked straight at me before forcing a smile across my face. There. I hadn't stopped smiling, see. I could do anything for Andy. Anything at all.

I stepped off the edge of the platform.

CHAPTER
FOURTEEN

"Are you sure about this? I feel awful not coming with you."

"I told you," said Mark, taking my hand. "I want the right to be a complete wuss in private."

"Well if you change your mind, call me. I'll come straight to the hospital, OK?"

"Sure, but I won't. Come down tomorrow like I said and I can bathe in the glory of it all and you'll have no idea what a fuss I made about the whole thing."

"Oh I don't know. I think the nurses will probably fill me in on the details."

Mark smiled and pulled a face at me. He didn't fool me though. I could see how terrified he was.

"Has Frankie told Emily yet?" he asked.

"She's going to tell her this morning. She wanted to wait as long as possible in case there were any last-minute hitches."

"Like me doing a runner, you mean?"

"You'll be fine."

"I will now," he said. "It makes it easier. Knowing it's for Emily."

"We still don't know for certain."

"I do," Mark said.

I smiled and kissed him on the lips. Knowing it should have made things easier for me too. And feeling wretched about what I might end up doing after he had left.

"Thank you," I said. "I think you're doing an amazing thing."

"It's OK," he said. "Just be aware that I'll milk it for all it's worth for years to come." He grinned as he walked out of the door.

"Text me when you get there," I said.

He nodded, climbed into his car, waved once and was gone.

I cried as I got ready. Hating myself for not having the willpower to resist. And hating the fact that Andy still exerted such a hold over me, all these years on. Every step towards the train station felt like I was trying to walk the wrong way up an escalator. When the train came I hauled myself on. The journey had begun. I read a book on the way but had no recollection afterwards of the story. Only of seeing the words on the page. By the time I walked across Bradford to Forster Square station I was resigned to my fate and had submitted myself to what was about to happen. I would be carried to Andy. He would be waiting for me. He'd already texted me to ask what train I'd be on. And when I stepped down on to the platform, that would be it. I would be his. Just like I'd always wanted to be.

The train came to a halt at Saltaire station. When I saw him on the platform the grey flecks in his hair threw me for a second. I realised I had been half

442

expecting to see the old Andy standing there. I still wasn't used to the new one. He smiled as he caught sight of me. My body tensed, as if recognising the forces which were at work here. Knowing the destructive qualities they possessed.

"Hi, Claire," he said as he reached out to touch my arm, bent to kiss me on the cheek. I didn't move this time. I didn't seem to be able to resist any longer. A frisson of excitement ran through me. The familiar churning sensation started up inside. Andy was here. I was not in control any more. "Good to see you again," he said. "How's things?"

I couldn't begin to answer truthfully. To say that actually my boyfriend had just gone down to London to donate bone marrow to my best friend's teenage daughter who had leukaemia and might die if it didn't work. It was all too real, too scary and not part of this at all. I used to be able to talk to Andy. He used to be the only one I could talk to. I realised that wasn't the case any more.

"Fine, thanks," I said instead.

"Did you hear anything about that job?"

"Yeah, I was offered it."

"Great. When do you start?"

"I don't. I turned it down." I'd sweated on it for almost a week before deciding. But the evening after I got back from visiting Kaz at the rehab centre in York, I'd finally written the letter. Mark had been right. It wasn't what I wanted any more. Not at all.

"Oh, why?"

"I guess I realised how much I love what I do now. You know what it's like, you moan and grumble about it like everyone does. But when it comes to leaving, well, it's a different matter altogether."

Andy nodded. I had no idea if he understood. Or if he was simply being polite.

"So where's Titus?" I asked as we walked across the road towards Salts Mill.

"At home. Safely shut up in the kitchen. I'm afraid his table manners are appalling. I took him for a really long walk this morning to tire him out. He'll be fine."

We reached the entrance to the mill. Andy held the door open for me. Just as he'd held open another door once before. When we were leaving court. When everything had been about to change.

"Have you ever been here before?" he asked.

"Once, a few years ago. Not to eat, just to look around."

"It's a great place. It'll be good to have the chance to chat properly as well. Without any distractions."

I decided to ignore his reference to our last meeting and its rather abrupt conclusion.

"So, are you a regular here?" I asked.

"I often used to come here for Sunday lunch quite a bit. Haven't been for a while." I guessed he meant he used to come with Jennifer. Going out for Sunday lunch wasn't much fun on your own. I could remember that much.

It was heaving when we got up to the diner, a huge open room with the kitchen on view at the heart of it. We queued for five minutes before a waitress had a chance to show us to a table. Andy pulled the chair out for me before sitting down opposite and smiling at me. The air around us was filled with clatter and chatter. This was clearly a place for talking. It was simply a matter of knowing what to say.

"What are you going for?" asked Andy, after a few minutes of perusing the menu.

"The asparagus risotto, I think."

"Are you veggie?"

"Yeah, have been since I was a teenager."

"Oh, right. I don't remember." He wouldn't, of course. Because we'd never gone out for meals together. It hadn't been that sort of relationship. It hadn't been much of a relationship at all.

"What about you?" I said.

"The salmon fillet, I think."

"Not the chicken?" I smiled.

"Why do you say that?"

"It used to be your favourite pre-match meal, chicken and beans."

"Was it?"

"Yeah. You said so, in one of those fact files in *Shoot!*"

Andy laughed and shook his head.

"Jesus. Did anyone actually take any notice of those things?"

"I did," I said.

Andy looked at me. I wondered if he was seeing the sixteen-year-old me again. Or the one sitting here, beginning to feel I didn't really know him at all.

"Do you keep in touch with any of the United players?" I asked.

"Only Thomo. And only by e-mail, really."

"What's he doing now?"

"He's a sports physio. He loves it."

"What happened with his wife?"

"She's fine. She's been in remission for a long time now. Though I don't think he's ever really stopped worrying about it coming back."

I nodded. Thinking how long ago it all seemed. Almost another lifetime.

"Do you go to any matches these days?" I asked.

Andy shook his head.

"No. My heart's not in it any more. Football got spoilt, didn't it? It's all about big business now. I spend my days negotiating clubs' sponsorship deals and drafting television rights agreements. The actual football doesn't seem to matter any more. How about you? Do you ever go and see United?"

"No," I said. "I haven't been since the Milk Cup Final."

The waitress returned with our wine and to take our order. Cutting through the awkward silence which had descended on the table. Neither of us wanting to talk about what had happened after the Milk Cup Final.

Andy raised his glass.

"To new beginnings," he said. His eyes were searing into me as he said it. Looking for any chinks in my armour. Any way he could get past my defences to the girl who adored him. Who would have laid down her life for him. Who very nearly did.

I clinked my glass against his but I took only a sip. Everything had been churned up inside. Things which had lain dormant for a long time. All these years I'd dreamt of this. Of seeing him again. Of carrying on from where we left off. But now I was here. And now I remembered exactly where we had left off, I wasn't so sure. My phone beeped twice from my bag.

"Excuse me," I said, bending to pick it up. I thought it would be Mark, letting me know he'd arrived. It wasn't though. It was Emily.

"Mum's told me. Mark's my donor. I know he is. He's a real live hero. You must be so proud of him. Thanx. Em X"

I put the phone back into my bag and looked up at the ceiling as I struggled to blink the tears away.

"Are you OK?" asked Andy. "Was that your boyfriend? Is he making this hard for you?"

I stared across at him. Seeing everything so very clearly for the first time. The top of the volcano blew.

"You weren't worthy," I said.

"Sorry?"

"Of being my idol. You treated me so badly."

"Claire. I said sorry at the time."

"And do you think that was enough for all the pain you caused me? You used me. I was sixteen, for Christ's sake. You were lonely and you thought you'd screw me to give your ego a bit of a boost."

Andy put his glass down, glanced anxiously around the diner in case anyone had heard. A frown creased his forehead. "It wasn't like that," he said, his voice soft and low.

447

"Well it wasn't far off. You were in my bedroom. The fucking walls were plastered with pictures of you. And you still carried on."

"I thought it was what you wanted."

"The Andy I wanted was the one on my wall. The one who would never let me down. Always be there for me."

"I didn't know it would end up in the papers like that."

"I know. But you could have given me a bit of support when it did. Instead of buggering off and leaving me to deal with all the crap."

"It wasn't up to me. The club told me what to do."

"And you didn't have the guts to stand up to them."

"My career was on the line."

"My fucking life was on the line." My voice broke as I struggled to control the pent-up anger which had festered away for so long. I was aware that other people were looking at us. Thinking we were having some sort of lovers' tiff. Having no idea of the enormity of it all.

Andy looked down at the table, his face long and drawn.

"I behaved like a bastard, I know that. It's been eating away at me all these years. The reason there was nobody serious in my life for so long was you. I knew I could never find someone who loved me as much as you did. You were special, Claire. You really were."

"Well you had a bloody funny way of showing it."

Andy looked up at me, his eyes dark and heavy.

"When you did what you did, I realised what a bastard I'd been. I didn't see how I could put things

448

right so I figured it was best for everyone if I kept well out of the way."

"I so needed you," I said, shaking my head. "So needed to know that you cared."

"I'm not proud of my behaviour, Claire. But as much as I wish I could, I can't change what happened. Can't make things better."

"Unless I turn up out of the blue, at a point when you're lonely and feeling a bit down. And you decide to start the whole thing up again."

"Hey, it was your idea to come and see me."

"It wasn't. It was my boyfriend's. Mark had the guts to do that, to give me your address and to trust me to come back to him."

"He's a fool then, isn't he?"

"He's not a fool," I said, shaking my head and pushing my chair away. "I'm the fool for taking this long to see how appallingly you treated me. And for agreeing to come and see you again today."

"You came because you wanted to," said Andy. "You want this every bit as much as I do."

"I thought I did. But I thought wrong. Mark's worth ten of you. I can see that now. And I'm not going to let you screw up my life a second time."

I stood up, aware that my voice had been louder than I intended. That everybody in the diner was looking now.

"Claire, please don't be like this. Please don't go. Give me a chance to make it up to you."

"I did," I said. "Twenty-two years ago. I lay there for a very long time. You didn't come. Now if you'll excuse

449

me, there's someplace else I need to be." I turned and strode off past the startled waitress who had just arrived at the table with our meals. I hadn't meant it to be so public, for everything to come out in that way. But now it had, I at last felt free of him.

Tuesday, 22 April 1986

I can hear Andy's voice calling to me. Telling me how much he loves me. Willing me to stay with him. My eyes are shut. I have no idea where I am. Maybe floating somewhere between heaven and earth. I don't care which one I go to, as long as Andy is there.

I drift in and out of consciousness for a while. But Andy is with me all the time. Wrapping himself around me. Love like antiseptic, healing my wounds. Whenever his voice fades, when he seems to be drifting away, I fight harder and bring myself back to him. Closing the gap between us. I draw strength from him. Draw oxygen. Feel him breathing life into me, pumping my heart until I am strong enough to do it myself. I can hear the blood rushing around in my head. Begin to feel a tingling sensation in my fingers and toes. Life flooding back into me.

I am aware that he is holding my hand, asking me to squeeze it if I can hear him. My brain squeezes but the message gets stuck somewhere along my arm. I try to smile. I have no idea whether it is showing on my face. After a while the fog starts to lift but reveals only blackness behind it. I lie still, fearing I have lost him. Until his voice echoes inside my head. The blackness starts flickering. And I realise it isn't blackness at all, but the inside of my eyelids.

With a huge effort I haul them open only for them to fall shut again as the light streams in. Andy responds, the tone of his voice rising, sensing I am nearly there. I wait while my batteries recharge. Then slide my lids half open, letting them get used to the light, before opening them fully. And seeing Andy's face inches from me. His eyes moist with tears but shining brilliantly.

"Hello," he says. "I knew you'd come back to me."

I smile, knowing he can see it this time. I open my mouth to say something but he puts his finger to his lips.

"Rest now," he says. "We can talk later."

I do as he asks. Shutting my eyes then opening them again a second later, to check I still can, before sleeping properly. Knowing I can wake again when I want to.

When I do wake, Andy is still smiling down at me, love pouring from his eyes. I lie for a long time just looking at him. Studying his face. Making sure I know every inch of it so if I slip away again I will be able to see it. Even with my eyes closed.

The rest of the picture around him begins to fill in, shapes, colours and smells. A huge bouquet of lilac and purple flowers stands in a vase at the end of my bed.

"Thanks for the flowers," I say, not needing to ask who sent them.

"It's OK. It was the least I could do. From now on," he says, "I'm not going anywhere. I'm looking after you, that's all that matters." I smile as I rub my eyes. "You get some more rest," he says, stroking my face.

"There's one thing I want you to do," I say. "Before I go back to sleep." I point to the plaster cast on my leg. Andy smiles, picks up a pen from the bedside cabinet and writes in large, sprawling letters across it, "To my darling Claire, all my love, Andy", and signs a huge kiss after it.

"Thank you," I say, smiling while trying to stifle a yawn at the same time. "That's made it feel better already."

Andy watches as my eyelids slide ever lower.

"Claire," he whispers. "I'll love you for ever."

"I know," I say, without even opening my eyes. "I love you too."

He sits there for a long time afterwards. I can feel his breath, warm against my face. And his love enveloping me, keeping me safe.

It was when I smelt Mum's Yardley perfume that I realised I hadn't died after all. I wasn't exactly sure what heaven would smell of but I knew it wouldn't be that. And I couldn't imagine they'd have any perfume at all in hell.

The initial relief was tempered by an overwhelming sense of failure at my inability to carry off what should have been a straightforward suicide. How typical that I couldn't even get that right.

How much damage I had inflicted upon myself in the process, I wasn't sure. All I knew was that I was hurting in a hell of a lot of places. Although considering I should have been lying in bits on a train track, I realised that, for the first time in ages, things could have been a whole lot worse.

But I was still miffed that I hadn't come round to the sound of the players singing a rousing chorus of "United We Stand". I'd always thought it must be the best thing about being in a coma — knowing that your favourite stars would be desperately trying to bring you back to life.

It gradually dawned on me that I had no idea how long I had lain unconscious. It could have been an hour, a month or an entire lifetime. I was almost afraid to open my eyes in case I found myself on a geriatric ward, but in the end, curiosity got the better of me.

It took a few seconds for the world to come into focus and for Mum's face to materialise in front of me. She was smiling a big, watery smile. Beneath it she looked tired and drawn but she didn't appear to have aged significantly.

"What year is it?"

"It's nineteen eighty-six, love. Why? Don't you remember?"

"Yeah, I was just checking. Is it still April?"

"Yes, of course."

"And what day is it?"

"Tuesday."

"So I've only missed a day or so?"

"Yes, love, only a couple of days. They've been very long days, that's all."

I nodded, noticing the catch in Mum's voice. A nurse came over to check on me, smiling, chatting away as if nothing had happened, and went off in search of a doctor.

"How are you feeling?" Mum asked.

"Like I've been hit by a train." I said it with a smile on my face rather than sarcastically, somehow taking comfort in the familiarity of Mum asking stupid questions. I surveyed the array of monitors around my bed and looked down at my body, much of which appeared to be swathed in bandages or encased in plaster.

"How bad is it?"

"Are you sure you want to know?"

"Yeah, go on."

"Well, you gave your head a bad bash, although the scans don't show any lasting damage. You've broken your left leg, fractured your collarbone, smashed part of your left arm and fractured a few ribs. The rest is just cuts and bruises. The doctors say you might be left with some scars but you've been very lucky."

"Right." I didn't feel particularly lucky, but I knew what Mum meant. The thing I didn't understand was how I'd even survived. But I wasn't sure how to ask without sounding ungrateful.

"So . . . what happened? Why didn't . . . I mean, how come I'm still here?"

Mum gave a long-drawn-out sigh and shut her eyes for a moment.

"The train hit you as you fell but it pushed you into the pit at the side of the track, love; it passed right over you."

I nodded, trying to picture it all in my head.

"What happened to my shirt?"

"What shirt?"

"My United shirt."

"I'm not sure. I expect it was in a bit of a mess, like you."

"Oh."

A doctor came over and examined me, looked at all the monitors and wrote something on the clipboard on the end of my bed.

"You're going to be fine," he said. "No more questions. You need to rest. Try to get some sleep."

I shut my eyes again, but not before registering the warmth in Mum's smile. A warmth I couldn't remember seeing before.

When I opened my eyes again Mum was still there, sitting beside me with the same expression, a mixture of relief, anger and guilt, etched across her face. She reached out and squeezed my hand. I noticed that her nail polish was scuffed and flaking. Normally you could see your own face in it.

"Well, you're here, that's all that matters. You gave us all quite a shock."

I wasn't sure who the "us" was supposed to refer to, as Mum appeared to be on her own and I couldn't imagine that anyone else would have been particularly bothered about what had happened.

"Your father was in yesterday. He said to give you his love. He brought you those." She nodded towards a huge vase of flowers that was squeezed on to my bedside cabinet, surrounded by an array of get-well cards.

"Who are they are from?"

"Oh, your nan, Auntie Barbara and Uncle Bob. There's some from your friends at school. Oh and one from Mr Aspland, the newsagent."

I was confused. I didn't have any friends at school and I hadn't realised Mr Aspland even knew my name.

"So everyone knows, then?"

456

"Well, yes, it was all over the news again. What do you expect if you go and do these silly things?"

I wondered what other silly things I had done that ranked up there with trying to commit suicide. I supposed Mum meant the Andy thing.

"Has Andy sent a card?"

"For goodness' sake, Claire, don't start all that again. That's what landed you in this state in the first place. When we get you out of here, I'm going to take you on a little break, give you a chance to get away from everything, forget all about it."

I had visions of another wet week in Great Yarmouth.

"It's all right, you don't need to do that."

"I do. I need to do a lot of things that I didn't do before. I should have listened, I should have been there for you, I should never have let it come to this."

Her voice was trembling — as was her hand. I felt I should say something.

"It wasn't your fault," I said. "It was just one of those things."

"It wasn't though, was it, Claire? Teenage girls don't go around throwing themselves in front of tube trains for no reason whatsoever."

"I couldn't see any other way out. I'd messed everything up. I thought everyone hated me."

Mum shook her head and looked up at the ceiling.

"Why would I hate you?"

I hesitated before replying.

"Because of what I did with Andy. And because I ran to you that time and told you about Dad, about what I'd seen when I came home from school."

"You thought I hated you because of that?"

"You never said it wasn't my fault that he left. All you did was give me a Finger of Fudge to eat. It wasn't very much."

Mum started to cry.

"Oh, love. It wasn't your fault. You did me a favour. Stopped me burying my head in the sand, pretending it wasn't happening."

"You knew about it?"

"I didn't know but I suspected. She wasn't the first, Claire."

"So why didn't you do anything before?"

"Because I didn't want to lose your father. I loved him so much I wasn't sure I could cope without him. And I knew how much you idolised him."

"So how come you told him to leave then? After I came to see you."

"Because he'd hurt you. Because you're the most precious thing in the world to me and I wasn't going to let anyone hurt you like that. And now look what I've done, I've ended up hurting you myself."

Tears started rolling down my cheeks, dripping on to the crisp white bedsheets.

"I just needed someone to talk to," I said.

"I know. I should have listened, I should have realised what you were going through. I suppose I didn't want to hear it because I was so scared of losing you . . . scared of you growing up."

"I do love Andy, Mum."

"I know."

458

"No, I mean really love him. Like . . . I dunno, maybe like you used to love Dad."

Mum smiled. It was a sad smile. That was when I realised.

"You still love him, don't you? You still love Dad."

Mum looked down and nodded slowly.

"I know I shouldn't do. But it's not easy."

"So when I told you about him remarrying . . ."

"It came as a bit of a shock."

"Is that why you started seeing Malcolm?"

"Partly. It made me realise I've got to get on with my own life."

"Do you love Malcolm?"

Mum hesitated.

"He's a good man, Claire. There's a lot to be said for that." She gave a weak smile and tightened her grip on my hand. "I couldn't have coped, you know, if I'd lost you. I don't know what I'd have done."

"It's OK," I heard myself saying, realising how drained Mum looked. "You haven't lost me. I'm still here. You should go home and get some sleep."

"Are you sure you'll be all right?"

"I can't do anything stupid in here, can I? Not in this state."

She managed a smile as she bent to pick up her handbag.

I had been awake a good ten minutes the next morning before I noticed the envelope, the one which had been left on my bedside cabinet by the post lady. It was pale blue and bore a Potters Bar postmark. I asked a passing nurse to open it for me. She ripped the top with her finger and tipped the contents out on to my bed. There was a get-well card and a letter on lined notepaper. The sort of notepaper great-aunts get you for a birthday present. I picked it up with my one good hand and started to read.

Dear Claire,

Hope you're feeling better. You scared the shit out of me, you silly cow. Don't you ever dare do anything like that again.

You never let me finish when you came to see me. I was going to say "I don't hate you, I could never hate you. You're the best friend I've got." But you never gave me a chance. I thought I'd lost you, when I heard about what you'd done. I'm so relieved I've got the chance to finish my sentence. I thought I'd do it in a letter. That way you won't get the chance to interrupt like you usually do.

I didn't mean all that stuff I said. I was hurting and I took it out on you. That was mean of me. I know you love Andy. I never loved Matt. He was just a lot safer than a boyfriend.

I told my mum about what happened, to me I mean. It was hard but I feel better now it's out in the open. She cried at first and said I was making it up but I think she believed me in the end. She's been all right since. Just a bit quiet. I don't think she's told Dad. I asked her not to. I'm not going to tell anyone else. Especially not Tara. She's a right gossip.

I'll come and see you soon. Bring you some Cadbury's Creme Eggs instead of all those crappy grapes. I love you and I'm really sorry.
Frankie XXX

I wiped my eyes and put her card right at the front of my bedside cabinet. In the space I'd been saving for Andy's.

CHAPTER
FIFTEEN

I phoned Frankie from the train down to London.

"How is she?" I asked.

"Pretty groggy. The chemo was really tough. But the doctors says she's strong enough. And she says she's ready for the transplant." A train hooted as it went past. "Where are you?" asked Frankie.

"On the train down."

"I thought you weren't coming until tomorrow."

"Last-minute change of plan. Who's looking after the children tonight?"

"They're with Joe's parents."

"And where's Joe?"

"Sitting with Emily. We're doing shifts."

"Will he be OK for a double shift this evening?"

"I guess so. Why?"

"We're going up West, as they used to say in *EastEnders*."

"Are you crazy?"

"Certifiable."

"Are you going to explain what's going on?"

"No. Just meet me at Leicester Square tube station in two hours' time. Phone me when you get there because it's going to be packed. Wear your glad rags. Or something black at least."

"I don't understand. Is this another one of your cunning plans?"

"Sort of. All you need to know is that it's for Emily. Something to cheer her up, OK?"

"OK," said Frankie, still not sounding convinced. "But this had better be good, Claire."

"Believe me," I said. "It will be."

I stepped off the escalator, hurried through the ticket barrier and stopped abruptly outside the tube station. My senses being assaulted by the bright neon lights, cacophony of noise and rancid hot-dog-stall smells of Leicester Square. I'd expected it to be busy, but nothing had prepared me for this. Hordes of teenage girls, all of them dressed in various vampire guises: a uniform of black eyeliner, pale faces and artificially unkempt hair. It was bloody freezing too. The first time for years I'd gone out in stockings and a miniskirt and the chill factor must have been well into the minus figures. I checked my mobile, deciding despite being in central London to keep it in my hand, the level of noise being such that I'd never hear it ring otherwise. I was aware that it was the wrong sort of mobile, of course. The bright young things around me were flashing the latest tiny camera phones around as they took pictures of each other. I was probably the only one here who had a separate camera tucked away in her bag. It was at least digital though. The film one had been left to rest in peace at home.

I turned to watch the crowd of girls behind me, laughing and joking, the thrill and anticipation of it all sparking from their bodies. And then I saw Frankie. Gliding up the escalator in a long skirt and boots, a low- cut top and a flowing black coat. Style oozing from her pores. I shook my head as she approached.

"You really piss me off," I said.

"Why?"

"You still look bloody hot, even at your age. And I bet you threw it all together in two minutes flat."

Frankie grinned at me. "It was pretty much the only decent outfit I had with me. I chucked it in the case in the vain hope we might manage to get out for a meal later in the week. If everything goes OK."

"Little knowing that I'd be taking you out for a night on the town."

Frankie rolled her eyes. "Don't think I don't know what you're up to. I worked it out on the way."

"Oh," I said. "It was going to be a surprise."

"What, with thousands of teenage girls squealing about their love of Robert Pattinson all over the tube station?"

"Yeah, well. I didn't reckon on it being quite this busy."

"So I take it that's where we're going," she said, pointing at the massive *Twilight* sign in red lights above the Odeon across the square.

"You've got it," I said, taking her arm and starting to march her across the icy pavement to where the crowd had gathered outside.

"And what is the plan exactly?" asked Frankie.

464

"We're going to get Robert's autograph."

"Right. Just like all these girls are, you mean?" she said, waving her arm at the throng of devoted Pattinson fans already massed behind the barriers.

"Aah, but we've got an advantage over them, haven't we?"

"What?"

"We're experienced autograph-hunters. We know all the tricks. We were getting signatures from gorgeous guys when they were still in nappies."

Frankie laughed and shook her head. "But they're younger and fitter and can probably scream more loudly."

"Nonsense," I said as we reached the back of the crowd. "We'll wipe the floor with them. Now, elbows at the ready, and if any of them protest give them one of your dirty looks."

We started squeezing our way through, row by row.

"Sorry," I said to the first girl who blocked my path and refused to budge an inch. "We've lost our daughters. We think they're somewhere down at the front." She stepped grudgingly to the side. I started calling, "Emily, Sophia, where are you?"

"You devious cow," whispered Frankie with a wicked grin on her face.

"Just remember," I said. "We're doing this for Emily."

Frankie started calling too. "Emily, don't worry, hon, we're here. Hold on tight to Sophia."

"The little one's only eleven," I said to an older girl who was looking daggers at me. "First time in London as well." She stepped aside to let us through.

Ten minutes later we were standing triumphantly at the front of the barriers, next to a girl with a "Bite Me Rob" banner, in a plum spot right outside the cinema. Still pretending to have lost Emily and Sophia but packed in so tightly that having got there, those around us could see it was impossible for us to move.

"What happens now?" asked Frankie.

"We wait."

"It's freezing my fucking tits off."

"Sshh," I said. "You're supposed to be a responsible mother."

"We're not very responsible if we've lost our kids, are we?"

I started giggling. Frankie took one look at me and started giggling too.

"I'm so glad I'm not their age," I said when we finally stopped laughing. "All that teenage angst and heartache. The pain of unrequited love."

"What's brought this on?" said Frankie. "Where have your rose-tinted spectacles gone?"

"I saw Andy today," I said.

Frankie stared at me hard, as if worried I might be losing it again.

"What do you mean? Where?"

"In Saltaire, where he lives. It's less than an hour from Todmorden."

"You mean you just bumped into him?"

"No. We had a sort of date."

Frankie's eyes bulged wide.

"Claire, I'm not getting this. Your boyfriend is lying in hospital about to donate bone marrow to my daughter and you're pissing around with the guy who nearly cost you your life."

"It's OK. It's not like that. Mark gave me his address. He told me to go and see him. Well, the first time at least."

"Whoa, you're losing me here. You'd better slow down and explain."

So I did. I told her everything. From the first glimpse outside his house to me storming out of the diner earlier that day. Frankie stood open-mouthed, sporadically shaking her head.

"I can't believe all this has been going on and you haven't told me about it."

"I didn't want to bother you, you've had enough on your plate. The last thing you needed was me bleating on about Andy again."

"You mean you knew I'd say you were being a stupid cow."

"Well, yeah. Probably that as well. But I had to figure it out for myself. I'm glad I went to see him. He's dominated my life for so long. It feels good to finally have some sort of closure."

Frankie shook her head again.

"You could have ended up with him. How weird is that? It's like the whole thing went full circle."

"I know. If you'd told me when I was fifteen that I'd be blowing Andy Pailes out at thirty-eight, I'd have said you were mad."

"But it is finally over?"

"Yeah. Mark's seen to that. No one's ever loved me that much that they've set me free."

"Have you told him that?"

"Not yet. I will do later. I'm planning to go to the hospital when we're finished here."

"He's a great guy, Claire. I know I would say that because of what he's doing for Emily. But even without that, he's solid gold."

"Like your Joe then. We did all right between us, didn't we?"

Frankie smiled and gave me a great big hug.

"We did bloody brilliant."

We had to wait another hour before he arrived. I couldn't actually feel my feet any more. Or my fingers, come to that. The dry ice was pumped along the black carpet laid out in front of us. Lots of people walked past, most of whom I had no idea who they were. The film appeared to have a cast of thousands, but we were only waiting for one man. The flashes went again as a young woman in an off-the-shoulder dress with startled cat-like eyes arrived. I guessed she must play Bella, because the girl beside me hissed in a jealous rage. Then through the ice a tall figure emerged. Black suit, white shirt, hair all over the place. But the eyes. Jesus, the eyes. A thousand girls screamed in unison as he strode towards us. Frankie was one of them.

"Oh my God. He's gorgeous," she shrieked.

"I told you Emily has better taste than you did."

"Quick. Where's the picture?" Somehow I managed to yank the poster I'd brought of Robert from my bag and thrust it towards him, pen held out in the other hand. He didn't see it though. His head was bent, and he was busily scrawling signatures on the mass of photos in front of him.

"It's no good," I said as he started to edge away. "He's going to go past. You have to do something."

Frankie opened her mouth wide and screamed.

"I'm a big mamma, Robert, and I want your babies." He turned instantly, a bemused smile on his face. "I don't really," said Frankie, grabbing the poster from me and holding it out. "I want you to sign this for my daughter. Her name's Emily. She would have been here herself but she's having a bone marrow transplant tomorrow. She worships the ground you walk on."

Robert scribbled something on the poster before glancing up.

"I hope it goes well," he said, his voice just audible above the screams which filled the air. And with that he was gone, whisked away to pose for the photographers hollering his name. Only his wild hair visible through the dry ice.

I looked down at the poster, realising that my hands were shaking, and read the words out loud.

"To Emily, live the life you've dreamed of. Love Robert." Frankie looked at me and screamed again. "And he's put kisses," I said. "Three of them. She's going to love it."

We stood hugging each other and crying for a long time. Oblivious to the screams and comings and goings around us.

"She's going to be all right, isn't she?" asked Frankie. I nodded and gently wiped the tears from her face.

"She's going to be just fine."

It was gone nine by the time I got to the hospital. Fortunately they were very relaxed about visiting times. I hurried along the corridor, hoping Mark wouldn't have decided to get an early night. He hadn't though; as I peered through the window of his room I could see him watching Sky Sports on his television screen. I turned the handle and stepped inside. He looked up with a start.

"Hi. You're a day early. It hasn't happened yet."

"I know. Last-minute change of plan," I said.

"But you agreed."

I bent to kiss him and sat down in the chair next to his bed.

"Sometimes people ask you to do something that you know isn't what they really want. Or what they need. You're scared. I'm here for you. It's how it should be."

Mark nodded slowly and turned off the TV with the remote.

"Thank you. What's with the get-up?" he said with a grin, looking at my boots and short skirt. "Is that your idea of boosting my spirits?"

"It was my failed attempt at blending in with a bunch of teenage vampire groupies, actually."

Mark frowned at me.

"I took Frankie to that film premiere Emily wanted to go to. We managed to get Robert Pattinson's autograph. She'll be well chuffed."

"You're always so bloody competitive. I give her my bone marrow and you have to go one better, don't you?" He smiled.

470

I looked at him, knowing I had to tell him but not wanting to turn things serious just as he was beginning to relax. It had to be done though. I didn't want to lie to him for a moment longer.

"I saw Andy Pailes again today. He didn't send me packing last time. Quite the opposite. I'm sorry I didn't tell you before but I didn't want to worry you."

Mark's face dropped. He looked as if he was bracing himself for bad news.

"It's OK. It's over. It's finished now. That's why I'm here with you."

"I don't understand. Why would you go and see him again?"

I sighed and took hold of Mark's hand.

"It wasn't like a normal teenage idol thing. I met him lots of times. We became friends. Well, more than friends, actually."

"You mean . . ."

I nodded quickly. Not wanting Mark to say it.

"Yeah. A couple of times. It was all pretty sordid. Although of course it didn't seem like that to me at the time."

"How old were you?"

"Sixteen. Just."

"Fucking hell."

"I know. That's what my mum said."

"She found out?"

I nodded again, looking down at the bed.

"Everyone found out. It was on the front page of the *News of the World*. They were tipped off by one of his teammates."

Mark raised his eyebrows and blew out. Clearly struggling to take it all in.

"So what happened?"

"He didn't want anything more to do with me. United put him on the transfer list and England dropped him."

"And what about you?"

I shut my eyes and squeezed Mark's hand tight.

"I did a really stupid thing. I tried to kill myself."

I felt the tremors radiating out through Mark's body. His hand went cold in mine. He was quiet for a long time. When I finally opened my eyes he was staring at me, his face unusually pale.

"How?" he managed finally.

"I threw myself in front of a train."

Mark winced and shut his eyes.

"Fortunately I made a complete hash of it. Ended up in hospital. I was unconscious for a couple of days and pretty badly injured but, well, it was nothing compared to what could have been."

Mark opened his eyes. A tear ran out one corner. He shook his head again and again. Something clicked inside his head. "So your scars. It wasn't a car crash?"

I shook my head, embarrassed at the lie I'd told to explain away the physical evidence on my hip and shoulder.

"Why didn't you tell me all this before?"

"It never seemed the right moment. It's not the sort of thing you can casually come out with. I told David not long after we got married and it kind of freaked him out. I guess I came to the conclusion it was one of those things that was best swept under the carpet."

"So why are you telling me now?"

"Because I want you to understand why I went back to see him. How deep this all ran. I know I should have told you when you gave me his address. And I feel bad that you had no idea what you were dealing with."

Mark thought for a moment. "And what about him? What did he want?"

"I don't know. He's a bit of an enigma," I said with a smile, remembering the first time I'd said it. "He's single; he struck me as pretty lonely. Which is probably why he asked to see me again. I know I shouldn't have and I feel really bad about it, but it's like I revert to a sixteen year old in his presence."

"Did you want to get back together with him?"

"I don't know what I wanted, to be honest. The whole thing with finding the list left me pretty mixed up. But when I saw him today it was like I was seeing him through a grown-up's eyes for the first time. All the anger about how he'd treated me came out. Anger I didn't even know I felt. I told him what a bastard he'd been. I said you were worth ten of him. And I meant it as well."

I started crying. Mark leant forward and took my head in his hands. Stroking my hair. Holding me as I rocked to and fro.

"It's all right," he said. "Everything's all right."

"You don't hate me?" I sobbed.

"How could I hate you? You're the most precious thing in the world to me and I've just found out that I nearly lost you years before I even met you. I don't care what happened in the past. All that matters is what happens from here on."

"Good. Because I want to be with you. I've never been more certain of anything in my entire life. I'm sorry I've put you through all this. I know I've been hard work these past few months. But it's all over now. It really is."

Mark nodded slowly. "That's all right then. And I'm sorry too. Because I probably brought it all on by putting you on the spot like that about the house."

"Hey, you were doing something really nice."

"Just going about it the wrong way."

I smiled as he brushed the soggy strands of hair from my face.

"Do you know what?" I said. "I quite fancy you in those pyjamas."

"Watch it," said Mark. "It's against hospital rules to take the piss out of patients the night before an op."

"Sorry. I haven't done a very good job of trying to calm your nerves either, have I?"

"Oh, I don't know. You've certainly taken my mind off the transplant."

"I ought to go and let you get some sleep."

"What, after coming out with all of that stuff? It'll be going round in my head for hours."

"Let me sit with you then." I shuffled on to the bed and snuggled in next to Mark. My hand stroking his leg.

"I'll probably have some more questions," he said. "Things I want to know about what happened when it all sinks in a bit."

"That's OK. There are no more secrets. You can read my diaries when you get home if you want to. I've got a stack of them in the loft."

"What, and know what was going on inside your head at fifteen? I think I'd rather be blissfully ignorant."

I smiled. We sat like that for a long time. Both of us thinking. Waiting for everything to settle so we could see what the land looked like after the earthquake.

"I'm glad you came," he said eventually.

"Good. So am I."

"You know tomorrow? There's something I'd like you to do for me."

"Of course. What is it?"

"Keep that outfit on. Something to look forward to when I come round."

"I love you, Mark Parry," I said, digging him in the ribs with my elbow. "I probably shouldn't, but I do."

Tuesday, 22 July 1986

Every morning I wondered if this would be the day when people would stop being nice to me. If they would think that my broken bones had healed, the scars had faded, I'd left school and was therefore old enough to know better, so they could go back to treating me normally again. I would have understood it if they had done. Part of me would have been relieved; I found the constant concern about my state of mind and the care people took to avoid mentioning anything remotely connected with suicide, depression or trains a bit wearing at times.

But when I went downstairs, Mum was sitting at the kitchen table beaming the same "Thank God she's alive" smile that she'd been sporting for the past few months. We sat and had breakfast together, Mum making cheery conversation in between each mouthful of toast.

"I was thinking of going into town tomorrow, see if I can find a new sofa for the front room. It's about time we had a change. I don't suppose you want to come with me, do you? To help me choose."

"OK," I said, "as long as it doesn't take long. And you don't drag me to Laura Ashley."

"Oh no, I wasn't thinking of going there. I was thinking of getting something a bit more modern."

I tried not to laugh as I took a quick slurp of tea.

"Oh, one more thing," Mum continued, hesitantly. "Is it OK if Malcolm comes round for tea this evening? Say if you don't want him to."

I thought about it for a moment.

"No, it's all right. He can come if he wants to. He's all right, actually."

I got up from the table and glanced back over my shoulder before I hurried upstairs. Mum had a huge smile on her face. I couldn't remember her ever looking that happy before.

For once, I knew exactly what I wanted from the wardrobe. It had to make me look good but not desperate. My blue summer dress would be perfect. Well, not perfect perhaps, but good enough. I spent ages doing my make-up. Putting on a brave face. When I had finished I stepped back to admire myself in the mirror. The slick of shimmering honey-coloured lipstick stared back at me. It was a long time since I'd seen that. I'd made an effort today, a real effort.

I caught Andy's eye in the mirror. And turned to see not one pair but a dozen others staring down at me from the wall. As they had done every day since Andy had been here with me. He hadn't gone away because I hadn't let him. Mum had threatened to tear the pictures down. But I knew she wouldn't. She was too scared of upsetting me.

I picked up the scrap of paper with the scribbled directions on it and popped it into my bag. Then I floated downstairs, the cotton dress cool against my bare legs.

"You look nice, love," said Mum. "Where are you meeting Frankie?"

"Round hers," I said. I felt bad lying. But I knew if I told her the truth she'd freak out. And I didn't need a big scene. Not today.

"See ya later," I called over my shoulder as I pulled the door to behind me. I walked to the end of our road, checked over my shoulder and turned left towards the station.

It was cool in the shade on the platform. I wished I'd brought my jacket. I felt goose bumps climbing up my arms and across my shoulders. I started walking up the platform, as close to the edge as possible. I didn't see the point in confronting something unless you were going to do it head on. A couple of people glanced at me as I walked past. I wondered if they recognised me. If they were racking their brains, trying to remember where they'd seen me before. I was half expecting someone to come and grab my arm as the train came in to the platform. Just in case.

The end carriage came to a halt directly in front of me. I waited while an elderly lady got off, then stepped on board and found myself an empty seat next to the window. It felt weird, travelling in the opposite direction to normal. Away from London. Further into deepest darkest Hertfordshire.

I got off at Welwyn Garden City. It smelt of warm Shredded Wheat. I couldn't understand it until I remembered seeing the address on the side of my cereal

478

packet. I hurried up the platform stairs and down again the other side. The single-decker bus was standing outside the station, engine running. Within a few seconds of me getting on, the driver set off. As if he'd been waiting specially for me. The other people on the bus looked like regulars. Elderly ladies in blouses tucked into elasticated trousers and mums with fidgeting toddlers on their laps. My age, clothes and lack of a shopping bag gave the game away. I didn't normally do this. I had some particular place to go.

The sun was streaming through the windows now. I could feel the backs of my legs sticking to the plastic seat. Stretches of green flashed past the window as we started to leave the rows of neat semis behind. It was another fifteen minutes or so before the driver called out that we were at my stop. I peeled myself off the seat.

"Thornley Lane's just there," he said, pointing to the other side of the road.

"Thanks," I said, stepping from the bus, glad to be on my own at last. I started walking. My feet already sticky in my sandals. The wetness creeping from under my arms. I hoped there'd be a cool air dryer in the loos, so I could dry my armpits Madonna-style. As I drew nearer I felt my breath quickening. My legs kept walking; I don't think I could have stopped them if I'd tried. But my steps were less certain. The nagging doubts in my head grew louder. I wasn't sure it was the right thing to do any more. Never go back, they said. But I wasn't going back. I was going somewhere new.

The piece of paper in my hand was shaking when I looked at it. Left at the bottom and the white gates are straight ahead. That's what the lady on the switchboard had told me when I'd rung, pretending to be a loyal fan.

I turned the corner and caught sight of a concrete clubhouse. It was small and drab. As I drew nearer I noticed the peeling paint on the gates. Even a letter missing from the sign. "Luton Town Fo tball Club Training Ground" it said. That was what it had come to. I walked through the gates. It was so not United. Even the players' cars were cheaper-looking. My heart started thumping as I caught sight of Andy's Golf. The only familiar thing in the whole place. I stood looking at it for a long time. Remembering being inside. Being with him. Kissing him. And everything that had come after it. It seemed like a lifetime ago now. As if it had happened to somebody else. Which, in a way, I guessed it had. When my legs felt strong enough to move again I crept towards the clubhouse, from where I could see over towards the training pitch.

The players were still out there. Though they appeared to be warming down. I picked Andy out straight away. Just by the way he was standing. He had his back to me. It was so weird, seeing him in a Luton strip. Like watching your mum looking after the kids next door. I wanted to shout at him that he'd made a mistake, got the wrong place. He hadn't though. This was where he belonged now. Beggars couldn't be choosers. And as he'd said in the papers, it was very good of Luton to give him a chance to resurrect his career.

I hid behind the wall as the players walked back towards the clubhouse. I didn't want Andy to see me. Not until I was ready. And I hadn't even worked out what to say yet. I had practised it in my head countless times. But now I was actually here, it had all become scrambled. Nothing seemed to sound right any more. A dozen or so Luton fans drifted across from the training area to congregate outside the clubhouse. A girl a couple of years younger than me came and stood a few yards away. She smiled at me; I looked away. I couldn't afford to enter into a conversation. I didn't want my cover blown.

I stood facing away from everyone else. Looking out across the car park. Waiting. A few players came out. I recognised Brian Stein as he walked past. I hoped the others wouldn't think it strange. That I wasn't asking for any autographs. That I wasn't even looking at them.

"Excuse me." It was the girl's voice from behind me. "Can you take a photo for me, please?"

I turned round to see her holding her camera out to me. And Andy standing a few feet away from her, wearing a Luton Town sweatshirt and looking at me with wide, staring eyes. I stood paralysed. My mouth opened to say something but no words came out.

"You just press that button," the girl continued, oblivious to what was going on.

I took the camera from her. As I held it up I could feel it shaking against my nose. I looked through the viewfinder. The girl leant in towards Andy. His hands were firmly behind his back. And he was staring straight at me. His face decidedly pale.

"Thanks," the girl said.

I handed the camera back to her. Knowing she'd hate the photo, even if it did come out. She moved away and it was just the two of us.

"What are you doing here?" Andy said. It was not the welcome I'd hoped for.

"I wanted to see you."

"I understand that but this is hardly the place," he said, glancing over his shoulder.

"Where else could I find you?"

"I'm very lucky to have been given another chance, Claire. I can't afford to screw this one up."

"Is there somewhere we can go?" I said. "To talk."

Andy nodded in the direction of the far corner of the car park, where his Golf was. Beyond it was a low wall, hidden from the view of the other fans and players. I sat down on it a few feet away from him, feeling like a kid all over again. I wanted to touch him but pushed the thought away. I waited for him to speak, to hear what he might say.

"Are you feeling better now?" he said eventually.

People asked you that after a cold. Not a suicide attempt. I looked across at him, frowning.

"I meant have your injuries healed?" he said.

"Yeah, fine, thanks." I looked away. All the time trying not to think. That the last time I'd seen him was when we were having sex.

"I feel such a shit," Andy said.

I didn't say anything. I wasn't going to argue and I wanted him to carry on talking. I'd waited a long time to hear what he had to say.

"I couldn't believe it when I heard what you'd done. I thought you were dead at first. And then when I got your letter . . ." He looked up at the sky and shook his head.

"I bet you wished I had died."

"Don't say that, Claire."

"Why?"

"Because it's not true."

"Why didn't you come to see me in hospital then?"

"With all the press outside? They'd have had a field day. Anyway, the club barred me from going anywhere near you."

"Is that why you didn't ring me, or answer my calls?"

"What calls?"

"I phoned you, loads of times."

"I wasn't at home. They told me to stay at Skip's. Till all the fuss died down."

I nodded. We sat in silence for a bit.

"Why did you come here, Claire?" he said at last.

"I wanted to know if I meant anything to you at all."

Andy sighed and ran his fingers through his hair.

"Look, Claire. I'm not proud of what happened. You're a lovely girl but . . . I never meant for it to turn into, you know, a physical thing."

I shook my head. This wasn't making sense.

"Oh. So why did you do it then?"

Andy shrugged. "I guess I let my heart rule my head again."

Frankie said it was his prick that he'd let rule his head. But I wasn't going to tell him that.

Andy blew out his cheeks.

"Look. I behaved like a complete bastard. I know that. I was lonely. And I was flattered by your attention. I went out with Annie to get the lads off my back about not having a girlfriend. Then when she dumped me for Clubber . . ."

"You never said she dumped you."

"I never said she didn't either. You believed what you wanted to, Claire. You idolised me. I realised that when I saw all those pictures in your room. I should have left then."

"Why didn't you?"

He shrugged again. Avoiding eye contact again. I waited for him to say "Because I loved you, because I couldn't resist you." He said nothing. It was my turn to sigh.

"I'm sorry about what happened to you, Claire. Really I am." He blew out his cheeks again before turning to look at me. I thought he was about to say something else, but he didn't.

We both sat for a bit. I dragged my toe repeatedly across the gravel. After a while I realised my heart had stopped thumping. And that my palms weren't sweating any more.

"You'd better go, before anyone sees us," I said. And with that I got up, brushed the seat of my dress and walked out of the car park without looking back. Because I knew if I did he would see the tears streaming down my face.

★ ★ ★

When I got home, Mum was busy in the kitchen preparing tea. I went straight up to my room and slowly, one by one, started taking Andy's pictures down from the wall.

CHAPTER
SIXTEEN

The signed poster of Robert was up on the wall behind Emily's bed when I visited her in hospital the next morning.

"Thank you," she grinned. "Mum said it was your idea."

"My idea but your mum pulled it off. Did she tell you how she got it?" Emily shook her head. "Ask her later, when it's all over. It'll make you laugh. Or maybe cringe with embarrassment."

"Was he just as gorgeous in real life?" she asked.

"Better. Your mum's got the hots for him. Just don't tell her I said so."

Emily giggled. I sat down on the edge of her bed and gave her a hug. Not that there was much of her left to hug. She'd lost a lot of weight. One of the side effects of the last round of chemo. Her hair was starting to grow back. Which was a shame in a way because she'd just get used to having it and it would all fall out again.

"Do you know the best thing about him though?" I said. "He's just the guy on your wall. It's the best place for him, because that way he can never let you down. Never be a disappointment."

486

"I know," said Emily. "I wouldn't want to go out with him. Not really. He can't possibly be as nice as I imagine he is. So it's better that I just imagine."

I smiled and shook my head.

"What?" said Emily.

"You're so much more sensible than I was at your age. It took me a long, long time to learn that."

"That guy Andy who you liked. You had a thing with him, didn't you?"

"How do you know?"

"I didn't. I guessed. Something in the way you talked about him."

"Yeah. I did. I got it all mixed up, you see. The real Andy and the imaginary one. I so much wanted them to be the same person but it turned out they weren't."

"Did he hurt you?"

"Yeah. He did. I don't think he meant to, but he didn't understand how special he was. Or that the Andy I wanted was the one in my dreams."

"I can still dream though, can't I?"

"Of course you can," I said, reaching out and holding her hand.

"All I dream of," said Emily, "is being well again. Of being able to go on holiday with Alia next year and taking Sophia shopping when she's older. Of Joe walking me down the aisle one day."

I smiled and wiped away the tears from her cheeks. "And all those things can still happen," I said. "Your Robert was right. You can live the life you dream of. You simply have to remember that dreams can change and

487

it's important you don't let the old ones get in the way of the new."

Emily nodded. I passed her a tissue from the box on the bedside cabinet.

"Anyway," I said. "Listen to me going on. I must sound like your mother."

Emily smiled. "I hope me and Alia are still best friends when we're your age. And I hope I end up with the man of my dreams like you have."

"How do you know Mark's the man of my dreams?"

"Because you couldn't have wished for anyone better, could you?"

I shook my head. Wishing I'd had half of her wisdom when I'd been her age.

"I'll tell him that," I said. "Now you get some rest. Everything's going to be fine. And I'll come and see you again later, OK?"

"OK," said Emily, still clinging on to my hand. "Will you tell me all about last night, about seeing Robert? That's what I'll be wanting to hear."

"Sure," I said. "I'll tell you every single detail. Even the bits your mum said not to."

Emily grinned. I left her lying on the bed. Gazing up at Robert on the wall.

It was a long time before Frankie came down to the waiting room. I'd gone through most of the contents of the drinks machine and still not found anything which tasted good.

She looked tired and washed out. But most of all she looked happy.

"Emily's fine," she said. "The doctor said it all went well. It's just a matter of time now. It will be a while before they know if the graft has taken. And whether her body will reject it."

She started crying. I wrapped my arms around her and let her sob into my shoulder.

"She'll be fine," I said. "She's a tough cookie, like her mother. She's also got more sense than the two of us put together at her age."

Frankie managed a watery smile. "What do you mean?" she said.

"All the things I wish I'd known at her age. She's got them all sorted. Knows exactly what's important. Exactly what life's all about."

"That's good," said Frankie. "Maybe, once she comes through this, she'll have a smooth ride, for a few years at least."

"Just remember," I said. "Don't you go trying to fix her up with any nice Italian boys."

"I promise."

"Anyway, I'd better get over to the other hospital to see Mark."

"Of course," said Frankie. "Will you do something for me?"

"What?"

"Give him a great big kiss from me."

"Sure," I said. "I'd be delighted."

I peered in through the window before going into Mark's room. The nurse had warned me that he was still a bit groggy but I could at least see him. He was lying on his bed looking like a real patient this time. His face a dull shade of grey. His body lying awkwardly. I slipped into the room and sat down on the chair, pulling it up close to the bed. He turned his face towards me and managed some sort of smile.

"How's Emily?" he asked.

"She's fine. The doctor says it went well. She's in with a chance."

"Good. Let's hope it stays that way."

I nodded. "Oh, and this is from Frankie," I said, bending to kiss him softly on the forehead. "And this is from me," I added, planting a kiss on his lips.

"Thanks. I needed that."

"How are you feeling?"

"Like someone whacked me over the head, drilled a dirty great hole in my back and took out half of my insides."

"You were right. You are going to be a lousy patient."

"I hope you're going to be a good nurse."

"I'll do my best," I said. "But I draw the line at dressing up, OK?"

"Damn, you're no fun at all."

He lay quietly for a moment. I fiddled with the strap of my watch.

"When you're ready to go home, you're coming back to my place. I'm off until Christmas."

"You didn't have to do that."

"No. But I wanted to. Give me a chance to move all your stuff in and get some decorations up."

"A dog's for life, you know. Not just for Christmas."

490

"I know. And that's why I won't be chucking you out in the New Year."

"But what if you're sick of me by then?"

"I won't be. And your place will be easier to rent out until you find a buyer."

"What, so we're going to live together?"

"Yep. That's what you wanted, isn't it?"

"Yeah, but I haven't had a chance to draw up a pre-nup yet, just in case you try to run off with my Chili Peppers albums in ten years' time."

"We'll be living somewhere else by then."

"What, with a thatched roof and roses in the front garden?" he said smiling.

"No. Something a bit more sensible but maybe with a bit of character thrown in."

"Something we both like, you mean?"

"Yeah. With four bedrooms, just in case I change my mind about having kids."

"Do you think you might do?"

"Maybe. But only if you promise not to buy any of those poxy little Blackburn Rovers romper suits."

Mark laughed. "I'll make you very happy, Claire," he said, reaching out for my hand.

"I know you will," I said, squeezing it tightly. "Emily reckons you're the man of my dreams."

"Must be all those drugs they've pumped into her."

"I don't know," I said. "I have a feeling she's right."

Acknowledgements

Warmest thanks to the following people: my editor Sherise Hobbs for her professionalism, enthusiasm and for being thoroughly nice to work with; the great team at Headline for all their efforts; my agent Anthony Goff for his expertise, support and advice; everyone at David Higham Associates; Martyn Bedford, for advising emergency surgery on an early draft of Claire's story when I was knee-deep in rejections, helping me turn it around and providing invaluable advice and encouragement over a number of years; Alex Elam for believing in my writing and Claire's story a long time ago; Michelle Hurst for editorial services (with a pink pen) way before I had a book deal, being on the end of the deputy editor's hotline in Grimsby and for bone marrow transplant advice; Rebecca Sutcliffe, Steve Connor and Vincent Carr for legal advice; The Anthony Nolan Trust (www.anthonynolan.org.uk), especially Victoria Moffett, Rochelle Roest and Sameer Tupule, for expert medical advice; Amarah Bashforth for being my teenage consultant and telling me everything I needed to know about Robert Pattinson; Lance Little for the great website (www.linda-green.com); Alia

Mahon Henson for lending her name and Grainne Mahon Henson for her generosity, the players of Tottenham Hotspur Football Club 1983–86 for putting up with a certain teenage fan's autograph requests (especially Gary Mabbutt for being infinitely nicer than Andy Pailes and a wonderful ambassador for the game); my friends and family for their ongoing support and PR efforts; my gorgeous son Rohan for all his help with my book and for allowing me time off from the Wizard of Oz birthday party preparations to get it finished; and, most importantly, my husband Ian for his unstinting support and belief over a number of years, for getting me out from under the table when the rejections kept coming, promoting my book to the wives and girlfriends of photographers in the north and for working tirelessly on the Emerald City and the Yellow Brick Road sets while I wrote this book. Neither the party — nor this novel — could have happened without you!

Also available in ISIS Large Print:

10 Reasons Not to Fall in Love

Linda Green

Jo Gilroy gave her heart away once. She won't be making the same mistake twice. In fact, she's got 10 reasons not to fall in love . . .

1. I'd have to shave my legs — even in winter; 2. Couldn't get away with wearing big knickers; 3. Or having spaghetti hoops for tea; 4. He'd have to meet my mother; 5. My boss is my ex and no man could accept that; 6. Single mums are about as attractive to men as syphilis; 7. "I'll Never Fall in Love Again" is my theme tune; 8. Last time I was dumped for a weather-girl; 9. I no longer trust men;

And most importantly . . . 10. Can't risk Alfie getting hurt again.

Then Dan Brady comes along, with some reasons of his own . . .

ISBN 978-0-7531-8440-0 (hb)
ISBN 978-0-7531-8441-7 (pb)

I Did a Bad Thing

Linda Green

Sarah Roberts used to be good. Then she did something bad. Very bad.

Now, years later, she's living a good life, working as a local newspaper reporter and living with her saintly boyfriend Jonathan. She has no reason to think her guilty past will ever catch up with her.

Until Nick walks back into her life. And suddenly what's good and bad aren't so clear to Sarah any more.

ISBN 978-0-7531-7912-3 (hb)
ISBN 978-0-7531-7913-0 (pb)

ISIS publish a wide range of books in large print, both
fiction and non-fiction. Any suggestions for books you
would like to see in large print or audio are always
welcome. Please send to the Editorial Department at:

ISIS Publishing Limited
7 Centremead
Osney Mead
Oxford OX2 0ES

A list of ISIS ... is available free of charge from:

Chivers Large Print Books Limited

(Australia)
P.O. Box 314
St Leonards
NSW 1590
Tel: (02) 9436 2622

(Canada)
P.O. Box 80038
Burlington
Ontario L7L 6B1
Tel: (905) 637 8734

(New Zealand)
P.O. Box 456
Feilding
Tel: (06) 323 6828

... complete and unabridged audio books
... able from these offices. Alternatively ...
... local library for details of their collections
... and unabridged audio books.